Starry Nights

FOUR CHRISTIAN CONTEMPORARY ROMANCE NOVELS

A SUMMER TO REMEMBER
BOOK TWO

ANGELA RUTH STRONG   CARRIE PADGETT
TABITHA BOULDIN   BELL RENSHAW

TWO DOGS PUBLISHING, LLC.

eBook ISBN: 979-8-88552-246-5

Print ISBN: 979-8-88552-247-2

Published by: Two Dogs Publishing, LLC. Idaho, USA

Cover Design: EAH Creative, Emilie Haney, eahcreative.com

Do you love anthologies?

Sign up for the Two Dogs Newsletter to stay up-to-date on upcoming collections and releases, as well as news from our partner authors that have been included in previous releases!

Out of Play

ANGELA RUTH STRONG

Dedicated to every mom who feels guilty for reading this book when there are a million other things she "should be" doing.

Bex

Play is the beginning of knowledge. –George Dorsey

When I gave up my professional soccer career due to an unplanned pregnancy and the responsibilities of single parenthood, I thought my life was over. I never imagined my daughter would become my greatest accomplishment, but here she is at the age of eight, dribbling down the field for tryouts like a mini-me, thin headband included.

I run alongside in the warmth of sunshine, clipboard in hand, plastic whistle between my lips. Tryouts are basically skills tests to help make teams even. Or more, a chance to show off my kid.

Other parents turn to watch, and I want to take a bow. I don't, of course, but I let her run a little longer than required before blowing my whistle.

"She's superb," calls a random dude on the sidelines. He sounds shocked enough that he must be new to our summer league. Except he looks kind of familiar with soulful dark eyes that could come across as sad if there wasn't a smirk playing on his full lips. Perhaps he's another military dad, finally home from deployment. His brown hair is longer and messier than allowed for Marines however.

I drop my whistle to respond, "She's got the moves, huh?"

She should. She hasn't missed watching one of Ceasar Navarra's games with me since before she was born.

He laughs wryly.

But the show's just getting started. I motion for Mia's bestie to join her on the grass for a passing drill.

With her blonde ringlets and rosy, dimpled cheeks, Treva is as cute as she is shy. Four years ago, she wouldn't even have gone on the field without holding her mom's hand. Jacqueline ran around with her during every game, but after getting pregnant again, Treva's dad put a stop to that. My daughter volunteered to take Jacqueline's place.

I'd been perturbed at first. I didn't want anyone holding Mia back. But her compassion is her strength. After a couple games of running next to Treva like they were in a three-legged race, the two began to pass the ball back and forth with the kind of synchronization only seen in the Olympics. Okay, I might be exaggerating a bit, but that's what proud mamas do.

Treva charges out to the field. The two little girls race toward the net together. Treva gives one final pass, lining up the ball perfectly. Mia kicks it in for a goal.

"Woo-hoo!" I jump and pump my arms in the air. Even though I'd known exactly what would happen, I'm still Mia's biggest supporter.

Mia flies around the field with her arms spread like airplane wings. It's her victory lap. Besides compassion, she overflows with joy.

She has nothing to prove and simply plays the game for fun. It's what I want for her, but it's also what I wanted for myself. I can't help being a little envious. So I'll just live vicariously through my kid.

I grin at the dude I assumed to be a military dad to catch his response, but he's not watching anymore. He can't. Dance Mom and Influencer Mom are demanding all his attention.

I roll my eyes because I know what it's like to put up with those ladies. Poor guy.

Along with Mia and Treva, their daughters are on my team. Dance Mom has skinny twin redheads she's practically raising alone because their dad runs an independent film studio. Influencer Mom's athletic husband coaches their son in soccer, so the parents go their separate ways for games. Riley, her daughter, is good at soccer too, but she loves animals more. Every year, they bribe her with a new pet to get her to play. It works out well for me, but I'm not the parent with a tarantula living in my house.

So which kid does this new dad belong to?

Treva runs between Dance Mom and Influencer Mom to get to him. He lifts her in the air and spins her around.

The Moms giggle more than the little girl.

I squint to get a better look. Treva doesn't run to just anyone. In fact, she's more likely to run away from people.

Jacqueline appears beside me. Her friendship is as comfy and soft as she is with her big blonde curls and leftover pregnancy weight. The latest baby rides behind her in an infant backpack. If having one kid can make me feel accomplished, this woman must feel like the most successful woman on the planet. "That's Caleb's brother," she explains in her thick, southern drawl.

We may live in California, but we also live near a Marine base, so we get all types of people from around the country. I wonder what type her brother-in-law is.

"Gotcha. It all makes sense now." No wonder the guy looks familiar. He's got the same height, thick eyebrows, and dark coloring as Jacqueline's husband. But while Caleb only seems to come home from deployment to impregnate Jacqueline every year, this guy is helping out with Treva. "Nice of him to join you for tryouts."

"Yeah." She pauses. "Unfortunately, the Moms can get more higgledy-piggledy than the kids."

I think she means they're nuts. They're certainly demanding a lot of her brother-in-law's attention. "Pfft... Moms."

We both chuckle, mostly laughing at ourselves. Sometimes being a mom is like living in a cartoon world. Jacqueline is Super Mom, and I'm Soccer Mom.

"You ready to make more giant cutouts of their heads for the championship game?" she asks. "That was my favorite part of last year's season."

"If my principal lets me use the school printer again," I answer automatically.

Yeah, I make eight-year-old soccer the event of the season. For other coaches, it's probably nothing more than a hobby. For me, my day job is teaching P.E. and, more importantly, coaching high school soccer, but the best part about my profession is that it gives me summers off to coach my daughter in this special league.

One day, Mia will attend Oceanside High, and we'll get to win the state championship together. Until then, we'll rule summer soccer.

Jacqueline beams, causing me to wonder if she's got that pregnancy glow again. "Because of you, watching my daughter play soccer has become the highlight of motherhood."

Her words make my heart beam right back. "That means a lot."

Not all parents feel this way. Some think I take the game too seriously. Of course, they'll thank me later when their girls earn soccer scholarships, saving them thousands in college tuition.

Jacqueline gives me a side hug, which is the most contact I've had from another adult in a long time. Part of being a mom, I guess.

She adds, "Treva's normally such a wallflower that it's rare to see her bloom."

It's a good day for watching children bloom. The distant mountains haven't dried up yet and are still a pale green to coordinate with the palm trees surrounding our outdoor soccer complex. The sky is the kind of clear baby blue we normally only get with aid from the Santa Ana winds during fall ball, but there's no wind today. It's hot in the sunshine, cool in the shade, and just right for getting sock tan lines because we forgot our necessary sunblock.

Staff hides from the sun underneath a tent canopy.

"I wonder who they're putting on our team to replace Shanti," I muse.

The Ladybugs lost one of our superstars when her dad was relocated to North Carolina. Hazard of being a military town.

Jacqueline nods toward a bigger Hispanic girl repeatedly kicking the ball out of bounds with the kind of force that broke my nose and gave me black eyes in middle school. "*She* could use your guidance."

There's also a tall girl who runs like a gazelle, but the director would never give me another good player.

"Yep. That's who we're getting," I refer to the girl with boundary issues.

Dylan will claim it's to balance out teams and make the competition fair, but I'm pretty sure he secretly wants to see me get a ball to the face. I cringe and touch the bump on the bridge of my nose from an old injury.

Jacqueline gives me an encouraging nod. "You'll be fine."

She's aware I had to overcome PTSD from flying soccer balls in a similar fashion to her husband overcoming trauma from US intervention in Libya. When our daughters turned into BFFs, she became my bestie by proxy. She knows more about me than most people.

"Let me find out for sure." I trot toward the folding table covered in lists and scoresheets.

Dylan Elliot, the director and rival coach, sees me coming and crosses his arms. He's all buzz cut, bulging biceps, and bad temper. It irks me that he coaches the other good team in our division, because he doesn't even like soccer. He wants to be a football coach, and by football, I mean *fútbol Americano*. Not the original *fútbol*. But somehow his bootcamp drills pay off.

The two young assistants glance at me then scamper away. Maybe because I yelled at one of them for making a bad call as a ref last year. Even if I was right, I shouldn't have yelled. My passion gets the best of me at times.

"Hey, coach." I greet Dylan respectfully then hold out my clipboard of tryout scores. "Have you picked a player to replace Shanti on my team yet?"

He takes the clipboard. "*Your* team?"

I blink. Being coach, I'm not sure why I shouldn't refer to the team as mine, but maybe it isn't politically correct anymore. If not, that would certainly offend PC Mom and her senator husband. "The Ladybugs," I clarify.

His gaze cools, or maybe it's the shade of the tent causing goosebumps on my arms. "The Ladybugs are going to be disbanded since no one has stepped up to coach them this year."

I suck in a breath. The board did threaten to remove me from my position if I got a third red-tag for winning by more than seven points last year, but I'd called Shanti off. "Just because I beat you in the playoff game—"

"You were warned, Rebecca."

"Bex," I automatically correct with my nickname even as my heartbeat studders. Pin pricks explode from my joints like the time I had to slam on the brakes to keep from hitting a mountain lion on the freeway. "It was the playoff game. That shouldn't even count."

"Of course it counts."

Is he for real? "I specifically told Shanti not to score. That has to count for something too."

"It doesn't say much for your control as a coach."

The fact that I haven't punched him in the face yet says a lot for my control. "She wanted one more goal because she knew her family was moving away, and she'd never get to play with us again."

"She was a first grader. She wanted to make her coach happy, and I have video footage of you giving her a high five afterward."

"What was I supposed to do? Spank her?"

"Not funny."

"I know."

We face off.

My chest rises and falls as if I'm running laps. I imagine having to tell Mia I won't be her coach this year, and tears spring to my eyes.

Mia has already been deprived of so much. She won't ever have a dad to be her coach, and now she can't have her mom coach her either. She doesn't deserve this.

Not to mention, I don't deserve this. I gave up my dreams to be here for her. I *will* be here for her.

"Please," I beg pitifully. My voice cracks.

It makes me angry. This guy doesn't even like soccer, yet he has the power to keep me from coaching my daughter in the game I love. All because of his own wounded ego.

A corner of his mouth curls up. "What would it say about this league if we allowed coaches to break our own rules?"

He's enjoying this too much. No wonder his goal is to coach football where they're encouraged to cause pain.

"You're making an example of me?" I try to sound challenging. Demanding. Maybe even scoffing. But my tone comes out weak. And broken. All over again.

"You made an example of yourself."

I try so hard. Yet it's never enough.

Then it hits me. This isn't only affecting my little family. This is affecting all the Ladybugs.

"Oh no." I cover my mouth. "Will Treva still be on Mia's team?"

Dylan shrugs and looks away like he couldn't care less. Though I bet he wants Mia on his team simply to punish me even further. "We'll evaluate each of your old players and disperse them between teams, according to their strengths."

Mia and Treva's strengths are playing together. They looked forward to being on the same team more than the sport itself. What would happen if they had to play against one another?

"The Ladybugs will find a new coach," I vow. My mind takes a moment to catch up to my mouth, but when it does, it agrees with the plan. "Nobody has volunteered for the position because everyone assumed I'd be coaching. I mean, Jacqueline would even coach if it meant keeping her daughter on my daughter's team."

She would, right? I imagine Jacqueline on the sidelines, surrounded by her five other children. The baby could be on her back, and the oldest could act as nanny. Except the oldest is nannying for PC Mom this summer.

Dylan arches an eyebrow that is way too sculpted for a man's eyebrow to be. "You're going to babysit for Jacqueline on the sidelines?"

"No." I stand taller. Because I won't let him get me down. "I'm going to serve as assistant coach. That's not against your rules, is it?"

He snorts but doesn't say no.

I got him. I found a loophole.

"The Ladybugs have one week to come up with a new coach or be disbanded."

My heart surges with hope. Because for all I care, Dance Mom or Influencer Mom can be head coach. I'm going to assist, and we're going to beat Dylan's team in the playoffs. By at least seven points.

Skylar

Play is not a luxury. Play is a necessity.
–Kay Redfield Jamison

"How'd I let you talk me into this?" I sit in the passenger seat of Jacqueline's minivan, facing the fields overrun by soccer families attending their first practice of the season. I'd once aspired to be a soccer dad. Now I have no such aspirations, yet I'd come with her today so she could introduce me as a coach.

"Because you love your niece." Jacqueline shifts into park and shuts off the ignition. "And it's only a five-week season."

Yeah, probably the most important five weeks of my career.

I don't speak my thoughts aloud because said niece bounces in the backseat along with all my other nieces and nephews. Well, except for Olivia who's escaped from watching this brood in favor of nannying for someone else.

"There's Mia." Treva bolts from her seat and points past me out the windshield.

She used to be the quiet one, and I feared that with my brother so often deployed, she was going to get overlooked. But then I watched her come alive at her soccer tryouts last week. Treva is exactly the reason I'm here.

"Can I go join Mia? Can I, Mom?"

Jacqueline pushes the buttons to open all the doors of the vehicle, releasing the scent of stale French fries into the fresh air. It will take her some time to gather all the backpacks and wagons and children.

"I'll take her," I offer to keep Treva safe in the parking lot.

I need to set up for practice anyway. I've never coached before. In fact, I've never played soccer before. My childhood didn't accommodate any public activities that weren't planned publicity. On the other hand, I'd starred in more than one movie montage where kids prepared for "the big game." So that's what I'm planning to offer my team. I've even brought a playlist and speaker.

Part of me wonders if I'm being set up for some practical joke television show, but the reasonable side of me sees no other option for the Ladybugs.

I'm not going to let Treva be split from the teammate who's pulled her out of her shell. And who else is available to coach? The moms who cared more about getting a selfie with me for their social media pages than about their own daughters' tryouts? Or worse, my sister-in-law, who I strongly suspect to be pregnant with her seventh kid?

Treva jumps to the asphalt before Jacqueline has even unbuckled her seatbelt. "Thanks, Uncle Skylar."

Grabbing my backpack of equipment, I look once more to the field with trepidation. I knew to expect girls on this team, but I'm surprised to see that most of the parents accompanying them are female, as well. Thankfully, I stop myself in time before asking where all the dads are. If they're overseas like my brother, I don't want to bring up that sore subject.

"You're welcome," I force out grudgingly. Caleb owes me.

Treva's satiny fingers slide inside my palm, and she tugs me toward her friend.

Not only is Mia jogging in our direction, but so is the sporty-looking coach who'd been running drills during tryouts and outed my identity. Probably hoping for an autograph.

Now that I look closer, I notice she and Mia share the same muscular build, olive coloring, expressive features, and golden-brown ponytails slicked back with matching tiny headbands. If this is Mia's mom, why isn't she coaching the girls' team?

Suddenly, I feel used. And I should know because I've been used before.

"I'm so thankful you stepped up to coach," the sporty mom gushes. "You're my hero."

Ugh. Hero worship.

"Just doing my duty as an uncle." I stride past her, pulling my niece along. "Do you know which field we're on?"

"Field four," Mia's mom answers for Treva.

"Thanks." I almost successfully keep sarcasm out of my tone. I don't need her complaining to the media that I'm rude.

"So I have some ideas." She bounces beside me, way too excited for this not to be about my childhood fame.

I glance at her left hand. It's tanned with clean, oval fingernails. And, unsurprisingly, her ring finger is bare.

Here we go again. My sister-in-law is trying to set me up despite my insistence I'm done with women. Jacqueline doesn't believe anyone can possibly be happy without a spouse and a million children. Though I'm not entirely convinced such a lifestyle has fulfilled her.

"Let me line up the cones, okay? Then we'll talk."

"Okay," says Mia's mom, but she follows me around, still talking. Something about their rival team, the Butterflies.

"I'm terrified."

And how she wants to beat them by more than seven points even though it will get me red-tagged.

"Bring it."

Because their coach is a jerk who probably wants to take her daughter for his own team.

At this point I stop and stare into her silvery-blue eyes. With the way she's pitting me against the other guy, it feels like some kind of weird love triangle. And I don't need any more entanglements.

"What's your name?" I ask. Fans love it when I address them by name.

"Rebecca. Though I go by Bex."

I'm going to start calling her Rebecca if she doesn't leave me alone. She's worse than the other two moms combined. "Would you like a selfie, Bex?" It worked with them.

She blinks. Probably in shock that I would offer such a gift. "A selfie?"

I'm onto her. "Maybe an autograph?"

She tilts her head as if to see me from a different perspective. Her forehead furrows.

Either she's an actor too, or she's authentically confused. Though it can't be an accident that she quoted my famous movie line to me at tryouts. Well, it wasn't an exact quote. More of a rephrasing from "I've got da moves," made famous by my role in *The Water Fight Professional* series of movies when I was fourteen. As soon as she said it, the other moms nearby instantly identified me.

"You don't know who I am?" I challenge.

Her eyes wander the field as if looking for answers to my identity before frowning back at me. "You're Treva's uncle?"

She isn't interested in me or my autograph after all. She's simply this excited about soccer. I'm an idiot with a huge ego.

"Yes." I soften. She doesn't want a piece of me. She wants the best for her daughter. "And I'm the coach."

It's nice to be unknown for a change. To be judged entirely on my current performance rather than things I'd done as a younger, more immature version of myself. To be seen as part of a team instead of set on a pedestal.

"Oh..." She laughs self-consciously. "Sorry. I've just been Mia's only coach up until now, so I naturally want to take over."

I press my lips together and nod slowly, trying to follow. "Why aren't you coaching anymore? Jacqueline made it sound like the team lost its coach."

"I was trying to explain." She holds her hands wide. "The director removed me from my position because I beat his team by too many points."

So that's where this other guy came into play. It's not a love triangle, it's a coach triangle. "The red-tags."

She claps in triumph, as if we're on the same page now. "Exactly."

I do remember the other moms mentioning Bex to me. "You're the crazy one."

Her forehead wrinkles again. "Who called me crazy?"

Whoops. "I've got to finish setting up."

I turn toward my backpack to grab more cones and find twin ballerinas dancing my way in tutus. Their rust-colored hair is pinned to the top of their heads, and by the dark eyelashes and shiny pink lips, they must be wearing makeup too. Ironically, it's their mom who called Bex the crazy one.

"What's up, girls?" I shoot my questioning look to their mother. Maybe they're all crazy.

The woman trills in glee and touches my arm with her pointy fingernails. "Sorry, coach. It was dress rehearsal for their recital, and we forgot to grab cleats for soccer practice afterward. It won't happen again. Dance is over until fall. We need soccer to keep them conditioned for when ballet starts back up."

"Well." I nod along as if I agree with anything she just said. "We're going to do a dance for warmup anyway."

"We are?" Bex demands from behind me.

I glance over my shoulder to find her hands on her hips and her eyes narrowed.

"As soon as everyone gets here." The sooner, the better. "Who else are we waiting on?"

"I'm here." Another girl charges our way, black cornrows flying. "Guess what animal I'm gonna get for playing soccer this year. A shark. I'm getting a real baby shark."

As I suspected, all the parents are crazy.

Though everyone else seems to think this is normal behavior. Her announcement ignites a round of *Baby Shark*. Shark Girl's mom films the whole thing on her phone like she'd planned this for her social media account, and by the time the girls finish with "grandpa shark," we're joined by the rest of our team.

My oldest niece's charge is a tiny Asian girl who runs around with her arms straight down by her sides as if she's never heard of pumping them before. There's a Hispanic girl who's big for her age and could prove to be a powerhouse on defense. And last, a theater kid shows up, as recognized by my own childhood. She sings the shark song with a fake British accent and adds extra flourishes to the moves. If I introduced her to my agent, she'd soon be playing a young Zooey Deschanel.

I much prefer these crazy kids to the adults watching me. Even parents from other teams snap pics as they walk by. I try to ignore them.

Bex paces. "Are we warming up now, Coach?"

"Yep."

Most folks retreat to their camp chairs and cell phones. Not Bex. She watches with rapt attention as if longing for a whistle.

Her intense scrutiny makes me almost feel silly when I shout, "Give me an L!" and make an L shape with my arms.

The girls mirror my actions. "L!"

I lead them in spelling out "lady," then follow up with a simple dance to a cheer based on the role that won me my first Kid's Choice Award. "We are the ladybugs, the lovely, lovely ladybugs."

The girls eat it up.

"Nice touch," my sister-in-law calls from the sidelines.

My team in the film referred to themselves as mighty, not lovely. But "mighty" just didn't seem to fit with ladybugs.

My back is to both her and Bex, but I overhear Bex say, "That cheer reminds me of an old sports movie."

"He was in that movie," Jacqueline responds, destroying all anonymity. We'll see how Bex's attitude toward me changes.

I hit "play" on the theme song from Rocky to drown out Bex's response and demonstrate different drills in a circuit. The girls go for it with gusto, rotating stations every time I whistle, and it's even better than a movie montage. Even with a couple of players in tutus.

It's real life. And it's not bad.

Music is blaring. The sun is shining. My endorphins throw a party.

"Are you going to run a practice game?" Bex's voice is the scratch of a record.

I glance at my watch. We've been having so much fun that we only have about fifteen minutes left.

"Of course." I truly had been planning to play a game.

"They need to know every position because even though they tend to run around like a herd, they're supposed to rotate through them. I've got it all organized in a binder if you want to borrow it."

I smile over because she must be joking. Nobody needs a binder for eight-year-old soccer.

Her face is completely serious. It's a pretty face except for the bump on the bridge of her nose, which, in this case, reminds me of the horn on a charging rhino.

I wrangle the corners of my lips down to answer without jest. "We'll play four on four without goal keepers since they already practiced goalie drills."

"Aww..." Paloma groans. "I wanted to be goalie, so I don't have to run very far."

"I like running." Kendall zooms by, arms stick straight.

I'm hiding my smile again. It's been a while since I've smiled this much.

I cut the team in half, put the soccer ball in the middle of the field, and blow my whistle. Paloma is closest. She winds up her leg and kicks the ball directly over the parents' heads. Bex ducks before chasing it down.

"Paloma." I drop another ball in front of her. "The goal is to get the ball in the net. That's why it's called a goal."

Paloma grins mischievously. "But if I kick it out of play, I get a break."

Okay then. "Let's rotate."

I bring Mia and Treva into an offensive position and blow the whistle. They do their thing like a couple of pros, but they're turned around and score a goal on themselves.

Bex steps up beside me. I don't look at her, but I can feel her energy. Also, she smells like green apples. I doubt it's perfume because she's not the perfume type, so it must be her shampoo.

"Before every half, you'll need to ask each girl individually to point the direction she's supposed to take the ball," she states. "It's the only way."

I look at her then, and she apparently takes it as an invitation to offer more suggestions.

"Jacqueline said you're an actor. Do you know any cameramen who could come film practices so we can show the girls their mistakes?"

That's what she gets out of the fact I'm an actor? She doesn't care about my fame, only my access to film equipment. With what I know of her, it makes sense. Filming the girls, however, does not.

"They're eight."

"They've come a long way since I started with them four years ago. I bet they're ready for some trick plays."

I can't hide my smile this time. But I'm able to turn my face toward the mountain range in the distance before laughing. "You realize you take all the fun out of playing?"

She presses her lips together, though with the way her eyes glaze over, it's obviously not a smile she's hiding. "You won't have to worry about getting red-tagged after all," she says.

There's no doubt it's the worst insult she'll ever give a person. And on that somber note, an enjoyable practice comes to an end.

As soon as Riley's mom distributes fancy soccer snack packs and pulls out her camera to commemorate the moment, Bex takes off with Mia.

I watch her walk away, wondering if I should apologize for hurting her feelings. I didn't say anything that wasn't true. She'd ruined my fun, but maybe fun for her is winning.

I take a couple steps after her and am about to break into a jog when a flash blinds me. I hold up a hand to block the light and turn to see where it's coming from.

Influencer Mom. She hands the camera back to Dance Mom. "Will you get my picture with Skylar and my snack pack?"

Before I know it, there's a line of players and parents wanting pictures with me like I'm Santa Claus. Strange this didn't happen while Bex was next to me. Or should I say crazy? Perhaps Bex's craziness scares everyone else away.

Which means she has something to offer me in exchange for letting her help coach after all.

Bex

You can discover more about a person in an hour of play than in a year of conversation. – Plato

I watch Skylar Hayes's little sports movie, and though it's based on a true story, I learn through IMDB that the ridiculous cheer they did was added for effect. It's all Hollywood, as was his using it for our warmup at practice. He has no idea what it takes to win.

Of course, I know him from the *Water Fight Professional* series too. But his film bio shows he hasn't been acting for the past decade. He's simply another child star who's trying to get back into the limelight by doing foolish things.

Having him coach the Ladybugs is certainly foolish.

Yeah, I was thrilled we'd found a coach at first. It pains me to remember the way I called him a hero. I even found his sad eyes sexy in a tragic sort of way.

Okay, I may have even admired Skylar's physique, but that's because he has the long build of a soccer player. The way the corners of his lips kept turning up also reminded me of the guys on the soccer team in high school. They were the ones with a good sense of humor. While the football team just liked to grunt and drink beer at parties, the boys on the soccer team attended other sporting events to cheer on their classmates, or they served on the student council.

Take, for example, our senior class president, Benji Morelli. He stood next to me in line for our Annual Can Toss where we tossed all the cans collected in the Thanksgiving food drive down the hall from student to student to a waiting truck. I wasn't very good at catching the cans, and I blamed it on being a soccer player, therefore never learning how to catch. So Benji rewarded me with one of the M&Ms he'd been eating for every can I caught. I haven't seen Benji since, but the candy still holds a special place in my heart.

All that to say, after I realized that Skylar didn't know much about soccer, I'd still had hope he'd make practices enjoyable the way Benji did for feeding the hungry. But then Skylar blamed me for ruining his fun and being the crazy one. Not to mention the way his oversized ego simply assumed I wanted an autograph. Unbelievable. I'll bet he went home afterwards to grunt and drink beer.

Skylar may be a hero in old movies, but he's not my hero anymore. I'm taking matters into my own hands by bringing a megaphone to Mia's first game. Even if I can't coach, I can shout directions from the sidelines.

I'm brushing Mia's hair into a ponytail in the parking lot as an excuse to spy on our "coach" before joining him on the field this brisk Saturday morning. Today's high should get into the low 70s, but according to my five-year-old Kia Soul's temperature gauge, it hasn't yet reached sixty degrees. Perfect for running around on the field. Not so perfect for parents sitting in lawn chairs. I shiver, realizing this includes me now. For the first time, I lament not bringing a thermos of coffee.

I sharpen my glare across the buzzing fields at the man taking my place. As I watch, he looks both ways then bends down to talk to Kendall. She points toward the net on the far side, and I realize he's following my advice.

He must have asked her which direction she's going to try to score for the first half. There's no way she would have moved her arm otherwise.

This bodes well for Skylar listening to my instruction through the megaphone, but it makes me mad that he's acting secretive about it. Like he wants to call my coaching techniques crazy then take the glory for himself.

My fingers curl into fists with Mia's hair clutched inside.

"Ow."

"Sorry." I release my grip and snap her headband into place to keep stray hairs from sticking to her sweaty face and possibly preventing her from seeing the ball.

"What's this?" Mia pulls my new megaphone from the backseat, squeezing the handle and making it squeal.

"Since I'm not your coach this year, I thought a megaphone would come in handy if I have something I want to say to you during the game." Yeah. That's not too crazy, is it?

Mia grins. "Like a cheerleader?"

I never imagined myself a cheerleader, but at least the powers that be can't stop me from cheering. "I'm your biggest cheerleader."

Mia squeezes the handle again and holds the megaphone to her mouth. "Give me an L." Her voice echoes across the open space.

Skylar looks over from where he's stooped in front of Riley. Riley is also pointing at the far net, meaning he knows I caught him red-handed. My turn to smirk.

Riley sees us and lifts her arms to make an L-shape. She yells in response though I can't hear her from here.

I grab my dumb lawn chair and lead Mia across the parking lot.

She squeezes the megaphone handle to activate it again. "Give me an A."

The twins join Riley, responding together. It does my heart good to see them act as a team even when I'm not their coach.

We step up into the grass.

"Give me a D."

Paloma and Charlotte make the motions. Kendall's mouth moves, though her arms stay by her sides.

"Give me a Y."

We've gotten close enough that I can hear them now. Even quiet little Treva joined the cheer. "Y."

"Why?" Skylar echoes, but his voice holds a groan, so I know he's not cheering but questioning my megaphone.

I love that I can get under his skin the way he's gotten under mine. I grin in triumph. "I thought you liked cheers." I mimic his dance moves from practice. "We are the Ladybugs, the lovely, lovely, Ladybugs."

He crosses his arms as if he's Dylan Elliot. Maybe I just have this effect on men.

Except he's not looking at me. He's looking at the surrounding fields and other teams.

I follow his gaze to see almost everyone else focused on us. Movement has stopped. Jaws hang low. Cell phones rise, likely in camera mode.

If he appreciates cheers, then he must adore attention. I'm getting him what he wanted. My plan backfired.

"Okay, crazy lady," he says.

I stomp my foot indignantly and open my mouth to defend myself.

He cuts me off. "Here's the deal."

I close my mouth. If he's offering a deal, there might be something in it for me. In which case, I'd allow him to think me crazy in exchange.

"After you left on Wednesday, I got swarmed for selfies and autographs."

I frown. Not sure how this pertains to me. Except that I'd turned him down when he offered both. And apparently my presence kept others from asking while I was there.

If he loves that kind of attention, then maybe he wants distance from me. Meaning he wants my kid off the team.

My pulse surges. Mia and I are back where we started before he was hired. I'd dethroned him as my hero, and now he's becoming the villain.

I grab one of his forearms folded over his solid chest, ready to do battle. We didn't make it this far for nothing.

His gaze drops to my hand then back to my face. "I need you to stick close to me to scare away the public."

I'm stunned. First, by the discovery that he doesn't want attention. Secondly, by how hard I've been digging my fingernails into his flesh. After I release my grip, there are crescent moon-shaped indentations in his skin. I rub them gently as if that'll wipe away all hostility between us.

Okay, the hostility was all on my side, but the way he's been brushing me off as a psychopath made me hostile.

I swallow the lump in my throat. If he needs me sticking close to the coach, then that might make me—dare I hope—Assistant Coach? "How close?"

He presses his mouth shut for a moment like it's going to pain him to answer. "Assistant Coach close."

"Yes." I pump my arms in the air and jump up and down like Mia just scored a goal.

This draws more attention from strangers.

"What did she say?" one stranger asks.

Jacqueline is there to answer. "She said yes."

Skylar holds out a palm to stop my celebration. He leans toward the strangers. "I asked her to be my assistant coach. That's all."

I laugh. What else would they think "she said yes" meant?

Oh.

I laugh harder, then share my joke with the strangers. "Coaching is so much better than a marriage proposal."

"Thanks for that," Skylar deadpans.

Like he doesn't already have enough women pining after his soulful eyes and smirky-smirk. For all I know, he's married with more children than his brother. Or worse, unmarried with more baby mamas than my dad. I'm just here for the game.

"Okay." I clap my hands, ready to go. "I say we start with Paloma at goalie. The twins are great at defense. Treva and Mia can run offense."

I look around for my daughter. The team is all in one big dog pile. They really are like puppies sometimes.

I grab the abandoned megaphone and bark into it. "Paloma. You're goalie."

The large girl at the bottom of the pile rolls over, knocking off everyone else. "My dad said goalies wear a special jersey. Do I get a special jersey?"

If I was head coach, I'd have brought a long-sleeved jersey to offer extra protection. I look to Skylar who is standing way too still for a coach that should be getting his team ready for a game.

I lift the megaphone to my lips, even though he's directly in front of me. "Do you have a goalkeeper's jersey, Coach?"

He twists a finger in one ear at my ridiculous amount of volume, then holds out the hand, palm up, fingertips beckoning.

If he thinks I'm giving him my megaphone—

"Give me your megaphone if you want to coach."

Sadly, he's got the power of Arnold Shwarzenegger telling me to come with him if I want to live. I sigh and hand it over. But my megaphone wasn't any more ridiculous than the music he turns on his Bluetooth speaker to repeat the same warmup from practice.

The twins lead the dancing.

I jump in as soon as the song ends. "Now we need to stretch to prevent knee injuries."

I demonstrate how to stand on one foot to stretch their other quadricep.

The girls all fall over dramatically, which I should have expected. Besides being eight, their coach *is* an actor. I demonstrate a seated quad stretch.

"While you're down there..." Skylar drops into half a burpee to end in a pushup position. "Let's do some planks to shred our abs."

The girls collapse again with overdramatized pain while the moms ask Skylar to prove he knows about shredded abs. To his credit, he ignores them. The moms, not the girls.

And I'm happy to report that I hold a plank longer than our fearless leader. Core strength came in handy when performing my famous flip throw-in.

Skylar flops to his belly.

I take an extra second to gloat.

He gives a small shake of his head, though I swear there's also a flash of admiration in the depts of his dark irises.

As if burned by the spark, I jump up. Though I'm simply demonstrating how to stretch hamstrings in a forward fold. I'm more concerned about preventing knee-injuries than the opinion of Skylar Hayes.

The team joins me in touching our toes, though nobody is as bendy as I am. Whereas having stronger abs made me look tough in the plank competition, being more flexible just means my bony bum sticks up the highest in this stretch.

I'm watching from between my legs and waiting for Skylar to take over again, when the young ref I yelled at last year wanders toward our team.

"You guys ready?" he asks Skylar then turns my way. I can tell the moment he recognizes my fanny because his cheeks turn pink, and he backs up. "No rush. I'm here to help your team."

I jolt upright fast enough that stars sparkle in my peripheral vision and my hearing fuzzes.

"That was weird." Skylar's words break through before his face comes into focus. He's aiming a thumb over his shoulder at the retreating ref. "I know he's a kid, but I'd expect him to be unbiased rather than here for our team. I hope it doesn't have to do with me."

No need for me to confess last year's temper tantrum that led to one too many points and a red-tag. I'm still learning my lesson. "It's probably you."

"Well, whatever. We're not here to win. We're here to have fun."

Did he just say we're not here to win?

I stare at Skylar, waiting for one corner of his lips to twitch at the joke, if not cracking into a full-fledged smile. But he's already moved on as if he was completely serious. He meant it. And I realize that for us to win, he and I are going to have to continue to play the roles of good coach/bad coach.

He'll be the fun one. Meanwhile, I'll lead the team to another victory.

Skylar

Always aim to play the long game. Instant gratification cannot build a legacy.
—— Andrena Sawyer

Bex leads the team to victory, losing her voice in the process as only crazy coaches do. More importantly, the kids have fun. I make sure they don't win by more than the allowed seven points, and Paloma gets to pick flowers inside the goalie box. Now the girls all wear dandelion crowns, and they seem prouder of the flower chains than their first win.

My assistant coach opens her mouth to bark orders but ends up squeaking instead. She taps her neck à la Little Mermaid and looks to me for help.

I cross my arms and grin at her predicament. If only a hoarse voice lasted five weeks, this season would be perfect. "Speak up," I tease. "How are you going to be my assistant if you're too timid to talk?"

She rolls her eyes to heaven and shakes her head, but the corners of her mouth lift toward heaven too. My goodness, she might have a sense of humor after all.

When she makes eye contact again, it's with a mix of indulgence and purpose. She points to where the other team has formed a line, facing us. We're apparently supposed to high five them the way we did in my old sports film. High fives must be a real thing.

"Line up, girls."

Mia spreads her arms like airplane wings and soars to the front of the pack. The rest follow suit. Except for Kendall, of course. Her arms remain glued to her sides. Those are going to be some low fives.

Bex steps behind them, so I join the line too, holding my hand at a height the girls can reach.

"Good game. Good game. Good game." It's a chorus of tiny voices and one adult whisper.

I can't resist. "Come on, Bex. Be a good sport. Tell the other team 'Good game.'"

She halts without warning and rams an elbow backward toward my gut. I grab onto her shoulders to both avoid her attempted assault and keep from knocking her over.

"Playing dirty?" I'm close enough that only she hears my question. And only I smell her fruity shampoo.

We've reached the other team's coach now. She's a grandma who crocheted all through the game and is still holding what looks like a Harry Potter scarf-in-progress attached to her crochet hooks. Perhaps she should be coaching quidditch instead.

Rather than simply high five us, the gray-haired granny grasps our hands with her frail bird bones. Her voice warbles. "Good game."

I echo the sentiment, releasing one of Bex's shoulders to let the little old lady congratulate me on kicking her booty. "Bex, don't be rude. Tell our opponent 'good game.'"

Her elbow gets me this time.

I may have deserved the sharp jab to my ribs, but it just makes me want to tease her more. "Hey now. Throwing elbows isn't allowed in soccer. If you want to get physical, you'll have to slide tackle me."

She turns her head to glare, but something else catches her attention, and her eyes bulge.

I completely release her in order to pat the top of the other coach's hand. "I must apologize for my assistant coach. She's a shy little thing."

"Young man." The grandma titters. "That means she's taken with you."

"I had my suspicions." I grin over at the normally boisterous woman who is most definitely not taken with me. She's so not taken with me that she doesn't even hear the conversation we're having about her. She's too busy watching our team as I should be doing.

"Treat her well," Grandma advises, and this joke isn't funny anymore.

"Yeah, I'd better..." I point the direction Bex is facing and jog over to see what the fuss is about. By "fuss," I mean she's being suspiciously quiet, even for having lost her voice.

I step beside her and follow the direction of her gaze to find a guy with a big camera on his shoulder interviewing the girls on our team.

My pulse surges. Paparazzi. I'm not sure what the law is on filming at a public park, but I do know he can't air footage of children without parental consent.

"Hey." I take a step forward. That's when I see my agent.

Craig stands out because he's a string bean but also because he's wearing a sports coat on a Saturday morning. We've been waiting to hear back on an audition for a big role, and the only reason he'd have come down here in person is if he has good news.

My heartbeat hitches for a whole different reason this time. I did it. My career is going to make a comeback.

Craig strides over in brown leather shoes that are designed to look like dress shoes but feel like sneakers. I've seen them advertised on social media and wondered if they're worth the hype, but, at the moment, they're not my biggest concern.

"Did I get it? Am I the Scarlet Pimpernel?"

He squeezes my shoulder. "No, no. They went with a British actor for an authentic accent."

I run a hand through my hair. "Sink me."

I really thought I had the part. I mean, I could relate to being married with a wife trying to interfere in my success. But maybe my failure isn't Gretchen's fault after all. Maybe nobody wants to see me act anymore.

Craig chuckles. "I'm here because you mentioned your assistant asked for film of the games like a professional sports team."

"What?" Oh yeah. Soccer. Bex. Crazy. "I wasn't serious about that. The girls are barely out of second grade."

Bex joins our conversation. Or rather, she claps her hands, points at the cameraman, then presses a palm over her heart.

I rub my throbbing temple. While the other coaches are crocheting Halloween costumes for their grandchildren, we're the team training like the pros to beat up on them.

"You know, we could have filmed on an iPhone rather than bring out an actual cinematographer."

Bex shakes her head as if I'm the ridiculous one. She extends a hand in a silent attempt at introducing herself to Craig and thanking him for what she seems to consider the greatest gift she's ever received.

Craig grips her palm. "You must be Bex. I've heard so much about you."

She lifts her lashes to look at me with a flash of surprise in her grayish eyes.

"Don't worry. It was all bad," I reassure her.

There's her lip tilt again.

Craig waves the cameraman our way. "Damian, get over here. Meet Bex. She's going to tell you what kind of footage she wants you to take at future games."

I exhale and check on the team. They're sprawled out with their snacks, and Paloma is giving a demonstration on how to hook dandelions together. They don't seem at all interested in the cameraman or the idea of watching themselves play soccer.

Bex pulls out her phone and starts tapping away. She holds the screen up for Damian to read. Losing her voice isn't going to keep her from bossing people around.

"Okay, here's the deal." Craig pulls me to the side. I should have known he had an angle. He wouldn't have come simply for my niece's benefit. "I got you an audition for a soccer film."

I nod slowly. Playing in a soccer film won't get me away from the roles I've been typecast into, but it can reintroduce me as an adult. Could be a smarter way to go. As long as I'm not wearing a mascot costume. "Is it a leading role?"

"Yes. Think Ted Lasso in the States."

"Right-o. The States is good since my British accent apparently needs improvement," I say this in my awful accent.

"Moving on." Craig nods toward the team. "Damian will film the girls playing to make your assistant happy, but we're also going to leak some footage to the press. Whet viewers appetites so they hunger for more of you."

My accent disappears. "Craig…"

He holds up his palms. "I know you don't like press. You're not in this for fame."

As compared to Gretchen.

My eyes wander the field and catch on Bex. She may be crazy, but that's a sign of not caring what others think. She's doing what she loves because she loves it. We should all be so crazy.

As a kid, it was fun getting paid to throw water balloons and snowballs. It was fun to play an angel on a skateboard in *Angel Warz*. I did things nobody actually does in real life. Then I watched and listened to viewers laugh and cheer. I made them feel good. That's movie magic.

Making movies is about the viewer. I'm there for them. Not the other way around.

"I'm here to coach the team. They aren't here for me."

Craig spreads his arms wide. "It can be a win-win."

"No."

"Your assistant would understand. She likes to win."

I lower my eyebrows in warning.

"You realize you're self-sabotaging again, right?"

I didn't self-sabotage before. I willingly sacrificed my career to travel to sets with my ex-wife. When she started getting offered bigger roles, I didn't want the distance to come between us. I don't regret my support. I regret finding out the hard way that she cared more about my stardom than me.

I'll never make that mistake again. And I'm not making a mistake now.

"If I get the soccer role, it will be for my acting, not for exploiting a bunch of kids."

"Don't use the word 'exploiting.' It makes me sound bad."

"You're making yourself sound bad, Craig."

He huffs, meaning I've won the argument. Now for more important topics...

"Are your shoes comfortable?"

"So comfy. Listen." He juts his head forward in the kind of bad posture only tall, skinny people have. "The public thinks you abandoned Gretchen out of jealousy. They don't adore you anymore, meaning casting directors won't adore you either. If you want to work, you have to show your audience how lovable you are. You must play the game."

I want to act for a living. I want to be genuine in real life. Never the two shall meet, and I must make that clear if Craig is going to continue representing me.

I cross my arms like the good coach I am. "Soccer is the only game I'm playing."

Bex

Work and play are words used to describe the same thing under differing conditions. -Mark Twain

The warm rain blasts us like we're riding a log over a waterfall on the old Splash Mountain ride at Disneyland. But this is better. We're at soccer practice.

I thread my slick ponytail through the hole in a ballcap to keep water out of my eyes then lead Mia through the soggy grass toward Field Four and our fearless leader. I have to hand it to Skylar. Besides getting a cameraman to film our first game as I requested, he's the only coach who hasn't cancelled today's practice.

"This is perfect weather for teaching slide tackles," I call as soon as we're close enough for him to hear over the splatter of precipitation.

He faces me from under a red and white umbrella. "Slide tackling is illegal in our division."

Semantics. "It'll prepare the girls for their future. Besides, it's fun." This is the guy who warms up with dance moves and teased me when I lost my voice. "You like fun. Remember?"

"I prefer the kind of fun that doesn't involve hospital visits."

I harrumph. "There's risk involved in any sport."

His eyes narrow to study me through the waterfall cascading off his umbrella. "Have you been injured before?"

Feeling exposed, I realize I should check to make sure I'm not wearing a white t-shirt. Whew. It's my navy Under Armour jersey. Though my hesitation in responding to Skylar's question could still be revealing. So I shrug. "Hasn't everyone?"

His lips part. Presumably for a follow-up question.

Thunder rumbles in the distance then growls loud enough to make the base of my skull tingle.

Mia's hand slides into mine. "What's that?"

It's just the distraction I need.

I squeeze my daughter's hand. "That's the starter pistol. Ready to run?"

"Bex..." Skylar uses his warning voice for my name, per usual.

"As long as the lightning is outside a ten-mile radius, we're fine to stay on the field."

Jacqueline appears, her and baby dry underneath a polka dot umbrella. Treva is with her, but I assume the rest of her kids must be hanging out in the minivan. "I'll download a weather tracker app," she offers.

Skylar nods. "Thank you."

Treva wears a sweatshirt with the hood up over her head, but as soon as she sees Mia, the two of them jump in puddles together, so the hood doesn't really do much good.

Their teammates race from the parking lot to join them. A line of cars faces our field, windshield wipers running. Apparently, all the other parents decided to skip the fun in favor of staying dry.

The driver's side window of a black Cadillac Escalade slides down. Kendall's distinguished father sticks his salt and pepper head out the window. "This doesn't feel safe," he yells.

Jacqueline holds up her phone. "I'm tracking the storm," she shouts back. "If lightning comes within ten miles, I'll send the girls back to their cars."

He nods and ducks inside.

Finally. We can get going. I clap my hands and turn to see if Skylar is closing his umbrella long enough to lead the girls in a silly dance or if I should warm them up by running suicides.

Skylar continues to face the line of cars. "Was that Senator Thomas Kopf?"

Kendall bounces in place, looking like Larry from VeggieTales—a cucumber without arms. "That's my dad."

Tommy is a good guy. I may not agree with him politically, but I appreciate him for adopting his little girl from China. She's got more of a father than I had. She's got more of a father than Mia ever will.

"Let's get started, Coach. Want me to lead them in a lap?"

Skylar glances at me and blows out a breath. "No slide tackles."

"No promises."

"If anyone gets tackled, it's going to be you."

I laugh because that would totally be fun. "Come on, girls. If you beat me around the field back to this net, Coach Skylar will dye his hair red like a ladybug."

The girls take off ahead of me.

I jog backwards to catch Skylar's reaction.

His mouth hangs open, but once we make eye contact, he snaps it shut. By how hard he's pressing his lips together, I think he's trying to hide a smile. "If you lose, I'm canceling practice."

Lightning flashes in the distance as if putting an exclamation point on his threat.

Jacqueline reads from her phone. "Twelve miles and headed this direction." She grins up at me. "Looks like we're going to have to cancel anyway, so go ahead and let the girls win. I'd love to see Skylar with red hair."

"Hey." Skylar shakes his head at her, and I'm a little jealous she just stole his attention. But only because I don't have siblings of my own and thus will never have a brother-in-law like him.

I turn and jog after the team. My long strides easily catch up, passing Paloma first. The girl isn't even trying. But she cheers for the rest of them. "Go, Ladybugs. Don't let your mom beat you, Mia."

Mia is definitely the fastest. I'm only a little tempted to throw the race and let her win. As much as I'd enjoy forcing Skylar to dye his hair, I don't want to waste a minute of practice. The faster we get around the field, the sooner we can play a game, and there's nothing like playing soccer in a storm.

Thunder booms as we round the final corner. My pulse thrums in response. I've always loved to run, and soccer is simply the most fun way to run. I surge ahead, dots of water cooling my face.

The girls giggle and push each other, trying to pass me. Except for Kendall. Pushing someone would require her to lift an arm.

Almost there. Five more steps. I grin up at Skylar, expecting to see relief in his eyes, but they flicker with wariness.

Four more steps.

I push off through my back foot. My front foot lands in the mud. It slides sideways.

My arms fly wide to counterbalance, but before my back foot can catch my weight, I'm down. My hip hits the mud first. Thankfully the ground is too spongy to be jarring. A puddle splashes up, tasting bland.

Skylar charges forward, and I expect him to rescue me like the hero in a fairytale. I tense in preparation of human contact. It's been a long time since I've been touched by a man.

I can't let him rescue me. I can't let myself enjoy being saved. I'm not a princess. I'm a soccer player.

Before I can even finish my self-talk, he's past me. He whips his umbrella down and slides it shut. Then he uses it like a barrier to hold the girls back.

"Go, Bex," he calls over his shoulder to me. "Crawl to the net if you have to."

He's not concerned for me. He's concerned for his hair.

I should be relieved.

I roll to my hands and knees and lunge forward like a track runner on the starting line. Mia's sturdy frame charges into my peripheral vision. She's broken free and about to beat me.

Skylar drops the umbrella and scoops her up from behind, turning to block Treva who's hot on her heels. The little blonde giggles and attempts to dodge her uncle.

Mia wraps her arms around Skylar's neck as if to keep from being jostled. "You can do it, Treva," she yells.

Skylar sticks out his leg to hold her back. But now the rest of the girls have caught up. Fortunately for him, they're laughing too hard to put up much of a fight.

If he's going through that much effort to help me win, the least I can do is finish the race. I bound forward the last three steps to the net and raise my muddied arms in victory.

"Yes," Skylar shouts. He scoops Treva up in his other arm and spins the girls around.

As soon as he sets them down, the rest of the team surround him. I'm impressed he's able to stay upright. I certainly hadn't been.

He shakes his head at me in mock disapproval. "So much for trying to throw the race."

"I wasn't trying to throw the race." I wipe as much mud off my slick arms as I can. "Thank you for your concern about my fall, by the way."

"You're too insolent to be injured."

Little does he know.

A lightning bolt zigzags through the far side of the dusky blue sky.

"Eleven miles," Jacqueline calls.

I clap my hands together. "We've got a practice game to run."

He tilts his head. "Are you serious?"

"I didn't win that race for nothing." I retrieve a ball from the bag and head out to the middle of the field.

Thunder crashes.

The girls jump then giggle. They follow me the way I trained them to over the past few years, warming my heart despite the chill of being soaked.

"Fine." Skylar follows too. "Annie and Aby, you're defense behind Mia and Treva. You're going that way." He points toward the far net. "Which way are you going?"

Mia and Treva point. The twins spin like ballerinas and amazingly finish by pointing the correct direction.

"Good." Skylar positions the rest of the girls as he gives directions. "Paloma and Charlotte, you're defense on this side. Riley and Kendall, which way are you trying to score?"

Riley points. Kendall nods.

Skylar lifts the whistle to his lips, waiting for me to set the ball on the center line.

I squat and place the ball in the middle of the field. Before I've even stood up, the wind blows it away.

Annie and Aby do ballet leaps after it.

Skylar gives me a look. I look right back.

The sky crackles.

Goosebumps pop up on my arms. From the lightning, not from the look. Even if Skylar could have played Noah in The Notebook with that look.

"Ten miles," Jacqueline yells from the sidelines.

"Ten miles," he repeats to me.

"I heard." Though I wish I hadn't. At the very least, I wish I could schedule a make up practice. But why can't I? Skylar might not want to, but that's okay. I've coached without him for years. "You get the equipment, and I'll make sure the girls get back to their parents."

He studies me for another moment as if suspicious of what I'm about to do. But how would he know? "Thank you," he finally says.

My heart hammers, though I'm not doing anything wrong. I'm helping out. Assistant coaches run practice all the time when the head coach can't make it. "You're welcome."

We go our separate ways. And as I lead the girls to where their parents are waiting and lean into each vehicle to inform various moms and dads that we're meeting here again tomorrow, I justify my decision with the fact that I can still tell Skylar.

There. Anxiety eased. It won't be my fault if he already has other plans for his Thursday evening or doesn't get my message until it's too late for him to make it. He's not a bad coach. He's just not serious enough. Though the girls do seem to love him.

Mia trails behind me, dribbling a soccer ball against the wind.

"Ready, hon?" I ask.

"After I return Coach Skylar's ball."

I do a double take. The ball she's kicking isn't her favorite pink ball. It must be the one Annie and Aby went after, and Skylar forgot to grab it when he packed up. He's probably gone already though.

I look across the parking lot to find him slamming the trunk of his silver Tesla. Unless he hops behind the wheel and takes off like a Formula One driver, we're going to have to pass him to get to my Kia. That means there's no excuse not to drop off the ball. Hence, there's no excuse not to tell him about tomorrow's practice.

I bunch my lips together but follow Mia his direction. Wind whips strands of wet hair into my eyes. Maybe I can claim I didn't see him there. Except I'm intently watching him take off his wet jacket.

Mia picks up the soccer ball. "I've got your ball, Coach."

"Great. Stick it in the front seat." He runs his fingers through his slick hair as if trying to squeeze out excess moisture before climbing into his luxury vehicle.

He disappears inside, and she pops the passenger door open.

I cringe at the idea of tossing a dirty ball inside his pristine car without wiping it off first. "Wait, Mia."

She pauses and turns toward me.

I reach for the ball and rub it against my belly, using the wet jersey to clean off bits of grass and mud. I guess now is the time to tell Skylar about tomorrow's practice. I'll spin it like I just thought of the idea and offer to run the practice if he can't make it.

Thunder booms God's judgement. It's close enough to feel like a door slamming. My hair stands up on end with static electricity. Mia leaps unbidden into Skylar's car.

"Get in, Bex," he barks, and my first reaction is that he knows what I've done.

But no. That idea isn't a logical thought but comes from a belly full of guilt. Skylar is simply inviting me to seek shelter from the storm.

I slide into the front seat, lifting Mia to my lap. The leather is chilly against my bare thighs but smells clean and new. "I'm dripping all over your upholstery."

Skylar pushes a button, and though I don't even hear the engine rev, warm air blasts from the vents. "It'll dry."

"Do you have any napkins or anything?" I pop open his glovebox as if he's the kind of guy who goes through drive-up windows of fast-food restaurants and saves the napkins. By the emptiness that greets me, he's apparently not. He's the type of guy who will likely pay to have his brand-new car detailed while eating caviar in his beachfront condo.

"Sorry," he says as if more concerned about my well-being than the mess I'm making.

Wind rocks the car, and sheets of rain run down the windshield. Lightning explodes at almost the exact same moment thunder roars. But we're safe.

Mia angles the vents to dry our wet faces.

"Have you played in weather like this before?" Skylar asks.

I smile at a memory.

"Oh boy."

I turn my smile to beam at him. "Is playing in a blizzard better or worse?"

He twists his full lips in thought. "You wouldn't run the risk of getting struck by lightning, but you could get frostbite."

Mia turns to grin back at me. She knows this story well. "It was mom's favorite game ever."

Skylar arches his eyebrows to question my sanity, but he lets them drop before I even respond. "Figures."

I shove his shoulder. "Hey."

He rests his forearms on top of the steering wheel, settling in. "Well, you are known as the crazy coach, and only crazy people would enjoy playing soccer in a blizzard."

His tone is as cozy as the seat warmers, so I'm not offended this time. "I think that's *why* I enjoyed it so much." I lean back and sigh. "Only the people truly passionate about the sport were at that game in Minneapolis."

His expression softens, telling me he can relate on some level.

So I continue. "Since the snow kept covering up the boundary lines, the refs didn't make as many calls, and we just played for love of the game. I've never felt so free."

His dark eyes study me, and their sadness is truly sad for some reason. Maybe he's never felt that kind of freedom. Or maybe he's sorry I haven't felt it since.

Mia squirms on my lap. "Look, Mom. There's an app on Coach Skylar's car called Toy Box."

"Because he's a big kid," I quip. Then I hug her tighter. She's the kid that matters, and I won't let anything get in between us.

"I do like to play." Skylar's lips turn up. "And I guarantee the way we played at today's practice will be a memorable one for all our Ladybugs."

My heartbeat pounds louder in my chest. I know what a pounding heartbeat means. It means I have to do something I don't want to do. I have to tell him about tomorrow's practice.

Mia looks up from where she's been messing with buttons on the screen. "I wish I'd beat Mom in the race, and you had to dye your hair red."

Skylar wouldn't really have dyed his hair red. He never agreed to that bet. He simply played along like a good sport, making today's practice even more memorable for the girls, like he said.

"That was a little too close for comfort." Skylar chuckles then sobers. "You didn't hurt yourself when you slipped, did you, Bex?"

I palm my hip where I'd fallen, and for the first time notice it's a tender to the touch. But that's not what concerns me in this moment. What concerns me is how much I care that he cares. "I'm fine."

But am I? I want to see Skylar again. I want to coach with him. I want him to tease me and play with my daughter. I want him to ask how I'm doing.

My pulse pounds louder, though this time it's not because I have to tell Skylar about tomorrow's practice. It's because I want to. So I can't.

"Let's go, hon." I open the door, but as Mia and I walk away, the strangest thing happens.

An orchestra launches into the Carol of the Bells, accompanied by the flashing of lightning from behind. I turn in confusion to find it's not lightning. Skylar's car is putting on a Christmas show.

The driver's side window slides down. Skylar shoots me a huge grin. "Mia must have turned on my car's light show when playing with the buttons."

Mia laughs in delight. "I did this?"

I want to scold her, but the moment is too magical. Rain might as well turn into fake snow like we're a part of Hallmark's Christmas in July programming.

I smile back at Skylar. Well, until I imagine snow becoming a blizzard and blurring the boundary lines around my heart.

Skylar

Play gives children a chance to practice what they are learning. – Fred Rogers

The field is a different place today. The sky is blue, the sun is shining, and Bex can't get us killed by playing in a lightning storm.

I glance toward the parking lot in search of my crazy assistant coach. Not that I miss her. She's just usually the first one here. Plus we've come to a truce about coaching, meaning I understand her a little better now. She loves soccer the way I love acting.

A whistle blows, and I look toward the sound in expectation. But it's not Bex. It's some military-looking dude leading our opponents in calisthenics.

He whistles. His team drops into a pushup. He whistles. They jump to their feet and reach toward the sky. Nobody giggles.

Poor girls. They'll be so jealous of our Ladybug dance warmup.

Jacqueline leads her gaggle of children my way. She nods toward the other coach. "That's Dylan Elliot. He's Bex's nemesis."

"Ah…" I nod in comprehension. He's the one who tried to disband our team. He's the one she wants to beat by seven points even though it'll earn us a red-tag.

Jacqueline brushes crumbs from her hair—the result of letting your baby eat crackers while in a baby backpack. "I think our girls are ready for him. Treva's been practicing the trick play at home."

"Trick play?" When did they learn a trick play? The only trick I know about is when Bex tried to trick me into dying my hair red. Of course, her daughter is besties with Treva. They could have been practicing trick plays on a play date. A trick play date.

"Yeah, Bex taught them a trick play at Thursday's practice."

My spine shoots rigid. I squint to study Jacqueline closer. Did I hear her correctly? If my team had a practice without me, then it's because Bex called a secret practice.

Jacqueline continues as if she didn't just out my assistant as Benedict Arnold. "It was a bummer you couldn't make it."

"I would have loved to be there," I answer mildly. I don't trust myself to say more.

Just when I thought the two of us had formed an alliance, Bex does this behind my back. Unless she sent me an email and it ended up in my spam folder.

I pull out my phone to check. I type her name into the search bar. Nada.

Could I have missed a voicemail? I scroll to the app I rarely use and find a message waiting. Relief washes over me. I click on the icon and hold my phone to my ear, expecting to hear Bex's intense tone.

"Hey, buddy…" It's my agent. "Since you don't want me sending clips of your coaching to the press, I signed you up for a celebrity soccer tournament to get you the attention you need."

I'll deal with that later. For now, I hang up and stare out at the parking lot again, willing Bex to arrive early so she has time to explain. Though what explanation could she possibly come up with?

I know she has my number. I gave it out to all the parents despite the chance it could be leaked to crazed fans. Despite the chance they *are* crazed fans.

Perhaps make up practices are standard, and I just missed the memo? "Is a make up practice standard?" I ask.

Jacqueline shrugs, jostling my nephew hooked over her shoulders. "We've never needed one before, but Bex offered it to parents when practice was cut short Wednesday night."

She offered it to parents. Wednesday night. Before getting in my car with me. And she didn't say anything.

The timeline doesn't fit. Unless this had been Bex's plan all along. Unless she sent me to take care of the equipment while she returned the girls to their cars with the intent of betrayal.

"Let me get this straight. She offered the make up practice Wednesday night when returning the girls to their parents?" I probably sound like a broken record, but I don't want to believe it. I don't like thinking Bex didn't want me at practice. Especially after we played in the rain. Even if she didn't want me then, I would have expected her desire to change after warming up in my car.

What? Did she think I would be too busy cleaning her mud off the vehicle's leather seats to attend my own team's practice?

"Yeah." Jacqueline answers nonchalantly, too busy corralling her kids to question my inquiry.

My sister-in-law doesn't notice me rock back on my heels like I've just been slapped. She doesn't see my jaw set. She's not aware this is how I felt when I discovered my wife had married me to make a name for herself. I'm being used again.

"Kendall was the only one who couldn't make it besides you. She had a violin recital."

At least Kendall knew about the practice. Though she plays the violin? My eyebrows jump. "She plays the violin with her arms?"

Jacqueline grins at me from where she's wiping peanut butter off her toddler's face. "Maybe her arms are too tired from all the violin playing to pump when she runs."

"At least she had a good reason not to attend practice." I rub a hand over my face, unsure why I'm even here, not to mention how I'm going to get through today's game.

"All right, Coach." Bex jogs up beside me as if we're on the same team. "This match is going to be a lot tougher than last weekend's, but I've worked up a trick play." She holds out her handy dandy binder to display a page marked with Xs and Os.

While I was looking for her earlier, I can't even look at her now. I fold my arms and stare across the field at our opposing team doing jumping jacks. I'd rather be paired with Coach GI Joe. "Too bad we didn't get time to practice the play. If only we'd scheduled a make up practice for Thursday."

"Uh..."

Jacqueline stands upright, forehead creased with new awareness. "I'll go get the girls warmed up for you two."

"Thanks, sis." My gaze slides to lock with Bex's. To accuse her. "You didn't think I'd find out about your secret practice?"

Her lips pinch. Her metallic eyes dip. "Not this quickly."

At least she's honest. Maybe even contrite. But that doesn't make me feel any more wanted.

She closes her binder and hugs it to her chest. "It wasn't like everyone attended."

I roll my eyes. Lame excuse. "Kendall had violin. I heard."

"Can you believe Kendall plays violin?" She looks over to where Jacqueline leads the girls in spelling out L-A-D-Y. Kendall yells the letters as if not even aware her arms aren't forming the shapes. "With her arms?"

Here's hoping the little girl never goes deaf and needs to communicate in sign language. And here's hoping Bex learns to communicate at all. "Not the point."

Bex takes a deep breath. "I should have told you."

That's a given. I mean, Jacqueline even assumed I knew about the practice. It's not a question of whether she should have told me or not. The question is, "Why didn't you?"

Bex's eyes wander the field, as if looking for answers. Or avoiding the truth. "I like being in charge."

Another given. Maybe I shouldn't take her rejection so personally. I knew this from the start. But it doesn't solve our problem.

She can't be head coach anymore. I agreed to let her be my assistant to keep the fans at a distance, but I'd started to enjoy our relationship. That's the problem. This isn't fun and games for her. This is serious business.

For that reason, we might truly make a good team. We could balance each other out. "Are you willing to work with me?"

"Yes." She says this automatically. Robotically. Like she doesn't have a choice.

"You'll let me be in charge?" I challenge. Because it's *all* about her choice.

"Yes." She glances up with as much hesitancy as sincerity. She's willing, but she doesn't want to be.

"You'll prove it by not saying a word today?"

"What?" This time her response is aghast. Pained. Screechy. "You don't know who you're up against. You don't know the trick play. This is the one team I want to beat by seven points." She's finally opening up.

"All right. Here's the deal."

She stills, awaiting her fate with the kind of petulance I enjoy. If she's not open to having fun with me, I'll have fun at her expense.

"The girls have to know I'm in charge. So you can talk, but only to me."

Her gaze darts around as she processes. I give her time to consider her options. Her huff is all the answer I need.

"If you yell to any girls on the field, even once, you're done being my assistant."

Her eyes squeeze shut.

I may have taken her megaphone away last week, but this week I'm completely silencing her.

"Is this only for today's game?" She opens her eyes to read my expression. To beg me for understanding.

I almost want to give in. But last time I thought I understood her, it turned out I was being played. "It's a trial. We'll see how it goes."

Her chest rises and falls. "I agree to a trial. That means I'll try my best not to yell at the girls on the field. But this is new to me, so I would appreciate some grace. Like a reminder if my mouth gets away from me."

* * *

I wrap my arm around Bex's neck to clamp a hand over her mouth. Her muffled lips tickle my palm, and her stiff muscles radiate tension. We're behind by one in the fourth quarter, and she's stressed enough for both of us.

She turns her face my way, freeing her mouth and speaking directly into my ear. "Sorry. But you should call a timeout. We need to refresh the girls on our trick play."

I look down my nose at her, inhaling her apple scent. Maybe she's sucking on a Jolly Rancher, and it's not her shampoo I smell after all.

She's inches away, and I've got my arm around her shoulders like we're a couple, but the only thing she's thinking about is soccer. Which is how it should be. It's probably what makes me feel so comfortable with her.

Yeah, I'd been hurt when discovering she didn't want me at practice, but there's a little relief in it too. Like when Paloma kicks the ball directly off the field so she can take a break. I'm also out of play.

I unravel my arm from around her to form a T with my hands. "Timeout." Thankfully, timeouts are allowed in our league.

The young ref blows his whistle. Coach GI Joe glares across the field. Our girls jostle each other while dancing back to the sidelines.

Riley pumps her fists overhead. "Are we winning?"

"I feel like a winner," Charlotte sings to a Broadway tune I can't quite place.

Mia grabs her water bottle. "We're behind by one. Right, Mom?"

Bex shoots me wide eyes as if asking permission to talk to her kid. Does she think me a monster?

If it were up to her, I'd be a monster with red fur. So I embrace the persona and answer Mia's question. "Yes, we need one point to tie the game. But this is where we're going to pull out that trick play Coach Bex taught you at your secret practice."

Bex scrunches her nose bump at me, and all is forgiven. Not that I'll tell her so.

"We had a secret practice?" Paloma asks. She's probably wishing it had been a secret from her.

"Not me. I had a secret violin lesson." Kendall.

"It's not a secret if you tell people." Annie.

"Was it a secret violin lesson because you don't want anyone to know you can move your arms?" Aby.

"I move my arms all the time. See?" Kendall's arms don't move.

I drop to one knee to join them on their level and hopefully draw their attention. "You girls are doing great. Riley and Charlotte, you're on offense now, which means it's your turn to score."

Riley pulls an elbow to one side. "My mom loves taking pictures of me when I get a goal."

"Getting a goal makes me want to sing." Charlotte demonstrates by humming the scales.

I'm pretty sure everything makes her want to sing, but hopefully I can harness that energy. "Now the other team is going to try to stop you, so remember the trick. When one of their players comes after you, kick the ball backward to your teammate. Then stand in your opponent's way, helping your teammate to dribble around them and score."

Charlotte hums louder. The rest of the girls join in.

Coach GI Joe shakes his head at us, and now I want to beat him by seven points too. Though I'll be lucky if we tie.

The ref whistles.

I hold out my hand into the middle of our huddle. Bex's strong yet surprisingly soft fingers rest on mine. The girls pile their sweaty hands on top of ours.

I count them down. "One...two...three..."

We throw our arms in the air. Even Kendall, though our muscles probably did all the work for her. "Ladybugs."

I name the five players needed on the field.

Bex shouts after them. "Which way are you—?"

I pull her into another smothering hug. With as much as I've had to remind her to be quiet, one might think she likes being in my arms. Though we're both focused on the field, of course.

"Ladybugs," I yell. "Which net are you trying to kick the ball into?"

They look at us dumbfounded as if they've never heard the word "net" before. Mia stands in front of us on the sidelines and points for her friends to see. She's a miniature version of her mother.

The girls take their positions, except for Aby and Paloma who need to trade places. We're supposed to rotate them evenly through positions even if Paloma prefers being goalie and Aby wants to run defense with her twin. We could get a red-tag for not rotating.

"Aby," Bex tries to shout through my hand over her mouth.

"I got this." I soothe then raise my voice to be heard on the field. "Aby, you're goalie."

Aby's eyes grow to the size of soccer balls. Paloma groans but trudges forward to switch positions.

"Aby, you get to wear the special jersey."

A smile flickers over her face, but then she glances worriedly toward her twin as if she thinks Annie might be jealous.

Annie grabs her hand. "I'll miss you."

Bex twists out of my hold to hiss in my ear. "If you let me coach, we'd be winning right now."

I hate to admit that she's probably right, so I don't. "If you'd let me coach on Thursday, we'd be winning right now."

She rolls her lips inward and turns from me in what I'll consider acknowledgment. I wonder if she gets in her own way with every aspect of life or simply soccer.

Finally, the girls are in position. The young ref blows his whistle. We focus on cheering for our team. Well, Mia and I do. Bex is finally keeping her mouth shut, but she still grunts and points and jogs in place.

As if by magic, Charlotte dribbles down the field, faces off with a player from the Butterflies, kicks the ball backward to Riley, and positions herself to help Riley score. I hold my breath, willing the sporty girl to wind up with all the strength of Paloma and slam the ball past their goalie.

Instead, Riley runs with the ball. She casually jogs right into the net. I blink in surprise, but the whistle blows. That's a goal.

Our crowd goes wild. Especially Bex who shouts "Yeah!" before remembering she's supposed to refrain from shouting words and turns her cheer into whoops.

Riley's mom replays the video footage on her phone for the rest of the parents in case they missed her daughter's brilliance. It's sure to end up on Instagram later. As it should. Not only did Riley make an awesome play, but she tied the game.

Mia spreads her arms like airplane wings and flies a circle around Bex and me. The other girls on the sidelines follow.

I hold up a hand to offer my assistant a high five. She may be crazy, but that's what makes her crazy good at what she does.

When her palm strikes mine, I close my fingers around hers in thankfulness. Even though she snuck behind my back for Thursday's practice, I'm glad she had it.

My continued hold draws her eyes to mine, and for the first time she follows my instructions in staying silent, though there's a question in her curious gaze. And that's when I know.

I need her to coach me for my celebrity game.

Bex

It is easy to work when the soul is at play.
–Emily Dickinson

That extended high-five from Skylar makes me think he might have forgiven me for holding a secret practice, though the only reason I'm willing to forgive him for making me stay silent during this game is because Riley ties us up in the last minute.

Coach Dylan calls a timeout like he's actually scared of us.

My stomach has been churning with the dread of losing to him and his Chargers ball cap. Now I can breathe again.

"All right, girls." Skylar motions our team into one final huddle where I'm not allowed to talk.

Losing my voice at our last game was less painful than this. At least I can show him the timer I set on my watch so he'll see we have less than a minute left.

He drops into a squat to be on their level. "It would be great if we score again, but more importantly, we need to keep the Butterflies from scoring."

I want to say it would be great if we score seven more times, however I bite my tongue. I can't risk getting relegated to watching the game back with Influencer Mom. I want real influence.

Aby pulls her arms inside her special jersey, ready to shed the layer. "Am I still goalie?"

"Yes." Skylar helps her untangle her sleeves in order for her to wear the shirt properly again. "Goalies can use their hands, so you rush the ball and grab it whenever it comes near you."

"It's awesome," encourages Paloma.

Mia grins up at me. "Mom says good goalies have to be a special kind of crazy."

I cringe at the idea Paloma might think Mia's calling her crazy, though I stand behind the sentiment.

Skylar arches an eyebrow. "Coach Bex would know." He's calling me crazy, but that's nothing new.

Paloma laughs. Thank goodness. Every team needs a crazy goalie.

Mia grabs my hand. "Mom stopped playing goalie when she had a ball break her nose."

Everyone turns to study my schnozz.

I smile politely, not saying a word. Both because I'm not supposed to and because we need to get back to talking about the game.

Skylar's eyes lift from my nose to my gaze. They lighten from a bitter espresso to delicious mocha, and I turn away before drinking them in. Somehow, my skin still buzzes with his unique brand of caffeine.

Aby gasps. "That's why you have a big bump? I don't want a bumpy nose."

"It's not that big," Mia defends. Though she never saw me with a normal nose.

"Just grab the ball before anyone can kick it." It's good advice, but I'm not supposed to be the one giving it. I release Mia's hold to clamp a hand over my own mouth before I find Skylar's strong arm around me again.

Skylar stands to my level, but keeps his head bowed as if trying to hide his smile. He smiles a lot for a guy with sad eyes. "You'll be fine, Aby." He pats her on the head. "A little bit longer, then you won't have to play goalie again until the end of the season."

"I have to be goalie again?" she wails, totally missing the point.

He looks to me as if expecting help. Am I allowed to talk now?

Mia steps in as Mia does. "How about we just make another goal? Then the ball will go the other way."

Riley grins. "I'll do my trick play again."

Skylar takes a deep breath as if attempting to regain control. "Which way are we scoring, girls?"

They all point toward the correct net. We've got that going for us, at least.

He reaches his hand into the middle of our circle.

I wait for the girls' hands to pile on his first, so I'm not touching him. We've touched enough this game, and I don't want to get used to it. I already mourn the end of summer soccer as it is.

Skylar counts us down.

"Ladybugs."

Half the girls run onto the field.

We can end in a tie. It'll be okay. We'll just have to beat Dylan Elliott in the playoff game when I'm allowed to coach again.

The teams take their positions. I hold a palm to my trembling middle. Our game should never be this close. Even worse than my nausea is the joy Dylan must be getting from it. I refuse to look at him.

Maybe Riley will even score in that time, and I can go puke with relief in a port-a-potty.

The ref whistles.

Their tall girl kicks off, but Charlotte intercepts.

"Go—"

"Goatheads are weeds," Skylar yells louder as if finishing my sentence for me. Though why would I say something so ridiculous?

"What?"

"Would you rather I put my arm around you?"

Maybe. He does smell clean and musky. "Only if you want to get bitten."

Just like before, a defender blocks Charlotte's path. Just like before, she checks over her shoulder and kicks the ball backwards toward her teammate.

Now my arm wraps around Skylar, hugging him with excitement. In normal circumstances, it could be taken the wrong way. Under these circumstances, it's preparation for celebration.

The ball rolls directly to Riley.

"Smile, Riley," calls Influencer Mom from behind us with her camera.

To my horror, Riley smiles and waves. The soccer ball rolls past her. It rolls toward our net.

Thankfully, Aby sees the ball coming. Whether she runs toward it the way Skylar instructed or not, she's in position to stop it. All she has to do is bend down and grab the ball. The ref will blow his whistle, and the game will be over. We're not going to win, but we're not going to lose either.

"Aby, get—"

"Get down tonight," Skylar finishes as if I was singing a disco song.

Unfortunately, I've positioned myself close enough that his arm can wrap around my neck and muffle me.

I watch in muted horror as Aby squats, screams, then jumps into the air, performing an almost perfect toe touch that she must have learned in dance class. Does she think she's playing dodgeball?

The ball rolls directly underneath her into the net. The Butterflies scored. The game is over.

Cheers erupt from the other side of the field.

Skylar releases me. I have nothing to say now. Though I could if I wanted to since the game has ended.

All my feelings drain down to my toes. I'm numb.

"I don't believe it," Skylar mutters.

I'm sure Influencer Mom has the moment on film if he needs to see it again. I want to blame her for ruining the game, but she's not the only one to blame. Aby jumped over the ball so she wouldn't end up with a bumpy nose like mine.

Of course, it wouldn't have come down to that if I'd been allowed to coach the way I used to. Though that's my fault too, isn't it?

I run a hand down my face. I let my team down.

"We didn't win, Mom," Mia announces in shock. I guess her team has never lost before.

How do I coach a losing team? "Now we know how the other teams feel when we beat them."

No wonder we're not supposed to win by seven points. Just one point is brutal. Maybe it's more brutal. We thought we had a chance.

Aby has her twin to comfort her, but Riley runs off the field bawling.

"Uh..." Skylar places a hand on my back to gently press me forward. "Coach?"

Oh, now I'm a coach? I want to say. But it's more about me being a mom.

I reach down to hug Riley. "It's okay, hon."

But she's not okay. "I lost the game." Her voice warbles like she's an old lady who knits scarves.

I lift her little body into my arms, and she buries her wet face in my neck. I try not to think about all the snot and focus instead on the scent of coconut oil I know from her mom's social media account is used on her braids.

"We're a team. We win together, and we lose together." I rub Riley's bony spine. "You still made the outstanding goal earlier. That's something."

Her sobs quiet into gurgles.

Influencer Mom joins me, reaching for her daughter. "Sorry," she mouths to me. But then, like she's not even sorry, she says, "Riley, you looked so pretty in my picture."

Riley releases me to cling to her mother. Which is fine. I've got seven other little girls to line up for the walk of shame, not to mention a neck to wipe dry.

Skylar motions us to facing the happy team trooping our way. "Girls, I'm proud of you."

Mia looks to me as if to verify it's okay for her coach to be proud of a losing team.

I smile and nod. Because this isn't on them. This is on how well we coached them.

Mia smiles back bravely, and my heart really does swell with pride. I love that kid. I have to do better for her.

Skylar catches my eye like he's coaching me too. "Let's go congratulate the Butterflies for a good game then meet back here for snacks."

Riley lifts her head from her mom's wet neck. "Snacks?"

"My mom made us *cortadillo*," Paloma announces, her all-American accent turning Spanish when she pronounces the one word.

The rest of the team stares at her in confusion.

"Court of what?" Annie asks.

Paloma's smile shows off a missing tooth. "It's cake with pink frosting and sprinkles."

Charlotte singsongs, "Pink ca-aaake," and just like that, the Ladybugs feel like winners again. The players anyway.

They fall into line, facing the oncoming Butterflies. Riley even scrambles down from her mom's arms to join us. Skylar leads the way, and I pull up the rear.

"Good game. Good game. Nice toe touch. Good game."

The closer I get to Dylan Elliott, the more my guts sink with dread. But I choose to hold my head high and meet his gloat directly.

I recite the compliment and slap his hand. "Good game."

He catches my hand and doesn't let go. Kind of like Skylar did earlier, but not. Whereas Skylar's touch was congratulatory, Dylan's grip is an invitation to arm wrestle.

"Good game." His overly warm tone scorches my ears. "Don't worry about losing. It's not like you're playing professionally."

I freeze in my tracks. Is that a random jab, or a knowing dig?

He winks before turning away. He knows.

Oh, how I'd love to dropkick a ball at his behind. Or at least come up with some kind of scathing remark about how at least I'm coaching the sport I love. Though he'd probably twist it to use against me.

"Mom," Mia calls.

I turn to find my team already sprawled out on our sidelines, awaiting their paper plates of pink cake like it's a birthday party. Mia motions me to join the fun. At least nobody is sobbing anymore.

I take my time strolling back. I don't have an appetite for sweets.

Skylar stands with hands in his pockets, watching me. Paloma's mom offers him her homemade snack.

"Thanks." He accepts then turns to pass it to me.

I hold up a palm. "That's okay." I look around to find something else to do. Like gather balls or fold chairs.

"What did that coach say to you?" Skylar takes a bite of cake, though his dark eyes appear extra serious in contrast to the pink icing he licks from his lips.

I shrug off the question. Dylan's words themselves might have sounded kind if not for the undertone that I don't want to have to explain. "Good game."

Skylar harrumphs. "Not as good as if I'd let you help coach."

My gaze snaps to his. If he believes that, then why did he hold me back? Why would he do that to our team? "Did you want us to lose to teach me a lesson?"

He grimaces. "I thought we'd still win. I didn't realize what a difference you make."

At least he realizes it now. And acknowledges it.

I sigh. "Can I help for the rest of the season?"

His arches an eyebrow. "Are you going to have any more secret practices?"

I had that coming. We both learned something today. "No."

His lips curve up slightly. "Will you give me private soccer lessons for an upcoming celebrity soccer tournament?"

This request I didn't see coming. I tilt my head. Frown. Study him closer. How long has he known about his celebrity tournament? Maybe he didn't think our team would lose today, but he'd known I'd hate having to keep my mouth shut, and he figured he could use the horrible experience as a threat if I don't coach him. "Is that an ultimatum?"

A laugh bubbles from his chest. He's too lighthearted to issue ultimatums. Even today's attempts at silencing me had been playful. "It's a compliment. Flattery. You're such a good coach that I want you to help me coach The Ladybugs, *and* I'll pay you to coach me."

I meet his gaze for as long as I can before my heart revs its warning that I have to do something I don't want to. My head drops backwards in defeat. The whole reason for my secret practice was to avoid extra time with Skylar. But now, because of it, he wants to pay me for one-on-one time.

I'm available because it's summer vacation.

I could use the money to upgrade my mid-century modern home into this century.

Plus, I love coaching, so I'd take him up on this offer if it was anyone else offering.

But it's him. Which shouldn't mean anything. Except I like the way he looks at me with his soulful expressions. As does the rest of America.

"I'll let you run the next practice," he sweetens the pot.

I can't be bought. And flattery will get him nowhere. But now he's speaking my language.

My pulse pounds in argument. But it's going to lose like I lost us today's game.

I'll coach Skylar so I can coach the Ladybugs back to victory. This will only benefit my dream of someday coaching Mia's college team. Maybe even her professional team. While I'm dreaming, why not the World Cup?

Mia is my one and only priority. As I wish I had been to my mom.

Skylar

"Time is a game played beautifully by children." ——*Heraclitus*

Asking Bex to coach me was humbling, but I'm sure it won't even compare to the humility of letting her whip my rear into shape. I've got two weeks to prepare for Soccer in the Sand. The tournament is held every summer on Coronado Island, but this year they added a celebrity expo to draw more spectators.

My agent seems to think I need wholesome exposure if I'm going to pick up where I left off. As for me, I don't think I've changed much since my starring role at the age of fourteen when I just wanted to have fun and entertain.

At least, we're practicing on the beach, so I'll be in a beautiful location for the humiliation. I drive down from my home in San Clemente once again to meet Bex on her turf. I'd have invited her up to my private beach club, but Jacqueline is watching Mia, and I'm not going to make her bring her whole litter. Instead, I'll meet Bex there.

My brother's Mediterranean ranch screams 1990s with a bay window and basic garage doors, but it features five bedrooms and a big backyard in a family-oriented development, so he knows Jacqueline and the kids are comfortable when he's deployed. I open the iron gate to the courtyard, step over abandoned chalk and bubbles, then knock on the set of double wooden doors as a courtesy. After bare feet slap past a couple of times without letting me in, I thumb the lever on the rubbed bronze handle and enter the open concept living room with vaulted ceilings and honeyed wood trim.

"I'm here," I call to whomever might be within hearing range.

Treva charges out, but when she sees me, her double dimples disappear. "Oh..." she moans. "It's just you."

"Just me?" I scoop her up and toss her on the denim sectional so I can tickle her belly. "You're going to pay for that."

She tries to push me away, but her dimples flash again, and giggles choke her pleas for mercy.

"Don't you mean, 'Hooray, it's Uncle Skylar?'"

She attempts to slither to the floor like a snake. "Yes... Yes..."

I roll her back into the corner of the couch and wiggle my fingers in her tiny little armpits. "Then let me hear you say it."

"Hooray." She laughs and squirms and fights for breath. "It's Uncle Skylar."

"That's what I thought." I let her go.

She runs toward the archway leading to the hall. "Hide. Uncle Skylar is here to tickle us."

Her warning is followed by a chorus of screams and foot slaps in what will be a one-sided game of hide-and-seek.

Jacqueline appears in the archway. "This is the most peace I've had all day. The kids have been so higgledy-piggledy." She pads across the travertine tile and collapses onto a chaise lounge. "Thanks, Skylar."

I chuckle and lower myself onto a cushion across from her. "You going to be okay with another kid showing up soon?"

"Another kid?" Her eyes bulge. "Oh, you mean, Mia." She chuckles to herself and relaxes. "Mia will keep Treva entertained. And Oliva will be home soon from her nannying job to help."

My sister-in-law may get help, but she never gets a break. "Can I order you a pizza or something? A bunch of pizzas?"

She closes her eyes like a cat in the sunshine. "Have you ever had jalapeno poppers on a pizza? That sounds good." She's definitely prego. If the alarm at me knowing there's another child on the way didn't convince me, her craving for jalapenos did.

"I'll see what I can find." There's no jalapeno popper pizza to be found—if that's even a thing. But I order enough pepperoni and Hawaiians for the family to have leftovers.

"You'll make a good husband and father someday," Jacqueline murmurs, apparently too sleepy to remember I've already tried and failed in that arena. "I'm so happy you're getting to know Bex."

My suspicions that she'd originally been plotting to set me up with her friend are confirmed. "Bex is coaching me to play in a celebrity soccer game. We're not dating."

"I know." She smiles as if she thinks I can't see it because her eyes are closed. She must have learned that from her two-year-old.

Maybe in her dazed state, I can get some info out of her too. "Where's Mia's dad?" I ask.

Her smile droops. "That's a sad story."

I imagine Bex went through a divorce similar to mine. Except she got a kid out of the deal, so her story has a happier ending.

"Bex was drafted into the National Women's Soccer League and celebrated by partying a little too hard. She got pregnant without ever learning the father's last name."

Whoa. That's a lot of info to take in. I'm glad Jacqueline has her eyes closed so I don't have to worry about hiding my reactions to multiple revelations.

I'm stunned Bex made it into the pros. I knew she was good, but not that good.

As for Bex's one night stand? I'm tempted to judge her for it, but at the same time I feel compassion. How might her life have been different if the dude had stuck around?

Not to mention, she must have given up her dream career for her daughter. In my mind, that both redeems her mistake and explains her obsession.

I catch Jacqueline watching me from under hooded lids, and I take a quick inventory of my body language to imagine what she sees. Or what she thinks she sees.

My forearms rest on my thighs like I'm leaning forward in rapt attention. My eyebrows are lowered as if brooding. And I'm nodding for some reason.

"She won't mind that I told you. Mia knows. It's not a secret."

I sniff. "Unlike last week's practice?"

She smiles her small smile and closes her eyes again. "You two."

A knock jolts me to attention. I rise and answer the door since nobody else in this house seems to answer knocks, and it's probably Bex and Mia anyway. I just hope these wooden doors are solid enough to muffle the conversation I'd been having.

Before I can grip the handle, the door swings open, revealing Bex's big, surprised smile. In this moment, I have two realizations. First, she's surprised to see me, so thankfully, she must not have overheard the discussion I was just having. Second, even though she's got a bump on her nose, it fits with all the large features on her face. Without the bump, she'd be pretty. With the bump, she's expressive, and her expressiveness is what makes her beautiful. She doesn't hold back, unless, you know, I've got my hand clamped over her mouth.

She scans me from head to toe, and I wonder if perhaps she's having similar realizations about me. But then she asks, "You ready?" revealing she was simply checking out my soccer gear.

"I'm ready, but I'm not so sure about my sister-in-law." I shoot a thumb over my shoulder at a sleeping Jacqueline.

Bex twists her lips. "Hmm…"

Mia has yet to enter the house and cause a stir with Treva because she's been distracted by bubbles in the courtyard. She's creating a surreal scene in which iridescent orbs float around Bex and me.

I spend the magical moment wondering whether we should stick with our original plan or try to usher the kids down to the beach quietly to give their exhausted mom a break. I wouldn't get much practice in, but that's okay because there's two more weeks before the celebrity match.

Except… "I ordered pizza."

The iron gate clangs shut. Olivia sashays in, a teen version of Treva with longer blonde ringlets and glittery eyeliner flashing above her light eyes. She's got Kendall in tow.

"Pizza sounds great as long as there's no jalapeno poppers on top. Mom craves jalapenos whenever she's pregnant."

Bex's unplanned pregnancy might not have been a secret, but Jacqueline's is. And I'm not going to be the one to reveal it. My sister-in-law is probably waiting for my brother to come home on leave in July so she can tell him first, in person.

I evade a direct response. "Pepperoni and Hawaiian only."

Kendall bounds forward to pop the bubbles Mia's blowing. Only she pops them with her head rather than her hands.

Olivia drops onto a bench next to the girls. "Kendall heard Mia was coming over to play with Treva, and she wanted to join them. I can take care of them all, Uncle Skylar." She snickers. "You go practice your soccer skills. I wouldn't want you to make another team lose."

Bex's laughter joins in, guttural and infectious. And it's at my expense. At least she can laugh about Saturday's game now.

I shake my head at her then respond to my niece's jibe. "Thanks, kid."

Bex kisses Mia goodbye before climbing into my passenger seat.

I join her, wondering if she's also remembering the last time she'd sat here. When I'd thought we were becoming friends.

"Did Jacqueline ask for jalapenos on her pizza?" She breaks our silence with a doozy of a question.

If she shares my suspicions, then I'm not spilling any secrets. "You know it."

"Okay then." She tightens her ponytail to make it stick up higher on her head. "We're working you out extra hard today because next practice we'll bring Mia and Treva to the beach with us."

I groan. Not about bringing the girls but about what "extra hard" means to a woman who'd once made it to the pro level of her sport. "What am I getting myself into?"

She turns her radiant smile my way. "Nothing a little Advil and Epsom salts can't cure."

* * *

Running on the beach may look peaceful, but the way the unstable sand challenges every single muscle in my legs is the exact opposite of peaceful.

Were I to google antonyms, my run would be described as chaotic, disturbed, and lawless. Or as my southern sister-in-law has been known to call it "higgledy-piggledy." I've never used the term before, but I will now. It sounds like something eight-year-olds appreciate from their soccer coach.

Eight-year-olds would not appreciate the warmup Bex gives me. Such a grueling run would normally be considered my entire workout. And it only gets worse from there.

After two hours of dribbling and passing drills, Bex allows a drink break. I wait for my panting to slow before slurping liquid down my sandpaper throat. I slurp and slurp and slurp. The more I slurp, the longer my break will be.

Finally the light-headedness passes, and I stand from the drinking fountain. Lifting my damp t-shirt collar to mop my face, I'm disgusted by the ammonia scent of my sweat. Definitely not *People Magazine's* Sexiest Man of the Year material. Though I bet Chris Hemsworth can get pretty stinky too.

Thankfully the golden sun dips toward the ocean, and it'll soon be too dark to practice passing drills without the concern of taking a ball to the face. After Mia revealed the reason for the bump on Bex's nose, I would assume she's averse to such risks.

"We about done?" I hope.

She's still jogging in place but has the grace to look at her watch. "Is it eight already?"

"Feels like eight a.m." I'm gonna sleep well tonight.

"I was hoping to get into shooting drills, but we'll have to save that for next time."

"If I'm able to walk after today."

She cackles with a little too much glee. "We'll cool down and stretch. You'll be fine."

If her cool down is anything like her warmup, then we're going on another five-mile jog. I point to the pier. "Let's cool down by walking out there."

She finally stops bouncing and puts her hands on her hips to study our gorgeous surroundings. "It's been a long time since I've watched a sunset from the pier."

I'm curious if she's thinking of a past romance, but with what I learned from Jacqueline, I'm not going to ask. The memory might be sad.

"Come on." I stroll through the sand at a leisurely pace.

She rolls my soccer ball next to her orange cones and scans the boardwalk. As if satisfied there are no soccer ball bandits around, she falls into step beside me. "Why are we doing this?" she asks.

I glance at her out of the corner of my eye. Does she think I'm leading her on one of those long walks on the beach that people mention in their online dating profiles? If I let her think that, then I'd definitely be leading her on. Yeah, she's beautiful in her strong, determined way, but I'm not looking for any kind of relationship other than that of coach/assistant soccer coach. If we can get past the tension that came with our positions, then maybe we could become friends. That's it.

I shrug as nonchalantly as possible. "I'm not trying to create a romantic ambiance. I just thought it would be relaxing."

She stops. Tilts her head as if she has no idea what I'm talking about. "Romantic?"

Well. There I go sticking my cleat in my mouth again. She's not looking for love any more than she was trying to get my autograph when we first met.

I cringe. "Sorry. I'm just not dating right now, and I don't want to be accused of leading anyone on."

"I appreciate that." She takes off toward the pier. "Though I'm more concerned with the threat of you pushing me off the edge as revenge for the workout I just gave you."

"Not a bad idea." I attempt a light jog to catch up, but my right calf cramps. I have to slow enough to shake it out. "Oh, yeah. I would absolutely love to take you on a long walk off a short pier."

She watches with a wry smile.

Some ladies leaving the pier glance at me too, do double-takes, squeal, and pull out their phones to film me hobbling along. I do my best to resume a normal stroll and give a friendly wave. Wouldn't want to undo all the work I'm putting into repairing my reputation by walking like a zombie for a recording they're sure to post on social media.

Bex's eyes flick to their camera app screen, and she intentionally walks behind the women so as not to end up in my zombie footage. When we reunite on the wooden planks, she asks, "I suppose if you get that a lot, I can't ridicule you for assuming I wanted something more than the chance to help coach the Ladybugs."

I splay my arms in exasperation. "Thank you."

"I mean..." She looks me up and down, her silver eyes flash coyly. "You're a sweaty mess who walks the beach like you just crawled out of a grave. That's every woman's dream."

I chortle in surprise. "You should be so lucky," comes out before I remember she's not lucky in love at all. I'd planned to avoid the subject like I'm currently trying to avoid stepping on seagull poop.

But she continues forward toward the cotton candy clouds, and a breeze blows stray hairs away from her smile. It's not one of her huge smiles. It's small. Easy. And I appreciate that as crazy as she is on the soccer field, she's at peace with being single.

We make it to the end of the dock, at which point, I rest my forearms on the wooden railing and lean against it to take some weight off my aching soles. Naturally, she kicks a leg up on the railing to demonstrate a stretch. It's not a skinny or sleek leg. Rather, it bulges with strength and is decorated in bruises. If I hadn't realized she was beautiful before, I would have in this moment. She's a butt-kicking ballerina.

She motions to my tender calf. "Come on. I told you we're stretching."

"You're so getting pushed in." I balance on one foot and lift an ankle to the lower railing with a groan. Though my hamstrings protest louder.

She reaches for her toes easily. "When I asked why we're doing this, I was talking about training for the soccer tournament. You've never played before. Why now?"

I extend my arm toward my toes and lean forward the one inch my tight hamstrings will allow. Perhaps if I focus on the fire in my leg, I won't feel the pain of sharing my story. I don't normally tell it, but Jacqueline told me about Bex's past, so it only seems fair.

"I'm trying to get back into acting, and I'm auditioning for the role of a soccer coach."

Her foot drops to the wooden planks, creating an echo in the space below us. "Is that why you're coaching the ladybugs? To experience the role for real? Method acting or whatever?"

"No." I hold up a hand to calm her. How dare I have any goal but to beat Coach G.I. Joe by seven points. "I'm coaching for Treva. It wasn't until after our first game that I was offered the audition."

She studies me as if weighing my honesty. Her chest rises and falls.

"In fact," I add to my case. "My agent brought the cameraman to film the way you requested, but with the goal of leaking footage to the press. I refused to let that happen and agreed to this tournament instead."

Bex's chin lifts with the lightness of understanding. "When I suggested filming the girls, I didn't consider the public's interest in your involvement. Thank you for protecting them."

Man, she's emotional, but this emotion of gratitude brings me much satisfaction. "You're welcome."

She swings her other leg on the top railing and folds forward in silence. After a moment, she glances over, and I know she's about to ask the question I've been preparing for. "Why'd you stop acting?"

I hang onto the railing to switch leg without falling over. "My wife."

Her slate eyes squint then slide toward my left ring finger.

"I'm not married anymore."

Her gaze lifts to meet mine with the softness of empathy that can only be offered from someone who has experienced similar pain. "I'm sorry. Can I ask what happened?"

Bex

Play is the highest form of research. – Albert Einstein

I gave up playing soccer for Mia because giving up Mia was unfathomable. Meanwhile Skylar gave up something he loved for someone he loved, yet he lost both. My heart twists as I wait for his sad story. If he'll even tell it.

Maybe I shouldn't have asked. It's just that seeing someone in a good place then learning they've been through something bad gives me hope for my own future.

Also, Skylar's still in the overcoming stage. I'm helping him train for an event that could affect his career. His dreams. If he needs some encouragement to go along with the rear-whooping I just gave him, I could offer that too.

He lowers his leg from the pitiful little stretch and turns to lean against the railing. He stares out at the golden line of light reflected off the water from the setting sun. I let him, though I pull my own leg back to demonstrate a quad stretch. He really should lengthen his tight muscles if he wants to be able to walk tomorrow.

"You know I was a child star, right?" he asks.

"Right up there with Shirley Temple."

He drops his head and chuckles. "I'm usually compared to Zac Efron, but okay."

"I can see Zac, as well." Yeah, that's probably a better comparison, but not the point. When do we get to the wife part?

"I grew up fast and married young."

Oh good. He's not going to make me wait. I prompt him with, "I didn't know that."

I wouldn't be surprised if most people he interacts with already know his personal life from the tabloids, but I'm a single mom. I'm too busy surviving to follow updates on the rich and famous.

"Yeah." He huffs. "She played my girlfriend in the football movie."

I think I remember. If she's the actress I'm thinking of, she's become a lot more famous since. She has a reoccurring role in all those superhero movies. Might have even won some big awards. But I can't recall her name. "Strawberry blonde?"

He turns his head to study my expression. As if he wants to read my thoughts. Or maybe he expected more of a reaction out of me. I cheer for sports and freak out about protecting my daughter, but when it comes to celebrities, I've got nothin'.

"The strawberry blonde. Though usually people know her name now."

I shrug. "The most interesting thing about her is that she married you."

"Hm." He studies me some more.

It makes my palms itch. I release my quad stretch to curl my fingers in and scratch them.

"If only she agreed with you." He sighs. "Acting pulled us in two different directions, so I quit to stay close to her. She lost interest in me when my fame faded."

I shake my head at a loss for words. At a loss for his loss. "She said that to you?"

"She didn't have to. She simply left me for a bigger star."

I release my fist to splay a palm over my chest. Of all the reasons to leave that I've experienced, this might be the worst. While "the strawberry blonde" had unconditional love from her husband, it wasn't enough to satisfy. She gave it up for the world's conditional love. And one day, they'll turn on her like they do on everyone. Like they did on Skylar.

As for him? "It's no wonder you're not dating. How do you recover from a relationship where you have to compete with the whole world?"

He nods in thought. "I made a lot of embarrassing choices at first. I tried to numb my ache. I attempted to fill my emptiness. Mostly, I tried to prove myself as a man and ended up looking like an idiot in the process."

This is where he can be glad I don't watch Entertainment Tonight. Perhaps my lack of knowledge is why Skylar feels comfortable opening up to me. Whatever it is, I admire his transparency, accountability, and humility.

Thinking of my own mistakes and what it would be like to have them displayed for strangers to judge, I shudder. "We probably all try to prove ourselves in different ways at some point of our lives. What helped you through?"

He shakes his head at himself. "I can't believe I'm about to tell you this."

"You don't have to." I hold my breath in hopes he does.

"I went on a date where I thought I could impress this girl by bragging about all my old acting jobs and name-dropping celeb friends. Well, I went on lots of dates like that."

That sounds like the worst date ever. But it also sounds like he was a different person then. "Why does the one stand out?"

He rubs a hand over his face as if to hide his embarrassment. "She said she was going to the bathroom in the middle of dinner and never came back."

A laugh bursts out, and I smother my mouth the same way Skylar had during the last game. Why do I have to have such a big mouth?

Once I get my mirth under control, I move my hand away from my lips to apologize. Because this man has gone through some serious pain. It doesn't excuse his actions, but it makes them understandable. "I'm sorry. It's not funny." Except I contradict my own words by laughing again. At his expense.

He laughs along, relieving me from guilt. "You would have left the date too, huh?"

I picture the two of us at a romantic dinner, and my laughter dies down. Because it's a cozy image of the kind of relationship I'll never have. Even if I wanted it with Skylar, he's already set a boundary about not dating.

But that's not the image he asked me to imagine. He's a nice guy now who coaches his niece's soccer team and orders pizza for his pregnant sister-in-law, but I'm supposed to be imagining myself on a date with the jerk version of Skylar. Would I have snuck away? "No. I would have called you out."

One corner of his full lips curves up. The smile reaches his not-as-sad eyes. "I believe it."

I lean over to shove his shoulder with mine, and it's a good thing he's not still balancing on one leg.

"I would have deserved your tongue lashing." He shoves back. "But I would have defended myself. I needed this woman to leave me, so I had no one else to talk to but God."

Now we're getting to the life-changer. And I respect him even more. "What did you say to God?"

As he considers his conversation with the Almighty, the golden glow of sunset outlines his chiseled profile. Rather than stare in awe, I turn to join him in watching daylight drown in the glimmering sea.

Have you ever noticed how the sun sinks behind the horizon the way a credit card reader asks for a credit card? Slow...slow...slow...super-fast and done. Only sunsets are prettier.

Now we're alone on the pier in the afterglow of twilight, which is exactly what I worried about when Skylar asked me to coach him. However, he might need the shadows in order to open up. Plus the dim lighting will hide any longing that could possibly spread from my heart onto my face.

"It took me a while to talk to God," he finally admits. "First, I tried to woo the other women at the restaurant. Then I walked through the carnival, posing for pictures of people who recognized me. Finally, I ended up by myself on the beach in the dark."

A breeze ruffles his hair. He's at the beach again, but in a completely different place emotionally. Okay, now I'm definitely staring in awe at his profile. Or more accurately, the face of a changed man.

He slides his eyes to meet my gaze for a second. Like checking to make sure I'm interested before continuing. Or maybe my obvious interest was a little too much for him to face head on. Either way, he's looking out at the horizon again while I gape at him.

"Once I got away from the noise and had nothing to listen to but the crashing waves and the sound of my own thoughts, I got angry about my loneliness. I blamed God for letting my wife leave me. I asked him why he would make me so unlovable."

The light pales and the air cools. He turns my way for real this time.

I blink away my gape. Followed by any loneliness Skylar might be able to read in my eyes.

I don't blame God for my situation though. I blame myself. Skylar's the opposite, and I'm fascinated by hearing his side.

Well yeah, he made mistakes, but that was after his wife cheated on him. Though does anyone make mistakes from a place of fulfillment?

His wife must have had her own pain she'd been trying to ease with fame. But her selfishness caused pain for Skylar. Then he likely caused pain for the date who'd deserted him, among other people. Where does this cycle end? Why did it have to begin?

"Did God give you an answer?" I bite my lip.

"He gave me the answer a long time ago." Skylar shrugs. Not with nonchalance but as if what he'd been looking for had been right in front of him the whole time. "I don't know if you go to church or what you believe about God, but I was raised in Sunday School. I loved it because when I started acting, I couldn't attend a normal school anymore, so Sunday school felt like the most normal part of life."

I take a deep breath of salty sea air before responding. Most memories from childhood are painful, but not this one. "My mom didn't take me to church, but the neighbor lady did. It was my normal too."

He smiles in his understanding way. Who would have thought I'd have this in common with a famous movie star? While he was making his millions by throwing water balloons and snowballs, I was throwing myself into soccer to avoid a toxic home life among other things. Yet, we both found peace in the same place.

Skylar arches an eyebrow. "What's the very first song you learned in Sunday school?"

I don't have the heart to ruin his story by telling him it was a Silly Song with Larry, so I give him the standard answer. "Jesus Loves Me."

He nods like, *enough said*. "When I yelled, 'Why did you make me unlovable?' I immediately heard the words to Jesus Loves Me in my head."

I swallow the painful lump in my throat. It hurts for him. It hurts with the realization that his life was changed by a song he learned when he was Mia's age. My coaching position, ahem, *assistant* coaching position, is more than the opportunity to win. It's an opportunity to show a bunch of little girls what love is. While I'd thought I was failing them by losing to Dylan, I was actually failing them by caring more about winning a game than about being there.

Skylar continues, unaware of the current revelation he's inspiring. "At first, I laughed with cynicism at the idea Jesus loves me. I mocked the idea of a grown man needing reassurance from a silly song. From an ancient book."

"Hm…" I murmur. Because it's a popular perspective in our culture.

"But if I was going to blame God, then apparently I believe in Him, right?"

That's a quandary a lot of society has yet to face. I admire his willingness. "Right."

"So I asked myself what I believed about God. Did I believe the Bible? I didn't necessarily want to because there's a lot of insane stuff in there."

I nod in agreement. Jacqueline invited me to read through the entire Bible with her last year, and if you think *Game of Thrones* is bad, then you haven't read the book of 1 and 2 Kings. As for Queen Esther? She'd be a soccer player if she was alive today. She might even beat me.

"But the beginning and ending of the Bible make sense." He motions to the vastness before us. The silhouettes of birds flying over the sea. The waves rushing in and out. "There's no other good explanation for life on this planet other than creation and heaven."

I study the endless ocean now reflecting the full moon above. Perhaps long walks on the pier should be known more for their invitation to discuss theology than for romance. Though if one believes the Bible, then they're both about love.

"So I confessed right there that I believe in Jesus. Of course, if I believed Jesus came to earth and died for me, then I had to believe he loves me. Which meant I wasn't unloved."

Skylar makes it sound so simple. He's answered the questions I didn't voice earlier. This is where the nasty cycle of hurting each other ends. In being fulfilled by God's love.

He laughs. Not with the mockery he mentioned earlier, but with freedom. "I sang right there on the beach. I laughed, I cried, I sang Jesus Loves Me."

My eyes blur with tears as I visualize it. A broken man willing to admit he's broken and unable to put himself back together. Perhaps like a team of eight-year-olds who don't know the direction of the goal if they don't see their coach point it out.

"That's beautiful." While I'd intended to avoid contact tonight, I have to support Skylar's courage. I reach a hand to his forearm resting on the railing closest to mine.

He meets my gaze hesitantly. Hopefully. As if he revealed more than he'd planned and wasn't sure how I'd respond. I'm not sure what he sees in my response, but one side of his mouth lifts while his shoulders drop. The muscles in his forearm unbunch, reminding me that I'm still touching him.

My breath catches. While he's relaxing, I find myself tensing up. I need to back away. I need to lighten the mood.

I pull my hand off his arm, but what do I do with it? I'll stick it in a pocket. Oops, soccer shorts don't have pockets. I wish I was wearing that cute sundress I just bought with the pockets. But then this would really look like a date. Not that this looks like a date at all. We're just talking about love. I mean God.

Yes. Let's get back to Skylar's conversation with God and why we're even here in the first place. "Then God said, "Let there be soccer'?"

"And there was soccer." Skylar chuckles. "No, actually, I found direction in a scripture verse that isn't quoted often, but it should be."

My chin tucks into my neck with that. "Do tell."

"John 3:16 is powerful, but it's Philippians 3:16 that's personal." He quotes, "*Only let us live up to what we have already obtained.*"

Focusing on what one has already obtained seems like the opposite of pursuing dreams, which he's doing. It's the whole reason we're here. I have to ask. "How so?"

"I don't have to prove myself anymore. I'm already loved."

Okay. Rather than doing things to prove he's lovable, he's doing things out of love for others. He's living from a place of abundance instead of a place of need. "What does that look like for you?"

Half shrug. "I focus on what I already have and ask myself what I can do with it. I have a passion for acting. So now I'm looking for ways to use it."

He's not learning soccer to look good. He's learning soccer to be the best at an opportunity he's been given. Plus, he's free to turn down offers that don't fit this goal, like leaking Ladybug coaching footage to the media.

My toes curl in anticipation for him. With his mindset, he's going to live a grateful life whether he makes a fool of himself at Soccer in the Sand or not. Whether he lands the role he's hoping for or not. He's already a winner.

I wonder how I could apply his philosophy to my own life. In some ways I have. Like, rather than try to prove I'm lovable to men, I just love my daughter.

I consider sharing my story, but I'm not prepared to be as vulnerable as Skylar has been. I'll save it for another time. If ever.

For now, I'll simply enjoy standing on the pier with Skylar Hayes in the dark. If I focus on this moment that I've already obtained, I'll be living a life of awe for a long time to come.

Skylar

Play is training for the unexpected. –Marc Bekoff

I sip my creamy protein coffee and watch Bex lead the Ladybugs in a warmup lap. This is the practice I promised to let her run, which is good since I can barely move after the workout she gave me Monday. Calf cramps woke me up repeatedly that first night and my thighs still sting like I'm army crawling through shards of glass. But for some reason I feel light and energized at the same time.

Bex slows and lets Mia and Treva pass her in the race. She smiles at me in a way that shows she might be a little more okay with not winning. Apparently sharing my backstory with her on the pier helped us connect. And that's a good thing for two coaches to do.

The rest of the team reaches me and falls to the ground panting. Except for Paloma who refused to run the whole way and is currently cutting across the field to join us.

Bex claps her hands. "Let's stretch out, girls. We don't want to end up like Coach Skylar."

I narrow my eyes in a mock glare.

She gives a sassy scrunch of her bumpy nose before demonstrating a hamstring stretch.

The girls on the ground sit up to touch their toes.

Paloma continues to lumber our way. "I want to be like Coach Skylar," she calls. "He didn't have to run the lap."

I lift my paper cup as if in a toast. "I ran five miles for my warmup on Monday, kid. You really want to be like me?"

Mia frowns in confusion. "So did Mom, and she still ran the lap."

"I'm not going to win this, am I?"

Bex bends a knee to stretch her quad in a way that makes me want to wince. "I thought you were okay with losing."

"Brat."

She laughs. "You know stretching will help you recover. Come on, Coach. Join us."

I lazily sip my coffee. "You're the one who wanted to lead practice today."

Aby jumps up and grabs my free hand with her tiny little sweaty one. "You at least have to lead us in the dance."

Annie joins her, though with my coffee in the other hand, she can only grab my elbow. I flex to keep from spilling on her.

Even with the small contraction required to keep balance, my thighs scream in protest. I'll be picking up some of those Epson salts Bex recommended on my way home tonight. I need to recover for the practice she'll be putting me through again tomorrow. "Sorry, girls. I'm out of play."

Paloma sprawls on her back. "Lucky."

Riley jumps up. "When I don't want to play, my mom offers me treats. Something special. Like a baby shark."

Treva rolls onto her belly and lifts to her elbows to look at me with angelic blue eyes. "What treat do you want, Uncle Skylar?"

They're resorting to bribery, huh? "I want to go home and sit in my jacuzzi."

Bex switches legs to stretch her other thigh and clicks her tongue with disapproval. But her eyes also shine when they meet mine.

"No." Treva laughs as if I told the funniest joke ever. "What can we give you to make you lead us in the Ladybug dance?"

I'd do anything for that little girl, but I can't let her know it, or I'll end up dancing like a Ladybug when I'd rather curl up like a potato bug.

Bex pushes to her feet and snatches the coffee from my hand before I can stop her. Of course, with as slow as I'm moving, that really didn't have to be very fast.

She sips my beverage. "Mm... If you want this back, you're going to have to dance, Skylar."

"Hey." I swipe an arm, but without moving my legs, I can't reach her. "I thought you wanted to be head coach."

"You're the one who's—" She circles her hips. "—got da moves."

"Not today, I don't."

"Da...ance," sings Charlotte with a dramatic sweep of her arms.

"Dance. Dance. Dance," the twins chant.

"Dance. Dance. Dance," the rest of the girls join in.

I let my head fall backward and offer a dramatic wail as if I'm playing Snoopy in a theater.

Bex joins the chant I never would have expected from her. "Dance, dance, dance."

I don't know if I want my coffee back that bad. But I'll dance for them. "All right."

They cheer, and it's my favorite applause ever. These girls aren't fans I've never met. They know me, and their innocent enthusiasm reveals they enjoy spending time with me as much as I enjoy spending time with them.

I pull my phone out of my pocket to hit play on my Ladybugs playlist. Then I do my painful ladybug wiggle along with my mini flashmob toward Bex to retrieve my coffee.

She lets go of the paper cup with a chuckle. "You really do have the moves." The glimmer in her eyes sharpens to a flash. "Hey. That day of tryouts when you saw Mia play for the first time, I said the same thing about her, didn't I?"

I sip the perfect blend of cream and espresso as I drink her in. "Yep."

She runs a hand along her ponytail. "No wonder you assumed I knew who you were."

"Not only that." I tilt my head toward the Moms watching us from behind their camera apps. "I blamed you for revealing my identity to the team parents."

She shakes her head. "What are the odds?"

I shrug. "Doesn't matter now because I'm done moving."

"You know I just worked you out that hard to get the team for myself, right?"

"I had my suspicions."

She hits me with another one of her guttural laughs before turning back to the team. "All right, girls. You're mine for the rest of the hour."

They groan good-naturedly.

Riley crosses her arms. "Coach Skylar got a coffee. What do we get?"

"What do you want?" Her mom yells from the sidelines.

"Ice cream," Riley calls back as if she's been waiting for this moment.

"I'll take you out for ice cream afterward," Riley's mom agrees a little too easily. Bribery is going to backfire on the woman someday.

"All of us?" Paloma joins their conversation across the field.

And that time is now.

Riley's mom hesitates.

Mia dribbles a ball around the rest of her team, practicing without them. "I want something better than ice cream. I want to watch Coach Skylar play soccer in his tournament."

Shouts of excitement fill the air, and Influencer Mom's shoulders relax. She's off the hook, but I'm not.

Bex glances over and arches her eyebrows. "Are you able to get us tickets?"

I have no idea how tickets work, but I'll figure out a way. It'll be fun to have my own cheering section, even if I fall on my face. Especially if I fall on my face.

Once again, I experience the power of living up to what I've already obtained. I'm not going to be trying to earn the crowd's adoration the way my agent wants me to. I'll be playing my heart out for these girls because they already love me.

"Done." I agree. Then I point to centerfield. "If you want to come see me at Soccer in the Sand, you'd better get out there."

* * *

The team gets off easy compared to the drills Bex puts me through Thursday. I'd been hoping with Mia and Treva joining us for my training that Bex wouldn't be able to challenge me as much. I mean, we couldn't just leave them to build sandcastles while we ran five miles along the beach. But Bex showed up with their bikes in the back of her boxy little crossover SUV. I had to race even faster to keep up along the Strand, aka A Strand of Paradise, which is Oceanside's famous beachfront path.

I've never hated paradise so much, but everyone else has a great time. We run to the beach playground where the girls swing and climb monkey bars as Bex and I run drills around them. There are no faux-romantic sunset walks along the pier or vulnerable moments of sharing our hearts. Though that's probably a good thing. While she'd seemed to scoff at my mention of not dating last time, it kinda felt like a date. Only better since, you know, she didn't take off in the middle of it.

We're two halves of a coaching staff. Fellow Jesus followers. And, dare I say, friends.

Well, we're not friends right now. In fact, I'm pretty sure she hates me.

"Get those knees higher."

I'm performing what's called a mountain climber where I kind of run in place but from a pushup position. Sand is flying.

"I feel like a dog digging a hole." I also feel like a dog with as much as I'm panting, but I don't need to point that part out. "How is this going to help me win a soccer game?"

"Core strength, of course. Ten more."

I'd thought I had core strength until Bex came along. I perform the required ten then roll onto my spine to let my abs heal from having been ripped in half.

From this position, I can't help but stare up at the woman now bathed in the golden glow of a summer evening. My memories are flooded with an interview of Alec Baldwin talking about being cast alongside the great Sean Connery. He said all his shots were of him squatting down in the mud while Sean was filmed in front of gorgeous backdrops like waterfalls and mountains. I'm the muddy one here. If I fall for Bex it will be because of the way all these sunsets highlight her as the star of the show.

"You just going to lie there?" she asks rhetorically then motions toward her daughter and my niece who are performing some kind of gymnastics move on the high bar. "The little girls are still going."

"They're playing," I argue, though their play consists of exercises I could never perform.

Bex watches them drop from flips over the bar into a hang. They then lift their toes to touch the bar above their heads. "It does look fun. Come on. We'll do it too."

Before one could even say "higgledy-piggledy," the four of us are in a toe-to-bar competition. I didn't think I could do it at first, because my lack of bendiness, but if I curled up from my abs, it's not so much about flexibility as it is about strength.

Treva drops to the sand first, landing like my ex used to in all her superhero movies. Then Mia.

"Come on, Mom," Mia yells. "You can win."

Treva counters. "Don't let a girl beat you, Uncle Skylar."

I grunt between leg lifts. "Brutal."

Bex has the breath to laugh, which doesn't bode well for me. Her legs are also flying up and down at double my speed. But if slow and steady wins the race, then I'm Paloma.

A few passersby stop to watch. Followed by a few more. Next comes pointing and whispering. Now cameras are pulled out.

If I lose, it's not going to be a small embarrassment. It will get me trending on TikTok.

Bex is strong, but she's also smaller. If I use my body weight against her, I'll have the upper hand. So rather than lift my legs straight up like we'd been doing, I swing one leg in front of her body to block her leg lift.

"No fair." She tries to sound angry, but a giggle gives her away. It's not the guttural laugh I'm used to, but that's because her guts are too busy exercising.

I can't keep my leg up there forever, so it drops, sending me swinging from side to side. I swing away from her, and as I swing back, her legs wrap around my waist. The extra weight strains my shoulders. My finger joints cramp to hang onto the metal bar. I won't be able to hold on much longer.

The little girls on the ground clap and jump. Flashes pop. But my focus remains on this game of chicken.

I rock my legs back to swing farther away from Bex's position. My goal is to break free of her hold, but she's a determined little thing. Her legs hook at the ankles to stay locked around my waist. Unfortunately for her, my body is longer. Swinging away from her side rips her grip right off the bar.

Victory is mine. Except Bex's legs are still tangled around me. If she falls first, her head will hit the sand. That's not the way I want to win.

I let go of the bar to catch Bex's torso. Somehow, I land on my feet, holding her.

Bex's arms instinctively cling to my neck. I know it's instinct because her blue-gray eyes are wide with the fear of falling. Or is that the fear of falling for me?

Either way, they're only a few inches away, and I get lost in their depths like a sailor on a stormy sea. Our heaving chests crash against each other in angry waves. Skin is slick.

Little girls laugh and shout. "It's a tie."

"It's a tie," she repeats.

My brain remains in the fog. "What?"

She drops her hold and glides away as if in a lifeboat. "It's a tie," she repeats over her shoulder.

I sacrificed myself to save her, just like I did with my ex-wife. Also like my ex-wife, she doesn't appreciate the effort.

This is why I stopped dating. I'm choosing for God to be enough. Because even if I wanted something more with Bex, she'd never let me win.

Bex

It is a happy talent to know how to play.
–Ralph Waldo Emerson

I haven't been held in a man's arms since before Mia was born. But it's not Skylar's embrace that left me shaking. It's his sacrifice. Nobody has ever done that for me. Nobody.

Such a realization hurts. Even more, it's ignited a longing that can never be satisfied. Because I refuse to let Mia grow up like me—not feeling like a priority.

When I decided to raise her as a single mother, it was with the understanding that I'd have to give up my pro-sports career and romantic relationships. I'm protecting her from what my mother should have protected me.

Rather than let myself be affected by Skylar's touch, I'm going to be affected by his words. The way he let God fulfill his heart's desires.

While my longing for another human to find me worth sacrificing themself will never be fulfilled, Jesus loved me that much. That's what I'll focus on and live up to. That's what Skylar sang about alone on the beach when he quit dating.

Which means he's not available anyway. Even if he was, he'd have many more appealing prospects than a crazy soccer coach and single mom.

He's just a good guy. He would have sacrificed himself at the beach for anyone who was about to fall on their head. Even someone who deserved it as much as I did for playing dirty and almost making him look bad in front of all those people with cellphone cameras.

I may not have gotten what I deserved by falling on my head, but now the internet is full of video footage of me staring up at Skylar like a lost puppy. Or more like a hungry baby bird with the profile of my beak taken by amateur videographers.

Aside from the emotional upheaval and the unwanted infamy on social media, I had a great time running drills with Skylar. He'd pointed out how the girls weren't as tired as he was because they were playing, and I surprisingly fell into the same category. Coaching has never been more fun.

I'm enjoying our coaching sessions too much. It's going to be hard to give them up after next week. It's going to be even harder when the Ladybug's season ends.

For example, right now I'm in charge of ushering players in front of the cranky old sports photographer one at a time while Skylar keeps the rest of our team entertained with impressions of Disney characters, but I'm listening more to their conversations than the photographer. To be fair, I'm not sure how anyone can have a normal conversation when it sounds like Mickey Mouse is leading the Ladybug cheer. As if that's not enough, Skylar holds up a big soccer ball with two smaller soccer balls as ears so that the three of them form the outline of Mickey's face.

"Did you hear me, Bex?"

I blink and turn to Jacqueline who's taking her own photos of Treva from behind the cameraman's back. "Sorry. What?"

"I asked what you're doing for the 4th of July."

I take a deep breath of my favorite scent—freshly mown grass. Holidays are always tricky for me. I want to make them special for my daughter, but we don't have family to share them with. I have no parents or grandparents in the picture. No in-laws. Sometimes we'll attend church events or neighborhood block parties, but I hate being a burden that anyone must accommodate. “I’m planning to grill burgers, and I bought a Slip ‘N Slide.”

“That sounds dangerous. The Slip ‘N Slide, not the burgers.”

I shrug off her worries. “It’s a safer way to practice slide tackles.”

“You’ve got me there.” Jacqueline turns her camera and continues clicking. With all her kids, she prefers to take her own snapshots rather than pay for professional photos. She might be the reason our professional photographer is so cranky. “You can bring the Slip ‘N Slide over if you want to join us. Caleb is going to be home, so we’re inviting all our friends to catch up at once.”

Huh. That means Skylar will probably be there. In the background, his Mickey Mouse voice turns into a raspy Donald Duck and is accompanied by all kinds of giggles.

I smile at the sound. It makes me want to celebrate Independence Day with the Hayes family even more. Which means I probably shouldn’t. Of course, if Mia finds out we’re invited, she’ll beg me to go.

“Thanks for offering. I’ll have to get back with you.”

“If you come, bring your famous jalapeno poppers.”

Does she seriously think she’s keeping her pregnancy a secret? I’ll create an opening for her to tell me she’s expecting in case she wants to.

“My jalapeno poppers are not famous. I’ve only made them once, and they sent you into labor.”

“That made them famous.”

Okay then. “I’m glad your hubby is going to be here soon.”

“Me too. Hopefully for good this time.”

The photographer turns and catches Jacqueline taking her own shots. “Next,” he deadpans.

“That’s all the individuals.” I force my cheerfullest tone then turn to motion for the entire team to line up in front of the camera equipment.

Be still my heart, Mia is on Skylar’s shoulders. I will not make a big deal out of this. There’s no big deal to make. If I can wrap myself around him like a monkey at the playground and pretend it’s normal, then why can’t she go for a shoulder ride? He’s her coach. Her best friend’s uncle.

Skylar holds onto Mia’s ankles to keep her safe as he twists back and forth to herd the rest of the team forward. “Ladybugs, let’s go. It’s time for our team portrait." He shoots me a mischievous wink then asks in the most innocent manner, "Has anyone seen Mia?"

If he hadn't winked, I might believe he's forgotten where Mia went. It's the oldest trick in the parenting handbook, but he's not a parent. He's an actor, and a good one. While I'd been impressed with the Donald Duck voice, this performance is much more personal.

The team squeals with glee and points to Skylar's shoulders. Except for Kendall who we now know saves all her arm energy for playing the violin.

Skylar spins in a circle. "What? Where?"

Mia grins at me from her perch then pats the top of Skylar's dark hair to get his attention. "I'm right here."

"Look u...up." Charlotte sings.

Skylar throws his head back with a dramatic arch of his spine, knocking Mia upside-down to hang from her ankles.

I gasp.

She cackles like she might never stop.

The photographer frowns at his watch. "Any time."

I'm not sure whether I'm helping the photographer or attempting to save my own sanity, but I rush behind Skylar and scoop my baby into my arms. "We need to pose. Other teams are waiting."

Skylar lets her legs go then turns to face us. "Yeah, Mia. Stop fooling around."

She wraps her arms around my neck and kicks her legs in delight.

I shake my head at our coach. We haven't even played today's game, yet he seems to think this is the after party. "I miss the days when you were so sore you could barely drink your coffee. I'm going to have to work you out harder this week."

He lifts his chin to better show off his signature smirk. "Why don't you yell at me during practices. Then maybe you'll lose your voice again. I miss those days."

"It would be my pleasure."

"Hey y'all?" Jacqueline draws our attention. "If you want to be in the team picture, this is your chance."

She's lined the girls up in two rows, the front row kneeling. They're already showing off all their missing teeth in smiles for the camera.

Mia reaches their way. "Mom," she scolds like I'm the one holding us up.

I'm faster than Skylar, so I rush to the far end, depositing Mia in front of me. I paste on my grin, the camera snaps, and the grumpy old guy motions us away. I think Skylar made it into the shot, but if not, that's okay.

Next year he'll be making his movies, and I'll have my head coach spot back. We won't miss him. If he's not in the photo, we might not even remember him.

Skylar snaps to attention. "All right, Ladybugs. Let's go warmup."

That's right. He'd better start warmups. I narrow my eyes, so he knows what I'm thinking.

Jacqueline sidles up next to me and holds out her phone to display one of the pictures she took. "Look. Isn't it great?"

I'm still looking after Skylar to make sure he's getting back to business. He salutes me, does an about face, and leads the team marching toward Field Four. I don't know whether to be relieved or suspicious, but I let them go in order to compliment Jacqueline's camerawork.

My obligatory glance is followed by a double take. She's perfectly captured a moment of joy as Mia rode on Skylar's shoulders.

"Men usually play a little rougher with kids, but it's okay." She pats my arm encouragingly, knowing I don't have experience with a father or even a baby daddy. "I think sometimes it's even good for them."

And that's the problem. I want to give my daughter all the good things in the world, but no matter how hard I try, I'll never be enough. She's going to have to rely on God to fulfill her emptiness too.

* * *

After all my complaining about Skylar, it's *my* head that's not in the game. The team we're playing isn't even that good, but we're only ahead by one.

"Kendall, you're goalie," Skylar points out positions.

A groan escapes my lips. Thankfully the little girl is already running onto the field and doesn't hear me.

Skylar plants his hands on his waist and turns to ask me *really?* with his eyes. "You want me to start covering your mouth for you again?"

I scrunch my nose. I like having my own voice even more than having his arm around me. "Sorry. It's just that this is the worst time to put in a goalie who won't use her arms. Can't you save her for later?"

He looks at his list of players. It's not in a binder like my list would be, but at least he's trying. "She's the only one who hasn't played goalie yet. If I don't put her in, I could get a red-tag."

I shrug. "You don't get removed from coaching until you have three red-tags."

He tilts his head, playfully suspicious. "Are you trying to get me removed so you can have your position back?"

That's actually a good idea. Not because I want him to leave. But because I don't. "You'll be gone next year anyway."

Smirky-smirk. "I might return simply to torment you."

"Such a motivation explains a lot of the decisions you make."

A whistle blows, drawing our attention to the field. Okay, Aby and Riley are defense. We can work with that. As for offense, Charlotte is paired with Paloma.

Charlotte gets the ball. Dribbles. Passes to Paloma. Who turns and kicks it directly out of bounds. The whistle blows.

"I'd take the red-tag to switch their spots."

"That would make two red-tags."

Charlotte throws in. Their team beats Paloma to the ball. They kick it toward our net. Aby blocks. She kicks it back downfield. And Paloma's there to aim for the sidelines once again. The whistle blows.

A parent from the other team jogs to retrieve the ball.

Skylar runs a hand down his face. "We could be here all day."

"Paloma!" I yell. "*You* throw it in this time."

She grins and nods like this was her plan all along.

Skylar huffs a breath that ruffles his bangs. "If we can just hold onto our lead, we'll survive this one."

I glance at the timer I set on my watch. "Five minutes left."

"It's going to be fifty minutes at this pace."

"That's a long time for Kendall to defend the goal without using her hands."

Skylar crosses his arms and shakes his head. "Maybe Paloma will keep kicking it out of bounds, and Kendall will never have to make a stop."

"The dream team."

He chuckles. But our dream turns into a nightmare as the Bumblebees take possession. Their defender sends it toward our net, and all the little girls fly after it like a swarm of hornets.

"Come on, Riley," I shout. Then mutter, "Make Instagram proud."

Riley kicks and misses. Her momentum swings her around in a circle. Not to be outdone, Aby performs a pirouette of her own.

Both Skylar's hands fly to his head. "What the nutcracker?"

My hands cover my mouth to prevent me from saying something worse. Because with our two defenders twirling about, Kendall is the only one who can stop the swarm.

Their star player charges the ball. Winds up. Kicks.

The ball soars directly for the net.

Skylar points in case our goalie doesn't see it coming. "Kendall!"

Oh no. It's going to sail directly over her head.

But wait. She's running toward it.

"You can use your arms," I shout. Because Skylar isn't the only who yells obvious things. Except this might not be so obvious to her.

Kendall's arms don't rise. Instead she jumps. She's going to get a concussion like I did as a kid. Who made the rule about everyone playing every position? We all have different strengths and weaknesses. This is why we have teams. So we can learn to improve our strengths and become better together. But now the Ladybugs are going to be visiting Kendall in the hospital.

Just as a scream rips from my throat, Kendall arches back then powers her tiny body forward to slam her forehead against the ball. She does a perfect header, sending the ball flying the opposite direction. She really is Larry the Cucumber.

I stare in shock.

Fans jump to their feet.

The whistle blows.

Skylar looks around in confusion. "What just happened?"

My arms hang limp at my sides. I'm not sure how to feel. "Headers are illegal. If any player gets hit on the head, the game is over because she has to be checked for a concussion."

"Kendall looked like she knew what she was doing." He turns on me. "Did you teach her that in another secret practice?"

"Absolutely not."

Mia zooms onto the field, arms wide like she just made a goal. Kendall follows behind her except without her arms spread.

"Oh no."

Skylar looks from me to the girls. "What?"

"Mia must have taught her headers that day at Jacqueline's house."

"You taught Mia?"

"With Styrofoam balls."

He takes a deep breath. "I hope she's okay."

Even though Kendall doesn't seem to be in the kind of pain I went through when breaking my nose and getting a concussion, my heart clogs my throat. Thankfully, a mom from the other team identifies herself as a doctor and checks our goalie's pupils.

"Mia." I motion my daughter over to hold in front of me and keep her out of trouble. This isn't her fault. It's mine.

The doctor looks up and nods toward Senator and Mrs. Kopf. She's okay. Kendall laughs and grins, apparently still feeling like a superstar. Maybe because Riley's mom is filming her. Thankfully she wasn't hurt because this is going to end up on social media, if not the news.

"Did you see that, Mom?" Mia twists to look up at me in pride. "She did a header like Ceasar Navarra."

I cringe all the way to my toes. "She could have gotten really hurt, honey. You're not allowed to do headers yet."

"I know. I taught her with bubbles, but she did it with a real ball."

I close my eyes. I owe the Senator a huge apology.

A whistle blows, and I open my eyes to catch the young ref glancing hesitantly at me before announcing, "We're ending the game early. Ladybugs win four to three."

Skylar lifts his eyebrows at me. "That's one way to win."

"I deserve the red-tag."

The corners of his lips soften into a smile. "How about I just take everyone out for ice cream. Since we have the time."

Once again, he's making a sacrifice for me. Once again, I wish I didn't need saving.

Skylar

Whoever wants to understand much, must play much. –Gottfried Benn

I want to see Bex again, but at the same time I'm afraid of my growing attachment. In a similar fashion, I want to play in the celebrity tournament for fun and not have my career depend on it. These are both things that give me enjoyment but could lead to things I don't enjoy. Like divorce.

How dumb is that? I'm not marrying anyone. I'm simply driving down to Oceanside to jog on the beach with my trainer and her daughter. And perhaps eat more ice cream because it's summer. Because I'll be famished after one of her workouts.

It doesn't necessarily mean I'm looking for an excuse to hang out longer. Even if I am.

Gah. I roll my eyes at traffic on I-5 so I have something else to blame for my frustration.

The phone rings through my speakers. Bex's name flashes on the screen. Actually it says, "Crazy Coach," but after her taking the blame for Kendall's illegal header on Saturday, I need to change her name in my contacts. She wants the best for those kiddos. Same as she wants for me in the upcoming tournament. But why would she be calling?

Maybe she's canceling our training. Maybe I need her to.

I can jog by myself. I can dribble a ball down the beach by myself.

I won't have anyone to practice passing to. Or to argue with. Or to wrap themselves around me like they just escaped a dinosaur in Jurassic Park.

But I'm an actor. I should save the drama for the screen.

Tapping the green phone icon, I answer. "Hex, Bex. You okay?"

"I am. It's Mia I'm worried about. She's running a fever."

Oh no. Even if I truly wanted her to cancel, it wouldn't be for this reason. "You think it's serious?"

Bex sighs. "She says she feels like she's going to throw up. I'll take her to the doctor in the morning if she isn't any better. But I'm going to have to cancel tonight."

"Of course." I've helped Jacqueline out with sick kiddos before. When there's only one parent, there's nobody to run to the store for medicine or chicken soup. "I'm already on my way down. Can I get you anything?"

Silence. Meaning she doesn't want to ask. We'll just have to play the guessing game.

"Children's aspirin?"

"I have some. Thanks."

Okay then. "Vitamin C to boost your own immunity."

"Already doubled up."

I shake my head. What might she not have? "A foosball table so Mia can practice soccer when she's not healthy enough to run."

Bex chuckles. "Now you're talkin'."

Flipping on the blinker, I change lanes to take the next exit. I don't know where she lives, but I know where there's a pharmacy. Because she obviously needs something. "Do they sell foosball tables at Walgreens?"

"If not, maybe you could pick up some Ginger Ale?" Her tone rises with the question then squeaks with discomfort, and she rushes to justify the request. "I only let Mia drink soda when she's sick, so it's a special treat."

"You got it."

Rather than a simple thank you, she adds, "And not unless you still have time to do your training."

"Text me your address, Bex." I say this to end our conversation, though my intent is twofold. First, I'm okay with getting out of training. Second, Bex needs to know I want to pick up the special treat for Mia. Maybe I'll even throw in a baby shark for good measure.

On my way into the store, I give Jacqueline a call too. Might as well see if she needs anything while I'm down here.

Once in line with two care packages for a sick kid and a secretly pregnant sister-in-law, a DVD display catches my eye. It's advertised as "old favorites," which makes sense since nobody watches DVDs anymore. I wonder...

Yep. They've got the whole Professional Kid series. My nieces and nephews have seen them, but I don't know that Mia has. I grab the set and let the checkout lady take a selfie with me and the movies before hunting down Bex's house.

GPS directs me up a hill into a well-landscaped neighborhood. The area is nicer than I expected for a single mom who teaches high school and receives no child support. The house itself is older with lots of sharp angles and trapezoid windows. Imagine if the Brady Bunch had wanted their home finished in stucco with a red tiled roof. It's in need of some updates, but the covered patio above the three-car garage looks like it offers a view of the distant ocean.

I double check the address. This is the place.

Maybe Bex got a signing bonus before she had to drop out of the pros. Maybe she had some sponsorship deals. Maybe she has a roommate.

If she owns this place, then she probably didn't agree to coach me for the money. Not that her motivation to train me means something. She'd do anything for soccer.

I hook all the plastic bags of treats on my elbows and head up the flagstone path to the door boasting three random horizontal windows. I knock and try not to noticeably peek inside.

Bex's golden brown ponytail pokes above the top window and her bare feet pad into the bottom. She swings the door open and gives a small smile before noticing all the bags I brought. Then her face does its normal overly expressive thing. "How much Ginger Ale do you think Mia needs?"

I hold out the bags. "I bought Gatorade too. Electrolytes."

She takes the first bag to peek inside. "And DVDs? That's thoughtful, but I don't even know if my DVD player works anymore." She pulls out the first movie case, revealing the face of a younger me. "Wow, look at this kid."

"He had quite the fauxhawk going on, didn't he?" I ask about my outdated hairstyle, hoping she'll defend me.

"I like it. I'll bet it made his head more aerodynamic. Which is how he —" She does a side-to-side head bob, imitating the character I played. "—'got da moves.'"

I chuckle at her impersonation. "Should I style my hair that way for the celebrity tournament?"

"You could." Her eyes sparkle like freshly polished silver. "Or you could just use the moves your trainer taught you."

I guess we're both talking about ourselves in third person now. "My trainer cancelled our session tonight, so I might not be ready in time."

"Wait." After holding up a finger, she disappears inside the house.

I look down at the rest of the bags I brought, unsure of what I'm waiting for. If Mia wasn't sick, I'd finagle an invite to join them. The vintage home smells welcoming like grilled cheese, and I'm curious if it has a Brady Bunch orange kitchen. All I can see from the entryway is terracotta hexagon floor tiles, a floating staircase with railing that can't be up to current code—not to mention a nightmare when raising a baby, and a cluster of glass globes hanging from the vaulted ceiling by a yellow enamel light fixture.

"Look what Coach Skylar brought you." Bex's voice carries through the house along with the rustle of plastic.

"Old movies?" Mia murmurs, lacking her usual vibrancy.

I'm not *that* old.

"Look who's in them," Bex encourages.

I hold my breath.

Pause. "Coach Skylar as a kid. With a weird hairdo."

I press my lips together to smother a laugh that threatens to drown out the rest of their conversation.

"Why's he in movies?" The little girl sounds as confused as she is sick.

"He's an actor."

"That's strange."

So much for impressing the kid with my fame. Of course, that wasn't my intention. The role I played was part of something much bigger than myself. Something with the power to make Mia smile even while her tummy hurts.

Bex reappears with Adidas on her feet and a three-ring binder in her hands. She stops when she realizes I'm still holding a bunch of bags. "Trade you."

Looks like I won't be taking the night off after all.

We make the exchange, and she peeks at the rest of the stuff I bought. "Stuffed animals? Books? Art tablets?"

I shrug. "In case she's not entertained by the movies of me with a weird hairdo."

"It takes a lot to impress kids these days. You should have dyed your hair red like I suggested." Her smile flashes. "I'll be right back."

She disappears again, so I flip open the binder. The thing holds pages and pages of typed notes, workout plans, and illustrations of soccer drills. It would take me months to get through all of this, though she's probably expecting me to go finish it tonight.

From the other room... "Hey, look what else Coach brought you."

"I want to watch the movies."

There it is. I let myself smirk since nobody can see.

The conversation I've eavesdropped on is followed by the scrape of furniture being moved, the clatter of what sounds like a remote falling to the floor, and a couple of G-rated expletives. Finally there's the tune of trumpets announce my film's production company. The delay gives me time to rifle through the binder and plan my workout for the evening. I also snag a training drill or two to use next practice.

Bex jogs back and joins me on the walkway then closes the front door. "Sorry that took so long. Do you have any questions?"

I know she wants to demonstrate soccer moves, but as I lift my eyes to meet hers, there's a lot more I want to know about. Jacqueline filled in some gaps, but Bex hasn't told me anything about herself. "How long have you lived here?"

Bex bounces in place to warmup but looks around as if seeing her home through my eyes. "I grew up here. Moved away for college then came back when I got pregnant with Mia."

"Oh, so you live with your folks?" If her parents are here, wouldn't she have asked one of them to pick up ginger ale?

She gives a dry laugh and stops bouncing. "I inherited this place when my mom died."

Not sure what's funny about that. "I'm sorry."

Bex shakes her head and looks away. "In the relationship with my mom, I was the parent. She never really grew up. We only had this house because my dad was married to someone else when Mom got pregnant with me, and he paid her off to keep from revealing the secret."

My eyes bulge before I'm able to use my experience in acting and pretend like her upbringing didn't just send me reeling. But wow. When you grow up in a boring family of four, you expect everyone to have supportive parents and an overprotective older brother. Especially with all Bex has accomplished. I mean, she had the opportunity to play professional soccer.

Instead, Bex's existence is a secret. From her stepmother. From her half siblings.

"Did you ever meet your dad?"

She looks down. Scuffs the rubber toe of her shoe. "No. Though I believe he saved my life. If I didn't have a wealthy father for Mom to extort, she probably would have aborted me like her other pregnancies."

I blink at the bluntness. At the deep undercurrent beneath her shallow words. She still hasn't mentioned Mia, but her past had to have affected how she dealt with an unplanned pregnancy of her own. And here she is, nailing it. "I'm...I'm surprised you wanted to stay in this house."

She shrugs. "If I hadn't been living here with an infant at the time Mom overdosed, I would have sold it."

The tale just gets more and more tragic. I point to the front door. "Did she die here?"

"No. She was barely ever here." Bex waves her hand as if brushing away the idea. "Now that Mia and I created beautiful new memories, I don't want to leave. It's the only home she knows."

I've never been more in awe of a person. I thought I had it bad with my wife leaving and taking my career with her, but Bex lost her career,

Mia's dad, and all possible relatives. "My goodness. I don't know what to say."

She shakes it off. "You don't have to say anything. Just pay me for training you. I'm planning to use that money to replace my avocado shag carpet."

So, she *is* training me for the money. Though if I'd known how much she could use it, I'd have offered her double. If not triple. "Oh, I'm paying you, but are you sure you want to replace the shag? Avocado green is making a comeback."

She huffs, and a tiny smile flickers. "I don't want to be that trendy anymore."

I nod. I still want to say something encouraging so she knows it means a lot to me that she shared, that I admire her, and it's okay to ask for help. She doesn't have to do everything alone. As I circle the target, looking for the right words to say, I end up pulling the trigger on, "You're a good mom."

Her wet eyes glisten like the ocean when the sun streams through the clouds. Subdued yet strong. Private and powerful.

My throat clogs.

She dabs at her bottom lashes. "Stop it."

"Stop what?"

Stop caring? Stop wanting to make things better for her and Mia? Stop staring at the most beautiful woman I've ever seen?

"Stop talking. You're supposed to be practicing." She laughs off the painfulness of authenticity.

"Timeout." I tuck the binder under my arm to form a T with my hands. "We're both here today because you're a good mom. Now before we go any farther, you need to claim it."

Even if she's come to terms with the fact that her mom and dad were awful, she hasn't yet accepted that she's a good parent. And she's going to keep running herself ragged by trying to prove it the way Jacqueline does with pregnancy. The way Influencer Mom does on social media. The way Dance Mom does with ballet performances, and the other moms with baking cake and hiring nannies.

Don't get me wrong. These are all good things, but the women don't seem to be living with the joy of already obtaining them. They're doing these things for love instead of out of love.

Like Bex plays soccer.

"Say it. Say 'I'm a good mom."

Bex gives my chest a little shove with her fingertips, then strides past toward the front lawn. "I'm a *crazy* good mom. Now get out here so I can demonstrate the drills you're going to practice without me."

Crazy good works. It's how I feel when I'm around her.

Bex

This is the real secret of life -- to be completely engaged with what you are doing in the here and now. And instead of calling it work, realize it is play.
—— Alan Watts

Mia has a virus. That means the doctor can't offer a cure, and we're going to miss the Ladybug's practice. At least Skylar possesses my playbook now and has access to all the secrets of being a good coach.

As for being a good mom, there's nothing I can do but medicate Mia's symptoms and join her for a movie marathon. I cuddle her hot little body to mine, caress her hair away from her sweaty forehead, and watch a younger version of Skylar onscreen for over eight hours. It would have been less, but every time Mia falls asleep, she insists on rewinding the film, so she doesn't miss anything.

Ironically, the more I watch, the more I feel I'm missing out. It's like the time I saw Princess Diaries in elementary school then went home and cried because I wanted to be Mia Thermopolis. Everyone always assumes I named my daughter after soccer legend Mia Hamm, which is valid, but she's truthfully named after my childhood hero.

I grew up dreaming one day I too would discover my dad's royal family wanted me. And now I'm tempted to dream about Skylar, which is just as much a fairytale.

Anyway, watching his movies as an adult gives me a much different perspective. My heart swells with pride for Skylar's talent, but even more for his humility. If his goal is to live up to what he's already obtained, he's doing that. He's caring for his family and his team. He's using his gifts to bless those around him. He's the kind of guy who would still do that even if he had nothing to offer except the shirt on his back.

Mia rolls to face me on the overstuffed microfiber sofa I bought to replace the stiff, low-backed furniture Mom preferred. "Is Coach Skylar famous?"

I wonder what fame means to her. "Some people recognize him."

"Did you?"

I feel her forehead and note the fever reducer is doing its job. It's good with how much she's cooled down, but maybe not so good with how much she wants to talk about Skylar. "He looked familiar, but I figured he was a player's dad I'd seen at games."

She nods seriously. "I think when people tell him he's got 'da moves,' it's because they recognize him."

I smile at her logic and at the memory of him mistaking me for a fan. "Usually."

"I wouldn't have recognized him from seeing his movies. Do you know why?"

I'm already entertained by whatever deep thought she's about to share. "His weird hairdo?" I guess.

She shakes her head against my bicep being used as her pillow. "No. It's because at soccer practice we only kick the ball, but in the movie, he's always throwing things."

Images of Skylar throwing water balloons, snowballs, pillows, and food pop into my head. She's not wrong. I chuckle. "He's like Superman wearing glasses as a disguise."

She nods, either too sick to laugh at my silly comparison or because she now thinks of Skylar as a superhero. "Since he's good at throwing, you could teach him how to do a flip throw in."

I twist my lips to show consideration of her suggestion. Then I actually consider. After all the tricks Skylar has pulled out of his sleeve, it wouldn't surprise me if he could do a front flip when throwing the ball back into play. But I won't be inviting him over to jump on the trampoline I bought Mia to train her in the special skill. "I'm not teaching anyone else how to do a flip throw in until you master it. You're my first priority."

She grins. "I'll just have to teach him then."

Time to change the subject from Skylar. We don't need both of us mourning him after he's gone. Or more appropriately, mourning every time we see him with Treva's family after his life moves on from ours.

I boop Mia's nose. She's enough for me, and I try to be enough for her. Skylar claims that makes me a good mom, but how would he know? He hasn't heard the story of how I became a mom.

* * *

Thursday, Mia's better, but I've caught her bug. Usually when I'm sick, I tell myself it's a mental thing and try to push through. I might have done so with training Skylar, but then I puke. I wouldn't want to end up barfing in front of him during a run on the beach. Or worse, making him sick right before his celebrity tournament.

I plan to text him to cancel training, but I must have fallen asleep because I wake up to a knock on the door and, after a moment of confusion, realize it's probably Skylar.

"I'll get it." Mia charges to answer.

"Wait." I call after her. "Let me text Skylar to make sure it's him before you open the door." I don't know who else it would be, but I would have expected him to meet us at the beach. Unless he figured we could save on gas by driving down together.

I open my text app but don't have the energy to type, so I tap the phone icon.

The phone rings on my end then Skylar answers with concern. "Bex? I'm at your door. You okay?"

"I'm sick," I croak.

"I worried that would happen."

Mia fumbles with the lock on the door, and it swishes open outside my view. "Hey, Coach," echoes from my entryway then through the phone. "You got da moves."

I start to laugh but my stomach cramps and it turns into a groan. I roll to one side and bury my face in the couch cushions to ease the ache.

Skylar laughs at my kid. "You watched the movies."

"Yeah. You should have played baseball since you like to throw things so much."

He chuckles again. "But then I would've missed getting my rear kicked by your mom."

Yeah, every actor's dream. "How was last night's practice?" I ask him over the phone.

"Higgledy-Piggledy," he answers in a southern drawl.

"What?" I ask over Mia's giggles. He sounds like Jacqueline.

"That means the opposite of peaceful."

I groan. "It sounds the opposite of effective."

"Actually, I got Kendall to pump her arms when she runs."

I'm relieved to hear it's not as bad as I'd feared, but then I pause in a moment of silence for my coaching career. Skylar is both more fun and more effective than me. "Really?"

"No." I can practically hear the smirk in his tone. "We really need you there to keep us in line. I hope this Saturday's team isn't as tough as the Butterflies."

"They aren't. I'm more worried about your tournament." I close my eyes and sink deeper into the cushions. "Sorry I didn't call this time. I was hoping to push through."

"Ridiculous. Anything I can get you from the store tonight?"

"No." He came down here to train. "You need to practice."

"And you need to sleep."

I grunt in agreement.

"Let me take Mia to the beach with me. The fresh air will do her good."

My eyes fly open. My deep breath rasps. "No." Nobody watches Mia except certified daycare and Jacqueline who has the experience of a certified daycare. With all the stuff I saw as a kid…

There's a long pause before he draws out an "Okay…"

I didn't mean to hurt his feelings. He's trying to help.

"Mom won't let me go to the beach with you?" my daughter asks him knowingly.

"It's okay," he whispers to her. "Maybe you can watch my movies again."

My eyes sting at the idea of watching more TV. I let them drift closed again now that I know Skylar and Mia are both understanding of my need to keep Mia safe even when I can barely get off the couch.

"Or maybe," her tone rises with mischief. "I can teach you to do a flip throw-in on the trampoline."

"You have a trampoline?" He sounds a little too intrigued.

I drop the phone to raise my raspy voice loud enough for both him and Mia to hear me from the doorway. "You'll break your neck."

"That might be bad right before my tournament," he reasons with my daughter.

I don't have the energy for a chuckle, but my lips smile of their own accord.

"We have other ways to practice in the backyard." Mia is undeterred.

I don't know that Skylar wants to run drills with my eight-year-old, but I'm out of arguments. She'd get exercise and sunshine rather than sitting in front of the television for another eight hours. I'd know she's safe. And I'd be able to rest.

"Do you have a net?" Skylar asks. "My shooting needs work."

"Yeah." Her feet patter on the floor as she runs to ask permission. She leans over me to get my attention. "Is that okay, Mom? Can Coach Skylar practice in our backyard?"

I reach for her hand to remind her how special she is. How I treasure her. How I'm not trying to disappoint her. "Yes. Just take him in through the side gate so he doesn't catch any sick germs in here."

"Goodie." She grabs her shoes on the way back to tell Skylar the plan.

He could still turn her down and go jog five miles. But he doesn't. The happy sounds of their play is the lullaby needed to put me to sleep. How can I possibly repay him for such kindness?

Skylar

We win because we play together as a team.
–John Havlicek

My agent even wore his dress shoes to Soccer in the Sand. Meanwhile, I'm barefoot and digging my toes beneath the hot top layer to find cooler earth underneath.

"You know you're at the beach, right Craig?" I look past him toward the crowds lining up their camp chairs and blankets alongside playing fields marked off by ropes and bookended with nets. There's a light breeze but not a cloud in the sky, and the sun blinds me to the team I'm looking for.

"Yes." He snorts. "I'm at the beach, but I'm heading directly to a meeting afterwards."

"You know it's Saturday, right?"

I had to rush straight over after the Ladybug's game this morning. We destroyed the team who beat the Butterflies, meaning, as Bex keeps reminding me, we totally could have won our match against Coach G.I. Joe if I hadn't held her back. And as I keep reminding Bex, she'll get her vengeance next week when we face the Butterflies in the championship game.

"Not all of us have the luxury of getting paid to play," Craig counters.

I'm not getting paid anything to be here. But it's promotion for the kind of roles I want to play. As for Craig, I don't think you could pay him enough to take a day off.

"Well, thanks for coming to cheer me on."

"I'm leaving before your game starts." Figures. He's only here to get me some glory so he can bask in it. "You need to head to the VIP tent for the meet-and-greet with those who bought special tickets. After the game, you'll have press interviews. Then you'll finish with signing autographs and taking selfies. Oh, and I heard there are some pro players here who want to meet you too."

There's only one pro player I'm interested in. The one who gave up her career to coach little girls. They're the real VIPs.

"Skylar." Craig uses his admonishing tone.

I lift a hand to shade my eyes and peer down the beach at what looks like a giant cutout of my head bobbing through the crowd. Multiple cutouts. Except the giant cutouts are sporting fauxhawks. They're teenage me.

"Skylar."

My heads are waved around by little girls not much bigger than the cutouts themselves. A grin spreads across my real face, and I search for a signature ponytail to be leading the pack.

"Skylar, are you listening to me?"

"Yeah, you said my name three times." I can listen without looking, which is good since I just spotted Bex's eyes sparkling brighter than the sun off the waves. "Did you have anything more interesting to say?"

"You might not find it interesting, but it's important. I'm reminding you that your audition is this week, so don't worry as much about performing in the game as about how you perform with the press. Look for photo op..." He's struck speechless by what I'm sure he considers the photo op of a lifetime. "We need a photographer pronto." He takes off, sportscoat flapping.

Bex marches to a stop about ten feet away. She isn't holding a cutout, but rather her megaphone. The rest of the Ladybugs surround her in a triangle formation and lower their giant cutouts so I can make out every one of their toothy grins.

"Ready?" Bex calls through the megaphone, drawing attention from more than just our team.

"Ready," they echo in unison.

"One, two, who's got da moves?"

They all raise their cutouts. Even Kennedy. "Coach Skylar."

My mouth falls open. It's only been a few weeks since Bex ridiculed my cheer during practice, and now she's made up one of her own. In my honor.

"Three, four, who's going to score?"

All eight images of me shoot into the sky. "Coach Skylar."

The crowd around us collectively angle their phones to catch the scene. If my agent ever thinks about heaven, this is probably his very definition. But while he only cares about the media, Bex is cheering for my athleticism in the game.

"Five, six, who can both throw and kick?"

"Coach Skylar." The crowd joins in.

I chuckle at the inside joke and shake my head at Bex. "Don't raise expectations too high."

"Seven, eight, who's coaching is great?"

"Coach Skylar."

"Only because I have your playbook now," I shout back.

Professional photographers scramble to angle their cameras my way. Then at Bex. Which worries me a little, but I'm not going to let it ruin this moment.

Her laughter rings through the megaphone as she finishes, "Nine, ten, who can bend it like Beckham?"

"Coach Skylar."

Bex holds the speaker on her phone up to the bullhorn to amplify our warmup music. The girls perform the line dance I taught them while holding cutouts of my head in the air. They look like those Elf Yourself videos where you can put your friends' faces on dancing elves.

Bex joins me and turns to point the megaphone at the girls so we can both watch them perform.

I'm still incredulous. "I can't believe you did this. You're a cheerleader now."

"I'll cheer. You dance," she retorts. "Get out there with the girls."

Craig returns in time to give me a shove. "Get out there. Your old fans need to see how much you're still loved."

Craig doesn't get it. I'm not here to earn anybody's love. I'm here out of my love for them. Out of my love for my fans. Out of my love for the girls. Out of my love for Bex.

This last one stops me.

I love Bex as a person. I love being with her. But am I in love with her? And if so, what does that mean? What kind of sacrifice would loving her require, and would she even accept such a sacrifice?

Questions for another time. This is a time for dancing with a bunch of giant cutouts of my teenage head.

I take my position between Aby and Annie to ham it up like Dick Van Dyke with the penguins in Mary Poppins. They add their extra leaps and spins while I fake pass and shoot an imaginary soccer ball. As the last note fades away, we all strike a final pose. Of course Charlotte takes a knee in front of me, lifting her imaginary top hat.

While these girls came to cheer me on, the whole crowd cheers for them, drowning out the pop and whir of cameras.

"Who's that girl in front?" Craig shouts to be heard over the applause. "She could play a young Zooey Deschanel."

I pull Charlotte to her feet to bow beside me then make a beeline for Bex. Photographers cut me off and request our team pose together. I strain my neck to find Bex around them and wave her forward to join us.

She brushes me off. "You're the coach."

"You're the assistant coach," I argue.

"Come on, Mom," Mia yells.

I think she responds, but her words are overridden by a conversation taking place beside me.

An unfamiliar female voice asks, "Is Coach Skylar seeing your mom?"

After a pause, Mia answers, "Yep."

Bex's daughter just told someone I'm seeing her mother. Probably because I'm looking directly at Bex right now. The two of us are not dating, and Mia didn't mean to infer we are. But unless I keep her response from becoming tabloid news, Hollywood is going to consider us a couple.

No matter how I feel about Bex, I don't want any kind of relationship between us to drag her through the mud. Yet before I can even consider asking her out, she's becoming a target for mud pies.

Not to mention, this could affect my upcoming audition. I'm supposed to be rebuilding my family-friendly image after the end of my marriage, not stirring up more scandal.

I turn to track down whoever Mia was talking to and clear up the misunderstanding, but there's a whole wall of reporters. The voice had to come from a woman, which narrows my suspects down to about half.

In the pandemonium, I didn't convince Bex to join us for photographs, and neither did I track down the rogue reporter. I'm having the success of a swimmer trying to make it to shore during a riptide. Like that swimmer, my best avenue of survival is to go with the flow until I can make my escape.

I smile for the camera then somehow end up in the VIP tent, shaking hands with strangers and quoting my infamous line repeatedly. "I got da moves."

I smile and nod and text Bex.

I need to talk to you.

> Crazy Good Coach: You don't need anything else from me. I showed you the basics, now you get to go do what you're best at. Have fun.

She's talking about the game. She thinks I'm nervous like she probably would be.

I could care less about whether I win or not. What matters is that Bex is here to support me.

She brought the Ladybugs. She made up a cheer. She designed giant cutouts of my head.

All I can do is pull out my trusty life verse and go live up to what I've already obtained.

* * *

My teammates all played soccer for years before becoming famous. To be specific, a famous chef, musician, late night show host, and action hero. I don't have their precision and finesse, but I've got stamina and training in the sand. And I've got Bex shouting direction through her bullhorn from the top row of the bleachers. I feel like her avatar on Wii Soccer.

Jason wipes his bald head and asks in his British accent, "Who's the crazy lady taunting our opponents? I like her."

I grin. What Bex can't get away with in the elementary school leagues is welcome at exhibition games. "She's my secret weapon."

Gordon crosses his iconic arms. "She's being too nice. We're losing by one."

Nice is not a word I ever would have used for Bex. My mind rewinds through the month of coaching together. From practice in the rain to her secret practice.

What she taught the girls without me could benefit my team right now. "I have a plan."

The trick play may have been designed for children, but nobody will expect an action hero to pass to a gray-haired talk show host. Yet could anyone do it better?

Our team runs back into the sand, granules flying behind us. We line up, Jason facing off with a comedian who takes the game much more seriously than expected.

The whistle shrills, and we're off. I hang back on defense. Funny man dribbles toward the net. I shuffle in front of him and kick the ball straight through his legs. He might not find the move as hilarious as I do, so I'll laugh later.

Jason traps the ball with his instep then dribbles downfield. Their defender charges to stop him. Jon smoothly moves in behind Jason, giving him the opportunity to pass the ball backward with his heel. Just as planned, Jon takes off around him toward the net, and Jason gets in the way of the defenders. With one perfect kick, Jon scores.

My arms shoot into the air.

Jon and Jason chest bump.

"Three, four, Jon scored." Bex's voice echoes over the screaming fans.

"Coach Skylar," the team yells.

Bex shakes her head at them, and prompts them to shout, "Jon!"

The talk show host turns to me with a laugh. "You should definitely get some credit for that too, Coach Skylar."

"You can interview me about it next time I'm on your show."

He walks by and slaps my rear. I assume this is a positive response to my suggestion, though I've always considered it a weird sports thing to do. I hope nobody commemorated the moment with a photograph.

We're tied with less than a minute to go. A tie is not a loss, so I'm okay with it. Of course, Bex is not.

She leads the team in chanting, "One more goal. One more goal."

Our last point energized me in the moment, but now I fold forward to rest my hands on my knees and catch my breath. If my muscles are Jello, then my lungs are filled with pudding.

Gordon calls a timeout and leads the team in huddling around me. "They want another goal, and you're going to have to score it, Skylar. I'm trading you positions."

Jason grunts. "Yeah. Give those girls a reason to cheer."

"Oh man. The pressure." I think I prefer coaching.

Gordon shakes his head. "If you can't stand the heat..."

Point taken. "Yes, Chef."

Julio claps his gloved hands. "Break."

I jog to my forward position and bounce in place to shake off the stiffness starting to set in. I play defender because I can kick the ball far but not with precision. I might be able to get the ball in the net if there's no goalie, but in trying to kick around the goalkeeper, I'm likely to miss the net completely.

I guess I'll just do my best. It's not like I can lose us the game. Right?

"Smile, Coach." This photographer has a throaty voice like Influencer Mom. Because it *is* Influencer Mom.

I give her a wave to help make her Instagram famous. As she points her phone my way, I'm reminded of the game where Riley stopped playing to smile for this very woman. It was right after she'd scored by dribbling into the net.

I don't know if her camera flashes needlessly or if a lightbulb just popped on over my head, but I know exactly what I'm going to do now. If I get the chance.

A whistle blows. They kickoff.

Gordon intercepts the ball and passes to me. I push it forward through the lumpy drifts of sand.

Channing, from the other team, charges to intercept. He's got his shirt off, and his shiny sixpack receives a lot more cheers than I do. But the Ladybugs are supporting me, and that's what matters. I can't let him steal the ball.

Passing to Jason, I distract Channing's focus and give myself the opening to run around him. Both defenders and the goalie charge Jason, expecting him to shoot. Without even looking, he passes it to me.

They should have learned their lesson last time.

The goal is wide open on this side. But I'm not going to embarrass myself by missing a shot. I pull a Riley and dribble right into the net.

Jason reaches to pull out non-existent hair. "What?"

Fans in the bleachers jump to their feet.

"One, two, who's got da moves?"

"Coach Skylar!"

My little Ladybugs go nuts in the stands. I beam at Bex who beams right back. No wonder she loves winning. This is the best feeling in the world.

Wiping my slick forehead dry, I exhale excess euphoria. My team surrounds me for a giant, sweaty, group hug. Then we're mobbed by cameramen and ushered to a podium to take turns answering questions.

My mind is with the Ladybugs who are already waiting at my autograph table in the distance. Thankfully, this is what reporters want to know about.

"Skylar, you scored the winning goal even though you're the only celebrity team member who didn't play soccer while growing up. To what do you attribute your success?"

I smile down at the microphone, feeling uncharacteristically sheepish about the extent of my happiness. "This summer, I had the pleasure of coaching my niece's soccer team. They inspired me. As did my assistant coach who trained me for Soccer in the Sand."

I glance toward the autograph table in the distance for a glimpse of

Bex. To see if she can hear me talking about her. She's too busy keeping an eye on our team.

"She did her job well." The reporter checks her notebook in hand. "What's been your favorite part of this experience?"

They might be getting tired of my gushing, so I start with, "As delightful as I found Channing's abs..."

Uproarious laughter. Especially from the still shirtless actor.

Now I can gush again. "He can't compete with my Ladybugs, and I suspect they brought joy to everyone else who attended this event, as well."

After everyone else gets a turn to answer questions, we're released to find our spots in the autograph line. It's set up for me to meet strangers, but Riley's mom is there to take pictures too.

"You used Riley's move," she trills. "That means you got da moves from my daughter."

I pat her on the arm and side hug my sister-in-law. The girls jump around my legs, and I slap them high fives. Finally, I wade through the crowd far enough to wrap my arm around Bex in a celebratory hug. I realize that even while I'd been scoring for my team, this had been my goal throughout the entire day.

She fits securely against my chest. Her fruity scent makes my mouth water.

"Thank you." I stop there because if I listed everything I'm thankful for, we'd be here forever. Maybe I should list them as an excuse to hold her.

She pulls away, but only far enough to bless me with a radiant smile. "I'm putting the job of coaching you on my resume."

Probably the best compliment she could ever offer anyone.

"Skylar," My agent interrupts. He's apparently come back after his meeting to ruin the best moment of my day.

Again, I can listen without looking. I kind of rock Bex in my arms in a friendly way. "What is it, Craig?"

"I want to introduce you to Ceasar Navarra."

Bex gasps.

I recognize the man's name as the professional soccer player who married a British pop star and practically became European royalty. No wonder Bex's body just went rigid with shock. I'm about to be replaced as her hero.

I release her to grip his strong hand. "Skylar Hayes. Nice to meet you."

He gives my arm a couple of pumps. "You too. My daughters loved you in the Professional Kid series, but I loved watching you play today. You might have heard this once or twice already, but you got da moves."

I force a chuckle then step aside for Bex to fawn over the ruggedly handsome older man. His tanned forehead shows the kind of lines that come from a life spent in the sun. He still has a full head of dark hair, though the hairs of his trim beard have lightened as if to present his self-confident smile on a silver platter.

"If you think I've got moves, you should see this lady play."

Ceasar extends a hand to Bex, though she's too starstruck to respond. His mouth quivers in mirth at her frozen state. He probably gets this a lot.

"Nice job coaching the superstar." Ceasar shoots a thumb over his shoulder toward me, so he has something to do with his hand other than leave it awkwardly extended between the two of them. "It's nice to meet you. I'm Ceasar Navarra."

"I know." Her chest rises and falls. The olive complexion of her skin pales to match that of Olive Oyl's from Popeye. "I'm Rebecca—"

"Heads!"

A soccer ball flies out of nowhere, smashing Bex's face. Her arms flail wide to catch herself though there's nothing to catch herself on other than me. I grab hold and keep her upright, but blood pours from her nostrils and dots us both. Before anyone can even react, there's enough blood to connect the dots.

Bex's dream come true just turned into her worst nightmare. I need to get her to the medical tent.

"Excuse us. Jacqueline, you're in charge of Mia." Scooping Bex into my arms, I jog as best I can through sand toward the white awning with the red cross.

Bex clings to my neck but stares at the scene we're leaving behind. More likely, the man we're leaving behind. I understand her loss, but she needs to stop the blood.

"Pinch your nose if it doesn't hurt too much."

She does as instructed, but she also closes her eyes. In my peripheral vision, I see tears slide down her cheeks to mix with the red liquid already there.

I do a double take to make sure she's really crying. Her eyes could just be watering from the pain.

She's not trying to blink away the water in her eyes, however. She's squeezing them tighter as if holding in emotion.

"Oh, sweetheart. It's okay." I hope I'm speaking the truth. I hope she doesn't need surgery or end up with a second bump on top of her first bump.

"It's not okay." Her voice whimpers. "That was my dad."

Bex

Those who play rarely become brittle in the face of stress or lose the healing capacity for humor.
–Stuart Brown, MD

Pain gradually throbs into my numb face. You know that dumb game adults play with kids where they tuck a thumb between two fingers and say, “I got your nose”? I think I’m experiencing what it would feel like if they really did remove the child’s nose. But you know what hurts even more? The fact my dad never played such games with me.

You know what hurts even more than that? I don’t think my dad even realized he was talking to his oldest child. Would he have mentioned daughters if he knew I was one of them?

I tried to introduce myself. I even called myself Rebecca, as is printed on my birth certificate. But before I could finish with the last name passed on from my mother, I got a soccer ball shoved up my nostrils.

I’ve been so careful to never take another soccer ball to the face. Until now.

If I’d known this was how I was going to meet my father, I wouldn’t have played the stupid sport. Instead, I would've burned all the soccer balls I could find the way Sleeping Beauty's parents did to spinning wheels.

"What?" Skylar blurts, reminding me I'm in his arms. Not like a moment ago when he wrapped both arms completely behind my back and rocked us from side to side. No, he's now hobbling through the sand with me clinging to his neck and pinching the bridge of my nose.

I open my weepy eyes to stare at the blue sky while processing Skylar's question. He'd asked "What?" But I don't have the voice to explain.

Besides, who am I to claim the world's most famous soccer player as my dad? Mom kept our relationship hush-hush as part of their trade. She wanted money to buy her dream home, and Dad feared knowledge of my existence would wreck his.

For the first time I wonder if he made me more half-siblings. I could be related to anybody I pass on the street without knowing it. I could even be coaching a niece like Skylar is.

There's an online group for secret babies where we play "Who's Your Daddy?" on Fridays. When it was my turn, I posted three pictures. One of me, one of the boyfriend Mom first claimed to be my father, then a snapshot she took of dear ol' dad before he became a superstar. Every member of the online group guessed correctly, so I know our similarities are noticeable.

Surely Skylar sees our resemblance. Perhaps my misshapen nose threw him off. Ceasar Navarra and I share the same strong jaw, thick eyebrows, and our coloring matches except for his silvering facial hair.

Skylar's simply surprised. As am I. Though maybe I should've expected famous footballers to attend a celebrity soccer match.

I wish I hadn't come. Or I wish I'd at least avoided making a spectacle of myself with a bullhorn and giant head cutouts. Not to mention the soccer ball that smashed my face in.

A sob escapes. Tears puddle in my ears because I'm too busy hanging onto Skylar and plugging my nose to mop them up.

Blue sky gives way to white plastic. I'm jostled then set on a cot. I lift my feet to lay back, but small hands press me to stay upright in a seated position.

The emergency worker who held me up now offers me box of tissues. "I need you to blow your nose gently to get rid of any blood clots. Then you're going to tilt your head forward and pinch just above the nostrils for at least ten minutes."

These are things I'd expect to make a bloody nose worse. Blow my nose? Tilt forward? But what do I know? Everything I'd expected to make my dad proud of me has ended with the opposite result.

I soak the tissue then tilt my head forward and pinch my nose as directed. Looking down, I find my favorite jersey covered in blood. It's a murder scene of my hopes and dreams.

My shoulders shake with another round of sobs.

"Calm down, honey." The female employee smooths my crown with a palm the way I do for Mia. It's so nurturing. I can't remember if anyone has ever touched me like this before. "Crying can make it take longer for the bleeding to stop."

I nod because I don't want to cry anymore. But I seem to have even less control over my tears than the blood. I attempt deep breaths, but I'm gasping and sucking and shaking. I squeeze my eyes shut and see my dad's face all over again for the very first time.

"Here's some ice."

I don't feel any ice, but its sting must be minor compared to the throbbing pain of mangled flesh at the center of my face. At the center of my chest. Who notices a raindrop from underneath a waterfall?

"I'm going to step out to give you space. See if you can calm her down." The tent flap flutters.

"Bex?" Skylar's tone is soothing. Compassionate.

I open my eyes to find him kneeling on the ground to make eye contact. I imagine how I must look to him. Gone is the tough athletic trainer. She's been replaced by a giant baby.

Even the word baby guts me. Why don't all babies in the world get to be loved the way I love Mia? They should be.

Skylar takes my free hand. He doesn't lace our fingers together the way a boyfriend would. It's more the vibe of a priest visiting a dying patient.

His other hand holds an ice pack. The nurse had apparently handed it to him, which would be why I didn't feel it.

"Ceasar Navarra's your dad?" He asks evenly, the perfect balance of fact and feeling. Somehow it helps me balance too.

Sucking in a couple short breaths, I'm able to hang onto them this time. I nod, fingers still pinching my nose.

He licks his lips like he's really contemplating his next question. His dark eyes flinch. "Does he know you're his daughter?"

Still not ready to trust my voice, I shrug.

"I had no idea." He blinks. Blows out a breath. "Is he the reason you're obsessed with soccer?"

My lips squeeze together. My chin quivers. I hate feeling so weak.

This isn't the agony of defeat. It's deeper. For the first time, I understand there are worse things than losing. For example, playing your hardest only to discover your teammate planned to purposely throw the game all along.

My goal of becoming a pro soccer player was really the goal of making my dad proud. But I'd been set up to fail from the very beginning.

Skylar wipes a thumb over my cheek to dry yet another tear. "He's missing out, Bex."

This time I'm able to inhale long and deep. A cleansing breath. I want to believe my dad is missing out, but even more I want *him* to believe it. Hearing Skylar say he believes it isn't the fulfilment I'd been longing for, but it validates my longing while giving me permission to let it go.

"Thank you," I whisper.

"There's still a chance you can connect with him," he offers.

I roll my eyes to give them something to do other than sob. "He's not like other dads. I can't look up his contact info on LinkedIn."

"I know." One corner of his mouth quirks up. "Though I could have my people contact his people."

He makes the suggestion with a half-smile, which means the other half of him is serious. But I can't let myself think about meeting Dad again right now. Not when I'm still recovering from the panic attack from our first meeting.

"Hey." Skylar tilts his head. "Ceasar complimented you on your coaching and said it was nice to meet you. You impressed him."

"Right," I scoff.

"Right," he retorts.

His dark eyes burn me with their authenticity. The guy is watching my nose swell up large enough to get me mistaken for Beaker on The Muppets, yet he sees me as a better person than I see myself.

He doesn't stop there. "In fact, if Ceasar Navarra had known you were his daughter, he might have been the one to carry you up here himself."

I squint, trying to picture such a scene. I would have been a bloody, sobbing mess in my dad's arms. Even if he'd had a heart change since paying off my mom, even if he wanted to reconnect with me, that kind of reunion would have been overwhelming for anyone.

Maybe God's mercy allowed the soccer ball to hit me in the face before I revealed our relationship. Maybe He was saving me from something. Maybe I should be glad Skylar was the one to carry me and comfort me.

I don't say this aloud though. I'm vulnerable enough as it is.

Skylar narrows his eyes. Like he's also thinking deep thoughts. "Knowing you played soccer to earn your dad's love makes it even more impressive that you gave up the pro sports career to raise your daughter on your own."

My heartbeat stutters. I remember talking to Skylar about my parents but never about my pregnancy with Mia. Suddenly, getting hit in the face with a soccer ball while meeting my father for the first time is not the worst thing that could happen today. "How'd you know that?"

His eyebrows leap up and hang there. They're the Michael Jordan of eyebrows. "Uh…Jacqueline told me you don't know who Mia's dad is. She didn't think you'd mind."

I roll back onto the cot to lie down. Not for my nose this time. For my stomach.

"I'm sorry. I meant it as a compliment. No judgement here." He pushes to his feet from his kneeling position so he can make eye contact again. "Are you sure you should be lying down?"

My choices war within me. Not about sitting up or lying down but about revealing more truth. This one's never been a struggle before. But I'm raw. I'm scared. And Skylar seems safe. He let me bleed all over him.

As long as I'm telling secrets… "I know who Mia's dad is." I watch for his reaction out of the corner of my eye.

He pulls a folding chair over and lowers himself down. "Okay?"

I look to the white plastic awning, unable to face him. Though I didn't lie to him about Mia's dad, I did lie. I thought it would protect Mia from what I went through when I was her age. Unfortunately, she'll find out the truth one day. So what if I'm not saving her, but delaying her?

"It's my ex." The words come out squeaky. At least I'm getting them out. "We lived together and planned to wed. Since we were both driven in our careers, we agreed we wouldn't have kids. Then I took an antibiotic for a sinus infection, and it affected my birth control."

The story seems more ironic now than ever. My broken nose caused me to have issues with sinus infections. If I hadn't broken my nose, I might never have become a mother. It kind of makes me love my bump.

I also regret moving in with my boyfriend before we were married, yet God used that poor choice for good too. Through my greatest pain, He brought my greatest joy.

Sadly, Mia deserves better.

I choke down an excess of saliva. "My fiancé felt tricked. He said if I wanted to stay with him, then I had to keep my word and not have any children."

Skylar's chin lifts.

I brace myself for his judgment. Just when my tears had started to dry, this.

Skylar shakes his head. "Not only did you have to give up your career, but he made you choose between him and Mia?" He's incredulous.

I'm incredulous. I'd thought his chin lifted because he was sticking his nose in the air. But no. It lifted with the impact of having his mind blown.

Again he thinks higher of me than I do myself. I'm ashamed to admit keeping Mia was a tough choice. But he probably knows from his own life experience that the right choice is usually tougher.

I blink back unshed tears. Grateful tears. I've never been such an emotional mess. "My fiancé offered to take care of the pregnancy. I told him I'd be taking care of the child."

Skylar's hand grabs mine. He laces our fingers this time. "If he knows about Mia, why are you telling people it was a one-night stand?"

My throat clogs again. I motion out the tent flap. To the beach. Where I got my blood all over a man who probably doesn't know it's the same blood that runs in his veins.

Skylar nods slowly. "Because you don't want Mia spending her life trying to impress a parent who wants nothing to do with her. You'd rather she thinks her dad doesn't know about her than he chose not to meet her."

He understands, but that doesn't mean he agrees with my choice. I don't even know if I agree with my choice anymore. "Yes."

He lets me lie there in silence for a bit. Gives me time to acknowledge my dishonesty. I lied because I didn't feel like I'd had a choice, but the truth is that I had choices, I just didn't like them.

I still have choices, and I still don't like them.

"Do you know where Mia's dad is?" he asks.

I'll think about my choices later. "He's a team doctor for the Padres." What a different life I'd be living if I'd chosen him over Mia. Easier in many ways. But not better.

Skylar rubs his jaw. "Is he helping you out with child support?"

I shake my head a little too forcefully, and my nose slips from between my fingers. I still, suck in a breath, and dab my nostrils with a fresh tissue. It comes back mostly clean. "I don't want Mia to ever think I only kept her for child support."

"She would never think that," Skylar argues. "You're not your mom."

I grimace. I may not be my mom, but I brought my own baggage into parenting. My obsession with soccer, as Skylar pointed out, got me removed from my position as her coach.

Though, if it hadn't, I never would have worked with Skylar. Again, I'm blessed through a curse. I've yet to live up to all I've obtained.

Skylar taps his own nose. "How's it doing?"

I flare my nostrils, which feel okay, then scrunch the bridge, which does not. "Tender. I'm scared to see a mirror. Do I look like Bozo?"

Skylar chuckles then sobers to study my face. "Actually, getting hit today pushed your first bump back into place."

He surprises a laugh out of me. My nose throbs in response, so I cut it short. Who knew laughter involves nose muscles? "Nuh-uh."

"It could have. I can't tell with all the swelling. Here." He lifts the ice pack to my nose. It's cold, but the caress of his eyes is warm. "You might need to go to a doctor to get it realigned."

That gives me a little direction at least. I'm not sure what I'm going to do with Mia, but I'll take time to figure it out. First, I'll have to talk to the Father who didn't abandon her. Or me.

Skylar

In every real man a child is hidden that wants to play. – Friedrich Nietzsche

I want to kiss Bex's broken nose, but I learned from *Raiders of the Lost Ark* not to kiss areas of the body that have been injured. Right now, that's all of her.

Is it too late for me to catch Ceasar Navarra before he leaves? I wouldn't tell him Bex is his daughter, only that it would mean a lot for him to check on her. If he's already left, I'll try to catch Craig who has the network to contact him.

"Mom." Mia flies through the tent opening. The little girl doesn't know how loved she is, but she's so saturated that it just oozes out her pores. "Riley's mom took a video of the ball hitting you in the face. Are you okay?"

"I was until you said that thing about the video." Bex is better than okay. She's got her sense of humor back.

Mia charges to the cot. "Want me to kiss your nose like you kiss my boo-boos?"

Not fair. I cross my arms and try not to pout.

Bex winces. "You probably shouldn't touch it right now."

I nod in satisfaction that neither Mia nor I get to kiss Bex's nose. Not that it's a competition. If it was, I wouldn't stand a chance.

Mia bounces around, and I'm afraid she's going to bump Bex's nose accidentally anyway.

I stand. "Here. Take my chair."

Mia sits and wiggles. "Kendall said you might have to get a cast on your nose like she had when she broke her wrist."

Hmm... Yet another reason Kendall doesn't move her arms. I guess we all have reasons for the things we do, whether we know what they are or not.

For Bex, she needs healing from her past in order to be free from trying to earn love. I'm more determined than ever to track down Ceasar Navarra. Thankfully, my sister-in-law enters the tent, baby on her back. She still has a little pooch from her last pregnancy, so I can't tell if this one is showing yet or not.

"Skylar." Jacqueline motions me toward the entrance. "Will you let the team know how Bex is doing? They're waiting outside."

Great excuse to leave and chase down Ceasar. "Yes. One sec." I fold forward over Bex and smooth back her sleek ponytail. "I'm going to talk to the Ladybugs. You're in good hands."

Her eyes are silver bullets with the way they pierce me. Like they're wondering if I'll abandon her too.

Not a chance.

She grimaces. "Tell them I'll be at practice Wednesday, whether I have a cast on my nose or not."

Jacqueline clears her throat behind me. "Wednesday is Independence Day. They're all invited to our barbecue, so I guess you could practice in our backyard. That is, if you're coming."

Mia jumps up from her chair. "We have to go to Treva's."

Bex blinks a few times. "I guess we'll be there." She turns to me, and her forced smile softens. "Tell the team I'm bringing a Slip 'n Slide so we can practice slide tackling."

I am so tackling her. If she doesn't have a cast on her nose, that is.

"Will do." I pull myself away and head toward the tent flap.

Behind me, Mia asks, "Did Rudolph the Red-Nosed Reindeer play soccer?"

Oh no. The kid is replacing me at Bex's bedside, but without the comforting words. Hopefully Bex doesn't consider Rudolph too much worse a name than Bozo.

Bex doesn't miss a beat, nor does she sound offended when she responds with, "It was probably one of their reindeer games."

I smile to myself. I'm smiling because those two are so sweet together. I'm smiling at the depth of Bex's sacrifice and the beauty that has come from it. I'm smiling at how the day's tragedy doesn't feel tragic anymore. It feels like the beginning of something new.

I step into the blinding sunshine and hold up a hand to shade my eyes until they adjust.

"You're awfully happy for a guy covered in blood."

I recognize the crisp tone of a drill sergeant before lowering my hand and squinting at the silhouette of a man. Caleb is a shorter version of me with a buzz cut. And he's alone.

There are no Ladybugs with him. Not even his own kids. I assume he asked Olivia to take them to the minivan since that's what he normally does. As for Jacqueline, she tricked me.

"Hey." I grip Caleb's hand and lean in for a bro hug. "I didn't expect to see you until Wednesday. Welcome home."

He holds up a palm to hold me at a distance, so I don't smear blood from my jersey onto his white polo. "I couldn't miss my goofy little brother playing soccer with the best action hero of all time."

"Jason Statham?" I play along with his joke. "You came home early to watch Jason?"

"Precisely." Teasing is his love language. Though his troops might consider it taunting.

I click my tongue. "Sorry I had to ruin your experience by scoring the winning goal myself."

He stands with perfect posture, hands behind his back. "I'm surprised I was the only one who booed."

I chuckle at that but look around for Bex's dad. "Did you see which way Ceasar Navarra went?"

"Nine o'clock."

I scan the beach to our right. It's mostly teams and families. No women swooning. No cameras flashing. Not even an overdressed talent agent schmoozing.

Caleb pulls a wrist from behind his back to glance at his watch. "He left about five minutes ago."

Then he couldn't have gotten too far. I jog a step.

"Wait, Skylar. I need to talk to you." He follows, but he's not running.

I frown. Ceasar already has a head start. "Can it wait?"

"Is Jacqueline pregnant?"

My hands fall to my sides. I turn to face my big brother and take a deep breath of sunblock-scented air. "Why do you think that?"

"She asked for a hamburger with jalapenos at Burger Lounge on the way here." I can't see his expression behind his aviator glasses, but his tone comes out more clipped than usual, and his lips press together afterwards.

"Interesting..." I don't want to give anything away. Wish I had my shades with me, as well. "Why don't you ask her?"

"If Jacqueline's pregnant, I need to know before talking to her about re-enlisting."

Oh man. I rub a hand over my head. "She doesn't want you to re-enlist, does she?"

"With another kid to feed, we're going to need that signing bonus."

"With another kid to feed, she's going to need your help."

"So she *is* pregnant."

Big brothers are the worst. "I didn't say that."

"Refusing to answer is an answer in itself."

"Dude. Stand down. I don't know anything except that she's eating jalapenos."

He nods curtly then turns his head to stare up the beach. On an excitement scale of one to ten, he's not much higher than Bex's ex was about her pregnancy. It hurts my heart for his family. For Jacqueline. For his unborn child.

I shake my head at him. "I wish I had your problems."

He lowers his aviators to peer at me over the top of them. "You wish you had to work a job in one country to support a family in another?"

He doesn't have to. He could stay. "Do you want to be here?"

"Getting a lecture from my baby brother? No."

"Here." I motion to the coastline of San Diego across the harbor. "With your family."

He crosses his arms. "Of course I want to be here. But here is expensive. A family is expensive. Not that you would know."

I throw my arms in the air. "I *wish* I knew."

"Really?" he challenges. "You were making more money than both our parents combined before you were out of elementary school. You could probably live the rest of your life on interest alone. So don't fault me for worrying about retirement benefits, education, and, say, food."

I still. He has a good argument, and I'm going to have to set up college funds for his kiddos. But he's missing my point. "My wife left me."

His combat stance relaxes. As relaxed as he can get anyway. "I'm sorry, man."

"Thank you."

I heave a sigh. Because it's stupid that we're out here feeling sorry for ourselves over a lack of money or a significant other while Bex has neither and is currently in a first aid tent recovering from meeting her father for the very first time. Not that the man recognized her.

Caleb and I grew up with incredible parents. We're taking for granted a blessing we should be grateful for. As for my brother, he's soon going to have even more to be grateful for.

So I add, "And congratulations."

He laughs wryly. "I'm not really angry with you. I'm just scared."

My tough brother is admitting to being scared. And it's the most I've ever admired him. "You don't have to do anything alone, you know."

He claps me on the back. "I've fought in wars. I should be able to raise teenage girls, right?"

"I'm not sure I'd go that far." I attempt to flinch, but my lips curve up with memories from this summer. "I've been coaching Treva's soccer team, and...Ladybugs be crazy."

Caleb's rigid face cracks into the first authentic smile I've seen today. We grin across the beach at the games still going on in the golden glow of a setting sun. At the families cheering from the sidelines. At teammates learning about life through playing a sport.

There will always be more to learn.

"Jacqueline says you're a good coach," Caleb offers.

I know he appreciates the way I help out his family when he's gone, and it's nice to hear, but I'm not sure how to respond. "That might be the kindest thing you've ever said."

He grunts. "Well, if we have a boy, I'm naming him after Jason."

"Oh good. I thought you were getting sappy on me."

"Never."

"You weren't secretly disappointed I was covered in blood because you wanted a hug?"

"I secretly love bloody things and didn't want you to find out."

The blood is mostly dry anyway, so I wrap him in a bear hug. "Well now I know, so we might as well hug." I'll buy him a new shirt if needed.

Not to be outdone, Caleb wrestles me to the ground. It's squishy enough that I can body slam him without worry of injury. Well, until he forces me down a sandbank into the refreshingly cool surf, and my mouth is filled with salty water and gritty sand.

"Oh, hey." He says, as if we're just on a casual stroll down the beach rather than attempting to drown each other. "I meant to ask you about the woman with the bloody nose."

I groan and roll away from him to flop on dry ground. Now that I've had that talk with my brother, it's probably too late to chase down Bex's dad. But I won't give up. "What'd you want to know?"

Caleb sits up and is able to study me with a direct gaze now that his sunglasses are knocked off. "How long have you been in love with her?"

Bex

There is no passion to be found playing small –
in settling for a life that is less than the one you are capable of living. –
Nelson Mandela

The swelling went down so that my nose looks normal again. Well, normal for me. Not normal for other people. Thankfully nothing was broken this time, though I did get a couple of black eyes out of the deal.

Mia thinks it's cool, but that's mostly because Riley's Mom's video of me went viral. At least the general public doesn't know who I am. The clip is about a famous soccer player and a former child star. Hopefully Skylar's heroics help him get back into acting the way he wants.

I'm simply the comic relief. Like one of those TikToks where the grandma falls out of a boat, or the snowboarder flies off a cliff. Hilarious.

I don't even care anymore. Well, I care, but the non-relationship with my dad pales in comparison to the relationship with my daughter. I have to tell her the truth.

Every time I remember confessing to Skylar about Mia's real dad, my heart races. From experience, I know it will continue like that until I am honest with Mia too. I've been praying for days that I'm wrong, yet my heart continues to race. If I don't come clean soon, I'm going to end up in the ER, and I've had enough medical attention this week.

Tuesday night, I'm cleaning the kitchen from homemade macaroni (that I cooked to soften Mia up for the dreaded talk) when the embarrassing video actually airs on ESPN. I cover my mouth and step backwards so Mia can't see my face from where she's coloring at the orange breakfast bar.

Her little head lifts. She points to the television I tucked underneath the cabinets like a breadbox so I can feed my kid without missing any important games. Then she turns her face to find me, lips forming a tiny O. "You're on TV, mom."

My pulse pounds in my ears. I don't say anything because I'm straining to hear what the color commentators have to say.

"Can you imagine getting to meet Ceasar Navarra, then being interrupted by a soccer ball to the face?" the male announcer asks.

He doesn't even know.

The part where the ball hits my face plays on repeat, the last time in slow motion. I can almost feel the crunch of my nasal bone stabbing my brain all over again. Thanks, Influencer Mom.

The female announcer beams at her cohost. "I imagine it would be worth it if Skylar Hayes jumped in to rescue me like that. Though I don't think he'd rescue just anybody. It's been confirmed that the two of them are a couple."

My pulse races for a whole new reason now. This one could be worse.

Who confirmed such a rumor? Skylar and I have never been on a date. He laced our fingers together in the first aid tent, but nobody else was there to see it. In fact, sometimes I wonder if it really happened. I'd just been hit in the face with a ball. It's all a blur.

"Bex Lemaire is her name."

"Wah," I squeak.

Of all the places to air tabloid news, I never expected this from ESPN. They betrayed me.

If my dad watches the sports network and sees this clip, he'll know who I am. Will he feel bad we were interrupted, or will he be glad he avoided having to face the child he wanted to forget?

"Skylar Hayes coaches her daughter's soccer team, and she brought them all out to cheer him on."

Oh no. Our Ladybug cheer with the giant head cutouts. Dad's going to learn he has a granddaughter too.

Mia squeals. "Look, Mom. It's me."

I sink onto a stool beside her.

"Bex Lemaire's own daughter told reporter Emery Harrison that the two are seeing each other."

Okay, I'm not the only woman in this house with some explaining to do. Though I'm not sure who I should be angrier with—my daughter for telling stories or the reporter for relying on an eight-year-old source?

I turn to demand some answers from Mia.

She's still beaming her big toothy grin, crayon poised in one hand. Apparently, she's unaware she did anything wrong. Does she really think Skylar and I are dating?

I scrunch my forehead. "Did you tell a reporter I'm dating Skylar?"

Her wet lips purse in confusion. "No."

I point to the television. We just watched the same sportscast, right? "Well, that's what they said."

"No." Her eyes flash with worry. "The reporter asked me if Skylar was seeing you. He was. I checked. He was looking right at you."

My phone buzzes from its spot on the charger. I can't even imagine who all is calling, but Skylar is going to be at the top of that list.

I cover my face.

"Does seeing someone mean dating? Because that's silly. I'm seeing you right now." Mia's soft fingers circle around mine and pull. "Well, not right now because you're hiding behind your hands."

I drop my arms and give her a tremulous smile. She didn't do anything wrong. And if I've been waiting for an opening to talk to her about adult things, this is it.

"Come here, honey."

She crawls onto my lap, and I want to hold her forever. Just not on this stool. It's digging into my thighs and offers no back support. I stand and carry her into the living room to the one piece of comfy furniture in our house.

"The news lady thinks I told her Skylar is your boyfriend?" she asks again before I'm able to sit down.

The news? The country? The world? It's so ridiculous that it's hilarious.

Laughter takes over, and I drop onto the sofa. "Yes, she does."

She watches me in confusion then grins at my mirth. "Why's it funny?"

I catch my breath and blow it out slowly. "Sometimes it makes me feel better to laugh at sad things."

She tilts her head. "Why are you sad?"

I turn her to face me, so we're both comfortable and settled. The pudginess of baby cheeks is starting to thin, and I'm sad for a whole new reason. I want Mia to stay young and innocent, yet I have to tell her some not-so-innocent things.

I brush her maturing cheek with my finger. "There's some stuff about me you don't know."

"I know your favorite color is red like the Ladybugs."

Okay. That's a start.

"And your favorite number is five because it was on the back of your jersey when you played soccer."

"You have a good memory." I wonder how she'll remember this moment.

"Is your favorite letter M for Mia or L for Lemaire?"

My heart swells and slows a bit. If Mia feels this loved by me, then maybe she won't feel so unloved by her dad.

"It's I for ice cream," I tease.

"Noo..." She giggles. "That's mine."

"Oh, right." I tuck a stray hair behind her ear. "Mine is M for Mia because I love you so much. And I'm glad you know that. You're my favorite person in the whole wide world."

"You're mine too." She leans forward to wrap her little arms around my body.

I hold her there, smelling her cheesy macaroni breath and hiding my tears. "Here's what you don't know." I wipe my eyes dry and face her again. "When I was your age, I wasn't my mom's favorite person. She left me alone a lot and didn't like playing with me."

"She didn't play soccer?"

Hm… Maybe I should try playing other things with Mia if that's all I'm known for.

"No." I twist my lips. Probably best not to tell her my dad's identity since she's got a nasty habit of talking to the press. "But my father played soccer, and I thought if I could learn to play it well enough, then he would love me and come pick me up so I could live with him."

Mia leans back, eyes dazed. "Did he?"

"No."

"He should have. You're really good. Did you tell him that you could do a flip throw in?"

"No, honey." I measure my words. "He had other kids with someone else and he didn't want me in his family."

She gasps. She has no idea that her father isn't any better. Before I tell her, she needs to understand there's nothing she can do to earn his affection.

"Just so you know, nobody should have to do a flip throw in to be loved."

She nods somberly. "If they did, there'd be a lot of unloved people in the world."

So simple. So absurd. Yet most of us still try to earn love every day.

"You're a smart girl. It took me a long time to figure that out."

She smiles encouragingly. "Now you know."

I wish knowing in my head was as easy as feeling in my heart. But I think everyone must make that connection in their own way. For me… "The neighbor lady took me to Sunday School where I learned God loves us all. But I didn't really understand love until I had you. Until you came into the world crying, and pooping, and refusing to sleep, and eating all the time."

She laughs from her belly. "I still do that."

"You're actually worse now because you told reporters I have a boyfriend." I tickle her ribs, and her giggle brings me more joy than I'd known as a child. "But no matter how much you cry and poop and refuse to sleep and eat all the time—"

"And tell reporters you have a boyfriend," she adds a little too proudly.

"Or that. There's nothing you can ever do to make me love you any more or less. I love you just for being you. And you're the reason I know God loves me."

She presses my cheeks between her two hands. "I know God loves me because I have you."

My heart surges with hope this time. I prayed for an opening, and God gave it to me. Well, first he let ESPN air the most humiliating moment of my life and announce to the world that I'm dating a celebrity, but that got me here.

"Mia, I'm so glad you know God loves you, because I need to tell you something else. Something I don't want to tell you."

She watches me with wide, shiny eyes. "What?"

I wish I could kick a soccer ball right now. I'd kick it in Grant's face. But I shouldn't blame him. I knew where he stood from the beginning. It's on me now. "I know who your father is."

She stills. A China doll. Then her face lights up. She leans forward. "Is Coach Skylar my dad?"

It's one of those moments where I need to pray more than I ever have in my life, but I can't find the words. So I simply pray, *Dear, Lord*, and figure God knows what I need better than I do myself.

All I can do is answer Mia's question. "No."

"Is it Treva's dad?"

Dear, Lord, it's me again. "No, honey."

"Good. He's kind of mean."

In a Captain Von Trapp way, I guess Caleb can be mean. But that's for him and Jacqueline to figure out. "You haven't met your father, honey. That's why I didn't want to tell you. You deserve to have the best dad in the world, but your father doesn't want to be a dad."

My brain freezes, waiting for her reaction. I don't know what to say, think, or feel until I know what she says, thinks, and feels.

She holds her hands wide. "Then why'd he have a kid?"

Again she simplifies one of my life's biggest complications. We'll surely have this discussion again when she gets to sex ed, but until then, I need a simple answer. "Because God wanted a Mia on this earth for me to love, so He used your father to get you to me."

Her teeth flash again. "Okay."

She's smiling. She's happy. This is as unbelievable as Skylar lacing his fingers with mine.

Of course, Mia doesn't understand fully yet. Growing up with a single mom will be sure to affect her in many more ways down the road. I know because I've walked that path. But I'd like to think I'm paving her way.

Now that I've shared, there won't be a big dramatic reveal later. I won't have to worry about her doing a DNA search. The family tree projects at school could still be tricky with my dad's identity a secret, but maybe there'll be a time to share that with her, as well.

I'll save it for when she starts asking more questions about her own father. Then I can distract her with a, "Hey, did I ever tell you Ceasar Navarra is your grandfather?"

Nah. I'll be honest with her. As I'll have to be with people like Jacqueline, so they don't keep going around telling strangers I had a drunken one-night stand. Not that Skylar's a stranger anymore. I mean, Mia even hoped he was her dad.

She asks more questions, some serious, some silly. We laugh and snuggle late into the night. I figure it's okay for two reasons. First, it's been a big day, so she deserves a special treat. And second, tomorrow is the 4th of July, so it wouldn't hurt to sleep in as preparation for staying up late to watch fireworks.

As she falls asleep on my chest on the couch, my thoughts turn to Skylar. I wonder if he's heard the news that the two of us are a couple. If so, I wonder what messages he's left on my phone.

More importantly, I wonder how he feels about the idea.

Skylar

We are never more fully alive, more completely ourselves, or more deeply engrossed in anything than when we are play. – Charles Schaefer

I know seeing her dad face to face had to mess with Bex's emotions, but now I'm an emotional mess too. I'd overheard Mia tell the reporter I was seeing her mom, and I meant to do something about it at the time, then everything else happened, and it slipped my mind.

I apologized in my text. I asked how Bex was doing after the sportscast. I asked about her nose. And...nothing.

My ringer stayed on all night in case she couldn't sleep and wanted to talk. The notifications kept chiming and waking me up. Everyone else in my world messaged to ask about my new girlfriend. While said girlfriend ghosted me.

Now I'm debating whether to pursue my connection to Bex's dad. If he saw the clip—and I can't imagine that he didn't with how quickly I was contacted from viewers the moment it aired—he'll know Bex is his daughter. So whether I talk to him or not, the ball is in his court.

Would things have been different if I hadn't let my brother intercept me? I'm glad the two of us worked some stuff out, though his question about loving Bex left me reeling. If I'd really loved her, wouldn't I have gone after her father for her? Or am I wishing I had because I do.

My prayer is that she still comes to the barbecue tonight. I need to make sure she's okay. Then maybe I'll be okay.

The phone chimes again. I've been ignoring all my messages, but in case it's Jacqueline requesting I pick up ice or my brother needing another peptalk, I roll over in bed to grab the device from my nightstand.

A text from my agent.

Meh.

Crazy Good Coach

I scramble to sit up and give Bex's message my full attention.

> Crazy Good Coach: If I can't see you right now, am I still seeing you?

My chest practically explodes with a combination of relief and anticipation. She doesn't sound upset. Rather, she's making a joke about Mia's misunderstanding. And it's kind of flirty.

I could FaceTime her and ask, "Can you see me now?" Except then she'll notice I'm still in bed at ten in the morning. Which makes me either a lazy bum or reveals I'm exhausted from obsessing all night over not hearing from her. Not the impression I want when asking her out for the first time.

Yeah, I'm going to ask her on a date. Correction. I'm going to ask her and Mia on a date. Bex won't have to choose between me and Mia because I want to be there for them both.

Where should I take them? Disneyland? San Diego Zoo? Dinner cruise to Catalina?

All of the above.

I smile at my phone screen as I tap out my response.

> You'll see me at the BBQ tonight.

That's right. I'm flirting right back. And also making sure she's coming.

> Crazy Good Coach: Is everyone there going to think we're a couple?

I suck in a breath. Does the idea scare her?

That's the problem with dating when you're famous. Women either want to be with you or avoid you because of it. I sadly took advantage of my fame for a while, but the more I took, the less I had.

I didn't think fame would be an issue with Bex. She got to know the real me. Of course, that was before we were announced as a couple on national television. It could be a little tricky, but it will definitely be a lot of fun.

I take a deep breath to clear my head so I can figure out the right thing to say. I type, *It only matters what you and Mia think.* Then I stare at the words awhile, knowing if Bex is looking at the messaging app on her end, she'll see dots and be aware I'm putting a lot of effort into my response.

I'm not sure if I've said the right thing, but I believe it to be true. So I hit send and wait.

And wait.

> Crazy Good Coach: Mia and I had a long talk last night. Then she fell asleep on my chest on the couch. That's why I didn't get back to you right away.

I blow out a long breath. That makes sense. She wasn't avoiding me or hiding out to lick her wounds. She was taking care of business. *So it was a positive thing?*

> Crazy Good Coach: She took the news about her dad well. I was trying to make her feel loved, but in the end, she made me feel loved.

I shake my head in wonder. What a kid. She's stepping in and doing what I want to do—making Bex feel loved, offering to kiss her on the nose, telling the world we're together.

Because, what a woman.

I'm proud of you for telling Mia the truth.

I pause then add,

Do you want to talk about your dad at all?

It's a big deal. Kind of like the ball she took to the face. Bex had been hurt before, which made her fearful, but no matter how hard she tried to protect herself from the pain, she couldn't avoid getting hit again. She might need more time to process, but I'm here when she's ready. Also, for all I know, her dad saw the ESPN show, reached out to her, and they're planning a family vacation to his hometown in Italy.

Crazy Good Coach: Let's talk at the BBQ.

The barbecue can't come quickly enough. And I can't keep from texting back,

It's a date.

* * *

I would have been early to my brother's house except Jacqueline waits to request ice until I'm almost there. Then I have to run to three different stores before finding any. Finally I carry the cold plastic bags through a side gate into my brother's backyard, following the smoky scent of hotdogs.

I hear the party before I see it. Music, splashing, and screaming. I'm already smiling when I round the corner of the house.

My brother commands the grill. He spots me and points toward a couple of drink coolers that apparently need ice. Jacqueline chats with other moms as she pushes babies on the swing set I gave the kids for Christmas. Olivia and her teenage friends throw poppers at each other on the patio.

Then there's the woman I'm looking for. I watch her as I pour ice to clink over metal cans.

Bex kneels on a yellow Slip 'N Slide in front of the Ladybugs. Purple bruises circle underneath both her eyes, but she's not letting a previous defeat keep her down. With the way she holds a star-spangled soccer ball by her side, she looks to be leading our team back into battle.

The girls huddle around her in various combinations of swimwear and soccer gear, all soaking wet. Bex herself wears a black racerback suit with three sporty stripes down the sides. It's not much more revealing than the workout wear I usually see her in, but the most attractive thing about it is her body confidence. For Bex, apparel and health have to do with performance, not appearance.

I stuff my hands in my shorts pockets and stroll over to join the action.

Bex points out different parts of her legs as she speaks. "In a basic tackle, make sure you're sliding onto your hip rather than jumping onto it. You'll bend your bottom knee and extend the top leg to kick your opponent's ball away. Make sure you go for the ball, not your opponent. Now who wants to sprint past the end of the Slip 'N Slide so I can demonstrate?"

I step behind the girls and raise a hand. "You can tackle me."

The girls giggle and jump with excitement.

Bex's eyes lock on me and she arches an eyebrow. "All right. Who wants to see Coach Skylar get his butt kicked?"

Kendall shakes her head. "We don't say the B-word at my house."

"Can you say it in Spanish?" Paloma asks.

"I don't know Spanish."

"Mom," Mia reprimands. "You're supposed to call it a bum."

I smirk. "Yeah, potty mouth."

Bex stands and tosses me the ball. "Who wants to see Coach Skylar get his bum kicked?"

The girls cheer, though my brother cheers loudest.

I shrug off my shirt and kick off my flip-flops, depositing them on a lounge chair. When I turn around, I find all the adults have turned to watch, as well.

Riley's mom pulls out her phone, and my toes cringe. Jacqueline holds out her palm as if demanding the woman hand over her device, so Riley's mom stuffs it back inside her pocket. I catch my sister-in-law's eye and nod a small thank you.

Bex points to the corner behind her. "Start back there, dribbling the ball ahead of you. Try to sprint past the end of the slide."

I chuckle at her use of the word "try." It's like she took a taunting class from Caleb.

"Okay, girls. Watch my timing." She motions to me. "Whenever you're ready."

I tap my toes on the ball to hold it in place and look over at Bex like a rival on the starting block. She steps one foot in front of the other, leans forward arms ready to pump, and challenges me with her steely gaze. My pulse revs. This is the moment I've been waiting for.

Knocking the ball forward, I race across the soft lawn. Bex jogs about two steps behind down the yellow strip. Right before I'm about to intersect the path of plastic, she drops to glide in front of me. Her foot pushes the ball back the way I'd come and sweeps my front leg out from underneath my body.

Earth rushes up to meet me, I'm angled directly over her torso. I brace my arms to catch myself on either side of her and throw my weight sideways to roll away. With our legs tangled up, she's pulled along, and we tumble through the wet grass together.

"I can't believe you made me put my phone in my pocket," Riley's mom complains in the distance. "This is prime footage."

When the world stops spinning, Bex is on top of me, smiling face inches away. My appendages have flailed wide like I'm posing for a chalk outline in a crime drama while she seems very much in control. She simply needs to do a pushup to rise, yet she's taking her time. If we didn't have an audience, I'd take some of her time too.

Cheers from the peanut gallery fade in, bringing me back to reality.

Bex jumps to her feet and offers me a hand. "Are you hurt?" she asks as if I'm the one with black eyes.

"Just my pride." I gradually roll to a seated position before clasping her palm. No bones are sticking out of my skin anywhere, so I've got that going for me. "Do I get to tackle you now?"

"You go to the back of the line." She yanks me up then points to where the girls wiggle and dance. It's hardly a line, but I'll go wiggle and dance with them until my turn. "Paloma's next, so she's tackling me."

It's a rotation, though were this one of my movies, it would be a montage. I kind of wish Jacqueline allowed Influencer Mom to film because I'd love to watch back through it in slow motion.

Paloma proves to have a hidden talent for slide tackling. Maybe this will be the motivation she needs to enjoy running. She expertly kicks the ball away from Bex, though Bex demonstrates what I should have done by jumping over Paloma's leg.

Kendall's so tiny, that when it's her turn to tackle Paloma, she pretty much slides right under the bigger girl's legs. Riley can't keep her footing and ends up belly sliding to knock Kendall down like a bowling pin. Treva's timing is all off, so she doesn't even get close to touching Riley. Mia performs like the mini-pro that she is. Aby and Annie team up to take her down together. And Charlotte sings Wrecking Ball in her failed attempt at tackling the twins. As for me tackling Charlotte, I'm way too fast for her. She hadn't even made it to the spot of convergence when I ended up sliding off the plastic, through the grass for a nasty road rash, and almost into the fence. I basically tackled myself.

"I can't believe I'm missing this," Riley's mom complains again.

"You're not missing it, Mom," Riley yells. "You're here."

Her mom presses lips together and sits in one of the swings.

Bex and I are back up. Remember how I realized I could jump over her legs rather than rolling on top of her? Well, I don't.

Not that second time. Or the third. I just keep falling for her over and over again.

Round and round we rotate. Eventually, our audience tires of the entertainment. But we don't.

I can't remember a 4th of July I enjoyed more. Not when watching the Big Bay Boom from the flight deck of the Midway with my castmates in high school. Not even when attending a Padres game in college. And definitely not when riding in a stagecoach with my ex on the 4th of July parade. Playing on a Slip 'N Slide with a bunch of eight-year-olds in my brother's backyard is where it's at. Or maybe it's anywhere with Bex.

We're still taking turns tackling each other when my brother rings the triangle bell for dinner. I'm just drying off with a towel when I hear an unexpected voice.

"Skylar Hayes?"

The water from the Slip 'N Slide is nothing compared to this blast from the past. I turn to find the date who'd once deserted me. And apparently a new guy she didn't desert. In my brother's backyard. Is this real life?

"Charlee?" We'd made peace last year, so it's not as awkward as it could have been. It's just a shock.

She holds her hands wide. "I'd hug you but you're all wet."

"That's okay." I glance at Bex who is busy putting away the Slip 'N Slide, then I wrap a towel around my neck. "What are you doing here?"

She points to Charlotte. "I help with my niece when she stays with her dad for the summer. He's a fireman and got called out to work, and Charlotte didn't want to miss this barbecue."

All this time, I'd thought Charlotte was a miniature Zooey Deschanel when really she's a mini version of her aunt. Only I never heard Charlee sing show tunes. "Charlotte is a joy to be around. I'm surprised I haven't seen you at any games."

"I've been in Australia." She tilts her head toward the new guy. "Meet my fiancé, Maxwell."

I extend a hand. "Nice to meet you. And congratulations."

He shakes. "Cheers, mate." Ooh, he's got the accent and everything. Were he an actor, he could have beat me for a role in *The Scarlet Pimpernel*, as well.

I release his grip to stick a thumb at Charlee. "This one is quite the catch. Good jab landing her."

He chuckles. "I have heard the stories."

Charlee smiles then lifts a chin. "Hey, I saw you're dating again too. How did that happen?"

I rub my chin, wondering if I should explain that the tabloid news is fake, but the truth is that I am ready to date again. How did that happen? "Well, you know how selfish I was when we met?"

"Yeah," she huffs. Though I'd intended it to be a rhetorical question.

Anyway... "I'd been hurt by my ex-wife and afraid to sacrifice myself for anyone else." The realization washes over me of how things changed. "But then when my assistant coach, Bex, got hit in the face with a soccer ball, I realized I would have taken the hit for her."

"That's a great place to be in any relationship." Maxwell explains my choice like a psychologist. "It's love-based rather than fear-based."

"You're a new man." Charlee reaches past me. "And you must be Bex."

My guts clench like Charlee punched me. Did Bex overhear things that I should have told her myself when she was ready? I turn to look into her eyes and see if she is ready.

She shakes hands with Charlee, ignoring me. "Hi."

"Bex." Now what do I say? "Remember how I had a woman leave in the middle of a date? This is that woman."

Her eyes slide my way. Her smile flickers. "Nice of you to invite her to the barbecue."

I guffaw. Just when I'd avoided things being awkward with Charlee, I had to go and complicate things with Bex. I may be a new man, but I still talk too much.

"He didn't invite me. I'm Charlotte's aunt." Charlee grips Bex's hand between both of hers. "I'm so glad to see he has you now."

Bex bites her lip. "You saw on the news that we're dating?"

"Yeah," I answer for Charlee with a little too much enthusiasm.

Bex's gaze turns steady. She's waiting for me to explain our dating relationship. Or she overheard my claim about being ready to date again thanks to her, and she wants an explanation for that. Or both.

I'm saved by the triangle bell.

"Come on, Skylar," my brother singles me out. Apparently, everyone but our little group congregated on the patio to pray. "It's time for grub."

There's so much to say, but this isn't the time to say it.

I finagle a spot at the unlit firepit with Bex, not realizing I'm the only guy with a group of moms, but that's okay because I won't be expected to talk. I can just wolf down all the summertime salads in order to get her alone faster.

Bex leans over to inspect my plate. "You didn't get any of the jalapeno poppers your fake girlfriend made."

Rookie mistake. At least she's not angry about the fake girlfriend misunderstanding. I'll have to remember to eat the food she cooks for barbecues if she ever becomes my real girlfriend.

I tilt my head toward my sister-in-law who's passing around her baby, so she has time to chomp down dinner. "Jacqueline beat me to them." That's probably true, though I really just wanted summer salads.

Bex scrunches her bumpy nose. "Did she tell Caleb she's preggo yet?"

"I'm not sure," I whisper back. "When she ordered jalapenos on her burger, he freaked out a little bit and considered re-enlisting for the signing bonus."

"Oh no. She's been hoping he'll get out to spend more time with the family."

I know I'm supposed to respond in kind. I should be concerned about my brother. But it's Bex's concern that captures me.

She's been through a lot this week. She's still going through a lot with me proclaiming to strangers that her getting the ball to the face made me realize I'm ready to date. Yet she's concerned about my brother's family. She may look like the Joker with her black eyes, but she's beautiful to me. I'm about to tell her so when Dance Mom hands me my baby nephew. I guess it's my turn.

I set my plate on the ground so I can grip the little guy under his armpits and hold him up so we can study each other. His wisps of blonde hair have grown long enough to curl at the ends. The curly, blonde-haired gene is strong in Jacqueline, though this kid got my brother's dark, serious eyes.

Bex nods toward his kicking legs. "Look. He's going to be a soccer player."

"Or a martial artist," I counter. There are other sports that include kicking. "Or football."

"I entered a punt, pass, and kick competition in high school and beat the kicker for our high school football team."

I turn to stare at Bex in awe all over again. Though her opponent probably didn't share my admiration. "Poor guy."

"What about kickball?" Suggests the senator's wife. "I help out at Kendall's school during recess, and she beats the boys in kickball."

I imagine Kendall running the bases, arms by her sides like she's using Iron Man's repulsors to propel herself faster. "I can see that."

"He could be a dancer." Dance Mom crosses her legs toward us, settling in for what she seems to think will be a debate.

I seat the kid on my lap facing me for this conversation. We'll let him decide. "What do you think, dude? How are you going to use your kicking skills? Do you want to perform ballet or win soccer games with your little brother, Jason?"

"Who?" The voice is Jacqueline's, and it comes from directly behind me.

Oops. My mouth got me in trouble again. I scrunch my face before twisting to smile at her innocently. "Caleb joked that he's naming your next baby Jason."

She pops another jalapeno in her mouth then licks her fingers. "Oh, I'm done. And I told Caleb that with as fertile as we are, he should probably get a vasectomy."

My mouth hangs open, but my eyes slide toward Bex.

She shrugs, apparently also unable to explain how we'd all been wrong.

"Wait." Jacqueline plants a hand on her hip. "Did you think I was already expecting?"

Bex points to Jacqueline's plate. "You *have* been craving jalapenos."

Jacqueline guffaws. "I heard spicy food boosts your metabolism, and I'm trying to lose this pregnancy weight." Jacqueline pats her tummy pooch. Then she snaps upright and points a finger at her husband who also seems to be in shock. "Were you in on this? Is that why you were so hesitant to give up the signing bonus?"

He spreads his hands wide. "I've been right every other time I suspected you to be pregnant."

"Oh, babe." Jaqueline presses a hand to her heart. "You agreed to return to civilian life even while thinking we'd have another mouth to feed?" She crosses the patio to wrap her arms around him. "You're an incredible husband and father."

Caleb kisses her, then turns to tuck her under one arm while raising his can of soda in the other. "Here's to my lovely wife, all our precious children, and the hopes that they still love me even when I'm here to discipline them every day."

I want to add, *Or play with them*. But he'll have to figure that out for himself. So I call, "Here here."

Turning their youngest to balance against my torso, I grab my can from a side table and clink with Bex's bottle of lemonade. I'm proud of my big brother and expect Bex to be happy for her friend.

She taps her beverage against mine, but her eyes remain downcast.

Rather than celebrate the toast with a sip, she sets her drink on the fire pit table. "I'm going to go put on some dry clothes."

I watch helplessly as she disappears inside the house. Is she really just cold from being wet, or does seeing a dad step up to the kick-off remind her of how her father gave up the ball? I need to tell her personally that I would have taken the hit for her.

The weight of a six-month-old on my leg tips away from my torso, and I scramble to catch my nephew before he falls. Except he's being lifted from my leg. By my brother.

Caleb hooks the kid on his hip like a pro and nods toward the patio door. "Your turn, soldier."

Bex

We don't stop playing because we grow old; we grow old because we stop playing.
– George Bernard Shaw

It's a wonderful day. My friend is going to have her husband home for good. Mia is happy. I just had a blast teaching slide tackles. And Skylar claims he's ready to date again.

Yet there's this yearning for something more, and I want that something to be him.

I lean on the bathroom countertop and stare into the mirror. My damp ponytail, bumpy nose, and black eyes are the opposite of impressive. If I'm not enough for my own father, then why do I think Skylar might be attracted to me?

A knock at the door makes me jump.

"Just a second."

I wring my swimsuit into the sink then shove it into a plastic bag in my beach bag. At least I'm dry and comfortable now. I'll go help clean up the kitchen, serve homemade ice cream, and take turns holding babies inside the house so they're not scared by the booming of fireworks outside. Even if my dreams didn't come true, I've obtained the American dream.

I hook the beach bag over my shoulder and swing open the door. "It's all yours." I scan the tile floor for Legos and Hot Wheels before stepping into the hallway. I've learned to do this the hard way.

"I'm not waiting for the bathroom." Skylar leans with a shoulder against the wall, apparently waiting for me.

My heart jolts to a stop. I both regret staring in the mirror for long enough that he knocked to check on me and am thrilled he cared enough to check. "Sorry. I forgot I had pretend-girlfriend duties."

This is where my kicking skills could really come in handy. I need to kick myself for such blatant flirting.

Skylar rolls with it. "You've been doing great. I'm here to fulfill my pretend-boyfriend duties."

I peer into his dark eyes, looking for a flicker of something that isn't pretend. "Which are?"

He reaches for my free hand and holds it over my head to spin me around like I'm one of the twins in a tutu. "First, I want to make sure you didn't get hurt when tackling me repeatedly."

As my back turns to him, I realize he's looking me up and down. My collarbone tingles at the idea of being seen, but then I picture what he's seeing. Unfortunately, I'd been so busy staring at my bruised eyes in the mirror, I didn't think to check my legs or arms. "I may have a few scrapes, but that's not what hurts."

Did I just say that? I'm now fully dressed in cut-offs and a T-shirt, but I'm revealing too much.

My spin ends with me facing Skylar, but he doesn't let go of my hand. Rather, he uses it to tug me closer. "I know," he says.

My chest swells with the breath I suck in. He smells like chlorine and feels like sunshine. The beach bag slips off my shoulder, and I let it plop to the floor.

"That's really why I'm here." He tilts his head, and I think it might be to avoid bumping my poor nose when he kisses me. But then he says, "You texted that you wanted to talk at the barbecue."

Talk? I've forgotten how to talk.

He squints, really studying me. "I considered tracking down your dad for you, but they announced your name on ESPN, so then I thought maybe he tracked you down. Have you heard from him?"

A sigh of relief slips out. My shoulders relax. Funny how I've become more afraid of kissing Skylar than discussing my abandonment issues. Or maybe they're one and the same. I've just had thirty years to deal with Dad leaving.

I pull my hand from Skylar's and use it to wave away all my worries. "If he wanted to track me down, he could have done it a long time ago."

I'm almost glad ESPN announced my identity. Had Skylar confronted Dad, the rejection would have been so much more overt. God knows I don't need any more disappointments.

Skylar shoves his hands in his pockets but doesn't move away. His long torso is still bare. Probably because his shorts haven't dried yet. "So what did you want to talk about?"

"Um..." What *did* I want to talk about? I'm not going to tell him Mia asked if he was her birth dad. Though I wish.

Dear, Lord.

He prompts. "You said you tried to make Mia feel loved, but she made you feel loved."

"Oh, yes."

I melt a little inside. Others may have let me down, but my daughter has more than made up for it. She's enough.

"I was so afraid of hurting Mia by telling her about her dad. But she was just..." I throw my arms in the air, still dumbfounded by her response. "...so objective and considerate. She said she knows God loves her because he gave her..." My voice squeaks into nothing. I try again. "He gave her..." My throat clogs.

"You," Skylar finishes for me.

I nod, speechless.

His strong, warm hands slide up to cup my cheeks, and now I really can't swallow.

"I know how she feels," he says.

My skin goes numb and becomes extra sensitive at the same time. Skylar Hayes is cradling my face. He inferred that God must love him to bring me into his life.

But I'm not his. Well, I'm his assistant coach, that's it. Oh, and ESPN announced that I'm his girlfriend. But that's fake news. It's fake, right?

"You don't have to pretend to be my boyfriend here in the hallway," I whisper. It's the only volume I can get out, but also, he's so close that if I speak in a normal tone, it would probably sound like I'm using my megaphone. "Nobody's watching."

"I'm not pretending." His nose angles to one side again. "Are you?"

I've never been more real with a man. My gaze rises from his lips to my reflection in his eyes. He sees my bruises and knows all my secrets, yet he still wants to be with me. Maybe this can work. "No, I'm not."

His mouth lowers to mine. Sweet and savory. Soft and strong. Gentle and demanding.

My hands slide behind his back, embracing the newness. The rightness. The disbelief this is happening.

Pain evaporates. Joy bubbles within. I wish I could spend the rest of the night right here.

A muffled scream interrupts euphoria. I stiffen and pull away. I know that scream.

The back door swooshes open and Mia's cries threaten to strangle me. Something happened to my daughter.

Blindly, I shove off a wall to spin around and rush into the living room. Caleb carries Mia toward the kitchen.

Her eyes are closed. Tears stream down her cheeks. Her mouth opens wide to wail.

"What happened?"

He slides dishes out of the way to set her on the crowded counter with her feet in the sink and turns on the faucet. "The kids were playing with sparklers, and she stepped on a spark. I'm sorry. I should have had them put on shoes first."

He's sorry? She's my daughter. My responsibility.

I swoop in to take over. After holding Skylar, she feels so tiny in my arms. "Oh, Mia."

She burrows her wet face in my chest and whimpers.

I reach for her ankle to get a look at the burn on her sole. It's gray but small. "Should I take her to the ER?"

Caleb rifles through a cabinet, pulling out various tubes. "I'm going to ask Jacqueline where the ointment is. We've had a few burns over the years. This is a minor one. Mia will be fine." He jogs out the back door.

Whether Mia is fine or not, I'm not. My heartbeat pounds like a judge's gavel, ruling me guilty.

Skylar appears, fills a baggie with ice, and offers it to Mia. "Here you go, tough stuff."

She peeks out at him.

I'm afraid to meet his gaze. Afraid to prioritize his feelings over hers.

He lifts her foot from the sink to replace the water with his makeshift ice pack. "Are we going to have to change our team name from the Ladybugs to the Fireflies now?" he teases.

She laugh-cries.

I appreciate the way he's trying to help, but his presence is a reminder of how I failed my daughter. I'm my mom all over again.

I hug Mia to me and close my eyes to hold back the tears.

Skylar's palm presses warm against my back for a moment. When I don't respond, he murmurs, "Let me know if you need anything."

The back door creaks again, and he's gone.

I spend the rest of the night with Mia on my lap. I'm both comforting her and using her as a shield.

Her teammates stop by to ooh and aww over her wound. Jacqueline brings us bowls of ice cream. The sun sets on what was almost one of the best days of my life.

Skylar lights the fireworks. I try not to watch him because every time I look his way, his eyes are on me. I got lost in them once, and I can't let them suck me in again.

Mia squirms to be set down. "My sparkle-owie feels better."

I wish mine did.

Rather than let her go, I hang on. "You probably shouldn't walk on it tonight. Let's give it some time to heal."

All this time I'd been afraid falling in love would burn me, but Mia's going to be the one with a scar.

* * *

Finally it's time to pack up and go home. Mia passes out in her car seat before I even get my beach bag and Pyrex dish into the trunk. I slam the lid, shutting out the interior light, so that I feel rather than see Skylar waiting for me. Again.

My pulse revs, and I wish I could shift into reverse.

"How's she doing?" he asks.

"Better. Good. Thank you." I look down at the keys in my trembling hands, wondering how I'm able to sound so calm when my insides jitter. Thankfully the agitation is hard to make out with only distant porchlights and the sporadic colorful glow from rogue fireworks.

"How are *you*?" he prompts.

"Fine." I will be anyway. At the moment, I'm higgledy-piggledy. "And you?"

He doesn't answer. I'm forced to look up to find out for myself.

What I can see of his profile lacks all traces of the normal playful smirk. "Is this it?"

I can't say no. Even it if is. I need time to mourn so I can hold myself together when telling him. For now, I'll play dumb. "We have the playoff game Saturday."

A distant firework screams through our silence.

"I'll see you there." His voice is thick with the reminder of my morning's text. *If I can't see you right now, am I still seeing you?* He waits a beat as if making sure I caught the inuendo before striding away.

Does he hope coaching together again will remind me of what a good team we make? I wish it was that easy. But this isn't about us.

If I could choose to date any man in the world, I'd choose him. But I don't have that choice.

Another firework booms, taking me back to the rainy practice when Mia jumped into his car, and I'd been forced to follow. I knew at that time I needed to avoid him for my own good. Yet, I went and made everything worse by becoming best friends. By becoming more. By kissing him like I could keep him.

His Tesla steals away into the night.

I sit primly behind my steering wheel, waiting for the trembling in my hands to still before I drive. I might have to spend the night in the car.

Mia's already asleep, so she should be fine. I'm not likely to sleep, so it wouldn't matter anyway.

I lean forward to rest my head on the steering wheel. It's not like me to be melodramatic like this. I'll get over Skylar like I got over Grant. Like I got over Benji in high school. I can buy my own M&Ms.

That's what I did in high school anyway. Not sure what I can buy now to make myself feel better. Flooring? I can afford new carpet with the money I made from coaching Skylar.

Digging in my beach bag, I retrieve my phone to pull up the Home Depot website. My fingers automatically click on the email app first.

A few new messages greet me with their bold font, but it's the one from Dylan, the soccer director, that grabs my attention. It's not formatted like one of the many group emails he sends out. This one is addressed to me.

I shake my head. What more am I going to have to endure today?

Rebecca, I know it's bad timing, but I've been offered a position as offensive coordinator for San Diego State and must resign my position with the soccer league, effective immediately. My assistant director will fill in during the interim, but no one has yet stepped up to coach the Butterflies in this Saturday's final game. If they are forced to forfeit, the Ladybugs will be considered the winners. Congratulations. I know you love victory, so plan your celebration accordingly. Best wishes, Dylan

He forfeits? What a selfish jerk. Those poor girls.

I do like to win, but this doesn't seem right. At least I won't have to partner with Skylar any longer.

We'll simply plan a party together. Where we award trophies to each player for their strengths. And he'll make jokes about their quirks, at which I'll laugh. Then I'll have to give a speech about how wonderful it was to work as a team. Meanwhile, Mia's going to be riding on Skylar's shoulders and shouting to paparazzi that she wishes he were her birth dad.

But what other options do I have? Besides coaching the Butterflies myself?

Skylar

Play the game for more than you can afford to lose... only then will you learn the game.
–Winston Churchill

I got whiplash once. My stunt double was supposed to jump a golfcart into a sand trap, but I wanted to do it myself. I hadn't yet learned how to drive, and I certainly didn't have any practice relaxing my body on impact. But at the brash age of fourteen, that didn't stop me. I locked my stuntman in a port-a-potty and got behind the wheel without the director realizing it was me. Long story short, they had to delay filming until my neck healed.

Apparently, I didn't learn anything from the experience because I let Bex give me whiplash yesterday. One moment she's blowing my mind with a forever kind of kiss, and the next she's pretending it never happened.

Okay, I get that she had to take care of her daughter. She's a protective mother and has been put through the ringer lately. So I gave her space.

I'd been tempted to kiss her goodnight before I drove away. Remind her how she felt in my arms. But I figured it would be better to let her remember on her own. Mia will heal, and Bex will realize she overreacted.

She can't protect her daughter from everything. Mia could have stepped on a spark whether Bex was watching or not. All the kids had been barefoot while playing with sparklers. Any one of them could have gotten burned.

I fell asleep, expecting Bex to take care of her daughter then get back to me. The way she did yesterday morning after the news report. So when I wake up, I immediately reach for my phone.

No texts from Bex. Just Craig reminding me of today's audition. I have yet to look at my lines, but I hope they're of a jilted suitor, because if so, I'll nail it.

I open my email to pull up the script and find messages from that Dylan guy Bex doesn't like. We play him again this weekend, and I'm not going to hold her back from scoring seven points on his bum.

I flop onto my back to see what he has to say. Should he mock Bex in writing, these letters could give us proof. I open the latest one.

Coach Skylar, In case you haven't yet read my first message, I've been hired as a defensive coordinator for San Diego State.

In the sarcastic words of Adam Sandler, "Whoopity doo."

My departure has left the Butterflies without a coach.

All right, I feel bad for the players. They worked hard to get where they did. (Yes, I'm giving them all the credit.)

Your assistant coach, Rebecca Lemaire, has agreed to coach them in the championship against the Ladybugs.

What in the World Cup? I rip my covers off. I'm not taking Dylan's word for this. I have to hear it from Bex herself.

My anger simmers hotter and hotter as I brush my teeth and grab a pair of dirty jeans and the closest T-shirt. I should be dressing more professionally for my audition later, but if I'm going to stop by Bex's first, I don't have the time. Morning traffic doesn't help my mood.

I took this coaching position in the first place to keep Treva and Mia from being separated, but now Bex is taking Mia with her to our rival team and making them play against each other. Just to avoid me.

She's not protecting her kid like she claims. She's protecting herself. If she'd just finished out our season and explained to me reasonably that she doesn't believe dating to be in Mia's best interest, I'd respect her decision. I wouldn't like it, but I'd respect it.

But if she's just scared, this is the time for courage. I was scared about starting a relationship too. I was afraid my sacrifices wouldn't be appreciated. However that's not the issue this time. Bex is sacrificing me.

Does the team know yet?

By the time I reach Bex's outdated front door, the energy tearing through my veins would be enough to rip it from its hinges. I settle for pounding on the weathered wood. I'm pounding a second time when she swings it open.

She's dressed in soccer shorts and a hoodie, as usual. The blue circles under her eyes are fading to purple as a sign of healing, but I don't remember them being so puffy before. She won't meet my gaze but attempts a cheerful, "Hi."

I cross my arms to keep from pulling a Rhett Butler and kissing some sense into her. Don't need the neighbors mistaking my passion for meaning I'm the one who gave her the black eyes.

I lift my chin instead. "You want to play me in the championship game, huh?"

She glances inside the house then joins me on the stoop and closes the front door. "It's not that I want to, but the Butterflies lost their coach."

My shoulders shrug dramatically, arms still crossed. "So? We'll invite them to our celebration. Everyone wins."

She stares past me. "What's done is done."

Is she talking about the change in coaches or us? "I never took you for a quitter."

Her spine straightens. Her eyes snap to mine. At least there's still some fight left. "I'm not quitting. I'm protecting my daughter, okay? I'm all she has, and I can't let myself be distracted."

My chest heaves, inhaling compassion, exhaling fury. I'm sad for eight-year-old Bex who didn't have a mom to love her this much. I'm also sad she thinks of me as a distraction from her daughter. "You're not the only one Mia has."

"What?" Her tone dips in mockery. "You?"

"Why not me?" I demand. Though I'm not sure I want to hear her answer. There are lots of reasons why not me. I'm divorced. Never had kids. I've dealt with a lot of the insecurity issues common for child stars. "Never mind. I'm not talking about me. I'm talking about God."

The flash in her eyes fades. She tucks her chin. "Mia believes God loves her because he gave her me."

"As she should." I drop my arms so as not to appear so off-putting, but like a newbie actor, I don't know what to do with my hands. I run one through my hair to calm myself. "All good gifts are from God. If we lose them or they're taken away, God's still good. He still loves us. He still provides."

Her irises sharpen from steel to iron. She might not agree yet, but she's listening.

"You can protect Mia as much as possible, but you don't control the future. Something could happen to you tomorrow."

She shakes her head, looks away. Her throat flexes.

The idea gets to her, but I know her too well to believe she's worried about her own life. She's worried about Mia's. So I continue.

"Yes, you're a gift to Mia. But you're a gift from God. He's her Savior. And if something happens to you, He'll still be there for her."

She's quiet. Rolling the fears around in her brain. Afraid to let them go.

"Bex," I beseech. "If you had set a boundary between us yesterday before we kissed, I wouldn't have questioned you. I admire how much you care for your daughter and fully support it."

Her eyes finally flick my way. Wanting to believe, yet wary about where I'm headed.

"When we kissed, you were in a healthy place. You were hopeful about us. We wanted the same thing."

She huffs but can't deny it.

"It wasn't until Mia got hurt that your fear rose up. At that point, you made a decision based on fear rather than love. Which is not something I can support."

She blinks, and her eyelids push tears down her cheeks.

"Do you love God enough to trust Him with your daughter?"

She wipes her face dry. "You're the one who told me to live up to what I've already obtained. God has given Mia to me to take care of, and I'm going to live up to that."

Touché. "Does Mia know she's not a Ladybug anymore? That she's going to have to play against her bestie on Saturday?"

The water in her eyes seems to intensify their expression like a magnifying glass. Also like magnifying glass, they seem to be trying to reflect the sun's rays to set me on fire. "It's one game. You'll be gone next year, and I'll coach them both again."

I could be gone next year. I could be filming a show about soccer. It would be easier than this. I gave up acting for one woman and vowed I'd never repeat that performance. Why am I putting myself in this position?

Because it's what love does. It's what my brother did for his family. It doesn't make sacrifices to earn love, it makes sacrifices out of love.

I nod slowly, a plan forming. "What if I like coaching Treva? What if the Ladybugs want me to stay on?"

Her lips part with a little gasp. "You wouldn't do that. I'm the better coach."

"Are you though?"

"I coached you." She plants her hands on her hips. "And the Ladybugs only lost to the Butterflies because you wouldn't let me help coach that game."

I'm not going to argue. She's got great points. I'll simply use them against her. "So you think you can beat me in the championships?"

She shakes her head like a bull getting ready to charge. "Absolutely."

A corner of my mouth creeps up. I rub my jaw to hide it. "If you beat me, then I'll step down as coach."

She heaves a huge sigh. Her eyes close.

"But if I beat you, you'll let me take you and Mia on a real date."

Her eyes bulge back open. "No way."

I shrug with faux nonchalance. "Why not? You're certain you're going to win."

"Skylar, please," she begs.

The sound of her saying my name has the power to break me, and she knows it. She's still playing the game. But we're both here to win.

"What are you afraid of?" I challenge.

"Fine." She attempts a valley girl hair toss, but her hair is in its usual ponytail, so she doesn't quite pull it off. As if trying to coverup the gaff, she continues moving the same arm until it's extended between us to shake hands on our deal.

My heart leaps at the opportunity to connect again. I clasp my fingers around her palm and pull her forward, just like I did before our kiss.

Her eyes widen as if both excited and afraid I'm going to give her a repeat performance.

But I stop when we're face to face. When I can smell her sweet appley fragrance and hear her breathing intensify. "I have one more question for you."

Her fingers flex, tightening her grip on mine. Her eyes repeatedly dip to my lips then dart back up to glare. "What's that?"

"If you're goal is to live up to what you've already obtained, how are you going to live up to my love?"

Bex

Be glad of life because it gives you the chance to love, to work, to play, and to look up at the stars.
--Henry Van Dyke

My biggest regret about the deal with Skylar is that I shook on it. My second biggest regret is that my daughter overheard.

Never mind all the stuff about how much I love Mia and would do anything for her. The only thing she wants me to do, I can't do. I can't let her stay on one team when I'm coaching another. It's in the bylaws.

"You want me to coach you on the Ladybugs next year, right?" I try once more to reason with her on the way to our championship game.

"Yeah." She pouts from the backseat.

"Then we have to beat them today."

I ran a special practice with the Butterflies Thursday night. They're a well-oiled machine, and adding Mia is like giving them the latest upgrade. They ran their drills with efficiency and expertise. But there was no joy.

"It's not going to be fun," Mia states the obvious.

It's going to be torture. I took the position in the hopes of avoiding Skylar at a team celebration. I didn't think I could handle the tug-of-war between my head and my heart. But then he came over and pretty much tricked me into making a bet with him. A bet that could result in a date or worse—coaching with him again next year.

Would that really be worse, though? my heart asks. I've enjoyed every minute of our time together this season. He's taught me to play differently. He brought a lightness to a game I once considered a job.

Which is exactly why it's worse, my brain argues. You're too happy to be serious.

But that kiss... My toes curl in my cleats.

That kiss was a distraction. Yeah, Mia's fine, but next time it could be worse than a little burn on her foot.

And so it goes. My thoughts and feelings are so jumbled, I can't even figure out where God fits into it all. Skylar made some good points about trust, but trust doesn't make sense when everyone I've ever relied on has let me down.

All I know about trust is that I want Mia to have trust in me. Yet here I am breaking her trust.

Here I am, pulling up to a soccer field to face off with the team I want to be coaching. The man I want to spend life with.

Dear, Lord.

"Do we have a butterfly cheer?" Mia asks.

I scrunch my face. Even if I felt like cheering, I'm not good at the cheers. Except when there are giant face cutouts of certain child stars involved. "Do you *want* a butterfly cheer?"

She's quiet for so long I don't think she's going to answer. Which is fine. We'll consider it a rhetorical question.

But it turns out to be more a reminder of what she's missing. "Remember when we went to the fair, and Treva and I got butterflies painted on our face? I want to do that again."

"We will definitely do that again."

I pop open my door and climb out to the sound of Skylar leading my old team in his warmup cheer. At least I think it's Skylar. His hair has been spray-painted red with black dots like a ladybug. It's even better than

Mia's memory of butterfly face paint. Yet so much worse. He looks ridiculous, and I love him for it.

We grab our gear and trudge through the grass to the opposite end of the field from the Ladybugs. I should have swallowed ipecac to make me throw up this morning so I could have claimed to be sick and gotten out of today's game. Everyone would've been happier.

Except maybe Charlotte who is always happy. She breaks away from their team cheer as we pass to serenade us with Mama Mia. Because I'm Mia's mama?

I give her a hug and wave to all the rest of the girls before leaving them behind me. Oh, how I miss their wacky ways. To be fair, I'm sure the girls on my new team are sweet, as well. It's just hard to tell when they've been trained like the Russian in Rocky IV.

Despite attempts at remaining aloof, my gaze snags on Skylar's. I'm not sure what he can read in my expression, but his reads I'd-like-to-slide-tackle-you-right-now.

I turn my back on him to warm-up my girls. With the lack of joy Mia and I bring to the team, I'm really not one to judge their demeanor.

A little Indian girl tugs on my shorts. I mentally scroll through the roster in my head. I think her name started with a C-H like the last name of the Indian actress who married a Jonas brother. Champa, Chaaya, Chahna...

"Chandra?" It doesn't say much for my job as her coach if I'm excited over simply remembering her name. "What do you need, hon?"

She scratches her head and looks around at the other girls on the team. "Can I make a goal today?"

I blink. "That would be great."

A bigger girl laughs. Bobbi Jo. I remember her name because she was the best player on G.I. Joe's team. "She hasn't made any goals all summer."

Dear, Lord.

I *have* to win this game, and I'm supposed to coddle a player who can't score.

"Let me see what position I have you in." Thankfully, Coach Dylan's lineup has Chandra playing defense. If I move her around, I could get a red-tag. "You know what? You're playing defense today, but I had a friend in college who could kick the ball so far that she could score from the other side of the field. Why don't you try that?"

She nods, but as she walks away, her tiny shoulders sag in defeat. I wish Dylan had been more nurturing, so I wasn't stuck the remnants of her disappointment. I know Skylar would have been.

I glance over to where my old team has dog-piled on top of him. I would have thought that if he wanted to take me on a date so badly, then he'd be trying a little harder to get the girls ready for the game rather than goofing off.

We're definitely going to win. I only wish I could do so while getting Chandra a point.

The ref blows a whistle, and my girls rush to the field. Mia is on offense, since I was able to add her anywhere I wanted. She high-fives her old friends.

Skylar slides on his shades as if to hide his eyes so he can sneak looks at me, but then turns his head directly my way. So much for sneakiness.

I stare at him as I slide on my shades. And okay, I'm smiling a little bit.

Mia scores within the first minute and flies around the field. Her old teammates follow. Her new teammates watch in confusion. As do I.

Skylar shrugs at me like he's okay with his team celebrating my team's score. Like he's still playing just for fun. Like he trusts God with the outcome of this game. Or maybe he's got more tricks up his sleeve.

In the next rotation, he puts the twins in at offense. They do their thing and get a goal. It's tied.

My pulse ramps up. I put in Bobbi Jo. Score!

It goes back and forth, and by halftime, we're still tied. It shouldn't be so close. We have more players, so they should be worn out. Not to mention, this team already beat the Ladybugs once. And I have more experience coaching.

But I gave Skylar my playbook, didn't I? Of course. We need something new.

The girls sip their Gatorades on the ground.

"Okay, Butterflies." I squat to join their circle. "Remember when I mentioned my friend who could score from her defense position? That's what we're going to do. Mia's got a strong leg. I'm going to put her in defense. Everyone else's job will be to distract the Ladybugs. Once their players are on the other side of the field, pass the ball to Mia, and she'll score."

"We don't need to distract them," argues Bobbi Jo. "They'll let Mia score because they're her friends."

Mia sits up from where she'd been sprawled. "That's not true."

"Why do you think you got the first goal?" Bobbi Jo challenges.

Chandra hugs her knees. "They *did* celebrate with you when you got a goal."

Mia shakes her head. "It's a game. We play to have fun. Tell them, Mom." But when she turns to me for backup, her expression falls.

It's never been just a game to me. And certainly not today.

I place a hand on her sagging shoulder. "It's a sport. We all play to win because winning is fun."

"Not today, it's not."

"Mia..."

The whistle blows.

She jogs away. I hold a hand to my heart, more torn now than ever. What am I teaching her? What am I teaching any of these girls? Certainly not that Jesus loves them.

I've just got to get through this game so I can coach my Ladybugs again next year. So I can enjoy the game again. So I don't have to worry about a dashing movie star using "da moves" on me.

I glance over at my old team. Oh no. Skylar's put Kendall in the goalbox. Is his whole plan to get her to do another header so the game is cancelled? Nah. He has to put her in or he'll get a red-tag. Hopefully she's learned to use her arms since the last time she played goalie.

Time starts. The Butterflies execute my plan perfectly. Mia jogs slowly to stay on field right while everyone else chases the ball to the left. Bobbi Jo sends her the perfect pass.

Mia charges toward it. She's far from the net, but she's got a clear shot. She winds up and kicks the ball directly out of bounds.

I rock back on my heels, stunned.

Skylar looks over and holds out a hand to ask what happened.

I shake my head. Maybe she got turned around.

"It's okay, girls," I call. "Let's try it again."

Chandra jogs after the ball. She throws it in to Bobbi Jo. Again everyone but my daughter runs to the left. If we keep repeating this play, Skylar's going to catch on. We need it to work now while it's fresh.

Bobbi Jo passes. Mia races over. Winds up. Slams the ball out of bounds. She's turned into Paloma.

"Time out," I shout, then pace back and forth until the girls join me for a huddle.

Mia's the last to reach the sidelines. I wish I could take her off separately, but everyone is watching and listening. They've been trained well, and also this is some good drama.

"Mia." I start out a little too hot. I repeat myself in a calmer tone. "Mia. Why are you kicking the ball out of play?"

"Because I don't want to play."

She doesn't want to choose between her friends and her teammates. She's in a tough spot. But I'm only asking her to live up to that which she's already obtained. She's our star player. "You can't do that."

"Why not?" she challenges. "You have."

Ouch.

She's not wrong.

I've obtained the love of both my daughter and a good man. But in my fear of not being good enough for both, I refused to even try to make it work.

"You're right," I admit. Now what?

I look at the little girls surrounding me, and remember what Skylar said about considering love something to give, not something to earn. How can I best love this team?

I can teach them it's not about winning. It's about being there for each other. I drop into a squat. "Here's what we're going to do. We're going to get Chandra a goal."

"Are you changing her position?" the big girl asks. "You'll get a red-tag for it."

I'm no stranger to red-tags. "Yes."

Stunned silence.

Chandra throws her arms into the air like a referee. "Goal!"

The girls break into laughter then copy her.

Mia smiles proudly up at me. I might have to go on a date with Skylar now, but at least I'm living up to my job as mother. We'll see what happens next.

* * *

What happens next is nobody scores. There's lots and lots of shooting. But we've got Bobbi Jo playing goalie, which she's great at, and they've got Kendall defending Chandra.

The parents cheer with every shot. It's like they've joined us in trying to get Chandra her first point of the year. Maybe ever.

My heart roars in victory. It's won the debate with my head. Or maybe my head and heart tied. Everybody wins.

As for my deal with Skylar, we didn't make any agreements about what happens if the game ends in a tie. Does he still have to leave? Do I still have to go on a date with him? Or do we start our relationship over, coaching the Ladybugs together and dating when we feel like it? Well, not whenever we feel like it. I've got to go back to teaching high school in a month.

I glance over at him. He nods at me. He knows I could be winning this game if I wanted to. Well, if Mia wanted me to.

According to my watch, there's less than a minute left in the final quarter. I shrug my shoulders back in preparation of high-fiving the Ladybugs. Of high-fiving Skylar.

Whenever our hands have touched, he's pulled me close. I hope today is no exception.

Chandra throws in to Mia. Rather than kick the ball directly out of bounds, she dribbles it around. I assume she's just running down the clock until Chandra gets close enough for her to tap it backward to the little girl. Then she stands in Paloma's way so Chandra can kick the ball around her and have a clear shot.

It's our old trick play. The Ladybugs should have been ready for it, but Charlotte's too busy galloping around on an imaginary stick horse and pretending to lasso the ball while Riley is waving to her old teacher she'd invited to watch. Nobody can say they're not having fun.

But it's down to Chandra and Kendall. The world's worst eight-year-old shooter and goalie.

Chandra jogs with a giant grin on her face. She's free from anyone chasing her or getting in her way.

The crowd erupts. Parents clap and cheer. The Butterflies jump and scream. The Ladybugs point at the ball heading toward the net and demonstrate to Kendall how to lift their arms.

"Shoot it," I shout, wishing for my bullhorn.

Chandra stops the ball outside the goalie box to take better aim. Charlotte gallops toward her. Riley notices the commotion and runs to help so her mom can get a good action shot. Paloma's gotten around Mia.

"Kick it, Chandra!"

She winds up.

The defense converges.

Swinging her leg with all her might, she knocks herself over, but not until after she makes contact with the ball. It soars high toward the far end of the net.

Kendall may not use her arms when she runs, but she's fast. She charges to stop it. Only it's going to sail straight over her head.

Oh, wait. She lifts an arm. Both arms. She's not Iron Man anymore. She's Superman, soaring high.

The roar is deafening. Lightning could strike within ten miles, and nobody would be able to hear it above the noise.

My hands fly to my mouth. I lean forward in anticipation but am unsure how to cheer. I want Chandra to get her goal, but I don't want Skylar to give up coaching. He may not be crazy good, but he's good. He made me a better person.

Dear, Lord.

Kendall's outstretched arms connect with the soccer ball.

My stomach clenches, waiting for her to knock it away.

But she doesn't have that much control. Her hands spike the ball sideways like she's playing volleyball. It slams into the edge of the net.

"Goal!" My team shouts.

I'm frozen. The game is over, and I won. I beat Skylar. I get my team back.

Mia shows Chandra how to fly around the field in celebration. Then Mia offers Chandra the position of leading our team in slapping high-fives with my old team.

I take a deep breath and my place as caboose. "Good game, good game, good game."

Skylar and I watch each other over our players' heads as we're brought closer together. He must know I gave him every chance to win. Surely, he saw the change in me. In the way I was able to let go and enjoy this gift of life. Maybe he'll still take my hand and pull me close.

His palm slaps mine. "Good game."

He walks past.

I turn to watch him go. Is that a limo waiting in the parking lot for him? Is that why he's leaving, or is he respecting my boundary as he said he would?

Either way, I need to remind him the most fun I ever had playing soccer was in a blizzard when we couldn't see the boundary lines. When the ball rarely went out of play.

If I want back in the game, I'm going to have to throw the ball in. I scan the ground around me and find the game ball on the centerline. It's been a while since I did my flip throw in, but Mia seemed to think it impressive.

I line up a few feet behind the ball and call, "Hey, Coach Skylar."

He turns. Tilts his head.

Now or never. I run, fold forward to place a hand on either side of the ball, then grab it as I spring my legs up and over to land on my feet. My whole body propels the ball across the field with a snap.

It lands and skids to a stop at Skylar's feet.

A smirk spreads across his face. He taps the ball forward and jogs after it toward me. He picks up speed into a full sprint. Like he did in our slide-tackle practice.

Overjoyed, I jog on an angle to meet him at a point of interception. Bending my left knee I slip onto my hip and reach for the ball with my top leg. I push it out of the way and catch Skylar behind the ankle.

We go rolling through the grass, ending with him playing the part of a corpse again while I'm practically planking above him. Both sets of our sunglasses got knocked off, so I'm able to stare adoringly into his coffee-colored eyes. I know I'm staring adoringly because that's how I always look at coffee.

His hands brush my sides. "If you had something you wanted to say to me, you could have just grabbed your megaphone."

I love that he's teasing. It eases the tension building in my sternum. "I've said a lot of crazy things lately, so I thought it would be better if I demonstrated my change of heart."

His fingers curl around my waist. "Is slide tackling your love language?"

I laugh and roll to the ground on my side next to him, propping an elbow underneath my head. "Not the tackle. The throw-in. I wanted you to know I'm back in play." I wink one of my black eyes, fully aware it looks more silly than sexy. "In case you ever want to ask me out again."

"Hm..." He turns sideways to prop himself up facing me. "I'd planned to invite both you and Mia on a first date, but I've got a stretch limo waiting, so what do you say we take both our teams?"

This isn't the life I planned for myself. I could spend it being hurt that my dad rejected me again. Or fearful that having an unwanted pregnancy meant I'm going to make all the same mistakes as my mom. Or angry that Mia's dad abandoned us both.

But instead, Skylar taught me to focus on things I should be thankful for. I'll choose to see them as gifts. Blessings I couldn't obtain on my own.

It gives me freedom from needing to prove myself. The ability to give out of love rather than for love might be the only real love there is. Skylar's favorite verse could very well be the secret to happiness.

"I say you win." I'm going on a first date in a limo with a famous actor and, if their parents allow them to join us, both our teams. "Though a date with sixteen eight-year-olds sound a little...higgledy-piggledy."

He grins. "That's my favorite use of the term yet."

Nice to know I'm not the only crazy one in this relationship. "Where are you taking us?"

He reaches over to wrap a stray strand of hair around his finger. "I need some extras for this new soccer show I'm filming. The producers loved me so much, they agreed to work around next summer's soccer schedule."

A guffaw bursts from my lips. I'm happy for him, but I'm not the typical Hollywood starlet. "Maybe if you were filming a karate series, I could play someone who just got beat up. But they're not going to want me looking like this."

"They won't want my hair to look like a ladybug either."

"Yeah, it's almost as bad as the fauxhawk."

He chuckles and palms my cheek. "We'll let them clean us both up. And they'll be happy to because they're going to want you in the show. Do you know why?"

I shake my head in disbelief. We're still lying in the middle of a soccer field surrounded by families and fans, not to mention the limo waiting. I've never been so wanted. "Why?" I challenge.

His soulful eyes radiate a soul full of joy. "Because you got da moves."

About the Author

For Charlee and Maxwell's story, read Anxious for Love in the Bright Lights collection.

* * *

Angela Ruth Strong survived breast cancer, works as a flight attendant, and uses her own crazy life experiences as inspiration for the stories she writes. (Yes, she coached her kids in soccer, but not very well.) Her books have earned TOP PICK in Romantic Times, been nominated for a Christy, won the Cascade Award, and become Amazon bestsellers. She and her husband also got to play extras when her novel *Finding Love in Big Sky* was adapted for film. To help aspiring authors, Angela started IDAhope Writers where she lives in Idaho. Find out more at www.angelaruthstrong.com.

Lauren's Second Chance

CARRIE PADGETT

Acknowledgments

For the real-life Lauren.
You're missed every day.

Many thanks to Lisa Phillips and her crew at Two Dogs Publishing. You were a pleasure to work with! Thanks to the many friends and critique partners who have offered encouragement along the way. My editor, Rebecca LuElla Miller, gave thoughtful and spot-on feedback. This story is better because of her. Always, the biggest thanks to my family. They're my best cheerleaders.

Thanks be to God for giving me everything: this writer life I love. My family. My friends. But especially His Son, my Savior.

One

Applying for a spot on a stupid reality TV show, a dating show, of all things. What had Lauren been thinking? Obviously, she hadn't been in her right mind. Grief must still be making her do crazy things.

This was all Brooke's fault. Brooke, one of Lauren Bishop's best friends and the reason she was in Southern California, instead of home in Harts Leap, enjoying her summer break with swims in the lake, drinks on the dock with friends, and lazy days reading in the hammock.

Lauren slowed her racing thoughts as she shifted in the plastic chair, one of a dozen lining the hall of One Reality Productions in Hollywood, California. Mid-June sun shined through the building's windows, making squares of light on the white marble floors. Other women occupied the rest of the seats. Each one was more beautiful than anyone Lauren knew.

An adage floated into her head, something her bachelor Uncle Silas often said as he shuffled a deck of cards for gin rummy. "Lucky in cards, unlucky in love."

She lifted one finger.

Unlucky in love, lucky in ... jobs.

Yes. She had a great job, even if she'd never planned to teach fourth grade. Another finger inched up.

Unlucky in love, lucky in ... friends.

Also yes. Even if she was here thanks to Brooke-I found-love-on-a-reality-show-and-so-can-you Adler.

Unlucky in love, lucky in … family.

Should be an automatic yes. And had been, up until last fall. Her parents worked hard at the restaurant, providing a roof and food for her and her sister as they grew up. It had been enough for Lauren, for a long time. If only she'd realized the depth of Phoebe's despair before—

Enough. Phoebe was the whole reason for this meeting.

When all the pluses and minuses were added up, it was obvious she had a good and happy life, even if she was a complete and utter failure at finding—no, make that keeping—love.

A hallway door flung open, bounced off the wall, and a dark-haired woman hurried out, kitten heels clip-clopping on the floor.

"You wouldn't know a ratings goldmine if you were handed a map with an X leading to a Nielsen family," she called over her shoulder. She paused and leaned against a wall.

Everyone in the lobby and hall stared.

With a shuddering breath, she looked around, then straightened. "One Reality Productions is a sham, people. They don't care about helping you find love. They don't care about helping people find love. They only care about how many advertising dollars they can suck from corporations."

She headed to the door, but her low heeled shoe must have caught on something because she staggered a few steps, then dropped her enormous handbag. Lipstick, phone, wallet, coins, and pens tumbled onto the floor.

Lauren scrambled to her feet and hurried to help. She scooped up everything she could reach before it rolled under a chair. Everyone else seemed glued to their spots.

"Here." Lauren handed the items to the woman.

"Thanks." She stuffed them back into her purse and continued to the front door.

Lauren watched her leave, then she stood. Maybe she should escape too, before she was in too deep. What would she be getting into?

She'd gotten an invitation in the mail last week, promising the possibility of true love, travel to tropical places, and gorgeous dresses to wear. She called Brooke to laugh about the coincidence, since Brooke had just finished filming a show, and accidentally found love on a dating reality series last spring. Instead of hooting with hilarity as Lauren expected, Brooke encouraged her to apply.

"It's perfect," she'd said. "You'll have a platform to talk about your new foundation."

"Really? They'll let me promote a crisis hotline?"

"It depends on how you present it, but sure, very likely. You'll also meet people from all over. You get to travel to amazing places and have fun experiences." Brooke had hung up on that convincing note.

So, Lauren was alone in Southern California, while her friends, her family, her *life* were all back in Harts Leap, a small town nestled against a lake in the Sierra Nevada.

A guy who looked about twelve-years-old stuck his head into the hallway. "Bishop?" Lauren nodded and picked up her bag. One of the other women flashed Lauren a smile and mouthed *Good luck.*

Lauren followed Liam on stiff legs. As their steps echoed in the long hallway, one word—one name—seemed to follow her.

Phoebe. Phoebe. *Phoebe.*

Honoring her sister, and maybe helping others, would be her reward for subjecting herself to this interview.

Inside the room the intern escorted her to, six people sat scattered around a long wood table with lunch detritus strewn along the top.

The young man indicated a chair at the end and returned to his tablet. "This is Lauren Bishop."

She blew out a small breath. Brooke hadn't said auditioning would feel like being short ribs at a barbecue competition. The appraising glances of the interview panel hijacked her self-esteem and catalogued her attributes: hair color (natural—check—and she preferred to call it golden copper instead of red), her dress (new and cute—check—but from H&M, not a designer), and her bra size (none of their business).

"Nice to meet you, Lauren." A man she guessed to be a few years older than she, *may*be in his thirties, reached to shake her hand. "I'm Liam, assistant to the producer. This is Renee." He nodded to the woman on his left who was gorgeous enough to be on any dating show and guaranteed to win the love of the eligible bachelor.

Liam—Brooke mentioned him, said he was a good guy and could be trusted—looked a little like Joseph Gordon Levitt with tousled dark hair, twin dimples, and Harry Potter glasses. Nerdy and cute. Not her type, but maybe Angie, her other best friend, in Harts Leap—?

"Tell us about your first love." Liam looked up from his tablet.

Lauren froze with her mouth open, recovered enough to close it. Opened it again. Heat rushed to her cheeks.

"My first love?" she repeated. "What does that have to do with a dating show now?"

Liam's head bobbled back and forth, as if agreeing with her. "We'll see. Just tell us about him. Knowing who you were attracted to in the past helps with casting a contemporary show."

She drew a deep breath and considered. She hadn't thought of Mason in ... well ... a few days, most likely. And if just thinking about him made her face warm, maybe talking about him wasn't a good idea.

"My first love was Jake, my best friend's older brother. He got married when I was twelve, and he was twenty-five. He broke my heart."

Renee chuckled. Liam scribbled a note. "And after Jake?" he asked.

Rats. Evidently deflecting with a joke only worked with inquisitive fourth graders. "Well, I guess my first real love was Mason. We were seventeen."

Liam nodded. "Where did you meet?"

The air conditioning clicked on and blew across her head. Her heart staccato-ed against her ribs. Apparently, a decade wasn't enough to forget Mason and move on.

"I'm from a small town in the mountains, outside Yosemite. Summer tourism is our big business. Mason's family had—has a home in Harts Leap. Mason spent his summers there. We'd known each other since we were kids, but the summer before our senior year, we ..." She lifted one shoulder. "We saw each other differently. We fell in love. But we broke up the next summer. End of story. Pretty typical teen romance, I think."

Liam nodded. "Why did you break up?"

Lauren's jaw tightened. Why couldn't he drop the questions about her first love and get on with the real interview? Stuff like, what did she look for in a man? What were her hobbies? What were her goals and aspirations?

"Mason and I came from very different families. He's ... wealthy. They have homes in San Francisco and Boston. Vacation homes in Harts Leap, as well as Martha's Vineyard, and Maui. My family has lived in Harts Leap for three generations. Mason and I weren't just from different sides of the tracks, we were from different sides of the solar system."

"Mmm hmm, mmm hmm." Liam didn't look up from his notepad. "When is the last time you saw Mason Townsend?"

She glanced up and pondered. "Maybe ... eight or nine years ago? He didn't come back after spring semester, but a year or two later he visited for the Fourth of July."

Liam's full question penetrated her consciousness. He said Mason *Townsend.* But she hadn't given Mason's last name. Before she could dwell on that, try to remember if she'd mentioned it, the interview continued.

"Tell us what you loved about Mason." Renee leaned forward, her chin on one palm, elbow on the table.

Lauren stared at the group. "I don't see what my first boyfriend has to do with finding love here."

"You'd be surprised." Another man, a slightly more corporate type in a blue seersucker suit and loosened tie, spoke from the other side of the table. "You've heard the saying, 'Those who don't learn from history are doomed to repeat it'?"

She nodded.

"We're trying to ensure that what ultimately ended that relationship is no longer a factor that will sabotage your present."

She cocked her head. That made sense. Sort of. "I guess ... I loved his loyalty to his family, to his heritage. I loved that he was still trusting, despite so many people wanting to be his friend just for his money and connections. I loved how he made me laugh."

If that note of wistfulness hadn't crept in, anyone might believe she was over him.

"When did you break up and why?" This from Renee, who dragged her gaze up and down Lauren.

She drew a steadying breath. Nearly ten years and it still hurt to remember. "He said he met someone else." That was the short version anyway. No need to mention he'd broken up with her via a text from his condescending sister. "Really, I think we were too young, and we let other people have a say about our relationship."

“Who?” From the man across the table.

“His sister. My mother. Just … people.” She dredged up a smile and shrugged. “We were kids.”

The man leaned back, nodded. “Thanks for coming in today. We’ll be in touch.”

Message received. She’d blown the interview. No other reason for the curt dismissal.

“He loved me too much,” she blurted. “I didn’t know how to accept his love.”

“Okay. Got it.” Liam stood and held a hand toward the door.

Lauren sighed, gathered her bag, and stood. “Thanks for your time.”

She ignored the pain gathering in her chest. She was used to it by now. Used to letting down Phoebe. Used to not being able to help anyone. Used to this crushing feeling.

Back in the hallway, Liam hollered, “Holly Gilbert.” The blonde who’d wished Lauren good luck, stood and smoothed her floral A-line skirt, winked at Lauren, and followed Liam into the room.

Lauren sighed and looked for a sign to the restrooms. At least she’d experienced a trip to L.A. and a change of scenery. She hadn’t expected to find love. It was a shame though she wouldn’t get to talk about her new foundation.

After a stop at the ladies’ room, she retraced her path and headed to the front door. White light glared off the windows. A large masculine shape came through the door. She shielded her eyes. If she could focus, she could get out of his way.

The man—tall and broad-shouldered—stepped into the building, paused, then with a confident stride turned right.

Something in his form … she paused in the open foyer, gazing after him. The glare made a good look difficult.

She shrugged. It must be the interview. Questions about Mason brought him to her mind. Some random man had the same build, the same walk, and had entered the building.

“Crazy. You’re crazy,” she mumbled as she pushed through the door at last and headed to her Jetta, lonely among the BMWs, Teslas, and Range Rovers in the parking lot.

* * *

Mason Townsend drew a hand across his forehead, hissed out a breath, and risked a look behind him.

Shock had rippled from his toes to his eyebrows when he came through the door and saw *her*.

He hadn't seen Lauren Bishop in ... nine years, ten months, a week and a couple days. If he had to guess. What were the odds?

Hmm ... what *were* the odds?

He'd agreed—against his better judgment—to be on a dating reality show, and he "just happened" to see his first love at the production company offices?

No.

After a drink from his to-go coffee to collect himself, he strode down the hall then paused at the reception desk. "Liam or Renee, please."

The Blake Lively lookalike smiled broadly and picked up her phone. After murmuring a few words into the receiver, she hung up. "You can go to the conference room, Mr. Townsend."

He pushed away from the counter without a backwards glance.

Why had he listened to his sister? Jenna insisted he do this, to save the family company. The company his great-grandfather had founded. The company that supported three generations of Townsends. The company that seemed disastrously close to shutting its doors forever.

He shook his head, then entered the conference room. Liam didn't spare him a glance, but Renee—he sighed—Renee gave him a look of appreciation, one that would normally send him running. He knew too many other women who'd looked at him like he was a young wildebeest separated from the pack. Renee wasn't the first and wouldn't be the last.

He was here to save his company, plain and simple. He'd spend a few weeks filming, meet some nice women, garner lots of free publicity, and go back to his newly secure job. If this didn't go according to plan, maybe he'd get an offer to work for another hedge fund firm. He was still good at his job, whether at Townsend Management Group or somewhere else.

It was a genius plan. A plan with no room for memories of Lauren or for dodging aggressive women like Renee.

"What's up, Mason?" It could be his imagination, but Renee's smile felt more predatory than friendly.

He stopped by Liam, who looked up, surprise on his face. "I was asked to come by this afternoon. I'm not sure why. But I have a question. Why was Lauren Bishop here?"

Liam's gaze flicked between the door and his tablet. "I'm not sure who you mean. We've had a lot of women through the offices the last few days."

Mason just stared at Liam who finally looked away. Oh, yes. Something was up.

"Renee?" Mason tilted his head slightly.

She shrugged. "Like Liam said, we've talked to a ton of women."

"Okay." He'd drop it. For now. "What do you need with me?"

Renee stood. "Photos. Follow me." She ran her fingers along his arm as she passed.

He frowned but obeyed.

They made their way down a series of unfamiliar corridors until Renee finally flung open a heavy metal door. Inside, it looked like a Victoria's Secret photo shoot. Beautiful women in pink lingerie, wearing high heels and feather boas, were everywhere. Literally everywhere. He couldn't see anyone with a camera or tablet or even a light reflector.

Renee slithered through a gaggle of pink-clad women.

No way was he following. No. Way.

He took a more circuitous route, but managed to keep Renee in sight, and ended up next to her at a table along the studio side where she talked to a young woman with dark bangs hanging over her eyebrows. At least this one wore black leggings and a slouchy, off-the-shoulder sweater instead of the pink boas.

"Here's your business bachelor." Renee clutched his hand and pulled him next to her.

"He's here for a makeup test." The aide didn't look up from her tablet, much like Liam in the other room. "Sandy should be ready for him in a minute."

Renee tugged his hand, so he had to follow. He ended up in a chair in front of an array of mirrors. A woman, in a dress out of the 1940s, bent over another woman in the next chair.

"This is Sandy, the makeup artist," Renee said.

"I'll be right with you." Sandy brushed powder along the model's forehead.

Mason carefully detached his fingers from Renee's grip. "Thanks for the escort. I'll find my way out."

"I'll come back in an hour or so, to be sure you don't need anything."

He smiled but didn't nod. Whatever it took, he'd be out of there in fifty-five minutes. He'd do his own makeup if he had to. He'd holler for the models to move to the set. He'd even take the blasted pictures himself.

Renee finally wandered off and once he saw the giant door open and close, he turned to the busy makeup artist. "How long?"

Sandy turned the model's chair so she could see herself in the mirror. "You're next. Jessica is all done."

The model slipped out of the chair and disappeared into the pink mass that seemed to expand and shrink like a bubble-gum of ectoplasm.

"I'm in a bit of a hurry," he told Sandy.

She smiled. "I heard. Less than an hour." She put a paper bib-thingy, like what the dentist used, around his neck. "I'll be as quick as I can."

True to her word, in twelve minutes, she snapped away the protective paper. "They should be ready for you. Head over there." She stuck a thumb toward a backdrop of off-white shiny fabric draped over three partial walls forming an open room.

He made his way there, and only had to avoid looking down a woman's cleavage three times before he settled on a swivel chair upholstered in fabric that matched the walls.

Forty-six minutes and counting. He'd find his sister and tell her to come up with some other way to save the company. He couldn't do this. He couldn't pretend to be excited about being surrounded by women who ultimately would use him—his name, his money, his reputation—and walk away. Leaving him looking like a fool with a foundering company.

Nope. Not going to happen.

Two

Lauren parked in front of Brooke's apartment in Glendale. Scoring an empty spot in the crowded neighborhood must count as her lucky break for the week.

Lucky in parking, unlucky in avoiding old boyfriends who broke her heart.

From her phone in the passenger seat, Pharrell Williams erupted in song, telling her to clap along and embrace her happiness. She glanced down. A number from the 747-area code. The television studio? In a hurry to let her down?

Only one way to find out. "Hello?"

"This is Liam at One Reality Productions. Is this Lauren?"

"Y—yes." What now? After that abrupt interview this afternoon, there shouldn't be any more intrusive and awkward questions.

"You're on the show. Please bring one carry-on-size bag to the Beverly Essex Hotel Saturday morning at eight o'clock. Leave your phone and all electronics at home. Any questions?"

Only a billion of them. "Ummm ..."

Her mind spun, racing to keep up with his instructions.

"Okay then, see you Saturday." He disconnected.

She stared at the dead phone in her hand and let his words sink in.

Liam from the production company. She was on the new show. She had to go to a fancy hotel Saturday morning. Today was Thursday.

The Jetta door creaked as she flung it open. She dashed up Brooke's front stoop. As soon as Lauren pounded on the entry, her friend opened the door.

"What in the world?" Brooke's eyes widened.

Lauren must look like a mad woman, if her racing heart and hiccupy breathing were any indicator. She took a deep breath and exhaled slowly before dropping onto Brooke's gray microfiber couch.

"Liam just called. He said I'm on the show."

Brooke's face lit up. "That's great!"

Lauren shook her head. "I changed my mind. I don't want to do it. I have to call him back." She looked at the phone she still clutched and stabbed her unlock code.

"Wait—why? What happened?" Brooke, with wide eyes and raised brows, sat next to her.

"It was awful. I felt like everyone in that interview was judging me. And then when I was leaving, I saw ... Never mind. I just can't do it."

"Slow down. Don't forget, I've been there. I know exactly how it feels to be the token plain person in a room full of models." She paused.

Lauren's face heated. Talk about being kicked when she was down.

Brooke laughed, but with tenderness. "I was the plain one. You're gorgeous so I don't believe for a minute they said or did anything to make you think otherwise."

Lauren flashed her friend a quick smile. "You're delusional and forgiven."

She cast her mind back to the conference room. "It sure felt like I was being compared and found wanting. Especially in the figure department. Those women all had curves. I have to wear a padded bra and tight belts to not look like an adolescent boy. Not to mention killer heels just to be average height. Thanks to stilettos and underwires, I'll be crippled by the time I'm forty."

"You're exaggerating."

"I wish." She ran a hand through her bangs and pushed them to the side. "To top it all off, as I left, I swear I saw ..." Mason's silhouette filled her mind and she blinked to dispel the image.

"You saw … what? Or who?"

She shook her head. "It's crazy. I'm crazy."

"Lauren, spill it."

"As I was leaving … I thought I saw … Mason."

Brooke's brow furrowed. "Mason who summered in Harts Leap when we were kids?"

Lauren nodded. "I know I'm cracked. It must have been someone with a similar build. But during the interview—and I'm positive I never said his last name—Liam asked specifically about Mason *Townsend*. How long since I've seen him."

One side of Brooke's mouth tugged up. "The background investigations are really thorough." She searched Lauren's face for something. "So … how long since you've seen him?"

"July fourth, summer after our second year of college. He waterskied past the Lakeside Grill while I was salting fries and flipping burgers."

"But …" Brooke's head cocked to one side. "That summer, after high school graduation, you were inseparable. Then you two texted or emailed or called all the time, from Labor Day to Memorial Day."

Lauren nodded. "Second college summer Fourth of July was the last time I *saw* him. The last time I *talked* to him in person was Labor Day, almost ten years ago, right before he left for his freshman year at Colgate University. We made plans to meet during the holidays, but he had to cancel because of a family emergency. Then he promised to be back the day after he finished finals. Instead, his sister showed up at the Grill, said he wasn't coming back to Harts Leap after all and that he'd met someone else."

A pain stabbed Lauren's heart. The memory felt as fresh and sharp as the aroma of the Brookside Inn's grilled artichokes.

Brooke shook her head. "I still say something weird was going on. I saw the way he looked at you. The way he watched you when he pretended to trip off the raft into the lake. He loved making you laugh. He'd never do anything to hurt you."

Lauren studied her cuticles. "Except he did. He hurt me when he didn't tell me the truth. Even an email or text saying he changed his mind when he got back to New York would have been better than the lame voice mail about us being friends."

"I still believe something happened you don't know about. You're sure he never wrote?"

Lauren scoffed. "You think my mom or sister threw away his letters without giving them to me? This is reality, not a Victorian romance novel."

Brooke smiled. "I guess I'm just trying to make sense of it."

"Believe me, I've thought of every possible explanation—he bought a new phone when he got home and lost his contacts. But he knew where I lived and could have sent snail mail. He was in an accident and had amnesia—"

"Talk about a romance novel plot!" Brooke interjected.

"I told you, I've thought a lot about this. I Googled him and he finished at Colgate University then joined the family company." Lauren gulped the sudden lump in her throat. "I went to—to Fresno State. You—"

"Never mind me." Brooke was a little sensitive that she'd gone to Harts Leap Community College and then finished her degree online. But now they were both teachers at Harts Leap Elementary School, so they ended up in the same place, even if they'd taken divergent paths. Brooke didn't know Lauren's dream had been a different college, a different major, a different career.

"Maybe you really did see Mason." Brooke's voice pulled Lauren from her regrets.

Could it be? She was in L.A. from Harts Leap. He might have ended up in the same place, via a different path, just like her and Brooke.

"But why would Mason Townsend, scion of the Townsend family, President of the Townsend Management Group, a hedge fund manager worth more than the entire town of Harts Leap, be walking into production offices in Los Angeles? It doesn't make sense."

Brooke chuckled. "Take it from me, nothing in reality television makes sense. But his company could be advertising or sponsoring a program that films there. He could be advising someone how to make a million dollars in futures." Her phone chimed and she glanced at it before meeting Lauren's gaze. "There are literally a bazillion possibilities."

She picked up her phone and held it toward Lauren. "Fiction has to make sense. Real life can be crazy and illogical. Like me getting a text from

Austin, asking if I want him to bring over takeout when we hang out later."

"Why is a text from your boyfriend crazy and illogical?" Lauren asked.

"He's amazing. It makes complete sense that I would fall in love with him. But it makes no sense that he would fall in love with me, a fourth-grade teacher from a little mountain town. He grew up an only child with a famous mother. I grew up with apple trees and five brothers."

"Cut it out. You're talking about my best friend. You're the amazing one. He's lucky to have you." Lauren squeezed Brooke's hand.

Brooke smiled. "Thank you for proving my point. You are wonderful and Mason was a jerk for not coming back like he'd promised."

Lauren shook her head, her new dangly earrings bouncing off her cheeks. "I get it. Like you just said about you and Austin, Mason Townsend and I are from completely different worlds. It was doomed from the start. My romantic seventeen-year-old naïve self saw us as a twenty-first century Romeo and Juliet. And look how that ended. I'll take a broken heart over dying."

Brooke pulled her feet onto the couch and typed on her phone before looking up. "How was the rest of the interview?"

"When they asked about my first love, I said I was in love with your brother Jake, and he broke my heart at twelve-years-old when he married Anna."

Brooke grinned. "He broke a lot of hearts."

"But they kept on prying, so I finally mentioned Mason." She drew a deep breath and unlocked her phone again. "Now I have to call that Liam guy and back out."

Brooke grabbed Lauren's phone. "You'll do no such thing."

"Give me that." Lauren lunged for it.

Brooke leapt up and held the phone over her head. "Not until you promise you're going."

"Brooke."

"Lauren." Brooke imitated Lauren's exasperated tone.

"Gimme."

"No."

"It's my life! I'm not sure about going on a reality dating show. Especially one where they're going to make me talk about my first love."

She didn't dare voice the other even more terrifying possibility: that she'd see him.

Brooke lowered her hand but didn't let go of the phone. "What if Mason is on the show? What's the worst that can happen? You'll get a fun trip somewhere nice and tropical. And besides—" She gave Lauren a look of understanding and sympathy. "If you're serious about the foundation you want to start, this could give you amazing publicity, a real jumpstart."

"If only it was that simple." She wanted to curl into a ball on the corner of Brooke's couch. "I'd do it in a heartbeat for the Million Reasons Not To Foundation. But what about Mason?"

"You're over him, aren't you?"

She blinked, considered. "I thought so. Until I saw him. Or someone who looked like him."

Brooke handed Lauren her phone. "I know it's your life. But you've been stuck. Stuck in your job. Stuck in Harts Leap. Stuck in the past."

Lauren opened her mouth to protest, but Brooke kept speaking.

"You are, and you know it. Besides, you need the money."

She nodded. "About a hundred thousand dollars to start the hotline."

"The show can give you exposure. You can talk about suicide prevention, that it's a cause you're passionate about. People will be interested. They'll Google you and Harts Leap and learn about the foundation. And they'll send money."

"You think so? People—strangers—will send money to a small town to help set up a crisis hotline?"

"I know so. Besides, this is your chance to spread your wings a little. See a bit of the world."

"What if I don't want to see the world? I love Harts Leap."

"Lauren Kathleen Bishop. You've lived in one place your whole life. I know it's beautiful—it's my home too. But you've been tied to your family and the grill, helping out, doing for others in town, giving your life to your students. This is your chance to do something for yourself and see things beyond Harts Leap." Brooke handed her the phone. "When was the last time you went on a date?"

Lauren scrambled to come up with something less pathetic than the beach bonfire with Mason ten years ago. "Umm ... oh! Last week I went to coffee with Jace Keyser."

"Jace the attorney, who's at least a decade older than you and who's in love with Ms. Mendoza?"

"When you put it like that ..."

"Why'd you go to coffee with him?" Brooke asked.

"I had a—a legal question about the foundation and he was in line in front of me at Bean 'Em."

Brooke just stared at her a moment before her brows raised. "See what I mean?"

Lauren huffed a breath. "I've dated. Remember Mike? We went to dinner and a movie. His mom called me the next day to ask how it went and if I could give him tips on how to be a better boyfriend."

Brooke grinned. "I forgot about him. You told her he needed to shower and shave before his next date."

Lauren shuddered. "Some men can wear a five o'clock shadow, but not Mike. He texted me that if I wanted him to shave, I should've done something with my hair besides a ponytail."

"Okay, I get it." Brooke's gaze pierced Lauren. "But dinner with Mike was a couple of years ago. At least. Who have you dated in this calendar year? We're in June, so that's five-plus months to choose from."

Lauren floundered. Surely, she hadn't spent the last months at home with a good book every weekend. She snapped her fingers. "How about my double date to the movies with Henry? And his *parents*?"

"That's kind of sweet."

"They sat between us!"

"Yeah. That's unfortunate." Brooke's chuckle sounded forced.

"And don't forget Web. We dated a whole year after college. Then he decided to join the Peace Corps and left without saying goodbye."

Brooke held up her hands in surrender. "I give. You've dated. All I'm saying is why not do the show? So what if Mason is on it? You're gorgeous. You're a beloved teacher. You, my friend, are the one who got away."

Lauren sighed and sank back onto the couch. "I hear you. But what if I hate it? What if they hate me?" And the big one, left unspoken: What if Mason was really there?

"Then you'll be off the show and back in Harts Leap in a couple weeks, with the rest of your summer to enjoy."

Lauren covered her eyes with both hands. "What am I going to do?"

Brooke stood, gently pried Lauren's fingers away, and put her fists on her hips. "You're going to go. You'll have a blast. And who knows? Maybe we'll start a new show of our own? The Real Teachers of Harts Leap."

* * *

Mason strode through the lobby of the Beverly Essex without glancing around. He had to get to his room before one more person asked him a question or needed something from him.

So much for a quick photo shoot. Not only had it taken more than an hour, allowing Renee to come back and watch, but he'd been forced to smile and laugh through his tension while women cavorted around him, trailing pink boas across his face.

He grimaced, picked a stray feather off his lip, let it drift to the floor of the elevator as he inserted the keycard for access to his floor.

Finally, inside the suite, he paused. He didn't see his sister, but she was there. Her scent—some Oriental vanilla, rose, sandalwood, and mint concoction she bought overseas—tickled his nose.

"Jenna?" he called. "Where are you?"

"Living room," came her reply.

He loosened his tie as he walked through the entryway's tall columns to the room at the end.

His sister, in her signature pencil skirt and crisp button-down blouse, stood near a window holding a wine glass. She let the sheer curtain drop from her other hand. "How did it go?"

"What are you doing here? You're supposed to be in New York, working with the SEC and FBI."

"Something came up and I wanted out of town for a few days. This seemed like a good excuse." She seemed to find her manicure very interesting.

"What happened? Something with the investigation?"

She shook her head and finally met his gaze. "Dimitri called off our relationship."

Surprise tangled with resignation. "What did you do this time?"

"Why do you assume I did something?"

"That's your pattern. You meet great guys, date them for a while, then do something calculated to make them breakup with you."

She shot daggers at him from her glittering eyes. "I do not."

He held out a hand, touched his index finger. "Georgio. You invited his ex along on your trip to Majorca. Maurice. You stalked all his social media and tracked his phone. Alejandro. You drove the poor guy crazy, changing your mind about him every other week."

She shrugged. "You don't know the whole story."

"You're right. But you need to do some self-examination and figure out why you do this. Over and over again."

"Can we talk about something else?" She sipped her wine.

"Fine. What exactly is the premise of this show?" he asked.

She pushed a strand of her light brown hair behind one ear. "I don't know. It's top secret until filming begins. But it doesn't matter."

"Of course it matters! I need to know how I might be blindsided."

She set her glass down and crossed her arms. "You have to do this show, Mason. It's our only hope of saving the firm. So, no, it does not matter if you have to date Amish girls or Vegas dancers, you're doing it."

He rubbed the back of his neck. "There has to be another way."

She picked up her wine and sipped. "We've been over it a thousand times. When the embezzlement news breaks, you need to be off the grid, unable to comment. And we're going to need plenty of good publicity to mitigate the ugly. You, a wealthy and eligible bachelor, CEO of Townsend Management Group, surfing and skiing and sunning by the pool with a bunch of gorgeous women is what we need to get past this."

"Why can't you go on the female version?" Because really, there had to be another option, something that didn't make him feel like slime.

She just looked at him. "You're the face of the company. The youngest CEO in our one-hundred-year history. I'm only along for the ride."

He scoffed. "You have an MBA from Wharton. We might be a family company, but you earned your position."

"Back at you, little brother." She sat on the sofa, kicked off her heels, and folded her legs to the side. "Look. I know we could polish up the company image with charity runs and donations. But we must prove you had nothing to do with the losses and this show is our best option. There will be backstory videos, in-depth profiles in People and US Weekly. You will come out squeaky clean. Then when Millicent is charged, the focus will be on her and her crimes."

He dropped into the easy chair at Jenna's side. "I still can't believe it. Millicent Gresham, our CFO since the beginning of time, embezzled forty million dollars from the company, and we never saw it."

"It helped that she was sleeping with the auditor." Jenna's tone was as dry as the chardonnay she sipped.

He ran a hand over his face, a heavy blanket of fatigue settling across his shoulders. "I still don't like it. I think if we give the FBI and SEC some time, they could find Millicent and Gregory and the money."

"We don't have the luxury of time. This is going to be public knowledge in a week, two tops."

He sighed and shrugged. "Then, to top it off today, I think I saw —" He broke off, overcome by memories. The last summer in Harts Leap. Lauren, so small and petite, he always felt like a hero next to her. Lauren with her brown eyes, warm as Cook's chocolate lava cake. Lauren and her laughter which triggered his teenage antics. All so he could hear her voice, light and pure, dance across the lake. Oh, how he'd loved hearing those lighthearted giggles when he tripped off the dock to splash her.

Her home life was tough. He didn't know details, but her parents were always working, her sister always depressed, and Lauren often felt alone and overlooked. So he'd taken any opportunity to lift her spirits, even if it meant he looked a fool.

If she worked for the production company and he saw her while filming the show, maybe he'd finally get a chance to have some closure. And would it be so terrible if he could see her smile again? Hear her laugh again?

"You saw ..." Jenna prompted.

"I'm pretty sure I saw Lauren Bishop."

"Who?" Jenna ran a finger along her glass rim, smearing the lipstick smudge she'd left.

"Lauren. From Harts Leap."

"Not ringing a bell."

"You remember Lauren. We were a couple the last few summers."

"Oh, that Lauren. Didn't she break up with you?"

His smile soured. "Thanks for the reminder. Yeah. She turned out to be as loyal as every other friend I thought I'd made growing up."

"Then this show is a good thing. You'll meet lots of women."

"They all know my name, what our family does. There won't be a genuine woman in the bunch. Just out for what I can do for them."

"When did you become so cynical?" She finally met his gaze. "What happened to giving people a chance before leaping to a conclusion?"

"Never mind." He sat up, straightened his shoulders. "Where are you staying?"

"Here." She motioned to the room with her glass. "You've two bedrooms and you're only sleeping in one."

He stood. "I'm going to take a shower. Want to order us some dinner?"

She looked at him like he was a piece of jewelry in Tiffany's window. "I was going to suggest we go out, start building some favorable buzz, but you look fair knackered."

He smiled at the familiar expression, one their British nanny used often during their childhood. "I am."

"Go, shower. I'll take care of dinner."

Before he could head to the room, his phone vibrated. A glance at the screen had him grinning. He swiped to accept and put the phone on speaker so Jenna could hear. "What do you want, old man?"

"Nothing from a whippersnapper like you," Grandad replied. "Where are you?"

"LA. Where are you?"

"In the lobby of some monstrous pink hotel. Trying to get someone to let me into the elevator to go to my grandson's room."

Mason blinked. "You're here? Really?"

Jenna looked up, amusement on her face.

"I can't trust you alone with a bevy of beautiful women. Someone has to keep an eye on you."

Mason strode out the suite's door and stabbed the elevator call button. With Grandad here, everything would be all right.

Three

Lauren leaned her forehead against the window, watching the L.A. landscape blur by. The Uber driver had been quiet since picking her up at Brooke's at 6:30 that morning. Which suited Lauren just fine. No small talk. Watching signs and streets go by on the freeway was the perfect way to pass time in traffic. Some of the exits were familiar. Toluca Lake. Coldwater Canyon. Sunset Boulevard. Now they wended their way through city streets.

Last night, after two days of Brooke chattering about the fun outings on *Date My Son!* not to mention the friends she made, and the gorgeous clothes she got to wear, Lauren brought up her real objection to being on the new show.

"What if Mason is the bachelor?" she'd asked. "He's rich, drop-dead gorgeous, and eligible. Perfect bachelor material for any dating show."

"So what if he is? It's been ten years. You've been over him a long time." Brooke looked closer at her. "You are over him, right? You haven't mentioned him in years."

Lauren stuffed her feelings, ignoring the hurt and outrage that still lingered from those June days a decade ago when she realized Mason wasn't coming back to Harts Leap. He'd broken up with her *in absentia*.

"Of course. We were a teenage romance between a summer resident and a townie. We had a fun couple of months. Then we both moved on."

"Good." Brooke grinned at her. "So, no reason not to do the show, no matter who the bachelor is. It will probably be a complete stranger. And you don't want to miss the chance for free publicity for the foundation."

That last point had decided her. She owed it to the foundation to give it the best start possible. Not to mention, Brooke's happiness with Austin had spilled over and infected Lauren with optimism. Hope, even. Hope that lightning would strike twice in the love department for two Harts Leap women.

The car pulled up in front of a rosy pinkish building. There was a turnout at the curb in front with enough room for maybe three cars. Where was the huge porte cochere where she could step out of the car to wave at cameras and spectators?

A valet opened the door for her. "Thank you," she murmured, while adding a generous tip to the Uber app before closing her phone.

"This way, miss." The valet motioned her through an arched entryway. Inside, she paused. Here was the palatial greeting she'd expected out front. Shiny marble floors stretched in front of her. A table topped with a huge arrangement of lilies sat in the middle of the wide lobby. A dark wood registration counter stood across the way.

Liam waited inside. He saw her and waved. "Welcome to The Beverly Essex. Did you leave your phone at home?"

She drew a sharp breath. "I forgot." She fished it out of her bag. "I'm so sorry."

"I'll take it. Have it messengered back for you." He held out his hand.

She stood, frozen, gripping it in both hands.

"Lauren?" He wiggled his fingers. "Your phone?"

"I ... I can't let go. You'll have to take it."

He chuckled but tugged on the phone. Her fingers refused to release their hold.

"Really?" He peeled each digit up until he could slide the mobile out of her grasp. "There you go."

She watched her last connection with her real life disappear into a manila envelope.

Liam continued speaking as if he hadn't just tossed her security blanket into an abyss. "We're in the Penthouse suite for orientation, then you'll check into your room, get changed, and we'll reconvene in the Penthouse."

She nodded then did a double take. "Get changed? This isn't okay?"

The orange skirt and light blue top she'd topped with a yellow cardigan that morning seemed perfect for a late-June day. "Fun and bright colors. What's wrong with this?"

"The filming this evening will require something more formal. There are several dresses in the room for you to choose from. You gave us your sizes on your application. This way for now." He led her to an elevator, inserted a key card—she was going to an exclusive level? — pushed a button, then slithered out as the door closed.

Lauren's mouth felt as dry as the croutons the Lakeside Grill sprinkled on their tomato soup. This was a mistake. A huge mistake. No matter what Brooke said about needing new experiences. She had to get out of here. Maybe ... an emergency ... back home? But ... she'd already gotten rid of her phone, so how did she hear about it? What she really needed was an earthquake right about now. Not a huge, destructive quake. Just a moderate shaker that would leave people upset and jumpy and no one would question her decision to go home.

But the building remained unhelpfully motionless.

Finally, the doors slid open again to reveal a small room with a dark wood entrance. She'd barely stepped out of the elevator before the doors closed again, leaving her in the enclosed space.

She knocked on the closed entry and waited.

One of the women from her interview panel a few days ago opened the door and motioned her in.

Six other women, all tall and curvaceous—she could tell just by their long legs—already occupied the grouping of chairs and sofas. One was particularly striking: a silky blonde with deep blue eyes. She at least smiled at Lauren while the others continued to stare at their nails or the artwork on the walls. Counting the other blonde who'd winked at Lauren the other day, there seemed to be two semi-friendly women. She exhaled a breath.

The woman who greeted her motioned to the others. "I'm Renee.

Have a seat, get acquainted. The others will be along shortly, and we'll get started."

Lauren clutched the handle of her carryon and nodded.

"You can park your bag there." Renee motioned to an area near the door where six other small suitcases waited. All of them were covered in designer initials, proving again just how out of place she and her TJ Maxx bag were here.

"I ..." She placed a hand on her stomach. "I need a restroom?"

"Right there." Renee nodded to Lauren's left.

She hurried around the corner, opened the first door she came to. A row of hangers, one with a man's blue striped tie around the neck, greeted her. The next room revealed long granite counter tops, a wood-framed mirror, a toilet, and a walk-in shower. She shut the door behind her with an emphatic *click*, then leaned against the counter with a shaky sigh. She studied her reflection and shook her head. This was beyond crazy. She wasn't the right woman for this show. She'd text Brooke and demand she come pick her up. Except ... she rubbed her empty jacket pocket. Her phone was on its way back to Brooke.

She and Brooke had tried communicating telepathically when they were in middle school, but never had much success, except for the one time she'd brought Brooke a bag of Fritos after school and Brooke claimed to have sent the suggestion.

It was worth a shot if it would get Brooke to come to the hotel. She scrunched her eyes closed. *Fritos. Bring me Fritos. Please. Fritos.*

After a deep sigh, she stood and smoothed her skirt against her thighs. Okay. If no one was going to show up and rescue her, she'd have to rescue herself. She opened the bathroom door and strode back to the gathering of women.

Then froze.

A man had joined the group and sat in the middle of a sofa, surrounded by the other women. A man with white hair, a beaked nose, and a familiar gravelly voice.

"Mr. Townsend?"

He looked up, a grin splitting his creased face. "Lauren Bishop! How good to see you."

She took a step forward. "I really did see Mason the other day?"

Several women raised eyebrows and exchanged looks. Two of them scooted forward as another flipped her hair over her shoulder.

"I don't know about that, but I'm here today. Come sit by me." He scooted to one side and patted the cushion next to him. The two women on his other side stood with tight lips and moved to perch on the chair arms. "See? Plenty of room."

Lauren moved on autopilot and sat, cupping her elbows. If his grandfather was here, in this penthouse, Mason wouldn't be far away. This was bad. So bad.

Memories of walks on the beach, swimming in the lake, sharing fries on the restaurant deck crowded her mind. She steeled herself. She wasn't a naïve seventeen-year-old any longer. She could handle seeing Mason without falling apart. She could. She would.

"How have you been, my dear? It must be what ... ten years since I've seen you?"

She nodded. "Not since the summer after I graduated from high school."

"Yes, yes, that's right, you and Mason are the same age. What are you doing now? Did you go to medical school?"

Her breath caught in her chest. He remembered her dream. "No ... no, I didn't."

She cleared her throat. Despite shoving them aside, more visions pushed their way into her memory.

Eating tuna sandwiches on the Townsend boat dock. The older man wiping his hands on a stained towel after changing the oil and fuel filter in the family ski boat, then settling on the wood planks. They talked about nothing much. Until Mr. Townsend turned to her and asked about her college plans.

She'd never said it out loud before, but the warm sun, sparkling water, and his kind manner drew out her deepest, darkest secret: she wanted to be a doctor. She wanted to go into debt and work thirty-six-hour shifts. And she wanted to help people. What had she been thinking, saying it out loud? When she was from a hardworking family in a small town with zero chance of making it into medical school. It didn't matter that she had the highest GPA in Harts Leap High School. Girls who wore hand-me-downs, stained with grease from the fryer, didn't go to medical school. Except ... sometimes they did. She'd dared to dream back then.

She shifted on the couch. "I wasn't lucky enough to go to medical school. I teach fourth grade at Harts Leap Elementary."

Mr. Townsend patted her hand. "Luck has nothing to do with it. You made different choices. I'm sure you're blessed where you are. And your students are blessed by the best teacher they've ever had."

Lauren drew a deep breath. "I remember that about you. You don't believe in luck. Just blessings."

"God sends us blessings in different forms. Sometimes they don't feel right or good, but in the end, it is." He leaned forward. "Can someone find me an antacid?"

One of the other women leapt to her feet and hurried away, returning a moment later with a pink tablet she dropped into the older man's hand.

"Mr. Townsend." Lauren looked at him, chewing his pill, a thoughtful expression on his face. "Can you tell me what's going on?"

"I'm sorry, my dear. I'm sworn to secrecy." He pantomimed locking his lips and tossed the key over his shoulder.

"Are you on the show? Are you the ... bachelor?"

He guffawed. "I would love to be surrounded by so many beautiful and intelligent young women, but sadly, no. I'm just an old man brought in to say outrageous things and bring some comedic relief."

His words ratcheted her nerves. "So, Mason *is* on the show?"

He shrugged and winked. "I guess we'll have to wait and see."

The others giggled and one of the chair arm-perchers returned to his side on the couch. She ran a hand down his arm. "You're so funny, Mr. Townsend. Are you single?"

"The technical term is widower, so while I suppose you could say I'm single, my heart is still spoken for." He winked again at Lauren, and she smiled in reflex.

She'd seen in the paper when Mrs. Townsend, Mason's grandmother, passed away five years ago. She'd considered writing a condolence note to Mason but ended up not. She didn't want him thinking she was still infatuated with him or that she followed his life and his family in the media. She had, however, sent a card to Mr. Townsend. Both Mason's grandparents had always been kind to her, never treating her as anything but a friend of Mason's and his equal.

Unlike his sister Jenna who used to shoot Lauren, Brooke, and Angie ugly looks when Mason wasn't looking. Jenna had been a master of the insult veiled within a compliment. She could make even flattering remarks sound condescending. She'd once tipped Mom a hundred-dollar bill for a burger and fries at the Lakeside Grill. Then as she left the hut, she'd told her girlfriend, another rich summer resident, "I feel so sorry for that woman. Her daughter's clothes are always grease-stained when she's hanging around Mason, trying to get his attention." Jenna had spoken in a stage whisper, loud enough for every word to be heard inside.

Inside, where Lauren scooped ice cream for milkshakes and refilled sodas and drained the oil from baskets of fries. Inside, where more of Jenna's snooty friends sat, snickering. Inside, where Lauren's heart grew a little bit of a shell, trying to defend itself from the mean girls of Harts Leap's summer community.

Now, sitting on a couch in the Beverly Essex, next to Mason's grandfather, surrounded by several women who most likely defined the mean girl profile, she felt that familiar shell inch its way around her heart once again.

* * *

Mason stared at his mirrored reflection. "Tell me again why I can't shave?" he asked Liam.

"The women love it." He didn't look up from his tablet. "And the producers want the look."

"It's ridiculous. I'm in a tux and need a shave."

Liam shrugged. "I just pass on the orders."

"Speaking of which—" he turned to face Liam— "what's today's agenda?"

"The women are arriving now at the Penthouse Suite. Renee is taking care of them. They'll soon change into their evening wear, and we'll bring them to the Penthouse terrace where you'll greet each with a glass of champagne and chat for a few minutes, then send her off to mingle and get acquainted."

Mason nodded. Sounded pretty standard for these dating shows. "Then I make my picks of who's staying? How many do I have to get rid of?"

"Well ... there's a wrinkle."

"Isn't there always? What is it? I have to ask someone to bungee jump off the building with me first?"

Liam smirked. "No, but I'll file that for the future." He paused and looked Mason in the eye. "Remember the show we recently aired, *Date My Son!*?"

Mason nodded.

"It turned out to be more popular than we anticipated."

Mason squinted through one eye. "You didn't get my mother to agree to this. She's busy and happy in the Caribbean. Even hurricanes haven't been able to budge her off the island in the summer."

Liam shook his head. "You still get the final say, but ... we did bring in a family member to get to know the women also, and to advise you."

"Who ...?" Understanding hit him like a bug meeting a windshield. "Grandad. That's why he's here."

Liam nodded.

"I'm only the newest bachelor. I don't suppose anyone thought to ask my opinion."

Liam gazed at him for a moment then returned his attention to his tablet.

"That's what I thought." Mason sank into the chair and let his head drop into his hands. It was bad enough Jenna got him involved in this scheme, but to wrangle in Grandad? Why would she do that?

He pushed back against the chair. The company, of course. The public would love Grandad. Everyone loved him. It was all part of Jenna's strategy to save the company's bottom line and reputation.

After settling his elbows on the chair arms, he fisted one hand under his chin. Her plan had to work. If he put himself through this embarrassing display in front of the whole country, it better be worth it.

"How much time until I have to be dressed, unshaved, and up on the terrace?"

"Twenty-two minutes."

Dread gathered in his stomach and curled up like a snake waiting to strike an unsuspecting mouse. Except he was the clueless mouse. Which left Jenna as the snake.

Eighteen minutes later, he and Liam rode the elevator from the Washington Suite to the Penthouse. Grandad sat in the living room, alone, sipping coffee. He set the cup down and stood.

"You couldn't shave?"

"Don't start with me," Mason said. "You know this wasn't my idea."

Grandad grinned. "I kind of like it. I might even give up shaving myself."

Mason shook his head. "I just found out what's going on. You?"

"Not a clue, except Jenna said I needed to be here, and someone named Renee made me sign a ream of papers and wouldn't let me keep the pen."

"Gentlemen, we need to move outside." A young woman wearing a headset, a ball cap, and carrying a clipboard ushered them to the doors opened to a wide terrace. She directed them to the temporary bar holding two dozen champagne glasses.

"Don't mind if I do." Grandad snagged one and chugged the bubbly. "Delicious." He smothered a burp.

Mason had to chuckle. "Save some for the ladies."

"Who will be arriving in a moment." Liam followed them out. "They'll come in the door, walk through the entry with the columns, through the living room, and outside. They'll stop here. You offer them a glass of champagne. You introduce yourselves. You'll get about five minutes to chat. I'll signal you when it's time to send her on. She'll move down the terrace, and we'll film them all mingling."

Mason nodded. Sounded simple enough.

"We're ready," the woman in the ball cap said. She counted down from ten to four, then used her fingers. *Three. Two. One.* "And ... action!"

Mason straightened his shoulder and tried to quiet the roiling in his gut. Grandad gave another soft burp.

Could this get any worse?

Four

Lauren stood in the vestibule between the elevator and the door to the Penthouse Suite. Three women had gone in while the others waited, fidgeting in their heels and cocktail dresses. She'd been delighted to find one in her room that fit perfectly. Black lace overlaid a simple black slip dress and came to just above her knees. The mock neck made her body seem longer. The underdress had a higher hemline and lower neckline and a cutout just above the waist, all letting her show some skin but still look classy and elegant. Whether she and the bachelor hit it off or not, she and this dress were already in a lifetime commitment.

The door opened and Renee stuck her head out. "Lauren, you're up."

She gulped. Nodded. Wiped a sweaty palm on her thigh. "Okay."

Renee held the door, and Lauren threw back her shoulders and strode through. As she marched down the marble entry to the outdoor terrace, all she could think was *Fritos. Why didn't you bring me Fritos?*

A breeze ruffled the drape at the open terrace door. Three pairs of men's legs in black slacks showed beneath the billows.

She drew a deep breath, pushed the curtain aside and froze. Bile rose in her throat.

She'd been right.

Mason blinked at her, a blank look on his face. How could she walk out there, kiss his cheek, pretend they were strangers?

His grandfather smiled.

Another man, presumably the show's host, motioned her to come out.

She cast a glance over her shoulder, gauging the distance to the door. She could make a run for it. Stab the elevator button and get as far away from Mason Townsend as she could. Except for the production staff, equipment, and cables snaking across the floor, it was a clean getaway.

Except for all that and how much her non-profit needed the exposure a show like this could give it.

Fine. She'd go out there. She'd smile. She'd make small talk. She could do it.

The host motioned again, and Renee appeared at her side. "Show time."

The first step felt like dragging her foot out of the miry clay at the lake in early spring. The next was easier. Still, by the time she stood before the trio of men, her heart pounded and her hands trembled.

"Welcome, Lauren," the host said. "I'm Reid Allard. This is our bachelor, Mason, and his grandfather, Clarence."

"How do you do?" She extended a hand to Mason who took it. His mouth opened slightly, but he didn't speak.

Reid made up for Mason's muteness. "We hear you two are already acquainted. Tell us about that."

Mason's eyes closed briefly then he must have found his voice. "Yes, Lauren and I knew each other as teenagers." He pulled her in to kiss her cheek and whispered in her ear. "I'm so sorry about this. I had no idea. I thought you worked for the production."

Her brow furrowed. What the what? But she managed to keep smiling.

"Lauren!" Mr. Townsend opened his arms and she stepped into his embrace, feeling safe for the first time in days. After a moment, she reluctantly moved away. Mason's grandfather always smelled faintly of peppermint and pipe tobacco, and she welcomed the familiar scent.

"Lauren, do you remember Mason?" Reid asked.

"Of—of, course," she stammered. "Good to see you again, Mason."

"You two were an item once upon a time, weren't you?"

Lauren shot Reid a glare. Maybe he'd wither away into a toad and hop off into a hole.

Mason spoke first. "Lauren broke all the teenage boys' hearts back in the day. I was just one of many left in her wake."

Heat brewed in her chest. How dare he? He was the heartbreaker. He was the one making promises and then leaving. He was the one who never returned, who never looked back. *Back in the day.*

She opened her mouth to protest but Reid cut her off. "We'll hear all about that later." He gestured to the side where the three previous women stood, holding champagne glasses, and watching their group in front of the cameras.

Mason handed her a glass, bubbles clinging to the side. Their fingers brushed and she startled. Sparks? Really? Could this get any worse?

"It is good to see you, Lauren," he said.

She managed a smile at the three men, then turned and strode to the other women. One of them was the semi-friendly blonde who'd smiled at her earlier when she arrived.

"Hi," the blonde said. "I'm Philomena, but please call me Phil." Her smile seemed genuine. "This is Amelia and Keira." The other two women, another blonde and a brunette, both with pouty lips and drowsy eyes lifted their glasses in greeting.

"They blindside you, too?" Phil asked.

"Like I was a penny on railroad tracks and a steam locomotive heading my direction." Phil's question penetrated Lauren's consciousness. "What do you mean, 'too'? Did you—do you know Mason?"

Phil nodded. "We dated in college."

Lauren's breath caught in her chest. Of course. If the producers brought back Lauren, as Mason's high school romance, it made sense they'd include other women from his past.

"You?" Lauren raised her brows at Amelia and Keira. Amelia nodded, Keira shrugged.

"Mason and I interned together at the Townsend Management Group one summer. We were close," Amelia said.

"I've never met him." Keira sipped her champagne. Her gaze cut between the other three, seeming to appraise them as opponents. "My loss, apparently."

Lauren stood next to Phil, watching the next sacrificial sheep—er, ... contestant? bachelorette? ... woman walk out. Of the fifteen others, at least three seemed to already know Mason. The rest shook hands and exchanged air kisses without the shock Lauren was sure still haunted her face.

It took three hours, but after the last introduction, the assistant producer called everyone together into a corner of the terrace. "We're going to film another hour of conversations, then we'll break and head to the house where you'll all be staying. At least, where most of you will be staying. There will be an elimination at the end of the cocktail party." The women exchanged glances with each other, then looked at Mason. A few licked their lips.

Someone had fetched a chair for Clarence. He caught Lauren's eye and winked at her. She smiled reflexively. Whatever else was going on, seeing Mr. Townsend again made it bearable.

"Before we continue with the cocktail party, we're going to get some footage of the whole group, surrounding Mason, Clarence, and Reid. Ladies, this way."

More assistants appeared, leading the women into various formations around the Townsend men. Cameras would move closer or away. Clarence watched all the activity with a grin. Reid looked up every so often from his whispered conversations with Liam.

Finally, the AP called for quiet again. "Ladies, stand in a ring around the men. Reid is giving our intro."

Lauren, as the shortest in the group—as usual—was directed to perch on Clarence's knee. "Sorry about this," she murmured.

"Pffft. You're lighter than the New York Times crossword."

"Quiet! ... And ... action!"

"I'm Reid Allard," the host said, smiling with enough wattage to light up the sign in the Daisy's Cafe window. "With me is Mason Townsend, CEO of the Townsend Management Group. He's brought his grandfather, Clarence, to help him get to know the group of beautiful women behind us. In six weeks, we could be announcing an engagement live on our finale. But first ... our show is bringing first loves, rebound loves, and pity loves back together to see if there's more there than they thought the first time around. Welcome to ... *Re:United*!"

A crashing silence followed Reid's pronouncement.

Lauren turned to stone, unable to move.

"Dear? Are you okay?" Clarence jiggled his knee, and she startled back to reality.

"Yes, yes, of course." She stood. "Was I hurting you?" She managed a normal tone and words, but her thoughts raced around her brain like a circus motorcycle inside the wire globe.

Reuniting first loves? Rebound loves. *Pity* loves? If she was here as a pity love, she'd—she'd—well, she didn't know what she'd do, but it wouldn't end well.

Reid's little announcement also explained why several of the women knew Mason. Phil said they dated in college. Amelia claimed to have been close to him. Any of them could've ... could've ... She didn't want to think about what Mason could have been doing with those other women.

So. Lauren's "random" invitation wasn't so random after all. She'd been set up.

Her face felt hot, and she strode away from the men before she erupted.

At the railing overlooking the city, she gripped the cool iron and forced herself to take slow, deep breaths. "What a dirty trick."

She must have said it out loud because Phil joined her at the terrace rail. "How did they get you here?" Phil asked.

Lauren blew out a breath. "An invitation to travel, meet a man, have some fun."

Phil nodded. "Me too."

They looked over the view of downtown Los Angeles. City of Angels. What a crock. City of Lies, Spies, and Sighs.

* * *

Mason exhaled slowly and turned to his grandfather. "Did you know about this?" he asked.

When Philomena entered the terrace, he'd put it down to a coincidence. Amelia seemed familiar, but he hadn't time to think about it.

Then when Lauren appeared—his whole world shifted, and nothing was the same.

He'd been a single guy with a mission: to motivate viewers and the general public to absolute confidence in him and his company before the storm hit in a few weeks. He'd take beautiful women to various activities and chat with them. Then he could end the thing in six weeks with a rueful shrug and slip the ring back into his pocket. The announcement of his company losing forty million dollars to an embezzler would be a footnote.

Now, he was confused. Seeing Lauren stirred up something ... something he'd ignored for ten years.

Grandad gave him a steady gaze. "It sounded like some of these women ... you already know them? More than just Lauren?"

Mason led Grandad back to the chair. "I know at least six of them that I can remember. I feel like I took a wild pitch in the head."

"I'm sorry, son. It must be a shock."

Resignation seeped through Mason like ice overtaking a lake in December. He ran a hand over the back of his neck. "You have no idea."

"But ..." Grandad drew up one side of his mouth and thought for a moment. "Forget about the show and the company and all that. Is there anyone here you have unfinished business with? Anyone you want a second chance with? Or anyone you're sure you don't want to see again?"

Mason folded his arms across his chest. "Of course not. You and Dad always taught Jenna and me not to leave anything unfinished. 'Townsends have no loose ends,' remember?"

"We meant in business. Nothing comes back later to bite you or the company in the backside. But in our personal lives ... we're not quite so disciplined."

Mason scoffed. "Now's a fine time to tell me that distinction."

Grandad shrugged. "So, even Lauren? No loose ends there?"

Mason shook his head. "I got her message loud and clear. She met someone else before I got back to Harts Leap after our first year at college."

Grandad narrowed his eyes. "Are you sure? It seems to me—"

"There you are." Amelia appeared at his side and slipped her arm through his. "Let's go get re-acquainted."

"Re...?" Ahh. He'd been right. She was familiar, but he couldn't place her. The camera behind her shoulder had a steady red light, so he forced a smile. "Of course. Let's catch up. Where do you live now, Amelia?"

"I'm still in New York, where we interned together."

Of course! When he'd gotten Lauren's message not to come back to Harts Leap, he'd begged his father for an internship in the city. He and several of the other interns spent a lot of evenings hanging out. They were too young for bars, but someone always managed to get a six-pack. Or they'd get coffee. A few of them had hooked up. He'd been still reeling after Lauren and could barely recall those three months.

"It's good to see you again." He forced a smile.

"What I want to know—" she leaned close and whispered— "was I your first love? Please tell me I wasn't a pity love!" She batted her lashes and shifted so her already low neckline exposed more skin.

He ducked the question and averted his gaze. "I promise, there are no pity loves here. I'm not even sure what a pity love is."

"There are one or two here. Women you dated—or said you loved or wanted a relationship with—because you pitied them, felt sorry for them, or thought they needed rescuing. Like Lauren." Amelia's Cheshire cat grin made him shudder.

He pulled his arm away and faced her. "What do you mean, like Lauren?"

"She's so obviously not right for you." Amelia's gaze raked his face, leaving him feeling raw and exposed. "And you were young. Teenagers, right? It's pretty clear you felt sorry for the local girl and dated her for the summer to give her a boost and some memories."

His blood heated and rushed to his fists, but he stuffed them into his pockets. "I don't know what's going on here. I don't know what the producers hope to accomplish with this farce they're calling a show. I don't know what's a rebound love or a pity love. But I do know, I've never felt sorry for Lauren for even one minute. She was an amazing girl, and I'm sure she's grown into an even more amazing woman."

He turned on his heel and strode off. He needed to get out of here before he hit something. Impotent anger churned in his stomach.

"Hey, stranger." Phil appeared at his side. At least a friendly and familiar face. "Are you okay?"

He shook his head. "I—I don't think so."

"Let's grab a glass and sit for a minute. Tell me what's going on."

Phil led him to the bar then to a pair of chairs in the corner of the terrace. The other women were scattered along the two sides of the outdoor space while a few had moved inside. Amelia seemed to have recovered from his outrage and was perched near Grandad.

He sat and blew out a sigh of frustration. "I think I've been had."

"You didn't know about the whole *Re:United* thing?" She made air quotes.

"Not a clue. I saw Lauren the other day at the production studios and figured she worked there." He shook his head. "Something's going on, and I have a feeling my sister knows more than she's letting on."

"Jenna's here?" Phil looked around.

"She's down in the Washington Suite. Me on this show was her idea." A thought crossed his mind. "How did they know who to cast? How were you contacted?"

"Lauren and I both received invitations directly from One Reality Productions, asking us to interview for the show. I thought it sounded like a fun break. I didn't know you were part of it until I saw you." She nodded to where they'd stood and exchanged greetings a few hours ago.

"Lauren, too, huh. What about Amelia? Jordan, Emily, and Liz?" He named the other women he'd dated in the last eight or so years who also milled around the set.

"I only talked to Lauren and Amelia. Amelia didn't say." Phil put her hand on his. "I'm sorry you were caught off guard."

"Thanks." He smiled briefly. He and Phil had dated through their two middle years of college, then drifted apart as their final year got under way. He'd been concentrating on getting into an MBA program and she'd been focused on— "Are you a doctor? Did you go to med school?"

Her eyes lit up. "I am. Pediatric cranio-facial surgery."

"Geez." Admiration climbed in his chest. "And you joined a dating reality show, why? Saving children from disfigurement get boring?"

She glanced away. "Something like that. I'm ready for a break and the invitation came at a good time."

Another of his former "loves" approached, and he stood to greet Liz.

Phil stood also. "I'll catch up with you later." She set down her glass and wandered away.

Liz took Phil's seat, and he sat again. Liz put her hands on his knees. "Is this crazy or what?"

He stifled a groan as she gazed at him with wide eyes.

She had no idea. No idea at all.

Five

Lauren stared at her reflection in the bathroom mirror. The Beverly Essex's Penthouse Suite was as beautiful as you'd expect. She should probably feel awed at the palatial surroundings: marble everywhere she looked. A spa tub. A huge walk-in shower with four faucets arranged to rain water on soapy bathers. A long vanity with a stool in front. But all she felt was empty.

She sank onto the toilet seat lid and rubbed her forehead. This couldn't be happening. Could it?

Seeing Mason and his grandfather carved open the wound in her heart. The wound she'd spent a decade stitching up. Just when she'd thought she was over him, this had to happen.

The door into the bathroom opened.

"Occupied!" she said. Wait. She'd locked herself in. She looked up. The door was still closed.

"Lauren."

She swiveled her head. She'd missed the second door, entering from a bedroom.

Mason stood there, framed in front of a bed, still in his tux and looking better than he deserved.

She pointed. "Out."

He leaned against the doorjamb and crossed his arms. "You're in the master bath."

"Please, Mason." She looked away so he wouldn't see the emotion brimming in her eyes.

"I was blindsided too. I didn't know the premise of the show." He spoke quietly.

She shrugged. "It doesn't matter, does it? I signed a contract. Unless …" Her eyes widened as an idea occurred to her. It meant abandoning her plans to tell people about the suicide prevention hotline she wanted to start in Harts Leap. But there'd be other opportunities. There had to be.

She turned to him. "Unless you eliminate me. Then I go home, and we pretend this never happened." She clasped her hands, daring to hope, but wary. He could dash her optimism into the shoals of public humiliation.

He entered the room fully and propped a hip on the counter, folded arms showing impressive biceps through his jacket sleeves. She sat on her hands so she wouldn't run them up his arms, feel his tight muscles.

"I could," he said. She dragged her eyes up to his face. A smile tugged up one corner of his mouth. That was the Mason she fell for. Charming, funny, and thoughtful. "But why should I? You signed up for this, just like me. I might keep you all the way to the end, so we suffer together. Didn't we promise each other that, once upon a time?"

She ignored the question. Yes, they'd made that promise. Before she knew he was the kind of guy to break up with her via his sister. "I didn't know *you* were what I signed up for."

"Me neither. But …" He shrugged, looked away. "But maybe this is our second chance. Don't you want to stick around, see if we still have chemistry? Remember those summer nights out on the lake, in the boat?"

A spark of something ignited in her chest. Anger? No … attraction? Absolutely not. She shooed that thought away like an annoying fly and stood.

"Mason. You made it clear a decade ago that you were done with me. The least you can do is get me out of here."

She brushed past him and left the bathroom.

Turned out, even a huge penthouse suite wasn't large enough to get lost in.

* * *

Mason stared after Lauren, shockwaves rippling through him. Her words made no sense. He'd what? Made it clear he was done with her? How? He'd never ...

He glanced at the toilet. If only he could flush away his questions about Lauren, his reservations about this whole *Re:United* thing, and his worries about the company.

Maybe if he banged his head against the doorjamb. If it would help him understand what was going on, he'd gladly suffer a concussion.

Instead, he returned to the bedroom where he'd escaped for a minute to think. He snatched up the phone and stabbed the number for the Washington Suite. *Jenna, pick up.* He had a lot of questions and she'd better have some answers.

But the phone rang and rang until he replaced the receiver.

"Mason? We need you." A PA poked her head into the room. "It's time for the elimination."

"I'll be right there."

He had to do this show, so he would. But he'd do it his way and on his terms. He strode to the living room where Grandad, Renee, and Liam waited.

They explained the concept of the show in more depth. They spread an array of photos taken during the last few hours of filming. He'd pick through the pictures and discuss his choices with Grandad, then choose who he wanted to stay. He had to let four women go tonight. That shouldn't be hard.

He picked up Lauren's picture. She wanted to go. Nearly begged him to release her. An urge to do as she asked tugged his heart. He'd always loved making her happy, getting her to laugh.

Laughs were rare in her family, she said. Her parents were too busy working to put food on the table and had no time for fun. He'd made it his mission, that summer they fell in love, to give her smiles and laughter and memories.

He could make her happy again. He could toss her photo on the table and walk away. After all, she'd broken up with him via a message from Jenna. There had been no doubt back then that she was done, so he should cut her loose and move on with the other women who wanted to be here.

Except ... what *was* Lauren doing here? If she wasn't single, wasn't interested in a relationship, wasn't willing to date on television, she never would have shown up.

"You're keeping Lauren, of course." Grandad touched the picture Mason still held.

"She asked me to let her go."

"If you ask her to stay, I think she will." Grandad gripped his shoulder for a brief moment. "I'm not wrong about the unfinished business you both have."

Grandad moved back to the main room, leaving Mason with the array of photos.

He looked them over for a long moment, picked up some more.

Then he rapped a knuckle on the table, left Amelia's snapshot there, along with three other women he frankly didn't even remember meeting, and held out his selections to Liam.

"Ahem." Liam cleared his throat. "We want you to think carefully about your choices."

He nodded. "I did."

"You got rid of Amelia. She's one of the women you're reuniting with. That's the premise of the whole show."

Mason shook his head. "We never dated. She's an old acquaintance, not a lost love."

"Really?" Liam cocked his head. "You were never attracted to her?"

Mason shrugged. "She's pretty, sure, and I was eighteen. We probably flirted, but I was busy working and—" He stopped before he confessed that the summer he and Amelia had been co-workers was also the summer Mason spent thinking about Lauren, trying to understand what happened with her, why she'd moved on to some other guy without telling him. That sounded way too pathetic, even for a love-struck teenager.

"You and Amelia have unfinished business?"

"I don't think so. There's no chemistry." He looked at Amelia's picture again. She grinned at the camera, eyes dancing at some secret joke.

"The producers would prefer you keep the women you already knew. It'll make for a better show. More possibilities for conflict."

Mason groaned. "Conflict is what I want to avoid."

"In life, sure. But it's ratings gold. Don't you want the show to be a success? To be watched by millions of people rooting for you to find love?"

With a deep sigh, he picked up Amelia's photo, shuffled through the stack and plucked out another of the non-impressions. "Will that do?"

Liam grinned. "That'll work very well."

This was going to come back and bite him. He knew it as well as he knew the summer menu at Sushi Nakazawa in the West Village.

Six

Lauren took her place where Alison, the production assistant, directed her. Her telepathic communication with Brooke hadn't resulted in either Fritos or rescue, so she pleaded with God instead: *Please let Mason eliminate me. Please. I promise I'll go back to Harts Leap, and I'll never leave again. I'll never ask for more than what I have. I'll never try to be more than I am.*

Wasn't her desire to be more, really what this adventure was all about? But the truth was, she was and always would be the daughter of hard-working parents, a girl who grew up wearing grease-stained hand-me-downs from her older sister. A fourth-grade teacher in a small town where nothing much happened.

Please. She sent a final plea heavenward then waited while Alison positioned her and the others.

Mason, Clarence, and Reid stood several feet in front of the penthouse suite, the women facing them, arrayed in front of the terrace's half-wall, the lights of downtown Los Angeles gleaming behind them.

The sun had tucked itself into the horizon and a chill brushed up Lauren's arms. She rubbed them briskly.

Mason held a stack of something in one hand. Papers ... or ... she peered closer. Photos? Maybe snapshots. Clarence stood by a small table holding books. Small, brightly colored books, like journals ... or photo albums?

Her vision telescoped and blurred. She reached for the woman next to her, but Amelia pulled away.

Breathe deep. Inhale. Count to five. Hold it. Exhale. Again. After the third breath her heart rate slowed, and she could look around again.

Reid cleared his throat. A Steadicam's red light glowed, followed by the call: "Action!"

"Welcome to *Re:United*'s first reunion ceremony. Mason will invite the women he wishes to remain to accept a photo album and a picture of the two of them taken during tonight's party. If you—" he motioned to the group of women— "hear your name, come forward to take the album from Clarence and the picture from Mason. If he doesn't have a picture for you, you've been outcast, and the reunion is over."

Mason met her eyes for such a brief moment, she might have imagined it. Surely he would do what she asked and let her go. Right? She could leave with her dignity intact. He owed her that, at least. For breaking her heart without warning, without talking to her in person, without regard for her feelings.

She straightened. He'd let her go. Certainty filled her chest.

"Mason, who is your first choice to stay at the reunion?" Reid asked.

Mason flipped through his stack of photos, chose one, contemplated it, then looked up. "Amelia."

She squealed and dashed across the terrace to throw her arms around him. She took the picture and the photo album then hurried inside.

The process continued another ten times. Ten women heard their names, responded with a shriek, tears, or a big smile, received the symbols of being part of the chosen, and moved away.

Finally, only Lauren and four other women remained. She took a deep breath. He was really going to do it. He was going to let her go. She smiled her thanks at him.

"You have one last choice, Mason," Reid said. "Do you know who you're inviting to stay at the reunion?"

"I do." Mason held the last picture and glanced at it, a smile playing across his lips. "I certainly do."

"After Mason announces the final reunion attendee, the remaining women will be escorted out of the party and back to their real lives." Reid gave them looks of mock sympathy. "You'll be outcasts."

He turned back to Mason and his grandfather. "Clarence, did Mason consult you about his choices?"

Clarence shook his head. "I'm just the wrinkle in the process." He patted his lined cheek. "In my case, literally. Mason's a big boy. He knows who he is and who he wants." He shot Lauren a glance and—so quickly, did she imagine it?— he winked at her.

Dread knotted around her lungs, cutting off her breath. No. Oh, no.

"Mason, who is your last choice to remain at the reunion?" Reid waved a hand, inviting Mason to speak.

The ratfink had the gall to smile at her. "Lauren. I want Lauren."

* * *

Mason kept his tone even and his face pleasant as he asked Lauren to stay. She, however, gave him such a searing glare he wouldn't have been surprised to have spontaneously combusted right there on the penthouse terrace.

He held his breath as Reid invited her up to accept the photo book and snapshot. She could refuse. She could walk past him and out of his life. Again.

But she gave Grandad a smile that seemed genuine. She kissed his cheek as she took the album, then stepped in front of Mason. Her eyes held vulnerability.

After a long pause that bordered on uncomfortable, she extended her hand.

He covered hers with his and pulled her close enough to kiss her cheek, then released her. She took the picture and joined the remaining women.

He had to say good-bye to the four women leaving the show. They all looked dazed, clutching their consolation prize: a book on handling rejection.

He suppressed a grin.

It wasn't that they weren't nice enough or attractive. He just hadn't felt a spark. Come to think of it, he hadn't felt a spark with anyone. Except

Lauren. And she'd made it clear nothing would ever happen between them again.

Reid called the group back to order and closed out the episode. Before they could disperse, Alison took over, explaining the events for the next few days.

Mason was staying at the Beverly Essex, in the Washington suite, down a few floors from this penthouse. The women would be transported to a place in the Holmby Hills where they'd be living for the next few weeks. In the morning, they'd all be going to the Pacific Design Center for photo shoots, lunch, and more chats.

He rubbed the back of his neck as the women filed out and the noise level dropped.

Now, maybe he could find his sister and get some answers. He patted his pockets before remembering his phone had been confiscated. He'd have to hunt her down personally. Good thing he knew her favorite haunts were the pool or the bar. Which at the Beverly Essex meant the bar at the pool.

It took a few minutes for all the women to leave via the elevator, so he paced the penthouse's marble entryway until he could follow alone to the ground floor.

Finally, he emerged in the lobby, strode past the boutiques, to the exit out to the pool. He blinked in the sudden light and loosened his tie. The scent of something flowery tickled his nose.

After a moment adjusting to the brightness, he made his way toward the bar. Sure enough, Jenna perched on a high stool, a shapely glass with a paper umbrella in front of her.

He claimed the next seat. "Why does Lauren think I broke up with her? You're the one who told me she'd moved on, she had a new boyfriend in Harts Leap, and she didn't want to see me again."

Jenna glanced at him, sipped her drink. She shifted on the stool to face him. "I've no idea. I told you at the time, I ran into her the first day I was back in Harts Leap. She was walking along the lake with some dude, their arms around each other. She stopped me, asked me to give you a message."

He shook his head. None of that made sense.

The bartender approached and Mason ordered a beer. "Who was the guy? Did she introduce you?"

Jenna ran a finger down the frosty side of her glass. "She just said she'd moved on, and it would be better if you didn't come to Harts Leap that summer. And not to call her because she wouldn't answer."

A glass filled with amber liquid appeared in front of Mason and he took a swig. The cold brew slaked his body's thirst but did nothing to his need for answers about Lauren and that summer. The summer that was supposed to be theirs. They'd both finished a year of college. They were going to share every moment, swimming in the lake, eating burgers from the Lakeside Grill, watching movies in the restored theatre.

He'd planned to propose to her before fall. He'd go to Colgate in New York state. They'd get married the following summer and she'd transfer to Colgate too. Or wherever. There were two SUNY campuses within driving distance. Several other private and community colleges. And medical schools. With her grades, she would have had her pick. He had their lives all planned out. Until Jenna had called, spinning him into a daze that lasted months.

He finished his beer, placed the glass on the warped coaster. He'd respected her wishes. He didn't go to Harts Leap that summer. But he did call. True to her word, she didn't answer. He'd left a message, which she never returned. Which was answer enough.

He'd been forced to accept the unthinkable: Lauren had fallen out of love with him and moved on. Leaving him behind with a broken heart and no way to mend it.

"Mason." Jenna's quiet voice pulled him from the past.

He looked up. His sister—she looked about to cry. Jenna never cried. "What is it?"

"I—I have to tell you something ... about—" Her phone chimed. She glanced at the screen before accepting the call. "Hello ... *what?*" She listened intently for a few seconds before disconnecting. She stood, drained her glass, slung her bag over her shoulder. "I've got to go."

"What is it?"

"Just a work crisis. I'll handle it. You concentrate on being the perfect bachelor and wooing all these women." She kissed his cheek and disappeared down the path winding through the shrubbery.

"Wait! Jenna!" He raced after her, but she'd already disappeared. A door marked Ladies Locker Room clicked shut. He stood and stared at the barrier. Jenna had been about to tell him something. Something that would give him answers? Closure?

He shoved his hands into his pockets and strode back to the lobby and the elevator to his suite. Where he could toss and turn for the rest of the night and wonder why he was such a loser that he couldn't get over this woman who had so thoroughly gotten over him.

Seven

The next morning Lauren dressed in yellow shorts and a lacy top with shoulder cutouts. She pulled her hair into a high ponytail and stared at her reflection. She'd lain awake half the night, debating if she should just quit the show. Yes, she'd signed a contract, and yes, she'd had a chance to decline Mason's invitation to stay at the "reunion."

She'd been so sure he didn't want her there any more than she wanted to be there. But she'd felt caught.

The smart thing to do would have been to demur and ask to leave. Why didn't she? The dark circles under her eyes testified to the fact that she'd spent the whole night trying to answer that question.

She adjusted the rubber band holding her hair, easing some of the tightness in her scalp. Maybe that would help her look more rested.

A knock sounded at her door. "Ladies! Get on the bus or be left behind!" Her roommate, Holly, had left twenty minutes ago, eager to see the rest of the house. They'd both been exhausted last night and tumbled into bed without looking around. Their bathroom had granite countertops, a walk-in shower, and window shades operated by a remote with more options than her television remote back home.

Lauren followed the surge of women emerging from rooms along the hallway. They crested at the top of the stairs, then ebbed down to the living room. PAs and techs swarmed through the room.

Philomena walked a few steps ahead of her, so Lauren hurried a bit to fall into step. "Where are we going today?"

Phil greeted her with a smile. "Pacific Design Center. It's a group of buildings. There's a museum and restaurants. The rest is part shopping, part design showcase, part event venue."

"Like a mall?"

Phil cocked her head. "Not exactly, but I suppose in its simplest terms, yes."

Lauren exhaled. She knew malls. She could handle a mall. Lots of things to look at, shops to escape—er, wander into.

She and Phil settled into seats in the black Mercedes mini coach. She took a moment to observe the outside of her new home. On Brooke's show, the house had been a Mediterranean villa. This one resembled a European castle. There was even a small turret attached to one corner. Brick and stonework around the exterior added to the castle impression.

The van pulled onto Sunset Boulevard and Lauren settled into her seat.

"You were Mason's high school girlfriend?" Phil asked.

A knot formed in Lauren's stomach. So much for distracting herself with thoughts about architecture and shopping. She shrugged. "More like a summer of young infatuation."

"That's not the way I heard it."

"What do you mean?"

"I met Mason two or three months after you two broke up. He was ... well, shattered seems melodramatic, but it fits."

Something—surely not jealousy—snaked around the knot in her stomach and twined up her chest. "You dated in college?"

"We were in a study group as sophomores. We dated casually for the next couple of years. I went on to med school, he got an MBA."

Lauren ignored the twinge in her chest at Phil's words. Med school. Of course, gorgeous and sweet Phil was a doctor. She probably traveled overseas and did free surgery on kids.

Phil gave her a searching glance. "By the time we were seniors, we'd run out of things to talk about. Not to mention he wasn't over you."

Lauren felt her cheeks flush and looked out the window. Trees gave way to tall buildings, banks, or offices.

"I'm guessing it was mutual. The not getting over each other?"

Lauren turned to see Phil's quizzical expression and met her gaze. "I don't know what you're talking about."

Phil's lips tipped up in an almost smile. "My mistake." She grabbed the edge of the seat in front of her as the van made a wide turn onto a street lined with small shops and restaurants. A huge blue building appeared ahead. "That's PDC." She pointed. "Locals call it the Blue Whale."

"Wow. It's bigger than any mall I've been to." The coach shimmied as it turned into the huge parking lot.

After the bus stopped and they all climbed down, they followed Alison to a wide hall scattered with chairs and tables arranged in small groupings. Reid and Mason and Clarence stood on the bottom step of a staircase that ascended into an atrium.

It must be her imagination, but Mason seemed to be staring at her.

Lauren hardly heard the announcements. They'd be divided into small groups for "field trips" to various sites around the center. This atrium would be home base. Craft services—food and drink— available along the side. Chat and mingle before and after your outing with Mason.

"First up," Reid said, "are Philomena, Amelia, Holly, and Emily."

Lauren exhaled with relief. She needed to think about what Phil said, about Mason being shattered for months after he broke up with her. Something didn't make sense.

Jenna had delivered her devastating message with a smirk and a flounce as she left the Lakeside Grill, Lauren's heart in shreds. He'd called a few days later, but she was at work and missed the call. When she saw the voicemail, her fingers trembled as she stabbed the buttons. Did he call to apologize? To say he'd gone a little crazy. Was he begging her to take him back?

"Ummm ... hey, it's me. So, I wondered ... if maybe we could talk? I have some questions ... maybe you want to be friends ... I don't know ... call me?"

He thought he could break up with her through his sister and she would still want to be friends? She'd deleted the message and blocked his number.

Now Phil said months later he was upset. Why? If he didn't want to see her anymore, why was he upset? She'd been the one to drop two classes at Harts Leap Community College because she couldn't concentrate. She'd been the one to take extra shifts at the Lakeside Grill all that summer and fall, trying to keep her mind occupied. She'd been the one shattered.

* * *

Mason nodded as Emily chattered about the house they all lived in now, listing its amenities. A swimming pool and spa. A billiards table. A wine cellar.

Amelia walked on his other side while Phil and ... Holly? ... followed behind.

Amelia grabbed his arm and slipped her hand over his elbow. "It's a great place," she agreed. "But I want to show you this shop over here." With a tug she separated him from the other women as nimbly as a lion cutting a wildebeest from its herd.

She steered them into a store with various rooms of staged furniture. He glanced around. Not one of the groupings looked the least bit inviting. They were all hard angles, chrome, glass, and rough fabrics.

"Isn't this gorgeous?" Amelia stopped and gazed around. "I love it all. So sleek, so modern."

"Mmm hmm." If not for the ever-present camera behind them, he'd have removed his arm from her grip. But being open to all the women in all kinds of situations was part of his commitment to the show.

"Let's sit." She waved a hand at a nearby sofa of dark leather. He sat gingerly, in case the spindly legs couldn't hold both their weight. But once seated, the thing seemed sturdy enough.

"Tell me what you've been doing since our summer of love in New York." Amelia tossed her hair over her shoulder and raised one eyebrow.

If he'd been drinking coffee, he'd have spewed it all over the faux rabbit fur rug at their feet. Instead, he swallowed his amusement. "Did we have a summer of love? I remember fetching lots of coffee, collating endless stacks of paper, and eating late-night pizzas."

She leaned back and laughed like he was Jimmy Fallon. "Still funny as ever, aren't you. That was such a great three months, wasn't it? On our own for the first time, in the big city."

He murmured something that could be taken as agreement. His memories of that summer were a blur. Depression had weighed on his shoulders like one of the rocks from Devil's Slide trail in Harts Leap. He'd been on a hamster wheel of writing emails to Lauren then deleting them. Resolving to fly to California to demand answers, then deciding he had all the answers he needed and should move on. Throwing himself into being the best intern the company ever had, then shrugging off the menial tasks and asserting his privilege as a family member. He'd emerged into the heat of late summer in New York City, blinked at the blinding sun in downtown Manhattan, then moved to the central part of the state to start his fall semester at Colgate University.

Amelia still chattered as he dragged his focus back to her. "When I applied for this show, I never dreamed you were the bachelor. It's like fate or Kismet or something. Don't you think so?"

He rubbed the itchy stubble on his cheeks. How soon could he get rid of this perpetual five o'clock shadow?

"Mason? Did you hear me? That this was meant to be?" She leaned forward, gazing at him.

He let his hand drop from his face. "It's something all right."

"Oh, you." She swatted his arm. "Still silent and brooding, all these years later."

The women they'd left out on the savannah stampeded into the store and he stood. "Ladies," he called. "Over here."

A frown tightened Amelia's lips but was immediately replaced with a sunny smile. "Yes, come on." She motioned them over.

Emily and Holly joined them on the couch while Phil perched on a nearby armchair. A Steadicam hovered in front of them.

"This place is amazing." Emily gestured to the mall area.

"We should get back out there." Mason stood. "We've got things to see and—and rooms to design."

Three women giggled in response. Phil just looked at him, a small smile playing on her lips. They resumed their path through the center's shops and displays. This time it was Phil who hooked her arm in his, but she made no move to remove him from the others.

"I get the feeling there's more going on with you than searching for true love on a reality show," she murmured.

He forced his arm to stay loose and relaxed even as his shoulders tightened. "You were always too smart for me." He spoke softly then raised his voice for the camera. "I'm totally open to finding love. I want to share my life with someone special."

A production assistant waved from Mason's peripheral vision and gave him the *Time's up* signal. Finally. It felt like this date would never end. He steered their little herd back to the atrium.

The other women, assorted crewmembers, and Reid milled around the open area. Phil steered him to the X drawn on the floor with blue tape, kissed his cheek, and whispered into his ear. "Take it from an old friend. It's time for answers."

He pulled away and searched her gaze. "What do you mean?"

She winked, turned, and disappeared into the crowd.

The maelstrom of activity around him echoed the emotions roiling through his gut. He'd been remembering his summer of wanting—no, aching—for answers. What did Phil know? Had she talked to Lauren?

He searched the open space, looking for Grandad. He'd been a bit subdued this morning, not his usual jocular self. Instead of Grandad, he saw Lauren standing near the buffet table laden with lunch selections.

A familiar small orange-brown bag in a basket of various chips caught his eye. He snagged the bag and held it in front of Lauren. "Do you still love Fritos?"

Astonishment crossed her face.

"What?" he asked. "Have you given up corn?"

Still silent, she took the bag. After blinking at him, she opened it, and ate some chips. Finally, *finally*, she smiled, a real smile that crinkled the edges of her eyes. "Thank you."

A camera closed in, and a boom microphone hovered overhead.

"Watch it!" someone called.

Mason turned to see the boom operator stumble backwards, land on his backside, and kick the camera operator's feet out from under him.

It had to be reflexes honed on the basketball court that had him grabbing the camera before it hit the ground. A crowd gathered, asking if the two men on the floor were all right.

"I was backing up and tripped over a power cord," the boom guy said.

"Did you have to take me down with you?" The cameraman took his equipment from Mason and checked the lens.

"It was an accident," Mason said. "Could've happened to anyone. There are enough cords and wires here to string up a trapeze act in the rafters."

Lauren laughed and he flashed her a grateful look.

After everyone wandered back to their jobs, he and Lauren were left with the Steadicam operator and the mic guy again.

She offered him her bag of Fritos.

He took a couple before handing the bag back to her. "Have you seen my grandfather?"

She shook her head as a PA thrust a folded note at him. "For you."

Mason smothered a grin. So, this was how people communicated when they couldn't text, email, or call. He unfolded the yellow page torn off a legal pad.

Not feeling well. Going back to the hotel. Grandad.

"Excuse me." Mason touched Lauren's elbow and turned to search the crowd for Liam. Reid and Liam stood on the fringes of the activity, heads bent over tablets.

Mason hurried to them. "Is my grandfather okay?"

Liam looked up, slid his glasses to his forehead. "He said indigestion. I arranged for a driver to take him to the hotel."

"Can I call him?" Mason held out his hand.

Liam sighed and stared into his face before handing over a mobile phone. "One call to the hotel and you have to give it right back."

Mason nodded, found the hotel's number and tapped his toe until his grandfather answered in the suite.

"I'm fine," Grandad said. "I took some antacid and I'm stretched out on your sofa with the newspaper."

"Should I come back?"

Grandad chuckled. "You can't use my heartburn to get out of this. I'll see you later."

Mason handed the phone to Liam. Jenna had roped Grandad into this without a second thought. The man was nearly eighty. He should be golfing or playing bridge. Not traipsing around Los Angeles, tripping over power cords, and eating fried food from craft services.

"Here." The same production assistant who delivered the note now nudged him back to the blue X.

After the call for action, Reid gazed at the camera and spoke. "Next up for some small group time with Mason are Keira, Brandy, Liz, and Lauren."

Mason nodded once. Amelia was right. Maybe this was fate or Kismet. But as Phil said, it was past time for answers.

He retraced his earlier path through the design center and back to the showroom area, the four women surrounding him. Three of them chattered. Lauren lagged a step behind, and while she wore a tight smile, she didn't say anything.

This time, he recognized the predatory gleam in Liz's eyes and was able to hiccup his gait, walk next to Lauren, and take her hand.

She stiffened and tried to pull away, but he held firm. "Let's look over here." He steered her to a different shop than the one Amelia had lured him to and managed to keep a few feet ahead of the trailing camera operator.

Once inside, he let go of her hand. "I want to talk."

She folded her arms and gave him a look that could only be described as a glare. "So do I."

"Me first." He cocked his head toward a grouping of chrome director chairs with flamingo pink fabric.

She marched to the first seat and dropped into it. "I want to know—"

He raised a hand to stop her. "I've waited a long time for this." So long. Ten years of wondering. "Why did you break up with me through my sister? Didn't I deserve at least a phone call?"

Lauren drew back almost like he'd slapped her. "What are you talking about? You broke up with *me.* Through Jenna. Talk about cowardly. I'm the one who deserved a phone call."

Confusion had him scratching his head then he held up a hand again, this time so he could think. "I never ... I didn't—I wouldn't."

"You certainly did. Jenna told me the first day she got to town that you decided you were too young to be tied down, you'd accepted an internship in New York, and you wanted to date other people that summer and when you returned to Colgate." Her voice grew tight, and she swallowed.

He fisted his hands. He had to keep it together. Anger heated his blood until he felt like he'd ignite right here in the PDC.

Jenna. He should have known. It had been written all over her face at the pool bar last night. He knew she was hiding something. Why didn't she tell him? She had to know he and Lauren would talk, compare notes, figure out her treachery.

He reached over and took Lauren's hand again. She stiffened but didn't pull away. "Jenna lied. I was coming back to Harts Leap for the summer. I was coming back to my love, my girlfriend, with a ring in my pocket. I planned to leave in August with a fiancée."

All the color drained from Lauren's face. "You didn't—didn't dump me? You didn't decide I wasn't good enough for you?"

He banged his fist on the chrome chair arm. Then startled as a dimple appeared where he'd hit it.

Lauren burst into laughter, and he couldn't hold back his own chuckle. That was the carefree sound he remembered.

A memory of her laugh echoed through the years and into his head. "Remember the time we took Grandad's aluminum motorboat out to the fishing cove?"

She nodded, a light in her eyes. "You were showing off and ran it into the buoy and dented the boat."

"How was I to know the buoy was a last century left over and made of iron? I thought it was plastic and would bounce off the hull."

"Instead of leaving a dent the size of a basketball. Did you ever tell Clarence the truth?"

Mason chuckled. "A week later, the guilt was too much for me. He said he already knew, and I was becoming a man in front of his eyes."

She leaned forward. "I always loved your grandparents. I was sorry to hear about your grandmother."

"Thank you." He swallowed and stood. "We better get out of here before I destroy a couch or a credenza."

She got to her feet, and he touched her elbow. "Lauren. I never thought ... what you said." He ran a hand over his face. "I don't believe this, any of this."

Lauren looked away, blinking rapidly. He put a finger under her chin and drew her gaze back to his. "You've always been *too* good for me. Too sweet, too generous, too kind."

"Oh, Mason," she whispered. "What did your sister do?"

He shook his head. "She ... she destroyed me, that's what she did. I almost flunked out of college that next semester."

A red light wavered on his left and he squinted. A camera, not ten feet away.

He drew a breath, held it, then cleared his throat. "Let's walk around. I want to look at some ideas for my ..." He floundered for something plausible. "... for my home office."

Lauren canted her head to one side. "Um ... okay?"

He smiled and nodded toward the camera. She followed his gaze, then her eyes widened.

He tucked her hand into the crook of his elbow and guided her to a different area of the store.

They strode through fake kitchens, bedrooms, and bathrooms before reaching some ersatz libraries. He stopped and drew a deep breath. "Lauren, I had no—"

The ever-present red light appeared between the shelves of a bookcase next to them.

His jaw tightened.

Enough. He had limits, and this blasted show forced him to show them.

He held up a hand in front of the camera, blocking the view of Lauren's face. "No more, guys."

The camera didn't blink.

"I mean it. We need a minute."

Still no response from the crew and the light didn't fade.

Fine. If that's how they wanted to deal with him, he could handle it.

He grabbed Lauren's hand, and they hurried along the center opening. He glanced side to side down the aisles ... there. A beige door, no label, no nothing. He made for it, pulling Lauren close.

The door opened without protest, and they slipped in. A supply closet. Rolls of paper towels, a dust mop, and jugs of liquid soap surrounded them.

"I'm sor—"

"What's—"

They spoke at the same time, then both paused.

"I'm sorry." She shook her head, her copper hair swinging side to side like a hula dancer's hips.

"You." He gripped her shoulders. "You have nothing to be sorry for."

She looked at her feet. "I'm from Harts Leap. A small town in the California mountains. I don't want to live in New York, worrying about a Page Six mention. I'm happy in my town, my world, my school."

He shook his head. "I don't care about that kind of lifestyle either."

Her brows rose, and her lips sank into a frown that signaled her doubts as clearly as if she'd spoken them.

"I mean, I know about it, but I don't care. That stuff is all my parents' and grandparents' generation. We don't have to follow their stupid rules."

Her chest rose and fell in a deep sigh. "I wish that was true."

He gripped tighter and drew her close. "It is true." Before he second-guessed himself, he pulled her to his chest and pressed his lips to hers.

She tensed, but just before he released her and begged forgiveness, she leaned into him, relaxed her mouth, responded to him.

He savored her taste. Sunshine mixed with peaches. Until he couldn't resist asking for more. He darted his tongue to her lips, deepening their connection.

Heat raced from his toes to his scalp, and he struggled not to crush her in his embrace.

She pulled away, rested her forehead against his. "What are we going to do?"

The door cracked open. "Who's in there?" a man asked with an irritated tone.

Mason exhaled in frustration. They couldn't catch a break. Mason turned to see a store employee in the doorway. A camera hovered over his shoulder, the red light staring at Mason and Lauren, hiding in the closet like a couple of teenagers. "We need a minute—"

Lauren slipped in front of him. "We better get back to the others. Let's find Liz, Brandy, and Keira."

Mason smoothed down his tie and followed Lauren. He pulled her close and whispered in her ear. "As soon as this outing is over, I'll find Jenna. This time, I'm getting answers."

Eight

Mason climbed out of the limo in front of the Beverly Essex and strode through the lobby. He'd kept his temper in a tight hold. His words with the other women had been innocuous as he'd wandered through the Pacific Design Center's stores and atriums and galleries. He'd commented about abstract art and modern design and mid-century sensibilities in furniture. All while he wanted nothing more than to run to the hotel, find his sister, and demand answers.

He held his card to the reader and the suite door clicked open. He pushed through. "Jenna! Get out here! I need to talk to you!" he bellowed. "Where are you?"

Silence.

He hurried down the marble hallway to the living area. She was probably there with a glass of merlot. "Jenna!" he called again, but more quietly.

"She's not here, son." Grandad folded a newspaper. "What's got your knickers in a twist?"

Mason dropped into the armchair, let his head sag to the side. "How are you feeling?"

"Never better. And now I know to avoid the flatbread with tomatoes and cracked pepper." He held a fist to his chest and grinned.

"Where's Jenna? Have you seen her?"

"She wasn't here when I got back from the Blue Whale."

Mason stood again, toed off his Bruno Magli oxfords, and padded to Jenna's room. "Jenna?" He knocked on the closed door, waited for a three-count, then opened it and stuck his head in. Empty. He sighed and started to pull the door closed again before pausing. The room was clean. Too clean. No jars of lotion or moisturizer on the dresser top. No earrings or jewelry strewn on the nightstand. He stepped into the room to look in the bathroom. Also clean. The closet door stood open. With none of Jenna's power suits hanging from the rod.

His jaw tightened. She must have known he was getting close to hearing the truth from Lauren and she'd fled.

How convenient. For her.

Back in the living room, Grandad looked up from his paper as Mason snatched the room phone off its cradle.

He paused, a finger hovering over the keypad. "Dash it all. I don't know Jenna's number. I just call her from my phone's contacts and Liam has my phone."

"I have it." Grandad stood and crossed to the dining table where his suit coat hung over the back of a chair. He reached in, drew out a small address book, and tossed it to Mason. "Here."

Mason shook his head and grinned. "Old school, huh? You know I've heard of these things."

"Respect your elders, son, or I'll take it back and you won't have her number."

"I apologize." Mason thumbed through the pages until he found Jenna's entry, then dialed. He sighed. "It went right to voicemail. Either she's in the air, flying back to New York, or she turned it off, knowing I'd be calling to yell at her."

Grandad blinked twice. "Why do you want to yell at her?"

Mason returned to the chair, sat, and stretched out his legs. "She ... she lied, Grandad. To me. To Lauren. All those years ago."

Grandad set aside the paper. "She what?"

Mason recapped the information he and Lauren swapped this afternoon. "Jenna busted us up, which broke my heart."

"Are you sure? That doesn't sound like your sister." Grandad smothered a burp. "Excuse me. That flatbread thing is still repeating on me."

"I'm sure. There's no way to whitewash this or call it a misunderstanding."

"She may have had her reasons. You need to talk to her."

"Absolutely, I do. She has a lot to explain." Mason stood and paced. "She didn't just meddle, she completely changed the course of our lives. Both of ours. Lauren's and mine."

"How would your life be different? Would you have gone to a different college? Would you have a different job?"

Mason shook his head. "I was always headed to Colgate before coming into the company. But ..." His heart twisted with pain and longing. "But ... I'd have done it with Lauren. She would have gone to med school. Remember? That was her dream. And we wouldn't be here now, doing this insane show."

"I understand you're hurt and angry, but son, you're missing the bigger picture."

"What?"

"You *are* here now." Grandad tilted his chin down and eyed Mason over the top of his glasses. "As is Lauren. You can stomp around and shout about your hurt feelings from a decade ago. Or you can take this opportunity to get to know Lauren as an adult."

Mason opened his mouth then closed it again.

"Isn't that the reason for this show? Get to know some women?"

"According to Jenna, it's to build up goodwill and publicity for the company."

"Can you do both?"

The weight that had seemed glued to his shoulders all afternoon finally lessened, and he grinned. "You're right. Except—" He walked again. "The producers won't let me focus on one woman. I have to spend time with the others too or there's no show. Not that I care about that, but I did sign a contract. Not much good publicity will be generated by me leaving."

Grandad now stood also and patted his shoulder. "You'll figure it out." He disappeared into the kitchen area. Mason heard a cupboard door open. "Now, where will I find some Tums?"

"Look in the drawers in my bathroom," Mason called. He walked to the glass doors and stepped onto the balcony. Was it only four days ago he'd been—as Grandad would say—gobsmacked to see Lauren at the production studios? Then yesterday she'd emerged onto the terrace upstairs from the Penthouse Suite. He'd felt air inflate his lungs for his first deep breath in nearly a decade.

He gripped the railing and leaned back, looking up. Blue sky, white puffy clouds. A plane crossed the expanse, a dark blip moving eastward. Maybe Jenna was on it.

He shrugged. Or maybe not. It didn't matter anymore. Grandad was right. No amount of yelling at Jenna could rewind the last ten years. And now that Lauren was back in his life, he had the chance to redeem their past and look forward to a new future.

* * *

Lauren curled up on her bed, tucked her hands under her cheek. She had a few minutes of solitude while her roommate was in the shower. Her mind kept replaying the kiss with Mason earlier. His lips, warm and familiar ... His arms, strong and firm ... What had she been thinking, to kiss him back like that? The flutters in her stomach grew to a thrumming.

Despite her denials that they were over, her traitorous body had jolted from its decade-long coma and now yearned for Mason's arms and lips.

Then the Fritos. And saving the very expensive camera from dropping on the hard ground. He still seemed to be the same nice, genuine guy she'd known in Harts Leap.

She sighed, rolled to her back, and stared at the ceiling.

Jenna lied. To them both.

The shock that reverberated down her spine as they'd connected the dots had been mirrored on his face. She believed him. He had no idea what Jenna had done, all those years ago. Truths Lauren had lived with for a decade had been crushed into a bag of corn chip crumbs.

She ran a finger under each eye and inspected the tip for black smears. Nothing. At least her mascara survived intact, even if her heart and dignity were perilously close to being devastated.

He hadn't broken up with her back then. He'd loved her. He'd wanted to marry—No. She couldn't let her mind go there. It was a long time ago and a lot had happened since. How could Jenna ...? And why did Lauren believe her? She knew Jenna. She should have known better.

Sadly enough, she had no problem believing Jenna capable of destroying their relationship, their love, their future. Jenna had never tried to hide her disdain for Lauren, her family and friends, not to mention Harts Leap. Jenna believed only certain people were good enough for the Townsend family. People with names like Buffet, Gates, maybe Kennedy or Vanderbilt. People who went to schools like Harvard, Brown, and Princeton. People with homes on both sides of the continent and a pied-à-terre in Paris.

Lauren placed a hand on her chest to quiet the tsunami of regret welling there, then straightened her shoulders. Enough. She had a job to do: survive the filming of this show and get back to Harts Leap with her dignity—and her heart—intact. And if she could get some public notice of her foundation and the hotline, that would be a bonus.

Holly came out of the bathroom, a towel wrapped around her torso and another on top of her head. "What are you wearing tonight?"

"Tonight?" Lauren sat up, adjusted the pillows behind her back.

"The wine pairing dinner."

"Oh, right." She'd barely listened to Renee downstairs telling them about the next activity. There'd be another outcast ceremony after. "I don't know if I have anything."

"There are some darling dresses in the wardrobe room." Holly dropped her towel and pulled on a thong, then a bra. She slipped what looked like a raw chicken breast into each cup, then adjusted her bra to show cleavage. "You should go for something tight and short. Your legs will look longer."

Lauren blinked. "You're helping me?"

"Of course, silly. Why wouldn't I?"

"Ummm ... because we're competing for the same guy?" Lauren had already mentally removed herself from the competition, but Holly didn't know that.

She grimaced. "No, we're not."

"We're not?"

Holly pulled the towel from her hair as she shook her head. "I'm here to get my music noticed. I wrote a song for Mason that I'm going to sing to him tonight. But a relationship? Not for me, not now." She plugged in a blow dryer, a curling iron, a straightener—Lauren opened her mouth to ask why both but closed it again—then set out a yellow can of mousse, hairspray, a small pot of goop and a tube of more goop.

Lauren sighed, stood, and smoothed her shorts across her thighs. "I'll be back, I guess."

"Remember, short, one color, nothing boxy." Holly bent at the waist, turned on the blow dryer, and ran her fingers through her hair as it waved in the breeze.

Lauren returned twenty minutes later with a gorgeous dress. She wasn't sure it adhered to Holly's guidelines since it was long and had an embroidered bodice that was lighter than the skirt. At least it wasn't boxy and was somewhat form fitting.

"Let's see." Holly set down her hair straightener and stood.

Lauren held the dress to her chin, looked at her roommate over the halter-top neckline. "I can wear heels to look taller."

Holly nodded. "It's good. The bare shoulders and the keyhole in the neckline will also add the illusion of length." She returned to her array of hair products, picked up a squirrel tail and proceeded to clip it to the crown of her head.

"What is that?" Lauren pointed.

Holly met her gaze in the mirror. "An extension. You don't wear them?"

Lauren shook her head. "We don't have a beauty supply store in Harts Leap."

Holly chuckled. "Your stylist has them in stock, I guarantee." She continued parting her hair into slices, adding flat sections of fake hair. Lauren watched, fascinated. When she was done, Holly squirted her head with a healthy dose of hair spray, tucked her cans and pots into a drawer and pulled out a makeup case.

While Holly applied makeup in layers, Lauren shimmied into the dress and surveyed herself in the full-length mirror on the back of the closet door. Not bad. The navy silk skimmed her hips. The lighter mesh embroidered top had an empire waist, so she did look a little taller, a little leaner.

Holly had applied something that plumped her lips. Now she added individual lashes to her eye lids, then blinked at her reflection. With her hair and makeup done, she looked nothing like the young woman who'd stepped out of the shower an hour ago. She slithered into a short yellow dress with a deep V-neck, a gathering of fabric at the waist, and spaghetti straps.

Lauren dug through her suitcase and pulled out her favorite stilettos.

"Here." Holly held out a pair of dangly, sparkly earrings. "These will go perfect."

"Thanks." Lauren took the jewelry, set them on her nightstand. "You look—wow."

"Come, sit." Holly patted the chair in front of the vanity. "I'll do your makeup."

"I don't know, Holly. I mean you look fantastic. I'm just not a makeup and big hair kind of gal."

"Don't worry. I'm a professional performer. I know all the tricks. You'll be gorgeous and still look like yourself."

Lauren raised her brows at that but sat. If she hated it, she could wash it all off and do her own.

"First, a primer." Holly proceeded to apply makeup to Lauren's face, explaining what each layer did and why it was important. Primer, two different foundations, then blush and bronzer. That was just her face. Then her eyes. More primer. Three different shades of light brown shadow. Blending. Liner.

"I'll never be able to remember all this, much less do it later." Lauren blinked at herself in the mirror. "But thank you!"

Holly was right. Lauren still looked like herself, but ... better. Her eyes had smoky smudges above and below, darker liner, and a super-secret-formula mascara that made her lashes so long a Cocker Spaniel would howl with envy.

"You're welcome. Ready to go mingle and maybe watch a cat fight?"

Lauren laughed with a freedom she hadn't felt in a long time. Holly may use enhancements to play up her appearance, but who would've guessed she was the most genuine woman here?

Nine

Mason climbed out of the limo and held the door for Grandad. They had ridden to the mansion in silence, Mason still brooding about how he could make Lauren his priority while fulfilling his obligation to the producers. His grandfather seemed to respect Mason's need for quiet and hadn't uttered a word.

As they made their way to the front door, Grandad rubbed a fist against his chest.

"Are you okay?" Mason asked.

"Indigestion." Grandad cleared his throat.

"That seems to be happening more often. Are you sure you're all right?" Mason paused at the bottom of the stone steps to the house.

"I'm sure." His grandfather's tone said the subject was closed.

Inside, the living room was full of women in dresses of silk and lace and even a few feathers. The chatter quieted as they noticed him and Granddad. Mason smiled in greeting.

"Hello, ladies," Grandad said. "Don't let us interrupt."

"Oh, Mr. Townsend, you're not an interruption." One of the women —Liz? —took Grandad's arm and led him to the bar.

"Mason, we need a moment. This way." Renee guided him into the formal dining room that was being used as an office. The remaining women's pictures were scattered across a table. "You've got a couple hours to visit, chat, whatever, with the contestants. Then we'll do the wine pairing dinner. After that, just like last night, you'll come in here, look at the pictures, then make your choices."

He nodded. "How many do I send home tonight?"

"Another four. The next few eliminations will be two each."

He glanced at the array of snapshots, zeroing in on Lauren. Her picture had been taken this afternoon at the PDC. She was dwarfed next to Keira who must be six feet tall, or near enough. As always, when he was reminded of Lauren's petite frame, he had the urge to embrace her, to protect her, to shield her.

He winced. She'd hated being thought of as fragile. And he had to admit, she was stronger than lots of people he knew.

Another look at the pictures confirmed he'd been right a moment ago. It was Liz who'd taken Grandad to the bar. Phil had been caught in conversation with another woman. Amelia had a predatory expression on her face. Please don't let her be looking at *him* that way. He sighed.

"Time to make great television." Renee motioned to the door, and he dutifully left her.

Back in the living room, the party seemed in full swing. Music thrummed from speakers in the ceiling. Women were everywhere: perched on the backs of the sofa and chairs, leaning against the pass-through into the kitchen, sitting on bar stools. He'd just found Lauren, tucked into a corner of the sofa, talking with a striking brunette in a buttery yellow dress.

Before he'd taken a step in her direction, the woman who'd greeted Grandad slipped her arm though his elbow. "Mason, I'm dying for a chat. Let's step outside."

Liam and Renee had drilled into him the necessity of accepting every invitation like this. He had to remain open to each opportunity to get to know someone better. He stifled a sigh, pasted on a smile, and let her lead him outside.

They settled onto the swing overlooking the pool. The pungent scent of chlorine stung his nostrils, and he rubbed his nose. The mustache forming felt scratchy and rough.

"I just love your grandfather, Mason." Liz leaned closer so her shoulder touched his. He moved away a millimeter. Or ten. "He's so kind and funny. He reminds me of my grandpa."

"Tell me about him," Mason said, keeping the conversation going and ignoring the red light in his peripheral vision. "Do you see him often?"

Liz sighed deeply, then touched a fingertip to a corner of her eye. "We lost Grandpa last year."

Mason paused his chin rub. "Oh, I'm sorry. I can't imagine ..."

"It was awful," Liz agreed. "But I want to talk about us."

Mason turned his reflexive laugh into a throat-clearing. "Us?"

"Yes, us." She stroked his arm and leaned even closer. "It's been five years since our first date. We have so much to catch up on."

"We do?" Why did he keep parroting back what she said? And if he remembered correctly, it had also been five years since their last date. Five years since their only date.

"You're CEO of a Fortune 500 company now. You earned an MBA. I'm sure you remember I'm a dancer. I was always going on auditions, and you loved watching me rehearse."

"I did?" He rolled his shoulders, thinking. He had a vague memory of a woman who wore leg warmers and insisted he tag along to a studio in Soho. "Oh, yeah ... I remember." Sort of.

"I dance in Vegas now where *lots* of big corporations and CEOs come for conventions. I back-up a burlesque performer. It's great fun and very tasteful." Her voice lowered as she emphasized the last words. "Have you seen the show? At the Troposphere?"

"Nope, missed that one." He flashed a quick smile to mask the alarm flooding his veins at the thought of the repercussion if he took any clients to a burlesque show. Jenna would climb down his throat and pull out his small intestine. Not to mention Granddad's deep disappointment. "Our company doesn't do much entertaining out there." He kept his tone mild though, so she wouldn't pick up on his aversion.

She clutched his arm. "You've got to come! You'll love it! I wear a costume that's all feathers, but only in the most strategic placements, if you know what I mean. Oh!" Her eyes lit up. "I can show you some of my dance moves right here." She finally let go of his arm and stood.

"Imagine I'm wearing a bikini of bright blue feathers." She scurried to his right. "I don't have the music, so I'll have to hum. Is that okay?"

Was there a correct answer to that? "... um ... sure. I guess so."

"Da dah dum ... da *dum* ..." Liz sang at the top of her lungs as she gyrated from the edge of the pool into his vision.

He didn't know where to look. Not at her chest. She must have adjusted her neckline because it had been perfectly respectable a minute ago, but now threatened to turn this into an R-rated show. Or even X. Couldn't look at her hips, which swiveled like she wore a hula hoop and was terrified of letting it drop. The safest solution seemed to be her face or her eyes, so he kept his gaze fastened to her nose.

After an eternity that seemed long enough for an entire Broadway musical to be acted out in front of him, Liz finished with a flourish and a deep bow.

He clapped dutifully.

"We have to go to Vegas together and catch some shows. I can get us front-row tickets." She dropped in the seat next to him.

"That could be ... fun." The same way a root canal was fun.

Holly—finally, he was putting faces with names—approached them. "Mason, can I steal you away for a minute?"

"Of course." He stood, leaned down to kiss Liz's cheek. At the last moment, she twisted her head and his lips met hers. "Mmmmm. You're just too yummy for words, Mason."

He risked a quick glance around. Did anyone see that? No one had turned in their direction. Other than the cameras that were already there. "Thank you for the dance."

She pushed out her lower lip. "But we hardly got a chance to talk."

"Mmm hmm." And probably wouldn't. If he got to make his own choices tonight.

He put a hand on Holly's elbow and guided her to the fire pit. After they sat, she kicked off her shoes, pulled her feet up and tucked them under. "Are you having a good time?" she asked.

He considered how to answer. The ever-present red Steadicam light made the decision easy. "I'm enjoying getting to know all of you. Where are you from, Holly?"

"I live in Nashville now, but I grew up in Atlanta."

"Nashville, huh? Are you a singer?"

"I'm an instrumentalist, first. But I can carry a tune." She gave him an appraising look. "At least that's what I've been told."

He got a déjà vu feeling and an urge to find a cocktail. Holly was about to burst into song, just as Liz had danced for him. "Tell me what it's like living in this mansion." He gestured to the huge house behind them. "Do you have roommates? Dorms? Is there much privacy?"

"Two to a room with an ensuite bathroom. So, it's not bad. I only have to share with Lauren."

His eyes shot to her face. "Lauren's your roommate? How ... ummm ..." His mind raced. Holly could answer so many questions. "How do you two get along?" Lame, but while she talked, he'd come up with something better.

Holly nodded. "She's super sweet. A bit naïve."

He cocked his head. "In what way?"

"She's from a small town in the mountains. She teaches and she started some kind of charity, but she's never traveled or done much away from there."

"Does that mean ... are the women here mean to her?" The Lauren he remembered wouldn't let someone else's opinion bring her down.

"Not so's you'd notice. It's more like ... they don't think she's competition. That you're a bigshot New York City executive, so you ..."

"So, I won't be interested in a small-town gal who's loyal, kind, and trusting?"

Holly chuckled. "Well ... yeah."

He shook his head, barking a laugh. "Huh."

Holly shifted again and leaned closer. "I wrote a song for you."

He tried not to let his shoulders sag and kept a smile on his face. "Let's hear it."

She took a deep breath, hummed a note, then opened her mouth.

"A girl met a boy. He searched high. She searched low. Looking for love. Looking for love. Looking for love."

He blinked in surprise. Holly's voice was pure and strong and beautiful. The song continued for several minutes, a soft ballad about what brought the two of them to this place and time. In spite of himself, his heart softened. She was good. Really good.

When she finished the last phrase, he didn't have to prompt himself to clap.

"Brava!" He stood and reached out.

She untucked her feet, took his hand, and stood too. "Thank you." Her face glowed.

"You're an amazing talent."

She pulled him into a hug then whispered in his ear. "I owe you for letting me do that. Lauren is inside."

He hugged her back. "Thank you."

They walked hand in hand to the house. Inside the French doors leading to the great room, Holly kissed his cheek before disappearing into the milling crowd. He looked around, eyes darting like a heat seeking missile unable to find its target.

There she was. Sitting on the hearth in front of the enormous gas fireplace, in a navy dress that showed off her curves. As if she felt the warmth of his gaze, she looked up. Their eyes met and his breath caught in his chest.

He was such a goner.

* * *

Lauren felt her cheeks heat as she and Mason exchanged looks. She had to get a grip on herself. Learning the truth about their break-up and sharing a toe-curling kiss didn't change anything. They were still a high school summer fling. *They* were still ancient history. There wasn't an *us* anymore. She'd just seen him kiss Liz, after all. That was a clear signal he wasn't interested in revisiting the past. Something she'd do well to remember.

He smiled and darned if her heart didn't skip a beat. The collective sigh from all the women in the room could ignite a fire at her back.

Amelia's eyes narrowed, and she took a step toward Mason. Before she could think it through, Lauren stood, cut in front of the other woman, and approached him. He crooked his elbow, and she slipped a hand through.

"Come outside with me?" he asked.

She nodded, ignoring Amelia's glare and huff of displeasure.

Once on the rough slate patio, he guided her to a tall table with an ice bucket and an open bottle of sparkling wine. He poured two glasses, handed one to her, then held up his in a toast.

"Here's to ..." His gaze darted around the patio. He seemed at a loss of what to toast to.

"To a beautiful night in a beautiful city." She touched her glass to his and then sipped.

He did the same before speaking. "Jenna skipped town. Didn't answer my call."

"She's smart." Lauren shivered. "I'd run too if you were breathing down my neck."

He chuckled. "Speaking of heavy breathing. Remember making out on the dock?"

She felt her cheeks warm as she drew a sharp breath. "We were kids."

He held her gaze. "Teenagers fall in love and make it work. Youth doesn't mean a relationship is doomed. It just means there are more years together."

A lump worked its way up her throat like a knot through a needle. She swallowed. She was in so much trouble. She was falling in love with Mason all over again. Ten years too late.

They stared at each other for a long minute. She finally dragged her eyes from his and looked at the bubbles in her glass. One formed, clinging to the inside, then released, floated up until it burst as it reached the top.

"We're older now, but that doesn't mean the thoughts, feelings, dreams we shared with each other back then aren't still true."

Almost against her will, she nodded. He was right. She'd shared her dream about medical school, her insecurities growing up poor, struggling for grades, having to buy knockoffs to fit in with the other kids. She still felt less than women like Brooke and Holly and Amelia.

He'd told her his deep fear that he didn't really have friends, just people who wanted favors. Did he become isolated to the point that he had to go on television to find dates?

He tipped her chin up. "Lauren. Could we start over? No more talk about what might have been. Let's work on here and now."

She nodded, set down her glass, stuck out her hand. "Hi there, Mason. It's a pleasure to meet you. I'm Lauren."

He shook her hand. A whiff of something masculine—woodsy and clean—tickled her nose.

"The pleasure is mine, Lauren. Where are you from?"

"A little town outside Yosemite. I'm sure you've never heard of it."

"Really? My family has a cabin near the park. In Harts Leap."

"Harts Leap? No! Really?" She feigned shock and placed a hand on her chest. "I'm from Harts Leap. Born and raised."

His warm eyes danced with fun. "I've always loved that town. Is the Lakeside Diner still there? And Daisy's Café with the chocolate malt pie?"

She laughed, the first carefree sound she remembered making since answering Liam's call two weeks ago. Mason had been a friend before they fell in love. Now she remembered why. He was a genuinely nice person, fun and funny. She should just go with this ... whatever it was. A renewed friendship?

They chatted about Daisy's, about the famous radio talk show host, Dr. Ginger, moving back to town. About the new brew pub. They talked until the crew standing around began shifting from foot to foot, obviously ready for something more exciting to happen.

As if on cue, the doors opened again, and Amelia stumbled out. "There you are!" she cried.

Lauren forced a smile. "Hi, Amelia."

"Whas—*what's* going on out here? How come you're molopozing Mason? Huh?"

Another odor reached Lauren, this one sickly sweet. "Are you drunk?" she asked.

"Pfft."

Lauren fought the urge to waft away the breath Amelia expelled in her face.

Mason climbed off the high stool and took Amelia's elbow. "Let's go sit and chat." He smiled at Lauren. "Thank you for the talk. Can we meet up again later?"

She nodded, ignoring the twist in her heart. He was a gentleman. They were being filmed. Of course, he'd be nice to Amelia. She'd expect nothing less from him.

She sat in the dark a few minutes, as the crew trickled away, following

Mason and Amelia. The door opened again. This time, Phil appeared at her side.

"Is it safe out here?"

Lauren smiled into the darkness. "Mason and Amelia are off together. There are no cameras nearby if that's what you mean." One of Brooke's nuggets of experience that she'd shared danced into Lauren's memory. *Never assume you're not being watched or listened to or both. There are cameras and microphones everywhere.*

Phil climbed onto the stool Mason vacated. "Amelia had a lot to drink in there."

"It shows. She's slurring her words and staggering."

"Mason will take care of her." Phil swiveled on the stool to face Lauren. "Have you and Mason been able to chat and make up?"

Lauren shrugged. "We figured out his sister broke us up. We each thought the other called it off."

"Ah, the old my-brother-doesn't-know-what's-best-so-I'll-get-involved story. Didn't I see this plot on television?"

"It does sound more like a soap opera than real life," Lauren admitted. "If I was watching this in a show, I'd turn it off and go read a book."

Phil chuckled. "I can't remember the last book I read for pleasure."

Lauren gasped. "You're joking."

"I wish I was. Between office hours, surgeries, charting, and medical journals, there's not enough coffee in Boston to keep me awake long enough to read a paragraph, much less a chapter."

Lauren shook her head. "If I couldn't read, I'd go mad. Really, crazy. It's what keeps me sane. I guess it's a good thing I decided against med school."

"You wanted to be a doctor?"

Lauren lifted one shoulder. "Once upon a time, it was my dream. But I opted for a degree in education."

"Why? Why didn't you go for it?"

She couldn't tell Phil—smart, educated, gorgeous Phil—the truth: that she wasn't brave enough to make it in med school. So … "Money, mostly. I couldn't see going into that kind of debt."

Phil waggled her head. "It's not unsubstantial, that's for sure. But there are all kinds of repayment programs and grants. Money doesn't have to be the barrier. Did you take the MCATs?"

"No. It was a silly middle school dream. I'm doing what I'm supposed to do. I'm a teacher."

"Teaching is an amazing profession, but Lauren—" Phil put a hand on Lauren's arm—

"Medicine is a calling, too. You shouldn't give up on your dream because of numbers on a paper."

Spoken like someone born into wealth and privilege. Phil probably had no idea what it felt like, studying while flipping burgers, walking dogs, and babysitting Joanie Burnes, possibly the evilest child and diabolical manipulator ever born in Harts Leap.

"I'm not just saying that, you know," Phil said. "I had to work two jobs during college. I smelled like garlic and tomato sauce all four years."

"Really? I thought—"

Phil shook her head. "I'm from Nowheresville, Indiana. I'm the first person in the family to attend college, much less med school."

"I had no idea. You look ..." How to finish that sentence without sounding either incredibly shallow or dim?

Phil smiled. "It's okay. I get that a lot. For some reason, God gave me Upper East Side looks with a dishwasher's bank account."

Lauren chuckled. She liked Phil. Who would have guessed that she'd make friends on a show like this? Brooke said she would, but Lauren hadn't really believed her. She could call Holly a friend, and now Phil. Maybe one of them—one of the nice women—would end up with Mason. He deserved someone great. Someone genuine. Someone—her heart clutched. She didn't want to see Mason end up with anyone else. That knot was back, but now it tied her stomach into a bow.

A PA walked through the patio. "Ladies, it's time for dinner. Everyone inside please."

She and Phil picked up their glasses and followed the others. Mason stood behind a chair at a long table set for a banquet. A gold tapestry runner in the center of the table. Plates on gold chargers. Each plate had five wine glasses arrayed behind it.

Amelia sat on a chair next to Mason. Her mascara had run so she looked like a raccoon. Her hair trailed over her shoulders, falling out of its updo.

Lauren drew a breath, then joined the others milling around the table looking for their names. *Liz. Holly. Keira.* They all dropped into seats across the table from Mason. Nothing with *Lauren*. She started on the other side, working her way to the center.

Finally, she saw the gold-edged card with her name. Except ... Amelia sat there.

"Excuse me," Lauren said, forcing an upbeat tone. "That's my seat."

"Go to he—"

"Amelia—" Liam and Renee appeared at her sides. Liam gripped her elbow and slid her out of the chair. "Let's go to your seat."

She shook off their hands. "I'm in my sh—seeet. I'm sitting by Mason and rekindling our love."

Mason walked over and took Amelia's hand. "Let's go sit over here." He steered her to a nearby stool. It took her a couple of tries to perch herself up there. She crossed one knee over the other and gave Mason a lopsided smile.

He leaned forward and whispered in her ear. Amelia fisted her hands in Mason's lapels and—Lauren watched in horror—planted her lips on his.

Two kisses? In one evening? He'd kissed two other women after kissing her this afternoon.

Had this afternoon's encounter in the supply closet meant nothing to him? His lips had rocked her world—well, at least induced some toe curling and stomach flutters. While it looked like her lips hadn't done anything to him. Not the way he kept kissing the others.

Okay, she had to get a grip. This was television. He had to—she gulped—spend time with other women, talk and laugh with other women, kiss ... other women.

She turned, made her way to her now vacant seat, and set her jaw. Maybe she could talk Mason into letting her go. Her attempt last night had failed, but perhaps she could appeal to his chivalry. If they had no chemistry between them anymore, it would be a kindness for him to send her home.

This Mason seemed a man who cared more about himself, his

company, his status, than the teenage Mason she'd known back in Harts Leap.

It was a shame, really. That someone so nice could grow into someone so callous.

He slipped into the chair next to her, leaned close, and spoke behind the hand he held to one side of his mouth. "How much do you think she had to drink?"

She shook her head, settled into her seat and pulled her elbows to her side.

A PA called for quiet, counted down for action, then pointed at Reid.

"Welcome back to *Re:United*. Mason, tell us what we're doing."

Mason cleared his throat, then smiled into the camera. "Ladies, as the CEO of a large company, I often have to entertain clients. While I might prefer a diner or take-out at home, some of my guests are used to more gourmet fare, including fine wines. There are five different wines in the glasses in front of you. Each has been specially chosen to complement the meal. We'll pair each wine with the appropriate course. Feel free to examine the color, sniff the bouquet, and taste."

The women flashed smiles at him. Lauren turned slightly so she wasn't blinded by the light reflecting off all the whitened teeth.

Actor-waiters in cummerbunds and bow ties brought in plates they set in front of each of them. Three little dough balls huddled together on a nest of curly greens.

"Blue crab beignets," murmured the server.

Lauren gulped and eyed the five glasses. Two held white wine, three had red. She'd been raised in a beer drinking family, which she'd never enjoyed. If it came down to it, she could probably pick a pilsner from a stout, but that was about it. Wine? Forget it.

She cautiously picked up the first on the left, a white, and sniffed. Hmmm. Fruity. And sweet. More like dessert. She moved down the line and finally chose a light pink. It was also fruity, but not as sweet.

Amelia had slumped over on her stool and seemed to have dozed off. Every so often she would startle awake, look around, then drop her chin to her chest again.

The meal passed slowly. The mansion had entered some sort of time-bending dimension. She muddled through each course, certain she was guessing wrong. Every so often Mason would lean over and make a comment. She smiled with lips that refused to part for anything but a fork or a glass.

Finally, dessert was served. If she was going to appeal to be let go, it had to be now.

The waiter delivered a plate with a layered concoction. "Hazelnut-Chocolate-Meringue torte."

She picked up her fork and eyed the tower of fluffy whipped cream and crumbly, swirly white and chocolate meringue, topped with chopped nuts and chocolate shavings. She had one wine left. A very sweet red.

"Remember when Jenna and her friends got into your folks' liquor cabinet?" Lauren turned so she could see Mason's profile.

He grinned. "She got sick and was so hungover the next day, I thought she was going to puke up her guts."

"We share so many lovely memories." She leaned her shoulder into his arm, ignoring the tingles.

"We do. Although, I wouldn't call drinking until you throw up 'lovely.'" He covered her hand with his. "But remember? We're not dwelling on the past anymore. We're making new memories."

She drew a deep breath. "I want you to outcast me."

Shock spread across his face as his jaw dropped. A moment later his eyes grew hooded. "Why?"

She swallowed the sudden lump in her throat. "This isn't working. It's too hard. Seeing you with all the others."

Before he could respond, a commotion at the end of the table drew their attention.

Phil was leaning over Clarence. "Mr. Townsend! Are you okay?" She pulled him out of his seat and lowered him to the floor.

Mason stood. His chair clattered over backwards. "Grandad!"

Ten

Mason watched, his throat closing, as Phil loosened Grandad's tie, put her ear to his mouth.

"Call 911!" she yelled. She interlaced her fingers and placed her hands on Grandad's chest.

Mason hurried to them, threading his way around the women and production crew. He dropped to his knees. "Grandad!"

Phil started chest compressions, her hands moving in a steady rhythm. "Does he have heart trouble?"

Mason shook his head. "He's been complaining of indigestion for a few days."

Her lips thinned. "He should have gone to the hospital."

Guilt joined the fright in his chest, and he couldn't speak around the lump. "I didn't know ... I should have ... What can I do?"

Lauren appeared at his side. "The medical team has a defibrillator."

Phil looked up. "Bring it."

Lauren spun and disappeared into the crowd.

"Mason, stand back. I need room." Phil's bracelets clinked and clattered as she kept the cadence of compressions. "See what's happening with the ambulance."

He stood, searching for Liam or Renee. Anyone from the crew.

Lauren snaked her way through the crowd, holding a yellow and black plastic case, about the size of a ream of paper. She dropped to her knees at Grandad's side.

Lauren opened the case and pulled out a couple of plastic pieces. After she tore off some backing, she handed them to Phil, who affixed one to Grandad's left pectoral and the other to the upper right side of his chest. In a calm electronic voice, the machine instructed what to do next, but Phil was faster than the directions.

Liam dashed through the door, a radio in one hand. "The ambulance is coming up the driveway."

Finally.

"Stand back," Phil directed. The machine made a wheezing sound as it gathered the energy to shock a heart back to life. Grandad didn't move and Phil resumed the compressions.

Mason watched in a daze as two EMTs swooped into the room with black bags of gear. They took over from Phil, loaded Grandad onto a gurney, and rolled him out the front door. Mason chased after, but Liam grabbed his arm.

"We'll take you to the hospital. I have a car waiting."

He shook off Liam's hand. "I'm going with them." He reached for Phil, wrapped his arms around her and hugged tight. "Thank you," he breathed. "I don't know what I would've—just, thank you."

She pulled away and smiled. "Of course. Now, go!" She pointed at the door, and he obeyed.

He sprinted out to the ambulance and climbed in to perch on the narrow shelf next to Grandad.

The EMTs secured the gurney and took their places. Mason stared at Grandad and willed him to wake up. "I promise, I'll never let you get away with telling me you have indigestion again, old man."

Grandad's eyelids fluttered. "Who are you ..."

Mason leaned closer. "What?"

Grandad lifted his hand and raised the oxygen mask. "Who are you calling old?"

Mason's chuckle choked, and he swallowed a sob.

The EMT adjusted the clear plastic cover. "Leave this alone, sir."

"You do everything they tell you, hear me?" Mason peered into Grandad's eyes. "Everything."

Grandad's eyelids drifted closed again. He looked gray and frail and … for the first time in Mason's memory … old.

* * *

Lauren stood in the doorway watching Mason and Clarence leave in the ambulance. The flashing lights striped the whole entry area with candy cane red. Phil stood at her side.

"He'll be fine."

"Thanks to you." Lauren turned to face Phil.

"And you. You kept your cool." Phil's gaze searched hers. "You would be a great doctor."

Before Lauren could dismiss that, other women crowded around them.

"Oh, that poor man!"

"I hope he's all right."

"What happens now?" Amelia appeared on the edge of the group. She'd sobered up some and her hair no longer trailed down her neck.

Lauren tamped down her irritation. "The man's grandfather just had a heart attack. He has more important things to deal with than reality television."

Amelia just stared at her. "And they have a production schedule to keep."

Lauren pushed past her and into the house.

"Ladies, gather around, please." Liam shouted for attention.

It took a few minutes for the women to trickle back inside. They took their places around the table. Like nothing was wrong. Like nothing had changed. Like a man leaving in an ambulance happened every day.

Lauren stared around the room in disbelief. Phil touched her arm, shrugged, and took her seat. Breathe in, she told herself. Then out. Again.

It took a full minute, but her heartbeat slowed enough for her to speak. "What are we doing here? Going on like this? And don't say the show must go on!"

Liam held his clipboard up to the side of his face and spoke in her ear.

"I promise you, we're concerned. Renee is calling Jenna and their parents right now. The producer and an assistant are on the way to the hospital. But we do have to take care of some things."

She exhaled with a whoosh and sat. The chair Mason had occupied now seemed lonely and forlorn. The whole room felt emptier. Hollow and cold.

Wake up call, Lauren. She was fooling herself if she thought she could walk away from Mason.

Liam raised his hand and cleared his throat. "Our thoughts and prayers are with Mason and Clarence tonight. We'll keep you informed as we hear anything." He consulted his clipboard. "This does mean some changes to our schedule. Instead of the Thousand Words ceremony tonight, we're wrapping now. In the morning, we'll know more, but our tentative plan is to film the ceremony at nine a.m. sharp. Please keep your dresses, hair, and makeup consistent. Good night." He strode away.

Lauren watched in disbelief as conversations resumed, glasses lifted, and a few of the women even continued eating their desserts. She stood and pushed through the doors to the quiet of the backyard. The lights had been dimmed, so she walked slowly, feeling her way along the path to the pool.

"It's okay, you know." Phil materialized out of the darkness and sat on the chaise longue nearby. "It doesn't mean they're heartless. Some people cope with trauma by keeping things normal. Although, living and filming in this house isn't normal for any of us."

Lauren sat next to her. "I get it. I guess ... it just seems cold to me, that the production company wouldn't stop long enough for us to find out what's going on."

"It's too soon to know anything, so it's better to keep everyone busy and occupied."

"You sound like the voice of experience."

"Not my first medical emergency."

"I guess not." Lauren leaned back on the lounge and stared up at the dark sky, now dappled with stars. "How do you do it? Remain so calm? I was freaking out."

"Really?" Phil sounded doubtful. "You looked perfectly composed. You helped me with the defibrillator."

Lauren shook her head. "I wanted to run away and bawl." Her hands still trembled, and she placed them between her knees to still them. "You're the real hero. You probably saved Clarence's life."

"Yes, I did."

She chuckled at Phil's honesty. "No false modesty then?"

"I learned in med school the folly of not taking credit when it was due."

Lauren drew a deep breath to control her trembling. Mr. Townsend, the closest thing she had to a grandfather, nearly died tonight. Would have died if not for Philomena and her medical degree. The shaking intensified and Lauren shuddered.

"Are you okay?" Phil gave her an appraising glance.

Lauren shook her head. "I can't get the image out of my mind. He was so ... so still. And pale. My mind went to—" No, she did not want to go there.

"Went ... where? Did you know someone who died of a heart attack?"

Lauren took a deep breath. "I had to call 911 once." Maybe that was enough info for Phil to let it go. "Where did you go to medical school?" And if all else failed, distract and redirect. Just like she did with the kids in her classroom.

"Did the person die?"

How to answer that? When everything in her fought against the memories. "Um ... yeah." Short and simple.

"I'm sorry." Phil watched her with a steady gaze. "Was it unexpected?"

"You could say that." Why couldn't Phil just drop it?

"It might help if you talk about it."

"I did. Back then."

"Ah. Okay then."

Lauren's shoulders sagged. "It's not a big deal, but it's part of the reason I'm here." She drew a deep breath. In this far, she should just tell Phil the whole story, then they could move on. "My sister committed suicide last year. She hanged herself. I found her."

Phil gasped. "I'm so sorry, Lauren. How awful for you and your family. And that's a very big deal."

Lauren swallowed the familiar pain at the back of her throat. "I want to set up a crisis hotline in Harts Leap. I thought the show would help me get the word out."

"It will. That's brilliant."

"But now I just feel slimy. I'm the same as Liz and Holly, using Mason and this show, for my own purposes."

Phil adjusted her red silk dress across her lap. "We all have reasons for doing this."

"What are yours?" Lauren asked, suddenly curious.

"Not nearly so altruistic." Phil pulled her knees up, wrapped her arms around them. "I was ... burnt out. I've worked constantly for years, ever since med school. I got sick a few months ago, and I'm on forced time off for rest and rehab. The invitation seemed like a good way to pass some time without staring at the four walls of my apartment."

"You're burnt out from saving lives and healing people and helping children. It's hardly selfish to need some downtime."

Phil canted her head to one side. "It feels like I'm slacking off, not taking things seriously."

"We have issues, don't we?"

The bushes nearby rustled, and Lauren paused. "Who's there?"

"It's just me." Amelia staggered into view. Drunk, again. "Whash—what's going on?"

"We're chatting." Phil reached over and patted the bottom of her chaise. "Have a seat."

A memory Brooke had shared floated back. Someone had fallen in the pool ... or jumped? Brooke found her. The woman had to be rescued, Lauren remembered that much for sure.

"Yes, please, sit with us." Anything to keep a staggering Amelia far, far away from the pool.

Amelia sat like an obedient puppy, then turned toward them. "I hope Mr. Townsend is okay."

Lauren and Phil nodded.

Amelia hiccupped, then sagged against Phil's knees. "I messed up. So bad."

"How much have you had to drink?" Phil asked.

"Jus' a couple glasses of Chardonnay."

"How did you mess up?" Phil pulled a soft throw from behind her and spread it over Amelia's shoulders.

"I shouldn't be here. I'm a fraud."

Lauren wrinkled her forehead. "A fraud? Do you mean you didn't know Mason after all?"

Amelia scoffed. "I knew him. We were interns together. But we didn't really date. I made that up. Nah for lack of trying on my part though. But he wouldn't give me the time of day."

Lauren forced herself to reach over and take Amelia's hand. "You were young then, and he was a nice, good-looking guy."

Amelia nodded, woe written on her face. "His sister told me to help him forget."

"Forget?" Lauren sat up. "Forget what?" Or who?

"I dunna know. Someone he left behind."

"You knew Jenna?"

"She came by the office a week or so after Mason and I started interning. She took me ashide and said her brother needed to forget something and I should do everything I could to help him have a good time."

Of course. Jenna again. The woman was worse than a crop of July mosquitoes. She refused to be swatted away and extermination was impossible.

Phil caught Lauren's gaze and winked. "What did you do, Amelia, to help Mason forget?"

She stared up at the stars blinking overhead. "I flirted. I touched his arm, like a million times a day. I suggested we get pizza and beer every night we had to work late. But he shut me down every time."

Warmth flushed Lauren's arms and legs and she struggled to fill her lungs.

"Sounds like he wasn't interested in forgetting." Phil smiled at Lauren again.

"Tha's what I told his shis ... sister. When I left at the end of summer."

"Until—let me guess—you got an invitation to join a reality dating show filming this summer in Los Angeles."

"I thought we'd reconnect. It wash bad timing last time. But just my luck"—Amelia shot Lauren a venomous look— "he's *still* hung up on someone else." She stood and swayed but remained on her feet. "I'm going to bed. Have to be camera-ready and back in this dress in the morning." She tottered away a half dozen steps, stopped, cursed, kicked off her heels and then finished staggering toward the French doors.

"Amelia!" Phil called. "Drink a big glass of water. It'll help you in the morning."

Amelia turned, muttered something, then disappeared into the house.

"That was illuminating." Phil leaned against the chair's back and folded her hands in her lap. "Seems I'm not the only one who noticed Mason was pre-occupied for a long time after you two ended."

Lauren stood. "Amelia's right. We should get to bed. Big day tomorrow with filming first thing. I guess they'll let us know then how Mr. Townsend is doing."

Eleven

Mason strode around Grandad's bed in the emergency department cubicle. Because of the tight quarters, he could only get in two strides on each side before he had to turn and retrace his steps.

Grandad had been whisked away by a team of medical professionals as soon as they arrived at Sun Coast Community Hospital. They'd left Mason in the waiting room for hours, where he'd walked the square perimeter and gnawed a hangnail.

Liam had given him his phone so he could contact his family. Jenna still wasn't answering his calls, so he'd yelled a message on her voicemail and hung up. His parents were sailing the Caribbean and must be out of range. He'd left them a lower volume message and kept it brief. "Grandad had some sort of cardiac episode tonight. We're at the hospital. I'll contact you again when I know more."

They'd call him in a panic in a few hours or days, or even a week.

Grandad snoozed in the bed, his forehead creased, and occasionally plucked at the light blanket over his legs. His color looked better, less ashen, but Mason knew nothing more than he had when they arrived—he glanced at his watch—four hours ago.

He heard rapid footsteps and held his breath with the hope they were headed for him.

His prayer was answered when the curtain swept open as a woman in gray scrubs and a bright pink surgical cap entered.

"Mr. Townsend?" she asked, glasses riding halfway down her nose.

He nodded. "Mason Townsend. Clarence is my grandfather."

"I'm Dr. Potter." She pulled the curtain closed behind her. "We've done some tests. Your grandfather is a lucky man. I understand there was a medical professional on site who administered aid."

Mason's heart clutched. "My friend is a surgeon. She did CPR and shocked him with a machine."

Dr. Potter consulted the tablet in her hand. "She saved his life."

Mason sank onto the nearby chair. "He's been complaining of heartburn the last few days."

She nodded once. "That's quite common."

"Did he have a heart attack? Will he be okay?" Mason's brain raced to keep up with the doctor's words.

"Your grandfather's heart stopped without warning, due to an electrical problem. We call it a Sudden Cardiac Arrest. It's not a heart attack the way you think of one. He'll have to undergo some tests and take medication. I expect him to make a full recovery."

"He's going to be okay." Mason repeated. "What causes it?"

Doctor Potter nodded again and looked at him over her glasses. "It can be triggered by abnormalities in the heart muscle or its electrical system. He'll be in the cardiac intensive care unit for a few days while we sort it all out."

Mason stood again, stretched out his hand. "Thank you, Doctor."

She held up a finger. "One more thing. I understand you're both filming a television show."

Mason nodded.

"No trips. No flights. No leaving the city. Not until he sees a cardiologist, gets his meds stabilized, and is cleared for travel. And keep stress to a minimum."

"I understand." Liam and Renee and the rest of the production staff wouldn't fight him on it, but if they did, he'd refuse to finish taping. Simple as that.

The doctor left the cubicle and Grandad's eyelids fluttered open. "Meddling and officious woman, that doctor."

"Absolutely," Mason agreed. "And we will follow her orders to a T."

"I wanted to go to Aruba."

"You're going to a hospital room here, then maybe to the hotel, but that's it." He swallowed the lump in his throat. "You scared me, Grandad. I never want to feel that or see you that way again."

Grandad reached up a hand. Mason interlaced Grandad's gnarled yet still strong fingers with his. "Don't worry about me, son. I plan to stick around a good long time."

After assurances that Grandad wouldn't be dying that night, Mason allowed himself to be driven back to hotel.

He tried Jenna one more time. Yes, it was the middle of the night in New York—he guessed she'd fled to her high-rise condo there—but she never turned off or muted her phone.

This call, she answered.

"How is Grandfather?" she asked.

"He's going to be okay." Mason repeated what Dr. Potter had said.

"Good." Jenna exhaled in his ear. "That's good."

"Why aren't you taking my calls? I need to talk to you about Lauren—"

"Something came up with the investigation and I had to get back to New York. I couldn't babysit you any longer."

"Very funny. What's going on?"

A rustling noise sounded as she probably sat up. "It's too soon to be sure, but the authorities think they may have found our absconding CFO and auditor. We may be able to stay out of the news."

Mason's stomach growled. He was hungry for food, yes, but also for justice for his company. And someone to watch over his grandfather. "Do you have to stay there? Or can you come out for Grandad until Mom and Dad can get here?"

"I booked a seat on the first flight out in the morning. I'm packing now."

"Don't you keep a go-bag?" A teasing note crept in his tone. "For quick getaways? You were gone from L.A. so quickly, I saw the plane's takeoff contrails overhead spelling out 'So long, Mason.'"

"Ha ha. Have fun in Hawaii with Lauren."

She hung up before he could bring up her lies and how she broke them up. He touched the redial button, but knew she wouldn't answer again.

* * *

Lauren smoothed the navy-blue dress over her hips and stared at her reflection in the full-length mirror attached to her closet door. She had dark hollows under her eyes, but otherwise looked like she did last night.

"I still can't believe Mr. Townsend almost died."

"I know." Holly leaned closer to the vanity mirror and applied lipstick. "That was scary. You and Phil were amazing, though. You were so calm. And the way you shocked him with the defibri-thingy? Where did you learn to do that?"

"It has instructions. A voice tells you what to do and you do it."

"You were both great. If I didn't know better, I'd say you were a doctor, too."

Lauren closed the closet door with an emphatic click. "No medical school for me. I'm a teacher."

Holly glanced at her before twisting the lipstick down and tossing it into her makeup bag. "Do you want to be a doctor?"

Lauren shrugged. "I thought about it. Once upon a time. But it's too late now."

"It's never too late for destiny." Holly looked up. "Ooh, that's good. I have to use it in a song." She reached for the pad and pencil she kept near her bed and scribbled for a moment. With a faraway gaze, she stared at the corner of the ceiling, and wrote some more.

"Earth to Holly," Lauren called. "Time to go downstairs."

Holly tossed the pencil on the nightstand. "Let's get to this wine-pairing-dinner-at-breakfast time. Doesn't that sound like a hoot?"

They made their way down the stairs to join the others milling through the great room.

She searched for Mason. The conversation ebbed and flowed around her until she saw him in front of the study door. Then her head filled with buzzing and the chatter dulled until she thought she'd gone deaf. She blinked and shuddered. What the—

Mason smiled and lifted a hand in greeting. Her head cleared and the chatter resumed.

He threaded his way toward her, avoiding the women reaching out to him, scarlet nails raking down his arm or over his shoulder.

"Hi." He stood in front of her, looking good enough to eat, despite the shadowy circles under his eyes and his dark, stubbled chin.

Stop it. The man spent the night in the hospital. It wasn't his fault he wore exhaustion so well. "How's Clarence?"

"He had a Sudden Cardiac Arrest. He'll be okay. You and Phil saved his life."

She shook her head. "I just ran and fetched. Phil is the hero."

Mason opened his mouth, but before he said anything, Liam called for them to resume their places at the table.

"This is all new food and wine," Liam said. "We'll edit this footage with last night's."

The rest of the morning whooshed by like the Hogwarts Express headed to Hogsmeade Station. Lauren obediently sipped each glass and did her best to match a wine's flavor profile to the food in front of her.

Amelia seemed to have no ill effects from last night. She nearly glittered as she talked with the women on either side of her, only occasionally shooting glances at Mason and Lauren as she tossed her hair over her shoulder. She must have taken Phil's advice and hydrated well.

When the mock dinner finally ended, a PA herded the women to the great room, while Mason and Renee disappeared into the office.

Lauren drifted to Phil's side, and they stood behind the couch. Holly appeared to Lauren's left and the waiting commenced.

Last night, she'd barely gotten a chance to ask Mason to let her go when Clarence collapsed. Would he even remember her request?

Twelve

Mason followed Reid to their marks in front of the women. Liam gave an update on Grandad's condition and added that their thoughts and prayers were with Mason and his family.

Then Reid opened the segment, welcoming viewers back. He turned to Mason. "You have your pictures from the evening. Are you ready to ask the women to add them to their photo albums?"

He forced a smile. "We had a great dinner. It's been hard to think of saying good-bye to anyone, but ..." He drew a breath. "I'm ready." He was so ready. Ready to be done with this show. Ready to get back to Grandad. Ready to start the rest of his life with—

"Ladies." Reid interrupted Mason's thought. "Mason will say your name and offer you a photo of your evening. If you accept it, you'll be going with Mason to our next location."

The group squealed as one. Well, most of them squealed. Lauren, Phil, and Holly exchanged glances.

"Mason, it's all you, buddy." Reid clapped him on the shoulder and took a step back.

Somehow, Mason managed to get through the next hour. He proffered photos to Holly and Phil and two other women he'd had pleasant conversations with. Amelia and Liz watched him through slitted eyes until he had one snapshot left.

He gazed at the remaining women. Lauren. Amelia. Liz. Three others. No contest. Surely, they all knew that.

He swallowed. “Lauren.”

Her lips thinned, but she made her way to his side. He held the picture out to her. She reached for it, then paused, her fingers an inch away.

Her eyes met his. Something cracked in his chest. She had to stay. She had to. He couldn’t deal with losing her again, not on top of Grandad’s scare.

“Please, Lauren,” he whispered.

* * *

Lauren’s hand stopped in mid-air. She’d asked Mason twice to let her go. Both times, he’d ignored her. She was the one who kept accepting the pictures, kept adding them to the photo album that would end up being used on the show as a teaser at a commercial break. She was the one who kept going along with the program.

Why did she put herself through this?

One answer floated to the forefront.

For the hotline.

For Phoebe.

So other sisters, brothers, moms, dads—other *people*— wouldn’t come home to the same scene she’d found.

She swallowed, took the picture, kissed Mason on the cheek, and joined the group of women staying.

“What?” Amelia screeched from the great room. “What the —”

Liam appeared at her side, gripped her elbow and guided her to the foyer where several suitcases waited. She marched through the door and out of the house.

Renee motioned Mason to the entryway. The contestants he hadn’t chosen followed. He spoke to each for a moment, kissed her on the cheek, then she left, cameras filming every moment.

When it was Amelia's turn for the quiet goodbye, she threw her arms around Mason, laid a deep kiss on his mouth.

"Bye, Mason," she said. "That's just a reminder of what you're missing." She turned, shot Lauren a death-ray glare, and slammed the door.

The room erupted into nervous giggles. Mason met Lauren's gaze, swiped at his mouth with the back of his hand, and shrugged.

Renee raised her voice above the din. "Ladies, a moment, please." She waited a ten count, then spoke again. "We're ready to move on to the next phase of production."

The room quieted. Lauren sighed. She'd had her chance and instead of heading out the door with an empty prop suitcase, she was still there. Still sharing Mason with other women, still feeling like she didn't belong, still having to dress up and do her hair and makeup to fix a cup of coffee.

She'd make the best of it. This was her choice, after all.

"We have a slight change in plans. To accommodate Mr. Townsend's illness and to give Mason some time with his grandfather while his family comes to L.A., we're delaying taping for two days. Tuesday morning, have your bags packed and ready by eleven. We have a one o'clock flight to ..." Renee glanced around the room and smiled. "Maui."

Holly and Phil and the other two—Keira and Bree? —gasped and turned to chatter with each other.

"There are still beautiful parts of the island that weren't affected by the fire," Renee said. "We're going to show the world that Maui is open for business, and we'll give them some tourism dollars."

Hawaii. Lauren had never visited. Although once, she'd been invited. But Jenna got sick, and Mason's family canceled the trip.

She started toward the others but stopped at the touch on her arm.

"Hawaii, huh?" Mason's cheeks were still flushed, presumably from Amelia's goodbye.

She forced an upbeat tone. "It'll be great."

The women headed upstairs. Holly stopped by Lauren and Mason. "We decided to take advantage of the day off and spend it by the pool. You coming?"

"Be right there."

Mason met Lauren's eyes with a steady, unblinking gaze. "That thing with Amelia—you know how I feel about her. About everyone here. Everyone, except—"

"Mason, we need you in the office," Liam called from across the room.

Mason's brow furrowed. "We'll talk later?"

"Sure."

Lauren continued to her room where Holly had an open suitcase on her bed that looked like it had erupted in a lava flow of orange, yellow, and purple prints. Bathing suits, shorts, skirts, and tops were swirled together in a blinding mass.

"I cannot find my ..." Holly's voice trailed off as she dug through the pile.

"Your what?" Lauren plopped on her bed. "And why are you packing already?"

"I have a really cute turquoise halter top with a built-in shelf bra and a bandeau twisted bodice."

"I have no idea what you just said." Lauren stood and moved to her dresser.

"Here it is!" Holly held up a wisp of fabric and settled it over her head. After three gyrations worthy of a carnival contortionist, she emerged from the folds, tied some strings behind her back, then stepped into a pair of shorts. "Whew. I'm ready, I think, for a day at the pool."

Lauren pulled her tankini suit out of her drawer.

Holly sat on her own bed. "Did you see that kiss Amelia gave Mason? She couldn't go gracefully, could she?"

Lauren shimmied out of her dress and into the bright pink bathing suit. "I guess anything for a few more minutes' screen time."

"I hadn't thought of that, but quite likely." Holly cocked her head with a quizzical look on her face before shaking off the pensive moment and digging through her suitcase again. "Good thing we're not so desperate. I had my moment with my music last night. You've already mentioned your foundation and the hotline, right?"

Lauren sank onto the bed. "Oh, Holly. I'm—" Amelia's confession to her and Phil at the pool last night echoed— "I'm a fraud."

"What are you talking about?"

"I thought I wanted to do this show for publicity, for awareness of the foundation I'm starting. But every time the cameras are on me I forget to mention it. I've had how many chances, but ..." She could barely admit this part to herself, much less say it out loud.

"But?" Holly prompted.

"But ... whenever I'm with Mason, he brings up these feelings and memories, then all I can think of is him and ... an—and him."

"I get it." Holly stood, adjusted her hair in the mirror, then turned to Lauren. "Look, we all know you and Mason have it bad for each other. It's clear to anyone with an eye, an ear, a heart, and half a brain."

Lauren blinked. "It's that—um ... what?"

"From the second you reconnected at the penthouse, he's only going through the motions with the rest of us. You're the one he looks for when he walks into a room. He's the one *your* eyes follow. Everyone sees it. But we're not leaving. Because we all have other reasons for being here. Your other reason is being eclipsed."

"Like the sun by the moon."

Holly smiled at her reflection, then rubbed off a smudge of lipstick with a finger. "Or like a charitable foundation overshadowed by true love."

Lauren scoffed. "We're not teenagers. This isn't Romeo and Juliet."

"Isn't it? You said his sister's a snob who looked down on you and your family. That's star-crossed love."

"Neither Mason nor I tried to ..." Her voice trailed off as the reason for doing this rushed back at her. She cleared her throat. "Tried to kill ourselves."

"Mason buried himself in work and school. Sounds like he tried to kill a part of himself."

"You're awfully deep and analytical for a country singer."

"The best songs connect with hearts, not minds. And I have a degree in counseling."

Lauren chuckled. "Holly, you are a wonder."

Holly slipped her feet into strappy sandals. "And don't you forget it."

Thirteen

Two days later, Lauren gripped the armrests of the private jet. She didn't hate flying, but she'd heard the most dangerous points in a flight were takeoff and landing. The hummingbirds in her stomach didn't settle until the plane leveled off and the ground's features diminished beneath them.

When they had boarded, she'd tried not to gawk at the beige leather recliners, the walnut tables, or the flat screen television mounted on a partial wall. A couch and chairs made a conversational area under the television. Beyond the partial wall she spied a table with club chairs, all in the same buttery leather she now white-knuckled. Another group of recliners in the middle of the plane held Renee, Mason, and Liam. She and the other women sat in the rear of the plane in their own deep chairs.

The television flickered on, and the jaunty opening of *Murder, She Wrote* sounded.

Liam stood and called for attention. "We'll be landing in about four hours in Kahului on Maui. We'll load into our limos and vans and head to the resort. But while we're in the air, everyone will have time with Mason. And we'll film interviews." He gave instructions about where to sit, where to move to stay out of camera range during the confessionals taking place in the middle of the plane. They'd wait their turns in the front, and time with Mason was in the back.

Holly's name was called to be alone with Mason. She disappeared into the rear of the plane. Lauren was the first summoned for a private dialogue with Renee, the assistant producer.

After they sat, a PA set mugs of coffee in front of them both. "How's it going with Mason?" Renee asked, the red-light steady behind her.

"He's a special man," Lauren said, picking up her coffee. "I can see us ..." She faltered. "I can see us having fun in Hawaii." She would not lay her heart out on television screens around the country just to be trampled again.

Renee ran a finger around her cup's rim. "I get the feeling you're holding back." She sounded sympathetic. "It's crazy here, I get it. So many women, one man. Does your reluctance to show Mason your heart give the others an advantage?"

Lauren sighed. "I don't open up easily. If that's why he prefers someone else, so be it."

"You'd let him pick Holly or Bree rather than share what you're really feeling and thinking?" The producer sounded incredulous.

"Whatever's meant to be, will be." This woman would not get to her.

"I probably shouldn't say this ..." Renee glanced around, as if making sure they couldn't be overheard, which was ridiculous since they were surrounded by cameras, microphones, and crew members. She set down her coffee and leaned closer. "Before she left, Amelia said ... some things about you. She called you an avaricious gold-digger."

Lauren swallowed hard. "I've been called a lot of things, especially a gold-digger when Mason and I dated, but avaricious is a new one."

She'd thought she was over all that. The jealous looks from other girls at the lake. Jenna's whispered comments about greedy locals. She forced a chuckle. "Besides, I think that's redundant. It's like calling me a greedy mercenary. I'd take off points if one of my students wrote that in an essay."

Renee sipped her coffee before responding. "I was surprised she knew the meaning of the word and could use it in a sentence." She set down the mug. "She said you're only doing the show to get Mason's company to finance a business back in your hometown. That you're using him and his connections to further your own interests."

Lauren forced her tone to remain calm and even. "I'm a teacher. I don't have a business to promote." She ignored the tapping at her conscience. The foundation wasn't a business. It was to save lives.

"I know some of the women can be petty, and certainly Amelia wasn't the easiest person to get along with, I just thought you should know what she said."

The plane dipped and bucked, a perfect mirror of Lauren's stomach. She forced a smile as the turbulence faded and the engines resumed their steady hum.

"Are we done?" She half rose from her seat.

Renee glanced at her tablet. "One more thing. What's this about a charity you're starting? Could that be what Amelia meant? That you're looking for publicity and money for a foundation?"

Lauren sank into the seat. She'd told Holly she hadn't had a chance to mention the foundation, and Renee just gave her a gift-wrapped opportunity. It was her only reason for being here. Or had been until she saw Mason.

She leaned back, licked her lips. "Thanks for asking. It's not a business, but it is a charitable foundation I'm setting up. My sister died last year. She was one of over four thousand suicides in California, and one of over forty-four thousand in the nation. I'm starting a crisis hotline in my hometown, to help other people who feel hopeless."

"I'm sorry about your sister. That must have been incredibly hard. Tell me about her," Renee prompted.

Lauren paused to let the lump in her throat dissolve. The one that always formed when she talked about Phoebe. But if she was really going to do this thing, she had to get past the emotion.

She swallowed. "Her name was Phoebe, and she was amazing. She had strawberry blonde hair, Elizabeth Taylor blue eyes, and the sweetest smile in the world. She'd never hurt anyone. She used to carry spiders outside and let them go. She cried when Dad sprayed bug-killer on the ants in the kitchen. But she also suffered from depression. Some days she couldn't get out of bed. We thought she was doing better, but we didn't realize that her brighter outlook was because she'd already decided what she was going to do. I want to help other families see what we missed, so they don't have to go through what we did."

"Does the foundation have a name?"

Lauren creased the hem of her skirt across her knees, then smoothed it out again. "The Bright Help Line. Phoebe means bright or radiant and I want to honor her, as well as let others know their future can be brighter. I'm eager to get the word out. I'm applying for grant money and any good publicity I generate will only help."

"Commendable." Renee stood and motioned to where Mason sat. "Let's help you get the word out."

* * *

Mason watched Lauren stand in the mid-part of the aircraft. She must be done filming with Renee. Liam paused in his litany about making up for lost time and the fast pace they'd keep on Maui.

Lauren grabbed a coffee cup and made her way towards him and the small seating area where the other four women waited.

He flashed her a smile as the plane bucked. She stumbled, dropped the cup, and landed on her backside.

He rushed to her side. "Are you okay?"

"I'm so not okay." She chuckled though and reached for him. "Here, give me a hand."

He helped her stand. "What's wrong?" He ran his hands down her arms. "Did you sprain something?"

"I'm fine." She picked up the cup. "Good thing it was empty." She slipped past him in the aisle. "I need to let Phil know Renee and the crew are ready for her confessional."

He watched her join the others. Why did it feel like she was always walking away? Would they have a chance to finish a conversation? Linger over dessert instead of having to make sure the camera got enough shots of the food and the menu and the dishes?

Things were going to be different on this trip. They were going to Hawaii, for crying out loud. Talk about a place for romantic dinners, beach strolls, and falling in love.

Falling in love? Could it be …?

Yeah, it was sort of the point of the whole show, but everyone knew it rarely happened. Reality television love shattered when couples returned to the real world of work and bills and rainy days and flat tires.

Except he and Lauren had already tasted love in the real world.

Yeah. Remember how that ended.

He dragged a hand over his head and down his face. Yeah, Jenna broke them up, but they'd been nineteen years old. Maybe—probably—they would have broken up anyway. Who falls in love forever as teenagers?

His parents.

His grandparents.

He came from a legacy of finding love early and making it last.

Liam cleared his throat and called out. "Mason, I need a few more minutes."

He returned to the seat he'd bounded from when he saw Lauren stumble and fall.

"Where were we?"

"Going over the date schedule." Liam shuffled through some papers. "I've a list of possible activities. Pick a woman and what you want to do with her."

Mason smothered a chuckle as Liam turned bright red.

"Dude. Think about rephrasing that," Mason said.

"You know what I meant. Which activities with which woman?" Liam held out a paper.

Mason took the sheet and ran his gaze down the page. "Zip-lining with Lauren. Snorkeling with Lauren. Sunset dinner cruise with Lauren. Parasailing with Lauren. Paddle boarding with Lauren." He tossed the paper on the shiny table.

It slid back to Liam who picked it up with a sigh. "Come on, man. Work with me here."

"I'm tired of this."

"How about ..." Liam tapped his lips with a pen. "Keira is afraid of heights so let's say parasailing with Keira."

Mason sat up straight. "That seems kind of cruel ... or a peculiar kind of genius." He reached for the paper again and sighed. "Parasailing with Phil. Snorkeling with Keira. Paddleboards with Holly. That leaves Bree and Lauren."

"Sunset dinner cruise with Lauren, obviously for the romance factor, so zip-lining with Bree." Liam scribbled on his paper.

Mason expelled a long breath. The tightness that had gripped him since leaving Grandad at the hospital last night finally eased a bit. As much as he'd hated getting on this plane without Grandad, he knew the production company had gone to great expense and trouble to give him those two days. So, he didn't have a choice. He had to be here.

He'd given up trying to talk to Jenna. She'd become an expert at which of his calls to answer and which to ignore, so they'd only talked about Grandad and their parents' arrival. What she'd done ten years ago had gotten shoved to the back of the line of all he was dealing with.

Grandad. This show. Lauren. The company.

This delay would put the show on a collision course with the news of their huge losses due to fraud and embezzlement.

"Thanks, man." Liam gathered his papers and passed Philomena, making her way to him.

The next two hours passed in a blur. He played Spades with Holly, Slap Jack with Bree, Gin Rummy with Keira, and War with Phil. Now, Lauren would join him for a brisk round of Hand and Foot.

He leaned his head against the seat rest. How many more days of this did he have?

How many days of faking interest in other women? How many hours of inane conversation? How many minutes of longing for this to be over before he could scoop Lauren in his arms and kiss her like he'd yearned to do every day since he was seventeen?

Stop. He had to stop. This had to be done. Not just for his company, but for Lauren, too. She deserved the fairy tale.

Lauren dropped into the vacant seat across from him. The camera never blinked.

"How's Clarence?" Lauren asked.

"Jenna's with him in the CICU. My folks are on their way from Turks and Caicos. He's getting all kinds of tests and scans and charming everyone who comes in his room."

She smiled. "Sounds like he'll be okay. I'm glad for you."

"How's your family?" He reached for the cards to shuffle them. "I haven't had a chance to ask. Your folks still own the Lakeside? How's Phoebe?"

She shuddered, a fleeting tremble that was gone almost before he saw it.

He set the cards down and reached for her hand. "Lauren? What is it?"

* * *

Lauren stared at Mason. This was the moment she'd dreaded since she learned Mason was the bachelor.

She swallowed. "I—it's Phoebe. I guess you don't know."

"Know what?" His gaze searched her face, a furrow between his brows.

"She ... died. Last year."

"Oh, Lauren. I'm sorry. I had no idea." He gripped her hand.

"You couldn't." She managed a brittle smile. "I didn't expect you to."

"What happened? An accident?"

She pulled her hand from his and curled her arms across her chest. "Suicide."

Shock rippled across his face. "Phoebe killed herself?"

She nodded. "It's been a tough year."

"I'm sorry," he repeated. "It seems inadequate, but I am. I don't know what else to say. I wish there was something I could do."

She glanced down the aisle, to where the other women chatted. Her toes curled in her heels. She couldn't run away. This was why she was here after all. She'd already had this conversation with Renee. She could do it again with Mason. She had to. "Actually, maybe there is something. I'm starting a ..." She paused to swallow the pain.

"She had depression, didn't she?" Mason asked. "I remember her in your living room still in sweats at three o'clock in the afternoon, then curling up on the couch and falling asleep again."

He couldn't know what his memory did to her. Reminding her Phoebe had struggled for years, and no one had been able to help her in the end. Lauren should've done more, she should've insisted Phoebe get help, she should've badgered her parents until they drove Phoebe down the mountain to a counselor. Gotten her medication. Gotten her help.

Tears pooled in Lauren's eyes, and she blinked furiously, desperate to hide the guilt threatening to overwhelm her. She turned to look out the window. They were descending through the clouds, and she could see patches of blue water below.

"Lauren." He reached for her hand again.

She shook her head, laced her fingers together in her lap. If he touched her, she'd dissolve into a puddle. "It's okay. I'm okay."

"Of course, you're not okay. How could you be?"

Now was her chance. The whole point of this was to talk about the foundation. Her heart rate slowed from *Must Run Away!* to *It Might be All Right After All.* She could do this. She could talk about Phoebe and the foundation. She could pretend not to be an imposter with no idea what she was doing.

She drew a deep breath, held it a moment before speaking. "Actually, I want to tell you what I'm working—"

Renee appeared at her side. "We're about to land, so I don't have time for your interview, Mason. I'll need a few minutes with you in the lobby of the resort as we're checking in."

Lauren turned back to the window. She'd have to tell Mason about the foundation the next time they had a minute alone. Or as alone as they could be with a camera operator following.

Fourteen

Mason watched Lauren return to her seat with the others. The pilot came on the PA system and instructed them to take their seats.

Renee flashed a brief smile, and her fingers trailed over Mason's shoulder as she moved past him to her seat. "Prepare for landing."

It promised to be a rough one.

As Mason tightened his seat belt, he had a feeling he needed a safety belt for his heart as well as his body.

After the smooth-as-a-silk-tie landing, the group lined up to deplane. He touched Lauren's elbow. "Are you all right, after that fall? Any bruises? Soreness?"

She shook her head with a smile he didn't believe. "The only bruise is my lack of grace making itself obvious."

Lauren obviously still grieved her sister. As much as Jenna drove him crazy, if something happened to her, he'd never get over it. Your siblings weren't supposed to die. They were meant to pester you, be a support when you someday buried your parents, be doting aunts and uncles and provide cousins for your children. Lauren lost all that and much more.

He sighed. If only he could have been there for her. Taken care of her. Let her cry as much as she needed. Jenna robbed them of so much more than any of them thought. She'd stolen a shared past as well as their future.

He followed Lauren out of the plane and down the jetway, then moved to her side. They walked in silence, trailing Liam, Renee, and the rest of the television crew. He loosened his tie and undid his top shirt button. The air was warm and felt thick enough to chew.

Lauren ran a hand through her hair and shot him a glorious smile. "I love it here already."

"It's not your first time, though, right? We came to my folks' house in Kaanapali. They still have it. Kaanapali and Napili escaped the fire that demolished old Lahaina Town."

She shook her head. "That trip got canceled, remember? Jenna got the chicken pox and instead of coming to Maui for Christmas break, you stayed in Manhattan, and I shoveled snow in Harts Leap."

"That's right." He glanced at her skirt billowing in the breeze. "It looks like Jenna worked overtime keeping us apart."

Lauren flashed him a smile. "I'm sure she didn't get chicken pox on purpose. She was, what, twenty, at the time?"

"I wouldn't put it past her. When it comes to getting her way, Jenna's not above haunting a pediatrician's office until a feverish, itchy kid arrives, then asking to snuggle them."

"You're exaggerating."

"Didn't we figure out a few days ago that she told each of us a different story to keep us from contacting the other?"

Before Lauren answered, they arrived at a flight of steps leading down to an open walkway. They descended and were then herded to a curb where two limos and a fifteen-passenger van waited.

One of the PAs motioned Lauren and the other women to one of the limos, Mason, Liam, and Renee to the other. Mason started to object, but Liam shook his head. "We've got things to go over with you on the drive to the resort."

Mason grimaced but climbed in. He was able to tune out most of Liam and Renee's discussion and watch the island scenery through the window. It was his first visit since the devastating wildfire that demolished historic Lahaina. His parents loved the hustle and bustle of Kaanapali and Kapalua, while he preferred the south end of the island.

The limo turned left, almost as if the driver read his thoughts. Palm trees, a golf course up on the hill, and the orderly rows of a plantation rolled by. Puffy white clouds gathered over the mountain that bisected the island. By the time they parked in front of the light pink resort in Wailea, he'd removed his tie and his feet itched to feel sand.

Before he could grab his room key, Renee motioned to him. With a sigh, he followed the assistant producer from the lobby to a small couch flanked by two chairs, nestled between some potted palms. A huge vase of tropical flowers screened the seating nook from the rest of the area. Creamy tile stretched in every direction, with fixtures of white marble. A huge pond took up the center of the lobby. Dug-out canoes held a variety of plants. Tropical scents—plumeria, pineapple, and ginger—wafted around them.

He sat on the orange couch, his back to the pond and greenery. It took a few minutes for the camera and sound guys to get themselves and their equipment together. Renee sat opposite him and examined her tablet.

Finally, she looked at him. "What are you looking forward to doing in Maui, Mason?"

"This is a beautiful island, with tons of fun activities." Talk about bland and boring.

Renee must have thought the same thing because she gave him a quizzical look. "It's not your first time on the island, right?"

He swallowed. "Some of my favorite vacations have been here. I've loved zip-lining and visiting Haleakala, the inactive volcano crater. I hope to do all that and more with the ladies." *Sheesh, dude, cool it with the tour guide schtick.*

"Talk to us about the other night."

"My grandfather?"

Renee shook her head. "I mean Liz's dance and Holly's song. They both performed for you. Then you made Liz an outcast, yet you kept Holly. Talk to me about that."

He steepled his fingers. What to say without sounding like a total jerk? "Liz seems nice, but I got an impression she was more interested in performing for the camera than getting to know me. Holly and I had several conversations and we connected on a more personal level."

"Do the other women have ulterior motives that you're aware of?"

He glanced at the ceiling, let his mind go back in time. "I doubt it. I've known Phil and Lauren a long time. Keira and Bree and I are just getting to know each other, but they haven't mentioned wanting to perform or talk about anything in particular."

"You don't know Lauren's motive?"

He recoiled into the cushion slightly. "What motive?"

"Why she's here. Publicity for the charity she's starting."

Disbelief unfurled in Mason's chest, squeezing out his breath, pressing on his heart until it stuttered an uneven beat. "Lauren wouldn't use me like that."

Fifteen

Renee tapped her tablet, then held it out to Mason. A video of Lauren was paused. He pressed the play icon.

He heard Lauren's voice first. "I want to help other families see what we missed, so they don't have to go through what we did."

"Does the foundation have a name?" Renee asked.

Lauren gazed into the camera. She said something about Phoebe being a bright light. Then, "...any good publicity I generate will only help."

He shoved the tablet back into Renee's hands.

Lauren was here for a project?

Not to reconnect.

That wasn't the Lauren he knew. The Lauren he'd drenched with a cannonball dive off the dock when they were sixteen. The Lauren he'd thought he was falling in love with again. The Lauren who knew how he felt about people using him and his family.

He pushed against the armrest, hefting the rocks on his shoulders to stand under their weight, then walked away.

"We're not done!" Renee called.

Oh, yes, they were. He had to talk to Lauren.

* * *

Lauren followed Holly down an open walkway. A breeze ruffled her hair, and she lifted it off her neck with one hand while pulling her rolling suitcase toward the elevator with the other. As soon as she got out of these shoes, her hair was going into a ponytail. She hadn't expected the oppressive humidity. Hawaii was supposed to be balmy and pleasant, with gentle tropical air scented with orchids and coconut and frangipani. Not that she knew what frangipani looked or smelled like.

"We're on the fourth floor." Holly stabbed the elevator call button and handed her a plastic card. The elevator doors slid open, and Holly boarded.

Lauren paused.

"You coming?" Holly asked.

Lauren made her decision.

"I need to find Mason. You go ahead." She had to do what she should have done already. Talk to him. Tell him the foundation and the hotline. Before he found out from someone else.

"Lauren!"

She turned to see Mason striding in their direction, a camera and sound guy close behind.

She tucked a loose strand of hair behind her ear and tried not to let her happiness at seeing him erupt into a silly grin. With his shirt open at the collar and his jacket flapping as he walked, he looked every bit the high-powered executive he was.

"I need to talk to you." He stopped, and she noticed his pale face, tight lips, and veiled eyes. Anger oozed from him. But something else simmered under the irritation. He seemed ... hurt.

"What is it?" she asked, fighting the urge to smooth away the creases framing his mouth.

He stepped closer. "When were you going to tell me?" His voice was low, and he nearly growled the words.

"Now. Right now." Did he mean the same thing she did? "Tell you what?"

"That you're just like the others. Just like Liz. Using me."

She shivered in spite of the heat. "No."

"I didn't believe it, but I saw the video. You said you wanted all the publicity you could get. That's what this is to you? A chance to get yourself in front of cameras." He took a step back. "Are you really like all the others?"

"Mason." This couldn't be happening. "Let me explain."

"There's no need. I get it." He turned on his heel.

"Mason." She said his name again, but he was gone. The camera remained, its steady red light unblinking and reminding her what a fool she'd been, to think they could have a future. She'd always be the mountain girl with grease-stained clothes, not good enough for the rich, city boy.

The elevator doors opened again.

Their room. She had to find it. She could fall apart there. In semi-privacy. Not here in the lobby, surrounded by cameras, the crew, and tourists in flip-flops with towels slung over their shoulders.

She rode smoothly to the fourth floor, spied Holly ahead of her on the walkway, and hurried to catch up. "I'm coming."

"Everything okay?" Holly asked.

Lauren shook her head. "I need to get away from the camera."

They pulled their bags along the walkway, open on one side to lush foliage screening a parking lot.

With every step, Lauren felt Mason's sense of betrayal chasing her. The view and bird song couldn't distract her from the hurt and betrayal on his face. The shattered disappointment in his eyes.

She almost stumbled into Holly's back when they stopped in front of a pink door.

Holly waved her key card in front of the dark panel which flashed a quick green and admitted them with a soft click.

Lauren pulled her bag in. The door swung shut. The camera operator stayed outside.

Finally.

Her legs trembled, but they carried her to the nearest of the two queen-size beds.

"What's happening?" She buried her face in her hands. Instead of the expected tears, something else heated her face.

Holly sat beside her. "You didn't tell Mason about the foundation?"

Lauren shook her head. "I'd started to when we had to get ready to land." With the camera operators strapped into their seats, there had been no more chatting with Mason.

And now, judging from his reaction, there would be no more quiet talks, no more one-on-one dates. No more kisses.

"Why would he be so upset?" Holly asked. "It's not like you're married or had his secret baby years ago. You're starting a charity. To help others."

Lauren stood and moved to the window. Their room overlooked the grounds with the Pacific stretching beyond. Connecting pools lay below. Kids shrieked as they slid from one to the next. It was a perfect day in a perfect paradise. Or at least it should have been. Could have been.

Holly's question still hovered in the room. Lauren drew a breath. "He always hated it when people tried to use him and his family for personal gain. He said he could tell when someone wanted a favor because they became his best buddy." She rubbed her temples. "I promised I would never do that. That I would always be his friend."

Emotions surged through her. She stepped onto the small lanai. She would have called it a deck or a balcony, but when in Rome and all that. Or when on Maui. Lanai, it was.

She sat on a chair. Behind her, Holly moved around the room, unpacking, humming one of her beautiful songs. A brown crescent of land in the water to their left had a cluster of boats inside. A pair of kayaks moved slowly across her view.

The despair that consumed her in the elevator and walkway to the room evaporated like August morning mist on Harts Leap Lake. Instead of anguish and misery at Mason's reaction, something else rooted in her chest.

He immediately thought the worst of her. The very worst. The thing he knew—or had known, years ago—was her commitment to never betray him.

The only person she'd loved more than her sister just turned his back on her.

* * *

Mason's insides rolled like the surf outside his suite. The staff had commandeered one bedroom as an office, but he had the other room to himself. He paced, replaying that video Renee showed him, then Lauren's expression when he accused her of using him. Of being just like everyone else around here.

The back of his neck prickled, and he rubbed it. She wasn't, not really. And his heart knew it.

So why didn't she tell him about the foundation and needing money?

A knock sounded at his door before it opened a few inches. Liam's head appeared.

"We need you."

Mason sighed. "What now?"

Liam pushed the door fully open. Renee and several others milled around the living room. The sliding doors to the lanai had been opened and the sheer drapes fluttered in the breeze.

Mason inhaled. Sea, salt, sun. The perfect aroma for paradise. Instead of soothing him though, he just felt alone. Desolate.

He straightened his shoulders. All that mattered was he'd done his best to take care of his family and his company. As he'd been raised to. He had to be careful. He had to watch for opportunists. He had to put the company first.

Lauren showed she didn't trust him. Not enough to share about her sister until today, when he pressed her. The memory of their stolen kiss in the supply closet at the PDC emerged. Her yielding lips, her soft body. The memory waved from a corner of his brain. He ignored it.

He couldn't let himself be distracted from the hard truth. They'd been good together as teenagers, but they'd both grown up and they weren't the same kids, the same people they'd been back then.

"Our next filming with the women will be at four o'clock. Wear board shorts. We'll be at the Hibiscus Pool," Liam told him.

Mason nodded. He had three days of filming to get through and then he'd be free again. "When's my flight back to LA?"

Liam looked up. "In a hurry?"

He had no idea. But Mason just nodded. "My grandfather is hospitalized. Yes, I want to be with him."

The tips of Liam's ears turned red. "Of course. I'll check."

Renee motioned him to take a seat on the couch. She settled into the chair across from him. "Let's finish our conversation from the lobby."

This must be what torture was like. Never ending. No time to catch your breath before the next onslaught. "Fine. Where were we?"

"You'd just learned about Lauren's desire for publicity."

He shifted on the couch, rubbed the back of his hand along his chin line. "What was the question?"

"How do you feel about Lauren now, knowing what you do?"

He shrugged. "Everyone here has reasons for doing this. We've seen Liz dance, heard Holly sing, and that first night Katelyn brought cupcakes from her bakery."

"So, you're not angry with Lauren."

Angry, no. But hurt? That was another story. He schooled his face to remain impassive. "Like I said, everyone has ..."

"A motive?" Renee prompted.

"Reasons."

"What are your reasons, Mason?" Renee's brows rose.

His throat tightened. "What—" The word died on his tongue. He swallowed and tried again. "What do you mean?"

"You just said everyone has reasons. Does that include you?"

My sister made me wouldn't be a good response. *My family company might be hit with a blizzard of losses, negative publicity, and I'm trying to mitigate some of that* was also not quite right. "Mine are simple. As you know, I have some unfinished history with several of the women. It's been helpful to have closure. I feel ready to move on."

"Ready to move on with one of the women here in Hawaii? Or do you have someone else in mind?"

He gave a one shoulder shrug and a broad smile. "Everyone here is special to me." Give her what she wanted then he'd get out of there.

Renee spent a few minutes interrogating him about each woman and his feelings for her and if he saw a future for them. He dodged most of the questions with some of the agree-but-don't-commit statements he used in the boardroom when being grilled about objectively implementing future-proof best practices, or something else equally full of what Grandad called poppycock.

Renee nodded, a pensive look on her face, just like his board of directors.

Finally, she looked at her tablet, then raised her gaze to his. "Jenna was right. You've been a great bachelor for our *Re:United* show. Tell her thanks."

"I will—hey ..." A thought occurred to him. "I know Jenna played a part in all this, but how did it come together?"

"Jenna contacted the production company, said she had a brother who'd make a great bachelor."

"That's it?"

Renee nodded. "She may have indicated your company would be purchasing some advertising time."

Of course, she did. Because Jenna never did anything without a reason. Like Holly. Like Liz ... and like Lauren.

"Who told you about the women in my past?"

"You're from an influential family. It was easy enough to research who you've been linked with."

Renee left the room as the phone on the side table jangled. Liam scooped up the receiver, listened for a moment, then handed it to him. "Your sister."

Mason grabbed the phone. "Jenna? Is Grandad okay?"

"Everything is fine. Grandfather is resting comfortably. Mother and Daddy should be here in a couple of hours."

He drew a ragged breath. "Why did you call?"

Silence.

"Jenna? You still there?"

"Yes." She didn't say anything more.

He waited.

Finally, he heard a quick inhale, then words tumbled out of his sister like someone removed her inhibitor chip.

"I guess you know I've been avoiding your calls all week. I want to apologize for roping you into this, for getting you involved with all those women and not giving you a heads up that you had a past with some of them. I know it's been more than you bargained for. I'm also sorry for breaking up you and Lauren back then. I've watched you the last few years. You're not happy. I hope you can forgive me."

"As angry as I was with you a few days ago, it hasn't been all bad." Kissing Lauren, sharing memories with her—he'd enjoyed that. "I'm not happy with you, that's for sure. But, yeah, I forgive you."

She exhaled a soft breath. "Thank you. Also, it turns out, you were right ..."

"Let that be a lesson to you, dear sister. I'm always right." He chuckled. "But what am I right about this time?"

"Two things. I've done some self-examination as you suggested. I do sabotage relationships. I have an appointment with a therapist next week."

"Wow. I'll have to take a minute to process that. What's the other thing I'm right about?"

Jenna inhaled before speaking. "We didn't need you to do the show after all. Millicent and Gregory were found in Bermuda. The money is still in offshore accounts, but the FBI said we'll get it back eventually. We'll have a bit of a cash flow problem for a few months, but we'll be able to come through this okay."

He did a fist pump. "I knew it! I knew the SEC and the FBI would find them." He disconnected and sank onto the couch.

All this anguish, all this angst, all this agony for nothing.

No, not nothing. His heart was beating again for the first time in ten years. Grandad's voice echoed in his ears. *Everything can be a blessing if you use it correctly. Learn from it.*

Liam sat next to him. "You okay?"

Mason shook his head. "No. Yeah."

"Huh?"

"I need a minute to think." He leaned back and closed his eyes.

"Sure thing. It's just ..."

Liam's pause dangled in the air until Mason opened his eyes. "What?"

"Renee was right. We got most of the women's names from research. Except one."

Mason sat up. "Who?"

"Lauren. You were young and in the California mountains, so she was never in any of the magazines."

"So ... who? Who told you about Lauren?"

"Jenna. Jenna suggested we get Lauren on the show and reunite you two."

* * *

Several of the boats out in the crescent left its embrace. One chugged north through the water, the other turned toward Lauren and the resort.

Mason's words and haunted expression still hovered in her mind. He'd looked like his heart had been broken. She ached to run to him, to smooth away the wrinkles in his forehead, to kiss away the frown. His obvious feelings of betrayal kept her rooted on the lanai.

What had she really done?

Buried her sister.

Decided no other Harts Leap family should suffer as hers had, so she founded a charity to help lower suicide rates in California and maybe eliminate them in her little corner of the world.

Accepted an invitation to appear on a reality dating show.

Talked about the foundation and the hotline. Yes, hoping to generate some good thoughts in the viewing public and maybe a few donations.

Fallen for her leading man.

What had she not done?

Earned Emmy buzz for her acting chops. She allowed herself a small smile.

Used Mason or his family connections to further her own agenda. The show, yes, but not the Townsends.

She also hadn't compromised herself, her ethics, or her morals.

Resolve and determination sprouted from that certainty in her heart. She'd done nothing wrong. And if Mason couldn't—or wouldn't—see that ... Then he wasn't the Mason she'd known and loved and she was better off without him.

She'd be ready for the next taping, but given how Mason had stalked away from her, he wouldn't be offering her any more pictures. And if in some bizarre twist he did, this time she'd decline.

She'd go home. Home to Harts Leap. Home to her students. Home to the foundation and hotline and Phoebe's memory.

She stood. The greens and blues arrayed before her beckoned and she slipped back into the room. Holly had one hand on her hip, surveying the contents of the closet.

"When do we have to be somewhere?" Lauren asked.

Holly glanced at her. "We're not up until four o'clock. Then bathing suits at the Hibiscus Pool."

"I'm going to the beach." She hefted her bag on the bed, snagged her suit.

"Can I come with, or would you rather be alone?"

"Of course you can come, silly. We're friends and I need all my friends just now."

Holly smiled. "We're part of the reality dating television sisterhood. So, we're sisters. Better than friends."

They shared a handshake and a hug before moving to change out of their travel clothes. Lauren shucked off her skirt and top. Both now felt sticky and clingy, and she couldn't get out of them fast enough.

Dressed in her tankini, a flowing coverup, flip-flops and with sunscreen slathered on, she waited only a moment for Holly before they emerged onto the walkway outside their door. A camera operator fell in behind them.

They followed the paths through the resort, past the pools, to the sand.

Lauren stood at the edge of the beach and raised a hand to shield her eyes from the glare off the waves. Blue water stretched to the horizon, meeting a paler sky. Puffy white clouds dotted her view. Boats streamed steadily across the horizon, leaving wavy trails.

With the white foam bouncing along the waves and the deeper blue of the sea, a familiar ease crept into her soul. She always felt better near water. Something spoke to her soul from the lapping of the waves and the ebbing tides.

"What is that? Do you know?" Lauren pointed at the rocky formation.

"Molokini. It's a partially submerged dormant volcano crater, full of coral and all kinds of tropical fish." Holly tugged down the brim of her floppy hat.

"Molokini." Lauren repeated the name, the combination of vowels and consonants unfamiliar in her mouth. "Have you been here before?"

Holly shook her head. "I read the tourist info in our room while you were on the lanai." She pointed down the beach. "Do you want to walk or sit?"

Voices from behind prompted them both to turn. Mason strode toward them, still in his suit jacket, his tie flopping from the pocket.

* * *

Mason stopped at the edge of the sand. Lauren and Holly were a few yards down the beach. Lauren looked uncertain as her gaze flicked from him to Holly to the water. If she was deciding where to escape to, she didn't have many options.

He toed off his shoes, shrugged out of his jacket, dropped his doubts, and left everything in a heap. The hot sand burned the soles of his feet, but he ignored it.

"Can we talk?" he asked Lauren.

Her lips compressed as she turned and gazed at the horizon, then at Holly. "I'll catch up with you in a few."

Holly nodded and strolled in the opposite direction.

After a long moment, Lauren faced him again. "You said what you wanted to."

Her neutral tone gave him a little hope she'd listen to what he came to say.

"I need to apologize." He cleared his throat and reached out a hand. "Let's walk."

After another beat of silence, she turned and headed down the beach. It took him a few seconds, but he caught up to her. They continued walking along the soft ground but a minute of slogging through the unstable and shifting sand left them both staggering. His knees and legs felt shaky and weak.

"Let's move down there, to the damp apron." Mason took her elbow and they trudged to firmer ground. The camera operator skipped ahead of them, turned and walked backwards, keeping them in his viewfinder.

"Well?" she finally asked. "You wanted to talk?"

"I overreacted. I'm sorry." He glanced at her.

She nodded once. "Okay."

"Listen." He reached for her hand again. "I screwed up. I heard you on the recording and I just ... it brought back things."

"Things? What things?"

"Feelings ... about how people try to use me for favors. Things Jenna used to say about you. I saw that video and I jumped to a conclusion. I should have known—I *do* know better. I hope you can forgive me."

"Mason—"

He squeezed her hand before she could continue.

"It was totally wrong of me. To compare you to Liz and Amelia, to the others here. You're not like them. And I know you'd never take advantage of me or my family. I can't explain why I snapped like that. I'm sorry. I hope you can forgive me."

Her features softened. Did that mean she'd heard him? Heard his heart?

A wave rushed in swallowing their ankles. She stumbled as the water flowed out, taking the sand under their feet. Mason grabbed her arm.

"You okay?"

"This is the second time today you rescued me." She pushed a strand of hair out of her face.

"I only ambushed you once. Does that mean you forgive me?"

Her smile seemed tinged with something bittersweet. "We still need to talk. I was about to tell you about my—"

"It doesn't matter."

"It does." She stopped. "I was going to tell you about the foundation and the hotline when we were on the plane."

His brow furrowed. "The Bright Help Line? The one you mentioned in the video?"

Lauren nodded before meeting his gaze again. She swallowed then spoke. "I did come with a motive. But it was before I knew you were the bachelor. I started a charity, to reduce suicides. I want to help other people, other families, so they don't have to go through what our family did. Our first project is a crisis hotline in Harts Leap. I wanted—want to get out the word, start raising awareness."

Of course, Lauren was focused on helping people. What a complete jerk he'd been. "I'd be happy to help you."

She continued. "I've formed a non-profit corporation with a board of directors. We applied for tax-exempt status. As soon as that comes through, we'll shift the fundraising into high gear."

A pair of standup paddleboarders crossed into their field of vision. She shaded her eyes as she watched them glide effortlessly across the water.

"I can help," he said. "I know grant writers. If you need an attorney to look over your bylaws ..." His voice trailed away. "You've probably got all that covered."

"Most of it. I hadn't thought of hiring a grant writer."

A flicker of hope ignited in his chest. "We've always made a great team."

She dropped her hand and faced him. "I'll talk to Renee and ask her not to include footage about the foundation and wanting publicity."

"No, Lauren, you can't do that." He sounded strangled, all his emotions tangled in his throat.

"I think it's best."

An outcropping of rocks barred any further progress down the beach. Foam and waves tumbled and played around what looked like lava flowing down the mountainside to the water before cooling and petrifying.

Something moved in his peripheral vision. "Look." Mason pointed to the water, about fifty feet out. "A turtle."

She squinted, took off her sunglasses. Something that could be a small football floated on top of the water. "That?"

"Just watch."

The oval shape morphed into a head as it lifted its chin to the sky, then dipped below the surface.

"I saw it!"

"Keep watching."

Now that she knew what to look for, they spied several more, moving effortlessly in the water, poking their heads above, then disappearing below the surf.

"I love it." She breathed out slowly, as if savoring the sea air, the turtles, the blue water.

"We can go snorkeling at Turtle Town if you want."

"They have their own town?"

He chuckled. "It's an area just south of here, lots of them hang out there."

She shook her head, inhaled, and held it a long moment before speaking. "I'm quitting the show."

Sixteen

Mason stared at Lauren, incredulity spreading across his chest until it pressed on his heart with an intense pain. Was he having a Sudden Cardiac Arrest, like Grandad? After a long moment though, his heart resumed beating. “You can’t,” he managed to say.

“It’s for the best.”

“Lauren. I need you here.”

“You’ll have fun with Holly and Phil and Keira and Bree.”

He shook his head. “I don’t care about them.”

“They’re nice women.”

“That’s not the point.”

“What’s not the point?”

“That they’re nice. They’re all beautiful, kind, wonderful people. But they’re not ...”

She blinked rapidly before meeting his gaze. “They’re not what?”

“Not what. They’re not . . .” He had to get out the words before they choked him. “They’re not you.”

“Oh.” Her tongue flicked the edge of her mouth and retreated. He fought the urge to pull her into his arms and kiss her again, like he had at the PDC. He longed to feel her compact body in his embrace, to taste her sweet lips again.

He dragged his mind back to the beach and forced himself to speak. "If you really want to leave, I won't stop you. But would you think about it first? Your foundation—it seems wrong for you to leave without getting the word out."

Her head shot up and she met his gaze with a fierceness that made him take a step back. "I will not be talking about the foundation on camera again. If I stay—and that's a huge if—it'll be because we're still having fun and want to continue getting to know each other as adults. I won't let there be any speculation or gossip that the only reason I'm here is for personal gain. Your sister would love—" Her lips compressed in a grim line.

"My sister—" He grinned, he couldn't help it. "I think my sister will surprise you. She's the one who gave the production company your name. She helped reunite us."

"Your sister, Jenna Townsend? Tall and thin with an acid tongue and a will twice as strong."

He waggled his brows with a chuckle. "That's her."

Lauren shook her head. "I don't get it."

"I guess she could see my heart was still yours, and all the setups in the world weren't going to change that."

"Mason ..."

He took her hand in his, gazed at the sea. "Can you believe this view?" He watched the horizon where the deep aquamarine ocean met light blue sky and fluffy white clouds.

He turned back to Lauren. His heart felt like a basketball dribbling down the court.

She looked up at him, a slight smile on her lips. Her soft, pink lips. A decade ago, he couldn't get enough of her lips. He woke every morning, eager to see her again, to taste her again. If it was possible, he'd fallen a little more in love each time they kissed. And they'd been kids back then. The thought of kissing the grown-up Lauren, the woman holding his hand on a Hawaii beach, sent his heart into a downcourt-jump-shot rhythm.

What in the world was he doing? He was here, in one of the most romantic spots in the world, with Lauren. He loved her. Why was he just standing there, holding her hand?

He pulled her into an embrace. She lifted her face toward his, a smile —an expectant smile?—playing on her mouth.

"Lauren. I missed you so much. I missed your laugh. I missed your smile. But you know what I missed most?"

She shook her head. "What?"

He drew a deep breath. "This." He lowered his lips to hers. She tasted sweet and fruity, and he gave himself to the sensation. Lauren back in his arms again. Where she belonged.

Heat unfurled in his stomach and wove through his limbs until he felt weak. He pulled her closer, his hands on her waist.

Finally, she broke their embrace, stepped away.

"Lauren?" His voice was husky.

"What are we doing?" She raised a trembling finger to her lips. "Is this ..." She glanced to her right where a steady red light reminded him everything they said—and did—was filmed. For her parents, her friends, her neighbors, her students, to see.

"This ..." His gaze never wavered from hers. "This is me doing what I should have done a decade ago. It's me, telling you and the world, that I love you. It's always been you, Lauren. It's always ever been only you."

Epilogue

Six months later

Lauren scooted to make room for Mason. He settled next to her on the couch in her Harts Leap apartment and nestled the bowl of popcorn on her lap before helping himself to a handful.

Lauren pressed *Play* on the remote to start the recap of last week's episode of *Re:United*. Amelia appeared on the screen glaring at Lauren and Mason chatting across the mansion's pool.

"I didn't know she was there." Lauren shrank into the cushions. "Good thing, I guess, because she's scaring me now, months later and two hundred miles away."

Mason took her hand, rubbed a thumb along the top of her knuckles, before bringing them to his lips. "As I recall, you were a bit preoccupied with making me crave Daisy's chocolate malt pie." He sat up straight. "Which, by the way, you still owe me a slice of."

The shot cut to Amelia in her confessional interview. "I'll be the last woman standing at the reunion, I guarantee it. Mason and I have unfinished business. If you know what I mean." She winked broadly at the camera.

Lauren dug an elbow into Mason's side. "Unfinished business, huh?"

He yelped. "I had to remind her she was part of my past because my sister put her up to it back then. The production staff insisted I keep her for the drama quotient."

Lauren snuggled back into the crook of Mason's arm, contentment threatening to clog her throat. Last summer when Brooke urged her to accept the invitation to be on *Re:United*, never did she think she'd be here in Harts Leap, in love with Mason, and—she glanced at her left ring finger—engaged to him.

He'd proposed on the beach in Hawaii, the Wailea resort behind them and an audience of seven turtles. Along with Renee, Liam and a dozen assorted crew members.

Her phone chirped with a text from the hotline volunteer on duty that night.

> All quiet. I'll let you know if anyone calls or needs help.

She sent a thumbs up emoji and set the phone on the arm of the couch. "I'll be forever grateful to One Reality Productions and our *Re:United* family."

"Your confessional interview after our walk on the beach that first night, how you opened up about Phoebe and her struggles, that was amazing." He tossed a piece of popcorn in the air and caught it in his mouth.

"Still, they didn't have to air it. The outpouring of support and money made it possible to set up the technology and infrastructure in less time than I expected. I owe them."

"Liam and Renee are fine with the ratings we're giving them. No need to send them flowers. Or chocolates. Or cham—oof."

She elbowed him in the side. "I'm going to invite Liam to visit Harts Leap on his next break. So, he can meet the volunteers and see how the hotline works and the difference it's making. That'll be my thanks."

They watched the rest of the episode, occasionally guffawing at the editing which presented things not quite the way they happened. Mason only grumbled twice at something someone said. The show was airing episodes filmed on Maui and was gearing up for the finale next week.

Then, finally, the rest of the world would know that she and Mason had truly reunited in the best way possible.

Forever.

Lucky—no. Blessed in love and life.

"Stay tuned for a sneak peek at the next season of *Re:United*," the host, Reid, said.

Mason stood, stretched, and rubbed a hand along his clean-shaven chin. "How about a stroll to Daisy's for that pie?"

"Don't you want to see the teaser for next season?" She let him pull her to her feet.

"I barely tolerate watching our shows. You're the only person there I care to see again."

Reid appeared on the television screen behind Mason. Lauren gasped.

Mason whirled. "What?"

"Meet the next bachelorette looking to reconnect with her past loves." Reid motioned to the woman next to him. A familiar woman in a pencil skirt and crisp button-down shirt.

"No." Mason blinked. "It can't be."

Lauren tried to smother the giggle, but it fought its way to her mouth and into the sudden quiet.

"Jenna Townsend!" Reid motioned to a smiling Jenna, who looked relaxed and confident.

"Hi, Reid." Jenna kissed him on the cheek.

"Did you know about this?" Lauren asked.

Mason shook his head. "She said she was taking some time off since the cases against our accountant and auditor are settled."

They stood together and watched a kaleidoscope of images rush past. Jenna surrounded by men of varying heights and sizes. Jenna and Clarence —completely recovered from his heart issues—huddled together on a couch in the Beverly Essex's penthouse suite. Jenna and a tall man in a tuxedo dancing a tango.

"You got your wish." Lauren gave Mason a sidelong glance.

He still stared at the screen as if transfixed.

"What?"

"Jenna's getting to find out what she got you into."

He grabbed the remote and turned off the television.

"What she got me into was love and happiness and contentment." He lowered his lips to Lauren's and pulled her close.

She melted against him. Heat unfurled and spread to her chest. He deepened the kiss and she responded with a rush of emotion that threatened to overwhelm her.

Oh, how she adored this man. This man she'd known and loved for nearly half her life. This man who knew her inside and out, who loved her back, and who always found her to be enough.

He pulled away, rested his forehead against hers. "Jenna should be so lucky."

About the Author

A personal note:

As I wrote this story, sometimes I'd be questioned if suicide was an appropriate element to include in a "light" summer read. I thought long and hard about this and decided yes, it is. The longer we try to sweep away or ignore mental health issues, the easier we make it for those afflicted to delay seeking treatment.

If you, or someone you know, struggles with suicidal thoughts please call the National Suicide Prevention Lifeline at 1-800-273-TALK (1-800-273-8255). You can call confidentially, anytime, day or night.

Bio:

Carrie Padgett has lived in every part of California, and currently writes from her office with a view of the Sierra Nevada. She thinks nuts take up room where chocolate ought to be and chips and dip should be its own food group. She and her husband have been married for far longer than most reality shows last. She has two daughters, two sons-in-law, and six grandkids who call her Grammie.

Sign up for my newsletter:
https://carriepadgett.com/
Find me on Bookbub:
https://www.bookbub.com/profile/carrie-padgett

facebook.com/WriterCarriePadgett
x.com/carriepadgett
instagram.com/carpadwriter

Her Cowboy Champion

TABITHA BOULDIN

One

Sage Rhett had one purpose for sitting in the bleachers for the last five hours without so much as a moment to stand and stretch her legs. Pins and needles stabbed at her calves, and she rotated her feet to get the blood flowing again. The shutter button's steady click kept her focused as the horse and rider raced into the arena. An expectant hush tightened the tense atmosphere in the closed arena where emotions ran high and one shout at the wrong time could have a thousand people sending glares at the wrongdoer.

Dark hooves sank into the deep sandy dirt, the rider taking each stride with a steady seat and minimal movement with her hands. Of all the competitors she'd covered today, Lanie Nichols was a favorite to win. The mare's coat gleamed under the stage lights and Sage's breath caught when the pair executed a perfect sliding stop that sprayed dirt and grit on either side of them. After a series of clicks, she double-checked her camera screen. Perfection. She'd framed the mare in the center of the shot, the background crowd blurred so the sole focus rested on Lanie and her mount. Sage recognized the mare, thanks to hours and hours of studying today's competitors. Righteous Show Girl. She'd been in and out of the show ring since she turned three.

People cheered all around her as Lanie guided the bay mare into a loping circle on the left lead, then finished with a rapid spin that caused the rider's blonde braid to fly out in an arc across her shoulder. Sage rapid-fired a series of shots to catch horse and rider in motion. Her telescopic lens and acute attention to detail kept the mare in focus despite the flurry of movements in the open arena. Bodies surged upward, people lunging to their feet when Lanie finished the routine and patted the mare's neck. Shouts echoed off the twenty-foot ceiling as the crowd turned frenzied. Shouts the rider acknowledged with a tip of her hat while the horse didn't react at all. Sage flipped through the photos while she waited on the next pair and stretched out her legs. Her back ached and her stomach pinched with hunger. A cramp hit her left calf, forcing out a hiss between her teeth.

"Sage?" A male voice sliced through the air over her left shoulder.

She whirled, gripping the back of the bleacher to keep her balance. People flashed past in her hurried movement and her heart lodged in her throat in a sudden burst of fear. "What?" A lightning quick look around brought her attention to a tall blond man wearing black fringe chaps and a blue snap button shirt that brought out the brightness in his eyes. Sage blinked and focused on the face attached to those bright baby blues. "Remington?" No way. She glanced over his shoulder, both hopeful and fearful of who she'd find there. When she didn't spot Remington's older brother, Maverick, she lowered her guard.

A woman stood on Remington's right, her arm looped casually around his. Dark blonde hair hung in loose spirals around her face, and she grinned at Sage with the kind of casual acceptance that seemed to come easy.

"I thought that was you." Remington propped his booted foot on the riser beside Sage and rested his elbow on his thigh. His brown Stetson tilted forward to shade his face but something about the joyful grin had her returning the smile. "Where you been? Haven't seen you in twelve years."

Twelve years. Senior year and last time she'd seen any of the Pierce kids.

Her smile dropped. She blinked away the memories longing for release and focused on the camera. "Spent most of my time in Arizona. Came back to Colorado last year." After her ex stole her photos and passed them off as his own, ruining her photography business when the entire circuit took his side, thanks to his family's money. She was just a kid from the poor side of town. Why should anyone trust her when family and prestige always seemed to win the day? Not that she was bitter. Nope. Why bother?

Speakers squawked. "Next up is Denise Hart riding Goin' for the Gold."

"That's my cue." She motioned at the camera. "Time for me to get back to work."

"You do this for a living?" Remington invaded her space, leaning over her shoulder. "Can I see?" Remy never did understand what personal space meant. His hat brim brushed hers and his aftershave invaded her senses with a spicy aroma that mixed well with the anticipation brewing around her. Her fingertips prickled with the urge to click the camera button. She checked her tripod and adjusted the legs until they sat level on the concrete pad holding up the metal bleachers.

"Come on, Sage." Remington gave her a million-dollar smile, showing off his perfect teeth. "I'll beg, if that's what it takes."

She had a few seconds before the horse and rider would appear, and Remington was one of the few people from high school who'd treated her with kindness. "Sure. Why not." Not like he could steal them from her. Nodding, she pressed the viewing button and tapped through the last five photos. Pride roared up fast and thick, sending her pulse skittering as she examined the photos alongside Remington.

He whistled. "Holy smokes. You're good." Leaning closer, he pressed the zoom button, tracking the line of the horse in full motion.

She smacked his hand. "Don't touch."

Remington's eyebrows shot upward but he didn't comment on her lack of decorum. "Look at these, Violet. These are awesome." He pulled the woman down beside him.

"Yeah. Tell them that in Arizona." Her throat tightened as the memories flooded in. Nuh-uh. Blinking rapidly, she pushed the memories back into the locked box where they belonged. Nate couldn't bother her here. She'd come back to her roots for the sole purpose of starting over. That meant leaving Nate and his thieving ways behind her. Time to change the conversation. "You riding today?" She flipped the camera back into picture mode and adjusted the focus.

Remington eased backward, his gaze darting toward the arena. "Yup." He fiddled with the middle button on his shirt, then ran his thumbs into his belt. "Violet hasn't had a chance to see one of these big shows yet." He smacked a hand to the center of his forehead, knocking his hat askew. "Good grief. Sorry, Violet. Sage, this is my wife, Violet."

Wife? Sage blinked and tried not to gape at the youngest Pierce sibling. "You're married?"

"Yep." Remington pulled Violet in close to his side and kissed her temple. "Wish I'd known you were back in town. I'd have invited you to the wedding."

Uh, no thanks. She definitely did *not* need to see Maverick all dressed up in a tux on his brother's wedding day. "Gotta say, I'm surprised. Always thought Landon would be the first."

"Whatever." Remington made a rude noise in the back of his throat. "No one expected it. Least of all me." His gaze softened when he looked at Violet. "But when you know, you know."

Oh, yeah. She understood that. Least, she always thought so. After Nate...

Remington interrupted her musing with a sharp elbow to her ribs. The man really needed to learn to leave off from invading her space. He probably didn't even realize he did it. Not after all those years of being the youngest who always tried to shoehorn his way into the older kids' fun. "You shooting all the rides today?"

"You make it sound like I'm gunning for you or something." She snorted and punched his knee where it rested beside her. "I'm in charge of photos for the *AQHA Tribune*. They're running live coverage, but they asked me to photograph the rides for articles they'll be posting throughout the competition." As one of the qualifying rounds for the National Reining Horse Association, today's rides were important to every rider, horse, and spectator. They were all out to win enough points to make it to the Open Futurity Challenge in a few months.

Cheers pulled her attention back to the arena where another pair rushed in. She focused on her job and tried to ignore the cowboy lingering beside her. She could handle Remington. As long a–

"Hey, Maverick. Come look at this." Remington's eager shout and the shadow of his hand waving back and forth over her camera lens caused her to miss a shot.

She huffed and pushed Remington's leg. "Get out of my shot, Remy."

He shuffled sideways with a laugh. "You're as bossy as ever." The bleacher bounced beneath his weight, and she steadied her camera while shooting him a dirty look that only made him laugh. "Don't give me that look. I know I'm the brother you never had."

The mention of family locked every muscle and drove a dagger of pain through her heart. Once upon a time, they'd been her family.

"What's up?" A voice dark as molasses snapped her head up from the camera.

Maverick. Her throat convulsed as she took him in with quick, darting glances she tried to hide. Shaved dark hair peeked from beneath his black Stetson and a dusky beard attempted to draw her attention to his lips. Eyes fathoms deep and far too wise for their years grazed over her, widened, then returned to his brother.

Why? Why did Remington have to call his brother over? She'd rather face down a herd of wild horses than be in the same building with Maverick Pierce. Tall, dark, and brooding barely scratched the surface of the enigmatic cowboy she'd grown up with. She scowled and turned her back on the siblings. Not her problem. Whatever happened, she had to pay attention to her job. It was the only one she had, and she couldn't afford to lose it. She needed this gig to lead to the next one so she could keep paying her rent. Another month of noodles for dinner and she might have a chance to upgrade her portfolio.

Horse and rider finished their run and jogged out of the arena. Sage checked her camera. "Stupid cowboys." She muttered under her breath and palmed her eyes as she realized she'd missed the last spin.

Remington and Maverick talked behind her, their voices muffled by the crowd. She didn't care. Really. Violet shifted on the seat beside Sage and shot her an apologetic smile.

What would it hurt to be friendly to this woman who'd married Remington? Kindness was free and Lord knew the world needed more of it. "How long have you and Remy been married?"

"Three months." She spun a silver band around on her finger and a look of adoration crept into place.

"Hey, Sage?" Remington tapped her shoulder, interrupting her next question.

She knew it was him because her body didn't react to the touch. And the difference in his voice, gruff but too smooth to be Maverick.

However, when she turned and caught Maverick's dark smolder, fire lit up her chest and skittered down her arms. Nope. Not happening. She frowned and jerked her head back around. "What? I'm busy."

"Whoa." Remington held up his hands in a gesture of surrender. "I have a job offer for you."

Her ears perked up. "Job? What job?" Shoot. Way to keep cool.

If Remington heard the desperation in her voice, he ignored it. "Can you turn around and talk to me?"

She brushed off his hand where it lingered on her shoulder. "Nope. I can't miss these shots. Don't get paid if I don't do the work." Not like *he* would understand that. Not a one of them understood hunger or the fear of losing everything if a job didn't work out.

She pressed her lips flat to capture the words before they escaped. Remington was not her problem. Honestly, neither was Maverick.

But they were a distraction she couldn't afford. Literally.

"Okay." Remington stood and backed up. "Can we talk once you're done?"

She lifted a shoulder and let it fall. "Sure. I'll be here for a few hours after the last competitor." Her work didn't stop when the competition did. She'd have to go into the back barn and take photos of the horses and riders there. If her luck held, she'd get this job done in time to grab a meal from the food trucks outside before heading to her apartment. Fatigue weighed on her. How long since she'd managed a full night of sleep? A regular meal? She barely even had time to answer her sister's text messages before she fell into bed exhausted each night. She should stop in and see them before she moved on.

"You're up." Maverick nudged Remington's arm and jerked his head toward the open barn attached to the arena. He grew larger in her peripheral vision as he eased into the space Remington left and lowered to the bleacher. "Haven't seen you in a while."

She ignored him. Which was one of the hardest things she'd ever done. Tan chaps covered his long legs, the fringe brushing her knee when he stretched out and propped his elbows on the bleacher behind him. Dark brown boots and matching Stetson with a black long-sleeve snap button shirt made up the rest of his show ensemble. His shirt probably cost more than her whole outfit. It wasn't his fault. He came from money. The Pierces were among the richest and most influential in the quarter horse industry.

"Remington Pierce." The announcer called out Remy's name in that same calm voice.

But the crowd reacted like they'd been electrocuted. Screams and clapping hands created a rush of noise that made her ears ring. She angled the camera to capture his ride into the arena and continued to ignore Maverick by her side.

It was like ignoring a panther perched overhead. Silent. Powerful. Beautiful. He'd laugh in her face if she said that out loud.

And he didn't invade her space.

She homed in on Remington. Maverick's presence sang through her veins. Lord but she'd hoped the years apart would create distance in her heart too. No such luck. She'd loved him too long for that. The constant click from her camera grounded her to the action in the ring. Violet stood near the rail, her grip tight on the wood. Sage wasted a second or two and risked a shot of Violet's upturned face and broad smile when Remington's horse slid in a perfect stop. Money shot, right there. She'd captured a perfect moment between horse and rider, with his wife looking on, her face shining with love. It twisted her stomach, that look.

Remington completed his run with an almost perfect score.

"He overturned that last one." Maverick leaned forward, setting his elbows on his knees. The strong line of his back came into view, along with his broad shoulders.

Don't think about that. She shuttered her eyes and swallowed.

The intercom crackled. "We'll take a thirty-minute intermission to rake the arena."

Her stomach pinched and grumbled. Great. Thirty minutes. Not enough time to pack up her camera and grab a bite. No way she'd leave it sitting here unattended. Not after that near fiasco in Nevada where a man had tried to take off with her camera while she packed it up.

She turned off her camera to rest the battery and angled her head away from Maverick. Maybe he'd take the hint and go away.

"Are you going to keep ignoring me?" Maverick kept his face forward, but the words were for her, pitched low and slow in that gravely sound she found herself dreaming of night after night. No wonder Nate stole her work and dumped her. She had to be sick in the head to spend twelve years in love with a man who never saw her as anything but a bother.

She tipped her hat down over her eyes and scrubbed her scuffed boot over the bleacher. "Didn't realize you were talking to me." Iron infused her voice despite the lie.

His shoulders rolled back and he turned to face her, straddling the bleacher and giving her his full attention. "How about now?"

"What do you want, Maverick?" Bitterness coated the words. He was the last person she wanted to see after all these years. Their time together as kids taught her a lot. Mainly how to maintain her independence at all costs. The one time she'd lowered her guard, his father reminded her she didn't belong in their world, and especially not with Maverick. Then the whole thing with Nate...yeah, better off forgetting about men and relationships and all the baggage that came with emotions and feelings.

His eyebrows lowered as he took her in with a cool, assessing gaze. Dark brown eyes flecked with hints of gold masked a deep intelligence and a softness he hid from the world. Had twelve years hardened him? They certainly had done a number on her.

"Our team photographer is out on maternity leave. Remington saw your work and wanted to ask you to join us for the fall season." He spoke in crisp, clean words that held no affection or even a hint of familiarity.

Her breath hitched. "Join your team?" She splayed her hands out and waved them back and forth. "No way. Your dad would never go for that." Ugh. She shouldn't have said that.

One side of his mouth hitched up in a small smile. "It's not his call. I'm team manager. It's up to me, Sage."

Oh. Great. Her stomach pinched and tried to growl at the same time, causing a roll of nausea that burned her throat. Being part of the Pierce team was one of those once-in-a-lifetime opportunities. It would put her name out there. Could she do it? Could she re-enter their world?

Did she dare turn him down and risk the payday of a lifetime? "I have a few stipulations before I can make a decision." Her words were a breathless rush, and she sucked in air to calm her nerves. "I need a contract. One that promises I will be identified as the photographer on every photo I take. It will be noticeable and legible. Not some tiny little blip that's completely missed."

He nodded. "Done. You'll even have a byline on the website." A full smile emerged. "The job comes with room and board at Twisted Branch. You'll be responsible for documenting the entire process from here to the Open Futurity, along with the Futurity itself. Daily walks through the barn. Photo ops with riders and horses. Training sessions. And every competition between now and then. You'll be compensated with a five-thousand-dollar sign-on bonus and two thousand a week base pay."

What? She tried to process the numbers, but her mind stuck fast and refused to go any further than the mention of room and board. "I'd stay at the ranch?" Twisted Branch was the largest and most well-known ranch and training facility in Oklahoma. The horses living there were worth more than most houses. Her heart skipped into overdrive. "Where?" She met his smile with a calculated look. "Where would I stay?"

"The cabin on the lower forty. About a mile from the barn. It comes with full amenities and two-thousand square feet of living space. You'll have access to a maid, chef, and all the main facilities like the riding arena, pool, lounge area, and rec room. There are horses you can ride, if that's still something you enjoy." His eyes skipped to her boots and he frowned.

She didn't bother looking down, already knowing he'd noticed the small but annoying hole in the toe of her boot. No sense in trying to hide it. This was her life, one she could not say she was proud of but had created for herself.

His toe tapped against the metal and the frown lines deepened when he swept his eyes over her again. Maverick saw too much. He always had. And yet, he'd missed the biggest, most obvious thing. Her.

"I need to think about it. And take a look at the contract once it's drawn up." She fiddled with the camera strap and checked her watch. "I have to get back to work."

Maverick stood, forcing her to crane her neck to look up at him. “I’ll have the contract ready tomorrow. Come by the ranch anytime between noon tomorrow and Friday afternoon. We leave for another show Friday night. If you’re on board, I’ll need you with us.” He squeezed her shoulder in passing. “It’s good to see you again.”

He walked away, leaving her breathless and empty, with her shoulder burning from his touch. She rested her cheek on the space where his hand had rested and closed her eyes. Going back would be a huge mistake. Monumental. She left her heart back there at Twisted Branch twelve years ago. Going back meant facing the Pierce siblings, but above all, it meant being close to Maverick again. The man who broke her heart without even trying. But the risk was worth the reward. Room and board. Those were enough to lure her in. The cash advance and weekly salary sealed the deal. As long as the contract was legit and she received full credit for her work. She was *not* going down that road again.

She couldn’t resist turning to watch Maverick maneuver his way to the bottom of the bleachers. He nodded here and there, a steady but standoffish smile twisting his lips. He managed to look approachable but out of reach all at the same time. He slipped out of sight, ducking into the barn where his family and his horses waited. Same old Maverick. His hard-core family values were one of the many qualities that had drawn her to him as a kid turned young woman.

Maverick was good all the way down to his bones. Strong and confident, he displayed every ounce of integrity without a hint of remorse.

She’d trusted him back then. Trusted him with the glow of a dewy-eyed schoolgirl with her first crush. He’d never known. Nor would he ever find out.

Two

"Maverick." His dad's voice carried through the barn, harrying Maverick into jerking his chin up from where he looked over Goldie Boy's hooves.

Lord, give me patience. He'd need it. "In here." He lowered the palomino's hoof to the thick bedding and straightened while grabbing his hat from the hook beside the door.

Heavy steps carried his dad down the barn aisle, his boots thudding as hard as Maverick's heart. He'd been expecting this, dreading it.

"I told you to warm that mare up before you hit the arena." Thick brows lowered over eyes as dark as midnight. His dad slung a hand out and pointed at the mare Maverick had ridden three days ago in the mid-week proving competition.

He held on to his temper and met Dad's stormy gaze. "I did warm her up." Shoot. He knew better than to argue.

Hooves struck concrete and the sound of grooms working around horses crashed into the empty space between him and his dad.

Jaw working side to side, Dad crossed his arms and leaned forward. "Not like I told you to. You let her get away with that left lead on a right lope for three strides."

It had been one and a half, a proper amount for a lead change at full speed. Maverick locked his jaw to keep from pressing the issue. The longer he stayed quiet, the more likely Dad would run out of steam and leave him be. Until he messed up again.

"You were this close." He held his thumb and forefinger a few centimeters apart. "This close to getting it right. If you'd listened to me." He shook his head. "You'll never win the Open if you keep making rookie mistakes."

"You're right." Maverick tightened his control on the anger rushing through him with enough force to knock him onto his heels. Dad had a point. He did make a rookie mistake. He'd let Sage distract him, something he tried to ignore even now as his watch ticked down the time. He'd watched it wind closer and closer to her arrival, his stomach tightening with each passing hour.

Seeing her had knocked the breath clean out of him. Getting kicked in the sternum hurt less than seeing the discomfort and annoyance in her eyes when she looked up at him with those molten irises.

Dad lowered his arms and jerked his chin in a nod. "You should take her out again today. Ride her until you both get that lead change under control."

The mare needed rest after her performance, but a slow trot around the indoor arena wouldn't hurt. "I'll take her out this afternoon. I have business in the office."

Dad's eyes narrowed. "What business?"

"Hiring a new photographer to take Melinda's place." He propped his elbow on the gelding's half door and watched Dad's face. "Remington and I asked Sage to take over."

Red infused Dad's cheeks and his lips spluttered together. "Sage Rhett?" He spat her name like a curse.

He'd never understood Dad's animosity toward the Rhett family. They'd grown up together, with Sage and her sister Rosemary visiting Twisted Branch every weekend during summer break, and often staying for days on end when their mom needed them out of the house. Old memories rose in a wave that blotted out everything else. He'd missed Sage something fierce when she left without a word. He'd tried to track her down and looked for her at every show for years before giving up.

"She's not working here. I refuse." Dad slashed a hand through the air.

Maverick's blood boiled and he fisted his hand beneath his chin while staring Dad dead in the eye. He would not back down on this. "The photographer is my responsibility. Sage is one of the best I've seen in a long time. Even better than Melinda. We're lucky she can work for us."

A muscle ticked in Dad's jaw. "She's bad news. I wouldn't let a woman like her within ten miles of this place. They're all a bunch of money-grubbing thieves."

The vitriol surprised Maverick into stunned silence. He'd known Dad didn't approve, but this went deeper than he'd ever expected.

"Sage isn't like that." Neither was Rosemary, as far as Maverick was concerned. He didn't know their mother well enough to make a judgment call on her. "And I'm hiring her. The contract is already drawn up and ready for her signature. I'm letting her move into cabin three. She'll go with us to every event." He dared to add one last caveat. "And you'll leave her alone. This is business. I won't let you turn it into a personal vendetta." The words poured out of him, from some place deep in his heart that demanded he defend and protect Sage.

Dad's eyes narrowed and his lips parted.

Maverick braced but held resolute.

"Maverick, I need you to sign off on the feed order." Ross stepped out of the barn office and waved a clipboard.

Dad snapped his mouth shut, but Maverick saw the fury hiding beneath the surface, the unwillingness to let this go.

Too bad, because Sage deserved a chance to come back. She used to love it here. And based on how she'd looked, she needed the respite. The holes in her boots and the deep shadows under her eyes kept him awake these last two nights. Whatever she'd been through in the last twelve years, it had worn her out.

He exited the stall and locked it behind him, giving Dad his back as he made his way to where Ross waited. "Great timing."

The old cowboy smirked. "Sounded like you needed a break."

"It's not that bad." He could handle Dad's temper. He'd been doing it for years.

Ross wagged his head side to side. "Don't need to defend him to me, son. I've known that man longer than you've been alive."

"Any chance you'd tell me what he has against Sage?" He'd poked around the subject long enough. Dad would rather die than tell him, and he hesitated to bring it up with Mom.

Ross took the clipboard once Maverick scribbled his signature on the paper and tucked his thumbs into his belt. "That's one thing I can't say I know. Alls I can say is that your daddy took a dislike to Sage the minute he found out her last name. Only time I've known of him dealing with a Rhett was forty years ago. Far as I know, he used to be friends with Sage's uncle. Man by the name of Carl."

Landon popped his head around the corner of the double doors where sunlight streamed into the barn. "Need you up at the lodge. Tried to call but you didn't answer." And he'd run down to find Maverick instead of calling the barn phone.

What he wouldn't give for a single minute of peace and quiet. Maverick removed his hat and threaded his fingers through his hair. "What's wrong?" He shot the question at his middle brother.

Landon rocked on his heels and jerked his head toward the lodge. "Nothing. Sage is here."

Sage. His heart thundered so hard his ears rang. He'd not forgotten, but the thought of seeing her again punched him straight in the solar plexus. "Great." He slammed his hat back on and tugged the brim down low to combat the blistering Oklahoma sun. "Can you take Roxie to Arena One and get her warmed up?" He motioned at the mare's stall and hurried down the immaculate barn aisle. "And remind Remington that he's supposed to work Locomotive today." A dozen other tasks needed his attention, something he'd come to accept as the oldest of the Pierce siblings. Everyone looked to him to get things done. And he wouldn't let them down. Unlike how he consistently disappointed Dad.

Landon swung into a long lope on his way to the stall. "Hurry back. Peter had a question about the farrier schedule. Told him to find you and ask."

Great. One more thing on his endless list. "I'll take care of it after practice." He *had* to work Cosmic Gold aka Goldie Boy today if they were going to have any chance of winning the Open Futurity. This was his year to prove he could win. He spun on his heel, passed his dad's office, and threw up a quick wave at Mom's curious expression.

Dad met his gaze for a flicker of a second before he jerked it back down to the books spread across his desk. The automatic response proved his rejection. Until Maverick won the Futurity and proved himself, he wasn't getting any respect from his three-time champion father.

His jaw clenched so hard his teeth ached. This year was all his. To win or to lose.

Leaving the barn, he hopped into the UTV and zoomed toward the lodge. Made of massive split logs with broad bay windows across the front and an elegant, sloped roof, the lodge completed one of the main attractions for visitors looking to explore Twisted Branch. It also contained the guest house, dining room, and general get together place for all the employees.

Sweat slicked his palms and trickled down the back of his neck. A wild breeze tore across his skin, whipping his shirt against his chest.

Sage stood on the porch, her arms crossed and her head turned toward the barn off to his left. The smallest barn where they'd all grown up riding. He had fond memories of that barn, even if they were soured by Sage's twelve-year absence. He wanted nothing more than to hug her, but one look at her face warned him to keep his distance. She'd changed. That much was evident in the recalcitrant twist to her lips. The old Sage would've jumped at the chance to join his team. This one seemed reluctant to even be in the same building as him. Why? What had changed to eradicate the genuine sunshine and rainbows attitude he remembered?

Killing the engine, he climbed out of the narrow vehicle and jumped up the steps. "You came."

She lifted one shoulder and let it drop, almost like it didn't matter to her either way. "Do you have the contract?"

"Yep." He pulled the door open and ushered her ahead of him. "I think you'll find it to your liking." He hadn't missed the way hunger clamped her teeth at the arena as her stomach roared or how ragged she looked when he offered her the job. He had no idea what happened to her in the last decade, but he had a feeling it wasn't pleasant.

The old Sage was a bright beam of happiness and easy smiles. This one...well, this one looked more jaded, rough around the edges.

Sage stepped into the lodge and looked up. Her eyes clouded with an emotion he couldn't name. "This place hasn't changed much. I wondered when I saw the new barn." She took in the space with a quick, darting gaze.

He'd become accustomed to the lodge with its enormous open living room. The three couches spaced evenly around a fireplace large enough to flood the room with warmth, and the low counter that separated the kitchen area from the recreation rooms. The wood glowed a soft gold, the overhead beams catching the light and reflecting it back onto the walls and polished hardwood floor.

"I left the contract in my office." He made his way around the open living space, his boots sounding hollow in the cavernous room. "It's this way," he called out when Sage remained still.

Arms still crossed, she followed him through the lodge, down a narrow hallway, and into a second, smaller building attached to the back.

"You call this an office?" She shook her head and a tiny smile crinkled the corners of her eyes. "Welcome back to dreamland."

The words were so low he almost missed them. "What do you mean?"

Her expression closed off, leaving him in the dark. "Nothing."

It was obviously something, but he'd let it go for now. He slid around his desk and dropped into the leather seat. The brown leather portfolio sat in the center of his desk, and he pushed it toward her. "Take your time."

She shot a look at him and flipped the portfolio open. "Are you going to sit here and watch me read it?" Her fingers tapped along the page as she examined the five-page document.

He'd read and reread every single word to ensure it would meet her criteria. Lacing his fingers together, he leaned forward and set his clasped hands on the desktop. "Yes."

She snorted out a laugh that reminded him of long days in the saddle with her by his side. Stolen moments at the pond when they'd all abandoned their chores to lay in the tall grass and talk about their dreams. He'd always wanted this. To raise, train, and ride the best reining horses in the country. He was so close to proving himself that he tasted it with every breath. Or maybe that was the dirt from the arena. They were kind of the same thing at this point.

Her eyes narrowed as she read, but she nodded along. Her posture remained stiff, her shoulders and spine straight as fence posts. Her long, elegant neck curved into a pointed chin framed by long, straight brown hair. Her t-shirt had a hole near the seam. And unless his eyes betrayed him, she wore the same hat he'd given her ages ago.

"Got a pen?" She held out her hand.

He withheld the breath of relief that pinched his lungs and passed her a fountain pen.

Her eyebrows lifted as she uncapped it and she did that little head shake again. What was that all about?

"There." She slapped the portfolio closed and handed it back to him. "When do I start?"

"How about now?" He shot a look at the clock on the wall behind her. The crystal shone in the sunlight pouring in through the open shades and the running horse background reminded him of his grandfather on the day he'd given Maverick the clock. "I'm about to start practice. I'd like some shots of me and Roxie to add to the website. She's going up for sale during the next show."

"Okay." She pushed back from the desk and stood. "I'll grab my camera."

He hurried to follow her back outside and paused at the UTV. "I'll give you a ride to the barn."

She looked ready to argue, so he tipped his head. "It's a long way to the barn. You can drive down if you'd rather. It's the white one. Right there." He pointed at the barn furthest away, and Sage's shoulders lowered. "You have full use of the UTVs. Once we're done today, I'll show you around. Get you reacclimated."

She stalked to her truck, her silence deafening as she opened the door. It squealed loud enough he halfway expected it to fall off the hinges, and when she slammed it shut with a kick, he barely resisted a laugh and held out his hand to take the suitcase from her.

"I got it." Her independent streak snapped into place, and she yanked her hand back, slamming the oversized camera case into her legs.

He rolled his eyes. "I'm not going to steal your camera."

A hard look crashed over her face, a muscle feathering in her jaw. If he didn't know better, he'd think he nailed her exact worry. What use did he have for her camera? Her fingers tightened on the case handle, but then she blew out a long breath and held it out to him.

Victory.

Why did that feel so good? It shouldn't matter that Sage handed him the case and walked around the UTV to get in the passenger seat, where she tucked her hands between her thighs and stared straight ahead.

He forced the thought away and strapped her case down tight where it wouldn't jostle around. "Your cabin is on the other side of the barn." He jerked his chin. "You'll see it once we reach the outdoor arena."

* * *

What was she doing here? She tried to take it all in, but Twisted Branch reminded her of a fairy tale. Long stretches of crisp grass interspersed with massive buildings stretched out on either side of the gravel path where the UTV sat. She counted three barns. Two she remembered. The yearling barn and broodmare barn. Non-competition horses lived in the third. An outdoor arena big enough to host a show all on its own sat between the main competition barn and the house, and the lodge they'd just left could've been some millionaire's home.

But not the Pierces. Oh no. They lived in a three-story monstrosity up on the hill. A house so large it could have its own zip code. A person could get lost in a house that size. She'd done it before. Years ago.

Maverick finished strapping her case to the UTV and climbed in beside her. A chill washed down her spine and she swallowed hard to ease the sudden rush of nerves. She'd agreed to this. She could follow it through to the end. Only a few months. That's what the contract said. Once Melinda came back from maternity leave, she'd be on her own again. Back to scraping for jobs and wondering if she'd lose her lease. "Who are you riding today?"

"Roxie." He shot a look at her. "Fixin' to Rock."

"Nice. I know her." Her cheeks flushed as she realized that it might sound like she'd been following him since Maverick showed the mare. "She's a fan favorite. I'm always getting requests for more shots of the two of you."

Maverick didn't respond except to tighten his grip on the wheel.

They wound their way down a gravel drive toward a tan building with an oak brown tin roof. "Her stall is always the busiest when we're at a show. Had to get her a guard last week." Maverick grinned, crinkling the corners of his eyes. Thirty looked good on him, she realized with a pang. He wasn't the tall and gangly cowboy she remembered. He'd aged. Matured. But that smile...that smile still sent her heart into overdrive. Stupid. Stupid. She had no interest in Maverick. Even if she did, his father would never allow it. And Maverick wanted his father's respect too much to risk it for someone like her.

They arrived at the barn with a small spin of gravel spitting out beneath the tires. She jumped out and ran to the back, where she grabbed her case. "It'll take me a few minutes to set up. Any particular shots you'd like me to get?"

"Whatever you think will look best on the website." His lips pursed. "I almost hate to sell Roxie. Great horse."

"Yeah. But she's no Moonlight." She slipped easily into the cowboy banter, falling back into that place she never really left. Horses were her life. Even if she sat and watched them from behind a camera. "He's your winner."

A stunned look crossed Maverick's face. He recovered quickly and scrubbed a hand over his mouth. "Yeah. Listen, I've got to run. Landon is warming up Roxie for me. And I have a full day of practice ahead. You can come and go as you need to, just try to get as many shots as you can. Couple dozen of each practice, maybe?"

"Do you want to review them at the end of the day?" She hefted the case and lugged it toward the barn. Sunshine warmed the back of her neck and made her skin prickle.

"Aspen will do that." He threw up a hand and hurried into the barn ahead of her, his steps sending up little puffs of dust until he hit the cold concrete aisle.

Focused. The one word she'd always attributed to Maverick. At least one thing stayed the same. She stepped into the open barn and stopped in her tracks. The ceiling rose twenty or thirty feet overhead, and a long cascade of lights and fans filled the space with bright light. Soft sandy dirt sank beneath her heels the first foot or so, then nothing but pristine concrete. Twin rows of stalls marched down either side. She counted six stalls per side, each one big enough for two or three horses. A roan horse occupied one stall, but the others had their doors open and shavings leaving tiny paths where the horses had been led away. A young woman with a broom and long-handled dustpan rushed up and down the aisle, sweeping the shavings back into place. Wood gleamed with polish, the iron railings along the top of each stall and door a muted black. Gold name plates decorated each stall door. Money. The whole place screamed of money.

Not her business. She forced her feet to move past the stalls and into the arena. More stalls lined one side of the massive space, each one occupied by a horse in the process of getting tacked up. She recognized the Pierce uniform on the grooms and bit her lip.

Would Maverick make her wear a uniform too? She dared a look at her ratty t-shirt and winced. Might not be a bad idea if it saved the rest of her clothes. It wasn't in her contract, but the Pierces bought uniforms for all their employees.

The Pierce money was no concern of hers. She needed to find a Maverick-proof focus. Breathing in the deep, earthy tone of horse and leather, she found an out of the way spot near the rail where she could set up. She moved through the motions automatically, no longer having to think about the process of setting the camera on the tripod and adjusting the angle. She clicked a few test shots to check the lighting.

Maverick trotted in small circles on the far end of the arena. The dark brown mare held her head low, her hooves shuffling along in perfect rhythm. She zoomed in and shot a series of rapid-fire photos of Roxie's head. The silver conchos on her bridle contrasted with the dark hide and brought out the sheen in her coat.

Maverick sat perfect in the saddle. Reins in one hand, the other a closed fist near his side. His heels pointed down, the spurs on his boots rounded smooth. No one here used a pointed spur. They didn't need them. Everyone knew that a Pierce horse came trained to respond to a soft touch. A single roll of the spur's wheel over Roxie's side sent the horse spinning hard left.

Her mane fanned out, forelock draped over one eye in a perfect arc. She snapped another series of pictures.

"I heard you were here." Remington looped his arms over the rail beside her and thumbed his hat away from his eyes. "How's it going?"

"It's going." Nothing else she could say. "You riding today?"

He jerked his thumb over his shoulder at the lone horses in the stalls.

"Testing out that one. The black gelding on the end. They call him Locomotive. Big engine. Hard to stop once he gets going. But getting him fired up is a story all by itself." He chuckled. "Maverick sees the potential in him, even if Dad doesn't."

Movement flashed on her other side, and a woman stopped beside her. "Look what the cat dragged in." Aspen, Remington's twin, smiled widely and threw an arm over Sage's shoulders. "Girl, I have missed you something fierce. Can't believe you left me with all these boys." She pouted, then laughed, ruining the effect. "It's good to have you back."

"Can't really say that I'm back. Remy offered me a job." A job she neglected as she chatted with the twins.

"Ah." Remington waved a hand. "You're back."

"My contract expires once your other photographer comes back from maternity leave." She turned her attention to the camera. She'd not missed that little detail in the contract. Few months. That's how long this golden goose laid golden eggs. Then she headed back to the rat race. But at least she'd have the prestige of being the photographer responsible for documenting Maverick's rise through the Open Futurity this year. If he won, it would be even better for her.

Remington clicked his tongue and pointed at Maverick. "Roxie is still starting on the wrong lead. Every time. That kid does not like going right on the right lead."

Sage glanced at the horse but pulled away from the conversation. She wasn't here to worry about riding or training. It didn't matter that they all seemed happy to see her again. This place wasn't home. She didn't have a home anymore. Just a month to month lease on a place with leaky pipes, no hot water, and a stove as likely to burn the place down as cook a pot of noodles.

Maverick switched Roxie to the right lead and circled her around the arena at a lope. They passed the camera, and she held off on her next series of shots until Roxie made it to the far side where the fencing helped line up her form and show the pretty mare to her best advantage.

"We'll be packing up tomorrow." Remington gripped the top rail and leaned forward, his left foot hooked on the bottom rail. "Make sure you talk to Maverick about who you're riding with. Don't want to leave you behind."

Aspen hugged her before she knew what was happening. "You can ride with me. No way you want to ride with one of the boys. We have too much catching up to do. Violet's coming with us, but she's riding with *Remington.*" Aspen made kissing noises at her brother, who swatted his hat at her.

A breath of relief whooshed out. She couldn't imagine being trapped in the truck with Maverick for hour after hour. Talk about torture. Just the ride down to the barn set her nerves on edge. She hoped he'd stay far away from her. Being close to him hurt with a kind of gnawing ache that made her want to carve out her heart with a spoon.

Maverick rode toward the gate, and Remington backed away from them. "That's my cue." He strode away without a backward glance.

Aspen ducked around to look Sage in the eye. "Where have you been?" Her blue eyes sparked. "Twelve years, Sage. You up and left without even a goodbye. No way to track you. Nothing."

That had been the hardest part of all, leaving without a trace. "It was for the best."

Her former best friend narrowed her eyes. "Best for who? Not for me. Not for Maverick. You broke his heart."

"No." She barked out a caustic laugh. "Whatever I did, it didn't affect Maverick at all." She knew that for certain. He couldn't have cared less.

Aspen's eyebrows lowered. "You're wrong. He missed you. We all did, but Maverick?" A dark look lingered in her eyes. "He mourned like you'd died."

Her heart pinched. That couldn't be right. She'd talked to him the day she left. She'd asked him point blank what he dreamed of for his future. He'd wanted prestige and money. He didn't say one single thing about her.

"We were friends." She forced the words out. "I had to find my own way."

"No. You didn't." Aspen always pushed her to admit the truth no matter how much it hurt. She glared at Sage without remorse or a hint of backing down. "You chose to walk away from all of us. Not because you needed space or whatever other ridiculous story you told yourself. Something else happened. Something you didn't think you could tell us."

She'd never considered Aspen saw that much. Words lodged in her throat, and she pulled away from Aspen to check her camera. "It's not important now."

"Not..." Aspen made a sound that was part scoff, part laugh. "You always were too stubborn for your own good." She hugged Sage, not even bothered that she didn't return the embrace. "But you're back now. I'll find out what happened. Just you wait and see." She bounced away, her blonde ponytail slapping her back.

Leave it to Aspen to call her out like that. She wasn't too worried about her finding the truth. Only two people knew about the conversation that had sent her running away. And she knew for absolute certain that Mr. Pierce would never admit to his children that he felt threatened by a poor kid from the wrong side of the tracks.

His secret was safe with her. Just like her heart was safe from Maverick. As long as she kept her distance. He never needed to find out she'd been head over boots in love with him back then.

Three

She'd underestimated how familiar it would feel standing alongside Maverick and his siblings as they prepared to enter the arena. After a long drive with Aspen at the wheel, she'd fallen asleep in a plush hotel room and then dragged herself down to the barn before daylight to start capturing pictures.

Controlled chaos ruled the barn, the sight as comforting as breathing when men and women walked horses up and down the aisles. Some stopped at the bathing stalls for one last wash before the horse hit the arena. A low buzz of energy permeated the air alongside the blend of leather cleaner, hoof polish, and the overall smell of horse.

The whole process and sheer amount of prep work that went into these shows blew her mind.

Maverick stood in a horse's stall in front of her, his wide hands smoothing the horse's forelock between his eyes while Ross removed the braids from the stallion's mane.

"We should have a braiding competition." She held the camera to her eye and zoomed in on Ross's hands. "Not on competition day, of course. But maybe once we're back home." She winced at the word, wishing it back. Twisted Branch was not home.

Maverick's head tilted toward her, but he didn't respond except to watch Ross's fingers speed through the flaxen mane at warp speed.

Landon led his mare from the stall, her hooves striking sharply on the concrete. "I'd take that challenge." He elbowed her in passing. "But you have to join us."

No. She wasn't part of this family. Her stomach clenched and she clicked another picture to distract her mind from the sudden yearning twisting through her.

Maverick remained silent, his hands in constant motion. He wore brown chaps today, the designer label for Cowboy Corruption—one of the brands sponsoring today's competition—branded high on the left thigh. Did they sponsor the Pierces too? Or was this just another of Mr. Pierce's moments where he flashed his money around? Cowboy Corruption chaps cost thousands of dollars. She couldn't imagine forking over that amount of money for something she couldn't eat or drive.

Aspen joined Landon, her own mount still two doors down in his stall. She crossed her slim arms and leaned in close to Sage. "Maverick's nervous."

Yeah, she knew. For a quiet man, Maverick never said much, but the complete stillness in his body betrayed him. To the casual observer, it might look like confidence. Twelve years away from each other and she still recognized the worry in his brown eyes.

It wasn't her problem. She forced her body to turn away and hooked her arm through Aspen's. "Come on. I need to get shots of you and... what's your horse's name?"

"Cobalt. His registered name is Midnight Comes a Running, but I prefer Cobalt." Aspen chuckled and led the way to the stall where a coal black horse stood in the crossties. His mane hung down below his neck in a silky sheet.

"Hey, big guy." She held out her hand to the gelding and let him snuffle along her palm. His lips wiggled up her arm and he raised his head to her shoulder, then moved down to rest his forehead in the center of her chest.

She wrapped her arms around his head and cradled his jaws in one hand while her other held the camera. Cobalt sighed, his entire body relaxing.

"He's a sweetheart." She caught Aspen's eye and grinned. "How long have you had him?"

"Two years." Aspen made her way to Cobalt's side and patted his shoulder. "He'll be entered in the sale next year. Maybe at the Futurity if he performs well today. I'll be sad to see him go, but he's a great prospect. Excellent potential and a cool head."

She nodded along, hearing exactly what she expected. Twisted Branch excelled as a breeding and training facility. They took great horses and made them exceptional, then sold them for profit. A lot of profit. Not to mention the money they brought in if they won the Futurity. Even placing brought in significant cash. She cast a look over her shoulder. Was that why Maverick tensed when she mentioned riding?

Nah. That couldn't be it. The Pierce family didn't depend on him to win to bring in money.

So why did he keep standing there looking lost and alone in a sea of familiar faces? He must have felt her gaze, because he lifted his head and met her eyes. He blinked, and a slight grin broke free before worry snatched it away again.

Mr. Pierce stalked down the hallway, his long legs chewing up the distance with harsh strides. His presence cast a gloom over the entire barn. One man should not have that kind of power over emotions, but one look from him and the Pierce siblings scurried to put themselves to work. Aspen grabbed her saddle pad and slung it over Cobalt's back. "We'll be ready in half an hour."

"Good." Mr. Pierce stopped in the middle of the hallway. "Sage, are you set up in the arena?"

She backed away from Cobalt. "Not yet."

"Best get a move on." Cold laced his tone and his eyes sparked with that dark anger she knew so well. He was a hard man. Hard to please and hard to ignore. "Would hate for you mess up your first big day on the job."

Bingo. The threat landed square between her eyes.

Her spine jolted straight and she met his gaze head on. "Right. Wouldn't that be terrible." She continued stroking Cobalt's jawline, his horse scent bringing back memories she'd tried to bury for years.

He took another step, closing the distance. His presence lifted the hairs on the back of her neck. "Careful. My son brought you on for a job. That's it."

She refused to let him rattle her. After all she'd been through, that scared little girl he used to intimidate no longer shrank in his presence. "Exactly. Maverick hired me. Not you."

Aspen's head snapped in their direction, her face hidden by Cobalt's body. Her sudden stiff posture sent warning bells ringing in Sage's head.

Apologize or not? One look at Mr. Pierce's cold eyes and she lifted her chin. No. She would not apologize to him. Maverick's contract protected her, stating plainly that no one had the ability to fire her except him. She'd caught that line in her contract, and it gave her hope that things might be different this time.

Stepping back, he tugged his hat over his eyes in a move so like Maverick that her heart squeezed. "Aspen, you need to use the Grooveline tack today." He walked around Sage and moved into the stall, ripping the saddle blanket off Cobalt. "I told you that before we left the house."

"Sorry, Dad. I forgot." Aspen hurried to grab the blue and white saddle pad that he'd thrown aside and carried it to the tack room at the end of the hall. Each group had their own tack room, with enough equipment to supply an entire generation of riders.

Sage winced for her friend and finally backed away into an unobtrusive corner where she managed a few more shots before heading over to the arena. It wouldn't hurt to have another camera already set up, but her budget didn't allow that, unless she asked Maverick about her sign on bonus and used it to purchase a second camera.

Might be worth it.

A childish giggle burst from her left as a young girl in overalls and a long ponytail raced past. "Catch me, Nicky." She laughed again, her voice rising higher. Footsteps pounded down the alley coming toward Sage.

Horses lifted their heads. A few snorted and followed the activity with curious gazes.

A boy joined the chase, darting out from a nearby stall, his boots drumming a rapid staccato. He raced past Sage. "I'm going to get you, Grace."

"Kids. Stop." A man in jeans and a battered hat stepped into the aisle to cut them off. "You shouldn't be running in here."

They ignored him. Grace cut left while Nicky went right, tearing around the man before he could grab them.

Sage lowered her camera, setting it on top of the Pierce crates that housed all the halters, leads, and supplements that would be required this weekend. A quick look showed no one else following the kids, and even the man who'd tried to stop them shook his head and went back to work wiping down a bay mare in a nearby stall. His voice grumbled out a low litany of anger. Things about kids being kept under control when in a high-risk environment. He meant the horses, not the kids. If those kids kept going and stirred up the horses before they were supposed to enter the arena, there would be some almighty mad riders coming to complain. She followed the boy and girl at a distance. They banged into a stall door further ahead, then careened off to the side and hit the opposite stall.

The stall doors on this side of the barn were nothing more than woven ropes attached at the top and bottom. They were easier to move and caused less fuss than a wooden door swinging open and closed a hundred times a day.

Nicky caught Grace around the waist and they tumbled into an open door where a horse stood tied. It snorted and jerked its head up. White ringed its eyes and socked hooves shuffled a nervous pattern. Sage broke into a run.

"Ow, Nicky." Grace whined and the sounds of scuffling boots drove Sage faster.

The horse–a mare–pranced as far as her crossties would reach, lifting her hooves high and setting them down with sharp snaps that sent shavings flying.

"Easy." Sage gripped the nearest crosstie. "Kids, get to the back of the stall."

They looked up at her, eyes as wide as the mare. Their roughhousing stopped as they realized they'd fallen on the ground right behind the mare. "Uh-oh." Grace shoved a hank of brown hair from her face. "You're in so much trouble, Nicky. Mom told us to stay out of the stalls." She cowered less than a foot from the mare's rear hooves. Tears welled in her eyes.

"Come on." Sage ducked beneath the ropes, her hand sliding along the mare's side and down her hindquarters. "No crying. It's okay. We just have to get you out of here." She held out a hand. "Go to the back of the stall. Stay still until she calms down."

The mare danced away from Sage's hand, swinging her hindquarters around toward the kids.

All thoughts stopped. She tore around the mare, threw an arm around each kids' waist, and dove for the corner. Hooves struck the wall above her head with enough force to rattle the wood.

"Hey, what are you doing in there?" An angry male voice cut through the ringing in her ears.

Sage lifted her head and peeked at the kids tucked in front of her. Trembling bodies pressed tight to her stomach. "Could you walk the mare out of the stall?" Her voice came out clear but breathless.

"You shouldn't be in there." The man continued. "I could have you arrested."

Sage swallowed the anger burning in her gut and forced out a smile for the kids. "It's okay." She whispered too low for the man to hear. "You're going to be okay."

Grace nodded, her throat working in several hard swallows. "Mom's going to be mad."

"Forget Mom. Dad'll have us mucking out stalls for a month." Nicky rolled his eyes. Fear lingered in his voice, but he took Grace's hand and straightened.

They were older than she'd first thought. Probably seven or eight. Old enough to know better. "These horses are trained to deal with all sorts of stressors, but you both need to be careful, yeah?" She gave each of them a pat on the shoulder. "Come on. Let's get out of here."

Still grumbling about people not respecting the sanctity of the barn, the man clipped a lead to the mare's halter and guided her out into the aisle. "You're lucky, you know." He shot the words over his shoulder. "Blanche here is a sweetheart. But she does *not* like people coming into her stall unless I'm around." He paused while turning Blanche around. "You could have been hurt bad."

Sage ran her thumb over the black mark on the soft wood a couple inches above where she'd crouched. A shiver snaked down her spine. One second slower and she'd be standing before God Almighty right now. Wouldn't that be a hoot. She had *no* desire to meet Him just yet. *Sorry,*

Lord. Life down here might make me grumpier than a rattlesnake, but I'd like to stick around a while longer.

Nicky took Grace's hand and walked ahead of Sage. "Sorry, Mr. Masters. It's my fault. I tackled Grace and she tripped. I didn't mean to upset Blanche."

Grace sniffled and swiped her hand under her nose. "We won't do it again."

"Nicky. Grace." A man and woman jogged down the aisle. Their eyes darted from the kids, to the horse, and back. "What happened?"

Nicky and Grace fell over each other trying to explain.

Sage rubbed her shoulder where she'd banged it into the wall and moved out of the way. "Sorry for the trouble." She motioned at Blanche. "Is there anything I can do to help you calm her back down before you ride?"

They were all in the prep stage of the day, so she knew he'd not been in the arena yet.

Mr. Masters shook his head. The anger bled out of his expression and his shoulders lowered with the release of tension. "Naw. That's okay. Thanks for the offer." He ran a quick hand down Blanche's neck. "Sorry I got a little heated. This girl is my one shot at the Futurity this year."

Discomfort made her clear her throat. "I understand how important that is. I wish you the best." She resisted the urge to pat Blanche, respecting the man's space and his horse.

"They said you saved them." The man who'd approached Nicky and Grace cut in front of her. Sharp blue eyes clouded with the reality of what could have happened. "Thank you."

Their mother stepped up behind him, an arm around each of her children.

"Anyone would have done the same thing." She shrugged off the thanks as the discomfort returned. She wasn't the savior type. "Right place at the right time." She'd run like mad to be in the right place at the right time, but that part mattered about as much as the manure caked in her boot treads.

"If there's ever any way we can repay you, let us know." The man held out a business card.

Sage took it between her fingers and slipped it into her back pocket without even looking at the black script. “Sure thing.” She thumbed over her shoulder. “I have to get back to work. Be careful, you two.”

Nicky and Grace grinned and waved at her, causing her to shake her head. Kids really did bounce back from deadly situations far better than adults. She hoped the close call would give them a better appreciation for the dangers of bursting into a strange horse’s stall.

Some could argue that Mr. Masters should keep Blanche behind a real door. But that was not her problem to solve. She picked up the pace as she rounded the corner and spotted Maverick holding her camera. He looked up at the sound of her boots on the concrete. Deep frown lines marred his face and he held out the camera with a puckered frown. “You missed the interview with *Saddle Weekly*.”

“Sorry.” She opened her mouth to explain, then snapped it shut. It didn’t matter. “I’m going to set up in the arena.”

Maverick’s hand skimmed along her arm, the feeling so feather light she almost missed it. The touch nothing more than a memory. A thought. But it shook her to her core as it dredged up years of their connected past.

“I thought you’d left.” Maverick sighed. “Again.”

Her head snapped up from the camera, her eyes finding his. Was she crazy or did he look at her like the thought hurt him? “I’m not going anywhere. You hired me to do a job.”

His frown deepened. “Is that the only reason? The job?”

“What else is there?” She took the camera from him and looped the strap around her neck. People bustled up and down the aisle in a perpetual state of controlled panic. Things were about to get interesting as the rides began. Maverick and the others lived for the competition. They loved the horses, and the thrill of the ride. She smelled it in the leather and sweat that came at her from every side.

His thumb skated along her inner elbow and his fingers wrapped around her arm.

Heat skittered along her skin in a breathless rush. She longed to lean into the touch and let it take her back to how things used to be. Back before she let Mr. Pierce convince her that she didn’t belong at Twisted Branch. Before Nate ruined her career.

“You used to look just like that before you rode.” Maverick dropped his hand. "You always looked so fierce. Ready to take on the world. Ready to take anything that came at you right on the chin."

Yep. And look where that had gotten her. Right back where she started. Older. Wiser. But still poor. She'd learned a long time ago about the difference in poor and *poor.* She'd grown up the latter. The kind of poor where she worried about using too many paper towels because she didn't know if she'd have the money to buy another roll before payday. "I'm not the same person, Maverick." His name rolled off her tongue with the sweetness of first love.

He shrugged. "Who is?" His eyes crinkled as he finally smiled. "It's good to have you back, Sage. I missed you." He walked backward, tapping his index finger to his hat brim. "Maybe this time you'll stick around."

"I'd like that." She let the confession fall between them. She could tell him she'd stay only as long as the contract allowed. She resisted the lie. She'd come home to Oklahoma to lick her wounds and rebuild her life. Twisted Branch might be a stopping point on that journey, but Oklahoma was still home. She could rest here. Even after she left the ranch, she'd stick around.

A pause lingered between them. Maverick nudged the toe of his boot against the hay where he'd stopped. "Do you have everything you need for the Champions Rein Awards Gala?"

Her nose scrunched. "I'm sorry?"

A crooked smile emerged. "You're supposed to go with us to the Gala. Photograph the event for our page. And in case any of us win an award." He said it all with the kind of calm detachment he'd always shown for these black-tie events.

Meanwhile, her heart stuttered with fear and panic. "I can't go to the gala." Nope. No way. Hours at a fussy dinner with fancy plates and way too many forks. Not her idea of a fun night.

"You have to." He took a step closer but stopped when she retreated. "It's one of the events laid out in your contract."

Shock jolted through her. "I never read anything about that."

"It reads that you will attend all functions deemed necessary for the betterment of the Pierce brand. This is one of them." He gave a casual shrug like he hadn't just ripped the rug right out from under her. "I thought you knew."

"Maverick." His name felt like a curse in her mouth. "I hate the gala. I always have." He knew that.

"I'm sorry." He met her gaze without a hint of relenting. "But I need you there. If it's about the dress code, I have a stipend set up at the boutique. You can use it. It's what our other photographers did."

"Oh, well that makes it so much better." She resisted the snort but clamped her arms over her stomach as another protest built on her lips.

Could he be telling the truth? Would he use the contract to manipulate her? Her grip tightened.

Maverick gave her one last calm look before he turned on his heel and walked away.

Aspen walked past leading Cobalt. She nudged Sage in passing. "Somebody still has a crush." Her voice rose and fell in a sing-song.

"Not me." She held her hands up and backed away. This thing with Maverick definitely was *not* a crush. Not even an inkling of romantic feelings remained in her. If it tried to take root again, she'd dig it out. Burn it to the ground if she had to.

"He's right about the Gala. We always have a photographer there." Aspen's laughter followed her when she turned. "He never stopped talking about you. Once we're home and we have a break between competitions, he'll want answers. I hope you're ready to give them."

Nervous energy flooded her, and she hurried away with Aspen's warning ringing through her head. Answers. She could not give Maverick the answers he wanted. They'd been friends back then. Nothing more. Even though she'd loved him. He'd never let on she meant anything to him.

Four

He didn't have time to think about Sage. She distracted him, and distractions were dangerous. His lack of concentration in the arena and the resulting low score proved it. He'd hear it from his dad when they made it back to Twisted Branch. He wished he could reverse time. Go back to that night and find her before she left. What if? The what if drove him crazy each and every day since she took off. What if and why?

He wanted to believe that she'd come back to stay, but then reality barreled in and knocked every molecule of air from his lungs. At the first sign of trouble, Sage would disappear.

Scowling and tunneling a hand through his hair, he faced the barn aisle where the horses dozed. Night had fallen hours earlier, but sleep eluded him. The peace and comfort from the barn offered his only sense of refuge. Quiet shuffles from one stall drew him down the dim corridor.

Sage's voice trickled out, her tone soothing even as it sent his pulse skyrocketing. What was the matter with him? This was Sage. They'd been friends forever. Up until the night she took off without a goodbye. He resented her for that. She hadn't bothered to say a word that last night when they'd talked about their hopes and dreams. He'd poured his heart out to her, telling her everything about his mission to become as famous as his father. And better liked to boot. People brought their horses to his dad because he trained great horses, not because he gave off warm and fuzzy vibes.

Stopping outside the stall, out of Sage's line of sight, he closed his eyes and took a deep breath.

"That's it," she crooned, her voice lilting high, then low as she hummed. "You're okay, sweet girl."

The mare in the stall chuffed and fidgeted, her hooves shuffling the shavings around. He had better things to do than stand there and daydream about years long gone. Opening his eyes, he crossed the aisle and draped his arms over the half door. "Everything okay?"

She startled at the sound of his voice and spun around, her hand on her heart. "Don't do that." Pink flooded her cheeks and she jerked her head back around. "What are you doing out here?"

"Couldn't sleep." He locked his fingers together and tipped his head toward her. "You?"

"Same."

He waited for more, but she rolled her lips together and busied herself with fixing a braid in the mare's mane. "You didn't answer my question."

Silence. Frustration welled up and spilled over, driving him to pull the door open and step inside. "Is everything okay?"

Her frown stayed firmly in place, but she met his eyes before shifting away from him. "I heard her pacing in her stall and came to check on her." She patted the smooth back.

"We call her Mox. She's one of Colt's projects." He flashed a smile that faltered when he caught her solemn stare. "She'll be okay. It takes her a few days to settle in at a new place."

"By the time she settles, it'll be time to go back." Sage pointed out with a tap of her fingers on the mare's mane.

Right. Mox turned into Colt's problem when he took over her training.

Another horse snorted and poked its head out over the door two stalls down. The white face and blue eyes beckoned him closer.

Quiet descended on the barn. He stayed in the stall with Sage, uncertain what to say or do.

Sage ducked beneath the mare's neck and popped up beside him. "What happened in the arena today?"

"Nothing." He ground his teeth. Of course she'd noticed his lack of composure. He waited for the criticism, his muscles coiling tighter with each passing second.

Her hand skated over his, her smooth skin catching on his calloused index finger. Years of holding the reins created the rough spot that never went away.

She shifted closer, bringing her fresh from the shower floral scent to his nose. Her hair hung in damp waves around her face, and her lack of a hat gave him a clear view of her eyes when she tipped her head back to look up at him. "You're a great rider. Today's one day in a long line of days. You'll still get into the Futurity." Her confidence in him sank deep.

How long had it been since anyone talked to him like that? Had he gotten so used to disparaging remarks that he couldn't enjoy her praise? It felt wrong to feel okay with having a bad day.

"I'll never prove myself and become a million-dollar rider if I have bad days." The words rushed out in a deluge. He wanted them back the instant they passed his lips.

Her eyes shadowed and she took a step back. "Right. I forgot that's all that matters to you. Getting the title. That's what's important." She shook her head, obvious disappointment in the motion. "I remember when you were in it for the horses." She searched his face. "What happened to that guy?"

What indeed.

"He grew up." His jaw locked in a tight clench that sent an ache along his neck. "You can't run a business on hopes and dreams."

Sage snorted. "That's your dad talking. And it's my cue to say goodnight." She walked out of the stall without a backward glance. Quick strides carried her down the aisle, her boots clicking a soft cadence.

"I'm an idiot." He hurried from the stall, closing and locking the door behind him. "Sage, wait."

She stopped in the doorway leading out to the parking lot. Their hotel stood next door, one of the biggest ones available for housing during these events. He blew out a breath that emptied his lungs and scrubbed a hand over his face. "I'm sorry. I don't know what else to say. Dad may have problems."

She snorted and crossed her arms.

"But he's a great rider and businessman." He forged ahead, not understanding why he needed her to understand. "It's like when people say a man's a great surgeon, but his bedside manner is terrible."

"Yeah, but that guy saves lives." She never backed down.

He knew that, but he pushed anyway. "Dad made a name for himself in the AQHA industry. It's our obligation as his children to keep that name going."

"Doesn't mean you can't fix your bedside manner." Her head tipped to the side, and she watched him with a deep, assessing look that speared through him. "Can we not have this conversation? We're never going to agree. He's your dad. I get it."

"Get what?" Genuine confusion pulsed through him.

"That you have to defend him. That he can do no wrong. Whatever it is that has made you act like his way is the only way, when the Maverick I used to know had ideas of his own on how he wanted to live his life." She lifted her arms and let them fall to her sides with soft claps as her open palms hit her thighs. "There's more to life than winning."

"The only thing I ever wanted was to make him proud of me." The admission pained him. He should have higher aspirations in life, but after chasing this one dream for so long, it made his entire existence feel pointless if he gave it up now. How could a thirty-year-old man crave his father's blessing so much that it guided every second of every day? If he knew the answer to that, maybe he'd learn how to stop the need to please the unpleasable man.

A pained look crossed Sage's face. She lifted a hand to his cheek, cupping her palm over his stubbled beard. Her mouth opened but no words emerged. They stood in silence, breathing each other in with millions of stars as witness to the charged air rippling around them. Her thumb brushed the corner of his mouth and every thought he'd ever had about Sage roared to the surface. Once upon a time, he would have closed the distance and risked a kiss.

Before she abandoned him.

Shock jolted him back and he followed it until her hand fell away.

"The Sage I thought I knew would talk to me instead of shutting down." With nothing to gain and everything to lose, he challenged her to give him the same courtesy she'd asked of him.

Her throat convulsed and she swallowed hard. "It's not a nice story."

"Nights like this are the best time for the worst stories." He lowered his voice to a soft whisper. "We used to be friends. Can't we pick up where we left off?" Maybe then he could reconcile this Sage with the old one.

She shook her head side to side, her brown hair fanning out in the breeze. "I'm not the same person anymore. Being friends with you is like trying to hug a porcupine. It can happen, but not without some pain and scars."

Ouch. "I'm not the prickly one who's always shooting quills at people."

One eyebrow arched high. She let out a low chuckle that sang through him. "Okay. Okay. You got me there. I've been a terror this week."

"Yeah." No sense beating around the bush. He walked over to a stack of hay and sank onto the closest bale, then patted the remaining space. "Why?"

Sage rocked on her heels, her hands deep in her pockets as she stared up at the night sky. Minutes ticked past with nothing but the rustle of wind between the buildings to keep them company. A guard walked around the corner. He twitched when he spotted them. "Need to see your badges." He shuffled over, eyes dark and cold until they fished their badges out of their pockets and showed them to him. "Have a pleasant night." He ambled off with a tip of his hat.

"Glad to see the security is tight." Sage stage-whispered to him with one hand cupped around the side of her mouth. Relenting under his silence, she moved to sit beside him and let out a deep sigh. "I spent the last five years building up a professional photography portfolio. I've been all over the US, taking pictures and documenting the horse industry for some of the biggest names in the world."

Okay. That was unexpected.

She toed the ground and plucked a piece of hay from the bale. "Turns out, I should have read my contracts better." A wince tightened her features. "I let myself get swindled. Five years of work flushed down the drain because I didn't realize a single clause in my contract allowed my partner to lay claim to every photo I'd ever taken. He claimed them as his own, used my portfolio, and took over my business."

There were no words for the sudden rush of anger that turned his vision red and tightened his hands into fists. White-hot rage unfurled in his stomach and he gripped his thighs so hard his fingers popped from the pressure. "How did it happen?"

She did that one shoulder shrug thing he despised. She used it when she wanted to make it look like her response held no meaning. When, in fact, it mattered more than he cared to admit. "I loved him. I thought he loved me. We were supposed to build the business together." She let out a noise of such raw anger that it notched her chin up until she looked him square in the eye. "I let him lie to me about what he wanted out of life. That's a mistake I'll never make again."

He had no words for that. Nothing that could even come close to making things right. She deserved so much better. He started to tell her, but she held up a hand.

"I don't need your reassurance. I can handle it all by myself." Standing, she brushed hay from her jeans and turned her back on him. "I'm going to get some sleep. You should too."

He followed her across the gravel drive, the two of them stopping at the road as they waited for the crosswalk sign to light up. Maybe he couldn't change what had happened to her, but he could make sure that nothing like that ever happened again. His jaw set and he resisted the urge to put his hand at the small of her back as the walk sign flicked on and she bolted across the street.

Headlights illuminated her slight frame, sending it stretching across the road ahead of her. He'd only just gotten her back in his life, but she felt further away than ever.

What kind of friend wanted to find the little weasel who'd hurt her and make him regret every last minute of their time together?

* * *

Why had she told Maverick about Nate? A week had passed since that night in the barn. They'd both been run ragged by the show and the drive back to the ranch. Once there, she'd spent her days taking thousands of pictures and her nights editing them for the website. Aspen turned into a small tyrant when it came to getting the right shot, especially if it involved a product from a sponsor. Sage understood her fanatical obsession and had figured out Aspen's style by the third day, which helped them both breathe easier.

A bird chirped outside her window and hopped among the oak tree's thick branches. She sipped her coffee while forcing her attention back to the laptop where yesterday's photos scrolled past in slow motion.

Her doorbell rang, followed by another screen popping up on her computer. Aspen's face appeared in the ring camera and Lord help if she didn't look bright-eyed and perky for the early hour. She waved and grinned. "Hey. I wanted to stop by and see if you wanted to go to church with me."

Church? Sage slapped a hand over her mouth to keep from spewing coffee across the laptop. It wasn't even her laptop. She'd found it on her porch the day after they came back from the show, with a note in thick scrawl that she vaguely remembered as Maverick's from the few times she'd ever seen him write anything down. She traced the letters on the note, a smile teasing her lips. "There's working hard, and there's working hard because of bad equipment. Hopefully this helps."

He'd obviously seen her struggling with her old laptop and bought her a new one. She should be offended, but this one time, she accepted the gift because it benefited the business. And she'd leave it behind when she moved on.

"Hello?" Aspen sang into the doorbell camera. "Sage, are you awake?"

She tapped the button on the screen that would unlock the door and allow her to talk to Aspen. "I'm in my room. I can be ready in half an hour."

"Good." Aspen opened the door and disappeared from view. Her voice carried through the house and the camera. "I'll be in the kitchen."

Why was she doing this? She didn't go to church anymore. Sure, she talked to God from time to time, but nothing serious. Curiosity. Plain and simple curiosity. She wanted to see if anything had changed in the big ole church where she'd spent half her Sundays between the ages of ten and eighteen. The Sundays at home with her mom until Aspen pestered her into joining them. She'd enjoyed church back then. The music and preaching were always entertaining, but the friendly gatherings and chats afterward had her coming back time after time. Had anything changed?

One way to find out.

Thirty minutes later, freshly showered and dressed in her one and only maxi skirt with tiny blue flowers and matching blue shirt, she yanked on her boots and thumped down the hall to the kitchen.

Aspen met her there, holding out a bagel slathered in strawberry cream cheese and a travel mug of coffee. "Let's go." She shoved the items at Sage and snatched her keys from the counter while slinging a tiny purse over her shoulder.

The drive passed in a flurry of rapid conversation, most of it from Aspen. She filled Sage in on what had changed through the years. The church had a fire five years ago and they'd rebuilt the vestibule. She'd helped them paint and put down flooring. Even Maverick had helped.

His name sent a rush of heat to her cheeks. She tightened her grip on the travel mug and gulped the scalding hot liquid to keep from asking if he'd be there. It was none of her business.

"Dad tried to get Mom to stop going." Aspen rolled her eyes and brushed hair from her cheek. She rode with the windows down, letting the wind tear through the cab and send her hair flying in all directions. "He says it's a waste of time." Her hands tightened on the wheel.

No way she'd admit she felt the same way sometimes. She would never, ever admit to having something in common with Mr. Pierce. "But you didn't stop going?"

"Nope." She popped her lips on the P sound and grinned. "I figure as long as some of us keep going, keep praying, maybe someday he'll change his mind, you know?"

No. She didn't know. She'd never had the kind of relationship with God that she remembered Mrs. Pierce having. A soul-deep sense of belonging radiated from the older woman. She was loving and kind. The opposite of her hateful husband who looked down on Sage because she grew up poor. He acted like it would rub off on him and his family. She blocked out the other reason, desperate to keep her thoughts clear enough that she made it through the day without too much anger.

Ugh. There she went again, letting what he thought of her dictate how she felt about herself. He wasn't worth the angst. Something she tried to convince Maverick of last week. It hurt her to see Maverick so desperate for his dad's affection.

How had Mr. Pierce landed such a loving wife and kids? Talk about not deserving it. Conviction pierced her heart. She had no right to judge Mr. Pierce. Or anyone, for that matter.

The small town of Apple Creek appeared as they rounded a curve. Sage sank her teeth into her bottom lip.

Aspen wheeled into the parking lot beside a large white church building. The bell tower rose high overhead, the bell tolling in crisp rings that rolled across the land. She straightened her shoulders and pasted on a soft smile that had fooled more people than she cared to remember.

Now that the church stood in front of her, her heart raced and her palms grew damp. She'd believed in a loving God before. But then her life fell apart and she let herself slip away from that hopeful presence that had been the only calm in the raging storm of her life.

Five

Sweat trickled down the center of his back. Maverick rubbed his palms together to make sure they were dry and approached his family where they stood lined against the wall amid a group of familiar riders. The hotel's ballroom spread out around them in an array of black and white. Black tablecloths covered the tables, while white plates and crystal glasses caught the bright light from the chandeliers.

His tuxedo collar pinched the back of his neck, and his tie threatened to choke the life out of him. He resisted the urge to run his finger under the collar or loosen the button.

"Stop fidgeting." Dad glared until Maverick stilled.

Anger rolled up and blotted his vision. He wasn't a kid in need of correcting. Landon eyed them and lifted an eyebrow in a silent question. Maverick shook his head. Not now. Not in public. He forced out a smile and crossed the room to talk to a cowboy he recognized. "Scott."

They shook hands, with Scott offering a cheerful grin that made his eyes sparkle. "Maverick. Nice ride last week. I almost had you."

"I was surprised I beat you. That new mare of yours is something else." They'd been competing against each other for years, but he'd always gotten along well with Scott and several other competitors mingling with the crowd. Tonight would be a good night.

But where was Sage? He scanned the room in hopes of spotting her. Women in evening dresses and men in tuxes mixed together in a vivid display that contrasted with the drab tan walls. His sister and brothers split off from their parents and mingled with people they knew.

Men and women in sharp tuxes and black evening gowns played soft music on the nearby stage. A stage that would soon be overtaken by tonight's guest speaker before the awards ceremony began.

Two more men joined him and Scott. "Any interest in mixing it up this year?" A tall cowboy whose name Maverick couldn't remember angled a look at him. "I have a mare who's showing great promise."

The almost silent click of a camera jerked his attention to the right. He lost all hope of following the conversation as he spotted Sage in a midnight blue evening gown. She'd done something to her hair, piling it on top of her head in a nest of curls. Light makeup brought out her eyes and drew his attention to her mouth, where a hint of pink brightened her lips. She lifted the camera, her eyebrows pulling together as she concentrated and clicked.

His heart battered against the cage of his ribs, threatening to burst loose at any second. She'd always been beautiful. But this...this Sage dressed to fit his world blew him away. That realization shamed him. He shouldn't like her more now that he saw her here among his peers. How she dressed had nothing to do with the state of his heart. But the sight of her dressed up brought his initial attraction to a whole new level.

"Close your mouth, Maverick." She grinned at him over the camera. "Otherwise, your pictures are not going to help your brand at all."

The Sage he knew and loved roared up. Same snark and wit. Same cold way of staring him down like she dared him to say one word about her dress. He snapped his jaw shut at the reminder of why he stood in shoes that pinched and a tux that made him long for sunshine and hard work. Tonight focused on business. He couldn't afford any distractions. Not even Sage-shaped ones. Especially not Sage-shaped ones. His casual smile in place, he turned back to the conversation and tried to ignore Sage's presence. She floated around them, snapping several pictures before she moved away. He followed her with his gaze, not meaning to but unable to stop. She moved over to Aspen and Landon and snapped a series of shots then disappeared behind a potted plant that towered over her.

The music stopped and conversations dried up as a man stepped onto the stage. He waited until the musicians left to lean into the microphone. "Thank you all for coming tonight. We are proud to host the Champions Reining Awards Gala again this year." He held out his hand. "Everyone, please find your seats and we'll begin momentarily."

He said goodbye to Scott and the other man whose name he'd never remembered and threaded his way through the crowd to the Pierce table. They were right in the center this year, a place of honor that his dad had probably paid serious cash to acquire. His family flocked to the coveted space and settled in. A flurry of staff rushed around the room to fill the delicate crystal glasses with ice water. Another set of staff rolled out covered carts and began distributing plates of aromatic greens, steak, and golden potatoes. Not the fanciest food he'd seen here, but something they were all familiar with and enjoyed.

Remington cleared his throat beside Maverick. "Where's Sage?"

His head swiveled to take in the table once again and found every seat occupied with members of his family. Remington sat on his right, and Mom on his left. Followed by Dad, Aspen, Landon, and Colt. No empty chair for Sage?

* * *

She seethed as she took a seat on a wooden bench in the corner. Out of sight. She must've been out of her mind to think tonight would be any different. They relegated her to the sidelines. A few trainers she knew from her years following the industry joined her. Their tuxes were a little worn at the elbows and their boots were a little banged up. Her jaw worked as she attempted to tamp down the injustice scorching through her. Just because they didn't have as much money as the muckity mucks sitting out there, these men and women were pushed aside. Literally.

Meanwhile, Maverick paid her to photograph the night in all its illuminating glory with the intention of making the Pierce family look good online. They were cornerstones of the industry, and she liked all of them, with the exception of the man who'd made her life miserable.

Her foot jigged up and down, her heel tapping the floor at a blistering pace. She ground her teeth and took the photos, but then she turned and focused on the party happening behind the scenes.

"Could I take your photo?" She hefted the camera and directed the question at a man and the woman tucked in close to his side.

They sat at a little table to her left, just the two of them. Smiles lit up their faces and they laughed. "Sure." The woman leaned in close and draped her hand over the man's shoulder, bringing their faces side by side.

Sage clicked and then turned the camera around to show them the picture. "That's a perfect shot. Have you been to the Gala before?"

The man nodded. "I'm newer to the reining circuit, but we were here last year."

Patting his shoulder, the woman grinned. "He rode cutting horses before I found him and turned him into a reining guy. He's never looked back."

The two disciplines were alike but different in enough ways she appreciated the distinction. "Isn't there a cutting and reining horse championship?" Sage risked another photo of the couple, enjoying the way the light played off the sequins on the woman's dress. And the way they supported each other, smiling and living their lives their way.

The man raised his eyebrows. "Is there? Too bad I didn't bring my phone or I'd look it up."

"If there is, you have to join. We'll never be at that level, though." The woman continued with a sharp jerk of her head toward the Pierce table.

"It should be more about skill and less about the money spent," the man added. Frustration lined his face. "Although, that's me being bitter because I still can't afford to buy the horses I really want. The ride itself is skill based, as are the points we earn. But stuff like this" —he spread his hands wide— "just proves that not every rider is counted equal among his peers. We prefer to spend our money elsewhere, and we're looked down on for not paying a fortune to sit and rub elbows with the elite this one night out of the year."

She completely understood his sentiment. At the arena, anyone here could talk to another on equal footing. But not tonight. They might all be in the same room for the same reason, but there were clear lines between those with money and those without. The low anger kindling in her belly grew to an inferno. Life wasn't fair, but this, this could be fixed.

She ran her thumb along the seam of her dress where it draped across her hip in a swath of midnight. She'd picked this dress with the intention of thumbing her nose at the Pierces after buying it with her own money from a second-hand store downtown. Forget Maverick and his stipend and his fancy boutique. Why pay thousands of dollars for a dress she'd wear this one time, when it would hang in her closet as a constant reminder of the core values she'd given up? She'd come tonight because Maverick insisted and the contract held her in an obligation. That didn't mean she did everything his way. And the look in his eyes when he'd seen her for the first time made it all worthwhile. That shocked look would live on in her mind forever. Too bad it took a fancy dress to get his attention. If he couldn't like her in her busted boots and tattered hat, he didn't deserve her.

Not that it was ever an issue. Maverick would end up with someone rich. His father would see to that. One way or another.

The weight of a heavy gaze landed on her, lifting the hair on the back of her neck. She angled a look over her shoulder and caught the man in question scowling at her. He flicked his fingers in a gesture warning her to get to work.

A wolfish smile bared her teeth and she set the camera in her lap, daring him to walk over and tell her himself. If her actions didn't speak for her, the look she shot him did well enough.

His face purpled and he pointed a long finger at her.

Malice resonated in that look, and again she wondered how a woman as wonderful as Betty ended up with a tyrant like him.

Maverick shifted then, his attention scouring the room. He lingered on his dad, then followed the man's gaze to where she sat. Anger tensed his features, drawing them together in a scowl.

"It's with great honor that I present tonight's awards." The host droned on, his voice a muffled background noise blotted out by her ringing ears.

Her courage threatened to falter, but she'd given sway to this man years ago. Never again.

Maverick pushed back from the table. Men and women all around the room watched in silent interest. Forks stopped moving, some holding them aloft as curiosity drove them to follow the tall cowboy dressed to kill in his black tux and Stetson.

The man at the table beside her let out a low whistle. "That's Maverick Pierce."

Yep. None other. And he stormed toward her like his boots were on fire.

She relaxed her posture and tipped her face up to hold his gaze. She refused to jump to her feet for him or anyone else.

He slid into the empty space beside her and stretched out his long legs, crossing them at the ankle.

"What are you doing?" Curiosity drove her to ask the question pounding in time with her pulse.

He leaned into the bench seat and draped his arms on either side of the low back. "Enjoying the Gala. What about you? Having fun?"

"Oh, tons." It didn't take a rocket scientist to hear the sarcasm in her words. She cleared her throat. "Actually, I was having a wonderful conversation with..." Shoot. She'd never asked their names.

"Trent and Vicky Williamson." Trent held out his hand, and Maverick shook it without hesitation. "Pleasure, Mr. Pierce."

"Maverick, please." He returned his arm to the bench, brushing her bare arm in the process.

Delicious heat ran along her skin and burrowed deep in her heart. She ignored it as best she could, knowing he didn't mean anything by the accidental touch.

"They'll start the awards soon. Shouldn't you be with your family?" Part of her wanted him to leave. The other part—a bigger part—wished he would stay.

He twisted one of her curls around his finger, pulling it straight then letting it go so it sprung back into place. A shadow of something flickered across his face. "They don't need me. And if I win something, I can get to the stage from here."

His solid presence at her side caused a riot of emotions to light in her chest. Why had he come over? His dad shot look after piercing look at them, all of which Maverick ignored. "You're upsetting your dad," she whispered after a particularly long glare. The poor man appeared beside himself at the obvious breach in protocol. No one else gave them a second look once Maverick sat down. Mr. Pierce, however, drew several scowls from men and women alike.

"It's none of his business." Maverick's voice darkened. "I'm not a kid anymore. He has no say over my actions. Who I speak with. Or who I sit beside. If I have to be here, then I'm going to enjoy it the best I can."

And he'd chosen to sit beside her. What did that mean? Her heart and her mind went to war over the potential implications.

Six

A yawn cracked her jaw and made her eyes water. Sage scrubbed a hand over her face and laughed at the mare when she wiggled her upper lip in Sage's direction. "Yeah, Sweet Pea. You're adorable. Now stand still." She tied the palomino mare in the crossties and ran a curry comb over the golden coat. Sweet Pea nosed Sage's arm and wiggled her lip again. "I'm not giving you a treat yet."

The sun had barely risen when she forced herself out of bed and down to the riding barn—not to be confused with the professional barn—with every intention of taking Maverick up on his offer to ride. He'd given her free rein of the lower barn where the non-competitive horses lived. The barn itself didn't look like anything special at first glance with its darkened wood and high roof. But that all changed when she stepped inside and saw the updated tigerwood paneled stalls with iron railings running vertical across the upper halves of the stalls. It gave the barn an open, airy look that almost matched the prosperity in the upper barn.

Sweet Pea stole her heart right away when the mare trumpeted a greeting and stretched out her pretty head. The golden hide twitched when Sage ran her hand along the mare's spine. She repeated the motion to make sure Sweet Pea wasn't experiencing any discomfort, then resumed her brushing before moving on to picking out the mare's hooves.

"Want some company?" Maverick's deep voice snapped her body straight so fast her spine popped.

She released Sweet Pea's hoof and worked to conceal the shock radiating through her.

He stood in the open door behind her, his forearm resting against the frame and his Stetson shading his eyes. He didn't move, but his presence shrank the barn until she could barely breathe.

"What are you doing here?" Why did she sound breathless?

"You asked me that last night." He dropped his arm and moved to the first stall on the right. "Kind of obvious, isn't it? I'm going for a ride."

But...he had elite horses in the upper barn. Her question remained. What was he doing down here with the regular horses kept for casual riding?

Without another word, he led a sorrel gelding from the stall and clipped him into the crossties.

They worked in silence long enough for her heart to settle.

"Congratulations." She ended the silence on her way to the tack room to grab a saddle and bridle. He'd won two awards last night at the Gala. Both well deserved. Neither a surprise to her.

He dropped his brush into the grooming box and followed her into the tack room. "Which trail were you planning on taking?" He ignored her congratulations with all the grace of a newborn foal standing for the first time.

"Why? Are you planning on going another way?" Don't think about the alternative. Riding alongside Maverick led to trouble. She'd learned that years ago.

His dark laugh sent shivers down her spine. "No. It's so I can follow you and pester you into telling me why you were sitting on the sidelines last night."

"Good luck with that." She grabbed a saddle with Sweet Pea inscribed on the brass plate where it hung and slung the matching bridle over her shoulder. Even down here in the *cheap* barn, money showed up in the gear and the quality of the horses. "Better yet, here's your answer. I sat there because that's where I belong."

"You belong wherever you want to be." He stopped her with a hand on her arm. “Those events are a hassle for everyone. We show up because it helps the NRHA.”

“I’m not getting into this with you.” She backed away from his touch before it muddled her mind even more. “We never agreed on this before. I doubt we will now. You’ve seen how money paves the way for a lot of people in this industry. You ignore it because it doesn’t affect you. Well, it affects me.” She hefted the saddle higher on her hip and stormed out of the tack room.

His steps echoed behind her on the rough concrete. “Is that why you left before? Because of the disparity between us? Because I have money and you didn’t?”

“Still don’t.” She muttered under her breath, needing the spoken reminder but not wanting him to hear her admission. Yes, he paid her well to work for him. By the time she sent money to her sister Rosemary to help her and their mother, her bank account screamed for mercy. If not for his generosity with room and board, she’d still be living in an apartment with holes in the floor and eating rice and noodles every meal because they were cheap and filling.

Sweet Pea bobbed her head, jangling the ropes that tied her in place. Sage swung the saddle pad onto her back and followed it with the saddle. Movement from Maverick caught her eye when she ducked to grab the girth dangling on Sweet Pea’s far side.

He stood beside his horse, his arm beneath the gelding’s jaw while he stroked his other hand down the horse’s face. Soft eyes closed and the gelding leaned into Maverick’s touch. He’d always had that way with horses. A quietness that soothed them and made them want to perform for him. Confidence like his could not be bought or sold. He earned his place in the reining community because he rode amazing horses and possessed an incredible skill for bringing out the best in them. None of that was his fault, yet she continued to punish him for growing up with the proverbial silver spoon in his mouth. Her quiet sigh caused Sweet Pea to turn her head and nose Sage’s side. She finished reaching for the girth and brought it up through the buckle but didn’t tighten it all the way.

Instead, she crossed the barn to stand in front of Maverick. “I’m sorry.” Time for a little truth. It burned bitter as bile in the back of her throat, but it needed to be said. "I've always been jealous of you. All of you."

His eyebrows lifted. "Because we have money?"

"That. And because you have each other. Your dad might be a major thorn in my side, but he loves all of you." In his own weird, twisted way.

The look in his eyes said he didn't believe her. Well, she didn't care. She forced herself not to care. Getting lost in their world again set her up for another stabbing loss when she left. And she would leave.

"The happiest I've ever been is on the back of this horse." He thumped the gelding on the shoulder. "I bought him for a thousand bucks at a local auction after working all summer hauling hay for my grandpa. I rode him everywhere. Never cared that he couldn't lope to save his life. Even now, I don't care that he doesn't have a pedigree and will never win a single dollar. He's the only horse I've ever truly loved."

His words spoke of more than the horse. She hesitated, afraid to look too deep for fear of what she'd find. Now wasn't the time. It might never be the time. Too many obstacles stood between them. She held his money against him and didn't know how to stop blaming him for letting his father push her away twelve years ago.

Even though he'd never known what Mr. Pierce did to convince her to leave. She'd wanted Maverick to save her, but learned through her disappointment how to save herself. Trusting him again meant giving up part of that control and opening her heart to another potential heartbreak.

Maverick led the horse back into the stall. "I can't ride him anymore. He's too old to carry my weight, but I still come to see him. It's good to remember the amazing rides we had in the past."

Her throat constricted. "Not my past." She shook the emotion from her face. "I've never owned a horse. The only ones I've ever ridden were the ones you let me ride. There's a difference between you and me. We both might've worked hard, but you always had something to fall back on. I didn't."

"You had me."

Why did those three words rip her insides apart? Once upon a time, they might have been true. If she'd told Maverick about his dad back then, he would have done everything to protect her. Fear told her that he'd fail her, but Maverick—sweet, hard-headed Maverick—would have tried to fix the situation. He would have done it because it was the right thing to do. Not because he had any feelings for her. She knew that in her heart of hearts. But it would have pitted father against son, and he would have grown to hate her for forcing him to make that choice. She'd seen it play out in real life between her parents.

Her father resented her mother for taking him away from his parents. And his brother, the man Mr. Pierce accused her of being like, took out his anger on everyone around him.

Tears gathered and threatened to spill over. She focused on returning to the mare and removing her halter to ease the bridle into place. Sweet Pea took the bit without hesitation and held still while Sage tightened the jaw strap and moved around to cinch the girth. "I'm going out on the Old Pine trail. You can come if you want." She offered the smallest olive branch toward friendship. She'd rather keep the lines between them clear. They stood on opposite sides of a divisive line. Boss and employee. Once friends and now nothing more than acquaintances. She came here for a job. Nothing more. Maverick was not the type of man who could be ignored. He wormed his way into her life every single day with his gentle smiles and quick humor.

They were not kids anymore. They could face the hard things that life threw their way and keep going. She could use a friend like Maverick, as long as her heart understood that it would never be anything more.

She led the mare from the barn and stepped into the saddle. Her weight settled into the smooth leather like she'd never left. Even the reins felt familiar. The yard stretched out in a sheet of green grass. To her left, the main barn and the outdoor arena sat limned in hazy sunlight, with the indoor arena peeking out from the far corner of the barn. A row of crepe myrtles marched down the long drive. All the glitz and glamour of money sitting high on the hill. She reined in her jealousy and turned her attention to the horse beneath her. Sweet Pea stood quietly waiting for her command. She moved forward at a tap from Sage's heels and they set out at a slow walk.

Minutes passed before Maverick rode up alongside her on a bay mare whose coat shimmered in the sun. He held the reins in one hand, in the same position as when he competed. She eyed him, then smirked. "You won't find a challenge out here, cowboy."

"I disagree." His head dipped forward as he ducked under a pine bough, and they stepped into the quiet of the woods.

It was a different world here. Most ranches had nothing but clear land as far as the eye could see. Not the Pierces. They'd kept this one stretch of dark beauty. "I always loved coming here." She breathed in the heady dampness of moss and oak mingled with pine and cedar. So many trees mixed together in a bouquet of varying shades.

The trail angled to the right, cutting around an old pine tree that had fallen during their teen years. The split trunk lay torn open with bark littering the ground in every direction. The pine needles had disappeared, but the trees around it loaned the space a heady scent. Birds and squirrels quieted once they drew closer to the Old Pine Trail that twisted deeper into the woods until it spit them out at an old pond encircled with weeping willows.

"I miss this." Maverick's entire body relaxed. He closed his eyes and let his horse pick her way over the thin trail. "I haven't had a chance to get out and ride for fun in a while."

The reality of his life crashed over her. She picked at him for his money without ever really paying attention to the price he paid to keep it. Competition steeped in his blood. He'd been raised in the show ring, competing since his dad first put him in the saddle.

"You should get out more."

His sigh spoke volumes. "Wish I could. With the Futurity coming up, I need the practice more than ever."

"What happens if you don't win?" She realized how the question sounded as soon as it left her mouth and gripped her reins in a tight fist. "There's every chance you will, but what are the consequences for you if you lose?"

His shoulders lifted toward his ears. She hated that the question put him in such a state.

"I always wanted to win the Futurity. It's been my dream for so long I barely remember a time when I didn't think about it." His fingers worked up and down the reins, his free hand still fisted near his side like he had no choice but to sit that way after so many times in the ring. "It's all Dad talks about. The next generation of Pierces to win. Starting with me." His voice changed, growing dark. "As the oldest, it's my duty to set the bar for the others. If I don't win, then why should they bother to challenge themselves?"

"They have the same goal. Win or lose. It shouldn't have anything to do with you winning." Courage pushed her forward. "You should be allowed to compete because it's what *you* want to do. There's already pressure to win. You don't need more."

"I want him to be proud of me." Maverick spoke with the quiet brokenness of a little boy. "It's the one thing I've wanted from him my whole life. For him to look me in the eye and tell me he's proud of me. Or that I did a good job. That would work too."

She had no answer for that. His need and her reluctance to trust that her life could change mattered. They were stuck in this perpetual loop, always searching for the one thing out of reach. She could tell him his dad would never utter those words. Not without a serious change of heart. The kind that came from turning his life over to God. The elder Pierce would never relinquish that kind of control.

Maverick knew that, but he continued to hope.

How dare she shatter his dream?

Seven

What on God's green Earth had driven him to admit his deepest secret to Sage? The quiet ride through the woods loosened his tongue like the secrets of the world were free to roam without consequence.

She'd not argued with him, which he appreciated. The look on her face screamed she thought him foolish. She might not say it, but she thought it. Did he trust her instincts?

In thirty years, his dad had never, ever told him he'd done something right. Even when he did, Dad found something to improve. The first time he won a reining competition and beat his highest score, Dad told him he'd picked up the wrong lead on the lope for half a stride before catching it. If he'd fixed that, he might've gotten a perfect score.

Nothing ever pleased him.

So why did he push himself so hard for those few words?

He contemplated it through the rest of the week. It kept him awake that night after his and Sage's ride and dogged his steps through every practice. Hour after hour of practice, where he executed perfect turns and exceptional control over himself and his horse. They were ready for the Futurity. Even if he didn't win, they'd accomplished spectacular performance growth.

Mom stopped outside the stall where he tacked up Gunny—one of his three allowed horses—for the Futurity. Each one needed to be perfect, but he feared nothing when riding Gunny. He moved one of Gunny's platinum braids away from his withers and settled the saddle pad in place.

"How's he doing?" Mom's blonde bob framed her oval face in a classy look she'd kept for years. She held out her hand to Gunny and brushed the back of her knuckles between his nostrils.

He heaved the saddle into place and ducked to grab the girth. "He was great yesterday."

Gunny snorted and pawed at the concrete while tossing his head up and down. "Been throwing some attitude today."

Dad poked his head out of a stall across the aisle. "Make him work through it. No way to win on a sullen horse."

"Or with an attitude in the rider." Mom shot back with an arch of her brow. "Horses are allowed to have bad days too, Randall. They're animals, not machines. Same as humans."

How many times had he heard this argument over the years? It always ended the same.

"Don't preach at me." Dad retreated to his horse, his muttering loud enough to reach across the distance. "All that nonsense about God wanting to help us be better people. I don't have to be better. What could God give me that I don't have already?"

Some compassion? A heart? Maverick had a few choices picks if Dad ever deigned to darken God's doorway.

Mom's face pinched, her skin whitening as the color drained away. "One of these days."

He couldn't tell if the words were a warning or a prayer. Her smile slid back into place. The same smile—according to her—that won Randall Pierce over when he first heard her sing in Nashville. Back in her glory days of country music. She still had the voice of an angel, though he didn't hear her sing nearly as much anymore. Mostly on Sunday when she sang the hymns alongside him and his siblings.

"He'll figure it out." Maverick drew her in for a quick hug. "We keep praying, and one day, he'll realize what he's missing." Lord, please let it be so. His frayed nerves couldn't stand the constant agony much longer.

"I just worry he'll wait too long." She sniffed and patted his shoulders.

"Don't let his bark cut too deep, son. He loves you the only way he knows how. He doesn't show it. His father taught him never to reveal a weakness, but he wants what's best for you."

"Winning isn't the only thing that's good for us." He let the admission breathe between them. "How many times have I fought with Remington or Colt because they did better than me? Or the other way around. Competing like this drove a wedge between us for a long time until we figured out how to deal with our pride." Gunny grunted again when he tightened the girth but he followed Maverick into the closed arena and stood still while he hopped into the saddle.

Colt loped his horse in a smooth circle on the far end, his mare's nose almost brushing the ground as she moved. She had nice form and enough potential to be a contender next year.

A familiar surge of jealousy tried to roar up, and he tamped it down with a forceful breath.

Mom stayed on the other side of the fence and draped her arms over the top rail. Her keen eye raked over him, then flicked to Colt. "I thank God every day that the five of you found Him early." What might have been remorse tightened the lines around her mouth. "I wish your father had stayed in church with me. Maybe things would be different. He's a hard man."

"But he loves us," he finished for her. He locked his teeth and blew out a breath that matched Gunny's. "I know, Mom. I try to give him grace, but it's getting harder every day. There's more to life than this. I live in this arena, riding like my life depends on it." How much longer could he hold back before he let it all go? He held his own life in tight control, but the reins were slipping.

The Pierce legacy could continue without him. Dad's contacts, his ability to turn horses into cash, would ensure the family money continued and kept everyone secure.

Money. Did it always come back to that? The wedge between him and Sage, a problem he had no idea how to overcome, or why she turned it into an issue at all.

He liked her in a way that had grown stronger since her return. His chest ached when she stood beside him. All he wanted was to prove that she could trust him. He would never let her fall. He reined Gunny around and set him at a walk around the rail to get him warmed up. The stallion's head lowered, and he scuffed his hooves over the thick dirt and sand mixture.

They rode closer to Colt, who watched their approach between circles. He nodded at Maverick. "I'm bringing Lucy Belle in after this one. She's still hot-headed, so I'll wait until you're done with Gunny."

"Thanks." Maverick finished his first circle and turned Gunny, prompting him to pick up the left lead even though they held a slow walk. Gunny gave a little buck to show his annoyance. Maverick sat hard in the saddle and tightened his grip with his legs. Gunny's actions were more playful than dangerous, but he tightened his focus before Gunny tossed from the saddle in the middle of a warm-up.

He smoothed Gunny's braided mane and kept him going forward. "Come on. You're not getting rid of me that easy."

Dad shuffled up to stand beside Mom. His piercing gaze landed on Maverick. "Told you to make him work."

"I am." He forced the words through gritted teeth. He knew how to ride, and he knew his horses. Gunny's workout yesterday left him feeling fresh. Once he got through this little spell, he'd be fine.

One look at his dad and he knew he had a short amount of time to get Gunny settled before he tried to take matters into his own hands. Dad's method of training created great athletes. He'd never hurt a horse, but he also didn't like to be disobeyed and he had other ways of breaking through a horse's attitude than resorting to harsh spurs or a whip.

"It won't come to that." Maverick rolled his smooth spur along Gunny's side, setting the horse into a rapid spin that flung his braids out in a wide arc. He ignored everyone around him and focused on Gunny's needs.

The horse settled and let Maverick guide him through the routine. He did it once in order, then moved Gunny through a series of spins and loping circles that stretched his legs and gave him something to think about other than trying to anticipate Maverick's next request.

* * *

She busied herself with shots of the arena while Maverick warmed up. They'd look great on the "about us" portion of the website and she needed the distraction. The tan metal walls mixed with olive green support beams in a pleasing backdrop against the dark dirt and short wooden wall that separated the riding area from a walking path where another horizontal fence split the walking path from the bleachers lining the side where she sat. She allowed herself to admit the truth. This beautiful space called to her.

Maverick leaned forward and the palomino stallion burst into motion. They were beautiful. Sage sank onto the cold bench with her camera angled just over the bottom rail on a short tripod. Maverick and Gunny whirled in a perfect spin. She angled the shot to catch both horse and rider and clicked. She'd set up this morning to capture Colt and Flicker, and she'd done that, but now that Maverick sat atop the golden stallion everyone loved, she couldn't resist a few more minutes of uninterrupted work.

The board behind her shuddered with a groan. She snapped a look over her shoulder and found Remington perched on the bleacher. "Nice." He leaned forward and cupped his chin in his open palm. "Knew you'd pull it off."

"Just doing my job." His tiny bit of praise worked through her, allowing a crack in the thick walls she'd built around her heart. If those mild words could give her that much pleasure, no wonder Maverick craved his father's approval. The impossible man demanded perfection. Gaining words of encouragement from him had to be as good as...well, she couldn't even think of a comparison.

Remington stayed close without invading her space. "Where's Violet?"

"Working. She's finishing her rounds with Dr. Benton this year." A small smile tipped his lips. "She's a great vet." He lowered his voice. "We plan on opening our own practice once we both finish our schooling. It'll take me a little longer since I can only attend classes between competitions."

"You're leaving the ranch?" The idea clanged around as a sense of desperation took hold. "Does your dad know?"

"Not yet." Remington kept his face impassive, but his eyes hardened.

How weird to be back in this place with the people who had defined her developing years. Remington was almost like a brother to her, and the fact that they'd played endless pranks on the other Pierce siblings through the years bonded them together. The tension built to an unbearable level, so she did the only thing she could to distract him. "When's the last time you glued Colt's boots to the porch?"

His grin burst out, lightening the atmosphere. "Month ago. Dude left them outside. No way I'd pass up an opportunity like that. Never seen him that mad. Turns out, I'd picked his favorite pair." Remington's rich laugh trickled out.

Colt rode over and stopped his mare in front of them.

Sage used the moment to shoot an image almost vertical, giving the camera a chance to capture the long lines of the mare's legs and Colt's easy smile. It wasn't a picture that would draw most people's eyes, but she loved the artistry involved in finding odd angles and perspectives that many people overlooked.

"What are you two conspiring over here?" He adjusted his reins and swept a hand down the mare's neck.

Sage took another shot. "Put your hand back."

Colt raised an eyebrow. "Why?"

"Trust me." She stood and grabbed his hand, placing it on the mare's neck where she wanted it. "Now, lean forward and smile."

Colt grimaced and crossed his eyes.

"Not like that." She huffed from behind her camera. "Come on, Colt. Cooperate or I'll put slugs in your pillow again."

He shuddered. "How am I supposed to smile when you bring that up?"

"Pretend you're looking at the woman of your dreams." She shrugged. "I don't know. Surely you know how to fake a smile."

"Never had a reason to learn. Maverick is the front man for the Pierce name."

Jealousy? Her mind scrambled back through the pages and pages that filled the Pierce website. Almost all of them showed Maverick with a horse.

"Time to learn." She adjusted the focus on the camera. "Remington, give him something to smile about."

"I stole all of Maverick's remotes and hid them in the loft."

Colt snorted a laugh that brightened his brown eyes and made dimples pop in his cheeks.

She clicked a series of shots and grinned up at Colt. "Perfect."

"What's going on over here?" Mr. Pierce stomped over, his eyes shooting sparks at the three of them. "Colt, you're supposed to be practicing, not flirting with the help."

"Sage is a friend, Dad. And Flicker is done for now. I'm waiting on Maverick before I bring in Lucy Belle." Colt met his dad's cold gaze with one of his own.

A muscle popped in his jaw. "You shouldn't have to wait on him. Teach that mare to mind her manners."

"I am." Colt stayed right where he sat in the saddle. He relaxed his hands and settled his wrists on the saddle horn. "And I'll do it my way."

Teeth ground together so hard she heard the man's jaw crack. She wouldn't be surprised to see smoke pour from his ears.

"Sit up straight." Mr. Pierce continued to frown.

Colt shook his head. "Find someone else to bother. I'm busy."

Her mouth fell open with a pop. She'd never, ever expected to hear anyone talk to the older Pierce that way. From the heated glare that eclipsed his face, neither did he. His lips turned white from the pressure, but instead of arguing, he spun on his heel and stomped away.

"You shouldn't do that." Remington scratched the back of his neck. "He won't forget it."

"Good." Colt showed zero remorse. He straightened and picked up his reins. "I'm sick of it. He thinks we should fall over ourselves to do what he says." His smile turned feral. "Not me. Not anymore."

Her heart twisted hard at the fury sparking in his eyes.

Mr. Pierce was losing Colt. He couldn't see it, but she did, and if things didn't improve, she worried he'd lose them all. Except Maverick. No situation seemed dire enough to push Maverick away from this life and his father.

Maverick rode behind Colt and angled a look their way. Curiosity burned there as he took in the three of them sitting around. He'd missed the showdown, but the way he watched them said he knew something happened.

Colt turned his horse and trotted over to Maverick. The two had a short, hushed conversation that caused Maverick's body to tense.

Remington's breath rushed out behind her. "Not good." He stood and ducked between the rails, leaving Sage as nothing more than a bystander to their drama.

Eight

He didn't have time for this. He should be in the arena practicing for the Futurity. The last few weeks proved they had potential, but he didn't feel certain enough of their chances to win. The call from his siblings snapped him out of the reverie and brought him back to the billiard table.

"Come on, Mav. We're not waiting much longer." Colt pointed a pool stick at his chest and laughed the deep rumble that made more than one woman swoon through the years.

He grabbed a matching stick from the holder mounted to the wall. "Don't call me that." Ever since the new movie released, everyone thought it was hilarious to call him by the famous nickname. "Rack 'em up, Remington."

His brother slid the balls into place and eyed him over the table. "One week left. How you feeling?"

Like a miserable failure. He hid those words behind a shrug and worked on chalking the end of the pool stick. This end of the week bonding experience they'd started years ago never failed to lighten his mood, but with the weight of his entire career resting on what happened during the three week long competition, he struggled to keep his emotions from stampeding across his face and out his mouth.

"Wow." Colt slapped his back, sending him rocking forward. "Don't hold back on us or anything." His smile faltered when a heavy tread stomped down the hallway. Their dad passed the open door without even glancing their way. Colt's long sigh and shaking head made Maverick's heart clench until his vision swam.

Something had to give. Soon. They'd all tried to uphold the "respect your parents" aspect of the Bible, but at what point did that count as enabling their dad's horrible behavior? Most of their clients would have found somewhere else to go rather than put up with Randall Pierce if they saw him in his true form. But he trained the best horses.

Almost the best.

If put to the test, Maverick would put Colt's training skills above even their dad. His little brother could get a horse to do anything.

"Let it go." Remington rolled his stick between his palms.

"Let it go. Let it go." Aspen belted out the words in a high falsetto, her hands clasped beneath her chin.

Remington rolled his eyes and lined up the first shot. In one swift move, he cracked the cue ball into the stack. Balls rolled all over, but Maverick stopped watching when Colt backed away from the table.

Colt dropped onto a nearby stool and rested the stick across his lap. His close-cropped hair made his expression even more severe than usual, and all the laughter fled from his face when he looked at Remington. "I can't take much more."

Remington glanced at Maverick, then lowered his pool stick across the corner of the table.

Aspen walked around from the backside of the bar area where they stocked drinks and snacks and handed each of them a bottle of water. She hopped onto the stool next to Colt. "I'm with Colt. He's getting worse. I didn't think it was possible, but..." she shrugged and left her words hanging.

"Mom keeps saying we need to have grace. And I agree to a point." Colt twisted his bottle open but didn't drink. "I feel like we're all beating our heads against the wall."

"We can't stop." He knew deep down that Dad could change. Would he?

Colt's eyebrows snapped down as he frowned. "I never said we stop praying for him or hoping that he comes to his senses."

He'd missed the argument between Dad and Colt in the arena earlier, but he knew by the way they both stalked off that things were going south fast.

"I won't let him keep putting me down, Maverick." Colt met his gaze head on, no remorse or hesitation. "It's emotional abuse. The way he talks to us. No one should have to live with that in their head all the time."

Right. They were adults, not kids. They could fend for themselves. Still. Colt had a point. How often did he lay awake at night reliving all the terrible things he'd been told throughout the years? Too often. They were living, breathing things that lodged in his heart and told him he wasn't good enough. Would never be good enough. His thoughts ran backward to Sage and their ride.

She'd never said it, but the unspoken had been stamped on her face. Would he never hear his dad say he'd done a good job? It hurt to consider after all he'd put himself through. After all the hours of practicing and striving for those three words, that "Good job, son" that he wanted so desperately. To think it had all been a waste made him want to puke and punch something.

Remington leaned a hip against the pool table and crossed his arms. "What's the plan, then? Do we all just quit? He'll disinherit us if we walk away from the ranch."

"And money is more important than our emotions?" Aspen stood. "Is that what you're saying?" She held up her hand when Remington started to reply. "I'm not done." She might be the only girl in the bunch, but they'd all raised her to be tough and speak her mind. "You have no idea the emotional scars I carry because of the things he's said. I love him. Really, I do. He's our dad and I'd do just about anything to make him love me. But I can't keep turning myself inside out to make him happy when I know good and well it will never happen. He's never going to be happy or tell us he loves us. He'll never admit he's proud of us." She shot a meaningful look at Maverick. "Not until he gets right with God. I'm willing to lose my inheritance. I can make it on my own."

They all could. They had the skills and the Pierce name. Even if they didn't have his understanding or his blessing, the horse industry wouldn't turn away from them if they split up and started their own businesses.

Remington's arms tensed and his jaw worked side to side for a long minute. "Violet and I are leaving once we both have our degrees. We talked about opening a vet clinic nearby, but we might take a year or so off to travel."

Violet walked in and crossed to Remington's side. Her arms went around his waist and she pulled him close. "Despite all the traveling he's done for riding, Remington has never really seen the world. We can give each other that before we settle into a career."

Giving up on the ranch had never been his dream. "We always swore we'd be here forever." Exhaustion curled his shoulders and sent him sideways onto the nearest stool. "Foolish kid dreams, maybe. But we've made it this far." He spread his hands out, the right still clutching the pool stick. Failure tasted sour on the back of his throat. "We were going to make this the best horse facility in the US."

"We still can." Remington leaned forward and gripped Maverick's knee. "We're all tired and irritable. Dad gets on our nerves, especially when we're close to a competition."

Aspen made a noise in the back of her throat and stood. "I'm going for a ride." Of all of them, she preferred solitude over bonding. Maybe because she was a girl. He'd never bothered to ask. She walked away before he could bring it up this time, Violet going with her.

The four of them sat there, staring at each other, for a long minute.

"I really don't feel like playing." Colt returned his pool stick to the rack and scrubbed both hands down his face and over the back of his neck. "Let's do something else."

"We could go riding with Aspen." He straightened and rolled his shoulders back. The weight remained, but he could bear it. He'd been born to bear it. The oldest Pierce kid. They all relied on him to be the example.

Remington took the reins tonight and helped hold them so they didn't race off, scattered to the four winds. Time for him to take back the mantle of responsibility and guide them the rest of the way home.

They piled out of the lodge and jogged toward the barn. Man, it lifted his spirits to run across the dew-damp grass alongside his siblings like they used to as kids. His heart soared, the weight he'd been carrying forgotten for the moment as Colt slammed a shoulder into Remington, knocking him sideways with a loud laugh.

Light from the lower barn spilled out, cutting a swath of bright into the gloom. An owl hooted, then took flight as they encroached on its territory.

Remington shoulder-checked Colt, then the two of them came for Maverick. He dropped his weight onto his heels and anchored his boots to the ground. "Not happening."

Slow smiles crawled across his brothers' faces. They hit him from different sides, locking their arms around him and carrying him down to the ground. He hit with an oomph that drove the air from his lungs. Stars spun overhead and he pushed Remington off his chest only to have Colt replace him.

"Say Uncle." Colt's voice sounded light and free, like it did back when they were kids and the worst thing they had to worry about was getting home late from school.

Disappointing their dad. That guilt always hovered overhead. *God, will I ever escape it?*

He dug his heels into the ground and scooted backward, ripping his hat off and rolling it under his shoulder. "Get off. I'm not telling you again." The vague threat rolled off Colt. He knew he had Maverick pinned until they let him go. "Two against one, huh?" He smacked Colt's hat off his head and twisted an arm over his neck in a headlock.

Colt grunted as he faceplanted into Maverick's chest. He scrubbed his knuckles over Colt's shorn head until Colt bellowed and pinched his ribs hard enough to bruise.

"Get out of the dirt and stop goofing off." Aspen popped her head out from the barn. "I'm riding out and you're scaring the horses." She huffed and glared. "Brothers," she muttered under her breath.

"She's right." Remington rolled to his feet and pulled Colt from Maverick's grasp. "We'd better hurry if we want to ride out with her."

Still laughing and shoving each other, they ambled into the barn, where he staggered to a halt.

Sage.

Seeing her punched him in the gut, leaving him wheezing for air. She stood outside a stall, too busy tossing a saddle onto a bay mare to notice him gasping like a fish.

"I didn't know it was a party." Landon chuckled with a wiggle of his eyebrows.

Violet smirked from down the hallway and patted a black gelding on the ribs as she led him from his stall. "Good thing I got here before Colt took my favorite horse."

Sage snapped her head around, her eyes widening at him. Her mouth moved but no words came out. He'd avoided her the best he could, desperate to keep away from the distraction she caused. It wasn't her fault. He needed more dedication. Their history tangled him up inside and he couldn't afford to give it the time and attention it deserved with the Futurity riding him hard with its quick approach.

One more chance. One last attempt to win his dad's approval. Maybe even his affection. A ridiculous goal, but he'd worked at it for so long that he couldn't give up now.

He took a step back. Colt caught the motion and grabbed him by the arm. "Oh, no. You started this. You're not running away now." He stepped closer, cutting off Maverick's line of sight to Sage. A sudden seriousness twisted Colt's face into a frown. "Don't let her get away again."

Colt let go and walked away, leaving his words hanging over Maverick's head. They were a threat he'd do well to ignore.

Sage tightened her girth and moved to replace the halter with a bridle, giving him her back.

He doubled back to an Appaloosa gelding he'd ridden before and brought the horse out into the crossties.

"You want us to wait for you?" Aspen led her horse toward the door, her words carrying over her shoulder.

"No." All the Pierce brothers answered her at once. Their voices mingled together in a loud laugh.

Remington shook his head at them. "We'll catch up in a minute." He grabbed Violet around the waist and kissed her hard and fast.

Sage watched them, and he watched Sage, unable to look away from her as her cheeks pinked and she swallowed hard. Her fingers twisted in her horse's mane when she finally looked away, following Aspen outside before she swung into the saddle.

"You two need to sort this out." Landon popped around the Appaloosa and glared at Maverick.

He shook his head. "Nothing to sort out."

Landon spit out a word that would have their mother chasing him down with a bar of soap to wash out his mouth. "Don't lie to me. I know you better than that. You've been a mess since she came back."

"It's none of your business." He bit out the words. "I'm not letting anything distract me from winning the Futurity."

"Not even when your future is right there?" Landon pointed at Sage's retreating back. "Your career is not more important than love. Trust me." His eyes shadowed. Shaking his head, he stalked over to his gelding. "Forget it."

Pain lanced his chest. His brothers were hurting too, and he had no idea how to fix it. No matter how hard he tried, he couldn't fix their family.

They finished tacking up in silence and led their horses out one by one. He stuck his foot in the stirrup and swung into the saddle. The gelding lifted his head and scented the night air. Maverick did the same. Everything looked different at night. Softer but with lingering shades of danger lurking at the edges. It felt forbidden and delicious. A cool breeze brushed the back of his neck and a shudder rippled down his spine.

Feminine laughter drifted back to him and his stomach clenched. Sage. He knew her laugh. It was branded on his mind, steady and impossible to remove. He angled his horse's head in that direction and gave him a squeeze. The four of them rode into the dark, riding toward the soft lullaby of hope and peace that came with that gentle laugh.

Nine

She should have stayed home. Not home, she reminded herself fiercely. The ranch house where she lived until Melinda came back and resumed taking pictures of the Pierce family for posterity. A pang pierced her heart. She'd miss them.

Years of missing them didn't make leaving again any easier. If anything, it made it harder. She'd given up hope of being part of the family years ago.

So why was she out riding with them like no time at all had passed?

Aspen raised her hand and let it fall with a slap to her jean-clad thigh. "And just when I thought I'd made it, Maverick threw me in the horse pond." Her laughter rang out, begging them all to join in. She'd given in once already, more only tore at her heart, ripping open the wound she'd spent years patching.

Hoofbeats announced the boys riding up behind them. The four Pierce boys mingled among the three girls, Remington sidling over to ride beside Violet. Colt and Landon bookended Aspen.

Maverick lingered behind, his horse's nose in line with her stirrup. She'd have to turn to see his expression, which would give away her curiosity.

Moonlight spilled out from behind the clouds, bringing light to the night and pushing back the shadows to reveal the thin, winding trail Aspen followed. Their mingling hoofbeats created a rhythm of sorts, one that her heart met and matched.

Violet took Remington's hand. The two of them rode like that without either horse breaking stride.

What did that feel like? To have someone you trusted so implicitly. She'd never know. Her ability to trust shattered with Nate's betrayal. He was not the man to judge all men by, but she'd learned through the years that she sought out the ones certain to hurt her. Those who would abandon her in her hour of need. She'd run away from Maverick twelve years ago because she couldn't abide the thought of seeing him turn away from her when he chose his family.

He'd have protected her, but when push came to shove—as his father would've demanded—he'd have no choice. Family meant more than some ragtag girl with nothing to offer.

Talk about depressing. If she kept this up, she'd bury her own self in her thoughts.

A breeze rustled through the tall grass in the pasture to her left. The trail stretched out in front of them, a stark ribbon of tan against the grassy backdrop. Even without the moonlight, she'd know where to go. Her heart never forgot these twisted trails or the years she'd spent riding them alongside these same people.

"Do you have everything you need for the Futurity?" Maverick's voice rattled through her, the deep timbre solemn.

Aspen laughed at something her brothers said, but they'd ridden so far ahead their words were muffled.

Remington and Violet cut off to the side.

They left her alone with Maverick. The one situation they both seemed to want to avoid but found themselves constantly falling into. Lifting a shoulder, she scratched her cheek on her shirt's rough fabric. "What else do I need besides a camera and the computer?"

He set his free hand on his thigh. "We'll drive the campers and trailers to the arena. Have you been there before?"

"No."

"It's huge. Easy to get lost if you don't know where you're going. We bring enough horses that we'll have an entire barn to ourselves." He stared ahead, and the look on his face said he didn't see the night around them. He focused on winning to the point of exclusion, insuring that he missed out on everything else.

"Can we talk about something else?" She jiggled her reins when her horse slowed and started to fall behind. He caught up with a shuffling trot and she reined him back down to a walk. "I don't want to stress out about this. Not right now. We have a week. Can't we enjoy it?"

"Enjoy it?" He asked it like he'd never considered the notion.

Her horse sidled closer to Maverick's Appaloosa. Their knees bumped and another step almost tangled their stirrups together. "What happens after? Win or lose, what do you plan on doing when you come home?"

"Get ready for the next show." He rubbed the back of his neck. "I want to be a million-dollar rider. I'll never reach that goal if I slack off."

She debated her answer for a long minute, chewing on the inside of her cheek. "I always thought I obsessed over work. Out of necessity. If I don't work, I don't eat. You don't have that problem, but you work harder than anyone I've ever met."

"You make it sound like a bad thing."

"It is if you hate every minute of it. What's the point of all that work if you despise it?" She lobbed the question at him with a desperation that boiled deep inside. "You used to love riding."

"I still do." He shot back. His boots hooked deep in the stirrups, and he leaned forward a smidge. A hard breath rushed out. "I love what I do. The shows are stressful. I don't know a single rider who isn't a nervous wreck right now. This show is it, Sage. This show sets the bar for our future. All those horses I've been riding, their future in the business depends on how well I ride them."

He spoke with more passion than she'd heard in years. She didn't mention his dad. Why bother? They'd had that conversation already. No point in rehashing it all.

She sat deep in the saddle, letting the gentle motion work through her entire body one muscle at a time. Quiet conversations drifted back to them.

Aspen turned in her saddle. "Everybody okay back there?" She waited for them to wave before she continued. "We're almost to the creek. Anyone up for a race once we hit the other side?"

"Me." Sage shot Maverick a grin. "Come on, Mav. Live a little tonight. Stop obsessing over what you can't change and enjoy the moment."

Hearing the words out loud unleashed something in her that she'd held bound for years. She couldn't change the fact that she'd been driven away from Maverick. She couldn't change the fact that she'd had to scrimp and save for years while building her career. She couldn't change the fact that Nate had taken that career from her overnight.

She *could* stop living in the past and choose joy over anger. *I'm sorry, God. Sorry that I let myself drift so far away from the truth. Help me to cling tighter to You and not to the things of this world that I cannot control.* Tightening her legs around her mount, she reined him closer to Maverick.

His lips tightened into a flat line, then slowly relaxed into a smile that seared every neuron in her brain and turned her pulse into skittering wild horses in her veins.

"Let's go." He urged his horse into a trot, and they caught up with the others. Laughter burst out in a wild cascade as they rushed across the thin ribbon of water and up the small bank on the other side.

Sage kept her horse at a steady pace until they reached the second path where all the siblings lined up.

"On three." Colt held his hand in the air.

"You're not counting down." Remington pushed in close to Colt. "You cheat."

"Do not." Colt scoffed.

Violet patted Remington's shoulder. "I'll do it. On three."

She crouched in the saddle, her body poised for the burst of speed that came with quarter horses. Her mount gathered himself.

"One." Violet chanted in a soft, sing-song voice. "Two. Three."

They launched forward in a flurry of thundering hooves and whoops. Her mount shied sideways, knocking her into Maverick. He steadied her with one hand on her shoulder before they pulled ahead.

The race burned through her. She'd never won one of their races before. Tonight might not be the night either, but she could not sit back and lose on purpose. Her horse's strides lengthened, and he put on a burst of speed that carried them ahead of Maverick until they closed in on Colt. They were crammed in together, the smell of horse and midnight wrapping her up tight. Her pulse raced. Joy and excitement combined until every breath brought out more laughter.

"Around the trees and back to the creek." Aspen pointed at the copse of trees limned in moonlight and circled her hand around. She rode at the front of the pack, but Maverick pulled close, his mount in a flat run for the win. These horses might not be the ones who made flashy appearances in the arena and sold for tens or hundreds of thousands, but she loved the raw power of their strides and how each hoofbeat rattled through her chest.

She leaned closer to her horse's neck and ran her hands into his mane. "Come on. Let's show them what you can do."

They inched up Landon's side and passed him before chasing down Violet and Remington. Neither were riding to win but their mounts didn't realize that. They strained forward, grinning when Sage ran past. Maverick and Aspen were the only ones ahead of her now. The world shrank to this. Racing through the night surrounded by friends. She'd been alone for so long.

Maverick whooped and tapped his horse's sides with his heels. The sound of his joy worked through her in a heady wave. She rounded the copse of trees right behind him and asked her horse for another speed. He gave it, catapulting them past Maverick and Aspen and into the lead.

The creek came up fast. Almost too fast. She eased up on the reins but let the horse slow at his own pace. He jumped over the creek, much to her surprise and delight. She released the pent-up laughter. A moment of weightlessness held her up before they landed and wheeled around to wait on the others.

Maverick slid into a perfect stop, a wide smile wreathing his face. "Nice. Didn't know he could do that."

"Are you okay?" Aspen rose up in her stirrups. "You scared me to death."

"Obviously not since you're still sitting there. Alive. Talking and breathing." She couldn't help the snark rolling off her tongue. What a ride. "Where are we going now?"

Aspen huffed but a smile tipped her lips upward. "I'd love to keep riding, but we should go back."

Disappointment rounded her shoulders. She snapped them back and focused on getting home safely as the moon slipped behind the clouds again. She'd never really thought about the phrase "shrouded in darkness" but tonight reminded her of the phrase when she blinked and looked around. They were all shadows. There and gone again.

"Something on your mind?" Maverick settled in at her side again.

She crossed her wrists on the saddle horn and relaxed her reins. Her horse plodded along, not caring at all whether she guided him left or right. He kept his hooves on the trail. After his excitement at the creek, she'd almost expected him to show off a little. "Not a thing." She answered Maverick with an ease she hadn't felt in years. "Just enjoying the night and the reminder that no matter what, I'm a beloved child of a Heavenly Father."

They rode into the barn and dismounted. Conversations flowed, but Sage tuned them out, racking up tonight as yet another mistake. It made her want things she couldn't have. Things she'd given up a long time ago. She reiterated her prayer from earlier.

Her family needed her to help provide for them. Her sister and mother depended on her monthly payments. She couldn't risk losing this job for a hint of normalcy.

Ten

Why did he have this deep need to check on Sage? The quiet ride back to the barn should have eased his tension, but he'd been on edge since seeing her expression close off. She moved with careful, deliberate motions as she removed her horse's tack and carried it to the tack room.

He followed her, his saddle against his hip and the stirrups banging into his shins. It rattled and clanked when he heaved it on the rack alongside the dozen or so others, and she faced him at the rattle of leather. Her eyebrows arched and she fidgeted with the bridle reins, looping them in perfect circles and hanging them over the hook. Leather and spice calmed him with every breath, and he crossed the room before she ducked out the door. "What's wrong?"

"Nothing."

"Don't. Please." He wrapped a hand around her upper arm in an easy caress that he meant for comfort and not to control her. His thumb brushed over her smooth skin. "Don't lie to me. Or to yourself. I'm here to help."

"My problems are not your problems. They never were." Her chin lifted and she locked eyes with him from beneath her hat brim.

He wanted them to be his problems. The realization hit fast and hard enough to knock his breath loose. He wanted to be the one she came to when she needed help. “Sage.” Her name slipped between them with the softness of velvet. He slid his hand down her arm and set it on her hip. “You can tell me anything.”

Her immediate inhale brought them closer together. She shook her head, a tiny motion that snagged his attention when she bit her lip. “Some things are meant to be a secret.”

What was that supposed to mean? He lifted a hand to her cheek and brushed his thumb over the shadow beneath her eye. Her lips parted and he couldn’t stop himself from lowering his head and kissing her. He’d spent years wondering what it would be like, and the moment did not disappoint. This would live in his mind for eternity. It was the start of something new and beautiful. Forget trying to keep himself from her and the distraction she presented. He’d gladly let her take over his heart and everything that went along with this feeling.

She melted into him, her hands finding purchase on his shoulders. Those single pinpoints of contact burned through him. Life would never go back to before. Kissing her was the best thing he’d done in years.

She pulled away first, and he opened his eyes, enjoying the moment of watching her before her eyelashes fluttered and she lifted her gaze. “I’m not sure what you intended, but it can’t happen again.”

What? Of all the things he’d expected, that ranked last. He dropped his hands from her waist and stepped back. Rejection hurt no matter what form it took. But it was especially painful after such a tender moment that had awakened something in him.

* * *

Maverick kissed her. It should have been the best moment of her life, but all she thought about were the consequences if his father found out. She’d lose her job, and Maverick could kiss any hope of gaining his father’s approval goodbye.

But oh, how she hated the hurt in his eyes.

She took a step closer. “We work together. It’s a bad idea—”

“Sure.” He held up his hand and backed away.

Her phone buzzed from her pocket. She almost ignored the sound, but at midnight, any call meant an emergency and she fished the phone out, her heart skipping at the sight of her sister's name on the screen. "Rosemary? What's wrong?"

A heavy sigh gusted through the phone. "Thank goodness you answered. I didn't know what I was going to do if you didn't." Her younger sister had a flare for the dramatic, but she'd grown more levelheaded over the years.

Sage appreciated the change but still reined in her temper in moments like this when the old Rosemary popped up.

"It's Mom." Rosemary's footsteps echoed hollowly, like she stood in an empty room or hallway. "She's in the hospital, Sage. She's asking for you."

Her head snapped up, her eyes finding Maverick without a second's thought.

He tapped his ear, a signal that he'd heard. "Go." He mouthed the single word at her, concern etching deep lines around his eyes.

"I'll call you right back." Feeling like a horrible sister and daughter, she ended the call. "I can't leave." She'd not wanted Rosemary to hear this. "My contract says I'm to cover all events and training. I can't just go."

How would she get there? Her truck couldn't make the drive, and a plane ticket cost too much when compared to a four-hour drive. She chewed her lower lip as panic flared.

He traced his knuckle down her cheek, drying the tears she'd not realized trickled from her eyes. "Go. Don't worry about your contract. I'll take care of everything." He held out a set of keys. "Take my truck. The tank's full and there's cash hidden in a lockbox under the seat. This key opens it." He held up a silver key, then pressed the keys into her palm and curled her fingers around them. "It's your mom, Sage. Family comes first."

How could those three words be so painful? They were a double-edged sword, and he didn't even realize it. Family would always come before her in his eyes.

She had more important things to worry about than Maverick and her growing feelings for him. Nodding, she accepted the charity he offered. Not because she wanted to but because she had no choice to get back to her family. "I'll pay you back."

"No, you won't. This is part of the job package. Access to vehicles and cash when unforeseen emergencies arise."

He made it up, and she loved him a little more for trying to save her pride. "I'll be back before the Futurity." She made the promise with all her heart and prayed God would help her with the details.

"You can always bring your mom and sister here." He dropped his hands to his sides and shoved them into his pockets.

Noise from the hallway cascaded into the tack room. They were running out of time before his siblings filled the room with noise and laughter. Before they invaded the tiny bubble Maverick created when he took up all her vision and wrapped her up in a strong hug. The force of his embrace brought a few of her broken pieces back together.

A sob caught in the back of her throat.

"Do you want me to come with you?" His breath whispered over her ear, sending a tingle down her spine.

She shook her head. "I can't ask you to leave."

"I asked first," he shot back with a quiet chuckle.

Did he really mean it? He'd said family came first. Did he think of her as family? She couldn't deal with the confusion and the panic clawing at her, raking her heart into ribbons. Having him along would help one and encourage the other. "I'll be okay. I'm used to doing this by myself."

His arms tightened, then released. "Maybe someday you'll realize you don't have to. I'm not going to abandon you."

Not intentionally. She bit her cheek to keep from saying it out loud. His words echoed in the empty cavern where her heart used to live. They warmed up the dark space and threatened to punch holes in the wall she'd spent years building. "I have to go." For her own peace of mind, before she gave in to the urgent need to have Maverick by her side as she faced the unknown. She tapped Rosemary's name on her phone and brought it to her ear while smiling a goodbye at Maverick as she walked out the door.

His siblings stood around the barn, their voices expanding as they joked and laughed.

"What happened?" Rosemary barked out as soon as she answered. "Why'd you hang up on me?"

"I had to talk to Maverick about leaving." She winced even as she said his name.

Rosemary followed her sudden inhale with a screech. "You're back with Maverick? Sage Wisteria Rhett, you'd better tell me everything right now."

"You first. What happened to Mom?" She reeled in her sister's exuberance with the careful question. Their mother hadn't been well for years, but it rarely resulted in a trip to the hospital.

Rosemary sighed. "I don't know what to tell you. The doctors keep running tests but so far we don't have an answer except that her liver is toxic."

Cold rushed through Sage. She slid behind the wheel of Maverick's big 4x4 and stuck the key in the ignition. Rosemary stayed on the phone while Sage drove to her little house and grabbed a bag of clothes and her wallet. She listened with half her attention on her sister and the other half still rooted in the barn with Maverick.

Four hours and fifteen minutes later, she pulled into the hospital parking lot. The truck idled while she rested her forehead on the steering wheel. "Lord, give me strength to act in Your will." She'd prayed for her mom off and on throughout the drive, but seeing her face to face required a whole other set of skills and patience.

Prayer done and nerves skittering from the three coffees she'd drank during the drive, she eased from the truck and slid the keys into her pocket.

Rosemary bolted through the metal door, her boots peppering across the concrete in rapid-fire shots. "You made it." She grabbed Sage's arm and pulled. "Come on. The doctor is on her way in to talk to Mom. I asked her to wait for you."

"You shouldn't have waited." Caffeine and adrenaline kicked her into overdrive, and she let Rosemary haul her into the building and the nearest elevator. Sweat gathered on her brow as the doors whooshed open and the astringent smell assaulted her nose.

"This way." Rosemary pulled her hand. Brown hair escaped from her ponytail and trailed down her shoulders. They looked enough alike that people often mistook them for twins, but they couldn't be more different in personality. Rosemary barreled ahead at full steam while Sage preferred a cautious approach. Even now, she considered hanging back.

Her sister wasn't allowing that and dragged her into the tiny room with its white bed, white walls, white sheet, and their pasty, pale Mom lying still as death. The hollowness in her cheeks shocked Sage into a gasp that scorched her throat.

Rosemary shot her a look that filled her with guilt. She should have known things were bad when Rosemary's calls fell from once a week to every other week. She knew to look for the signs, but she'd hoped for more *this time*.

Her heart knew better.

"Mama?" Sage crept to the bedside and sank into the obnoxious green chair that squeaked with every move and reminded her of vomit.

Mom lifted her eyelids, the thin eyelashes fluttering to reveal her stark brown eyes. Recognition flashed and she scooted up in the bed. "Sage. You're here." A look passed between her and Rosemary. "I told you not to call her."

"Sorry." Rosemary shrugged thin shoulders. "She needed to know."

"I'm fine." Mom slapped her hand down on the bed. "I got a little carried away. Won't happen again."

Sage's heart—what was left of it—twisted hard. She cradled Mom's hand between both of hers. Words scratched and clawed at her throat. They needed to be said, but maybe not right now.

The door opened with a click and a woman in a white coat strolled in carrying a tablet and a stack of papers. "Ah, company." A warm smile lit up her face as she rolled the doctor's stool over and sat with her sneakers firmly on the floor. She settled everything in her lap and laced her fingers together on top of the stack. "I'm Dr. Watson. We need to have a serious conversation. Are you all ready?"

No. They'd never be ready. Sage forced her shoulders back and met the doctor's eyes. "We're ready." Hard was a part of life. Deal with it and move on. She'd used that motto for years and it never let her down.

Dr. Watson smiled her approval. "Great." The smile turned serious. "Mrs. Rhett, you're killing yourself."

Whoa. All three of them snapped away from the doctor's words.

She met them head on without flinching. "I've discovered through the years that truth is best spoken boldly. Your drinking is out of control. This is the third time I've seen you for alcohol poisoning in three months. That suggests an inability to drink casually and stop when necessary." She paused for a breath, or maybe to give them time to refute her claims.

Sage could do neither. Her lungs refused to move and words failed her. She'd known...had suspected alcoholism for a long, long time. But to hear the words said like they were blunt knives carving out her heart left her mind spinning.

"I'm fine." Mom tried to argue, but her hand shook when she lifted it from the bed. Her fingers curled into a tight fist. "I don't need some doctor to tell me how to live my life."

"Yes, you do." Dr. Watson kept her expression calm, but her voice hardened. "At the rate you're drinking, you'll be dead by the end of the year. Those are the facts. You can either choose to do something about it, or you can sit here and plan your funeral."

"You can't talk to me like that." Anger sparked in Mom's eyes, turning the dull brown bright for the first time in years.

Dr. Watson's smile grew wider. "I can, actually. I tried the gentle approach the last two times. You remember?" At Mom's tight-lipped expression, she reached over and patted her leg on the bed. "We laughed and talked and became good friends. The second time, I referred you to a psychiatrist and offered you some options for AA. You threw the papers in my face and stormed out. It's time you faced the reality of your actions, Mrs. Rhett. You are killing yourself one drink at a time."

Mom's lips whitened. She pressed them so hard together that they disappeared completely. A machine ticked behind her bed. Fluid trickled through the tubing and into her arm. Sage read the names on the multitude of bags but only one registered: Metadoxine. A medicine meant to help with the effects of withdrawal.

"What do you suggest?" Her voice sounded like something that crawled out of a cave. She cleared her throat and met Dr. Watson's kind but serious gaze. "What does she need to do?"

"Rehab is her best option." She leaned forward and put both her elbows on the bed. This woman cared deeply about her patient. "Ginger, you have to want this. It's hard work. Trust me, I've been through it. But you *can* do this."

Mom dashed a tear away from her eye and sniffed hard. She caught

Sage's hand, then brought Rosemary's over to rest atop the pile. "Okay. I'll give it a try."

Sage rested her forehead on her mother's wrist and prayed. Her mother needed to do more than try. *Lord, help her see that we love her and we need her.* A soft breath whispered past her lips and she lifted her head. "I love you, Mom. Rosemary and I will do everything we can to help you."

Eleven

He called himself every kind of fool for letting Sage go without him. Three days without her presence in the arena poked every last nerve until he turned into a mess of frustration. He checked his phone for the dozenth time. Nothing but the four voicemails she'd left him, each one timed perfectly with his training schedule, almost like she didn't want to talk to him. Her messages were short, terse things that made him want to race out of here and track her down. He didn't need an explanation. He needed to know she was okay, and none of the messages reassured him of that.

"Mom's going to be okay. Rosemary and I are getting her settled. I'll be back soon."

"It's going to take longer than I thought. Sorry I can't be there to shoot your ad with Saddle Guru."

"Rosemary says hi. So does Mom. She's out of the hospital."

The last one hurt him most of all. "Hey, Maverick." A long pause, followed by a sigh that cinched around him. "I'll be back tomorrow. I'm bringing Rosemary with me. Hope that's not a problem."

It wasn't. What about her mom? He remembered very little about Ginger Rhett. Except for her eyes. She always looked right through him, and through Sage, like she couldn't be bothered to notice that her daughter stood right there in front of her.

He'd called Sage back fifteen times and gotten her voicemail each time. His messages were short but sincere. He tapped her name as he stepped out of Rowdy Boy's saddle.

"Maverick. I'm pulling in now." She answered with a breathless rush.

He moved to the side door and threw it open. His blue truck rolled up the gravel drive and stopped near the corral gate.

Rosemary hopped from the passenger side and slapped a tattered straw hat on her head. She whistled, her hands on her hips, and turned a slow circle. "Things sure have changed around here. Wonder how many thousand that barn cost them."

The number popped up in his mind, and he squinted at the barn where Rosemary pointed. Several hundred thousand. His dad turned it into a pet project, saying the mare and foal barn would help them in the long run. It made good business sense, even if the price tag made his skin prickle with heat.

He made his way down the path, his boots crunching over the gravel. Sage slid from his truck and held out his keys.

"Here she is. Safe and sound. I kept track of the money I spent. I'll give it back to you out of my next paycheck." Shadows ringed her eyes and she looked past him, her gaze pained and distant.

He stopped just out of reach. "I don't care about the truck or the money. Are you okay? How's your mom? What happened?" *You didn't answer any of my messages.* That one sounded too whiny and petty to say out loud, though worry spurred him into calling so often.

Sage's hand fell to her side, the keys clanking against her jeans. "I'm fine." Her mouth puckered.

Rosemary scoffed and rolled her eyes while leaning her forearms over the back of the truck bed. "Mom's doing better than she has in a long time. If she'll stay in rehab, maybe she'll stay that way."

He'd missed that about Rosemary. She didn't believe in beating around the bush. If she thought it, she said it.

Sage made a hissing noise and smacked her palm against the side of the truck. "Rosemary."

"Sage." Rosemary hissed back with another roll of her eyes. "Come on. It's not like you can keep this a secret forever. Mom's an alcoholic. Get over it and help me help her so we can have a normal life for once."

The words, spoken in what sounded like love, knocked Sage back a step. He reached for her out of instinct when her boot hit a patch of grass and she staggered. Rosemary's confession lingered between them. It explained a lot about Sage and the history she never wanted to talk about. Warm skin met his fingertips, and he curled his hand around her elbow and tugged her closer. She didn't back away from him, but the distant expression disappeared and she gave him a look that dared him to say a word.

"I'm glad you're back." He released her arm and gave her a side hug.

Rosemary picked at a fleck of dirt on his truck. "What's a girl got to do to get some food around here?"

Sage's groan worked its way out. She covered her eyes with her hand and shook her head side to side. "Don't make me regret bringing you here."

"There's food in the lodge." He pointed at the large log building. "Your kitchen is fully stocked. I took care of that myself when I got your message you'd be back today."

"You didn't have to do that." Sage's immediate and expected response wove into the air between them. Her hand lowered. Gratitude filled her eyes with a softness he'd not seen in a long time. "Thank you."

He leaned in close and whispered, "I told you. I'm not going anywhere."

Asking for her trust was like throwing ropes at a wild horse. They might land, but that meant the fight had just gotten started. He released her and grinned at Rosemary. "You interested in a job while you're here?"

"Am I interested?" Rosemary grinned like she'd been given the best Christmas gift ever.

He'd seen that look on her face before. She darted around the truck and skidded to a stop in front of him. A slim finger pointed at his nose. "It's not just mucking stalls, is it? Not that I can't, or I mind it. But I can do more now. I have my equine massage therapy license. You could let me give your horses massages before and after practices."

She stopped for a breath, and he grinned. "You can start by helping Sage, and I'll see about getting you on the schedule for horse massages." He'd been reading up on the benefits anyway. Dad wouldn't approve.

He'd never been one for what he called "coddling" the horses, but Maverick trusted the research.

Rosemary squealed and bounced on the balls of her feet. "Thanks. You won't regret it."

Sage slid a hand down her face. She wore exhaustion as clear as the clouds rolling across the horizon in a thick mass.

"Storm's coming in." He tugged his hat lower. "I need to make sure the horses are all brought in."

"I'll help." Sage tossed her bag toward the back of the truck.

He caught it and held it out to her. "You and Rosemary head on home. You've been through a lot and could use some rest."

"That's a nice way of saying that you look awful and need to sleep." Rosemary bumped her elbow against Sage's. "Come on. Show me around so I'll know where to go."

Sage rubbed her hand down her face again. "Fine. Call me if you need help."

He wouldn't, but he nodded. She needed rest more than he needed her dragging around in the fields rounding up horses. "I'll see you both tomorrow morning." He turned away before Sage figured out a way to argue and waved down Ross. "Headed down to get the horses?"

"Yup." The old cowboy climbed into the UTV and grinned beneath a bushy mustache. "You riding along?"

He slid into the seat and grabbed hold of the metal frame. "Let's go. Those mares and foals need to get in first." They had priority over the riding horses in the lower pastures. He didn't like assigning worth based on their potential net payout, but this year's foals were next year's yearlings. And the yearlings were the bread and butter of their training operation and what made them the money to keep the ranch going. Still... "Who's bringing in the horses from the lower barn?"

Ross thumbed his mustache. "Colt and a new guy I brought on last week. The one your father asked for. Stanley."

He'd seen Stanley lurking around. Man kept to himself but seemed good with the horses. He tapped Colt's number on his phone and shouted to be heard over the sudden rumble of thunder. "You got enough people to bring in the herd?"

"Think so." His brother's voice garbled over the line. "Sage and Rosemary just showed up. They're bringing in the oldest ones first." The call ended.

His stomach dropped from more than the rut Ross bounced into. The UTVs shocks sent him flying off the seat, his head hitting the roof before he landed.

Ross eyed the sky, his brows bunched up together. "Not enough time. We need everyone up here." He pointed a gnarled finger at the clouds. "Only got a few minutes. Gonna be a wild one."

The mass of black clouds turned purple and green. Lightning raced through the clouds and crackled across the sky, lifting the hairs on his arms. A streak split the world in half and a boom of thunder sent horses in the pens around the lower barn scrambling with wild whinnies and snorts. Several of them reared and bucked, then they ran, the whole herd racing for the barn at top speed.

Colt stood near the door, his hand cupped around his mouth as he shouted. Wind tore his voice away, but the horses ran at him without slowing.

Ross stopped the UTV and Maverick jumped out to open the gate. His fingers flew over the phone as he called in everyone over the emergency alert system he'd had installed years ago.

Another crack of thunder shook the ground and he yanked open the gate for Ross. "I'll start on the west side. You get the east. Everyone is on their way."

His mom and sister bolted from the lodge, their racing feet heading toward the mares and foals panicking in their small fences.

"Please, Lord. Don't let anyone get hurt." His breath stuttered in and out in ragged gasps as he fought down the fear and adrenaline. "Don't let us lose anyone. Or one of the horses." Not even one of the little old ones that were only there for recreation and entertainment and cost more than they were worth keeping. His dad's words floated around inside his head. He understood the business aspect of that thought, but he loved the horses. Each and every one of them. They were all important.

He caught the halter on the black mare closest to him and led her into the barn. They never should have been turned out today with the threat of the storm looming over them. He usually kept a better eye on the weather and the turnout schedule. Sage's absence distracted him. His fault, not hers. Annoyance growled in the pit of his stomach. He had no one to blame but himself. Sage being there or not being there had no bearing on his abilities. He might not like worrying over her but having her in his life made it worth every worry and distraction.

He had to keep a better hold on himself, so his distraction didn't cause anyone else trouble.

The mare let him walk her into her stall and chuffed at him when he closed and locked the door. He barely spared her a glance before racing back out for the next one. They led them in one by one, passing each other in the field. The foals were too small to risk one of them getting trampled by having the mares too close together, so he and Ross staggered their arrivals.

Ross raced past with a mare and foal. "Three more. Betty and Aspen got the other two."

He tapped his hat, showing he'd heard and trotted outside as the first raindrops pelted him. They slammed into his face and hands like tiny missiles, stinging where they landed. He hunched his shoulders against the assault and ran for the mare and foal in the last pen furthest from the barn.

His mom and sister passed him but didn't stop for pleasantries. Wind gusted across the pasture, laying the grass flat and sending the weathervane careening around in a screeching circle. By the time he brought in the last mare and latched her stall, his boots squished with every step, spilling water onto the concrete aisle. He stopped outside the stall and put his hands on his knees. Every breath he hauled in scraped his throat raw.

"What about the others?" He sluiced water from his face and twisted more from the tail of his shirt.

Aspen shot a look at the gray sky. "We've not heard anything."

"What?" He snatched up his phone and called Colt. "Are all the horses in?"

"All but one." Colt shouted as thunder continued to rumble.

Lightning split the sky with a bolt so bright it left him seeing sparkles when he blinked. He peered through the sheets of rain, but the barn disappeared in the deluge. "Who's missing?"

"...boy....Sage." The phone line crackled and then beeped.

He crushed the phone in his hand. What good was the ridiculous device if it failed him when he needed it most? With a look heavenward and a prayer for swift feet and safety, he bolted into the rain. Slick gravels and soft turf sent him crashing onto his backside. He slid several feet down the hill, his body picking up speed and mud that covered his back before he regained his footing.

Mom's fear carried on the wind, her words lost to the storm. He didn't—couldn't—stop. He'd heard Colt say Sage's name. Nothing else mattered. He slammed into the closed barn door with both hands, gripped the edge, and peeled it open enough to slip inside.

Colt jumped up from where he sat on a hay bale with his phone to his ear. He raised his eyebrows at Maverick. "Okay. That's fine. Stay there and we'll come get you soon as the weather clears."

"What? What's happened?" Sage. He knew it in his bones, in the way Colt looked at him with sad eyes and pinched lips.

"Sage. Stay. There." He enunciated each word, shouting between claps of thunder. His brother held out a hand, palm up, like Maverick was one of the yearlings about to bolt and took the phone from his ear. "She's fine."

"Colt." His tone said everything his lack of words left out. Fear so pungent he tasted it ran up the back of his throat and threatened to choke him.

"Sage fell while bringing in Boycott. She's okay. Rosemary is with her, but they can't get back to the barn in this storm. They're down by the creek, in a little shelter made by some fallen trees. They're going to stay there until it's over." Colt grabbed his sleeve. "She's okay."

Then why couldn't he breathe? Why did every fiber in his body scream at him to go to her? She'd gotten trapped, maybe even hurt, saving his horse. Sage would lie through her teeth if it meant keeping them safe even if she suffered. "Who did you talk to? Sage or Rosemary?"

Brow furrowed, Colt twisted his phone in his hand. "Sage."

That did it. He brushed past Colt and ran to the far end of the barn. "I'm going to get her."

"Maverick, the storm's right on top of us. You can't go out there." Colt grabbed him by the collar and pulled him backward. "What are you going to do once you get there? You can't drag them out in this. You'd be stuck right there with them."

“Exactly.” He’d be *with her.* It beat this. It beat standing here like a knot on a log not knowing and unable to help. A snarl grabbed him by the throat, and he ripped his shirt out of Colt’s hands. “Close the door behind me.”

“I’m coming with you.”

“No.” Maverick pushed Colt back, but his brother held his ground.

Colt braced against the wind and dragged the door open. “Fight me or fight the storm. You can’t beat us both.”

Lord save them all from their intense, stubborn pride. He ran alongside Colt, their steps in perfect synchrony. Water sprayed up with every step, and the water in his boots ensured he’d have blisters by the time they made it back. Worth it.

An unholy sound tore through the heavens. Leaves ripped loose from trees and slapped him in the chest. Rain so thick it could drown a man ran down his face and into his gaping mouth. The tree line appeared in a flash of lightning and he diverted his course to intercept the path leading to the shelter Sage mentioned. He knew the spot, but they’d have trouble finding it in this rain.

As quick as it all started, the rain lessened. He almost didn’t notice at first when he stopped squinting to peer through the downpour.

The domed shelter stood down the creek, five fallen trees crossed over each other in a crisscross pattern that created the perfect hollow space.

Boycott—the gelding he’d brought out to show Sage that first night they rode together—nickered when he turned and saw them.

Rosemary and Sage stepped out, hands on their hats to keep them from blowing away. Lightning flashed, highlighting the shock in Sage’s face when she spotted him. “What are you doing?”

Words failed him even as he scooped her into a hug that made her squeak a protest. “I had to make sure you were okay.” It sounded foolish now that he looked back on the whole situation. He usually reacted better under stress.

The thought of Sage down here, possibly hurt, shut down every thought but one.

“Oh, Maverick.” She set her chin on his shoulder, her arms winding tight around his neck. “You didn’t have to do that. I’m fine.” The last word hitched higher and her arms tightened. Her voice was the sweetest thing he'd ever heard. "Thanks for coming."

"Always." He meant it. No matter what the situation or the need. Having her in his arms felt right. Natural. They belonged together like this. One shift of his head and he could kiss her again. Except...she didn't want that. How did he reconcile these feelings of longing now that they'd been let loose and left to wander?

Twelve

What was she going to do with these new feelings for Maverick? Not new, exactly, but deeper. Stronger. They wore her out and buoyed her spirit all at the same time. The panic she'd seen in his eyes warmed her even as she wanted to shout at him that his safety mattered more than hers. Fear clamped tight, the great motivator, and it rampaged through her for the rest of the night.

Long after the storm passed and they'd checked each and every horse on the property, she fought down the rush of fear. Fear of what, exactly, eluded her.

Losing Maverick was always a possibility. Once Melinda came back, she'd have no choice but to leave. A headache throbbed at her temples and pushed her up from the bed.

Soft carpeting muffled her steps until she reached the kitchen where the hardwood turned cool beneath her bare feet.

A light flicked on, bathing the room in a warm glow and catching Sage by surprise. She yelped and grasped her throat. "Rosemary. Don't scare me like that."

Rosemary leaned a hip against the marble counter and tucked one arm across her stomach with a shrug. "Sorry. Didn't know what else to do."

She blew gently on a steaming cup of what smelled like chamomile tea. "You want some?"

She sank into the closest chair and cradled her head in her hands. "Sure."

"You look awful." Rosemary moved around the kitchen, already comfortable in the new space. She'd always adjusted faster than Sage. Liquid splashed into a cup and the chamomile scent strengthened.

The comment didn't deserve an answer. Instead, she rolled her head to the side and peered over at Rosemary when she lowered herself into the chair across from her.

"I can't believe you." Rosemary sipped her tea.

Sage pressed her fingertips into her forehead and stared into her cup. "About what?"

"You're going to let Maverick get away again." Rosemary kept her voice quiet, but the words punched through the kitchen and straight into her heart.

"What are you talking about?" She knew. Oh, how she knew. Rosemary had been furious with her twelve years ago when she allowed Mr. Pierce to run her off. She'd done everything possible to try and convince Sage to come back. Even threatened to call Maverick and tell him herself what the man had said to Sage. But in the end, she gave in to Sage's pleas and let it go. Or so she'd thought.

Rosemary gripped Sage's arm with both hands, pulling her down to look her in the eye. "You've loved him as long as I can remember. That whole thing with Nate aside." She spat out his name, her lips twisting to the side. "Why won't you accept that he loves you too?"

"Because he doesn't. He can't." Because if he did, then everything she'd gone through when she left—all the agony of losing him—would have been pointless.

Rosemary's eyes softened even as she massaged Sage's arm. "You're wrong. He can. And he does. Didn't you see the way he looked at you today? He came for you, Sage. That man ran through the middle of the biggest storm I've ever seen in my life to see if you were okay."

"He thought I needed rescuing." She wanted the words to come out harsh and bitter, but a tinge of warmth bloomed in them. "I can take care of myself."

"Yes." Rosemary agreed with a grin. "But that doesn't mean you push aside a man as good as Maverick because he cares enough to want to be there for you. You *can* do everything alone. Doesn't mean you're weak if you let someone shoulder part of the load. You let God help, right?"

Sage raised her cup and took a sip to keep from answering.

"What's the difference? Other than the obvious." Rosemary plowed ahead, grinding Sage's silent objections into dust. "Nate hurt you and you've always had trust issues. But Maverick isn't Nate. He couldn't be Nate if he tried."

True. The pain intensified and she lowered her head to the table. "It's too late and I'm too tired to think about this right now. We leave for the Futurity in three days."

"Three weeks of nothing but cowboys, cowgirls, horses, and dirt." Rosemary chuckled. "I can't wait."

Three weeks photographing Maverick and his siblings as they competed for the coveted title and prestige that came with the challenge. Her heart lodged in her throat. Maverick was a few good rides away from winning the challenge of his dreams and hitting that million-dollar earnings milestone at the same time.

She'd thought there would be more time with Maverick. Now that her contract was ending, she found she didn't want to leave. Twisted Branch felt more like home than anyplace she'd ever lived. Her heart lived here, among the horses and the creek and the twisted trees that gave the ranch its name.

"Once the Futurity is over, we'll be leaving." Sage forced her head up and finished her tea. "Maverick might think he wants me here, but his father will never let us stay." The truth of it all came crashing down on her, bringing a level of exhaustion that threatened to knock her to her knees.

Rosemary stood. "You should tell him the truth. Tell him why you really left and let him deal with it."

"No." She barked out the word, her hands fisting at her sides. "I won't ask him to choose."

"It might not come to that." Her sister's eternal optimism bubbled up.

Sage refused to let it touch her. Rosemary could think sunshine and rainbows even on the worst day of her life. She'd found a way to deal with all their drama and keep a smile in place. Not Sage. She dealt with the hard truth the only way she knew how. She turned and walked away.

Leave first before they leave you.

* * *

Three days later, she helped Maverick unload the horses and lead them to their stalls. The barn was a hive of activity as owners, grooms, and riders led horse after horse inside.

"You really need eighteen horses here?" She eyed the mare she led, a golden palomino with a flaxen mane that hung well past the mare's neck even when braided.

Maverick walked at her side, a sorrel mare at the end of his lead. "Three horses each. Plus a few extras that are available for the sale. We almost brought more but I thought the exclusivity of only having a few for sale might drive up interest."

Everywhere she looked, she saw dollar signs. Horses raised and trained to compete at these high levels were worth their weight in gold. Once they proved themselves in the arena, Maverick would more than double his investment.

She dodged around a pile of manure and snapped at Maverick when he laughed. "What? These are new boots." Her first pair in six years.

Delight shone in his eyes and he shook his head. "Nothing. I'm glad you like your boots."

Yeah, well. He'd been the one to make her realize she could afford to buy herself boots now. And her old pair officially bit the dust after the storm. She'd gotten up the next morning, shoved her feet into them, and both soles peeled right off. "When will Melinda come back?"

Maverick focused on the last two empty stalls. His voice carried over to her in an almost apologetic tone. "Next month. But there's something I want to talk to you about."

A flutter buzzed through her stomach. Ugh. Feelings and emotions were not what she needed today. Ignoring the constant needling in her skin, she led the mare into the stall and unclipped the lead. "What?"

"Can yo—"

"Hey, Mav. We need you at the trailers." Colt jogged over, sweat dripping down his face despite the cool air. Deep lines creased his forehead. "Sunshine Girl won't leave the trailer."

"What?" Maverick stopped long enough to remove his horse's halter before he followed Colt down the long corridor and back into the sunshine.

They'd experienced cooler temperatures since the storm. Wouldn't be long before snow covered the ground and temperatures dropped for the winter.

She followed at a slower pace to better enjoy the brisk atmosphere and constant activity. They didn't need her, but curiosity drove her closer. Sunshine Girl, one of Colt's rides for the championship, huddled at the back of the trailer with her head down low and her legs locked.

"Get Remington. And Violet if she's nearby." Maverick barked the order.

He held his emotions in check, but she read the panic in his wide eyes and the rigid set of his shoulders.

She took off at a jog, calling for Remington with every footfall.

"I'm calling him." Rosemary panted beside her.

Where had her sister come from? She'd been so focused on Maverick that the rest of the world disappeared. That needed to stop. Now. A phone rang nearby, and Remington stepped out of a stall, raising the phone to his ear at the same time Sage waved. "Remington, they need you at the trailers."

He snapped a look over his shoulder and Violet emerged from the stall. "What's going on?"

"Come on." She spun on her heel and hurried back the way they'd come.

People filtered out of the surrounding barns, each of them going about their lives as they prepared for the upcoming three-week competition.

Sage's nerves fluttered for Maverick. He wanted to win, but so did every single rider here. She led Remington and Violet to the trailer and stood back while Maverick explained the situation.

"Might be colic." Remington deferred to Violet, who plucked her stethoscope from around her neck and held it to the mare's stomach.

Her brow furrowed as she listened. “Once I’m done, get her to the barn if you can. Keep her moving.” Violet ran her hands over the mare and moved to the other side for another listen.

Maverick’s grip on the rope tightened until his knuckles stood out in stark relief against his skin. A muscle leaped in his jaw. “Colt won’t be able to ride her.” Defeat dragged his voice to a rough rasp. When he met Violet’s sad headshake with a sigh, Sage climbed into the trailer beside him. The urge to hug him roared up and brought her arms around his waist before she thought better of it.

His arm looped over her shoulders and he pulled her tight to his side. “She’ll be okay, though, right?”

Violet’s attention remained on the mare. “I think it’s colic. And we caught it early. I don’t see why she won’t recover. But no. Colt won’t be riding her. Not this year.”

“You still have next year.” Sage rubbed a hand up and down his spine while meeting Colt’s gaze. Hard muscle stood out beneath her fingertips, the tension in his body drawing him straight as an arrow.

Colt stood at the mare’s head. “I don’t care about winning. Help her and we’ll go from there.”

“Right. Next year.” Maverick said it like a prayer and pain raced across his face. It disappeared in a blink and he rubbed his hand in the center of the mare’s forehead and down over her muzzle. “Come on. Let’s get you inside.” The mare shuffled forward at the click of his tongue.

Sage let go of Maverick and stood back with Violet while horse and man stepped into the sunshine. The mare’s golden coat gleamed with love and care, but even that couldn’t hide the dull way she walked or the heavy breaths that billowed with every step.

Rosemary waited for Sage at the barn door. Concern wrinkled her eyebrows, and her crossed arms offered a warning. “Mom called.”

Sage’s stomach nosedived straight through the floor and kept going. Pain battered her ribcage. Pain that echoed through her heart and pressed into the back of her throat. “How is she?”

“She sounded good. Wanted to talk to you, but I knew you’d say no.” Her sister’s glare could light water on fire. “How long are you going to blame her?”

"As long as I want." She shot the words at Rosemary with a sense of desperation. They fell flat before causing any real damage.

Rosemary dropped her arms and stared past Sage. "I don't blame you for taking off and staying gone. It's what you needed." She chewed on the end of her thumbnail for a long minute, and Sage let the words sink in. "Mom made some bad choices. Choices she regrets and tries to bury with her drinking. I'm not defending her." Rosemary held her hand out, palm up, to stop Sage from arguing. "I'm asking you to understand that she knows she's not perfect and she's sorry that she ruined your life."

"She didn't ruin my life." The words jumped from her heart to her mouth. They were honest. More honest than she'd been with herself in a long time. "She really thinks I blame her?"

Rosemary lifted one shoulder and let it fall. "You just admitted that you did. Maybe not for all of it, but for some things."

Yeah, okay. Fair enough. "I wanted her to choose me. To choose us over the alcohol." Memories of their childhood flickered through her mind. Moments Mom missed because she couldn't be bothered to put down the drink long enough to come see her daughters. School plays and basketball games. Riding lessons and competitions. Maverick's mother had been there more than her own, and that hurt even now. "She abandoned us."

Rosemary stepped backward and sank onto one of the many chairs that lined the barn. Emotions flickered across her face like pages in a book being flipped at high speed.

Voices mingled with the sounds of over a dozen horses. Tack jangled from the practice arena when a woman jumped into the saddle and started a practice run on a pure white mare. Sage focused on the pair and let her emotions carry her away. How different would her life be if she'd had a single parent who cared about her wellbeing? *Ugh. Get over it, Sage. What does it matter now?*

"I'll talk to Mom next time." She dropped into a matching chair beside Rosemary and crossed her legs. "You're a better daughter than me. You stuck it out all these years without complaining."

"Oh, I complained." Rosemary's dry laugh barked out. "Just never to you. You didn't want to hear it, and I was afraid if I said too much, you'd come home and then you'd really resent me and Mom."

"Good grief. Am I really that terrible?" She thought she'd done her best, but obviously, she had a long, long way to go.

Rosemary bumped her shoulder. "You're not terrible. You just got pushed into being an adult too soon. Too much responsibility."

Maverick stepped out of Sunshine's stall. His hat sat askew and the tight lines on his shoulders and hands on his hips betrayed his mounting concern. Hay dusted his knees, and he paced up and down the aisle until his dad cut in front of him.

"Uh-oh." Rosemary glared at Randall. "How did a man like that build the Pierce empire?"

The question knocked Sage back and scrambled her thoughts. How indeed. The haughty expression made Sage snarl and she slid from the chair.

Maverick stood toe to toe with his father, and the cold look that passed between them set her teeth on edge.

Randall pointed at the stall. "I warned you not to let her get too comfortable. She should have been ridden yesterday when we stopped."

"She's my responsibility. I've already spoken with her owners. We all decided that she needed the extra day of rest after being ridden every day last week. That's not what caused her to colic." Even with his voice pitched low and the general noise in the barn, Maverick's anger rippled through the air.

She hated this tension between them, the menace Randall Pierce represented to his children. He'd trained some of the best reining horses in the world, but that did not excuse his horrible personality and controlling tendencies.

Her hands clenched so hard they shook.

Remington and Colt took up matching stances on either side of Maverick. The three brothers created a barricade that blocked their father from the stall and the matching crossed arms and iron jaws created a family resemblance of stubbornness. It was the only thing any of them took from Randall, though it might have come from their mother even more so. The woman deserved sainthood for sticking things out this long and raising five amazing children despite her husband.

Cold fingers wrapped around her wrist and pulled her back. "Don't get involved. He's not worth it."

Rosemary's voice snapped Sage back and she realized she'd been walking toward the confrontation with every intention of telling Randall Pierce exactly what she thought of him. Randall Pierce might not be worth it...but Maverick was.

As though he felt her eyes on him, Maverick shifted toward her. The cold flatness transformed to a delicious heat that warmed the tangled knot in her belly and sent tingles of awareness jumping through her nerves. He dipped his head in silent acknowledgement, like he knew what she'd intended to do and appreciated the gesture. He had the situation under control. They all did. The realization zapped the energy from the moment.

Maverick did not need her help. Or her interference. He welcomed her back into his life and at the ranch, but he didn't *need* her.

Thirteen

Sage nestled her camera in her lap and checked the settings one last time as the rider loped a left-sided circle. Her pulse thrummed in her veins and caused her hands to shake so bad she almost dropped the camera.

Rosemary took mercy on her and pried the device from her hands, grinning all the while. "Sage and Maverick, sitting i—"

"Stop." Heat flashed into her cheeks and sizzled hotter than a fried egg in an iron skillet.

Rosemary rolled her lips together, but her shoulders shook as her laughter continued. The girl couldn't be serious about anything. Sage took the time to look hard at her sister. Purple shadows darkened Rosemary's eyes and when she lifted her head, a haunted look passed over her face. She shifted away from Sage as though to hide the truth and brightened her smile. "Mama Betty at three o'clock."

The sweet smell of Betty's floral perfume announced her approach ten seconds before she sat beside Sage and folded her hands in her lap. "Mercy but I still get all tangled up inside watching my kids ride." She patted her knees and knotted her fingers so tight the tips turned cherry red. "You'd think they were doing rodeo or something the way my heart's racing." She still spoke with the Nashville twang of her youth but the words were soft and pleasant, a reminder of years gone by.

Sage tried to speak but words failed her. What was she supposed to say, that this didn't matter? It did. Lord but it mattered so much to Maverick. Her heart ached for him. He wanted to win so bad that it seemed nothing else mattered to him. Her least of all.

That wasn't fair, and her heart knew it, but she had to make herself believe or she'd fall right back into that old place where she gave too much of herself and risked losing it all.

"You're ready." Rosemary squeezed Sage's knee. "I'm going down a few levels. I'll record video."

A grimace twisted her lips at the reminder of Rosemary's additional task to record every Pierce who rode into the ring. Part of her felt threatened. Maverick wanted video. Big deal. He'd watch it, obsess over it, until he found every single flaw in his performance. It wasn't a reflection on her work. She repeated it in her head while snapping a picture of Maverick riding into the arena.

Betty sucked in a sharp breath and planted her boots on the riser below her. "Help him, Lord."

The almost silent prayer reached Sage and burrowed deep inside. Silence fell over the arena as Maverick asked Roxie for a sliding stop. Dirt sprayed as the mare locked her hindquarters and skidded. Her front hooves pulled her along several steps and she sat down so low her legs disappeared beneath her. Her coat shone copper bright, the long black mane and tail hanging in perfect waves. Light flashed on the silver conchos that decorated the saddle and bridle when Maverick asked for a spin, and Roxie responded with a whirl that spun her mane out in an arc. She loved the concentration on Maverick's face. And Roxie. The mare knew her job and loved every moment of attention from the crowd. Her ears swiveled to catch Maverick's low voice. Sage continued to click and even zoomed in once on Maverick to capture the moment he grinned down at Roxie.

Betty's whispered prayers continued all the way through Maverick's ride. From Sage's perspective, he'd been perfect, but the judges would find something different. No one received a perfect score at this level.

Maverick thumped Roxie's neck on their way out of the arena, and his smile said he knew they'd done well. Sage snapped one last picture and sat back to wait for Colt, who would ride in half an hour.

Betty exhaled loud and long, then grinned at Sage while bumping her shoulder. “One down.”

“Four to go.” Sage reminded her with a chuckle.

“It never gets easier.” Betty rocked back on the bleacher and propped her elbows behind her. “Thought it would. Never does.”

An easy silence sat between them, the kind Sage had grown familiar with and even craved, thanks to the years sitting at events alongside Betty.

“How come you stopped riding?” Betty nudged Sage again, this time with a little more force.

The move pulled Sage sideways to take a long look at the older woman her sister had dubbed Mama Betty when they were teenagers. “You used to love challenging Maverick in those spins. I just knew you two would end up competing against each other.”

“I never wanted that life.” Sage motioned at the arena. “I like it here. There’s no pressure here. That out there…” She shoved her ice-cold hands between her thighs and held them there. “That’s not where I belong.” Out there or with Maverick.

“You sure about that?” Mama Betty could be ornery as an old Missouri mule when she wanted, and as stubborn as one besides. Once she took hold of something, nothing but herself could get her to let go.

Was she sure? She’d thought so when she left, but sitting here now made all those old wants roar up. She loved riding. Sitting in a saddle and riding through these patterns in the practice arena had made her feel on top of the world. But she’d never once ridden in a competition. That didn’t appeal to her. Being in the spotlight made her skin itch, but that didn’t mean she couldn’t train or help warm up the horses.

There hadn’t been a chance to try that life after Mr. Pierce ran her off Twisted Branch. After she *let* him run her off. Her biggest regret in life. Everything might’ve been different if she’d stood up for herself instead of running away. Even the thing with Nate. She’d confronted him, only to have her lower-class background thrown in her face. He’d told her she’d never win against him, and she’d believed him.

Who would listen to someone like her?

God does. The thought hit so hard she reared back with a gasp.

Mama Betty raised her eyebrows and grinned. “That a good thought or a bad one?”

"Good." She rubbed her chest in slow circles. "Just realized that I've been stumbling around in the dark my whole life because I didn't trust anybody but myself."

"I'd say that's a mighty fine realization. What're you gonna do about it?" The challenge in her tone slithered through Sage. She could keep going the same as before, or she could make a concentrated effort to change.

You are worth believing. You're worth fighting for. If she believed that, then everything changed.

* * *

Two weeks passed in a blur of riding, sleeping, and riding some more. With interviews, photo shoots, talking with other riders and potential buyers thrown in for good measure. The fast pace and constant motion wore him down. Maverick stopped outside the barn and yawned, stretching his arms over his head, then twisting his torso side to side.

"You look like I feel." Remington hefted a giant thermos of coffee and saluted Maverick with the cup. "If this keeps up, Violet has threatened to put makeup on me so I don't look like death warmed over."

He took the thermos from Remington and poured a cupful into the mug he kept at their station outside the barn. "It would be an improvement. Can't believe you haven't done it before now."

"Har har." Remington cracked his neck and slid a hand over his head. "Man, I'm tired. This doesn't get any easier."

Not when they were riding three horses each and going in and out of the ring constantly day after day. "I'm not doing this next year. Not with this many horses. It's too much."

"Don't ever let me hear you say that again." Dad stalked out of the barn and stopped in front of them. "The two of you will never win with that attitude. You're lazy. That's the problem."

"No, Dad." Remington's free hand tightened and he shoved it into his pocket. "This has nothing to do with work ethic."

"We're allowed to complain," Maverick added. "There's nothing wrong with slowing down a bit. If we only had two horses each, we could put more time into their training."

"If you didn't insist on coddling them all the time, they wouldn't need longer training." Dad folded his arms and glared. "I taught you both, and you're not doing anything with it. You're wasting time with all this nonsense."

Maverick locked his jaw to keep from saying more and reminded himself that it wouldn't do any good. Dad believed horses should be trained through more drastic measures. They could be effective if used properly, but they soured Maverick's stomach. No one should learn through fear, not even animals. Dad allowed them to train their way because he'd seen the undeniable results and steady trust. But any time a ride didn't go how he thought it should, he resorted back to their training methods as the cause.

Remington swirled the last of his coffee around in his cup, then downed it in a single gulp. "I have work to do."

"Me too." Maverick carried his coffee into the barn with him, shouldering past Dad on the way. He meant to stay far enough away that they didn't touch, but Dad moved into him, their shoulders colliding.

"Keep away from those Rhett girls. Saw one of them talking to Beckett Moore this morning. Looked awful chummy." He sneered the man's name, his entire face twisted.

"Beckett's a good man." Maverick didn't hesitate to defend Beckett. They'd known each other for years. He'd talked to Beckett himself yesterday.

Dad shook his head, the look in his eyes calling Maverick every kind of fool. "You're going to regret bringing those girls back here."

He highly doubted that. Sage's top-notch work gained more hits on their website than ever before. She belonged in this world as much as anyone. He bit his tongue until he tasted blood, but the words brewing inside refused to stay trapped. "The only thing I regret is that Sage didn't come back sooner. Better yet, I regret that she left at all." He walked away without another word, because if things kept going, they'd end up in a shouting match right there in the middle of the barn.

Sage met him at Goldie Boy's stall, her camera around her neck and a tentative smile firmly in place. "Everything okay?"

"It is now." He choked down his emotions and settled for subtle flirtation. She'd shut him down after their kiss, and he'd respect that boundary. But he loved the way her cheeks flushed and she suddenly found everything else in the barn interesting as she looked away from him.

She twisted the camera strap around her wrist and motioned at the palomino. “You’re going to do great today. Colt warmed him up for you, and I took some great shots. You want to see?” The last came in a breathless rush and she held the camera out away from her body. “Look at this one. I think it should go up at the primary shot on the for sale page.”

Her scent teased him as he leaned in close, the whisper of her hair touching his cheek. He left it alone. It tickled and caught in his short beard. The picture of Goldie Boy captured his attention. She’d caught him in mid-stride, his neck long and elegant and his wavy mane in motion.

Colt sat easy in the saddle, his reins loose and his smile a glowing reminder of his brother’s quick wit. “You’re amazing. That’s going on the front page as soon as we get back.”

His name rang out over the speakers and he pulled her into a quick side hug before she escaped.

“Good luck.” She lowered the camera and took the coffee cup from him.

Realization settled over him, and he shook his head. “I’m not going to win. Not this year.” He sucked air through his teeth. The weight of the competition lifted and he gave her a cheek-pinching smile. “And I’m okay with that. I want to show the horses to their best ability. That’s all.”

He picked up Goldie Boy’s reins and walked him toward the arena, where others clustered around and talked in voices that carried vivid excitement. Smiles spread like wildfire, and despite the tense competition and everyone hoping to win, they cheered him on when he swung into the saddle and rode through the gate.

Goldie Boy performed better than ever. His spins were tight and controlled, his lope elevated to a level the gelding had never achieved. He responded to the slightest cue and rode off on the correct lead every single time. Maverick finished the routine with a final spray of dirt and patted the golden neck. “That’s it. We did our best.” He had other horses to ride, but he stopped worrying about whether he’d win and focused on getting the horses to perform their best.

Colt, Aspen, Remington, and Landon met him at the stall.

“What’s that?” Aspen grabbed his face when he hit the ground and pinched his cheeks. "You're smiling. You never smile after a ride. You always grumble and complain about what you should have done."

Did he really? He racked his brain and the moments came to him in a wave of crushing pain. "Not anymore." He had better things to do. He loosened Goldie Boy's girth and led him into the stall. "He did great. I couldn't have asked for a better ride."

Remington's eyebrows shot to his hairline, all but disappearing beneath his hat brim. "Wow. Never thought I'd hear you say that."

"I think our big brother is finally coming to a conclusion about his perfectionism." Aspen crossed her arms and smirked at him. Her head tipped to one side. "And I think our friend Sage has a big something to do with Maverick's sudden change."

"Not just Sage," he corrected her. "God."

Colt slapped a hand to Remington's back. "Miracles do happen. Never thought I'd see the day ole Mav stopped trying to prove he could beat the old man."

"Respect, Colt." Maverick pinned his younger brother with a look that had him scowling. "Dad has his issues, but we still owe him respect."

Colt muttered under his breath. The words were too low to hear, but the look on his face said more than enough.

Fourteen

No. Heat raced up the back of her neck and flooded her cheeks as she scrolled the webpage. Image after image flashed past. Her pictures. But not her name. Melinda. That was the name scrawled in the right corner of each and every photo she'd taken for the last three weeks during the Futurity. Bile rose in her throat and she rubbed her neck to push it back down.

She was not letting this happen again. Sage snapped the laptop closed and stormed to the front door. Stopping long enough to shove her feet into her boots, she let the anger build until it filled her completely. She'd trusted Maverick.

Was she wrong about him? How could he do this to her? She pinched the bridge of her nose and took a deep breath. It might be a mistake. Her heart tripped, then raced away. It had to be a mistake. Maverick wouldn't betray her like this. What, then?

She narrowed her eyes against the sun's glare and situated her hat low over her forehead.

Maverick would be in his office this time of the morning. Jaw locked, she marched across the lawn, ignoring everything around her. Nothing mattered except finding the answer. And a solution. Maverick might be the son of one of the richest horse trainers in the western riding world. He might have the power to take all this away from her again. But not without a fight.

Her breaths came in ragged bursts as she tried to tamp down her anger so she didn't blow up at Maverick before they even had a chance to talk.

"Please." She breathed out the prayer. "God, please let there be an explanation."

The lodge door opened under her palm. Ross bustled out while tipping his hat. "Morning."

Her throat constricted too tight to answer him. She nodded instead.

The arched ceiling echoed her footsteps back to her, driving her into a jog toward Maverick's office. The place still amazed her, but she ignored the desire to look around at the opulent luxury. Her steps faded as she hit the carpeted hallway and she forced her feet to slow into a casual walk.

"I don't care." Maverick's voice barreled out of his office. Long strides thundered down the hall to her right. Maverick. She knew that step anywhere.

Mr. Pierce's heavy voice leaked out. "It's not that big a deal, son."

"Yes." Maverick boomed back. His steps slowed to a stop, as did hers. "It is a big deal, Dad. I promised Sage that she would get credit for her work."

Her heart leaped into her throat and took up residence there.

Mr. Pierce scoffed. "Why? What does it matter? Even if she hadn't broken her contract, it ends when Melinda comes back."

"Exactly." Maverick's voice lowered. He ignored the part about her breaking the contract. He knew why, and she thanked God he didn't mention it. "I signed that contract. And it clearly states that Sage will receive credit. You've broken the contract. And you're going to fix it."

Another scoff. "I'll do no such thing. That contract might be binding between you and Sage, but nowhere does it state that everyone with the ability to manage the website will abide by that clause."

"Unbelievable."

Sage crept closer and ducked into the office across the hall. She shouldn't eavesdrop, but no way she'd leave. The answers she needed were right at the tips of her fingers. Or...right across the hall.

Maverick leaned across the desk, his weight balanced on his palms. "You will fix this."

Mr. Pierce relaxed in his chair. The man wasn't at all bothered by his son's furious scowl. "No. I don't think I will. It's time for that woman to leave." He flicked a spot of hay from his knee. "She never should have come back."

Maverick's nostrils flared and his hands curled into the desk. "I'm not asking. Sage is back, and I have every intention of seeing that she stays here if that's what she wants."

"You forget yourself." Mr. Pierce's solemn facade cracked. "This is my business. I make the decisions here."

Maverick shook his head in a slow wag without ever dropping eye contact. "You have three hours to fix this." He stabbed a finger into his desk. "Fix it or I will walk away from you. From this. And you will *never* see me again."

Mr. Pierce lunged to his feet. "You would do that? You would choose that woman over your family?"

"That woman has a name." Maverick didn't back down. They stood nose to nose with nothing but the desk between them. "Sage has always been good to me. Sage believes in me. And I believe in her. You say she should have stayed gone. I say she never should have left. But if you insist on driving her away, then I go with her."

He defended her. He defended her when he had no idea she stood on the other side of the hallway listening in. He had nothing to gain and everything to lose.

She couldn't let him throw everything away like that. She didn't deserve his friendship, much less anything more.

Love for him swelled until her chest felt like it would burst. Could she walk away again? The joyful burst in her chest popped and she deflated.

Whatever happened next, she had to see it through. She slumped against the wall and brushed tears from her cheeks.

Quiet anger breathed from Maverick's office. His father seethed in silence.

"Three hours." Maverick straightened. He walked around the desk, past his father, and out into the hallway. His stride didn't falter as he strode away.

She stepped out of the doorway. He spotted her and froze. His throat worked in several hard swallows, then he moved. He rushed to her like he couldn't get there fast enough. Whatever he saw on her face, it didn't stop him. Strong arms went around her waist and he pulled her close enough to bury his nose in her neck and lift her off her feet. "I'm sorry. I had no idea, but I will fix it."

She tangled her hands in his shirt collar and held on as emotions raced through her too fast to name. "You can't turn your back on your family." Of all the things she could have said, things like "I love you" worry for him poured from her.

Maverick's arms tensed but then relaxed. "You're more important to me than his ridiculous ideas. I choose you, Sage."

The tears came in a burst that she worked to control. "That's the most romantic thing anyone has ever said to me. But I won't let you choose me and lose them."

"I'm not going to lose anyone." He eased back and stared into her eyes. "This is his chance to change. It's radical, but I'm willing to risk it. And I won't be giving up my mom or my siblings."

"So you think you can have it all?" She didn't know how she felt about that.

Maverick turned them around with a hand on her waist. His palm slid to the small of her back, and he guided her through the lodge and out into the sunshine. They kept going until they reached the barn.

"I let you get away once. Won't make that mistake again." His fingertips skimmed over her spine as they reached a stall and stopped. "I should have tracked you down years ago and told you how I felt. I was a coward."

"Don't say that." She framed his face in her palms. "You were respecting your dad's wishes."

"Why did you leave?"

She flinched at the unavoidable question but tried to deflect. "You don't need to know."

Maverick lowered his head so they were eye to eye. "Yes, I do. And the only thing that makes sense is he made you leave."

"Don't make me answer that." She couldn't stand the thought of being the reason Maverick turned his back on his dad. Yes, the horrid man might deserve it, but he'd ready lost Colt. Possibly even Remington. If he lost Maverick too, the others might follow his lead.

"I choose you." His hands slid up her sides. He knocked her hat back and skimmed his lips over hers. "I'm in love with you. Have been for years. It's time I followed my heart."

Her heart kicked a rapid beat that lodged in her throat. "I can't remember a time when I didn't love you."

She'd fallen for him almost as soon as they met. They were kids back then, but she'd known he was her happily ever after.

* * *

Sage needed to tell him the truth. All of it. "Tell me why you left." He framed her face and brushed his thumbs over her cheeks. "Please tell me why you ran away." Because that's what she did. She'd taken off without ever looking back, and if they were going to work, he had to understand.

Sage gripped his wrists. Her eyes closed and a tightness came over her features. "Can we go somewhere else?"

"Anywhere you want." He'd take her to another state if that's what she needed.

Opening her eyes, she turned her head and kissed his palm.

Heavy steps echoed down the hallway and Sage flinched backward, her gaze darting over his shoulder.

"Come on." He took her hand and strode to the door. "We'll go down to the barn." Their place, the one place in the whole world where he felt most at home and connected with Sage.

Once they ducked into the shadowed quiet, Sage pushed her hair back from her face and knotted it at the back of her neck. Pink dusted her cheeks as she looked over her shoulder, back toward the lodge where his dad stood on the porch with his hands on his hips.

"He hates me." Her voice dipped low, almost inaudible.

Maverick squeezed her hand. "Hate's a strong word. Dad doesn't like most people."

"But he has a special dislike for my family." She spoke like she possessed insider knowledge, and the need to know roared up once again.

"Come here." He pulled her in close and she settled her cheek against his chest. "You can tell me anything. Or nothing. As long as you know you can trust me." He wanted—needed to know—but he stopped trying to push for answers. She'd been pushed around her whole life, and that stopped. Right now.

Her arms went around his waist and clung to his back. "Your dad believes that my uncle sabotaged his ride in the Futurity forty years ago. When I started coming around, he saw me as a gold-digger, a liar, and a cheat. He expected me to do the same thing to you, even though I had no interest in showing horses."

Anger pulsed hot and heavy, beating against his temples and cinching the air in his lungs. "You would never do that. Not to me or anyone else."

Her head scratched up and down on his shirt. "I tried to tell him that. He didn't believe me." She leaned back and stared into his eyes. Hurt lingered there, years worth of desperation and a need to be heard. "I left because he threatened to make you stop riding as long as I stayed."

Every last particle of air rushed out of him in a whoosh, leaving him lightheaded.

"And I knew you'd blame me, so I left. I couldn't risk you losing out on the thing you loved most."

"And you were afraid I wouldn't believe you." He didn't blame her, even though he knew he'd have stood by her, even back then.

Her eyes brightened with the sheen of tears. She sniffed them back and knuckled the corners of her eyes while clearing her throat. "No one has ever stood up for me before. I learned that I can't rely on anyone but myself. Mom's an alcoholic who used to send us here while she went on benders. Then she'd lie about it to anyone who listened, telling them that me and Rosemary were half wild and she couldn't control us."

He remembered hearing stories like that throughout school. Teachers would give the Rhett girls side glances like they expected them to steal everything out from under them. "That's why the teachers always made you sit by yourself when we took tests."

She nodded. "They accused me of cheating every time I did well. Got to the point I quit trying and did just good enough to get by. Seemed to satisfy them." Her shoulders rose and fell in that casual shrug that he'd come to learn meant she cared a great deal more than she let on.

It explained why she ran instead of coming to him. It didn't matter what he said now. Words were useless, worthless, to Sage. Action mattered.

Soft footfalls sounded outside. Maverick lifted his head but kept his arms around Sage. She tensed but stayed within the circle of his embrace.

Mom closed the distance with short but powerful strides. Her face held a mix of anger and love, and when she stopped a few feet away with her arms loose by her sides, Sage lifted her chin.

"I'm staying this time. Wherever Maverick goes, I go. So if he plans on kicking Maverick off the ranch, that's his loss. And his problem. I refuse to be his scapegoat anymore." Her tone held powerful conviction and her words burst out in a rapid shot that held nothing back.

Mom's frown eased and she set her hands on her hips. "Well." A smile started, the slow creep of joy relaxing the tight lines around her eyes. "All right then. Welcome to the family, Sage. We're happy to have you."

"What abo—"

"Randall?" Mom swatted the air with both hands. "Don't you worry about him. God has that situation under control. And I'll make sure he doesn't do anything he'll regret." She slid forward a few steps and held out her arms. "I mean it, Sage. You're welcome here. Forever. You and your sister."

She fell into Mom's embrace with a soft cry.

He stood back and let them hug while he sorted through his thoughts and emotions. Dad had tried to get rid of Sage by making her think he'd betrayed her. She trusted him enough to stay and talk things through. *God, please let her running days be over. Where she goes, I go.* God had promised He'd never leave them nor forsake them. 'Whithersoever thou goest, I will go.' The verse worked the last of the anger from his bones and he shook out his clenched hands. Dad had his own issues to work on. Maverick could not fix those problems, but he could love him the way God loved and hope that eventually Dad's hardened heart would crack open and allow that love to soak into the desert plain of animosity he created.

Maverick had his own life to live, and it started right now with Sage.

THE END

About the Author

Tabitha Bouldin has a bachelor's degree in creative writing/English from Southern New Hampshire University. She is a Publishers Weekly bestselling author for her cowboy romances and drinks way too much coffee. When she's not homeschooling her kids, you'll find her curled up with a book. Tabitha's genre of choice is Contemporary Christian Romance which she describes as: Adventure with heart.

You can keep in touch through any of the following:
www.tabithabouldin.com
www.sendfox.com/tabithabouldin

facebook.com/tabithabouldinauthor
instagram.com/tabithabouldin

Love in the Lyrics

BELL RENSHAW

To horse camp and 4H where I became familiar with horses and fulfilled dreams as a kid!

One

Libby

Liberty "Libby" Taylor lived by the fact that there was nothing like the scent of oiled leather in the morning. Or hay, for that matter.

She hoisted her Dakota saddle onto the back of Butterscotch, her buckskin mare, before bending low to grab the back cinch. Bringing it up, she made quick work of securing the saddle.

"How are you doing this morning, girl?" She circled the mare and laced the bridle over her head, the bit settling easily into her mouth.

The horse, always docile, tossed her head once to adjust the hardware and then settled down as Libby put her left booted foot in the stirrup. She easily hoisted herself up and over, settling comfortably into the saddle, before she took a second to admire the reds and pinks of the sunrise.

Golden fields of grass stretched out before her to meet the dark green of the foothills in the distance. Beyond that rose the Big Belt Mountains. If it wasn't the middle of summer, she would have expected to see remnants of the thick blanket of snow that clung to them like grannies with their sweaters while sitting under the AC at church.

But spring had long since faded, bowing to summer's hot temperatures. Even today it was forecasted to be in the mid-eighties. Too hot for Montana this time of year.

"Come on girl, let's go." Libby clicked her tongue, and the pair took off down the winding path, trodden enough times to wear down the weeds and grass to pebbled dirt.

In the summer, it was best to get a ride in early and let the horses have the afternoons to themselves to laze in the shade of tall trees or near the river that bisected her father's little plot of land. It put a damper on her horse therapy business, but the clients who could afford to move up, or push back, their time slots always did so to accommodate the weather.

The sound of a gentle breeze through the tall grass accented the gurgling of the river—or stream really. They'd called it a river as kids, and maybe it had been then, but everything faded with time.

"Libby!"

She pulled back on Butterscotch's reins and turned in the saddle, one hand on the pommel, to see her younger sister jogging toward them. She wore tight running shorts and a sports bra. Never missing a workout, Victory, or Vicky as they all called her, was always on the move.

"I thought you said you could take me to work today."

Libby bit her tongue to keep a quick answer from slipping out and chose her words carefully. "I'll be back in fifteen, twenty minutes, tops. I'll take you after that."

She didn't point out that Vicky wasn't even ready yet—and wouldn't be for another half an hour at least—but she held that in too. A monumental task for so early in the morning and before coffee.

"You always say that, and then you come back and have to rub her down and all that stuff. I can't be late again."

Don't say it. Don't say it. Don't—

"Need I remind you why we were late the last three times?" *You just had to say it.*

"Uh." Vicky's hands fisted on her hips. "It's not always my fault."

Libby took a calming breath. With seven years between them, she tried to remember that her little sister was still facing the harsh realities of life as an adult, whereas she'd been there for a while.

"I'll be back in time. I promise."

Vicky looked like she wanted to argue but then nodded. "Oh fine."

Libby nudged Butterscotch forward. This was why Libby needed to get her own place. She loved her little sister, she really did, but with both of them living with Dad still, it was getting crowded. Not to mention the fact Libby *knew* she was enabling Vicky by always giving her rides.

She refocused on the scenery around her. The silence broken only by Butterscotch's hooves, the gentle gurgling of the stream, and the distant sound a dog howling—or was that a coyote?

They took the narrow path that wound along the stream deeper into government land. It wasn't exactly off-limits, but she wasn't sure there was an open invitation either. Still, it would take her past her favorite piece of land. The one she would never own due to the multi-million dollar price tag.

Sure, a girl could dream, but she still had to be realistic.

A chickadee fluttered out of a bush, and Butterscotch sidestepped to the right.

"Easy girl. Just a bird."

They were almost there, and Libby sensed the anticipation tighten around her middle like a roped calf. The path curved, and the gates came into view. They were tall things, ridiculous really since the front half of the land itself wasn't fenced—at least not fully. The poles jutted into the sky, their bases secured with cemented river rock, but something was different.

Nudging Butterscotch down the path, they exited from the wild lands onto the gravel road that she knew from experience ran all the way back to town. Hardly anyone drove this road so she didn't worry about looking right or left, she only kept her focus on what was missing.

The sign. It was gone.

In the last month or so, every other time she'd come this way to catch a glimpse of the massive mansion that rested on God only knew how many acres of prime Montana real estate, there had been a sign. Well, two. A long, grayed out wooden one that stretched from one pole to the other and showed evidence a name had been painted on it at one point, but was now lost to time and the wind. And then the real estate sign by one of two agents local to Winter.

Both signs were gone.

A sinking feeling dropped into her gut. The place had sold.

It was ridiculous. She couldn't even dream of owning a ranch like the one in front of her. The type of money it took to purchase, let alone keep up, that amount of land was beyond her imagination. But *a girl could dream*—and dream she had. Right down to the secret Pinterest board she'd made to pick out furniture and a porch swing, because every mansion needed one of those.

Then again, she'd never even ventured down the road to see if the house had a porch. It had to have a porch, right? What self-respecting Montana mansion didn't have a porch with a view of the mountains?

But the reality of her cowardice made it even worse. She hadn't risked it, and now she never would. She knew what could happen to anyone trespassing in Montana. Guns were a right, not a privilege, and she wasn't going to test that.

Tugging the reins, she turned them back to home. Back to reality.

"Come on, Butterscotch. Looks like this girl's dreams are dead in the water."

"Can't you go any faster?"

Libby pressed her booted toe down a little. "Can't risk killing the shocks completely." *Just because you weren't ready on time—again,* she didn't add.

"Ugh." Vicky blew out a breath. "This thing is a piece of trash. Can't you, I don't know, trade it in for a car or something that can go faster than twenty miles per hour without the risk of falling apart?"

They'd gotten off on the wrong foot from the start of the morning, and Libby wasn't sure that they were going to salvage things before she dropped Vicky off at the Bradley Diner where she'd just started work a month back. Still, Libby drew in air like it might magically give her patience and tried for an even tone.

"I like the truck. It was Grandpa's, and it works just fine. Besides, I don't need to get anywhere in a hurry."

Vicky didn't respond. Libby knew she wouldn't, but that was all right. She'd made her point without losing her temper or saying something she'd regret. That was a step in the right direction. They drove on, the gravel roads giving way to pavement as they wound into the heart of Winter proper.

It wasn't a big town nor did it offer a lot of the amenities Libby knew big cities afforded, but she loved it all the same. It had heart, as her mom used to say. And to Libby, that heart was worth having to drive an hour to visit any kind of *big* store.

"Oh. My. Gosh!" Vicky's shouted expression shattered the otherwise quiet ride. She leaned forward over her phone, glued to it like a fly to fly paper.

"Victory Taylor! What in the world? You almost made me drive off the road!"

"Sorry, it's just—no *way!* I mean, like, no way!"

Libby flexed her fingers on the wheel. "Care to enlighten me?"

"I just saw an article in my favorite celeb gossip site that says that Harland Grey—*the* Harland Grey—has moved to Winter! Like, *our town, Winter, Montana!* I'm shook. Nothing like this ever happens."

Libby signaled a left turn before shooting her sister a look. "Huh?"

"Please tell me you know who Harland Grey is."

At her blank stare, Vicky rolled her eyes hard enough to roll the car. "Do you live under a rock? He's only like *the* most famous musician ever."

"Vicky." Libby sent her sister a look.

"Okay, so yeah, that's an exaggeration, but he's totally hot and super famous, and he's living here. Gina is going to *flip*. We've got to stake out his house or something—he's got to come into town, right? I mean, I could go viral if I posted a photo of him and me together."

"Vicky, take a breath." Libby pulled up behind the diner. "If he really did move here—which I highly doubt, seeing as you got that information from a gossip site—then you should leave the man alone. I doubt he'd move to Montana if he wanted to be bothered for photo ops all the time."

Vicky stared back at her, mouth agape.

"What? News flash, sis. Celebrities are people too."

"Whatever." She put her hand on the door. "If I see him, I'm asking for a photo."

Vicky was gone before Libby could make her promise she wouldn't, but the reality was, if a celebrity *had* moved to Winter, Montana, it was likely she'd never see him.

Two

2 Weeks later

Harland

"I can't believe you bought this place sight-unseen." Winslow turned in circles, taking in the vaulted wooden ceilings, antler chandelier, and wall-to-wall windows.

"Are you kidding? The listing photos didn't even do it justice. It's perfect." Harland Grey spun in a slow circle in the dead center of what would be his living room. And dead was right. "I do think the antlers have to go. Not sure I'm at the 'let's hang up dead stuff' stage of my life quite yet."

"Give it a few months and you may change your mind." Winslow turned back from the windows to level *that* stare at Harland.

"What?"

"Are you sure about this, Har? I mean, I was on board with you getting a place outside of LA It's a madhouse there, you and I both know it. But then you listed your place in Malibu and...I guess I wasn't expecting a full-on, cross-country move."

Harland rubbed at the days-old growth on his chin. "It felt right."

"Oh yes, and that's how we make massive life decisions, based on feelings."

"My feelings are what make my songs good, and you know it."

Winslow laughed. "You've got me there. As a friend, I'm behind you, but as your manager, I'm concerned."

"What? Did they stop flights from Montana to LA, and I don't know about it?" Harland spread his hand across his chest.

Winslow's stare was his reply.

"Sorry." Harland dipped his head in deference and walked past his friend to the bank of windows.

If he could point to one thing that had sold him on this property, it was the view. The Big Belt Mountains in the distance with grassy fields stretched out before him and a sheer rock face just to the north behind the horse barn. Perfection.

"Are you okay?" Window stood next to him now, hands in the pockets of his chinos. He didn't look at Harland, just took in the view, perhaps out of respect.

After a full minute, Harland answered, "I honestly don't know."

"She's supposed to sign the agreement. She's not supposed to talk to the press or anything."

Harland ran a hand down his face. "It's not that. I mean, *it is* about that, kind of, but it's more than just what happened." He let his gaze travel the fence line where it ran into the distance. "I needed to get out. You know I haven't written in months, and I just...I can't do it with all that noise. Social media. News outlets. Interviews. Gossip. It's all so...stifling."

He thought back to the last month of his most recent tour, now almost a year past, and how he'd been so depleted, he'd gotten pneumonia and lost his voice and the ability to sing for weeks. They'd rescheduled the last few dates, but it had been a nightmare.

"I know the tour was rough for you, especially with everything that happened. I just think ditching Hollywood for Montana is a little, I don't know, extreme?"

"Are you looking at the same view I am?" Harland turned to his friend. "*This* is real life. This is a place where I can breathe. Where I can think. Who knows, I might even write some more music here." *Maybe.*

Winslow put on a fake glare. "You'd better. You know Pinnacle is waiting on your next record."

"You can tell the label I'm not turning in a thing until I'm sure it's good."

"You could sing a shopping list, and we'd get a million downloads in a day."

"Oh yeah, that'd really add to my legacy. I can see it now: "Harland Grey, The Shopping Files".

"I mean, there's a ring to it."

Harland offered a weak smile. "I appreciate your confidence in me, but I feel drained."

"I get it, man." Winslow turned back to the main room and tilted his head to the side. "You know I'm staying here, right? Are you planning on getting furniture sometime soon?"

Harland grinned. He knew his friend would come around to see it his way, even if the manager side of their friendship wasn't there quite yet.

"Yeah, but for now it's going to be a little like camping. You're going to love it." Harland clapped him on the back. "Come on. We've got to unpack the truck. You're going to work for your supper tonight."

The fire crackled in the pit just a short ways past the back deck. Thankfully, the previous owner had left a few old Adirondack chairs, and while Winslow had gone inside a few minutes before to head to bed—or to cot, more accurately—Harland had wanted some time outside by himself.

The stars were unreal. They blanketed the sky like a million tiny pin pricks, and he was certain he'd never seen so many in his entire life. Growing up in LA hadn't afforded him the opportunity, and while he'd toured all over the world, quiet time outside at night was never a priority. Free time was focused on getting sleep and being ready for either travel or another show.

He laid his head back and thought about the last few hectic months. He'd been through the wringer, and while he was the first to admit he'd had a hand in some of it, he still felt like a victim.

His phone vibrated, and he checked it.

"Hey, sis."

"Har, where the heck are you?"

He chuckled. "Montana."

"I was afraid you were going to say that. Do you know I had to read about your move in the tabloids?"

He winced. "Sorry."

"Sorry? That's all I get?"

"You're in—what is it now? The Netherlands? France?"

"Scotland, and you can call me any time. You know that."

"And interfere with the world's most renowned cellist? No way."

She snorted on the line, and he imagined her pixie cut dark brown hair and rounded nose she'd inherited from their mom. An ache seized his chest. He missed her.

"I'm sorry, Cadence. I really was going to call. I just didn't want to interrupt. I know how crazy touring can be."

She laughed. "Yeah right. My tours are nothing like yours, Har. We classical musicians are a refined bunch—no scandal here. Oh, gosh, sorry I—"

"It's okay." He knew she hadn't meant any harm, but the memory her words conjured caused pain nonetheless.

The silence drew out. "I'm sorry—about everything. You got a raw deal and—"

"Don't. It's okay. I moved to Montana, and I'm just looking forward to some peace and quiet, you know?"

"Tell me about the place." She sounded eager, and he appreciated that. Cadence was older by three years and, at thirty-eight, had a career most classical musicians would envy. It was odd that they'd both gone into the entertainment business knowing that their parents had tried to dissuade them after their own very public careers, but here they were, sharing their music with the world.

"I've got to name it—still working on that—but the ranch is about a hundred acres of land just fifteen minutes from the town of Winter, Montana. I think it's considered part of town still though."

"Winter? What a cute name."

"It's small—like, really small—but I hear they have some great festivals throughout the year, and it seems like a nice place to live."

"I've got to ask." She paused for dramatic effect. "How in the world did you pick Winter?"

"It's a long story, but a friend of mine is in the business—Brenton Matthews, not sure if you've met him?" When she said she hadn't, he went on. "He was just cast in a movie with LifeWorks under Reba Farwell as director, and she's from here. Or, well, not really. I guess she married an actor who is from here, but they live in Winter part time. He connected me with her, and we did a video call that convinced me to look into it. I did, and I've got to say, Cadence, Reba did *not* oversell this place."

"Pretty, huh?"

"Try beautiful. Picturesque. Inspiring."

"Someone's wanting to write."

He laughed but also sensed the warmth that spread through him. There was nothing like talking with someone who truly got you. "Maybe. I mean, I've definitely got the space for it, inside and out."

He went on to describe the house to her, his ideas for some of the rooms, and then the land that stretched out before him.

"Okay, when this tour is over, I'm coming for a visit. I'll need to drink in some nature by the time I'm done traveling."

"You're always welcome." His smile widened at the thought of sharing a space with his sister again.

"Are you really doing okay?" she asked after a moment of silence.

"Everyone keeps asking me that." He meant the words to come off as lighthearted, but there was a strain to his voice.

"It's because we care about you. I hope Winslow is doing a good job keeping an eye on you."

"I'm thirty-five. I don't need a babysitter."

"I didn't say you did. You need a friend."

He nodded but only to himself. "He's been a good support."

"I'm glad to hear it. I hope you can connect with people in town as well. Do you think they'll bother you?"

"That was another thing I'd asked Reba, and she said that most probably won't even know who I am. That's a refreshing thought."

"Good. Take advantage of that and find some friends, little brother."

"Yes, sir."

She laughed. "I've got to go, but I'm glad things are going well.

Remember, you can call me any time. I may not pick up, but I'll call back."

"Will do. And Cadence? Thanks for calling."

"You bet. Make sure my room is ready for when I'm back in the States."

He laughed and agreed before hanging up the phone. With a deep sigh, his eyes roamed the darkness. In the distance, he caught the faint sound of a coyote howling at the moon. If he listened really hard, he thought he could almost make out the stream that ran along the west edge of the property.

He'd told his sister some of his plans, but he had more. Like refreshing the stables, adding a swimming hole, getting cows, and even rethinking some of the landscaping. The stables, he knew, would take the least amount of work since the previous owner had run the place as a working ranch, but they still needed to be cleaned up. He already had a call in to a contractor in the area.

A tingle raced across his shoulders, and he twitched his right hand, fingers working back and forth. The movement surprised him. It's how he felt when he wanted to play guitar—which, before a year ago, had happened daily.

The lone guitar he'd brought with him while the rest were shipped rested in the house, but he decided against getting it. The feelings were encouraging, and he took them to mean that the music still lived in him, even if it had been forced dormant by circumstances and the harsh reality of life in Hollywood.

His eyes closed, and he drew in a deep breath of the sweet, grass-scented air and campfire woodsmoke.

Yep. He'd made the right choice by vacating his life in LA for something simpler. Something closer to who he *wanted* to be, even if he wasn't sure who that man was yet.

Three

Libby

"That's it, Gemma. Just relax into the trot. You're doing great." Libby stood in the center of the sand arena on her dad's property. She tried to ignore the weeds pushing up from the edges and the rust on the metal fencing, focusing instead on the young girl riding Butterscotch. "Okay, now gently pull back on the reins. We want to tell Butterscotch that we're done trotting and to go back to a walk. Nice and easy. Yes, there. Perfect."

She let them walk around the arena two more times before instructing Gemma to bring the horse to the mounting block. After helping her down, they walked Butterscotch to the fence line where Gemma tied her up. Libby held open the gate for her, and Gemma bounced out.

"You looked so good, baby." Gemma's mother said, coming out of the shade from her folding chair. "You had great control."

"Thanks, Mom," Gemma said, blushing. "Butterscotch is my favorite. But RJ's nice too." She sent Libby a wide-eyed look.

"Butterscotch likes you too," Libby said, meeting the mother's look. They conveyed a multitude of things though that look, but namely, it was encouragement on Libby's part. Gemma's mother had struggled to connect with Gemma's spectrum diagnosis a year before, but Libby had met the woman at church and suggested horse therapy.

Gemma was one of the many clients who couldn't afford to pay for their time with Libby, but it didn't matter. Seeing the young girl connect with the horse and the sense of accomplishment Gemma had when she left their lessons was worth more than any payment.

"See you next week," Libby called after them.

Gemma turned to wave at her, and then she waved goodbye to Butterscotch.

Libby entered the arena again. "Good girl, Butters." The horse snorted and nuzzled into her shoulder. "I know, you want to get out of this heat. You and me both. That was the last one so it's time to go. Come on, girl."

She led the horse out and back toward the pasture. After taking off the saddle and other tack, she brushed the horse down and turned her out to pasture with the two other horses she owned. She ran a small operation for now, but she had ideas on how to grow it. She just needed some time and the cash to do it.

Libby turned and trudged back toward the house. Once inside, she paused for a moment to enjoy the air conditioning. It had been on the fritz all last week, but it was working perfectly now and felt so good she could cry.

After a quick shower and hastily thrown together turkey and cheese sandwich, Libby opened her laptop and began running the numbers again. She was making progress, but nothing like she'd hoped. She'd had to fix her truck last month, JP had gotten an infection with a vet bill she'd rather soon forget, and part of the pasture fence had needed repairing. Normally, her dad would have taken care of it, but he was struggling as it was to make the monthly mortgage—though she helped by paying a small rent to him.

She was just about to update her website with new time slots opening up in the fall when her phone rang. The number was unfamiliar but had a local area code so she answered. You never knew when someone might have referred a client.

"Hello, this is Liberty Taylor."

"Miss Taylor? This is Etta at the hospital."

Libby's stomach dropped. *Hospital?* "Hi, Etta. Uh, what's going on?"

"I'm afraid it's your dad." There was a disturbance on the other end of the line, and the woman's pause drew out.

Libby's heart dropped to the floor. "Is he—"

"Sorry, dear. He's fine. Should have led with that. Well, I guess not *fine*. He's been in a bit of an accident."

"Can you tell me what happened?"

"It's better if you just come on down here. You free?"

"Yes. I—all right. I'll be right there."

"Good. See you soon."

Libby hung up and raced to the door. Skidding to a stop, she snatched her purse from the hook, grabbed her keys, and was back in the heat in no time.

She pushed the truck to its max limit of twenty-five miles per hour on the gravel road and thirty on pavement, and was at the hospital in record time. Rushing from the heat into the sterile cool of the hospital snatched her breath, but the two older women behind the table at the front merely smiled up at her.

"Hi, honey. You're James' girl, right?"

Libby notedly mutely.

"He's fine," the other woman added. Her name tag read Marge. "Don't scare the poor girl, Charlene."

"Sorry. He's just dandy. Well, mostly dandy. Go on back to room 203. It's to the right. We'll send Doc Fuller in when we see him."

"Th-thanks." Libby had questions—so many questions—but she knew the ladies were just docents and not able to tell her much. She bypassed them and reached room 203 in a tizzy of worry and anxiety.

Her mother had lost her life in this hospital. Vicky had gotten a cast for a broken arm in this hospital. And Libby herself had her tonsils taken out in this hospital. There were memories for them all here, but none were truly good. What could have happened to her father?

She popped her head in the room, knocking on the frame. "Dad?"

"Hey ya, honey. Come on in." He muted the TV and looked up at her with a big smile. It was a little *too* big.

"What happened?" Right away, she noticed the brace on his right wrist and the cast on his right leg.

"Bit of an accident."

She sank into the plastic chair next to the bed. "I can see that. *What* happened?"

"I was over at Melody Ranch. You know, my new job?"

She nodded. Her father was the type of guy who went from job to job like the changing of weather patterns. One day he was working in town at the local auto body shop, the next he was helping out on someone's ranch. He'd only just come home days before saying he'd gotten a new full-time position at a local ranch as a manager of the horse barn. He'd seemed happy enough, and Libby had learned through the years that it was best to let her father do what he thought was right.

Mom had tried to micromanage him, but that had never worked, so Libby tried a more hands-off approach. It seemed to be best for them both as long as she could cover her part of their mortgage.

"Yeah, Dad, of course. What *happened*?"

"A new horse was brought in, but despite what the seller said, it was *not* broken."

"You've broken horses before. How'd you let this one best you?" She softened her words with a smile.

"It was my stubborn pride is what. I thought for sure I could break him faster since he'd had some training. Wanted to show this new owner that I'm the right guy for the job and...the horse showed me instead."

"Oh Dad." Libby reached out and squeezed his uninjured hand. "I'm so sorry. You seemed to really like this job."

"About that."

The glint of caution in her father's eyes made Libby lean back. "What's that look for?"

"I know you've been wanting to get your own place for the therapy stuff you're doing."

Her eyes narrowed at his saccharine sweet tone. "Yes?" She drew out the word.

"And you've been saving so hard."

"Spit it out, Dad."

"Could you take my place for a few weeks while I heal? That way I can keep the job, and you can take in my pay and keep it for yourself."

She frowned. "How'll you pay your part of the mortgage?"

"I didn't want to tell you until I was sure I was going to stay on, but this job'll pay twice what I've been making over at Stubbins Garage."

"Twice?"

He nodded. "Will you do it?"

"I...I mean I've got my clients to manage."

"You'll be able to do both, I'm pretty sure. It's flexible hours and close to the house. There's just one thing."

Now Libby crossed her arms, waiting.

"You can't let the new owner know you're there." Her expression must have said more than words could because her father hurried on to explain. "He's pretty particular, and the housekeeper there, nice woman named Ruth, was the one who hired me. She said that no phones are allowed on the property, and I had to sign some papers about keeping things quiet."

"Are you working for the mob, Dad?"

He chuckled. "No, sweetie. Just a very private guy is all. I think you'll be fine since the stables aren't close to the house, and from my few weeks of work there already, I haven't seen the owner once."

"Why does he have horses then?"

"Who knows? Ruth didn't say *why* she was hiring me, just that the stables were going to be my responsibility. So will you do it?"

"I don't know, Dad. Sounds like a disaster waiting to happen. What if the guy comes to the stables?"

"He won't. I'm sure of it. Besides, I heard he travels a lot."

Libby knew it would help her dad, and the idea of getting his pay while he was out recovering was enticing, though she knew better than to think all of it would go toward her "property fund." But that was okay. It would be more than she was making with her spotty therapy sessions and the odd jobs she did around town.

"You sure he won't go down there?"

"Positive. You know the type. Buys a big ranch, spends one week a year on it. He may not even be there when you are."

She raised a skeptical eyebrow.

"Say you'll do it, sweetie." He flashed a hopeful grin.

"On one condition. You tell the housekeeper about me. I don't want to get shot going on to someone's property."

Her father's grin widened. "Perfect. I already did."

"You did what?"

"Told Ruth you'd be taking my place."

"Dad!"

"She's the one who drove me to the hospital so I wouldn't have to pay for an ambulance. She's real nice, and I convinced her you're not the type to talk out of turn."

"You're sure this guy isn't with the mob or something?

"Pretty sure." He laughed. "Yes, sweetie. I'm sure."

"Fine." Libby huffed out a breath. "Fill me in on the horses."

Four

Harland

Harland had never seen such blue skies. Big Sky Country, as the state had been nicknamed in the sixties, was spot on. His coffee released steam into the morning air already warming with the sunrise. It was supposed to be hot again, but the mornings often stayed at a reasonable temperature, and he could read on the deck for several hours.

He'd never done so much reading in his life. Now that Winslow was gone, and things were settled in the house, thanks to Ruth who had agreed to move with him from Los Angeles, there wasn't anything pressing.

Well, there was one project he'd considered starting, but he still hadn't made up his mind on it yet.

Shoving the thoughts away, he let his gaze travel over the fields. He'd talked to a landscaper about putting in some trees as a windbreak to the west and knew they'd be coming out later that week. Then he'd talked with another guy about the pond idea he had. Things were moving, but he was still restless.

A neighing sound from the stables and horse paddock drew his attention. He knew Ruth had hired someone to take care of them after he'd had the horse barn cleaned up, but he hadn't even been down there yet.

"Morning, Mr. Harland."

Try as he might, Ruth had never called him *just* Harland. "Morning, Ruth. How are you liking your rooms?"

"Two is too many." She gave him that look that always reminded him of his mother.

"You moved away from LA Giving you an extra room was the least I could do."

She made a *phhhsh* sound and flopped a hand in front of her. "I was happy to get out of that rat race. It's changed a lot since the days when I knew your mother. I think Montana suits us though." Her grin widened as she took in the land and then him. "You look more relaxed."

"I am. Though I'll admit, I may be going a little stir crazy."

"I see you haven't picked up a guitar yet or touched that beautiful grand piano." Her one raised eyebrow said more than her words.

"It's not the right time."

"I'm sorry about what you're going through." Her expression softened. "You don't deserve it, if I may say so."

He shook his head and took a drink of his coffee to buy himself time to respond. "I think I deserve some of it."

"I disagree. But boredom is something that can always be fixed. There's that project you were telling me about—"

"Not yet." He cut her off but kept his tone light. "I'm not ready yet. I was thinking of going to the stables actually."

Surprise and—was that worry?—flickered across her aged features. She was somewhere in her sixties if he did the math right. "I, uh—the stables?"

"Yeah. I saw them after they were cleaned up, and then you said you hired someone to take care of the horses, right?"

"Yes, I did." She pressed her lips together, and her hands fumbled with one another.

"I was going to, I don't know, see if that guy you hired might be interested in giving me some lessons. Is that something I'd pay him extra for?"

"I really couldn't say." She turned to look at the house. "If you're looking for something to do, I've got a few things you could help me with inside."

He narrowed his gaze. "What is it you aren't telling me?"

"Horses make me nervous, that's all," she blurted.

"I didn't realize." He'd never seen her look so flustered. Ruth Adams was a force to be reckoned with and had acted as his house manager for years after his mother passed. She was like family, and he trusted her with his life and his privacy, but something was off.

"I just...I'm worried. You know, about the horses. I heard one of them wasn't fully trained or something."

He hadn't heard that but shrugged. "How about I just look, not touch, for today?"

Her smile was forced as she said, "If that's what you want."

Harland considered pressing the issue with her, but he wanted to get out of the house and walk around. The thought of at least seeing his horses was the perfect escape.

"I'll be back in a bit."

"All right then." She dipped her head, took his coffee cup, and went back inside.

Five

Libby

Her father was a week into his recovery, and she'd been at Melody Ranch for five days now.

"Melody Ranch," she muttered to herself as she cleaned tack while sitting on a hay bale.

Her heart had shriveled a little when Dad had told her *where* he was working—her ranch!—but she'd tried to make the best of it. Ruth had met her at the stables the first day, reiterating the details her father had offered and explaining the no cell phone rule.

It was fine by her as she'd left it in her truck, but it was an odd request. Then Ruth had shown her into the stables, and Libby had nearly passed out. They were every horse-loving cowgirl's dream.

Stone pavers lined the main alleyway with stalls off to each side separated with wrought iron bars. Small lamps were hung at intervals, and the wooden railing on the top floor—yes, it was two stories—added a rustic charm she loved. With dual sliding doors on either end of the barn open, there was stunning natural sunlight streaming through and a perfect breeze to keep things somewhat cool in the heat of the day. But never fear, there were built in AC units for when it got really hot.

The owner had gone all out, but it baffled Libby. When she asked

Ruth about her duties, it was simply to keep the horses happy and healthy. It was clear she had no idea what to do with horses, but it seemed as if her employer didn't either.

Why have horses if you weren't going to do anything with them?

Libby finished her polish job and moved to the deluxe tack room to hang up the bridle. It smelled like leather and polish. She breathed in deep and couldn't help her smile. This was the kind of set up she dreamed of. A place to house her horses in comfort. Even the exercise arena just beyond the stables was practically begging for a therapy session. Her clients had to make do with her small set-up, but this place would be—

The sound of boots on gravel reached her, and panic ensued. Ruth had told her that no one came down to the stables. No one—not even her. So if she was hearing something...it couldn't be good.

Her father's plea echoed back to her. She couldn't be seen by the owner. He needed this job. She didn't want to get shot.

Heart pounding, Libby slipped from the tack room and glanced left, then right. She couldn't see the person. By the sound, they were still a ways away from the stables, but she didn't know where to go. The ladder to the second floor, probably the best place to hide, was across the main thoroughfare of the barn, and she'd certainly be seen running across.

So it had to be something on this side.

She bit her lip. The tack room was literally just that, a room with no cupboards or extra space, and there was no way to secure the door. The rest of the barn was just stables.

The footsteps drew closer, and she made her move. Shuffling light-footed across the stone pavers, she gently slid the well-oiled door sideways and moved into Buster's stall. He was the gentlest of all the horses and was most likely to ignore her—so she hoped.

She slid down to the floor, sitting on her butt, knees up, and prayed that whoever it was wouldn't look in. It was doubtful she'd be seen by anyone walking past, but one look in the open window of the stall, and she'd be visible.

Libby ground her teeth. Why had she let herself get in this situation? She should have said no to Dad. Then again, she didn't want him to lose this job. Not with the hospital bills sure to be coming in soon. It was sweet of him to say she could keep what she earned while he was out, but she knew it wasn't going to happen that way.

The sound of boots on pavers made her heart jitter. They were here. By the heavier sound of the footsteps, Libby guessed it was a man. As they drew closer, she chewed herself out for picking the first stall—the *only* stall—with a horse in it since Buster was recovering from a minimal leg wound. If she'd gone in an empty one, maybe she'd have been more likely to remain hidden.

She pressed up against the wall, trying to make herself even smaller. It was working. The footsteps passed. Then Buster decided he cared she was in his space.

He'd been contently chewing on some hay on the opposite side where there was another window open for him to look outside and create a cross draft of air, but now he turned toward her, mouth full of the grass.

Snorting and still chewing, he made a beeline for her. His head dipped down in friendly exploration and nudged her cheek. Drool mingled with hay smeared across her cheek and she barely managed to hold in a disgusted grunt.

Carefully, she reached up and rubbed his cheek, hoping he'd get the love he wanted and go back to his breakfast, but no. He nudged her again, this time almost knocking her over. He wasn't being mean. He just really wanted affection and to know why this strange human was hiding in his stall.

The booted steps had receded but now grew louder. Her person was coming back.

Gently, she shoved the horse's head away as he came in for another slobbery kiss. But he thought it was a game. Shaking his head, he gave a loud whinny.

"Hey there, fella." The voice spoke from the horse's window to the interior of the stables and sounded deep and calm.

Buster, seeing a new human option for affection, headed over to the window. Libby didn't dare look up. One move and she'd draw attention to her hiding spot. As long as this guy petted the horse and moved on, she'd be safe.

But Buster had other plans. He tossed his head a few times and then, unfortunately, turned back to her. Holding her breath, she heard a few booted steps and let out a low sigh just as Buster's wet nose made a move. He snuffled at her face, and despite everything she tried, she couldn't keep the giggle in.

The instant the sound was out, the footsteps stopped. Her hands clasped over her mouth. She didn't move. She didn't even blink.

But slowly, there was one step. Then another.

And then, "Who are you?" The earlier, softer tone directed at the horse was gone.

Libby didn't move. She didn't even take her hands down. Maybe it was foolish, but there was a part of her brain that thought, *If I don't move, he won't be able to see me.*

"You know I can see you, right?"

Rats.

She slowly dropped her hands and turned to look up from her awkward position on the floor. What she saw was not what she'd expected.

When someone owns a ranch like the now-named Melody Ranch, they tend to be old, rotund, and have a lot of money. She'd seen it time and time again in Winter and the surrounding towns. People from all over wanted a piece of land and thought they'd just come out to Montana and become ranchers, but they had no clue what they were doing.

This man was none of those things.

He was tall, really tall, or so she thought from her odd vantage point on the floor, with the type of stylish haircut that was short on the sides and longer on the top. He had a square jaw—the definition of chiseled—with expressive eyebrows and dark eyes she couldn't see the color of. Objectively speaking, he was extremely attractive, or "totally hot" as her sister Vicky would say.

She swallowed down her embarrassment and stood. She'd face this like a woman. Dusting off her hands on her jeans as she'd done a thousand times before, she met his gaze and said, "Hi."

"Who are you and what are you doing here?" His eyes bored into her, and now that she was a bit closer, she could see they were a vibrant hazel color. The green reminded her of the trees at the foothills with flecks of brown so light it was nearly gold.

His look intensified. Right, he'd asked a question.

"I'm your stable hand." She said it with as much confidence as she could muster.

"No you're not."

"Uh, yeah I am."

His head tiled to the side in challenge. "My stable hand is a man."

"Okay well, technically, my *father* is your stable hand, but I'm filling in."

His eyes narrowed even further. "You're not a reporter, are you?"

"What? No." She couldn't keep the offense from her voice. "I work with horses."

He gave her an evaluative look, and she felt heat rise in her cheeks. *Keep it together, Libby.*

She hadn't dated in a long time, let alone been around many men younger than Winter's median age of fifty-two years old or older. And certainly she hadn't interacted with anyone as attractive as this man, but that was beside the point. She was a professional.

"Why were you hiding then?" His tone implied hands on hips, but he remained unmoving.

She thought of saying something like it's part of the job, but she knew that wouldn't fly. He deserved the truth.

"There was an accident and," she twisted the end of her long blonde braid between her fingers, "my dad has to be off his feet for a few weeks. I'm filling in, but I was told to...stay out of sight?" She offered the last part as a question.

"I see."

"Look, I'm sorry, but Ruth read me all the rules. I don't hardly use my cell phone for anything but keeping in touch with clients, and I've left it in my truck parked off the ranch. I just take care of the horses and that's all."

"What kind of clients?" He looked skeptical.

"Equine therapy. I work with kids who have handicaps and other needs."

He made a noncommittal grunt and crossed his arms. It was clear he was still not convinced. "What happened?"

"What do you mean?"

"You mentioned an accident."

Libby didn't want to get her dad in trouble, but she wasn't one to lie either. “He was trying to break your new horse, Lyric, and he did it too fast. Got bucked off and broke his ankle and sprained his wrist.”

Emotion flickered across his face. “Why is this the first I’m hearing of this?”

“Probably because my dad’s pride was wounded. And he really likes this job, apparently.”

“Is he okay?”

Libby was surprised by the concern she saw wash over the man’s face. “He’s stubborn, and it’s not the first horse that’s given him heck. He’ll be fine once he heals.”

Silence descended, and she could tell he was weighing his options. Send her away and have no one for the horses, or let her stay. She needed to convince him to let her stay, or bills were going to pile up, but she didn’t know *what* to say that would change his mind. It was pretty clear he was about to give her the boot.

“Sorry, but I value my privacy, and frankly you don’t look old enough for this job.”

She huffed a breath. “Old enough? I’m twenty-eight, and I know horses better than most in this town.”

His eyes narrowed. “It’s personal.”

Just then, Buster remembered she was in his space and gave her a nice firm headbutt, causing her to stumble forward a few feet. She caught herself on the stall door, her hand brushing across his. He yanked his fingers back like her touch had burned him, and their eyes locked.

He had beautiful eyes. Libby told herself it was an objective observation, and when you were met with eyes like that, you couldn’t forget them. Her breath shallowed, and she swallowed. Frantic for anything that would convince him, she tried her last-ditch effort. Begging.

“I *really* need this job.”

Six

Harland

He was face to face with one of the prettiest women he'd seen in a long time, and he was mad about it. What was this woman doing in *his* stables, hiding with *his* horse, begging to keep the job she was never supposed to have?

Harland drew in a calming breath and couldn't help but notice the sweet scent coming from her. The scent of hay, yes, but was that sweet pea?

Even with a wad of hay glued to her cheek, no doubt thanks to Buster —as the name plaque read—she made it hard to draw in a full breath.

"I—I don't think it's a good idea." Not only could he *not* have her image on *his* property leaked to the press, he couldn't be sure she wasn't there for ulterior motives. What were the odds that he moved to a new state and suddenly a beautiful woman was offering to tend his horses? Right, like that seemed likely.

"Look, mister." She slid the stall door open, and he took a few hurried steps back. "I get that you're, I don't know, reclusive—I don't care about that. I'm not going to report on what I do here, though I'm *sure* someone cares about all the horse poop I shovel from these stalls and the kind of grain I feed for special occasions. I just want to do the job my dad was hired for, and after he's recovered, I'm out of here. Cross my heart."

Now that she was out of the stall, he saw she wore bootcut jeans over leather cowboy boots, a form fitting blue T-shirt tucked into the jeans, and there was a crease at her forehead where he guessed a cowboy hat often sat. She was country through and through, and something about her made him want to say yes to her.

It was the stupid part of him. The part that got him in trouble. When would he learn his lesson?

"No. You can't stay."

And with that he turned to leave.

"Hey, wait. Hold on!" She caught up with him, keeping pace. He'd noticed she was tall, maybe five eleven to his six foot four inch height, and she was determined. "Come on, mister. I promise you I don't care who you are. Wait, you're not with the mob, are you?"

That forced him to stop and face her. "What?"

"The mob. You know..." She made a motion across her neck with one finger.

"No, I'm not with the mob." Was it possible she really didn't know who he was? "Do I look like I'm with the mob?"

It was her turn to consider him, and she traced the lines of his face down past his loose plaid shirt over a white t-shirt and dark wash jeans. He had boots on too, but they were designer and worth more than a thousand dollars.

"No. Definitely not mob material," she faintly said.

"I'm not sure if I should be offended or not."

The corner of her lips twitched upward, and she looked down. "I promise you, whatever you're afraid of getting out, it's not going to leave with me. I've lived in Winter all my life, and I'm about as social as...I don't know, something that's not social."

"A chuckwalla."

"A what?"

"A chuckwalla lizard. It's one of the world's most solitary animals."

"Okay, then." She shot him a skeptical look. "I'm less social than *that*. I live a quiet life, and to be really honest, I just need the money, okay?"

"For what?"

"You're nosy, you know that?"

Harland's eyebrows rose.

"I want to get my own land so I can expand my therapy business. That's all."

He could tell there was something she wasn't saying, but at the same time, he believed her.

"So what do you say, mister? Hire me? It's only a few weeks."

"Harland."

She frowned. "Excuse me?"

"Every time you say mister, I feel like I'm in a John Wayne movie. My name is Harland." He looked closely for any indication she recognized the name, but either she was an excellent actor, or she honestly didn't know who he was.

"Oh. I'm Liberty, but you can call me Libby." She held out her hand.

He hesitated. It was a bad idea. He'd explicitly told Ruth he wanted to hire men, and they needed to be older. No one that would potentially know, or care, about who he was. And now this. Ruth had agreed though, and he wondered if that was a good sign. She tended to be an excellent judge of character.

"I'll let you stay on two conditions."

She held his gaze as if to say, *Go ahead, try me.*

"One, you keep my life private. You don't tell people you work here. You abide by the rules. What happens here, stays here." He flinched, realizing how that sounded, but plunged ahead. "And two, you teach me how to ride."

The minute the words were out, shame made his cheeks heat. Perhaps it was something about admitting he knew nothing to this obviously experienced equestrian, or maybe he just felt awkward talking with one of the only people even remotely near his age who didn't know who he was. Either way, he was blushing, and he wanted to bury his head in the sand.

"Done." Her expression never wavered.

He accepted her hand shake. Her palm was soft and warm, and the shake itself was firm. She pumped their hands once and then released.

"Did you, uh, need something?" she asked after he'd stood there for a moment longer. "Dad said you don't come down here, so I wasn't expecting you."

"Clearly," he muttered. "I just wanted to see the horses."

"Oh, well, you can still do that. I was just cleaning tack." At his expression, she explained. "Buffing the bridles and oiling the saddles, things like that to keep them in good condition."

"Maybe another time." His mood to wander the property had dimmed in the light of this new hitch to his seclusion plan. Even still, he worried that some adventurous photographer was hiding on the ridge and was going to catch him talking with a beautiful woman and plaster it all over in some type of new smear campaign.

"All right." She dipped her head again, hands in the back pockets of her jeans. "Say, what *do* you do? I don't care." She held up a hand as if to stay off any argument. "Just curious."

Yeah, he wasn't going there. "Sorry, that's classified. And you've got a little something on your face."

With that, he turned away and headed back to the house. He might have just made the worst decision possible, but there was something about Liberty—*Libby*—that made him cave. Whether it was her persistence or her matter-of-fact attitude, he wasn't sure, but he'd never been treated more normally, and he had to admit, he kind of liked it.

He glanced back to catch her wiping furiously at her face, and covering a grin, he continued back to the house.

Seven

Harland

"You know it's later here, right?" Harland reclined on his leather couch, a true crime documentary playing in the background on low. He stifled a yawn.

"Since when do you go to bed before midnight?" Winslow was at a party, or at least somewhere in public, if the chatter on his end of the line was any indication.

"I'm changing my ways. Trying to get a good eight hours and all that." Harland yawned again. Did this make him old? He pushed to a sitting position and rubbed a hand over his face. He'd done some yard work that afternoon despite the heat, and he was feeling an unusual ache in his body after the strenuous work.

"Right." The noise on Winslow's end quieted down. "I've got some bad news."

Harland's shoulders stiffened. "What is it?"

"There's no easy way to say it. Another article is dropping tomorrow."

Harland's gut clenched. *Article.* He knew what that meant. Either a tabloid or something close to it was going to "report" on his alleged misconduct yet again.

"Is there really anything different to say after what's already been published?"

"I only got the heads up that it's bad, not what the content is. I've got your lawyers primed and ready to read over it for slander, but—"

"Free speech. Yeah, I know." He'd faced this all before, countless times really, but even still, it bothered him. He knew that being famous came with the consequence of being in the lime light, but why did the light have to be so harsh? And why did they only ever focus on the supposed *bad* things he'd done and none of the good?

But pointing out the charities he donated to and the humanitarian work he'd been a part of was a sure-fire way to make him look like he was trying too hard.

"I'm sorry, man. I know you went to Montana to get away from all of this, but I'm not sure it's ready to blow over yet."

"That wasn't the only reason I left." His mind supplied the image of Libby, horse gunk on her cheek, and he *almost* smiled. "I wanted a fresh start. I know I'm not leaving the past behind, and I'm not trying to, but I want to be able to live without it staring me in the face at every corner."

"I hear that." Winslow covered the phone and said something on the other end of the line before coming back. "Sorry, at a party."

"Hey, thanks for letting me know."

"I'm sorry there isn't more I can do, but we'll see if anything is actionable tomorrow."

Nothing like a waiting game without anything to do about it. But Harland understood. "Keep me posted."

He sighed and ended the call. So this was it. Another article, another chance for people in Winter to see the ugly untruths from his not-so-distant past.

"That was a big sigh, Mr. Harland."

He jolted, a hand flying to his chest. "Ruth, you startled me."

"Sorry." She wore a matching velvet sweat suit in dark purple and perched on the edge of a leather end chair. She looked more relaxed than he'd ever seen her in LA "I was going to turn in for the night and wanted to see if you needed a nighttime snack."

He chuckled. "I'm not five. I can get my own snacks."

"I know you can," she said with an air of superiority. "But so can I. You know you're like a son to me."

Warmth from her words flooded his chest. "I do know that. Are you liking Winter okay?"

"I am." Her smile held mischief. "I already feel like I fit in. The church in town is nice too—if you ever want to go."

The thought of going anywhere in public right now sounded awful, but he appreciated the offer. "I'll think about it."

"And I wanted to apologize." She looked down at her knobby hands folded in her lap. "I knew about Miss Libby coming to the ranch, and I didn't say anything."

He propped his chin on his fist. "Why not?"

"I know I shouldn't meddle, so this isn't that, but I met her before agreeing to let her work here and knew she wouldn't be a problem."

He narrowed his eyes. "How could you be sure of that?"

"I couldn't. We never can be *totally* sure about anyone, but I had a good feeling about her. You know me, I've got good instincts."

"I do know that." He shifted back against the couch cushion and propped his feet up on the wooden coffee table. "But you know why I have the rules in place that I do. In fact," he let out a sigh and gave in to telling her what Winslow had shared. "I can't afford more bad press."

"It's all lies. Can't believe they get away with printing that trash."

"It's mostly lies." The words felt like ash in his mouth.

"It's all lies." She nailed him with a look. "And don't you go blaming yourself for any of this."

"But—"

"I won't hear it." She stood and leveled her gaze at him. "Don't forget, I know the truth. I know what really happened, and you aren't to blame. Don't let everyone else's opinions confuse you on what's right. You're a good man, Mr. Harland."

"Will you finally call me by my first name now that we're out of LA?"

Her responding grin released pressure in his chest. "I'll think about it. Good night."

He watched her saunter down the hallway toward her rooms on the opposite side of the massive ranch house from his space. Her support meant a lot to him, but he felt like she was too close to the situation.

Still, he trusted her instincts. After hearing Winslow's dour news, he'd considered letting Libby go and finding someone else to take her spot temporarily, but maybe Ruth was right. Maybe Libby wouldn't be a problem.

He thought of the way she'd hidden in the stall, pretending he couldn't see her until she knew the jig was up. Then how she'd embraced it full on. That seemed to be her personality. Bold. Brash. Going for what she wanted.

His smile grew wider despite how he tried to stifle it. There was something about Libby, something he liked, and that scared him more than anything else.

Eight

Libby

Everything hurt. Libby pulled herself up the steps of her childhood home, one hand over the other on the wooden railing like an invalid. She knew she was being ridiculous, but she hadn't been this tired in a long time. It turns out working three jobs isn't just as easy as one.

The smell of the pot roast she'd put in the crock pot that morning greeted her as she pushed the door in. At least that was one less thing she'd have to do. There was still her own horses to feed and water, the chickens to be put up and fed, her goats, and the donkey who would soon be demanding his flake of hay with loud braying if she waited too long.

"Hey ya, sweetie." Her dad sat at the kitchen table, his crutches resting against the counter and his foot propped up with a pillow on another chair. "Long day?"

"How can you tell?" She leaned against the door frame and dropped her satchel.

"You look exhausted, that's how. Can I do anything?" His beard was more gray than brown now, but his clear blue eyes, the same light shade as hers, held compassion.

James Taylor was a hardworking man who loved his daughters and had done everything he could for them when his wife—their mom—had died from breast cancer when Libby was fourteen and Vicky was seven. It had been hard living without a mom, but their dad had done everything he could for them.

Sure, she would have liked him to have a steady job, but perhaps she too was falling into the habit of taking on what she could, just like her father. Then again, Libby told herself it was just until she could have a facility that was all her own. Then she'd be able to expand.

"Libbs?"

She blinked out of her thoughts. "Sorry. No, Dad. You just rest up. What are you doing?" She took stock of the papers scattered across the aluminum Formica topped table.

"Balancing the check book, but for once, it's good news."

"Yeah?" She pulled out one of the vintage fifties chairs and sank onto its unforgiving and cracked cushion. "What do you mean?"

"You're never going to believe this." Her father looked positively giddy. "Mr. Grey paid for my medical bills."

Libby in confusion. "Mr. Grey? Who's that?"

"Libby, he's the man you're working for. You said you met him." He made a face. "Even though you were supposed to stay out of sight." He shrugged his shoulders as if to say, *Kids, what can you do?*

Libby put the names together. Harland Grey. Harland Grey? Where did she know that name from? Harland—she gasped. "Harland Grey?"

Confusion washed across her father's weathered features. "You said you met him? Then again, Ruth does always call him Mr. Harland."

Her father's faint smile that accompanied the name *Ruth* didn't get past her notice, but she was too focused on the name. "Harland Grey. Like the same Harland Grey Vicky's been talking about? The...what is he? Musician?"

"You didn't know?"

"No, Dad. Why would I know? I listen to good music."

"Don't you dare say that to Mr. Harland. He's a very talented young man." Her father's shocked expression made her laugh.

"He's not a country singer, or I'd have heard of him, that's all I'm saying." She shook her head as the pieces of the puzzle now aligned. Vicky had told her Harland Grey moved to Winter, but at the time, she hadn't been focused on that. And somehow, the name didn't stand out to her when it was just his first name, even though it was sort of unique.

She dropped her forehead into her palm. "I'm so out of touch."

"It's okay, honey. I'm hip to the new things."

She shot her father a look. "Just the fact that you said that proves you really aren't."

He chuckled. "Maybe not, but I do know this. Harland is a decent guy. He didn't have to pay for this. I didn't even report it to him. I wonder if Ruth told him." He pushed his reading glasses up on his nose and looked back down over his paperwork.

So *the* Harland Grey, music sensation and star, was living on *her* dream ranch, and she now worked for him. Talk about a small world. But more than that, he'd paid for her father's medical bills—probably because she'd outed her dad to him when they met.

"Well, this is a fine mess."

"What is?" Her dad didn't look up, scratching numbers on a notepad and then erasing every other second.

"I don't know how I feel about working for a celebrity."

"You're not. Well, not officially. Just for the next few weeks is all."

He had a point. "But, he's from *Hollywood*, right?" She made a face. "What is he doing out here?"

"Can't people in Hollywood want to live in our beautiful state?"

They could. She knew that much already. "I guess so."

"Besides, he's not been treated too kindly in the press. I bet he's just happy to be out of the hubbub of all that gossip."

"Gossip? What gossip?"

Now her father looked up. "It's not my place to say. I just know that Mr. Harland has been good to me—to our family—and that's what counts. I don't believe what I read about him. No way."

If Libby were a cat she'd be on life eight. It was not only curiosity that got the best of her most days, it was the inability to back down. With her father's words dangling between them, she knew what her next step had to be, but she needed to be coy about it.

"Well, I'm going to go relax for a bit. Dinner should be ready in an hour or so. I'll make some salad to go along with it."

"Don't bother."

"We're having salad, that's final."

He looked at her over his glasses. "Do we have to?"

"Since when did I become the parent?" She sighed and spun on her heel.

"I mean it, Libbs." She leaned back around the corner, her father's frown at the ready. "Don't believe what you read."

"I not going to snoop—"

"You most certainly *are* going to snoop on Mr. Harland. It's written all over your face. Just give him the benefit of the doubt. Don't judge lest you be judged type of thing the pastor's always talking about."

"I won't."

"Good." He winked, and she took the short staircase up to the second floor of the home. The brown carpet muffled her steps and held decades worth of memories. Sliding down the stairs on cushions. Crawling as she and Vicky pretend to be barn animals. The time the chickens got inside.

She shuddered at the last one. There were a lifetime of memories in the bare-bones walls of their small home. The good, the bad, and the ugly which often looked like her and Vicky arguing about one thing or another. Her life had existed in this house for twenty-eight years, and she'd be lying to herself and to God if she didn't admit she felt stifled by it sometimes.

Just being around Harland's estate—because that's what it was, not just a ranch, an *estate*—was enough to show her what she hadn't accomplished in those twenty plus years.

She slumped on her twin bed near the window that looked out across the prairie grass toward the mountains. It wasn't that she wanted all the money, though she could admit it would be nice at times. It was more the stability and assuredness of a paycheck she longed for. Of things to rely on.

It was a risk to get her own place. A risk to leave her dad and Vicky alone. And it was a risk to try her therapy business full time when she wasn't sure if it would earn her a consistent living. She couldn't go full-time with it until she cut off the other odd jobs she did around town—horse care, grocery runs, pet sitting. But she also couldn't afford to lose their steady income yet. All of it was money in the bank, but none of it was a guarantee.

Sighing, she pulled out her phone and navigated to the search bar.

She started with just his name, and millions of results popped up. *Millions.*

Multiple images of him filled the top of her screen, links to articles, and YouTube video links to his music videos and live shows.

And good golly if he wasn't handsome.

Libby tried not to stare, but his vibrant eyes stared back at her from promotional photoshoots and magazine covers. Perfectly messy hair, rolled up sleeves showing off a tattoo she hadn't noticed in person, and just the right amount of smolder. Yep, that's what it was. These photos showed off a smolder only celebrities could perfect.

She yanked her eyes forcefully to the articles below the mesmerizing photos and clicked on the first one. She didn't care what it was, she couldn't look into those eyes a minute longer without thinking of how he'd smelled like sandalwood and some type of polish she couldn't put her finger on. Something citrusy.

The headline banished all her thoughts as effectively as a bucket of ice.

HARLAND GREY: FROM BEACH PLAYBOY TO MOUNTAIN HOTTIE

Harland Grey has made a move—and no, not toward another woman. Yet.

In this article we're digging deep into all the rumors as we follow famous singer/songwriter Harland Grey and his exit from Hollywood in a cloying cloud of scandalous gossip. Our only question: Will he "find himself" in Montana, or just find another woman to victimize?

Libby dropped her phone to the bed, unable to read more from the gossip site. It was already so much worse than she'd expected. Sure, she knew that celebrities were put through the wringer when it came to anything interesting, but this seemed over the top.

She picked her phone up and pressed the back arrow. Quickly scrolling down to avoid his unnerving—and ridiculously attractive—stare, she read the article titles now. Most had something to do with his scandalous behavior and some Instagram viral post, but they all only hinted at what it could be.

She wasn't brave enough to read any more, at least not tonight, and her mind wandered to what he could have done to earn such scathing articles. And worse, if they might be true.

"Libbs, have a second?"

"Yeah, be right down." With a glare, she tossed her phone on her bed and made her way back downstairs. This was the reason she stayed off of social media and hardly went on the internet unless it was to look up new therapy techniques. It was all scandal and gossip and rumor. But what was true?

"I dropped one of my crutches." Her dad made a face where he stood at the table, his broken ankle held at an angle and one crutch supporting him.

"You okay?"

"Doing just fine. Was going to head to my chair for a bit. I figured we'd watch something with dinner." She nodded, her mind still lost on the articles about her new employer.

"Should I quit?" The words came tumbling out. Try as she might, Libby had a hard time keeping her thoughts inside.

"What's that now?" Her dad hobbled to the living room a few short steps away, Libby watching the whole time, and slumped back into his reclining chair with a sigh.

"Should I quit? I could find someone in town to take over—maybe a guy? I mean, maybe it's safest."

"What in the world are you talking about, sweetie?" Her father looked up at her like she'd grown an extra head. Then a light dawned. "You Googled Mr. Harland, didn't you?"

"You say that like you did too."

"I did, but that was *after* I'd met him. He's a good guy, Libbs. Whatever the news is saying about him's not true. It can't be."

She wanted to believe him. She'd met with Harland and walked away unscathed—though embarrassed, definitely embarrassed—but that was just one meeting. One meeting did not a friendship make.

"It seems like he...has problems with women." She flinched even saying it.

"There you go, judging. How do we know what those articles are saying is true?"

She had to admit she'd never heard of *PopStar Today* or *Top Celeb Culture*, some of the websites she'd seen the articles on. And the only other news about him that came from sites she recognized was about his last album which had been release almost two years prior.

Maybe her dad had a point. "You wouldn't send me into the lion's den, would you?"

"Sweetie." Her dad held out his hand. She took it. "I'd never have suggested you take my place if I thought it would put you in danger. From all accounts, Harland Grey is a nice man who wanted to get away from the lime light. He's spared no expense to take good care of his animals—you saw the stables. And to me, that speaks of a man with integrity."

She had to agree there. He'd shelled out when it came to the ranch from what she'd seen.

Then another thought occurred to her. "You haven't told Vicky."

Her father pressed his lips together. "I think it's best that, for now, Mr. Grey is our little secret."

Libby couldn't agree more. She knew what it would be like if Vicky found out they were working for Harland Grey. She'd be worse than a dog with a bone—whatever that animal would be. Harland would probably know.

The thought caught her off guard.

"I'm going to get dinner ready. I think Vicky has a later shift, but Gina's giving her a ride home."

"Sounds good. And Libbs?" Her father held her gaze. "Give him a chance."

"I'm just going to take care of his horses, nothing more." And she made that promise to herself. She wasn't some young girl who'd fawn over a celebrity—she wasn't like Vicky—she was a grown woman with her own business, kind of, and she was going to do a good job, get paid, and that was that.

Nine

Libby

Libby pressed her palm to her stomach as she approached the barn. Being back at Melody Ranch after her late night Googling was disconcerting. While she agreed with her father that she shouldn't judge Harland by what the media said about him, she had to wonder where they got all those stories if none of them were true.

She didn't dig deep, but she'd gone deep enough to see allegations from women about him at parties being overly flirtatious when they'd said they weren't interested, other women saying he'd used his power and influence over them, and other women still saying he was nothing more than a player and a flirt.

Part of her recoiled at that. She was a strong woman, and while Harland didn't exactly scare her, she didn't want to put herself in a dangerous situation either. But another part of her wondered...were there women out there who *wouldn't* want the attention of someone as handsome and talented as Harland Grey? And if he was such a womanizer as the articles had said, why had she needed to beg to have him keep her on at the ranch?

Maybe she wasn't his type.

Her thoughts trailed to the other part of her Googling. The part that had made her fall a little in love with his music. Okay, a lot if she were being honest. As a staunch country music fan, she didn't stray. If it didn't have twang, it wasn't for her.

And yet...

Harland's music was incredible. His lyrics were deep, his melodies complex and beautiful, and then there was his voice. The good Lord in Heaven had given him a voice of gold, or whatever the musical equivalent was. She'd fallen asleep to one of his haunting love songs, and her dreams had been as peaceful as his melody.

She shook her head and pulled back the barn door. Unlike her own barn, these wheels were greased, and it opened without much effort. The scent of sweet hay, fresh wood, and a hint of leather from the tack room greeted her. It was better than any perfume.

The barn itself was empty as she'd let the horses out to pasture. She'd been happy to see Buster doing better after he'd cut his leg and was relegated to the barn, but now it was empty and still.

Libby closed her eyes. Just for a moment. she pretended this was her barn. That the facilities were the realization of her dream to open her own therapy center where kids could come from all of the surrounding towns. Where grant money wasn't impossible to secure and where she had comfortable places for the parents to sit and watch the magic of what happened between horse and rider.

Emotion swelled in her chest, and her eyes felt wet. Libby cleared her throat, trying to yank herself back to reality. Cowgirls didn't cry. Well, that wasn't true, but she hadn't let herself give in to tears often. Not since Mom died. There was just too much to do.

Dusting off her hands even though she hadn't done anything yet, Libby moved toward the far end of the barn. She opened up the other side, letting in a delightfully cool breeze, and began moving hay into a wheelbarrow.

One of Harland's songs came back to her, and she thought about the words he'd sung with such emotion.

There's got to be more to this life
More than the worry, the pain, the strife

It was catchy, and she started to hum a few notes as she dug her hay hooks into a bale and began to heft it off the neat row.

"Need a hand?"

Libby jumped upright, letting out a muffled scream as the hooks went flying. Whirling around, she clutched at her chest as she came face to face with Harland. He'd ducked, likely to avoid the dangerous hooks as they sailed past him, and he wore an expression of shock.

"Goodness." Libby let out a loud breath. She pulled off her white straw Stetson and ran a hand over her hair for no other reason than she needed her racing heart to calm.

"I'm sorry." Harland had somewhat recovered, though he stayed several feet back from her.

"I didn't hear you come in."

"Clearly." His lips twitched in amusement, but he seemed to think better of letting the smile blossom.

"Need a hand?" he repeated.

Her eyes narrowed, assessing him. "I suppose now is as good a time as any to start your lessons."

Excitement transformed his face, making him appear younger.

"We're not starting with riding," she cautioned. "We'll begin with general horse management. Toss that bale in the wheelbarrow."

"Yes, ma'am."

She caught sight of that almost-smile again and forced her gaze away from his lips. They were unreasonably full.

She bent and reclaimed the hooks and handed them over. "Just dig 'em in."

He shrugged and did as she said. She watched as he lifted the bale, unable to ignore the way his light green t-shirt pulled taut against his arm muscles. He clearly worked out, but then, didn't everyone in Hollywood?

At least her build was thanks to a life of hard work and forgetting meals, even if the last part wasn't something she should be proud of.

"Now what?"

Hands on her hips, she nodded toward the open door. "We're heading to the feeders."

"Why don't you lead the way?"

"Follow me, Boss Man."

He bent and picked up the handles, and she sauntered past. "The thing about horses is this: they need to eat all day. They've got the type of system that all but demands they have something in their stomachs, or things get dicey." She held open the first gate for him. "During the winter, feeding is more crucial, but in the summers, depending on the pastureland, they won't need much supplemental feeding, if at all."

"Then why the hay?"

"I had a look over your pastures and talked with my dad. We both think that some supplemental feed will be good while they are in this specific pasture. There was a fire earlier this year that came through here. They mostly let those things burn, but due to lack of rain, we haven't seen the grass come back like we would have expected."

"Hence the hay."

"Exactly."

"I have a hundred or more acres. Couldn't we just move them to another pasture?"

She came to a stop at the first slow feeder and crossed her arms to look back at him. There were bits of hay clinging to his shirt and jeans, but the look suited him.

"We could, but you're going to need to bring in a fencer for that. There are too many downed poles and holes." He looked stricken. "It's normal. Keeping fence up can be a full-time job around here. It helps that you don't have cattle grazing. The horses will be fine as long as we keep these slow feeders stocked through the summer, and then you can decide if you want to fix up the other fences in the fall."

"How'd you learn so much about horses? Your dad?"

"My mom, actually." Libby smiled, her gaze traveling the distance to the mountains. "I mean, my dad knows everything you'd ever want to know about animals and ranch life, but my mom was the one who loved horses."

He looked at her as a gust pushed a lock of hair across his forehead. He shook it off with a move Libby assumed was habit.

"She passed when I was fourteen, but not before she shared that passion with me."

"I'm sorry to hear that." He held her gaze, no flinching, no awkward squirming. The depth of compassion he wore told her he'd faced loss like she had. "Hey, look."

Libby hadn't been ready for his full-blown smile. The way it transformed already handsome features to blindingly good looking made it hard for her to glance his way. Instead, she followed his line of sight to the horses slowly making their way toward the fence.

"They know when we're here. Especially Buster. He likes to eat, and I bet he knows I've brought him something special so I can get a look at his leg."

"He was the one who was hurt?"

"Yeah. He's doing great though. Doc Bradley did a great job with him."

"Good. She called the other day to check on him, but I didn't know what to tell her."

"It's all right. She was a few years ahead of me in school, and it's Winter. She called me after she talked with you."

He shook his head. "I guess that's small-town life for you."

"Exactly." She accommodated Buster as he asked for head scratches and then offered slices of apple as she inspected the injured area, happy with the progress.

Harland joined her and obliged Buster as the horse shifted focus with demands for more scratches with his insistent nudging.

"He's pretty friendly, huh?"

"He is." Libby turned and pulled hay through the fence to load the feeder. As she did, she thought of a question she'd been meaning to ask him. "I've got a question, Boss Man."

He peered around Buster, and she thought she caught a flicker of worry pass behind his eyes. "Yeah?" There was definite hesitation in the word.

"Did you name the horses?"

His deep chuckle surprised her, and she risked a glance at his perfect face lined with amusement. "You read the names?"

"I did. Now give it to me straight. They came named already, right?"

He shook his head slowly. "Buster did but not the rest."

"So Gandalf?"

"I mean, he's a dappled gray, right? So Gandalf the Grey seemed pretty appropriate."

"But Sirius?"

"Sirius Black. You can't tell me you've never read Harry Potter or seen the movies." There was a surprising amount of passion in his voice.

"Calm down. I've read the books. I guess I just didn't expect *you* to have."

"I don't look like a reader?" He came around the horse now and leaned up against the railing.

You look like a model, that's what.

Libby refocused on filling the feeders. "I don't know. I was just surprised was all. Well, not with Lyric though. That one made sense."

"Yeah?"

"Well, yeah." She looked at him from between floating bits of hay highlighted by the bright morning sunlight. "You named this place Melody Ranch, and Lyric is by far the most expensive horse you own. It seems...personal."

"You know who I am, right?"

She cocked her head to the side. "Tell me you seriously didn't just say that."

There was that laugh again, and he ran a hand through his hair, mussing it more. "I really did."

"Well, yes. I do know who you are."

"Then you know music is a big part of my life. Or it has been."

That last part caught her attention. "It's not anymore?"

"Inspiration is important when your job is creative. I've lacked the motivation for a while now."

"That must be hard." Libby almost didn't realize it, but she'd moved closer, leaning up against the railing as Gandalf the dappled grey came in for a snack. Sirius was also nudging his way toward the feeder but Buster stayed where he was, ever hopeful for more treats.

"I've been in the music industry since I was fifteen. Maybe it's time for a break."

"Fifteen?" She hadn't seen that in her research the night before.

"I did a lot of odd jobs, and my dad was a guitarist with a popular band. You could say I come by this work honestly." He chuckled and reached out to rub Buster's forehead.

"I've got to ask then, why leave LA? And why Montana? Are you done with music?"

A cloud passed over Harland's features, throwing them into shadow and hard lines. He shook his head and moved to slip back through the fence.

"Boss Man?"

"Sorry. I've got to get back to the house." He dusted his hands on his jeans.

"I'm sorry—"

"Don't be." He turned his back on her and walked away.

Libby blinked at the rapid descent their time together had taken. She knew she could be direct, sometimes *too* direct, but she hadn't demanded answers, only asked the kind of question anyone in town would.

Perhaps it was better this way. It wasn't that she needed to be friends with Harland. She only had to teach him how to ride and care for his horses. And if this was the type of mood swing she could expect from him, maybe it was better to keep her distance anyway.

She turned back to the horses and resumed filling the feeder. She might not understand men, but at least she understood *them*.

Ten

Harland

He'd handled that poorly.

Harland stomped his way back toward the house. He'd actually been enjoying his time with Libby and the horses. It was surreal to see one of his life-long dreams come true. He'd been standing there, just hanging out with horses!

But then she'd started asking invasive questions, and while he wasn't sure if she was just digging for gossip or truly wanted to know, they'd hit too close to home. Especially her question about music.

He was a musician. If he didn't have music, what did he have? What did that make him?

The thing was, he didn't need to answer anything. At least not yet. Money would never be an issue as long as he was wise with his spending, and that meant that his music—really, anything he wanted to do—would only happen if he *wanted* to do it.

There was a freedom in that. A freedom Harland hadn't realized he needed until recently. But no one seemed to understand that about him. No one was willing to give him that space so he'd had to take it himself.

Winslow tried to be sympathetic, but the guy just didn't get it. Ruth almost did, but she was mischievous and always thought she knew best.

Maybe she did, but Harland was pretty certain he needed time away from the pressure cooker of people's opinions if he was ever going to make music that was worth listening to again.

A gleaming black truck sat parked at the house, and Harland frowned. They didn't get many visitors out at the ranch since the moving company had come and gone and his first few work projects had been completed.

As he came closer, he saw that the cab was empty. Whoever it was had to be inside then.

He steeled himself. He didn't know who he was going to be meeting, but it was likely he'd have to put on some sort of front. Everyone expected to meet the "great Harland Grey," and he gave them what they wanted. Cool, aloof, and always just a little bored with everyone and everything. It was his Hollywood persona, as Ruth called it, but it had kept people at bay—especially after the bad press had started to snowball.

He went up the side steps that led to the sprawling deck but cut in to the house through an exterior side door. The scent of baking bread filled the house and triggered his stomach to growl. He'd been drinking coffee on the porch when he saw Libby arrive, and rather than eat breakfast, he'd taken a walk.

Despite how their time had ended, he was still glad he'd gone. Libby was nothing if not direct, and while it was somewhat disconcerting, he had to admit she didn't seem like the type to be out for a juicy piece of gossip about him.

His stomach clenched. He shouldn't have left like he did.

"There you are," Ruth said. She breezed into the kitchen with a smile on her face. "You've got a visitor."

"I see that. Who is it?"

"Someone here to help you. Come on. I've got chocolate chip banana bread and coffee in the living room."

She was plying him with food. He knew it, and yet his grumbling stomach demanded he give in. "Ruth," he muttered even while he followed her through the house. "What did you do?"

"Took some initiative, that's all. Let me know if you two need anything." She stepped back like a mother who'd set up a playdate hoping it would result in a friendship for her child. The twinkle in her eye was almost comical.

Harland moved past her into the living room and saw a man around his height with broad shoulders and a dark tan. He stood with his back to Harland admiring the painting hanging over the mantle. His blond hair was cropped short, and he wore jeans and a polo shirt with a thin-line tattoo sleeve running the length of his right arm to the elbow. Otherwise, he looked unassuming.

"This a Bama?" He didn't turn, just kept his focus on the painting.

"Well spotted." Harland came forward as the man finally turned around. "It's 'Ridin' the Rims.' I was lucky enough to get it at auction."

The man looked like he was a few years older than Harland, maybe early forties, and while he seemed impressed by the painting, he didn't look nervous to meet Harland. That was a good sign.

"I'm Dawson Walker."

"Harland Grey," he said.

"I figured." Dawson grinned and extended a hand.

They shook, and Harland gestured to the couch and chairs. "Have a seat. I'm afraid I'm at a disadvantage because I have no idea why you're here."

Dawson loosed a low chuckle. "Your housekeeper said as much. I was under the impression you were in need of my services."

Harland's eyes narrowed. "That makes it sound like you're an assassin."

"Goodness no, Mr. Grey." Dawson's laugh encouraged Harland to smile. Harland had to admit the man was easygoing which was a relief. "I'm a sound engineer."

Harland reached for the banana bread to give himself a moment to process.

"Ruth told me you were interested in setting up a home studio, and seeing as I live nearby, she asked if I'd come talk to you." Dawson leaned forward as if to make his point. "Believe me, I'm not trying to convince you of anything. If you've got a guy in LA that you work with, I get it. I think she just assumed that, knowing we run in similar circles and are both now in Montana, we might find common ground."

Harland chewed thoughtfully. "You relocated to Montana?"

"Yep. I've worked for all the big labels, but I got tired of it, you know?" He shrugged and picked up a mug, pouring black coffee in. "I've been just outside of Winter for about four years now, and I love it. Never leaving if I can help it."

"How does that work?" Harland knew he'd eventually be traveling back and forth to LA for work, but he'd manage to delay that until he felt ready.

"You'd be amazed the amount of people who are willing to come out to Montana to record." At Harland's surprise, Dawson pushed on. "I decided to make it an experience. I've got some land, though probably not as much as you, and I offer the artist a place to stay, studio time, and the experience of a working ranch. Horseback riding, swimming, campfires at night. The whole shebang."

"Interesting." Harland took another piece of the bread and followed it with his own cup of coffee. "And you make it work."

"More than. I'm booked solid through the end of next year."

Harland gaped. "Seriously?"

"Yep. So, you can see, I'm not here to try and poach you or whatever. The way Ruth made it sound, you're interested in setting up something for yourself. I'm all for that and would be happy to help advise or run the project or whatever you need. That is, if you're interested."

Harland turned to look out over the stretch of land that was now his. Was he interested?

"That Libby Taylor?" Dawson pointed to the truck slowly making its way up the graveled driveway toward the exit."

"You know her?" Harland turned to face Dawson.

"Sure. We go to church together."

"You know her well?" Harland studied his expression. Was there some interest there? It was obvious that Libby was stunning and confident in a way that would likely draw the attention of most men, but he hadn't even thought that she might already be involved with someone. Not that that mattered to him.

"Not that well. She kind of keeps to herself. She's a busy one with her therapy business and then all the other stuff she does. She working with your horses?"

Harland was caught off guard. What other stuff did she do? He realized Dawson was waiting on an answer and rewound the conversation to the question. "Uh, yeah. She works here for now. I hired her dad, but he had a bit of an accident."

"Heard about that. James Taylor is a tough old guy. I'm surprised a horse got the best of him."

"James Taylor? You're kidding."

"I know. He loves the association. Not only to the singer, but also to the guitars. You're a Taylor guy, aren't you?"

"Yeah, I mostly use Taylor guitars."

"You should get James to play for you sometime. He's great and will occasionally play at church." It was clear Dawson had fully worked his way into the community of Winter, and that fascinated Harland almost as much as Libby.

"Why Winter?" The question came out unfiltered, but Harland had a feeling that Dawson was an open book in most respects. Besides, he likely worked with stars as big as, or bigger, than Harland, and that made Harland feel comforted.

"Why did I move here? Easy. The people." Dawson sipped his coffee, and his head tilted to the side. "I came out to Bozeman first, kind of just to get *to* the state, you know? Then did some traveling. I'd found a few places I liked, but nothing that really struck a chord with me—if you will. Then I came to Winter for their Christmas festival that year, and I just knew."

"I've heard about the Christmas festival."

"Oh yeah," Dawson's excitement grew. "It's awesome. Draws people from all over, and they've got live music, tents for people to sell their home crafted goods, amazing food, and even an ice rink. It's like quintessential small town, but done well, you know?"

Harland didn't know, but he nodded anyway.

"After that, I started looking for land. Found my property, and it took about a year to get everything set up. Since then, we've been hopping."

"Nice, man. That sounds...amazing."

"It has been. I think you'll find that most people in town aren't going to care who you are. As long as you treat them with respect, they'll do the same for you and respect your privacy. I find that a lot of the celebrity musicians who come out here feel that way and leave having experienced a sense of normalcy. Or as close to it as they can get."

"I like the sound of that." He more than liked it. He craved it.

Dawson's phone rang. "Sorry." He silenced it before Harland could tell him to feel free to take the call. "We're gearing up for a big week, and I'm fielding a million questions from my staff."

"I bet." Harland bit his lip then purposefully met the man's gaze. "Here's the thing, Dawson. I don't know what I need. If it's a home studio, or if I should just keep it another empty room." He was saying everything *but* what he meant. And as much as he'd like to be fully honest with Dawson, Harland had learned the hard way that even those closest to you could betray you.

"I get it. I'm good either way. I just thought it wouldn't hurt to agree to come meet with you."

"I appreciate that." Harland teetered on the edge of a decision. He either sent Dawson away or admitted the idea of a home recording studio was something he'd considered. Was *still* considering.

He thought about Libby's question and whether or not he was ready to say goodbye to music forever. When he'd left LA, he'd admitted as much to himself, but that had been the pain and shame talking. Now, a month removed, he could sense the itch he felt to pick up his guitar or run his fingers across his grand piano. The bits of lyrics that leapt into his mind at inopportune times, begging to be released through pencil scratched on paper.

He questioned what his future looked like in the industry, but he wasn't sure he'd truly be able to give up music completely. Even if it was relegated to a hobby just for himself.

"You know what?" Harland's heart picked up pace. "If you've got time, I'll show you the room I'm thinking about. Not sure I'm ready to commit to a build just yet, but it would be good to get your thoughts."

Dawson's smile was that of a guy who understood, and that was a comfort all its own. "Lead the way."

Eleven

Libby

"You forgot your coffee," Vicky said. She rushed out the front door of the Bradley Diner with a paper cup in hand. She wore black jeans and a black shirt with a white apron over the top.

"Thanks, Vick," Libby said, accepting the coffee across the truck's bench seat and popping it between her legs due to the lack of cup holders. "You okay?"

She'd driven Vicky to work early that morning and decided to stay for a hearty breakfast of eggs, hash browns, and a flapjack as big as the plate it came on. Timon, the cook, had outdone himself, but she wasn't really surprised. Everything he made tasted like Heaven.

"Yeah, just tired. I got the advanced bill for school next semester. I was up half the night crunching numbers."

Libby rarely saw this side of her sister. "You doing okay? Money wise?"

"It'll be fine." Vicky said it with an air of someone who was convincing herself of the fact. "Got the job and all, so that's a good step."

"You're doing really great, Vick. I'm proud of you."

Her sister's smile wobbled a little, and she backed up. "Go on, now.

You've got your secret job to get to." She wiggled her fingers and closed the door.

Libby drove off, but a pang of regret pierced her. She hated that she'd kept her job—or more so, her employer—secret from her sister. They didn't always have the best relationship, but days like today proved that it was possible for them to be friends. At least most of the time.

Libby sipped the coffee watered down with cream and two sugars and hummed another one of Harland's songs to herself.

"I've got to be careful, or my radio's gonna get jealous," she said to the silence of the car.

With the windows rolled down to offset the lack of AC, the breeze threw her unbound hair around her face since she hadn't yet pulled it back in her customary braid. The wind made her feel carefree and alive. It was a new day, and while she somewhat dreaded going back to Melody Ranch and its moody owner, she had to admit she was excited to see the horses.

She'd spent some serious time with Lyric in the arena the day before, thankful when his owner hadn't made an appearance, but he was making progress. He was stubborn and had a fiery spirit, something she didn't want to break, but she needed to find the middle ground where the horse would trust her.

Her dad was a good horse trainer, but they took after different schools of thought, and she wanted to see if it was possible for her way to work when his hadn't. Not that she'd gloat or anything. Probably.

The truck skidded to a stop in the shade of the barn, and she opened the door. Draining the last of her coffee, she popped the cup on her dash and jammed her hat on before sliding to the ground.

It was already hotter than she would have liked, but she knew the hottest part of the day was still hours away. She walked around the barn calculating what she needed to get done. There was enough time for her to feed and water the horses, and if she hurried, she might even be able to ride—

She ran into a wall of muscle that smelled like sandalwood and lemon.

"Woah there."

Gentle hands gripped her bare upper arms as she fought to gain her balance. It was a good thing she'd already finished her coffee.

Slowly, so as not to hit Harland in the face with her hat, she looked up at him. "Sorry, Boss Man."

"Can we make it Harland?" This close to him, the brownish-gold in his eyes flared to life in the sun, and she was caught staring for a moment.

"I—I guess so." She stepped back, fighting for a fresh breath of air that didn't smell like him.

"I wanted to apologize." He jumped right in. No preamble, just a straight up apology. "I'm not the greatest when it comes to talking about my life. I may have overreacted to your questions, thinking they were more prying than you meant them to be." He reached up and rubbed the back of his neck. "I'm sorry."

Of all the things Libby had expected that morning, his raw apology hadn't been one of them.

"It's okay." The words rushed out automatically, but she took a breath. "Actually, it's not. I need you to know that I'm not some," she waved a hand in the air between them, "fan."

His eyebrows rose, but she pressed on.

"I mean, sure, your music is good, even though it's not country, but that's beside the point. I'm just not someone who's *into* those kind of details."

He looked amused now, that infuriating half-smile back. "And what kind of details are those exactly?"

Was she blushing? She was blushing. "You know. Gossip. Tabloids. Social media." She made a face. "I'm not on it, and I don't care about it. I don't like the insinuation that I'd be digging for information."

"Noted."

"And another thing." He was definitely trying not to laugh now. "This is Winter, not Hollywood. We don't care about what goes on there. Well, some people like my sister do, but the majority of us don't. I know you've got your rules, and I respect that, but here, in Winter, you're just not that big of a deal."

He burst out laughing. "Libby, I've got to hand it to you. No one has ever talked to me like that."

The blush was back. She felt her cheeks rival the heat of the sun beating down on her bare shoulders. Maybe the tank top had been a bad idea. She was going to get burned.

"But thank you for telling me that so...candidly."

"I say it like it is."

"I see that." He dipped his head, digging a booted toe into the ground. "Would it be possible for another lesson?"

Horses. Right. She shifted focus back to why she was there, and her embarrassment eased. "Yes. I think that would be okay."

He looked up, dark lashes framing those striking eyes, and offered a tentative smile this time. No humor at her expense, just honest gratitude. "Thanks. I really like being around the horses."

"Same. Let's go." She breezed past him, the now-familiar scent of him mingling perfectly with the hay of the barn.

Back in her haven, she felt more at ease with the rhythm of her job and the easy way Harland stepped in to help her. They restocked the feeders and swept out the barn. Then she decided he was ready for the next step.

"We're going to saddle up Gandalf."

He looked up from where he'd been sweeping the last few remnants of hay from the pavers and raised his eyebrows.

"Don't get excited. No riding for you today. I still want to see you more comfortable around the horses, but you can see the next step."

"I don't know that I like the slow approach." He propped the broom against the barn wall and followed her out to the pasture.

"Slow and steady gets things done. Besides, it's better to let the horse know you and sense that you're comfortable before you climb on top of them." She laughed.

"I guess you've got a point."

She slipped through the metal gate, and he held it closed while she used the lead to direct Gandalf. "Trust me, horses have great instincts. They can tell when someone is afraid, and it's better for all involved that horse and rider feel comfortable. Here, lead him to that shaded area there, and I'll get the saddle."

"You want me to take him?" Harland's eyes widened.

"He's the gentlest horse I've ever met. He'll go willingly, I promise."

"Okay." He cast a nervous glance at the animal that stood around sixteen hands high. A tall horse and the one she'd have Harland ride when he was ready.

"Remember, confidence. He's trusting you to lead him."

Harland nodded and walked off with the horse. She couldn't help but smile as he began to sing low and quiet to the creature. She caught herself wanting to stay and listen, but the point was for them to divide and conquer. She had another job to get to soon, but there was an eagerness she didn't recognize in her. Excitement to get back to Harland to show him the ropes—or more like the straps—of how to saddle a horse.

She tried to tamp down the feelings and how they distracted her, but the simple fact that Harland had made the effort to apologize to her had gone a long way to changing her mind about him.

Maybe he wasn't at all like she'd thought.

Twelve

Harland

The horse stood there patiently waiting, listening to Harland sing a lyric from one of his favorite songs that hadn't made the last album. The tune was low and gentle, likely why his producer hadn't wanted to include it, but the melody haunted him like a whispering ghost.

The horse shifted, taking a step, and Harland gripped the lead tighter before reminding himself to relax. He had to do what Libby said: project confidence and ease the animals fears if he had any.

"You're a good boy, Gandalf the Grey." He ran a hand across the horse's neck and down past its withers. Gandalf tossed his head, and he did it again. This wasn't so bad.

"Making friends, I see." Libby came out of a side door in the barn with a saddle in her arms. The tanned skin exposed by her light gray tank top arrested his attention as the muscles there strained with the effort. Clearly, the saddle was heavy.

"Should I take—"

"Just hold the horse." She curled around the back of Gandalf, walking close to its tail Harland noticed, and then gently pushed him to the side with a shoulder. "We always put a saddle blanket on first. Will you toss this up?"

She indicated the blanket he hadn't even seen pinned under her elbow. He placed it on the horse with one hand, and she gave him verbal directions until it was in place.

"Then next goes the saddle." With one stirrup looped up on top, she hefted the saddle up and into place. She was strong, but he was realizing that was a metaphor for Libby. Strong and confident. "Now we'll use these straps to attach it. They all have fancy names I can tell you, but for now, let's get the process down."

She first flipped up the stirrup then bent low, pulled a strap up, and began a fancy loop process through a metal ring. She replaced the stirrup and moved on to the bridle that had been hanging on her arm. She made quick work of threading it through the horse's mouth and brought the reins back over.

"And that's mostly it. We keep this strap loose until we're going to ride to keep Gandalf comfortable, but never forget to tighten it, or you're going to be riding upside down."

Harland knew she could tell what he was thinking by his wide-eyed look but all he said was, "Got it."

"I know it's not the most exciting part of horsemanship. Neither is feeding them, but it's all necessary."

"Are you going for a ride?" He nodded toward Gandalf.

She checked her watch. "Not sure I have much time. Maybe in the arena. I could show you a few things before I go."

"That would be great if you have the time." Harland looked down at her while her attention was on the saddle straps. He took in her light blue eyes, the scattering of freckles across her cheeks, and the way her blonde hair tossed about in the wind. She wore the same dusty white cowboy hat, but he'd never seen her hair unbraided.

"S-sure." Her eyes lifted to his, and his gut clenched.

He'd been caught staring. It was more an objective observation, or so he reasoned, but the resulting blush and warmth of her nearness was enough to make his heart pound. He purposefully stepped back.

"Great. Let's go." He started off in one direction.

"The arena's the other way." Her voice held amusement, and he made a quick about-face to follow her and Gandalf toward the sanded corral.

She let herself and Gandalf in, and he walked around to the far side where there was shade. As he watched, leaning against the metal fence, she tightened the strap she'd pointed out and then turned to face him. "You're tall so, unlike my therapy students, you won't need a mounting box. Just make sure it's the correct foot in the stirrup, or you'll end up facing backward." She grinned and climbed up on the horse like she'd been doing it forever. She probably had.

Then she directed Gandalf to the shade in front of him. "There are four stages of a horse's movement: Walking, trotting, cantering, and galloping. In this space, the most we can do is get up to a trot, but that's all I'd advise you do for a while anyway. It can be pretty jarring."

She grinned and directed the horse toward the outside rail, and he couldn't help but notice the way her body moved with the horse. He tried to observe as objectively as possible, but the motion was fluid and fit her so well. It mesmerized him, and lyrics started flowing through his mind.

Two in one, they work as a team
Horse and rider, always together
His will in her hands, her trust in his hooves
Horse and rider, always together

"You catch that?"

He blinked out of his thoughts. "Uh, sorry?"

She drew closer and gently pulled the horse to a stop. "Remember to keep your focus where you want to go. That'll help the horse." She scrunched up her nose. "Sorry, not sure I'm a great teacher when it comes to these things. I'm used to focusing on the rider not, shotgunning info."

She climbed down and walked in front of Gandalf, closer to the rail near him. Her hair tossed about in the wind and carried her scent to him. Sweet like hay but something flowery too. Her eyes didn't stray, holding his, and it caused his heart to thud in his chest. Warmth spread out, inching down his arms and coursing up his neck.

It had been a long time since he'd reacted to a woman like this. It was hard to ignore Libby's beauty. She was cover model worthy but with more soft curves, which appealed to him.

Snap out of it, Harland.

He broke eye contact, looking away, and asked the first thing that came to mind. "You've got other jobs?"

"Yeah." She sounded surprised, but she'd mentioned them first. "I do odd jobs around town for people."

Emotions more under control, he looked back. "Like what?"

"You don't want to know." She dropped her gaze.

"That bad, huh?"

"Nothing truly bad." She shook her head. "Just embarrassing to admit, I guess. I'm a grown woman, and I run errands for seniors and housesit pets to fund my dreams."

She took off her hat and shook out her hair. The effect was even more mesmerizing as the golden strands fell around her shoulders. He wondered if it was as soft to the touch as it looked.

He yanked his thoughts back. "It's not embarrassing to do what you have to in order to make a living." He said the words knowing how ironic they sounded.

"What would you know about it?" The words sounded harsh, but her tone was soft, not accusing.

"I have to get on stage and make a fool of myself."

"I bet your pay checks are bigger than mine." She laughed, and he found himself joining her. Normally, he didn't like joking about money like that, especially if it felt like the other person was jealous, but she was just being honest. It was refreshing.

"Maybe a little."

"Well, I've got something to admit to you."

His eyebrows rose as his pulse jumped again.

"I dreamed of buying this place one day." She turned in a half circle, Gandalf still standing obediently nearby. "We don't live too far away, just that way as the crow flies." She pointed behind him. "I'd ride out here and just...dream."

The way she said it formed an ache in his chest. He knew that kind of longing. Had felt it himself.

"What were you going to do with it?" He was actually curious, not just humoring her.

"Turn it into a therapy center. Though, I guess the house is probably a little bougie for that." She blushed. "Sorry."

He laughed, not minding her slip. "It's pretty big."

"Yeah, but I guess I just thought that the location was so perfect, you know? Well, of course you know. You bought it. Good taste, by the way." She bit her lip and looked back at the mountains.

A part of him was sad knowing that he'd taken something from her, even though he understood the distance economically between them. Or, at least he thought he did.

"Sorry?" He finally said, though they both took it as a joke.

"Yeah, you better be." She sighed. "I've got to get this guy back to the pasture and head out."

"Right. Of course." Some of the spell broke, but not enough that he didn't catch the faint longing on her features when she snuck one last look into the distance. He knew that look; found he wore it himself a lot as well. "Thanks for taking the time to show me all of this."

"Sure thing, Boss Man. Uh, Harland." Her smile was tight, but it didn't look faked, only hesitant.

"Maybe another lesson tomorrow? Or whenever," he added quickly.

"Tomorrow it is." Then she turned to Gandalf. "Let's go, Old Wizard. You've got an appointment with Helm's Deep."

He chuckled as he watched her lead Gandalf back to the pasture. She tied him up and worked on removing the saddle. He wanted to go and help, but their goodbye had felt final so he turned back toward the house.

The lightness in his chest worried him as much as the freedom of the feeling enticed him. He was playing a dangerous game, spending time with Libby knowing his own attraction to her. Then again, he'd only interacted with her a handful of times. Not enough to truly know her. Though, in those times, she'd never once treated him badly.

She'd been boldly honest, but he found he welcomed that. Anything to feel normal.

And maybe she had a point. He just needed to live his life here in Winter and do his best to forget about the past and the shadow of it that clung to him. He was here now, and that's where his focus needed to be.

He paused halfway up the road to the house, watching Libby finish her chores, and the tune came to him as quickly as they once had. Three quick notes followed by a long tone in the perfect rhythm of the lyrics he'd mentally penned. Maybe letting go of the past would also mean welcoming something new for his future.

Thirteen

Libby

"I'm *so* tired." Victory lay sprawled out on the couch like she'd been there for the last three hours. And, checking her watch, Libby knew she had been.

"Long day at work?" Libby hung up her keys, took off her dusty boots, and tossed her hat onto the coat rack. She was in desperate need of a shower and a quick bite to eat before her scheduled coffee date with Mallory.

"Yeah. Like, the longest ever."

"Make some good tips at least?" Libby thought back to the conversation they'd had earlier that day.

"Yeah, I did. Oh," she sat up so fast pillows flew from the couch. "You know who came in to the diner?"

The way she said it Libby knew she wasn't going to want to know who. Or that perhaps there was something behind her sister's words.

"Who?" Her tone was wary, but it didn't faze Vicky.

"Dawson Walker."

Libby's eyebrows shot up. She could admit there'd been a time when she'd had a huge crush on the man. Living in Winter, it wasn't every day a handsome man walked into church and wasn't already attached. But her feelings had cooled the moment she'd found out that Mallory had fallen hard for him. They'd dated, or something close to it, but as far as Libby knew, things hadn't worked out.

"Oh?"

"Yeah, and you've been a little liar."

Libby's blood ran cold. "What are you talking about, Vicky?"

"He said he'd been out at a ranch and saw you were working for *Harland Grey*. And you never said anything." Vicky was on the edge of the couch, leaning forward and telling the story with everything that was in her, former tiredness gone.

Libby noted her sister didn't look angry. Only shocked. "He told you that, hmm?"

"Liberty Mae Taylor, you tell me the truth right now, or so help me I'll —I'll—" She couldn't think of anything so she just reiterated her demand. "Tell me the truth!"

Libby slipped into her dad's chair, briefly wondering where in the world he was when WWIII was about to go down between his daughters, but she refocused on her sister.

"I signed a contract. I wasn't technically allowed to tell you."

Vicky's shoulders dropped. "But it's true? And you didn't say anything?" Vicky's excitement was replaced by hurt.

"I'm sorry, sis. It wasn't personal. This job is helping me save extra money while Dad is out. That's all."

"But...Harland Grey. *Harland Grey*. He's only, like, my favorite singer ever. I would kill to see him in person! Okay, maybe not kill, but I'd do some serious violence."

"Victory, don't say that."

"What? His music is *so* good, and he's *so* cute and—omg, he is *so* hot. You get to see him in person? Every day? How are you not, like, dying from his hotness?"

Libby felt her cheeks heat, but she tossed a hand to the side. "It's not like that. He's my boss. I take care of the horses. That's all."

You're a little liar, Libby.

Her stomach churned. Sure, they'd had some conversations, and maybe, just maybe, there had been a moment—or something—between them, but it was probably in her imagination and he hadn't noticed a thing.

Besides, someone at his level of "hotness," as Vicky called it, wouldn't ever need to look at her for dating material. She was Winter-chic, which was to say not chic at all.

"You don't get to see him then?" Vicky sounded bummed.

"Not really." *It's not totally a lie.* "Just every once in a while."

"Ugh. I'm so jealous. Please, please, please say you'll find a way for me to meet him. I promise I'll be so cool, but I *have to meet him,* or I might just die, Libby. I'm serious."

"You're not going to die, Vick. Chill out. I can't make any promises, but maybe if he comes into town or something, I can introduce you."

"Omgomgomg I'm going to meet Harland Grey!" Vicky jumped up and began dancing around the room, her exhaustion a thing of the distant past.

"What's all this noise?" Dad came out of his room leaning heavily on his crutches. It was obvious he'd been taking a nap, and Libby felt bad for waking him.

"Victory." Libby's voice warned her sister to play it cool. She'd signed the agreement, and so had their father, but technically, she hadn't told her sister. Still, Dad wouldn't be happy.

"Oh, nothing, Daddy. Just had a good day is all."

"I've got to shower. Meeting Mallory for coffee in a bit. Y'all are on your own for dinner."

"There's nothing in the fridge," Vicky whined, her former excitement fading.

"Then go to the store." Libby passed her family and went up to shower.

Pulling on soft jean shorts and a loose-fitting white t-shirt, she rushed out the door with a wave goodbye and slid into her truck. The windows got her first attention, rolling down with a squeak that was followed by loud rumbling as the engine powered to life. She pulled onto the road and let her hand dangle out the open window. The airflow not only provided coolness but also offered a way to quickly dry her hair. By the time she pulled up in front of Mountain Grounds and took a moment to run a brush through her long blonde locks, they fell into loose waves, and she called it good enough.

She spotted Mallory the moment she walked in the door, but that wasn't hard to do. Not only was her friend beautiful, but she had a bold personality that at times clashed with Libby's, though the friends were committed to working out any differences before anything went too far.

"Hey girl." Mallory pointed to a drink. "Got your favorite peppermint mocha."

"You are the *best!*" Libby said, sinking down into a chair across from her friend. "You didn't have to get it. I think this was my turn, right?"

"Forget it. I sold a Billy Royal today. Coffee is on me for a month."

"No way." Libby's eyes rounded. "Show?"

"Yes!" Mallory's grin widened at the clarification since a show saddle was categorically more expensive than an everyday purchase.

"That's got to be a great commission check for you."

"I needed it. It's been a dry month."

"I hear that." Libby leaned back. "Well, kind of."

"All right, I've been hearing things around town, and I need some confirmation. Are you really working out at this new Melody Ranch place?"

"First of all, where did you hear that?" She took a sip of the hot, chocolatey mocha with the perfect accent of mint and let a little groan escape. "Secondly, what do you know about the ranch?" She had to feel her friend out before spilling news that wasn't widely known.

"So it *is* true. Harland Grey owns Melody Ranch."

Libby gaped. "I didn't say that."

"Girl, your face said *everything.*" Mallory leaned back, dipping her chin as if to say, *Well, now you need to tell me everything, obviously.*

"I signed an NDA. I can't really talk about it."

"What? Someone needs an NDA in Winter? Wait," she leaned in, glancing around to make sure no one was listening. "Are the rumors true about him? Are you...safe there?"

"Mal, come on." Libby shook her head and took another sip to buy herself time. She didn't want to violate the NDA, but Mallory was her best friend. "I'm not going to say *who* I work for, but I will say that the person who employs me is very nice and has been very kind to me and my dad."

"Okay, go on." Mallory's expression shifted from concern to intrigue. "And, I mean, I've seen photos."

Libby laughed loudly and quickly covered her mouth. She knew Mallory was talking about photos of Harland, but even the thought of it made her blush. "Uh, yeah. So?"

"So, is he as attractive as they make him seem? Because dang, I just don't think that's fair."

Libby pressed her lips together.

"Wait a second." Mallory's dark brown eyes narrowed. "Girl. *Girl!*"

Libby didn't know what Mallory saw on her face, but she desperately tried to wipe any expression.

"You are totally crushing on him." Mallory folded her arms, the pink ruffled sleeves of her t-shirt swishing back and forth. "And you didn't tell me right away. I'm hurt. I told you everything about...well, you know who."

Dawson. Libby immediately knew who her friend meant and could see there were faint lines of hurt on Mallory's face.

"There's *nothing* to tell." Libby almost believed it herself.

"Come on. We're walking."

"But it's hot out," Libby protested.

"You're the one who always likes to order hot drinks. Besides, we'll stick to the shade." Mallory led them outside where, thankfully, the intense heat of the day had subsided. True to her word, she pulled them down a street lined with trees. "Okay. No prying ears here, and you *know* I take anything you say to me to the grave. So, spill it, Libb."

"There's nothing to spill. He's my boss. He just happens to be good looking and insanely talented. And he wants to learn how to ride."

"Wait, you mean you're spending time with him?" Mallory's voice jumped an octave.

"Just to teach him how to ride." Libby kept her face turned away, taking in the leafy green trees overhead and enjoying the slight breeze that afforded some break from the heat. It also helped to keep Mallory from scrutinizing her every emotion. It was like Mallory could read her like a book.

"Okay, so you'll totally *accidentally* drop my demo on his desk then, right?"

Libby turned toward her friend. "Absolutely not."

"Ha!" Mallory jabbed a finger at Libby. "That right there is how I *know* he's more than *just your boss.*"

"Mal."

"Don't Mal me. All I want is the truth, is that so much to ask?" She went into full-on Scarlett O'Hara mode and threw the back of her hand against her forehead. "Why won't you confide in me, Liberty Mae?"

"You really are dramatic, you know that?"

Mallory dropped her hand. "And you're worse than the vault at the bank."

Libby felt a pang of regret at not telling her friend what she was really thinking, but if she did that, she lent credence to the fact that yes, her boss was cute, and yes, she might have a little crush on him. And that was the very *last* thing she needed in her life right now.

"Look, I don't know what to tell you but—" Libby's phone rang, and she flashed a smile. "Saved by the call!"

"Totally no fair. Though I know you weren't going to tell me anything *interesting.*" Mallory crossed her arms, and Libby answered while they kept walking.

"Libby Taylor."

"Hey Libby, it's Sharese."

"Oh, hey. Sorry, I didn't look at the number before I answered." She sent a glare at Mallory, who only rolled her eyes. "What's up?"

"I've maybe got some good news."

"Oh yeah?" Libby's heart picked up pace.

"Don't get too excited, but I've been keeping an eye out for some property that would meet your needs. I might have found it, and it's really close to your price point."

"How close?"

"Let's talk specifics after you see it."

Libby groaned. "That means it's *way* out of range."

"I didn't say that."

"You didn't have to, you sly realtor, you."

Sharese laughed. "Just give it—and me—a chance, okay? Shoot me a text when you want to see it."

"Sounds good. And thanks. I appreciate your hard work on this."

"You know it. What you've done with Kayah is nothing less than a miracle. I believe in your vision and want to see this thing happen. It may just take some time."

"From your lips to God's ears."

They hung up, and Libby turned back to Mallory, who wore an expression that said Libby better tell her what the call was about or there would be more dramatics.

"That was—"

"Sharese. I know. Get to the good part."

Libby laughed at her dogged friend and filled her in on the call. "But you know if she won't tell me the price over the phone, it's got to be high."

"Most land in Montana is at this point." They had circled around a double block section, and Mountain Grounds appeared ahead of them two blocks down.

"True. If we didn't have all these out-of-towners coming in and buying up all the land, maybe I'd have a chance."

"Or," Mallory leaned in, "you could just ask your boss for a loan."

"You're the worst," Libby groaned.

"Whatever. Though you may not spill your guts to me when I demand, I know you will tell me if you need to talk. Right, Libby?"

"You know I will."

They walked the rest of the way in companionable silence and parted with a hug.

Back in her truck with the windows down, Libby thought back to Sharese's call. It was promising, but property was expensive no matter where you went in Montana. She'd joked with Harland about the land, but she really had held out some type of hope it was part of her future. With that hope gone, she had to shift to something more in her price range.

Maybe, just maybe, the land Sharese had to show her would work, and her savings would be enough to kickstart her dream. She only wondered if she'd have the guts to go forward with it.

Fourteen

Harland

The breeze that blew across the prairie drew with it the sweet, dewy scent of morning air as Harland sat on the porch, guitar in hand. It had been months—almost a year—since he'd picked up his guitar for anything more than a photo op or gig he couldn't work himself out of.

But this morning was different.

He'd woken early, the golden sunlight streaming through his windows as bold and effective as any natural alarm clock could be. Lying there in the sea of white sheets, he'd sensed the urge. It always started at his fingertips. They'd prickle and twitch, and then the sensation would race up his arms and spine, tingling as it went, until the back of his neck felt like a live wire had touched it.

This type of urgency was hard to ignore, and after digging one of his favorite guitars from the myriad of cases in the corner of what would eventually become his own recording studio—if Dawson had anything to say about it—he had the guitar in hand.

It was old, one of the first guitars he'd owned after selling his beat up Honda for just enough to cover the guitar itself. It was a Taylor, his preferred brand, with a creamy white rosewood top. The frets were worn, many times replaced, and the pick marks had eaten away at the wood where a guard would have been helpful, but it was still his favorite guitar.

He liberated it from his case and, with a cup of coffee in hand, made his way to the deck.

The mornings were chillier than he'd expected, and still wearing sweatpants, he snatched a hoodie to pull over his t-shirt. Bare feet met the deck's cold, wooden planks, but he pushed to the edge where the sun had just reached, drying out the damp.

The sun shone against his back, but it wasn't yet warm enough to truly heat him, so he sipped his coffee and let the silence of the morning draw out his creativity.

Try as he might, images of Libby wouldn't let him go. He'd written plenty of songs about women in his life in the past, or the idea of them. Romance and breakups were universal and always tended to strike a chord with listeners. He'd found a way to combine the emotions he'd felt without singling out any one woman—or at least he'd tried not to.

Perhaps that was why he'd stopped writing altogether after everything that happened last summer.

He drew down another gulp of coffee and began to strum. The chords were familiar; it was the way you aligned them that mattered. He often played in G, using a capo to change to another key while still using the familiar chord shapes, but today, he was feeling something in A.

He ran a few licks, letting the feeling of the strings familiarize themselves with where the indentations on his left hand used to be. The sad fact was that his calluses, which would always be there in some form unless he quit completely, had softened. The pain, while subtle now, would only grow the longer he played.

"You've got to practice, son. Practice more than the next guy. With that and your heart, you can't go wrong."

His eyes misted at the familiar words his dad had often told him, usually while they were jamming to one song or another. He missed him. Missed his mom too. What would they think of Montana and this land?

For some reason, the chords drew themselves into something that more resembled a country song than his usual, moody, singer-songwriter fare. While he liked it, he didn't do country. But this was decidedly that.

He began to hum along with the chords, the melody easily taking shape. And then he boldly hit an E for the chorus, and suddenly, the chords were coming faster than he'd anticipated. He ran through the set again, verse chords first, then the chorus, and then back to the verse. There was a bridge in there, he could feel it, but what he really wanted was some paper and a pencil.

He looked around as if somehow they'd materialized, but instead, he saw pink slippered feet.

"Looking for this?" Ruth held up his green notebook and pencil.

"Thanks, Ruth."

"I've got to say, Mr. Harland, it sure is nice to hear you playing again." Her smile beamed down at him and made him feel oddly self-conscious. Embarrassment and stage fright had never been things Harland understood. Anxious, excited tension before a show? Sure. But not fright. He'd always felt like his place was on the stage, even from a young age, but sitting here with the prairie grass and his house manager as audience, he wondered if he was worthy.

He blinked. Where had that thought come from?

"Can I get you anything? Another cup of coffee maybe?"

He looked down at his. It was still half full. "No, I think I'm okay. Say, Ruth..." He was about to ask her what she could remember about his mother's early years as a musician when the sound of rumbling drew their attention to the road.

While the entrance was a good distance from the house, you could still easily see anyone who entered. Beneath a cloud of dust from the gravel road, he caught sight of the bright red truck he'd come to associate with Libby.

"Looks like Miss Libby is early. You going down there for more lessons?" Ruth looked a little too eager.

"I might. I've actually got something I want to work out first though."

She smiled knowingly. "You get those lyrics and chords down; you know what your mother always said."

"Write it or you'll forget it." They said it in unison, and she smiled. "I miss her, Ruth. I miss them both."

"Your parents were some of the finest people I've known. I'm sorry that you and your sister have to live this life without them now, but you both are fine examples of their legacy."

He could agree to that. His mom had been a rising musician in the vein of Janis Joplin, and his father had played the music circuit in LA for most of his career as an electric guitarist. He was always in high demand....until the car crash.

"I suppose that's true. I just wish they could be here to see it."

"I know. I do too." He knew Ruth's son had passed away due to a drug overdose a few years before she'd met his mother. Harland often felt like she'd taken quickly to their family out of a need to pour her compassion into something in order to fight off the shadow of grief.

"But don't stay out here too long," she said, regaining her smile. "Those lessons have been doing you some good. You'll always have music, I know that, but you won't always have this opportunity."

She turned and headed back to the house, but her words stayed with him. Would he always have music? He'd been fairly certain he was at the end of his career the previous summer, but here he was, working on something new.

Well, if he'd learned one thing from his parents' death, it was to take every moment life gave you and live it to the fullest.

He pulled the notebook close and gently placed his guitar down on the deck next to him so he could write out the chords. When he'd done that, the melody still played in his mind, and lyrics began to form as his gaze sought out the barn. He wrote those down too.

The dust keeps rolling, rolling, rolling on by
Her red pickup's just caught my eye
I pull on my boots, and I pick up my smile
This country girl's got a heart for the wild

The prairie grass keeps rolling, rolling, rolling on by
And my luck's just turned in the blink of an eye
I pull on my boots, and I pick up my smile
This country girl's got my heart all riled

. . .

She's got the smile of the sun
Hair like gold
Eyes like sapphires and mine to hold
With my heart on my sleeve
And a love that's free
We'll be lost forever
In the country

Fifteen

Libby

At first, Libby had thought she was hearing things. The most beautiful melody reached her on the wind, and she stopped sweeping the floor long enough to know it wasn't her imagination.

Moving to the entrance of the barn, she peered out and up toward the house. It wasn't close, far enough that she could tell someone sat on the porch, but not who that someone was. Then again, she didn't really need to guess.

It wasn't extremely clear, but she thought she caught the telltale voice of her employer, and she smiled. He was working on a song. Not many could say they'd heard Harland Grey composing music, but she could.

She pulled out her phone, the one she'd forgotten to leave in the truck, and zoomed in. The feature worked better than she'd thought, and she captured a rare glimpse of him as he bent over his guitar, bare feet dangling and a hood pulled up.

Her heart did a little flutter and she shut off the recording. She shouldn't have done that. But it wasn't like she was going to be showing it to anyone. It was for her. Though why she thought she had a right to take a video was something she wasn't going to let herself mentally work through. At least not now.

She went back to her chores with gusto and soon she'd worked up a sweat as the sun rose higher in the sky. She pulled off her chambray shirt and tossed it over a stall railing, leaving just her black tank top already stained with dust and clinging hay. Her hair felt sticky on her neck, and she considered exchanging the low ponytail for a braid when the sound of footsteps greeted her.

Turning, her breath caught. Harland stood there, backlit by the sun. He wore jeans, a crisp white t-shirt, and new cowboy boots. He held a brown Stetson in one hand but wore the look of uncertainty.

"Good morning, Mr. Cowboy." She pushed past her initial reaction to seeing him and strove for normalcy. "Time for a lesson?"

"If you've got time?"

"I do. Nice boots." She picked up her hat, smoothing back her hair, and replaced it before clapping her hands. "Okay, first we get the horses, then the tack, and then you ride."

"Ride? Today?"

"Don't worry." She grinned at him as she reached for leads. "I'm not going to send you off into the sunset—or sunrise. Just a little riding time around the arena. You've got to get used to the movement of the horse and vice versa."

"The horse has to get used to me?" He looked incredulous, but she rolled her eyes.

"Let's get those horses."

Gandalf and Sirius stood ready to be saddled, and she watched as he did as she'd instructed. Saddle blanket down first, then the saddle, and then pulling the straps up. He halted here, long fingers fumbling with the straps.

"I'm going to need you to show me this one again."

Surprised he hadn't just tried to manhandle it, she stepped in beside him, reaching for the cinch. Their shoulders brushed, and she felt solid muscle there. With the way his t-shirt clung in all the right places, she didn't have to imagine he spent time working out, but he wasn't bulky. More the strong and lean type.

Focus, Libby.

Her hands had stalled, and she drew in a deep breath, fingers twitching with practiced movement.

"Hold on now." He placed a hand on top of hers, and everything came to a screeching halt. His hand was softer than she'd expected. And warm but not unpleasantly so. The press of his shoulder on her bare one and his close proximity made everything worse. Or was it better? "I want to learn."

Then she did the thing she shouldn't have done. She looked up at him.

Hazel eyes slammed into hers, and she caught his shock at the connection just a moment before he locked it away. There was something *alive* between them. Something that demanded space and air and also *no* air because she felt the overwhelming urge to kiss him.

It was completely ridiculous. Wholly unprofessional.

But it was true.

She quickly looked down. *Do your job, Libby. Nothing else.*

"Of course, sorry." Her voice came out breathy. She slowed her movements and redid the knot for him. It wasn't too difficult once you learned it, but she made him take it out three times and do it again.

Then she forced herself out of the confined space between horse and Harland and enjoyed a breath of fresh, warmed air.

"And don't forget to—"

"Keep it loose until it's time to ride. Got it."

She risked another glance, but he wasn't looking at her, just admiring his handiwork. He was acting normal, and she needed to do the same.

"Let's lead them to the arena." She went first, gently tugging Sirius with her and instructing Harland to keep a fair distance between the horses. Then she opened the gate and let him through, latching it behind them.

She ran through a checklist of things, most of which she'd told him the day before, and then, after tying Sirius to the fence, she held Gandalf as Harland pulled himself up into the saddle.

"Wow, he's, uh, tall." Harland had wide eyes and gripped the pommel with both hands.

"Don't worry, he's not going to go anywhere without you instructing him. He's a good boy like that." She rubbed the horse's forehead, white hairs flying off in the breeze. "Aren't you, Gandy?"

"You can't call him that."

She looked up and caught Harland's smile. "He likes it."

"The Fellowship would be horrified."

"Gimli would approve. Here, take your reins." She gently pulled the reins back over Gandalf's head and offered them to Harland, making sure not to touch him this time. "Don't worry if he shifts his weight. He's a patient guy."

"Okay." Harland looked a little uncertain, one hand still on the pommel while the other held the reins in a fist—another thing she'd have to show him—but he didn't move.

She made short work of climbing on Sirius and then directed him next to Gandalf. The horses were of similar height, and she made a mental nod toward whoever had done the purchasing for Harland. Probably her father. Harland being well over six feet, it made sense that he would have taller horses.

They were almost eye to eye, though Harland was still taller, and he looked relieved to see her come up next to him.

"Okay, remember what I said about horses sensing your energy? If you're nervous, you're going to translate that to them."

"I am like *feet* off the ground on a live animal."

"Yeah, and he's got some dude on his back. Y'all are both in awkward situations until you decide it's not."

Harland narrowed his eyes at her. "You've got a way with words."

"My daddy told me that once, and I've never forgotten it. Now, let's teach you how to hold these reins the right way."

His smile rivaled the sun, and she forced her gaze down to his fingers. It was getting harder and harder to not be distracted by this man. She knew he was in Montana for privacy, and she also knew there were some scandals that tabloids had blasted everywhere, but that wasn't the Harland she was seeing.

He was gentle, kind to the horses, and even a bit timid. How could *this* man be the one they wrote about?

Then again, she didn't know him. Not really. Sure, he was handsome in a distracting way, but the substance of a man was more important than his looks. Those would fade, or could change with any number of life circumstances, but his heart would remain.

What was Harland's heart like?

"Liberty?"

Her full name coming off his lips drew her back to the present. "Sorry, I forgot how to hold reins for a second there." She laughed it off and showed him how to hold the leather straps then directed him to encourage Gandalf into a walk.

The rest of the morning settled into the ease of slowly walking horses in circles. It was rudimentary to her but crucial for a new rider to learn how to feel the horse, work on his seat in the saddle, and get into the flow of directing the animal where it needed to go.

"So this is it?" Harland said after she'd pulled Sirius to the middle to watch him make the circuit himself.

"There's more to it, but for the basics, yes. You're doing well."

"Yeah?" He grinned.

"Yeah. Now bring him to the middle and ask him to stop."

He did so, and with a few extra sidesteps, she brought their horses together, nose to tail, allowing her to face Harland. "That was great."

He was giddy, the emotions bubbling beneath the surface, and Libby couldn't help but laugh. "I'm glad, Mr. Cowboy."

"It's Harland."

Her throat was dry as she met his gaze. "Sorry, can't help a girl who likes nicknames."

He looked like he wasn't sure what to say to that, but she wasn't about to admit that calling him by his first name made things feel much too personal. Too real.

"Thanks for taking the time to do this." He bent down and rubbed Gandalf's neck. "I dreamed of riding a horse as a boy. We did this family ride up to the Hollywood sign once." He shook his head. "But it wasn't real, you know? The horses just fall in line behind one another, and it was hot, and there were so many flies, and it just felt fake."

"You did mention Hollywood." The words slipped out, but thankfully, Harland merely laughed.

"You've got a point. They try to make it a fun experience, and I guess it is, but this feels real to me. Well, almost real." He gestured to the arena. "Once there's no fences."

"You're almost ready, but there are a few more things you'll need to learn before we go beyond the fences."

"So, you'll do another lesson?"

"Of course." It was easy to say yes to him. She wanted to see the responding smile.

"Thanks, Liberty."

"If you're insisting on Harland, you can call me Libby. Everyone in town does."

He chuckled. "Got it, Libby. And besides, I'm not really a cowboy anyway."

"You've got the boots." She nodded down. "But a word to the wise?" His leaf and bark eyes met hers, and she stalled for a moment before recovering. "Wear them in good before you go walking places. Your feet will regret it otherwise."

"Noted." His forehead wrinkled. "It should be fine. I don't go many places."

"Why not?" The question felt as natural as breathing, but she could tell it pressed a button for Harland.

"Isn't it obvious?"

"What? Are you agoraphobic?"

"No."

"House bound?"

"Clearly not." He was looking less amused.

"Allergic to people?"

Now he laughed. "No, not that."

"You're going to have to spell it out to me then, because I don't see any reason why you can't live a normal life in Winter." She hadn't meant to put such a fine point on it, but at the end of the day, that seemed to be what he was afraid of. Winter.

"Don't you think people might, I don't know, invade my privacy?"

"Oh," she gave a mock grave nod. "It's because you think you're too famous for Winter."

"No." He huffed a fake exasperated breath. "Actually, maybe?"

She caught his grin but narrowed her eyes. "You know, you need to learn something about Montana. We know what famous people are, and, news flash, we don't care."

"You think no one in Winter cares about who I am?"

"You're not the only celebrity to live here. We know how to treat y'all. You just have to give us a chance."

Concern flashed across his features. Or was it fear? Whatever had happened to him in LA and whatever had pushed him to move to Montana, it still hung over him like a shroud.

"Let me prove it to you."

"Prove...how?"

"Come to the Bradley Diner with me for lunch. I vow on Sirius Black's life that no one will mess with you. If they do, they'll get the boot."

"That was a cruel vow." His expression was serious enough that she laughed, and he joined in. "But fine, *Libby*, I'll let you prove Winter's not a star-crazed haven. But I'm still wearing a hat. And shades."

"Whatever you feel you need to do, but I'm telling you here and now, it's not necessary. People in Winter respect privacy. You'll see."

Sixteen

Harland

Harland wondered if this was a bad idea. Sitting in the beat-up truck next to Libby, windows down and country music playing over the radio, he almost felt normal. Almost. But while he'd said he wasn't agoraphobic, he wondered if all his time at the ranch had turned him a bit anti-social.

They wound through the golden, grassy hills and down into a slight valley. Libby sang along to the radio, almost too low to hear, but he caught enough to know she couldn't carry much of a tune. Not that it mattered. In fact, it was kind of cute.

He turned his face to the wind and let the air cool the heat that resulted in that thought. He had to watch himself with her. Even agreeing to take her truck probably hadn't been the best idea. What if some photographer grabbed a picture and—

He had to stop the spiraling thoughts.

He'd opted for a baseball hat and aviator sunglasses, but rather than a disguise, he'd just felt like they were the right options for the outing. He wasn't up to wearing a cowboy hat everywhere just yet. It felt a little too presumptuous after only a few months in Montana.

"That's our place down that road," she said, pointing past him.

He caught sight of a log cabin in the distance that had seen better days. The porch roof sagged, and there was an old, clearly derelict car slumped out front, but the rest of the yard was tidy, and he caught a glimpse of yellow curtains at the window.

"You've got a bit of land?"

"Yeah. Dad's land. It's not much, but it's enough for Butterscotch, RJ, and Cootie."

"Excuse me?"

"My horses." She laughed. "Though my sister named Cootie. I just call him Coot. But yeah, I think I told you I do equine therapy, right? Well, they are the real therapists."

"Is that what you studied in college?"

"Kind of?" She kept her elbow on the rolled down window while her other hand rested on the steering wheel. "I studied child psychology with a minor in equine studies. I went on to get my certificate and am an equine-assisted mental health professional."

"I hadn't really heard much about that until I met you."

"It's more common in areas with horses, but we're all over. I've designed my program a little differently and end up helping all ages, not just kids, but I've found especially kids with disabilities or depression respond really well to equine therapy. That bond you're forming with Gandalf is an example. It's early days for you two, but I think you'll notice that he'll become a good friend." He caught sight of a faint blush on her cheeks. "I know Butterscotch is that for me."

"I think that's great."

"Yeah? I don't sound loony?"

"Only a little." He laughed and shook his head. "Kidding. I think animals can create a special bond with people. I used to have a dog like that."

"You should get another one." She turned onto the Main Street of Winter, and he self-consciously tugged the bill of his hat lower. "Dogs and cats are great on ranches."

"Yeah, maybe I will." His anxiety was growing, and as if sensing it, Libby turned toward him.

"On my honor as a therapist *and* a cowgirl, I won't let anyone near you." Her clear-blue gaze pierced him with its honesty, and he truly believed her.

"All right then. Let's get some lunch."

She pulled the truck over in front of the diner he'd only seen in passing, and they climbed out. Harland was hyper aware of being so exposed, but he coached himself to act natural. Being in Montana meant that, while people likely knew him, they may not connect who he was off the bat. Or so he hoped.

"This is some of the best food in Winter," she said as he held the door for her.

The scents of French fries and bacon greeted them, and his stomach growled. He hadn't had breakfast, only a cup of coffee, so at least he could get something good. Forget salads and the protein shakes he usually had for lunch; he wanted a burger.

"Two?" A young girl looked between him and Libby then back to him, a slight frown creasing her brow.

Harland's stomach clenched. She'd recognized him and—

"You gonna take those sunglasses off?" Libby asked. "People are starting to stare."

He hadn't even realized he'd kept them on. Pulling them down, the young hostess grinned back at them. "Right this way."

He picked a strategic seat, his back to most of the diner, and felt a little more relaxed. He was still in public, still exposed and eating lunch with a woman, but at least he'd been able to keep the hat on. One quick look around the place showed that most men wore hats which had made his less obvious.

"You're like a live wire over there." Libby held her menu in front of her with one elbow propped on the table, her head resting against her fist. "Forget fencing, we'll just stick you out in the pasture."

"What?"

She grinned, and his heart did a strange shifting thump he couldn't consider in that moment.

"You've got so much pent up energy over there, I'd think you were electric fencing."

"Oh." Only then did he notice his knee was bobbing up and down, a constant rhythm of sixteenth notes.

She dropped her hand over his, the contact brief and clearly platonic, but his mind jumped into *what if* scenarios. What if someone caught a photo of that? What if his new home was invaded by reporters? What if—

The touch lifted immediately, and he'd almost missed what she said, but the words filtered back through his anxious mind. "It's going to be okay."

It's going to be okay.

He drew in a deep breath, and rather than staring at the menu without comprehending it, he scoured the items listed for what he wanted. When the waitress came over, he saw that she was in her sixties with short-cropped gray hair. She offered them both a warm smile.

"Cora, what are you doing here?" Libby said. Her smile rivaled the light in the room, and Harland was momentarily blinded. She hadn't looked this happy at the ranch. Did she not like working there?

"I've started coming down to help Hoyt every now and then."

The name drew Harland's gaze up to the woman. "Hoyt Bradley?"

"You know my son?" Her lips stretched wide.

"A little. He actually told me about Winter."

"This is Harland Grey. He just moved here," Libby explained.

It was nice to know that the news of his arrival hadn't gone out to *everyone* in town. Maybe he was overplaying this?

Then it happened—the one thing he'd been hoping to avoid.

"OMG is that *Harland Grey!?*" The voice was high-pitched, girly, and on the verge of a scream.

He couldn't hide the audible groan and automatically looked back down at the menu. So much for anonymity.

"Sarah Lawson, you get that behind out of here right now. You *do not* disturb our guests, and you will *not* be served until you can calm yourself down. Go on, get."

Harland couldn't help it. He snuck a glance at Cora. She stood tall, back straight, and a no-nonsense glower replaced her earlier friendliness. The young woman, clearly a teen, blushed deeply and rushed out of the restaurant. The amazing thing was that no one seemed to pay them any attention. The crowd was mostly older folks with a few younger ones, some with kids. They just kept at their meals.

Cora turned back to him after making sure the girl had left. "I am *so* sorry, Mr. Grey. Seeing as my son is a bit of a celebrity and he brings friends from LA out here to experience a normal life, we've got a no-nonsense policy about all of that. And don't worry, Sarah is harmless. She's just young and doesn't know to keep her excitement to herself."

Harland stared back at her in shock. "I—uh, thank you."

"You deserve to live in peace along with everyone else, and don't you forget that." She offered a look that he could only describe as motherly, and he swallowed, only able to nod in response. "Now, what can I get you from the kitchen? Timon is in rare form today, and I think he's adding bacon to just about everything—something about the freezer going on the fritz and needing to cook it all before it goes bad?"

Harland grinned. "In that case, I'll do the bacon cheeseburger and fries."

"Excellent choice," Cora said with a wink. "And the usual, Libby?"

"Make it a BLT. When in Rome and all that. And remind Timon, extra crispy on the fries."

"You got it. Thanks again for coming to the diner, Mr. Grey, and I'm sorry about Sarah."

"It's all right. And make it Harland."

"Will do." She winked and turned back toward the kitchen.

As Harland leaned against the red vinyl covered seat, he sensed a shift in himself, and for the first time in a long time, he thought he might know what it was like to have a real home. A place he could be himself in.

Libby had been right. Winter was different, and maybe it was time for him to stop hiding.

Seventeen

Libby

Lunch with Harland the day before had been...surprising. When he'd finally calmed down enough to enjoy it, she'd started to see a different side of him. He was more talkative and less furtive. As if knowing he wasn't going to be stalked by a random photographer had opened up another side of him.

The problem was that she liked that side even more.

Groaning, she pulled into a parking spot on the street at the address of a potential new client with twins. That was all she knew from the web form the mother had filled out, but Libby always included a free consultation and sometimes even a first appointment in order to assure wary parents that it was more than just riding horses, it was actual therapy.

She tucked in the tail of her button up shirt and smoothed her hair back where the wind had tossed it back and forth. Then she climbed from the truck. Her boots hit the ground, and she turned toward the house with as much confidence as she could muster.

It was one thing to spend time with kids who needed help and another entirely to be the business face of her little operation. She much preferred her work with the horses to the business aspects, but she knew they came hand in hand while her practice was still small.

She heard the doorbell chime and two sets of feet pounding inside. Then the door opened to a weary looking mother.

"Libby?" she said by way of greeting.

"Yes. Hi."

"I'm Sue Kestler. Come on in." The woman stepped back, opening the door wide to showcase toys strewn everywhere, bowls of half-eaten oatmeal on the table, and the television running in the background.

"How are you doing this morning?" she asked, though she could guess the real answer.

"I'm tired."

Libby grinned. That *was* the real answer, and it made her instantly like Sue even more. "Well, you've got twins. I wouldn't expect anything else."

"Twins yes, but also a three year old and a six year old." Sue grinned and gestured to two chairs in the living room. "Let me turn off the TV, and we can chat before chaos erupts."

Footsteps grew louder, and two hurricanes rushed into the room. One blonde, one with fiery red hair, both completely naked.

"Oh my goodness. Aspen, Rose, what are you two doing?" Sue leapt to her feet and ushered the children back down the hall as Libby kept her laughter to herself.

A few minutes later, Sue came back. "I am so sorry. The older girls were supposed to be watching their siblings. We're in a difficult stage right now." She slumped back onto her chair. "Okay, so it's all been a difficult stage."

"I can imagine. The twins are the older girls, right?"

Sue nodded. "Yes, they are both thirteen."

"You offered some of the history in your contact email. They were adopted and came from a drug addiction situation?"

"Yes, the mother was on meth when she had them. It was...really tragic. They even had to detox as children. It was awful. Now that they are getting older though, we've noticed the effects of their birth situation are more than we'd initially thought."

They dove into deeper details of the girls' lives, and Libby was able to share her philosophy for equine therapy and how she thought it might help the twins. By the end of the meeting, she was fairly certain that Sue was interested, but she knew there was one aspect that needed to be addressed.

"I really think my program would be helpful for the girls, and some of the cost can be covered by insurance or the state, maybe both. I'll look into that. But one thing I want to mention here is that I'm a small operation. Just me and my three horses at the moment. While I think it would be best for the girls to be riding at the same time, I do worry that my arena isn't quite big enough for that. I usually work with one client at a time."

"I see. Do you have anywhere else you can go?"

Libby opened her mouth to say no, then an image of her and Harland riding in his expansive arena came to her. But no, she couldn't ask for that, could she?

Or could she?

The picture of him laughing at lunch, more at ease than any time she'd seen him, came to her. But he was so private. Surely the thought of having strangers on his ranch would be a hard no. Then again, like Dad always said, you never knew until you asked.

"You know what? I might have just the place. I'll need to ask about using it, but only if you think this is something that would be best for the girls."

"Honestly, Libby, I will do everything I can to give these girls the best chance in life. If you can find the space, we're in."

Libby grinned as the sun greeted her outside the house. It wasn't as hot as she'd expected, and, all things considered, she felt good. Another set of clients to add to her list—if she could work up the courage to ask Harland.

What would he say? Would he think she was taking advantage of him?

Her phone buzzed in her pocket, and she saw it was Sharese. *Shoot.* She'd forgotten to text her back the night before.

> SHARESE: You still available today, or do you need to postpone?

> LIBBY: Let's do it. Send me the address, and I can meet you there anytime.

> SHARESE: Now?

LIBBY: Sure!

A location popped onto her screen, and she tapped it. The land was only ten minutes away and back in the direction of Melody Ranch. She couldn't place it in her mind's eye, but she started the directions and climbed into the truck.

The engine roared to life, and she took off toward the property, but her thoughts spun out of control. If she wanted her practice to grow, she had to expand. But she couldn't expand unless she had assurances that she was going to be able to do things like make a mortgage. *Ha, just that, Libby.*

She could still live at home with her dad and Vicky, but her hope had been to find a property with a house and arena space. She hadn't gotten a clear answer from Sharese on what this current property had, but she'd soon find out.

The road was dusty and full of potholes. As Libby rounded a bend, she caught sight of Sharese's black Land Rover that looked closer to dusty gray after its trip on the poorly maintained road. The realtor stood beside the SUV, her calf-length dress whipping back and forth in the wind.

"Where's the house?" It was the first thing out of Libby's mouth.

"Remember when I said this was in your price range?"

"You've got to be kidding me. It's a patch of dirt."

"But it could be *your* patch of dirt." Sharese wasn't put off by Libby's assessment.

"How much are we talking?"

"Let me show you around first."

"Around what? More dirt?"

"Come on," she said with a smile.

Libby obediently followed her down a path and around a tree-lined bend where the land dipped. As it opened up, Libby could now see what looked like a pond next to a flat area of sanded ground.

"That is where I was thinking your arena could go. There's plenty of room, but then you've got the trees as a windbreak, natural shade, *and* fresh water."

"I wouldn't call that fresh," Libby said as they wound down the half-dirt, half-gravel road. "But it is a nice touch." Libby's voice softened.

That's when it happened. The inexplicable shift from being completely opposed to the property to seeing the options. She knew she came off as a skeptic, and maybe she was, but she wasn't above seeing something beneath the surface—whether in things or in people.

"It isn't as bad as it seems initially. Right?" Sharese turned to her, hopeful smile showing white teeth.

"Well, dust my boots, I see it."

Sharese laughed. "I knew you would. Now, hear me out." She turned back to the land before them. "I think you can clean up the pond, use your existing fencing from your dad's place and just add to it, and then, in the future, look at that spot over there." She pointed to another level area to the right of the pond where the tire tracks led up to and stopped. "It would be a perfect area for an office space or a house, though a small one."

Libby's pulse quickened. She could see what Sharese was saying. Maybe she could even save up and get an RV. Her mind swirled with the possibilities.

"You've convinced me. Now what would this set me back?"

Sharese told her, and Libby did her best not to break into tears right then and there. "That much?"

"I know. I think it's high, and I think there's room to negotiate, but I just don't see it settling into your comfort zone completely. Is there *any* wiggle room?"

Libby thought over her finances. With the money coming in from working for Harland, things were looking up, but not *that* up. She'd already talked with someone at the local bank so she knew roughly what she'd be approved for, but it wasn't that, even if it was close.

"I don't think so, but I'll go back to the numbers and let you know."

"I'm sorry, Libby. I've tried to find places that will match what you're looking for, but it's a tough market with everyone moving in from out of state."

"I know. It's not your fault. I'll either find a way to make this happen, or we'll just need to keep looking."

"All right, well, I've got permission from the owner to let you look around. Do you want me to stay?"

"No, but thanks, Sharese. You've outdone yourself. I'll just do a walk around the pond then go."

"You've got it. I'll message you if I hear anything at all about the price dropping."

"Deal." She watched the woman walk back up the slight incline and disappear around the corner. She knew better than to get her hopes up. She *knew* she shouldn't have let herself dream, but she couldn't help it.

Resolution pulled her shoulders back. She had multiple problems to tackle, but one thing was becoming clear. She needed more clients *now* if she were to justify the expense of a property like this. As ugly as she'd thought that it was, she was only seeing the potential now.

Her thoughts cycled back to her conversation with Sue and her solution.

It was time for her to buck it up and ask for help. She needed to go talk to Harland.

Eighteen

Harland

"Only one person?" Winslow's voice had an edge of static to it.

"Yeah. It was great." Harland picked his way carefully through the underbrush of the forest past the horse barn. He'd yet to truly explore the area as the heat had been daunting during the day, but clouds had rolled in and promised rain, though not immediately. He'd decided to take the opportunity and see what his woods held.

"Maybe we ne—ed to get some more pro—motion in Mon—tan—a."

"You're breaking up." He slowed to a stop.

"Wh—at?"

"Can I call you back?"

"Wait. I've got o—ne more thing to tell y—ou."

Harland sighed. He knew this was going to be about some type of promotion he wasn't interested in, but it was also what he paid Winslow to do for him. Harland backtracked until he thought the line sounded clearer. "Can you hear me?"

"Yes, much better." Winslow drew in an audible breath. "Now, don't hate me."

"What did you do?" Harland's gut clenched. Winslow was one of his best friends and knew him well. If he was worried, it had to be something Harland really wasn't going to like.

"We need promotion for the repackage of Homeward."

Harland closed his eyes. "No."

"Come on, man. You can't do that to me. First of all, aren't I your best friend? And second," he rushed on before Harland could reply, "you know I would never make you do something I know you hate if it wasn't *critical*."

"How critical are we talking?"

"I was threatened with legal action, though I want to say that Jet was joking."

Harland clenched his jaw. "What kind of promotion are we talking about?"

"Photoshoot. Nothing more."

Some of the tension eased. While he didn't *enjoy* photoshoots, they were usually one day, and then everything was done.

"I really don't want to come back to LA" He spoke the words that were his true worry. He'd finally escaped only to feel like the Hollywood claws were dragging him back.

"Then I've got good news for you." Winslow's voice was unnaturally high. "They're coming to you."

"What?" The volume of Harland's reply startled a bird from a bush a few yards away.

"It's the best of both worlds. They'll come to you, do the shoot in one day, per our stipulated contract agreement, and then they'll be out of your hair."

This was sounding more and more like torture. "You're saying it like it's a sure thing."

"I think the tickets are booked. And I'm sorry, Har. I wouldn't have agreed to this if I didn't feel like I had to. You know I go to bat for you, but I'm also not willing to sacrifice the future of your career."

"What future?" Harland wished he could retract the words the minute they slipped out.

"Nope. Not going there and neither are you. I've told you before, and I'll tell you again, you need a break. A hard reset even. We don't talk about your future until you've had that and I'm satisfied you're ready to truly discuss things."

Harland let his head fall back. His eyes reached to the tops of the trees where clouds were gathering but hadn't yet turned the sky dark. He took a deep breath and let it out.

"Okay. Send me the details. I'll do what I have to."

"Better. And Harland?"

He waited a beat, not sure he wanted to know what Winslow would say next. "Yeah?"

"I'm glad it sounds like you can have a real life in Winter. If it took moving to Montana for that, then I'm glad you did it. I want what's best for you, buddy."

"Thanks, Winslow. I mean it."

"We'll chat later. Keep an eye on your email."

"Yeah, yeah."

Harland hung up the phone but didn't take his gaze from the branches. He felt insignificant at the foot of the trees, just a small man in comparison to their towering height. It was refreshing. The bird he'd startled earlier came back, resting on a branch, and he thought of the verse his mother had told him once. That God fed the birds, and he was even more valuable than that.

That was hard to believe with everything that had happened to him from the past summer. The angst, the worry, his reputation being stripped from him. It had made him stop and think—truly think—about what it meant to be human. Not just Harland Grey the singer, but Harland Grey the man.

He looked back down and began walking again. There was no path, just a few small trails he was sure some animal had made since they weren't really big enough for him. He'd have to forge his own trails in the future, but for now, he just wandered.

The light grew dimmer the further in he got, but he couldn't seem to make himself turn around. Back at the house was responsibility, and emails, and Ruth telling him he should keep playing.

He laughed out loud at that. She was his best encourager now, but all he really wanted to do was ride a horse again. With Libby.

He felt hot then cold. Libby was an enigma. He liked her

straightforward approach to life, but she also intimidated him. It was a strange feeling since he'd always been the one whom girls were shy around. His fame or his looks or whatever always seemed to cause women to blush and bumble around him.

But not Libby. Nothing seemed to faze her.

He slowed to a stop, wondering how she'd feel if he asked for her phone number. For horse lesson purposes only, of course. Or maybe Ruth had it, and he could reach out, as her employer, to schedule the next few lessons?

Mister. Boss Man. Mr. Cowboy.

She liked nicknames, and he wasn't sure why it bothered him so much. Perhaps it was the distance it implied? Like he was somehow above her and not an equal, which was the furthest thing from the truth.

He spun around at the touch of the first rain drop. He'd gone further than he'd thought, and if the sky was going to open up, he needed to get back to the ranch, or at least the barn, for shelter.

He started walking only to realize he had no idea which direction was *back.*

A sinking feeling landed in his gut as he pulled out his phone and saw the *No Service* text at the top.

This was not the smartest thing he'd done.

He tried a text to Ruth anyway. Sometimes a message would go through with the barest signal, and if he didn't see the service come back, maybe it would send once he did get a signal. Then he decided he was smart enough to get himself out of the forest.

Half an hour later, Harland knew the truth. He was lost.

Sinking down onto a stump under a tree, he rested his head back against the rough bark. This time, the height of the trees wasn't comforting, it was defeating. The leafy branches loomed over him, and he wasn't sure how he was going to get himself out of this mess.

He could see the headlines now: CELEBRITY EATEN BY BEAR or CELEBRITY MUSICIAN LOST IN WOODS, NOT EVEN A SONG COULD SAVE HIM.

Okay, so they were terrible headlines, but either way, he wasn't sure what to do next. He'd closed his eyes for a second when he heard it. The sound of...hooves? Then his name.

"Harland?"

He jumped up, nearly falling on his butt as his foot rolled on a branch. "Here! I'm over here."

He moved toward the sound, and through the narrow tree trunks, he caught sight of gray and white, then a flash of yellow and blue.

"Here!" He called again.

"Stay put."

He was certain it was Libby now, the voice growing closer. He wanted to rush to her, but he wasn't sure if that would scare the horse or make things worse, so he waited until she came into view, a sour expression on her beautiful features.

"Are you out of your mind?"

He deserved this, he really did, but couldn't she be just a little sweet?

"It's good to see you." He offered a lopsided grin.

Her hard features softened, and she climbed down from Gandalf. "Are you all right? I brought a first aid kit."

"If you don't count my wounded pride, I'm fine." His eyes searched her face like a man coming up on an oasis in the desert.

"Do you need me to tell you not to go into the woods on your own? Or without a compass? Or walkie talkie? Or, I don't know, a *path* to follow back?" Her anger made her cheeks turn pink, and rather than menacing, the effect was adorable.

He grinned. "But you found me."

She shook her head. "Lord, give me locusts."

"Huh?"

"Nothing. Are you sure you're okay? How about some water, need that?"

"That'd be good."

She nodded and moved back to Gandalf who had dropped his head to sniff the ground, likely wanting his bit removed so he could nibble a snack.

She handed Harland an old-fashioned canteen, and he took a deep drink. "Did it take you a long time to find me?"

"Thankfully, no. But Ruth is worried as all get-out. She's the one who sent me out to look for you."

He grimaced. "I honestly didn't think I'd gone that far, and then I turned around and realized I had no idea where I was. She's going to be so mad."

"She'll be better when she knows you're okay." Libby accepted the canteen back and slid it onto a loop on the saddle.

"Don't take this the wrong way, but why are you here?" He stepped closer. He'd been alone for a few hours, but seeing Libby after his earlier thoughts drew him like a moth to a flame. And, just like a moth, he had to be careful lest he get burned.

"What? Don't like being rescued by a girl?" Her grin was back, and she propped a hand on her hip.

"I don't mind one bit. Rescue is rescue. But I thought you only came in the mornings."

She bit her lip and looked past him, like there was something more interesting in the trees than meeting his gaze. "I've got something to ask you. That's why I was at the ranch."

The way she said it made his insides clench. He was about to ask her what it was when the rain picked up.

"We'd better head back." She moved toward Gandalf, taking the reins from the horn. "And I guess today's your lucky day because we've only got one horse."

He blinked at her back. "Excuse me?"

"You get two lessons in one day." She turned around, looking at him with confusion.

He felt heat creep up his neck thinking she'd meant he was lucky enough to share a horse with her. Then again, maybe he was.

"All right. Tell me what to do."

She helped him like she'd done this a thousand times before, and it made him wonder if she'd had a boyfriend who she rode with like this. He was situated in the saddle, her explanation being that it would be easier, and ultimately safer, for him to be there, and then she'd climbed up right behind him.

They rode through the forest now, the rain reaching them despite the canopy of leaves above. Libby guided him with pointed directions, sure of where they were heading, but he found it hard to keep his focus. He was keenly aware of the warmth of her behind him. She sat right behind the saddle on the horse with her arms wrapped around his torso like it was the most natural thing.

Again, his thoughts went to the media, but he silenced them with logic. This was his property, it was in the middle of a storm, and they were in a forest. No paparazzi was *that* dedicated.

The rain drove down in sheets, bouncing off his baseball cap and her Stetson behind his neck, but they rode on. The sound of a thousand drops pounding the leaves and the ground made it impossible to talk and, instead, created a type of companionable silence. Still, between thoughts of what she'd come to ask him and him actively trying not to think about her arms around his waist and her pressed against his back, he found his mind was full. Overly so.

He had no reason to like the situation as much as he did, but that was the truth of it. He'd take riding through the chilling rain with Libby so close over most things his scattered thoughts could consider in that moment.

He started to hum, and soon, the lyrics were rolling in his head again. His fingers itched for a pencil and paper, but he stowed the urge.

When the tree line finally broke and he could see the barn, he angled back toward her. "Thanks, rescuer."

"We're not there yet." She grinned. "I'd suggest you hold on."

He only had a second to hear what she was saying when she gave a loud command, her heels moving in, and Gandalf surged forward. It took everything in Harland not to cry out, and as they raced across the slope to the barn, all he could do was hold on to the horn and laugh.

Nineteen

Libby

She would remember the look on Harland's face for the rest of her life. He wore pure and utter joy like a kid taking his first trip to the candy store.

"Careful now, it's muddy," she said as they pulled up to the barn. She'd closed the doors when she brought the other horses in, knowing it would rain. They could have stayed out, but they were already at the fence as if they'd sensed the storm, so she obliged, filling their hay slow-feeders and prepping for her morning chores the next day.

Then Ruth had come down worried about Harland, and Libby had gone on a rescue mission. The only good thing about the mission, aside from rescuing her boss and letting him experience a nice, though short, run, was the fact that he might be in a lenient mood and ready to grant a request.

"Ah!" He slipped as he slid off Gandalf, and his boots hit the mud. He clutched at her knee and hand so that he wouldn't fall, but Libby just laughed.

"I told you."

"Are you always right?"

"Just about." She slid off, no help needed, and pulled the door open while Harland held the horse. When enough space was made, she stood back so they could all shuffle into the barn.

"That was," Harland shook his head, water droplets flinging from his brown locks, "amazing."

"The rescue or the ride?"

"Both?" His grin was boyish and pulled another laugh from her.

"Fair enough. Now let's get something to dry ourselves off with." She disappeared into the tack room and came back with an old towel. "It smells horrible, but it'll work."

She offered it to him first, but he refused, gesturing for her to use it. She began drying off her face, neck, and arms, but had to press her lips shut when Harland lifted up his shirt to wipe his face. The skin beneath was tanned and ripped with muscles. Yep, he definitely took care of himself.

She forced her gaze to the floor, memorizing the pattern of the pavers.

"Here." Her chambray shirt appeared in front of her eyes, and she looked up at Harland. "I think you left this earlier today."

"Thanks." Pulling the wet shirt from her skin, she considered the over shirt and then changed her mind. "I'll be right back."

Stepping into the tack room, she quickly pulled off the sopping mess of her shirt and pulled the over shirt on instead, buttoning it up to the top. It wasn't super comfortable worn like that, but at least it didn't cling like she'd won a wet t-shirt contest as her other shirt had.

Then, given the privacy of the room, she fluffed her hair out. It had gotten wet, but her hat had spared some of it. She didn't know why it mattered in that moment, but for some reason she didn't want to stand in front of Harland looking like a drowned cat.

"Better," she said, stepping back out into the main barn area. The rain pounded on the tin roof, but despite the sound, it was kind of nice. Soothing in a way.

"Man, this is a crazy storm."

"Doesn't it rain like this in LA?"

"Sometimes, but that causes flooding, and it's a hassle because no one knows how to drive in it."

"In rain? I thought that was only snow."

"Any weather that's not sunny, really."

She laughed and tucked a strand of hair behind her ear.

"What were you going to ask me? Before?"

She looked up and caught him observing her. Was now the right time to ask? Would there be a better time? Probably not.

"Let's sit on the hay. We can prop the door open a little for the view."

He followed her lead, not pressing the question, and when they were seated on hay bales, backs against more hay, she took the plunge.

"You know about my therapy clients." She shot him a quick look, and he nodded. "I just met with the mother of twins today. The girls are really sweet, or at least I think so. I mostly talked with the mom, but she's interested in having them do sessions with me."

"That's great."

His gentle encouragement was so unfamiliar to her it took her off guard for a moment. The support felt like telling a good friend something. But this was Harland.

Blinking to clear her thoughts, she continued. "She wants them to have sessions together though. I get that. I mean twins are used to doing everything together, and these are a special case." She would respect their privacy, and also the law, by keeping their conditions private, but she needed him to know *why* it mattered. "The only problem is that my arena is too small." And here came the kicker. "I was wondering if I could maybe host the sessions...here."

His eyes watched the descending drops of water as they crashed to the earth from the roof above. She wanted to know what he was thinking, but she was beginning to see that Harland was the type of guy who only spoke when he knew what he wanted to say.

Libby found that tedious. It was best to just say it and get it out in the open.

Finally, he shifted to look back at her, his forehead creased. "I don't think that's a good idea."

"Your arena is almost twice the size of mine and—"

"It's not that. I love that you help people and will help those girls with your care, but I'm not comfortable having people on my property."

"I have my own insurance. If anything happens, it's on me, not you. And—"

"It's not the liability. It's my privacy."

"For the love of all that's good, no one *cares* about you or those stupid articles." The words flew out, unrestrained.

Harland looked like she'd slapped him across the face.

"What I meant to say," Libby began, moving into fix-it mode, but Harland held up a hand.

"What articles?"

She narrowed her eyes. "The ones about you and all the stuff in LA and blah blah blah." Now that she'd said her mind, she wasn't going to back down. "We don't care. No one in Winter does. I mean, *maybe* someone like Sarah Lawson does, but she's a teenager. You're just some rich guy who moved to town. That's it."

He leaned back as if waiting for her to say more. When she didn't, he took a breath. "Did you read them?"

She flinched. "Sort of."

He tilted his head. "What does that mean?"

"That I don't have much patience for gossip or stupid tabloids so, while I saw some of them and maybe read a little, I didn't dig in. I didn't care to." She wasn't going to add that she'd already met him by that point and thought there was no way half of what they claimed was true. Maybe not even a quarter.

"If you'd read them, then you'd know more about why I value my privacy."

"Enlighten me." She propped her elbow on her knee and gave him her full attention.

"You are something, Liberty." He rubbed a hand over his face and then through his hair. The wet strands made the brown almost look black. "I guess the long and short of it was that I toured with a woman last year. She's a talented musician and opened for me. We'd connected online because she has such a big social media following."

"Always about social media," Libby muttered.

"It's true. Her following was a big part of why my label wanted her to join us. Everything was fine until she claimed that I'd forced her into an unreciprocated relationship."

Libby gasped. "Like..."

"Like made her do things she wasn't comfortable with. All of which was a complete lie." He grimaced, the memories clearly painful. "But remember that following? Well, she decimated me online. Degraded my character, called me names, claimed a whole bunch of unfounded things, and by and large made me look like some kind of horrible guy who...well, you get the idea."

Libby shook her head. There was no way she could imagine Harland ever being that kind of guy. Granted, she didn't know him well, but she just couldn't see it.

"What happened?"

"Lawyers got involved because what she was saying was false, and it was a he said, she said type of thing. But it was already so widespread, the cease and desist order didn't do much good because the damage was done."

"So you moved to Winter?"

"There was a lot more to it than that," he admitted. He turned his gaze back to the rain. "But I'm careful for a reason. It's not that I think this mother or her daughters are bad people, quite the opposite, but I know what greed can do. One media outlet who gets wind of someone coming onto my ranch and guess what? They're a target. It happens all the time. It's why I had you and your father sign NDA agreements. I hate that. It's not who I want to be, but I love this house and this country, and I want to keep it safe. Protect it."

Her heart melted at his open honesty. It was the most personal thing she'd heard him say, and every word was measured and filled with thought. While she might say a lot, hardly any of it got much attention, and it made her feel like her earlier words had done irrevocable damage.

"I'm sorry, Harland." He looked back at her. "Yeah, about all that stuff, but more so about what I said. I don't really think things through before I say them."

"I think I got that." The corner of his lips quirked, and she yanked her attention back to his eyes.

"I'm trying to work on that about me, but clearly, I'm not doing a great job. But I'm also sorry that you feel such a tenuous grip on your life here. While it was poorly said, I meant every word. But I know that's no consolation." She tilted her head to the side. "What if I had Sue sign an NDA as well? The girls are too young still, but I think she'd agree. She just wants to help her kids, you know?"

His expression shifted. "You really need this space, huh?"

"You saw our house." She offered up a chuckle. "We're not going to win any awards for space or for being fancy."

"You don't need to be fancy." The way his gaze bored into her made her feel seen from the core of her being to the tip of her nose. It was clear that Harland thought deeply, but she also felt as if he could see past who she thought she was to who she wanted to be.

It was disconcerting and also electrifying.

"I suppose I'll never be called that," she said with a forced chuckle.

"I didn't mean it like that." Then, with a swift motion she'd not expected, he brushed her hair behind her ear. "You're just right. Like this."

The silence between them crackled like lightning while her heartbeat provided the thunder. She couldn't move. Couldn't draw in air. The tension zinged between them, and she had the strangest urge to reach out and trace his lip with her thumb.

Gandalf stamped his foot and drew their attention.

"Goodness. I completely forgot about him." She flushed. She didn't know what to say to Harland, but she knew how to take care of horses. "I should get him dried off and in his stall."

"Need any help?"

Was it her imagination or was Harland's voice a little husky? She pushed those thoughts aside. "No, I can get it."

"Then I should probably head up to the house. I bet Ruth is beside herself. Here's hoping she hasn't called the cops on us." He laughed, but it sounded strained.

"Wish I could offer you an umbrella," she said, keeping her back to him so she didn't have to interpret what his expressive features were telegraphing.

"It'll be fine. I don't melt."

She kept her focus on brushing down Gandalf until she sensed him behind her. Close, but not too close.

"You can use the arena, Libby. I get what you're saying, and I guess I'm willing to take a risk when it's on something good."

She turned then, knowing she'd see his true feelings in his eyes. "Are you sure?"

"Positive." Their gazes locked, and she felt that same zinging sensation.

Then he was gone, walking toward the end of the barn and into the storm.

Twenty

Harland

HARLAND: Are you ready for today?

LIBBY: Ugh. Do I have to be?

HARLAND: I think that's my line.

LIBBY: It's just…those LA people. They can be a pain in the rear.

HARLAND: Why do I feel attacked?

LIBBY: …

LIBBY: JK. Present company excluded.

HARLAND: But seriously, will you be ready for everything they're asking for?

LIBBY: I saw the email. It's all easy stuff, and if they need me to ride some, I can. I'll be working under protest. That's all.

LIBBY: And I think this constitutes hazard pay.

Harland laughed out loud and then clamped a hand over his mouth. He was still in bed, dreading the day ahead of him, but he'd needed to check with Libby about the photoshoot, something he'd asked her about days before, and now they were texting.

His stomach clenched as the three dots appeared.

LIBBY: Unless you just fired me for asking for extra pay?

He quickly typed his response.

HARLAND: Hazard pay approved.

LIBBY: Yessss

HARLAND: See you in a few hours.

LIBBY: I'll be the one *not* from LA

Harland sent a laughing emoji and closed his phone.

He fell back against his pillows and let his gaze roam the wooden ceiling, his heart racing and his mind trying to catch up.

Libby was...unexpected.

He hadn't planned on telling her most of the truth that day in the barn, but there'd been something so bracingly refreshing about her blunt words to him that he'd wanted to honor her with his side of the story. Yes, there was more he hadn't said, but she had the basics.

But then he'd touched her cheek like that and was sure she was going to push him away or at least demand he leave her alone. But she'd done neither of those things.

Was it possible she'd felt the same attraction he did in that moment? More than just that moment, but especially then. They'd been soaked and wild-haired, but he'd only thought she looked more beautiful. Definitely not fancy, but he was beginning to see that fancy wasn't all it was cracked up to be.

The people coming from LA today would be fancy. Violet had been fancy when she wasn't pretending to be something else. And every one of his other girlfriends had also had a bit of *fancy* to them, but none of them made him feel like Libby did. Cold and on fire all at once. Like every molecule in his body gravitated toward her.

His phone dinged.

> LIBBY: Also...good luck today. I know you're not looking forward to it.

He read the message three times. Sure, Libby was outspoken, but he was fairly certain her sweet side would be his undoing. He thanked her and pulled himself out of bed.

The few hours before the crew showed up flew by. He spent time prepping as much as he could, knowing they would bring their own makeup artists and stylists, but he'd had Ruth plan out snacks and drinks and spent time setting up the porch for the ease of his soon-to-be guests.

"I think we're almost ready," he told Ruth.

"They'll be late. They're always late," she said, taking the last bowl to the table and filling it with drinks that would get topped off with ice once the crew showed up. "Are you ready?"

"As I'll ever be, I guess. I'm already planning out a secondary location on the ranch where I can have all this stuff take place. I don't like the idea of people coming to my house."

"I know, Mr. Harland, but I'll be on guard. Thankfully, they aren't really allowed inside, and we've got the outdoor access bathroom."

"True." He'd noted that and asked his realtor about it, but the man had only mentioned something about the idea of a pool that never came to fruition. All that mattered to Harland was to minimize the access any of the people had to his personal space.

Fifteen minutes after they were scheduled to arrive, the vans showed up, and chaos ensued. Harland had seen Libby's truck drive in ahead of them, but he'd known better than to bother her while she was at work. She'd planned to bring up Sirius for part of the shoot per the emailed request that he have "country things" ready for the shoot.

Otherwise, he'd hoped to minimize her need to interact with the team. He told himself it wasn't about the media or rumors, but maybe a little of it was. She was stunningly beautiful, and despite the fact each team member had signed NDAs, he still couldn't trust them not to spread gossip like a California wildfire if they thought there was even the remotest possibility there was something between Harland and Libby.

But was there?

It wasn't the time to think of it, but he couldn't help but like the sound of their names together.

He snapped himself out of his reverie when he saw Mateo, the photographer, exit the first van. It was time to put on his game face to slip more easily back into the LA way of life.

"So we meet again. What a picturesque background." Mateo didn't really *look* at anyone. He simply looked around them. Harland had been put off by this at first, but once he saw the way the man worked, he began to understand it. Mateo saw the world from a different perspective than Harland did, and while Harland might write a lyric about something, Mateo was always going to be thinking about how he'd photograph something.

"Good to see you again, Mateo. And you are?" He turned to a younger man standing next to Mateo, his own black camera bag in hand.

"Hi, I'm Jamin Hill." The man's grip was firm, and he looked Harland in the eye, not like he was proving anything, but like he was genuinely glad to meet him. "I'm a fan of your music, sir. Really looking forward to being on this shoot."

Harland grinned. The young man looked to be in his mid-twenties if Harland had to guess, but he didn't appear star-struck. "Cut the sir and call me Harland."

"You've got it." Jamin had a calm confidence about him as he trailed after Mateo who was scoping out the best locations for the shoot.

After the photographers, a group of women and a few men flooded out of the vans and began to unload gear, outfits, makeup cases, and everything else they'd need.

"Let's get you into makeup," a familiar voice said. "Daylight's a wastin'."

He spun around. "Rose?"

"Hey ya, stranger." She accepted his hug and squeezed back hard. "It's been too long, Har."

Only a handful of people ever got away with calling him Har, and Rose Roberts was one of them.

"It's good to see you. I didn't know you were going to be here."

"I bribed Winslow to keep it a secret. Had to give you something to take your mind off of it all once we got here."

He laughed and felt one of the bands that had been tightening around his chest loosen. "You don't know how true that is."

"Good. Then let's get to it. The faster we start," she began.

"The faster we're done," he finished.

They'd worked so many shoots together in the past, her managing them like a pro, and now he felt like he could see the end of the day in sight. It was no longer a nebulous, unformed thing, but something with substance and shape. Rose would get things done, and he could trust her completely.

"All right, Har. Let's go."

He grinned at her and let his friend drag him across the prairie and into the day ahead.

Twenty-One

Libby

Libby had never been around so may snooty people at once. She'd joked with Harland earlier that morning about the "LA people," but she'd thought her words had been just that—jokes. Well, the joke was on her. She'd never been snapped at so much in one day, and that was saying something considering she lived with Vicky.

"One more time please. Horse girl—" The main photographer waved his hand around in the air.

"Libby," the other photographer, she thought his name was Jamin, supplied.

"Right. Her. I need her to race across the background again, but *on my mark*. Got it?"

"One sec, Mateo," Jamin said. He walked up to Libby, Sirius bobbing his head, seemingly as frustrated as she was. "I'm so sorry about him." Jamin kept his voice low. "I promise he is not as rude as he's coming off. He's just not good with words. Or people."

She huffed a laugh. "I get it. But to be honest, I think Sirius has about one more good run in him before he'll need to be watered and take a break for food."

"Totally get it. I think we can make this last shot work. What I'd suggest," he leaned in as if conspiring with her, "is to wait two seconds after Mateo says go. You've been right on cue, but I think his shutter speed is a little too fast, and he's missing you."

Libby grinned. She hadn't expected Jamin to help her. Some of her tightened muscles relaxed a little. "Will do." She offered a wink and then directed Sirius up to the mark Jamin had placed on the ground.

With one glance at Harland, who was much closer to Mateo, she readied herself for the man's signal. She understood the concept Mateo gave her about the shot. Harland would be in focus in the front, looking off into the distance holding his guitar, and the mountains would be his background. Then she and Sirius would race through the background. A blurred image, if they could get it right.

"On my mark," Mateo called out. "And...go!"

She hesitated just as Jamin had said and then spurred Sirius into action. He tossed his head, and then they raced across the prairie and into the shot. She'd let her hair blow freely in the wind and knew she was grinning widely. She loved the feeling of flying across the prairie.

They reached the end of what he'd marked the shot to be, and she slowed, turning Sirius around and heading back to the two photographers who were consulting their cameras.

"Yes!" Mateo pumped a fist in a very youthful action. "That was it. Wonderfully done." He caught sight of her and actually smiled back at her. "It was perfect. Thank you."

"Glad to hear it. We're done with this guy?" She petted Sirius' neck, and Jamin gave her the nod. Mateo was already on to the next shot, but as she looked back at him, she caught sight of Harland. He'd been suspiciously quiet toward her all day, but now she saw him talking closely with one of the women from the team. She had some type of title, but Libby couldn't remember it. As she watched, he burst out laughing, and their shoulders fell together.

Pushing down sudden feelings of jealousy she didn't want to admit to, Libby trotted Sirius down to the watering trough and let him drink his fill before she took his saddle and harness off, brushed him down, and set him free in the pasture.

There were a few more shots with horses, but Mateo had said they'd only get to them if they had time. Which meant she had to stick around but not get in the way. *Great.*

It was already mid-afternoon, and she had a feeling if they wanted the horses, the Golden Hour might be the time for them, which was still a ways off. Rather than stay at the barn, she decided to go up to the house.

Ruth had made a point to tell her that there was food for everyone, and Libby was welcome to it. Seeing as she hadn't packed a lunch, it was past time for her to eat something, though she found she dreaded the possible interactions with more of the crew.

"Put on your big girl pants, Libby. You can do this."

Pep talk ringing through her mind, Libby walked up the gravel road and cut across the manicured lawn to the pavers that led to the deck. She nearly turned tail and ran when she saw the huddle of stick-figure women hovering around the diet sodas, but she pushed down her discomfort and walked up like she belonged there. Because, gosh darn it, she did.

She reached for a paper plate and napkin then began to fill the plate with a half sandwich, a serving of chips, and two pieces of watermelon.

"Someone's hungry," one of the girls said. The other two snickered.

Libby didn't want to even acknowledge that they'd spoken, but they were standing right in front of the sodas, and she needed a caffeine boost if she was going to make it through the rest of the day.

"Excuse me."

She picked up a Dr. Pepper and turned, but not before one of the girls made a hissing sound. "You're drinking *soda?* Don't you know how bad it is for you?"

Libby had been around bullies in school, but she'd determined not to let them get to her or her friends. The temptation now was to walk off like she hadn't heard anything, but to her, that would mean they'd won. Still, that little voice inside reminded her that speaking her mind often got her in trouble.

Then again, she was used to trouble.

"I'm sure it's real bad," she said, turning to face them. They were a trio of lookalikes with long blonde hair perfectly styled, expensive clothing, and makeup that made them look more like dolls than humans. "But the fact of the matter is I don't much care. I'd rather live my life enjoying things like a soda now and again than to deprive myself and shame others for their choices."

Balancing her plate on her arm, she popped the top and took a long, cold drink before turning away and heading to the opposite part of the deck as far away from the trio as possible.

She turned her face to the mountains and tried to ignore the furrows of shame the woman's words had tried to bore into her. She knew better than to care what others thought, but that didn't mean she was completely deaf. They were probably still standing there making comments about her jean size and how she had a little extra around the waist she could get rid of if she stopped drinking soda.

Well, the joke was on them. She hardly ever had soda, but something about the crisp, carbonated drink appealed on the hot day, and she wasn't about to ignore that urge when she'd spent the day working. She was justifying it to herself, she knew that, but the women had gotten to her.

Libby's gaze went back to the tent the crew had set up to prep Harland. He sat in a high-backed chair, and the woman she'd seen earlier, Rose she thought her name was, was next to him. She had all his attention and was laughing like he was the world's greatest comedian.

Then she reached out and touched his arm, and Libby felt that spike of jealousy again.

Uh oh. No you don't, girl.

She knew she had no claim on Harland. One gentle face touch did not a romance make. He was just a kind guy who had experienced a moment of weakness, or something like that. She'd just rescued him from being lost in the woods. That had to count for something.

"You work for Harland, huh?" One of the trio walked in front of her. Since Libby was sitting on the deck, they were about eye to eye.

Libby looked back to see her two friends watching them from by the food table. Was this some sort of experiment? Send one of them to talk to the country girl?

"Part time."

"With the horses?" The girl was pretty, her blonde hair cut just above her shoulders, and she had freckles across her nose and cheeks that were slightly reddened by the sun.

"Yep." Libby munched on a chip, uncertain as to where this conversation was going.

"But like," she looked over her shoulder at her friends, "is there *more* going on? I mean, it's Harland Grey we're talking about."

"I take care of his horses. End of story."

"I don't believe you." She folded her arms across her chest. "I've read the stories."

"Then you know some journalists fabricated tales. Good for you." She shoved another chip into her mouth. She didn't want to have this conversation.

"So you're defending what he did?"

"Look, I work with Mr. Harland's horses, not his media team. Take it up with them. Or don't, if you want to keep your job." She flashed a pointed stare at the woman. "All I know is he pays a good wage, and he treats his staff well and with respect. That's what matters to me, and that's what matters in Winter." Libby had seen how he all but coddled Ruth, and she'd heard her father tell stories as well. Harland was a good boss, and it was clear this girl was trying to get gossip out of her.

"*Sheesh*. You don't have to be so rude."

Libby knew her cheeks resembled the sunset now, but she couldn't help it. "Me? Rude? You need to look in the mirror."

The girl scoffed and spun on her heel, tromping back down the path, and Libby fully turned her back on them. She should have kept her temper, but she couldn't abide the girl's prying and insinuation that Harland was anything less than a gentleman.

"Everything okay?"

Libby startled and nearly dropped her plate. Rose stood a few feet away, a concerned look on her face.

"Yeah. Fine." Libby was not in the mood to talk to the woman who'd been flirting with Harland and was likely friends with the other girls. If this was what Hollywood was like, she never needed to visit.

"You sure? Harland wanted me to make sure everything was all right."

The words landed like an anvil on Libby's heart. Harland had sent Rose to intercede on the girl's behalf? What was this, opposite day? She'd stood up for him, and this was how she was repaid?

"Everything's fine." Libby's tone said otherwise but that couldn't be helped.

"Bella looks upset. She's got a big social media influence, and we just want to make sure everyone on the shoot is getting along." To her credit, Rose looked like she wasn't happy to be broaching the subject with Libby, but the sheer injustice Libby felt was enough to stoke the embers of her anger into a roaring blaze.

"I'm happy to get along with anyone, but, social media following or not, Bella shouldn't have said the things she did about my employer." Libby drew in a deep breath and tried for a more even tone. "I don't abide people trying to spread gossip. If you're here to do that too, then I'll just see myself off the deck."

She jumped down, flashing a tightlipped smile at the woman, and turned toward the barn.

At least there she could sit in peace and quiet and enjoy her sandwich without interruption. It just proved to her again how much she wasn't cut out for this life. What was worse was the way Harland was acting. Like he enjoyed it all and was chummy with everyone. It left a sour taste in Libby's mouth.

She cut a look across the yard toward Harland again. He was laughing and joking with none other than *Bella*. If only he knew what she really thought of him.

Libby ducked her head and picked up her pace. The sooner she was with the horses again, the better.

Twenty-Two

Harland

Harland watched as Libby made her way back toward the barn after he'd sent Rose to make sure everything was all right. A pit formed in his stomach, and he wondered what would have caused her to leave. Had Rose said something?

He watched as his friend made her way back to him. While he tried to pay attention to everything the social media influencer, Bella, was saying, he'd long lost interest in the details of her last trip to Iceland and how she'd been on set of a popular band's latest music video.

He got it. She was well connected, and this was part of Winslow's not so subtle idea to bring Harland back into the positive limelight, but he would rather scrap it all and take a horse ride instead.

"And then I was like, this is so sus, you know?"

He looks down at the girl who had to be almost fifteen years his junior and realized he had no clue what she was saying, even though it was in English.

"Sounds...like it." He noted her closed off expression to his lame reply. If he wanted to salvage this he had to crank up the charm, but he just couldn't muster the effort.

Thoughts of Violet came back to him and made him feel physically sick.

"Excuse me, I've got to talk to Rose. Good luck with Coldplay next month." He caught her surprised smile at the fact he had been listening, at least at first, and left her to duck her head over her phone. They'd taken a selfie, and he was sure it was about to be plastered over every digital space imaginable. At least he'd drawn the line at doing a TikTok dance.

"Rosie." He gestured for her to follow him away from the tent. The sun was on its way to setting, and he could see Mateo out in the field with Jamin at his side, motioning with his hands no doubt to show the younger man his vision.

"Well?" he asked.

Rose narrowed her eyes. "Why do I get the feeling I'm some sort of middle-woman here? Like, if you two just had a conversation you wouldn't need me."

His brow furrowed. "What do you mean? What kind of conversation? What's wrong?"

"I guess I'm doing this." She rolled her eyes skyward. "I asked her if anything was wrong, saying that you'd sent me to talk to her, and specifically mentioned Bella like you said."

He nodded. He'd suggested that because of the conversation he'd had with Libby. She knew how social media had played a role in the past, and he thought that might clue her in to the fact that Bella, as young and seemingly naive as she was, actually held a good bit of clout.

"That was the wrong move."

His stomach dropped. "What do you mean?"

"She said, and I quote, "I don't abide people trying to spread gossip." And she made it very clear that Bella was trying to get private information out of Libby about you."

"Really?" She nodded. Harland winced and rubbed at his jaw.

Libby was gone now, likely inside the barn as her refuge, and a big part of him wanted to march down there and clear this up himself. But he couldn't do that. Not when there were critical eyes on him like this.

"If you want my two cents, which you're getting one way or the other, I like Libby. A lot. And I think you messed up sending me."

"You know why I had to."

"No, I know why *you* think you had to. And I do get it. Trust me, I do." She shook her head, and he knew she was thinking of other clients she'd worked with. "But there comes a time when you have to live your life and let the chips fall where they may."

"I'm not sure I follow."

"Harland, how long have I known you?"

"Over twenty years."

"Exactly. And in that time, I've approved of zero of the girls you've dated."

He rolled his eyes.

"Don't you do that. It's not that I didn't think they were beautiful or successful or sweet. It's that I knew they weren't for you." She held up a hand. "And before you ask how I know, just call it woman's intuition. But after five minutes—or less—of talking with Libby, I've got to say. She's something special."

His insides twisted into knots. This wasn't the conversation he'd expected to have. If anyone were to overhear it... But that was Rose's point, wasn't it? He cared so much about what others thought that he was letting them dictate how he lived his life, not deciding for himself.

"I don't know, Rosie. She might be too good for me." The words slipped out before he had a chance to think them over, something that almost never happened to him, but the moment they were free, he knew he meant them.

"And that's how it should be." She placed a hand on his arm. "Every one of the women you've dated so far have been the kind that are a dime a dozen in LA. Beyond beautiful but with no substance." She made a face. "That was harsh. I think what I mean is that their aspirations are to look like they have it all, even when they don't. But Libby? She's the real deal. She knows who she is, and she's not afraid to live that—or speak it, for that matter. I think that's good for you."

"I can't be in a relationship, Rose." The words drew heat at the back of his neck. He'd only known Libby for a few weeks, and while the word *relationship* sent a thrill up his spine, he shut it down immediately.

"I'm not saying act on it at this moment, but also don't miss what's right in front of your face, Har. You've been singing love songs for over fifteen years, and I think you've put a lot of ideas into your head about what love is. Maybe, just this once, you shouldn't look for it in the perfect moments but the imperfect ones."

She gave him a look that said she meant business and then turned to Mateo. "Ready for the last round?"

Jamin gave them the thumbs up, and she looked back at Harland. "We're almost done. Hang in there."

And he did, but all he could think of was the conversation he needed to have with Libby. He'd messed up sending Rose to talk with her, but now he had Rose's words in his mind, and he wasn't sure what to do with them.

She's the real deal.

Like he didn't already know that.

But the fact of the matter was he still had buried secrets and a heart full of pain, and he wasn't sure he could get past it in time to seize that imperfect moment if it came.

Twenty-Three

Libby

Libby jogged her knee up and down where she leaned against the fence eagerly awaiting her first lesson with Ash and Sage, Sue's twin girls. Three days had passed since the photoshoot, and Libby hadn't heard from Harland, but she knew from a quick call with Ruth that the arena was open for her use as they'd planned.

Sure, she'd been a coward by not reaching out to Harland herself, but after the debacle that was Bella and Rose and the rest of the photoshoot crew, all except for Jamin who had been unexpectedly cool, she wasn't sure she *wanted* to text him.

Liar.

Fine. She'd wanted to text him, but it had seemed like a bad idea.

Gandalf shifted closer to the fence, and she absentmindedly rubbed a hand along his mane. He was a sensitive horse, and she was certain he could feel her frustration and confusion bubbling just beneath the surface. On the other side of him, Butterscotch stood, waiting for her new young riders. She and Gandalf seemed to be getting along well, which made Libby happy. One bright spot in an anxious, gray morning.

If she could have, she would have asked Sue to meet at her dad's house, but she'd drawn the line at that. She was an adult, and she would handle the situation like an adult. She'd just ignore him, simple as that.

A cloud of dust rose up from the road before she saw the truck, but soon it turned into the driveway, and Libby stepped out from the shade on one side of the arena to wave Sue down.

"Made it okay?" she asked when the woman had parked and two gangling tweens got out. They chattered incessantly to one another, and one held a phone with earbuds going to each ear.

"Sure did. Wow, this place is amazing." Sue whispered it as if the fact they were there might be illegal.

Libby had made sure Sue knew whose house it was and had her sign the NDA, which she'd been happy to do, and she'd also made the girls promise they wouldn't share anything about the place on social media. They were a little too young for Harland's music, Libby thought, but that didn't mean they weren't on social platforms.

"Nope." Sue turned back to the girls, her tone leaving no space for argument. "Put the phone away. What did I tell you?"

She turned back to Libby. "It doesn't have Wi-Fi or anything, but it can take photos. I told them not to bring it. I'm sorry." She looked around nervously. "The music helps them sometimes."

"It's all right. Leaving it in the car is great." Then, turning to the girls, Libby put on her in-charge voice. "All right, girls. Let's go. Time for your first lesson with Butterscotch." She pointed out the buckskin who tossed her head as if to say hi.

"Who's that horse?" Sage asked, pointing to Gandalf who stood at the fence line. He was either hoping for treats or wanted to make a new friend in Butterscotch.

"That's Gandalf."

"Like the wizard?" Ash said.

"That's the one."

"Cool."

The girls followed Libby to the arena, and she started with safety instructions for when they were around horses. Then she showed them their helmets.

"We have to wear those?" Sage said with an edge of a whine to the words.

"The thing about horses is that they are safe, but they can be dangerous if treated in the wrong way. I know you girls wouldn't knowingly do anything to hurt Butterscotch here, or any of my other horses when you're both riding, but see how tall she is?" The both nodded. "Well, even horses get spooked sometimes, and I've seen them rear up for no other reason than they saw twig and thought it was a snake. Falling from that high isn't fun. We can't count on her never getting nervous or spooked, so you'll wear the helmets to protect you. Got it?"

They didn't look excited, but they nodded.

"Since this is just our first session, I want you both to get a chance to get to know Butterscotch, and I'll let you do a quick ride around the arena with me leading you. Sound like fun?"

"Yeah!" they both shouted in unison.

She started the session with her usual routine for new clients, teaching them about the horse, about how to interact with it and around it, and then finally ending on how horse and rider had a special bond.

"This bond," she explained, "means that Butterscotch can sense how you're feeling."

"Will she get sad if I'm sad?" Ash asked, eyes wide.

"It's not exactly like that, but if you're really nervous, sometimes that can affect a horse."

"Wow." Sage's mouth made an O.

"But at the same time, that helps us to think through what we're feeling, right?"

The girls nodded.

"Okay, who wants to ride first?"

Both girls looked at each other, nervous. Had she overdone it on the feelings talk? They were a little younger than some of her other clients, and she was just getting to know them.

She forced a smile and was about to ask again when a deep voice drew their attention.

"You ladies going on a ride?" Harland stepped out of the shadows of the barn—how long had he been there—and walked forward. "I'm a little jealous."

"Jealous? Isn't that your horse?" Ash asked.

Libby's stomach clenched even though she knew she'd done nothing wrong. She hadn't even told the girls who owned Gandalf, they'd just guessed.

"He sure is, but you want to know something funny?"

"What?" Ash said, the bolder of the two.

"I'm just learning how to ride too."

"No way," Sage said. She giggled, clearly charmed by Harland.

"Yes way. I'm a newbie."

"You could go first," Sage suggested, looking between Harland and Libby. "Couldn't he go first, Miss Libby?"

Libby felt Harland's gaze on her as she looked between the girls. It was clear they were nervous after her safety and emotions talk, and if Harland was willing to go first, it might pave the way for the girls to feel more comfortable.

"I guess it's up to Mr. Harland." She braved a glance in his direction and felt the weight of his gaze boring into her.

"I mean, are you girls sure? I don't want to take up your riding time."

"I want to see you do it first," Ash said with a firm nod.

"Yeah, me too." Sage was going to agree with whatever her sister said.

"All right then," Libby said, regaining control of the situation. "One arena loop for Mr. Harland."

He made his way into the arena and over to Butterscotch. She couldn't bear to meet his gaze as she adjusted the saddle for him, lowering the stirrups to land where she thought his feet might fit. She felt him behind her and her stomach clenched.

"Up you go," she said, stepping back.

"Libby." He said her name but there was a world of meaning behind the single word.

"You get one loop." She could tell he knew what she meant. That he had one loop to explain or else that was it.

"One loop it is." He pulled himself into the saddle, and she noticed he was more comfortable this time. And then, just like she'd do with the girls, she took Butterscotch's lead and began a slow walk around the arena.

"I'm really sorry. About the shoot."

She didn't look up, just kept her gaze ahead. "Oh?"

"I sent Rose to speak with you because..." He fumbled for words and she snuck a glance. His eyes were on her. "Because I was afraid."

"I'd *never* spread gossip or lies about you, Harland. I thought you'd at least know that about me by now."

He paled. "No, no, that's not what I mean."

"What then?" Libby wasn't following.

"I was afraid of what the crew would think if *I* was the one talking to you."

Her cheeks flamed red. "Can't be seen with the hired help, huh?"

"More like can't be seen flirting. With anyone."

His words landed between them, and she almost stopped walking, but Butterscotch kept her pace, knowing the drill, and Libby tripped along.

"You were talking with Rose the whole time." Yet again her boldness won out.

He laughed—actually laughed. "Rose and I went to high school together. We dated for two weeks my senior year, and then she cheated on me with the captain of the football team when she thought we'd broken up after a fight. They've been married since their first year of college. She's one of my closest friends in LA, and whatever you thought you saw, it wasn't flirting."

Libby swallowed. Was it possible she'd seen something that wasn't there?

"And I'm sorry about Bella." He practically spat her name out. "I'm sorry I was too much of a coward to see if you were okay myself."

They were nearing the girls, big smiles on their faces, and Libby wondered if she'd had it all wrong. If she'd thought the worst of Harland because she hadn't wanted to admit that seeing him with someone else poked at a sore spot in her heart. One that wanted him to look at *her* like she was special. Like she was worth talking to amidst a crew full of beautiful, model-like women she could never compete with.

"I understand."

"I'm not sure you do, but I want to make it up to you." They were almost back at the starting point.

"What do you have in mind?" She shot him a quick sidelong glance.

"I know you're busy and have other jobs, but are you free Sunday night?"

She was free most nights, but she pretended to think about it. "Sure."

"Good. Meet me at the barn at seven."

"That better be in the evening."

"It is." His smile warmed a part of her that had frozen over after the photoshoot. A part she was wondering if she needed to protect rather than give in to opening up.

The girls started clapping. "You did really good," Ash said.

"Yeah," Sage agreed.

"Now it's my turn." Ash stepped forward, hands on her hips.

"But I wanted to go first," Sage said.

"It's okay, girls. You'll each get a turn," Libby said, making sure the squabbling ended there. "Come on, then. You first, Ash."

She helped the young girl up and handed her the reins even though she would be leading Butterscotch. A quick glance told her Harland was staying right there to keep Sage company, and the sight filled her with inexplicable joy and full-on terror.

He was too good at this. Too easy to forgive and much too easy to like. But still, as her gaze sought him out past all the excuses she could muster, she could only look forward to Sunday and what he had in mind.

Twenty-Four

Harland

It was really happening. Anticipation sent tightening bands around his chest, making it hard to breathe. He looked over Dawson's shoulder at the designs spread out on his eight-foot dining table and knew there was no turning back now.

"I really think this will make the space functional but also comfortable," Dawson said. "Once we get the build going, I'll have the designer I work with send samples we can go over so everything matches your style."

"I don't know that I have a style," Harland said on a laugh. "But I'll pick out what I like."

"The great thing about Brynlee is that she suggests things that match so you really can't go wrong." He straightened and looked around the main room of the house.

"Sounds good to me. And before you ask, no, I didn't design any of this. Just picked a color palette and let the designer go for it. Ruth oversaw most of it."

"It works, but I'm sure you've added a few personal touches."

"What gave it away? The wall of vintage guitars?"

Dawson grinned. "It was a hint."

"Yeah, you've got a point. I guess I can add things to something that's already there, but I can't start it from scratch. Unless we're talking about music."

"I hear that."

"Do you record your own stuff?" Harland crossed his arms, leaning back on his heels as his bare feet sunk into the plush rug.

"Used to, but nowadays, I pretty much just work with other successful artists."

"In Winter, Montana." He didn't mean for it to sound as incredulous as it had, but Dawson seemed to get his meaning.

"Yep. You underestimate the need for those in the business to get away."

"Not sure I'd say that." Harland shook his head. "Hey, want a cup of coffee? Or do you need to be somewhere?"

"You were my to-do list item for today. I'm down for coffee."

Harland begged Ruth to make them two lattes, and then he ushered Dawson onto the deck where the shade was deepest. Settled in comfortable chairs, Harland realized this was the first time since leaving Los Angeles that he'd felt at ease with someone he'd just met. Well, aside from Libby.

"How are you doing, being here in Winter?" Dawson leaned back in the cushioned chair. "I remember my adjustment period took a solid six months before I was used to the lack of traffic, the need to drive an hour for any kind of real shopping, and the utter peace and quiet."

"I'm adjusting faster than I thought I would, but that probably has something to do with the fact that I was beyond ready to leave LA"

"I hear that." Dawson sipped his coffee, his gaze taking in the mountains and the few head of cattle that dotted the distance. "Mind if I ask a personal question?"

The gut clench was inevitable, but Harland found himself agreeing. "Sure."

"Have people in town left you alone?"

It wasn't the type of personal question Harland had been expecting. "Yeah. I mean, I can't say that I've gone into town much, but Libby took me to the diner, and it went relatively smoothly. Just a teen girl noticed me in a vocal way, but that got shut down quickly."

Dawson laughed. "That'll happen, but I'm glad to hear it."

"I expected more, actually." He cringed. "Not that I deserve that or anything, just that I've been hounded since the first articles came out, and I've become a bit of a hermit because of it. That outing was nice, but I guess I kind of doubt it'll stay like that every time I go out. I'm just waiting for the other shoe to drop."

"I get it, I do. But someone in your position has to make a choice." He shot Harland an apologetic look. "But I don't need to be telling you your business."

"No, say what you were going to say." He was genuinely curious.

"I'll admit, I was curious. I looked at some of the articles but could see them for what they were. Sensational and lacking any evidence."

Harland swallowed but held his tongue. He wanted to hear the man out.

"The problem with social media is that it's loud and it's widely used, so it spreads like wildfire in the summer heat, but it also leaves behind a wake of dead, black things that have no substance. Sure, you can go viral for anything, but is it lasting? Not usually because things move so rapidly. So people keep looking for the next big sensation." Dawson shifted in his seat, moving so his elbows were on his knees, mug cradled in callused hands. "When I talk about making a choice, I just mean about how you're going to live."

"Like never leaving the house?"

Dawson offered a wry grin. "That's one option. But I think you can choose to let it be something that happened, not something that happened to you, and move on from it."

"I'd like to believe that."

"Then do it." Dawson held up a hand. "Don't hear me saying that's easy. I know it's not. I'm just saying that I've talked with a lot of celebrities over the years I've had my studio open, and by and large, the ones I've seen come back from something like what you've faced are the ones who kept working on their craft and living a life that disproved false allegations. But you don't need me to tell you any of this. I'm sure you've got a team on it, and this is just a phase."

Harland leaned back and thought about the man's words. He did have people working on it. He'd put Winslow in charge of their actions, but ultimately, he was disconnected from it because he'd wanted to be. That was healthy for him.

So then, why was he not able to jump full force back into songwriting?

"Sorry. Did I overstep?"

Coming out of his thoughts, Harland shook his head. "Not a bit. I was just thinking. I'm a processor."

"A lot of songwriters are."

"I appreciate you being honest with me, Dawson. I've got to say, it's refreshing to talk with someone who isn't interested in the angle of how they'll tell my story."

"I know we're just business associates at this point, but I'd be happy to call you a friend, Harland. And I mean in secret."

Harland sent him a questioning look.

"I'm not looking to call you a friend on my Instagram stories. Just a friend in real time."

"I appreciate that." The sentiment dove to the depths of him and anchored there. Like a lifeline he could come back to if he strayed too far.

"And one more thing. Do you want to come to church with me?" Dawson held up a hand, laughing already. "Not for any other reason than I've met some great people in this town, and the majority of them attend the local small church. It might be a good place to meet others who don't see you as a celebrity but as a person. I know Libby goes, and I think I've seen Ruth there."

Harland had gone to church as a kid. His mother had taken him and his sister while his dad stayed home, but he'd always loved the music. Even the old hymns played on the piano with nothing added. They had words that were deep and meant something.

Then, shocking himself and possibly Dawson too, he nodded. "Sure. I'll go with you."

Twenty-Five

Libby

"Oh my goodness. That's him. He's here. In real life. I think he's even more handsome than his photos." Mallory said it all in one low, hushed voice, her eyes wide as saucers.

"Mal. Hush." Libby had seen Harland walk in next to Dawson and had nearly fallen off her pew near the front. Harland Grey was in church —her church—and he looked good in his collared shirt and black jeans. Though how Mallory could judge him from just the back, she wasn't sure, but she still agreed internally.

"And he's standing next to Dawson. What is my life right now?"

Libby sent her friend a conciliatory look. While they had never officially dated, when Dawson had first come to Winter Community Church, Mallory had fallen hard for him. They'd spent a little time together as Mallory was considering pursuing her music as a career, but then something happened, and they'd stopped being seen together.

Libby had asked, but in an uncharacteristic move, Mallory never told her what happened. Just that he was focusing on his business, and she was busy enough with her work and place on the church worship team every other Sunday.

The pianist moved on to the next song, and Libby tried to focus on the words. Her friend's strong alto rang out next to her, and she let her eyes close. What was *her* life right now? Tonight she had a meeting—or was it a date?—with Harland, and here he was at her church.

Then again, there were only two churches to choose from in Winter, and it made sense that he'd come here if he were working with Dawson on something.

Her mind spiraled down trails that led to thoughts of what he'd planned for the evening. Of what she should wear. Of what he might say.

When the song stopped and everyone sat down, Mallory had to yank her down by the wrist.

"What's up with you?" Mallory whispered.

"Nothing."

"Liar."

Mallory's voice sounded a lot like her own internal one. "I'll tell you after church."

With a self-satisfied look, Mallory turned around, and they focused on the pastor's message for the morning. Or, at least Libby tried to focus on it, but her eyes kept straying to the back of Harland's head and the memory of how he'd touched her cheek. How she'd almost leaned into the touch.

By the time the last song ended, Libby was ready to jump out of her skin from the stillness.

"Should we go say hi?" Mallory asked. She looked as hesitant as Libby.

When Libby turned to look, the men were already near the back of the church and about to hit a crowd of older women. They were the kind of ladies who would pick lint off your jackets and bake you a casserole just because.

"No, let's take the side exit."

Mallory latched on to Libby's arm, and they rushed outside and into the midday heat.

"I feel like a coward," Mallory said. "But why didn't *you* want to see Harland?"

Libby still wasn't sure why. It wasn't that she didn't want to see him, but something about him being there in the small community church that made his move to Winter feel real.

"Libby, what's going on?" Mallory pulled her into the shade. "You've been distant all morning."

So, she'd caught that. "Harland asked me to come to his place tonight."

"Like, as a date?" Mallory's dark eyebrows shot up.

"I mean, I don't know? I didn't think so at the time. He said he wanted to make it up to me."

"Make what up to you?"

Libby filled her friend in on what had happened the day of the photoshoot. "I believed him when he apologized, and I was happy to say yes. I like spending time with him." Maybe too much.

"But now you're having second thoughts?"

"No."

"You don't want to go?"

"No, I do."

"Then what is it?"

"I don't know. Seeing him here today just makes it all feel more real." She bit her lip. "This job has always had a deadline for me, and it's been just that—a job. But Harland makes me want it to be more."

"Oh yeah?" Mallory waggled her eyebrows.

"Like, an actual friendship, Mal. Sheesh."

"There's nothing wrong with wanting to be a friend, but also acknowledging that your friend is hot and totally dateable."

"Stop," Libby said on a laugh. "Okay, so maybe I have a bit of a crush on him."

"Duh. I already knew that." Mallory sent her an understanding look. "But I'm glad you can finally admit it to yourself and to me."

"So what do I do?"

"Go on this maybe-date and have fun. He seems like a nice guy from what you've said, and that's all you need to know."

Libby's mind raced with all the *other* things she wanted to know, but at the heart of it all, Mallory was right. All she needed to know was that she was going to see Harland that night. She'd have to face the rest—whatever it may be—when the time came.

. . .

"Are you going on a date?" Vicky lay on the couch, her phone in one hand and the TV remote in the other, a large bowl of chips on her flat stomach.

"No." *Was she?*

"But you look...nice."

"Thanks. Try not to sound too surprised."

Vicky bolted upright, eyes wide. "Wait a second. Omg. Are you going on a date with Harland Grey?"

"What would make you say that?" Libby asked, working to keep her tone even.

"You totally are. Dad!"

Vicky called out, but Libby tried to shush her. "Dad's taking a nap."

"Does he know? Like, is this even legal after that thing you had to sign or whatever?"

"Just drop it, Vick."

"I will not. If my sister is dating Harland Grey, I am not going to be quiet about it. This is the coolest thing to happen since, like, ever. Omg. Does that mean I can come over and see his house? I really want to see his house. Some online magazine says they're trying to get inside photos. But you've seen it right?"

"Vicky." Libby whirled around, purse and car keys dangling from her fingers. "Just leave it alone."

Vicky frowned. "You've got no chill."

"It's just," She went back to deciding on bringing a light sweater or her jean jacket. Without knowing where they were going, it was hard to know which would be best. "This is my life, okay? Not some tabloid or online magazine article. Give me a break, okay?"

"Okay. Fine."

She turned and saw that Vicky actually looked cowed. It was anyone's guess how long that would last, but Libby gave her a grateful nod. "Thanks."

"Have fun." She smirked and turned back to the television as Libby stepped outside.

Twenty-Six

Harland

Libby wore tight-fitting boot cut jeans over cowboy boots and a frilly white top that made her tanned skin glow. She had her hair down, no sign of a cowboy hat tonight, and she looked amazing.

Harland swallowed as she strode into the barn like she owned the place. He watched as her gaze took in the floors, stalls, and then landed on him. Her smile made his heart thud in his chest.

"Hey." *Great opening.*

"Hi." She tucked a strand of hair behind her ear, and his eyes followed the movement before he told himself to snap out of it. "Ready for your surprise?"

"Maybe? I'm not much of a surprise type of person."

"Don't worry, I think you'll like this one." She eyed him skeptically but followed when he turned and led her out the other side of the barn.

Sirius and Gandalf stood ready and saddled. He sent her a look. "Wanna check my work?"

"You know I will." She grinned and moved to the horses. She checked each strap and cinch, but the slow smile that pulled the corners of her pink lips up gave him hope.

"Well done, Harland."

She said his name, and warmth pooled in the pit of his stomach. It felt right having her here tonight with the sun dipping low on the horizon and the stars a whisper away. He'd tried to think of all angles for the evening, but Libby herself was the wildcard.

"Then let's go."

She pulled herself into Sirius' saddle like the seasoned cowgirl she was, and he followed suit, though less gracefully. Then he gently directed Gandalf onto the trail he should have used when he went into the woods the first time. He'd been happy to discover it after his embarrassing rescue, but it only made the evening more special. A trail on his land with this incredible woman.

As they rode through the stillness of the woods that bordered grassland to the east of his property, they stayed silent, enjoying the stillness of the evening. The only interruptions were the jingling of the harnesses, the skittering of small animals through the brush, and Libby's gentle exhalations.

When they got to a fork in the path, he had them go left, which led up the bluff that overlooked his property.

"I saw you at church today."

He glanced over at her, glad the trail was wide enough for their horses to walk shoulder to shoulder. "I saw you too."

"You did?" She looked genuinely surprised.

He almost said that she was the *first* thing he noticed when he walked in, but wasn't sure it would come out sounding right. "Yeah. Dawson mentioned you went to church there."

"Sorry I didn't come say hi. I thought about it but then saw you were meeting the local knitting group and figured it was better to leave you in their capable hands."

He grinned, shooting her a look. "Thanks for that. I got so many offers for "welcome to Winter" casseroles and pies, and I accepted them all because, I mean, what was I supposed to do?"

"Don't eat Martha Young's pies. Trust me on that." Her caution was followed by a girlish giggle, and he wondered if there was a story there.

"Have you always lived in Winter?"

Her gaze went to the distance through the trees. "Moved here when I was three. I don't remember anywhere else though. This was where

Vicky, my sister, was born, where we grew up, and where my mom died."

"How old were you when she passed?" He knew the question was heavy, but he wanted to know.

"Fourteen. Old enough to remember her well, but young enough to still not know how to do life without her."

"My parents died when my sister and I were in our early twenties. Car crash."

"I'm so sorry." She met his gaze, and her compassion softened the hard memories.

"You never get over something like that. Not really. You just learn to live with it."

"You do." She nodded and maneuvered Sirius around a fallen log halfway in the path. "So where are you taking me? Somewhere to bury my body or something?"

"What?" His startled response made her laugh.

"I'm kidding, Harland. Where are we going?"

"You'll see. And I promise, only good things for tonight." They slipped back into the companionable silence he found so comforting with her.

They approached the last slight incline, and as they rounded the bend, he heard her gasp. "What's this?"

"The surprise. Turns out, there's a road up here too, not just this trail. I had the landscaping kid who's been helping me haul up a fire pit here. We cleared the area and watered it down a bit, just in case, but I thought it might be nice to enjoy a fire and some s'mores with one of the best views Winter, Montana has to offer."

"You've got that right." She clicked her tongue and urged Sirius forward. Easily sliding to the ground near the pit, she used a random rock to tie up the horse and made her way straight to the edge of the cliff that looked out over the valley where his land rested.

He followed her example, tying Gandalf to another loose rock, and joined her.

"This is incredible."

"I've got to say, I lucked out with this land." He winced. "Sorry, I forgot you'd wanted to purchase it."

She laughed. "I'll never be able to afford something like this. Not even if I lived nine lifetimes." The words left a marring frown on her forehead he wanted to erase.

"Money isn't everything."

She nodded her head. "It's not. Sorry, that came out wrong. I just mean, I'm glad at least someone I know has it and is taking good care of it."

She shoved her hands into her back pockets, and he studied her profile. Rounded nose, soft chin, rosy cheeks tinted orange by the dying sun's light. She was stunning. The girl from a thousand love songs, and yet he didn't have the words to tell her how he felt.

Or he did, but he was too much a coward to speak them.

But maybe this was all they needed for now. Time to get to know one another. No pressure, only easy companionship and the truth that he could offer her.

He turned his attention to the view and decided on offering her what he could, the second part of why he'd brought her up here.

"I've been talking with Dawson," he started. He felt her look over at him, but he didn't want the distraction of her blue eyes to derail his courage. "He's helping me set up a recording studio in the house, but he's become something of a friend. One thing he said got me thinking."

"What's that?" she asked, voice soft.

"He said I need to choose the kind of life I want." He ran a hand over his jaw, only then realizing he'd gone a few days without shaving. "At the photoshoot, I realized I was trying to live a life with a foot in both worlds. In LA and in Winter. I don't like who that guy is."

He broke then, looking over at her, but she pursed her lips, making it clear she would let him finish his thoughts before she gave hers.

He forged on. "I'm sorry you got caught in the midst of that. As I said before, I handled it badly. I've been living afraid. Worried that more bad news will come out, or that another smear campaign will finally be the death of my career, but I haven't been thinking about my life. Not really."

How did he explain that he loved music, that it thrummed in his veins like a wild thing, but that he didn't know how to be Harland the performer and Harland the man at the same time?

"I don't want to live like Winter is temporary. I don't want to hide anymore."

His gaze had drifted to the tufts of grass at their feet, but Libby gently took his hands in both of hers. "You don't have to. I see who you are, here." She pressed a palm over his heart. "You're a good man who just happens to be a big, famous star, but that's not the Harland I know. I think you can be the man who is both a musician and just that—a man—without having to live in that constant state of fear. All it takes is courage."

His lip tugged up. "Oh, is that all?"

She laughed, her hands dropping as if she realized what she was doing. "I didn't say it was easy. I said it was possible."

"And what about you, Libby? What is it you want?"

She bit her lip, the motion distracting to him. So much so that, when she looked back up at him, his eyes remained on her lips for a moment too long. She stepped closer, the warmth of her nearness as comforting as the sun at his back.

"I'm not sure I know the answer to that, Harland Grey." She tilted her chin up, and the fire from the look in her eyes ignited his own.

Alarm bells set to ringing in the back of his mind. This wasn't part of the planned evening. He was only going to apologize to her and, hopefully, get to know her better.

The ringing moved to his ears, but all too easily, he silenced them as he shuffled forward a few more inches. Her eyes poured into him. Hope. Curiosity. And something that looked a lot like the desire to match his own.

Then she moved, her hand reaching up to his cheek. Her thumb trailed over the scruffy hair there and then ghosted across his lower lip. He suppressed a shiver, but then her fingers rested at the base of his neck. Heat seared where skin touched skin, and his lips parted.

"Libby."

"Well? Are you going to kiss me or what?"

He laughed, his head dropping near hers. Their lips lingered a breath apart, and he wondered, however briefly, if this was a good idea.

Then she leaned forward and pressed her lips to his. The warmth of her against him, the delicate sweetness of her lips, it intoxicated him. Kissing Libby felt like freedom itself, and he wanted more.

His worries lifted and he was wrapped up in that moment, knowing only the touch of this stunning woman. His mind went blank aside from his desire to hold her closer. To whisper his heart to her in the stillness of the mountain top as the last rays of sun left them in a quiet darkness.

Her arms encircled his neck, and he slid his hands down to rest lightly on the curve of her hips. She made a gentle whimper, and he deepened the kiss, thoughts of reason flying from his mind.

He wanted to be here in this moment, not worrying about anything else. No thoughts of LA, no thoughts of his career or the future, just Libby and the melody that they were making together. The sweetest lyrics he'd ever known.

Twenty-Seven

Libby

Her head was swimming, and her mind was numb. Kissing Harland was like fireworks at the Fourth of July parade and the comfort of a hand to hold in the dark.

When she pulled back, gasping for breath and yet yearning for more, she saw her feelings reflected in his eyes. They were more gold than brown in the semi-darkness, the green a gentle flicker, and she knew she could get lost in them forever.

"Well shoot, you're a good kisser, Mr. Grey."

He tossed his head back and laughed, though his hands still held her close. When he looked back down, she leaned in, and he obliged with another kiss before pulling back. This time, she saw reality sinking in past the fantasy their kiss had drawn them into.

"Harland." She pressed her lips together, but the words demanded to be let out. "I think I'm falling for you."

His expression clouded, and he dropped his hold on her, stepping back to create space. "I shouldn't have done that." He turned, and his gaze sought the horizon as it gave up the last rays of sunlight across the prairie grass. "I didn't bring you up here...for that."

"I didn't think you had." She was trying to follow his logic. "I'm just telling you something that's true. I—I know it's a bit awkward, but ever since meeting you—"

"Don't. Libby, please." He ran a hand down his face like a weary man trying to wake up from a dream. "I shouldn't have kissed you."

"Was it really that bad?" She meant it as a joke, but he sent her a look, and she shook her head, retracting the humor. "Of course it wasn't. We're two adults, and we're allow to kiss if we want."

"But we're not. Not really."

"And why is that?"

He sent her a pained look.

"Not this again. You just got done telling me that you don't want to be two men in one. Be here. Be now." She looked down. "Be with me."

"It's not just that." He paced back to the fire pit and lit the paper under the logs as if he'd been meaning to do it the whole time and kissing her was just a misstep.

"Then what is it?"

"It's, I don't know, everything." He spun around, flames leaping up to lick the dry wood. "I just moved here. I don't know what's going on with my musical career. I can't write songs anymore. I just—I don't know what my life is."

"What does that make me then? A complication? Is that it? You don't know how to handle me so you're going to push me away?"

"That's not—you're twisting my words."

"No, I'm making you think about it. I'm making you choose, like you just said you want to." She held up a hand to stay his argument. "I'm not saying we have to make anything official. I'm not saying you need to put me on your arm and parade me around the red carpet. The Lord knows I'd be a death trap in heels. All I'm saying is that you *should* give us a chance." She winced at how pathetic she sounded. "I mean, maybe not *us*, but at least the idea of us."

He sank down into one of the Adirondack chairs and stared into the flames licking at the dry wood. "I don't know if I can do that right now."

The fire matched the growing heat in the pit of her stomach. "Then what was this?" She gestured to the seats, the fire, even the guitar case sitting to the side.

"A kind gesture. I don't know." He wouldn't look at her, and that's how she knew she had him.

"No, it was more." She slid down in front of him. Her hand reached for his, and her courage was bolstered by the fact that he didn't pull away. "I'm not asking you for anything, Harland. No commitment, nothing official, but I am asking for a chance. Can't you give me that?"

The words tumbled out of her, and she wondered where they'd come from. She'd come to this evening trying not to have expectations, but his kiss had unlocked something in her that refused to be put away again. A desire, now free, that demanded satisfaction.

"I don't think I can right now."

Her heart latched on to the *right now,* but she shoved those hopeless thoughts away. She wasn't someone to be toyed with. She didn't want to live on false hope just waiting for Harland to come around. She'd had plenty of boyfriends in the past who had wanted a relationship with her on their terms. This wasn't going to be that.

It wasn't that she needed her way or bust, but she at least needed the security of knowing he felt what she did. That it wasn't just her imagination. That there was something there.

But he couldn't give that to her. Or, more accurately, he wouldn't.

"All right then." She dropped his hand and stood. Casting one last longing glance to the horizon, she moved toward Sirius. The horse shuffled back a few feet, sensing her pent up emotions, but she quieted him with a gentle hand on his neck.

"You're leaving?"

"It's not a good idea for me to be here." She untied the reins from the rock.

"Libby, wait."

"Look, Harland. I get it. You've got a new life you're trying to fit into. New experiences, career changes, and fears you've got to wrestle with. I think you see yourself as someone who walks alone and, when the dust is settled, then you can see your way through. I'd like to be the one to walk with you through those things, but I don't think you're willing to let me in, even for that." She frowned, a lyric from one of his songs coming to him. "Someone who's better with words than me once sang this:

What you see is not what you get

And it's so hard to forget the past
But who you are is not defined by that
You're moving on
And never looking back

"I want to be the one to move on with you, but I can't make you choose me."

The words fell to the dust between them, and with one last longing look at him, she climbed up and took off at a trot down the mountain.

She was almost halfway back to the barn when the soft sound of guitar flooded through the stillness of the night. He was playing the song she'd quoted, and she hoped, if nothing else, that he would find release from his past.

He might not be able to see her as part of his future, but she didn't wish anyone the kind of chains he carried.

Twenty-Eight

Harland

I see your broken heart
It's crying out for the start
Of something new

I see the tears you hide
They're shining in your eyes
Telling the truth

The words were bitter on his tongue, but the reminder of a song he'd written and the words he'd penned years ago was like a drenching bucket of ice water to his heart.

She'd pinpointed his issues and used his own music to do the talking. Just like he'd said in the chorus though, it was so hard to forget the past. Surely she knew that.

His fingers moved of their own accord across the frets, shifting from the key of G into C and playing a new melody that had been plaguing him. The music flowed out of him without much thought, but that left plenty of space for his mind to fill in the gaps.

Kissing Libby. Her sweet words. Her directness. Her calling him out.

All of it was *so* Libby, and yet, he'd shut her down. For good reason, so he thought, but had he just not phrased it right?

He hummed the melody, no words to fit it yet, and thought back over what he'd said. He *wasn't* ready for a relationship. At least he was pretty certain he wasn't. And he didn't know what he was doing with her other than the fact that he liked spending time with her.

And that he liked kissing her.

He hit a wrong note and winced, readjusting his fingers. It was unfair to expect her to be okay with spending time alone with him without anything by way of a commitment. He didn't think she was being unreasonable, and yet, he could see that he wanted his cake and wanted to eat it too. That he wanted to do things on his terms. That was unfair to Libby.

Maybe letting her go was the smart option. He could get his life in order and—

When the dust is settled, then you can see your way through.

She'd nailed him. He wanted things to be right. He wanted his words to be thought out, his life to flow logically, but was that what life was even like?

He finger picked a riff of Amazing Grace. The pianist at church had done a great job with it that morning, and the lyrics had stuck with him throughout the day.

'Twas grace that taught my heart to fear
And grace my fears relieved

Dawson had encouraged him to choose, but what if it wasn't that simple? What if he couldn't get past the fears? There was still a world of things Libby didn't know about his past. And the whirlwind that came along with dating a celebrity. Were those things enough to disqualify him from a relationship with her? And, more than that, when did the past expire? When would he be free from it? Or was he destined to be haunted by his failures like a dark specter following him around for the rest of his days.

He shifted to a new melody and let his thoughts drift skyward along with the sparking embers. The next time he saw Libby, he had to have an answer for her. It was the only fair thing he could do.

Twenty-Nine

Libby

Melody Ranch at sunrise was a different experience. She'd seen it late at night, thanks to Harland, and she'd seen it morning, midday, even in the afternoon, but she'd never been there as the sun reached out over the land in search of new territory.

She yawned, slowing the truck to a stop at the side of the barn. There was a slight chill in the air that made her long for fall, but she knew it would soon fade away as the sun rose. Until then, she'd keep her chambray shirt on.

There was a bitter taste on her tongue at the thought of the last time she'd worn the shirt. When she'd escaped from a deluge and hidden out in the barn with Harland. When he'd gently tucked her hair back like she was a porcelain doll worthy to be handled with care.

Naturally, thoughts of Harland led to the kiss they'd shared, and she groaned as she slid the barn door open. Being back at the ranch naturally made her think of him, but she'd tried her best not to. Not when Vicky had demanded how the evening went and not even when Mallory had texted her later that night.

She'd just done what she accused Harland of doing and avoided it.

Pushed it to the side so she could wait for the dust to clear. Except, she didn't know if that would happen.

The worst part was that she'd said so much, she'd dug herself into a hole. As if one kiss a relationship made. She hadn't meant to make that her point. She'd just wanted him to stand up and accept something that was out of his grasp and enjoy it as the gift it was.

It was a unique experience—one she couldn't understand—for Harland to be so consumed by what others thought of his life because it actually mattered. Maybe that meant she'd been unfair to him.

Her stomach churned as she made her way to the tack room. She'd been so focused on what she needed to do that she almost missed the note pinned to the door. The handwriting looked feminine, which instantly eased her worries, and she yanked it down.

It was from Ruth who wanted to remind her that her check was waiting up at the house. The thought of going anywhere where Harland might be made her queasy, but it wasn't his presence she worried about. It was having to face him with her words hanging between them.

Rather than make a decision, Libby folded the paper, shoved it in her back pocket, and got to work.

She cleaned out the barn, polished some tack that probably didn't need it, and then decided to work with Lyric again. She'd made some progress with the horse, but nothing she'd be willing to tell her father about yet.

When she'd exhausted everything she could, and it was still only just after seven, she decided on a ride.

"Sirius, come here, boy." She couldn't see him, but she knew he was near. Perhaps behind the dip in the landscape. Gandalf had come up, likely hearing her filling the feeders, and she guessed Sirius wasn't far behind.

"Sirius," she called out again and was rewarded with a whinny.

He came running up the rise toward her, black mane blowing in the wind. She saddled him quickly and set off to check the fences. It didn't take long to see that everything was in order, but the fresh air cleared her mind and eased some of her worries.

By the time she was back at the barn and had brushed down Sirius, it felt late enough that she could get away with finding Ruth at the house for her check. She only hoped that Harland wasn't up yet. Didn't musicians like to sleep in late?

She opted to walk up to the house, knowing the rumbling engine of her truck would make too much noise, and set off at a quick pace. It was slightly up hill, and she was able to step onto a path that wound toward the back side of the house, but by the time she reached the top, she was winded. That, and she had no idea which side held Ruth's rooms.

Thinking back to the photoshoot, she hadn't really seen anyone go inside. Likely Harland's idea to keep his privacy, which she agreed with, but she decided to take a guess and went to the right.

There was a door, and after a soft knock, she pushed it open. Stillness reached around her. She'd never been *in* the house before, but here she was. Was this foolish? Should she go back to the front and ring the doorbell?

But that's when she heard it. The faintest sounds of Harland singing.

His voice pulled her forward like a tractor beam in one of Vicky's favorite sci-fi shows. She felt powerless to leave because the longing in his voice made her ache.

He was a man who experienced life deeply. She'd known that the moment she listened to his quieter albums from when he'd first started recording. The thoughts he expressed were complex but also universal. Things everyone felt, but he'd found a way to put them into lyrics and their emotions into music.

She crept through the hallway, the wooden floors sturdy under her boots, until she came to an open doorway. The interior of the room looked unfinished, and she wondered if this was the studio Dawson was helping him with. Golden sunlight played across the floor creating a square pattern, and she watched as it danced back and forth in sync with the changes of chords.

When she reached the door, she listened for a moment, letting his smooth voice wash over her. It eased some of her worries, though they hadn't talked about anything yet, and it made her want to see his face as he sang.

She took another step, this time going fully into the doorway, but he was partially turned away, head down and eyes closed. He wore gray sweatpants and a black t-shirt like the first day she'd met him. Just under his sleeve, she caught the edge of a tattoo.

She watched his feelings play out on his features, not even really listening to the words, just the emotions behind them. He sang with everything in his being, leaning over the shiny guitar with dark wood on the front, fingers playing over the frets like her hands worked with tack. Sure, confident, familiar.

This was Harland in his element. The Harland hundreds of thousands of people paid money to see in concert. The man who topped charts and won awards and who had all but broken her heart the night before.

Or had she done that?

Just then, he looked up, and the words died on his lips. His hands fumbled, but he recovered, his gaze shifting to one of curiosity.

"Morning," she finally said, her shoulder landing gently against the door frame like she'd been invited, not an unexpected guest.

"I didn't see you there."

"I'm sorry. I was looking for Ruth," she held up the note, "but heard you first."

"Working on something new." He looked down and played a little lick. It was like the guitar was an extension of him and seeing him like this completed some of the picture of the man.

"I like it."

His grin was weak. "It's not done yet."

"I can still like something that's not finished." Her words held a weight to them she hoped he knew.

He played a few more bars then shifted to put the guitar down. "I think we need to talk."

That was something no one liked to hear, and yet, the way Harland said it made Libby stand up and take a closer look.

"Then talk." She said it soft and low, no malice there.

"Come on. The deck is best this time of morning." And, like that, she followed him back outside into the depth of the morning air.

Thirty

Harland

He hadn't imagined that he'd see her so soon. In fact, he'd been dreading the reality of going to the barn and not finding her there. He was by no means ready to take care of the horses on his own, but that wasn't what worried him. It was the lack of Libby in his life he didn't like the thought of.

She trailed behind him, her sweet pea scent just reaching him as she climbed the steps to the deck. He picked his favorite chair, but Libby surprised him by pulling over a lounger. She plopped down and kicked her booted feet up, crossing them at the ankles.

"This is what they call *the life*."

He laughed, enjoying the look of her on the deck. She wore the same chambray shirt he'd found in the barn during the rainstorm, and her hair was pulled back in a loose braid that dangled over her shoulder.

"I could have Ruth bring us some coffee."

"That's okay. Don't trouble her."

"It's her job." He felt her gaze on him. "Hey, she has a lot of leniency. I'm just saying this is literally something I pay her to do."

"If I need coffee, I can get it myself."

He didn't doubt that for one second. "But maybe you don't always have to."

She looked over at him, pulling her gaze from the view. "I guess you've got a point, but I don't need any coffee at the moment."

He nodded. "What do you need then, Libby?"

His question surprised him as much as it did her, but she seemed open to it. "I'm not sure I know. Perhaps a better filter?"

He laughed; he couldn't help it. She was the most outspoken woman he'd ever met, and yet, he came to expect it. Who would Libby be if not someone who spoke her mind?

"And on that note, I'm sorry about last night." His mouth went dry, but she continued. "I shouldn't have said...well, most of what I said, I think." He could see her replaying her words before his eyes.

"I'm glad you did."

"Are you?" She shot him a questioning look.

"I am who you said I am. I'm someone who likes to see things settled before I can move on. I'm someone who likes no dust in the air if I'm to feel confident. The whole thing with what happened in LA, well, it's not settled, and I think that's why I'm struggling with," he swallowed, "all of this."

"What aren't you telling me, Harland?"

It was the opening he needed and dreaded at the same time. "Please don't think I was hiding this from you, but as you might have guessed, I'm not the most open book when it comes to personal things, and I wasn't comfortable enough to share with you before."

"I believe people talk when they're ready to. Unless you're me, and then you just talk all the time." Her self-effacing humor was calculated to help him loosen up, and it worked.

"While everything I told you about Violet is true, there was a part I left out. A part I'm not proud of." He winced and wished he had his guitar to fiddle with. It always made him feel more comfortable. "While what she claimed was completely untrue, some of it had merit."

He thought back to the long bus rides where they'd talked. How he'd taken her out to dinner many of the nights. How he'd finally kissed her that fateful night and felt nothing.

"What do you mean?" Libby's tone was soft, patient.

"I led her on. At the time, I didn't think that's what I was doing, but looking back, I can see that I was. She was pretty, fun, and flirted right back. And I thought, why not? What could it hurt?" He rubbed a hand down his face. "But then I finally kissed her one night. It was a really romantic spot somewhere in the Colorado Rockies at this fancy hotel. The type with private Jacuzzis in every room."

Her eyebrows rose. "Swanky."

"Very." He shook his head. "Well, I leaned in, and I kissed her. It was dumb. An impulsive decision, but I knew—I just knew—in that moment, it was the worst thing I could have done."

"What happened?"

"I leaned back and told her I hadn't meant to do it. She told me it was fine; she'd been wanting me to kiss her. But the problem was, I'd felt nothing for her. It was just an impulse, and I knew I was going to pay for it." He swallowed, remembering how the events of the night played out. "She either didn't believe me or didn't care because she wouldn't stop. I kept trying to get away, but she wouldn't take the hint. Finally, I told her it was enough, and I didn't want to see her again. Maybe it was my tone or something, but she finally heard me that time, and I'll never forget the words she said when she left." He was living that moment now, the darkness of the poolside area and the anger in Violet's eyes.

"What was it?"

"She said I was going to regret it. And I did."

"Harland, that wasn't your fault. None of this is."

"But don't you see? It was. I was playing with fire. She was twenty-three, and I was thirty-four, and I lured her right into an awful situation because I wasn't careful." He swallowed past his guilt. "I don't think I deserve what she did to me, but I don't know that I don't deserve some type of punishment for my foolishness."

Libby let out a breath. "Harland, you can't punish yourself for something you didn't intend to do. Sure, you can feel bad about your part in it, that's fine, but you can't honestly think you deserve the bitter retaliation of a barely-adult young woman who lashes out on social media instead of solving her problems in a healthy way."

"I've said it before, and I'll say it again. You've got a way with words." He shook his head, her truth sinking in to the soft parts of his heart.

"As do you. And I'll tell you what else you've got." She waited until he looked at her. "Friends."

The sun shone on her golden hair and made her blue eyes sparkle like water diamonds, but the beautiful part of Libby in that moment was her belief in him.

"Yeah?"

"Oh yeah." She raised her shoulders then let them drop. "And if that's all this will ever be, then okay." She licked her lips, drawing his attention for the briefest moment. "I have no right to make you choose anything. Nothing at all. If you need time for things to settle in your life, then do that. I just know that I can't be suspended in mid-air while you do it."

She clapped her hands on her jeans and stood. His heart lurched at the finality of it.

"Libby, wait." He stood, but the motion put them toe to toe. A strand of her blonde hair escaped her braid and fell across her forehead, and without thinking, he brushed it away. The tender caress drew him even closer.

"Wait for what?" The sadness in her eyes tugged at him and began to unravel the carefully tied up knots he'd need to secure his heart. He'd spent hours twisting them, and with one yank, she'd caused them to slip free.

"I don't know." The sorrow of his words felt oddly final, and he hated that. He knew what he wanted—he wanted to kiss her again. He wanted to pull her close and say to the wind with his worries. He wanted to know what it was like to love Liberty Taylor with his whole being, but he wasn't sure he could. He wasn't sure that all of him was enough for all of her.

"Well then," she pressed her palm flat against his chest again, a sad smile on her lips, "call me when you do."

And with that, she walked off the deck and down toward the barn. His eyes trailed after her, wondering if he should follow, but he wasn't sure he'd know what to say even then.

Libby was like mist through his fingers. The more he wanted to hold her, the more she faded. Or was it him who was fading?

Thirty-One

Libby

Harland hadn't called. It had been a week, and she'd heard nothing from him. Not even a text.

To be fair, she had told him to call when he figured things out, and maybe she'd just been overly optimistic thinking that would only take a week. She'd even held her next lesson with Ash and Sage, but he hadn't shown, much to the girls' disappointment.

"Are you okay?" Vicky asked. She rode shotgun in the truck as they made their way to town to run errands.

"Fine."

"Sounds like it." Vicky's voice dripped with sarcasm, but she kept her gaze turned out the window.

Dad was almost healed. In fact, he'd done the chores that morning, though Libby had noticed he took significant breaks between feeding the various animals. She'd asked him if he was sure he wanted to go back the next week, and he'd just nodded in that solemn way he had.

She'd been afraid to push back for fear of why she was pushing. Was it to be near Harland? Or for her father's sake? She wanted it to be the latter, but she had her doubts.

They pulled into a spot near the park.

"Why are we parking so far away?" Vicky rolled up her window, shooting a questioning look at Libby.

"It's the most central location."

"You're the one who's going to be drenched in sweat when you walk back with all the groceries."

Vicky had a point, but Libby wanted the walk. She wanted the time to think. Seeing as Vicky had an afternoon shift that day, Libby had agreed to take her into town on her way, but there was something peaceful about the park.

"You're right. I'll be the one."

Vicky slid out of the truck and slammed the door behind her, and Libby joined, closing hers with a bit more care. She slung her purse over a shoulder and joined Vicky as they took to the sidewalk.

"Hey, Libby?" Vicky's voice was tentative which wasn't a good sign.

"What?"

"Did you see the article?"

Libby didn't know why, but her gut clenched. "What are you talking about?"

"The news about Harland." Vicky whispered his name.

"What news?" Libby pulled her into the alcove of a vacant store front. "You know I don't keep up on stuff like that. What did it say?"

Vicky rubbed her nose, a sign she was uncomfortable. "It was a lawsuit some girl in California is filing about him, but then there was a 'source,'" she made air quotes, "that shared details of his estate in Montana. They even mentioned you."

"What? Me?" Libby's mind was spinning. "Why are you just now telling me about this?"

"I asked you if you were okay. I thought you were stewing about the article."

"I didn't see any article. Goodness." She shook her head trying to dislodge the jumble of thoughts. "I'm guessing it wasn't a good article then?"

"It was about a lawsuit, sis. What do you think?"

"Yeah, good point."

"I've got to get to work, but I just wanted you to know...in case you didn't."

"Thanks." Though she was really thinking *thanks a lot.*

They stepped back out onto the sidewalk, and Libby trailed after Vicky, her mind swirling. Was that why Harland hadn't reached out to her? This resurgence of the trouble from the year before coming back again?

Her heart ached for him, knowing that he was going through this mostly alone. At least he had Ruth. Her fingers itched to pull out her phone and text him, but she held back.

It was one thing to be a friend in a time of distress, which she wanted to be, but it was another to push herself into a situation that was likely already turbulent. She worried her involvement would only be a worse distraction.

They neared the Bradley Diner, and Vicky made a choking sound. "Holy cow! What's going on at the diner?"

Libby's eyebrows rose when she saw what Vicky had. A line of guests stretched out the door, and the other hostess, Gina, was outside writing people's names down. As they approached, Gina caught sight of Vicky.

"Thank goodness you're here, Vicky. We're swamped. They asked me to stay late." She widened her eyes and then caught sight of Libby. "Hey, Libby. How are you?"

"Good. What's the rush from?"

Gina shrugged. "I have no idea."

"Excuse me." A man with a large gear bag shifted closer to them. He used his index finger to push up his wire-rimmed glasses as he looked from Libby back to Gina. "Did you call her Libby? Are you Liberty Taylor?"

"Liberty Taylor?" another person said.

Then Libby's name was being said through the crowd like she was some type of celebrity.

Celebrity.

Her heart dropped to her stomach.

"You know this guy, Libby?" Gina asked.

Libby wanted to smack her forehead. Gina clearly wasn't catching on to what was happening here.

"No. I don't know him. I'll see you later, Vicky. Excuse me." She tried to push through the crowd that all but blocked the sidewalk, but several people pressed closer to her.

"We're just looking for a quick sound bite. Do you have any comment on what's being said about you and Harland Grey?"

"How about any photos of his house? We'll pay—maybe better than he does." The crowd snickered.

"Liberty, just a quick comment—"

She was surrounded, and all she could think about was what a horse did when they felt cornered—lash out. She bit her tongue. If there was ever a time for her *not* to say what she thought, this was that moment. She'd only cause more harm than good even if she tried to defend Harland.

Channeling her pent-up anger and all the things she wouldn't say, she burst out with, "Out of my way!"

Surprisingly, the crowd parted, and she slipped through without another word. She didn't dare risk a glance back, but she sensed someone was behind her.

When she paused at the sidewalk, her fear was confirmed.

"Just a quick word, Miss Taylor." The man was well dressed, stood a respectful distance away, and had his phone out as if he were recording. "There are accusations that you and Mr. Grey are in a romantic relationship. Do you care to comment on that?"

She drilled into the man with a hard stare.

"Or, if you're not going to speak to that, what about the other accusations outlined in the article. That he made inappropriate advances toward a young artist touring with him."

Libby's jaw hurt she was clenching her teeth so hard. She hated to stand by while Harland was slandered like this.

"Has he ever given you cause to worry?"

"Never." It was one word, the only one she'd allow, but she made sure the reporter saw the determination on her face. She took a step forward and said it again, this time more firmly. "Never."

The man opened his mouth to ask another question. She could see hope in his eye now that she'd spoken to him, but she held up a flat hand and walked off, not even caring to look at the traffic. Whoever it was could stop for her, because she needed to get away from the crowd who was only out for blood, not the truth.

. . .

Later that evening as she whipped up mashed potatoes to go along with the roasted chicken, Libby still felt the weight of her encounter that day. She'd taken a ridiculous, overlong route back to her truck, groceries in tow, but it had meant she was left alone.

How did Harland handle the press? More importantly, she wondered how he was doing now.

Her phone pinged just as the door opened, and Vicky came in looking weary from her shift.

"Hey, ya, hun. How was work?" Dad asked from the living room where he watched the local news.

"It was bonkers." Libby caught the familiar sound of all of Vicky's possessions being thrown onto the floor by the couch. "All those out-of-town media people can sure eat."

"Libby mentioned them," she heard Dad say. "You didn't have to deal with them, did you?"

"Not really." Vicky popped her head in the kitchen just as Libby's phone pinged again. "It says Ruth. Oh, Ruth! Isn't that Harland's housekeeper?"

"Is that Ruth?" Dad called out from the other room.

Libby pursed her lips as she pulled the chicken from the oven. "She's probably just reminding me about my check. I forgot to get it the other day. I'll have to go over tomorrow."

"Can I come?"

Libby halted, one oven mitt off, the other hand stranded in mid-air. "What?"

"Can I come with you? I mean," Vicky dropped her voice, "you know Dad'll never let me go with him, but if you're going, can I just come with you? I want to see the house so bad. Please, sis? Just this once. It's the only thing I'll ever ask you."

Libby finished pulling off the mitt. "I don't think it's a good idea."

"Oh come on, why not? I just want to see the inside. He's not allowing people in, you know? Like magazines, which is where I'd normally see stuff like that. You know I'm interested in interior design."

"Since when?"

"Since, you know, a while ago." She tossed her hair over her shoulder. "Come on, let me come. Just this once. I'm not even asking to meet him."

Libby pulled three plates from the cabinet and called out, "Dinner's ready."

"Libby, *please*," Vicky begged. "Just this once. Don't you want me to get bit by inspiration or whatever, and then go on to be a famous interior designer? You know, follow my dreams and all that stuff you always talk about."

Libby shot her sister a look as she carved the chicken. "Are you trying to convince me that this is your *dream*?"

"I mean, it might be. I love to spend time on Pinterest, and this is just like real life Pinterest."

"That smells great." The girls looked over at their father as he stood near the kitchen table. "And maybe you should let her go."

Both Libby and Vicky turned toward him. "What?" Libby said.

"I mean, she's right. I won't ever let her go with me, but it's your last day there. What more could he do? Fire you?"

Libby made a face. "Dad."

"See? Even Dad agrees." Vicky resorted to a pout, and as Libby looked at the amusement on her father's face and the hopeful but whiny look on her sister's, she tossed her hands up.

"Fine, you can go with me tomorrow. We'll be in that house no more than five minutes, you hear?"

"Perfect! You are seriously the best sister ever."

Libby shook her head but couldn't help the smallest of smiles. "Now, let's eat."

Thirty-Two

Libby

Libby slid the barn door closed, leaving her hand on the wood for a moment longer than necessary. She'd miss this place and the horses. She knew her dad would do an excellent job, and she was going to ask Ruth about the possibility of still using the arena for the twins' therapy sessions, but for now, this was the end of her time there.

In the pasture, Gandalf, Sirius, and Buster grazed while Lyric ran along the fence, his black mane winging out. He had spirit, and while Libby had been close to taming some of it, her father would have to finish the job.

"Ready?" Vicky called out.

She'd been in the truck waiting for Libby to finish. Libby had offered for her to come in and help with the chores, but Vicky had just held up her textbook and said she needed to study.

But now it was time to go by the house, get her check, and say good bye to Ruth. Her stomach twisted into knots wondering if Harland would be there. When she'd driven in that morning, the garage door had been open, revealing a missing vehicle inside, something she'd never seen while she'd come to the ranch. She tried to remind herself that if he was getting out into town, that was a good thing.

Though she wondered about how he was doing with the renewed media attention on his life. She dragged her feet, giving a longing look out into the pasture and then to the bluff just visible from the truck. The spot where she'd kissed Harland Grey.

If anything, she worried that the media's presence in Winter would make Harland revert more into his shell, but it felt wrong for her to feel bad about that because of how it affected her, not how it must be for Harland.

"Finally." Vicky slammed her textbook closed and grinned at Libby. "Let's go."

"Calm down, Speed Racer." Libby turned on the truck and put it into gear.

"I'm just excited. You know, dreams and all."

Libby shot her a look, but she just grinned and stared out the window at the scenery. It was still early in the morning, not quite nine yet, and Vicky had to be at school by ten, but she'd told her sister they were staying no more than five minutes or less, and she'd meant that.

"Wow. It's seriously so big," Vicky said as Libby pulled to a stop near the side entrance that she now knew led to Ruth's quarters. She wouldn't make the mistake of going to the wrong side, but she could still hold on to that sweet memory of catching Harland singing in his half-finished studio.

"Keep your voice down," Libby chided.

"We're not even inside," Vicky said, but more quietly this time.

"No fan stuff. Okay? Just a quick look around and that's it."

"Yeah, I got it." Vicky gave her an annoyed look just as Libby raised her hand to knock, but Ruth was already there.

"Come on in. Oh, you must be Libby's sister. Vicky, is it? Your father talks highly of you both." The girls looked at each other.

"He does?" Vicky stepped in after the woman and turned to mouth, *She talks with Dad?* But Libby motioned with her head for her to keep following the woman.

This side of the house was different from Harland's side, at least to Libby's untrained eye. Softer colors. More carpet. And there was even a small sitting room where Ruth took them now.

"Have a seat, and I'll grab your check."

"Could I use the restroom?" Vicky asked.

Libby shot eye-daggers at her, but Vicky pretended not to notice. This wasn't part of the plan.

"Of course, dear. Follow me."

Vicky shot a wink over her shoulder, and Libby drew in a deep breath. No doubt the bathroom request was so that she could see more of the house, and Libby couldn't totally fault her sister. She wanted to see it too. Wanted to see the place that Harland called home. But she also knew how important his private space was to him.

She looked at the photos on Ruth's bookshelves. Most were of her and Harland or her and another young man. It was clear Ruth had been a much younger woman when the photos with the young man were taken and Libby wondered what the story was. Was he a son perhaps?

There were also stacks of non-fiction and fiction book titles and a vase full of fresh flowers. Libby could tell that every detail had been thought of, and it was obvious no expense had been spared to decorate the space. What he'd said about Ruth was true; she was well provided for. Yet another credit to Harland that the press could know nothing about.

Libby sighed and went to the window of the lounge space. It had a sprawling view of the other side of the ranch. Less mountains and more grassland, but it was no less beautiful. Ruth was lucky to be close to Harland like this.

Libby turned as the door opened again, and Ruth came in. Vicky wasn't with her, and Libby's stomach clenched. "I'm sorry about my sister."

"Nonsense. I'm happy you were both able to stop by. I'm sorry to hear you'll be leaving us but glad your father is doing better."

"We're both glad he's on the road to recovery. He's been a bit of a bear to live with."

Ruth laughed. "I could imagine."

Libby wondered just how well Ruth knew her father, but also felt like it wasn't the time to ask such a private question. She'd drill her father later that evening.

"Here is your check," Ruth said, coming forward to hand it over. "There's a bit of a bonus in there. Mr. Harland knows that working here has likely been a hardship on your own business, and he hopes this somewhat makes up for it."

Libby slid the check into her pocket, not wanting to look at it with the woman there. "Thank you. I—could you tell him that for me?"

"Of course." Ruth's expression fell subtly. "This mess with the media in town has been a bit bothersome. Just when he was getting settled in here in Winter."

"I can imagine." Libby bit her lip. "He's not...thinking of leaving, is he?"

"Oh no." Ruth shook her head. "Or at least he hasn't told me anything. And he usually tells me most things." She considered Libby. "Though not all."

It was clear the woman was trying to read her, and Libby could only shift from one foot to the other in front of her.

Thankfully, the growing awkwardness was shattered by Vicky's return. "Wow, nice bathroom."

Ruth laughed. "That tub is something else, isn't it?"

"Jets and everything." Vicky looked at Libby. "You really should see it."

"You can have a tour if you'd like," Ruth offered.

"No, but thank you."

"Libby," Vicky whined.

"We appreciate your time and have taken up enough of it already. Come on, Vick. You have to get to school."

Before Vicky could protest, Libby latched on to her elbow and all but dragged her through the side exit.

"Ouch," Vicky said once Ruth had closed the door and Libby let go.

"You were gone for way too long. Where did you go?"

The gleam in Vicky's eye caused heat to rise into Libby's cheeks.

"Relax. I just looked around a little. His living room is impressive."

"Please tell me you didn't go anywhere else."

Vicky just mimicked zipping her lips shut as she climbed into the truck. Libby felt her anger bubble to the surface.

"Chill out, Libbs. It's all good. It's not like anyone caught me."

"I know, but that's *his* space. You don't belong in there."

"Tell me again how you don't like him?" Vicky's words almost made Libby drive off the side of the road.

"What?"

"It's this whole protective thing you've got going on. You deny you like him or that anything is happening, but saying stuff like that makes it clear you either don't know your own feelings or you're totally in denial. 'Cause from my perspective, you've got it bad."

"Don't change the subject. This isn't about me and him, it's about you being in *his* personal space."

"Whatever." Vicky folded her arms over her chest and shut down all communication by rolling down her window and turning on the radio.

Libby wanted to duke it out verbally with her sister right then and there, but she knew she'd say things she might regret. Besides, was she angry at Vicky or angry that she no longer knew the next time she would see Harland again?

That wasn't Vicky's fault, it was hers, and there was no way around it now.

Thirty-Three

Three Weeks Later

Harland

Customers cycled through the doors of Mountain Grounds every few minutes. Harland had chosen an unobtrusive seat in the corner, his back to most of the shop, but he still felt the uptick of warmth as the door opened and closed, admitting the next patron.

The urge to check who was coming in every time distracted him from the book he was trying to get through. The autobiography of a musician he looked up to was interesting, but with every warm gust, he hoped he'd turn and see Libby.

He knew it was ridiculous. He was the one who hadn't reached out to her, but he wasn't sure he had answers for the questions she'd asked of him, and until he did, he didn't feel right reaching out.

It didn't mean he stopped thinking about her though. It made trips to church with Dawson thrilling and also torturous. They sat in the back, and he ended up spending most of the sermon memorizing the back of her head, wishing she'd turn and flash that bright smile at him.

He slipped out early so they wouldn't actually meet, but that was more for self-preservation because he knew if she did talk to him, he would cave, and then where would they be? Another article. A stolen photo of them together. Reporters hounding her family. The options were endless.

Smoothing a hand over the page, he tried to refocus on the storyline. He had just moved into a new section about the musician's time touring, and Harland wanted to assess how it was the same and different from how they did things now. He was finally getting in to the story, his focus narrowing despite the distractions, when his phone rang.

He had half a mind to let it go to voicemail, but he saw the caller ID register Winslow. Doing some quick math, Harland knew it was much too early for his friend to be awake.

"Hello?" He kept this voice down, conscious of the others seated in the shop, most reading, though some held quiet conversations.

"I'm guessing by your relatively calm tone you haven't seen it."

Dread dropped like a lead ball into the pit of Harland's stomach. Was it another article? Would his name be dragged through the mud again?

"Seen what?" His tone was clipped but low.

"I'll send you a link. Look it over then call me."

A buzz vibrated his phone, and he knew he'd gotten whatever link it was that his friend and manager had sent.

"I've got to get home first, okay? I'll call you then."

"Sure. I'll be here whenever."

Harland swallowed the rest of his latte, admiring the smooth but nutty taste of the coffee and then shoved his book into his satchel. Placing the now-empty coffee cup in the dishes bin, he nodded to the barista and slipped out into the warmth of the morning.

It was still early, but people drove past on their way to work, causing a higher rate of traffic than normal. He'd parked down the block, so he ducked his head and made a beeline for his black truck.

Even though it was still early in the day, the truck radiated heat as he opened the door, making him regret, yet again, that he'd picked black as the interior and exterior color and not a lighter option. He turned it on, engine rumbling to life, and let the AC wash over him.

His hand hovered over his phone, but he resisted the urge to look at the link Winslow had sent. He knew from his friend's tone that it was bad, or at least something he wouldn't be happy about. There was no sense driving in anger if he could wait ten minutes to get home and *then* be angry.

Despair wrapped around him in a cloying blanket almost as bad as the oppressive warmth of the truck. Things had just settled back to normal in Winter. He was finally feeling confident enough to leave the house and go places like a normal person. And now another article threatened to shatter that peace. Was this how his life would always be?

He pulled out into traffic and drove the now-familiar route back to Melody Ranch. The new, official sign for it crafted by a local metal worker hung between the tall poles, and he couldn't help the smile that tugged at his lips.

There was a lot that hadn't gone right since this move, but buying the ranch wasn't one of those things.

His eyes traveled toward the barn. A beat up silver truck sat in the place where Libby's red one used to be. James Taylor was back at work, and while Harland missed Libby like crazy, he at least had her dad to talk to. They'd even played a little guitar on the deck a few nights back, though more and more, he'd been finding James up at the house talking with Ruth. He wondered if there was something brewing there, but he wasn't going to be the one to broach the subject.

Then he looked to the arena. He knew from Ruth that Libby had asked about still using the space, and he'd told the housekeeper to tell her yes. It was the coward's way, using Ruth as a go-between, but as much as he didn't know what to say to Libby, he did know he wanted to enable her dreams.

He pulled into the garage and shut off the engine. Not bothering to go inside, Harland swiped open his phone and clicked the link Winslow had sent. The title made his breath catch.

Inside Harland Grey's New Montana Mansion

Beneath it, photo after photo of his house stared back at him. Clean, tidy, and flooded with morning light, every room vacant but cozy looking. The work of a special designer's eye and weeks of work.

There were closeups of his hanging guitars, the magazines on his coffee table, and even the half-finished project of his recording studio.

Harland felt a wave of nausea wash over him, but anger was quick on its heels as he reached a break in the article where a new headline took over.

But is the Hollywood heartbreaker back to his old ways?

Beneath it, he read the first part of the text, unable to stop himself.

"*On the heels of more controversy, Harland Grey seems to be up to his old ways. From photos sent to us by a confidential source, this image of Harland working on a new song comes from a personal friend—or is she more than that?*"

He scrolled past more text claiming he and Libby were more than employer and employee to a video clip. He clicked on it and saw himself on the deck, playing guitar. It was clear the video was taken from near the barns though zoomed in, but he knew the morning this had been shot. He'd gone to see Libby right after.

His anger bubbled over, but like a pot left too long on the stove, it ran out of steam almost as quickly. Had Libby sold him out? He'd known she was coming to the house to get her check, and rather than risk seeing her, he'd taken the coward's way out and gone for a drive.

But he was certain that had been the only time she was in the house.

He wanted to be wrong, but there was literally no other explanation for that video. Betrayal, cold and sharp, pierced his heart as he pressed the call button.

"I'm sorry, Har." They were the first words out of Winslow's mouth.

"You didn't send the photos in." His tone was bitter.

"I did not. But our legal team says we can take action against them as long as you didn't give consent."

"Of course I didn't give consent," he barked. "Sorry. I know this isn't on you."

"The way you just said that makes it sound like you know who it is on."

"I've got a pretty good idea."

Winslow waited, but when Harland didn't speak, he asked, "Who?"

"Libby." Her name, once so special to him, tasted like ash.

"The horse girl?"

He winced. "Yeah. I...I know she was at the barn when that last video was taken." He didn't mention the fact she'd violated her NDA by taking the video.

"Oh, man, I'm sorry. You haven't told me much about her, but, I mean I could be wrong, but she seemed...special."

Harland leaned forward and dropped his forehead to the steering wheel. *She was.*

"I'll talk again with the lawyers, and we'll see if we can at least get the site to take it down."

"It seems pointless. Won't it be everywhere by now?"

"I do see some other less-than-reputable places reposting it or cannibalizing it for their use."

"Great." Harland's shoulders drooped even more.

"What do you want me to do?" He took a breath. "Send a letter to this Libby woman?"

"No." The word slipped out too quickly, but no matter how much her betrayal hurt, he meant it. "I'll figure something out. You just work on your end of things."

"Will do. I'm sorry, man. I know this is a huge invasion of privacy. Any idea why she'd do something like this?"

Harland had no clue, but one thing did stick out to him. "Maybe it was the money."

"They were likely paid well, but it can't be *that* much."

"She's got a business she runs, equine therapy. Maybe she thought it would be an innocuous way to get some funding without hurting me." He didn't add that he was glad she hadn't shared anything about their personal connection. That would have decimated him, but not for the reasons he would have thought.

To him, their kiss had been special. Sacred even. He hated seeing his private life plastered over the internet, but he would have hated it more if she'd admitted to their relationship for personal gain. She didn't seem like the type to do something like that, but then again, she hadn't seemed like the type to share his personal photos either.

"Seems harsh, but money talks. Okay, I'll keep you posted."

"Thanks, man."

Winslow hung up, but all Harland could think about was the fact that Libby had betrayed him to the world. She'd used her connection with him for money. He'd like to think she didn't know what she was doing, but that last photo made it all clear.

And something else was equally clear: He couldn't trust anyone in the Taylor family.

Thirty-Four

Libby

It was early afternoon when James Taylor drove down the dusty road. Libby frowned as her gaze followed her father's truck to where he parked next to her red one. He was home early, and he looked unhappy.

"What's wrong?" she called out, hopping off the porch to meet him halfway with his cane. The one he refused to take with him even though the doctor had ordered it.

"I was just fired."

Libby tried to understand his words. "Wh-hat?"

"Harland just fired me. Well, actually, Ruth was the one that told me." She thought she caught a slight reddening in his cheeks. "She gave me my last check and said I had to leave. She wouldn't even tell me what it was about."

He was definitely hurt by this, but it wasn't making sense to Libby. "Did you even see Harland?"

"Nope. Hadn't seen him all day, though we were supposed to go for a ride this afternoon, and he'd mentioned another jam session soon. This is all very unexpected."

Something was terribly wrong, and she was starting to make worrisome connections. "I wonder if that's why."

"Why what?" James eased down into a chair on the porch.

"Ruth texted me earlier, said she had to cancel me using the arena space for the time being. I asked her why, but she never texted back."

"You get in a fight with Harland?"

Her father's words hit like a slap. "Why would you say that? Of course not."

She winced inwardly. While she wouldn't have called it a fight, they *had* discussed some very personal things. Though, as disheartening as those conversations had been, she hadn't felt anger, only disappointment with how things had ended.

"Then I don't know. He just up and fired me, and now I'm not sure what I'm going to do."

Libby's phone vibrated. She'd been ignoring it since she'd had to tell Sue their lessons were on hold until she could figure something else out. She'd put her focus into yard work at the house to take her mind off of everything. It was amazing how pulling weeds in the summer heat could take all of a person's attention.

She pulled out her phone. "It's Mallory. Hold on, Dad. Hey."

"Did you see the article?"

Libby's stomach dropped. Another article? Was this why Harland had fired her dad?

"No. What is it?"

"Photos. Like, lots of them of Harland's house. *Inside* Harland's house."

Libby's stomach dropped. "Send me the link."

"I did, like an hour ago. Where have you been?"

"Oh." Libby pulled the phone away from her ear and clicked on it. The photos showcased a stunning home, but they were nothing she'd seen in person. "I bet he's spitting mad."

"Did you read it?"

"No, I just looked through some of them." If he were angry though, did he think her father, who was supposed to be using a cane to walk, had taken them? Why else would he fire him?

"They level some accusations at him. I couldn't read the whole thing—I was on my break, and I'm sneaking this call now, but it looks bad for Harland."

"Thanks, Mal. Dad just got home and—I'll call you later, okay?"

She hung up, and Libby turned to James. "I think he thinks you sent photos of the inside of his house to the media."

"What? Why in the world would I do that?"

"I have no idea, but I'm going to go talk with him."

"Libb, you can't do that. It's trespassing if you go over there."

"What do you think he'll do? Have me arrested?" Even as she said it, she hoped it wouldn't come to something so impersonal.

"It's all right. I can make my peace with him once this blows over. He can't truly suspect me, can he?"

"I don't know." Libby rubbed a hand across her forehead. "He didn't have Ruth tell you why you were being let go. That seems like a logical connection."

"You might be right." Her father let a curse slip and shook his head. "Be careful, all right?"

"It's Harland. I'm not worried." But she was. Just not about any physical violence.

She was more worried about her heart. She hadn't seen or talked to him in over three weeks, and now she was heading over to his house with a head full of steam.

Rather than take her truck, she put a bridle on Butterscotch and hopped on the horse to ride to Melody Ranch bareback. The time to get there would give her a chance to settle down, or so she hoped.

When the house came into view, the familiar longing for the property surprised her. It was Harland's land now, but she still harbored the same dreams she had before. Though, after seeing what he'd done with the interior in the few photos she'd seen from the article, he'd decorated it better than she ever could.

The half smirk slowly faded as she renewed her purpose. She passed under the Melody Ranch sign and tried to see if the garage was open. It wasn't, so he could be home, but she wasn't sure. And then she spotted movement down by the barn and adjusted her trajectory that way.

Coming back, even though it had only been a few weeks, felt like a homecoming of sorts, though she reminded herself *why* she was there. She couldn't let Harland fire her dad for something he'd never do. Though, even thinking that now, it seemed implausible. What other reason could Harland have for letting him go?

Butterscotch tossed her head, and Libby directed her toward the back side of the barn where she'd seen movement. Sure enough, Harland leaned against the fence feeding Gandalf apple slices. Buster was making his way toward them, Sirius not too far behind.

"I hope you have enough apples for everyone."

Harland whirled around, his eyes going wide. She slid off Butterscotch and tied her to the fence before walking toward him, hesitation in every step. As she neared, the hope she'd had to see something like happiness at seeing her fled.

A blank expression had washed over his handsome features taking away all of the warmth from him. "What are you doing here, Libby?"

His tone was dry, but the cold response was even more shocking. "Doing? You fired my dad."

He huffed a breath. "Yeah, I did. I need to trust who I work with, and your family has lost my trust."

Her hands found her hips, she couldn't help it. The gall this man had of even considering her father would have a hand in anything underhanded irked her.

"Is this about that article?"

"You know it is."

"We don't know any such thing. I can't believe you'd think my father would do anything to harm you or his position in this job. He's a good, honorable man."

Harland's eyes narrowed. "It's you, Libby. You're the one I can't trust."

Her eyebrows shot up so far, she felt them disappear under the brim of her hat. "Me?"

"Yes. I saw the video you took. The whole world's seen it by now." He shook his head and then stepped closer. "And you want to know the worst part? I thought I might be able to get past all of this. I mean, having those reporters in town was awful, but it was like you and Dawson said. People in Winter don't want to be part of that. I almost believed..."

He trailed off, and despite her confusion, his words drew her closer. "Believed what, Harland?"

"That the dust was settling." When he met her gaze, there was nothing but sorrow in his hazel eyes.

"I don't understand."

"I get it." He handed over the rest of the apples to her, stepping past. "You needed the money. I guess I just thought you'd come to me and ask before selling out to the media."

"Money? What on God's green earth are you talking about?"

"The photos in the article. I know you sold them to the media and—"

"You think *I* did that?"

"You've been in my house, and I know the exact day you took the video. Do us both a favor and stop pretending you don't know."

Libby's mind was scrambling to put the pieces together, but one thing was clear. "You think I would sell you out. For money." She tossed the apples in the feeder and spun to face him. "You really think that little of me."

"It's not what I think that matters. It's what happened."

"And let me get this straight." Her anger was back, a wildfire blaze coursing through her veins, ready to take down anything in its path. "Before, I don't know, *asking me* if I did it, you went ahead and jumped to your conclusions, believing the worst about me."

"I—"

"Here's a newsflash for you, Harland Grey. Not everyone wants to profit off of you. Not everyone is willing to sell out *their friend* for cash. If you could really think so lowly of me perhaps it was a good thing you never called. Perhaps we're better off this way. I'll find another place for my therapy sessions, and you know what? I won't be needing *your* help to do it. In fact, I won't be needing anything from you ever again."

She moved past him, careful not to touch him for fear her anger might ignite him. Using a nearby stump, she climbed back up on Butterscotch and, with a skillful kick, urged the horse into a trot back up the hill and away from Harland.

If he thought so little of her, then he deserved to keep this big ranch all to himself.

Thirty-Five

Harland

"You still there, buddy?"

The room was spinning, and Harland had to reach out for the back of the couch to steady himself. "What did you just say?"

"I asked if you were all right."

"Before that."

"Your lawyers did a great job. They found out that the source was a young girl from Winter named Victory Taylor."

Harland rounded the couch and slumped down. "Victory?"

"Yeah…why does it sound like you know the name?"

"I don't. Well, I kind of do." This was bad. So much worse than he'd imagined. "She's Libby's sister."

"Libby as in the woman you *thought* provided the photos."

"Yeah."

"Is it possible they were in on it together?" Winslow sounded doubtful.

Harland pictured Libby, her cheeks flooded sunset red and her hands fisting at her sides, ready to throw a right cross when she'd realized he was accusing her of selling the photos for money.

And he'd been wrong. So wrong.

"Ugh." His groan echoed across the phone.

"I'm guessing you already confronted Libby then."

"I shouldn't have said anything, but she showed up and was chewing me out for firing her dad."

"Her dad?"

Harland shook his head. "It's the whole family. James Taylor works—worked—with my horses, and then I got to know his daughter, Libby, while he was healing from a broken ankle. I...I haven't met her sister though."

"Dodged a bullet on that one."

"Win, come on."

"You heard the figure she was paid. I mean, I get that's a lot of money to some, but it's pitiful compared to what a bigger outlet would have gotten her."

Harland frowned. He had thought the amount seemed low, but it was possible Vicky hadn't truly known the worth of what she had. It didn't matter though. What did matter was the fact he'd accused Libby, and there was no way she was going to listen to him apologize—again.

"Did I lose you there?"

"Sorry. Just...thinking of ways to salvage this."

Winslow *hummed* over the line. "Nothing's coming to mind. I can't believe you didn't just, oh I don't know, *ask* this Libby woman if she'd done it."

In retrospect, that would have been the smart way to go about it, but he'd been blinded by his emotions, and there was something about Libby that made him lose all reasonable sense. She made him talk when he'd rather think first. Her passion drove him to find his own, but it had backfired this time.

"Not that I know from personal experience at this point, but I hear women really like flowers. Maybe get her some roses and tell her you're sorry? It sounds like you care for Libby."

Harland swallowed. That was the tip of the iceberg of his emotions when it came to Libby. Like her, yes, admire her passion and drive, also yes, fear that same passion when it bubbled over into anger...well, that was another thing about her he'd taken note of.

"I'll think of something."

"What do you want us to do?"

Harland thought back over the legal actions his team had offered him. Some like a slap on the wrist and others with much heavier ramifications. "Let's stick with something lenient. Let her know it was not okay, but I don't want to ruin her future or anything."

"Got it. And Har?"

He stood up, pacing to the window where night had fallen. His reflection shone back at him, bright against the darkened night sky.

"Explain things to Libby. I think she'll understand."

Harland shook his head. Winslow didn't know Libby. Nor had he seen the vehemence in her gaze when she'd told him she wouldn't need anything from him ever again. The words were seared into his memory like a streak of lightning.

"Thanks, Winslow. Night."

The room descended into silence, but he heard a soft footstep in the hall and turned to see Ruth, mug in hand.

"I know it's summer, but I thought you might like some hot chocolate."

He shook his head, offering a chuckle. "You know chocolate doesn't *actually* solve problems, right?"

"Says you. Just try it." She offered him the mug and then took a sip from her own.

The flavor of sweet, dark chocolate cocoa warmed him at the first sip. It was as if something had gone cold inside of him despite the heat of the day. Memories of nights by the fire pit at their house in Malibu came back to him. It brought with it the sound of the seagulls crying in the distance and the scent of sea salt clinging to his skin, his hair, the very air.

"This is good." He took another sip as she joined him by the window.

"You know I'm not much of an eavesdropper."

"Since when?" he asked with a chuckle.

"But I happened to hear you mention Vicky's name."

Suddenly, the sweet was *too* sweet, and he licked his lips to rid the sticky feeling. "I messed up, Ruth."

"How so?"

He told her about his assumption and how he'd accused Libby. "I blew it with her, completely."

"Libby was never in this house, but Vicky was."

"You didn't tell me that."

Ruth's gaze dropped even though his words were gentle. "I didn't think it was important. She was just supposed to be using the restroom."

"Well, I didn't even give Libby a chance to defend herself." Harland ran a hand down the side of his face. "I was judge, jury, and executioner." He winced at the terrible analogy.

"And that bothers you."

"Of course it does."

"Because you like her." Ruth looked up. "Quite a bit, if I was to guess."

He opened his mouth but closed it, turning to look down at his house manager and friend.

Her eyes twinkled. "Oh, Harland. This is a good thing. This is life." She reached up, cupping his cheek in a motherly way. "And if this is what it takes to show you what your feelings are, well then, I say it was a good thing this happened."

"But my privacy—"

"Was violated. Yes. But you know what? They may get to see the house, but *you* get to live in it and make memories in it. And I think you should ask yourself if living in it alone for the rest of your days is really what you want."

He swallowed. Ruth's words hit their mark, and he dropped his head, the mug of chocolate still in his hands. "I'm a coward."

"No, you're careful. Cautious even. I think the world has taught you to be that, but it doesn't have to be how you choose to live."

"My life is complicated."

"Everyone's lives are complicated, my dear. Yours is just more publicly so. That's not a reason."

"But people will know if I'm dating someone and—"

"Let them know. For goodness sakes, you deserve to be happy. I don't think that is the real reason." She tapped his chest over his heart. "I think in here, you've set up for yourself what you think it will be like to fall in love. You write all of those beautiful songs about it, so how could you not romanticize it? But sometimes falling for the right person means they make you mad, or you say something to them that was hurtful. Sometimes love looks like your lyrics, but sometimes it looks more like accepting the ugly parts of each other along with all of the good."

There was a lump in his throat he couldn't seem to swallow past.

"My dear boy, you deserve to be happy, and Libby makes you happy. If you are to fear anything, fear losing her."

Harland took in a shuddering breath. "You're right."

"Of course I am." She smiled and took his half empty mug from him. "Now, think of a way to win her back. Maybe write her a song—you're good at that."

And with those words, she walked off into the kitchen, humming one of his love songs as she went.

He knew she was right, but that still left the gaping reality of what he'd said to Libby, and the fact that, even if he could find the words to give her, he didn't know if she'd listen to them.

Thirty-Six

Libby

"Victory Ann Taylor, you get your butt down stairs this minute." Libby was shaking, her sister's phone clutched in her fist.

"What's going on?" Vicky said. Her hair was tousled like she'd been taking a nap.

Their father sat on the couch, content to be an observer, but Libby didn't need him on her side. She had the truth.

"How *dare* you." The words were that much more dangerous in the ultra-calm way she said them, and she saw the instant Vicky realized things were serious.

"Wh-what's going on? Dad?"

He tilted his head once in a half-shake as if to say, *I'm not touching this with a ten-foot pole.*

"Hey, is that my phone?"

"It is. And you know, it's a good thing I always know your password, because I think it's only fair that I get to break into your phone like you broke into mine."

"I didn't—"

"Don't you lie to me, Victory Ann." She held up Libby's phone with the email typed out and sent to "contact@starsite" which included the video Libby had taken of Harland all those weeks ago on the porch. The one that had just been for her and was now plastered across the internet.

"Oh."

"Is that all you have to say? *Oh?* Vicky, you got Dad fired from his job. You also helped this stupid site plaster Harland's personal space all over the internet. I—I can't believe you'd do this. I trusted you, but ultimately, I'm the one that gets the blame."

Libby gasped, pressing the back of her hand to her lips. Tears flooded her eyes, and she turned away, unwilling to be so vulnerable in front of her sister. She ached to think that Harland had so quickly assumed she'd stoop to something like this, but to find that it was her sister who had done it almost seemed worse.

"I—I didn't think it was a big deal. I mean, I needed the money."

"Money? What could you possibly need money for that you'd be willing to stoop so low?"

"College, okay? Things are a lot more expensive than I thought, and, my GPA slipped a little so I can't use my scholarship until I bring my grades up, but to do that I have to study more, which means I can't work as much. But I can't go to school if I can't pay for it." She huffed out a breath. "Besides, StarSite is a small blog and—"

"And nothing." Libby's anger overrode her sorrow. "It's everywhere, and you knew this would happen."

"I swear I didn't." Libby bored her gaze into her the way their mother used to do, and Vicky wilted. "Okay, maybe I thought it might blow up a little, but I was careful. They said they wouldn't share my name."

"Guess again." Libby backed out of the sent folder to one of the latest emails Vicky had gotten. Scrolling past ads for BootBarn and Subway, she pointed to the ominous subject line. "That's from a lawyer, Vicky. You could be sued or even brought up on charges for trespassing. I don't know."

She thrust her sister's phone forward. "Here. Take it. You've already done enough damage. You're on your own."

Libby turned, ready to storm out, when her father called out. "Okay, Libby, that's enough."

She paused, hand on the door.

"Come here. Both of you girls." Libby had never heard her father so stern before, and like the child she used to be, she turned around and obeyed. Vicky did too, though they sat on opposite ends of the room.

"What you did was wrong, Vicky. I expect you to write up an apology and send it to Mr. Grey, and you'll accept any form of punishment his lawyers deem necessary. Plus, you'll delete every one of those photos, or I'm going to come in and wipe your phone completely when you're asleep."

Vicky frowned. "You don't know how to—"

"I'll Google it." Then he turned to Libby. "And I think your anger, Libby Mae, is about more than just this."

"She—"

"Did a very bad thing. Yes. And there'll be consequences. But what I want to know is why this is the first time Libby and I are hearing about you losing your scholarship, Vicky? I don't want you working so much if you need to be studying."

Libby felt part of her soften at the look of shame that washed over Vicky's features, so like her own.

"I didn't want to bother you guys about it. I mean, you've been out of work, and Libby's saving for that property. I should be able to figure this stuff out on my own, you know? So when that photographer guy saw me with you, Libby, he asked if I could get pictures and told me how much he could get for them. I honestly didn't think it was that big of a deal. They weren't of Harland, just his home."

"But why steal my video?" Libby's voice cracked, betraying just how special it had been to her.

Vicky's cheeks went pink, and she looked down at her hands. "He said he'd add on an extra five hundred dollars for an image of Harland. I didn't have any so...I looked through your phone. That was all I could find."

It made sense, but in a terrible kind of way. "That was personal."

"I know. I guess I just didn't think about it like that."

"You never think things through. You just go and do whatever you have a mind to and—"

"And nothing," their father cut in. "You turn that finger right around, missy."

Libby blinked, but Vicky had the sense to remain quiet. "Come on, Dad."

"Don't Dad me. I know you, Liberty, and I can guess you had some choice words of your own for Mr. Grey."

She blushed. He wasn't wrong.

"And I don't know what happened before all of this. You girls never talk to me about anything these days. But I'm no fool. I could tell there was something—a spark—between you two. But I could also see that something changed Sunday after you went over to his house. I don't pretend to know the ways of young ladies, but I was married to your mother for a blessed fifteen years, and I still know the look of someone whose heart is breaking."

The tears returned, but Libby tried to blink them away. "I like him a lot, Dad. And that's the truth."

"And let me guess? You told him that, and things didn't go well."

"Kind of." She dropped her gaze to her fingers laced in her lap.

"I don't know Mr. Grey well, but when I have spent time with him, I can tell he's a processor. He needs time to warm up to things. He's new to Winter, and I think he's still trying to find where he fits in. You can't go demanding things of a man like that, Libby. It'll only push him away."

She broke down into a sob, her father's words hitting at the heart of what she'd done. "I just wanted him to know where I stood. That I wasn't willing to be a someday-girl, but I pushed for an answer from him." She left out the words she'd said in anger at his accusation.

"Oh sweetie." He pushed off the couch and wrapped his arms around her. "You're strong, independent, and fierce. But sometimes a man needs space to know his own mind. You shouldn't settle or compromise, I'm not saying that, but you've got to...how do they say it these days? Read the room?"

Libby laughed, sniffing back tears. "I hear you, Dad."

"Good. Now here's the last thing I'm gonna say." She wiped her eyes and met his gaze while Vicky did the same. "We're a family. Sure, we get on each other's nerves and make poor choices," he looked at Vicky, "but we stick by one another. Through the good and the bad. We're going to make this right with Mr. Grey, but that might look differently than you want it to." He directed this at Libby.

"Honestly, Dad, I don't know what I want anymore." *Had she ever?*

"I know what you want." Libby's gaze darted to her sister. She flushed again but held her gaze. "You want that land Sharese showed you. And I think you should go for it."

Libby blinked. That had come out of left field.

"I agree." Dad hugged her tighter.

"But the mortgage here—"

"Nonsense. I'll find another job. It'll be fine. And if not, I'll sell, and we can move into an apartment."

"But the land," Libby said.

"It'll get to be too much eventually, but the point I'm trying to make is that things come and go, but family remains. You girls are my life, and I value that over land, or jobs, or anything else. I love you both so much."

Libby saw tears in her father's eyes that matched hers and her sister's. He was right, though. In her anger, Libby had lost sight of her sister, in the bond they all shared. Vicky had done a terrible thing, but no one was past the point of redemption. Everyone deserved forgiveness, no matter the wrongs they'd committed.

"I'm sorry, Vick. I was just mad."

"You had a right to be. I was selfish, and I didn't think how it would affect you—or Harland." She bit her lip, the spot running an angry red. "I don't know how to make it up to him, or you."

"We'll think of something," their father said. Then he pulled his girls close.

Libby felt the connection to her family deeper than she had in a long time. And she also knew that Harland wasn't the only one living afraid.

"I'm going to buy the land."

Vicky gasped, and Dad craned his neck to look at her. "You are?"

"I've actually had the money, but my worry was that I would buy it and then suddenly have trouble paying the mortgage each month, but if the bank's willing to fund me, I need to take the step. It's a risk, but if I don't do it, how will I ever know?"

"That's my girl," Dad said, beaming.

"I'll help you, however I can." Vicky held her gaze in a pledge and already Libby felt better about the choice.

It was time for her to take her own words and put them to use. She was going to choose her path and commit to it. Let the fear come at her, she had something greater than that. She had faith.

Thirty-Seven

Harland

"You sure about this?" Dawson double checked the generator and the last string of lights leading from it.

"Positive."

"I figured, but a guy's got to ask."

Harland stared back at his friend. "What about you? You ever consider bearing your heart and hoping you look less like a fool and more like a romantic?" He scratched at his neck, knowing how that sounded.

Dawson merely laughed, dusting off his hands. "There was a time, and a girl, who I thought was worth a grand gesture like this, but it wasn't meant to be."

"You'll have to tell me that story someday."

"Maybe. But I came out looking like the villain so, maybe not."

"I doubt that." Harland pulled his guitar strap over his head and let it settle comfortably across his shoulder and neck. His fingers found the strings like they were magnets drawn there, and he easily slipped into the chords he'd been playing over and over again.

"You're set to go, man. Everything else ready?"

Harland pulled his phone out and checked his messages. "Yeah. Mallory says they're on the way."

Harland thought he caught a slight flinch on his friend's face at the mention of Mallory, but he was too amped up to dig deeper there. If that was part of the story Dawson wanted to tell someday, he'd listen. Until then, he had to get in place.

"Okay, here goes nothing. Thanks again."

"Sure thing, man. I'm all for love, even if it's not for me."

Harland slipped into the darkness but double checked that he knew where the foot switch was for when the time was right.

If Mallory's estimate on time was accurate, they'd be there in minutes. Dawson flipped on his headlamp in the fast-growing darkness and raced off over the hill to the back road where he'd parked his truck. Harland's truck was there as well, but for now, he was positioned near the new building.

That's when he saw the lights.

"Turn them off, Mallory. Turn them off," he muttered.

They winked out, and he released a sigh. The sound of blaring country music came to him, and he almost laughed, but his nerves were live wires that wouldn't let him settle. His fingers met the strings again, but he muted them with his palm, playing but with little sound coming out.

He waited as the SUV came down the sloping road, skidding to a stop. Laughter erupted from the rolled down windows, and his heart threatened to hammer out of his chest. This was the moment, or almost, when he knew the next step was going to be a turning point in his life.

And yet, standing there in the dark by a freshly erected building and a swampy smelling pond, he knew it was the right choice. It was the same feeling he got when the perfect lyric came to him. A feeling of *rightness*.

"What is going on?" It was Libby. His palms began to sweat at the sound of her voice, and he wiped his hands on his jeans.

"I told you. A big surprise, just for you. Now, I'm going to help you from the car, and then you need to just wait. Okay?"

"You're not going to throw eggs at me or something, are you?"

"Eggs? What? No. Come on." The passenger door opened, and he saw that Libby was blindfolded. *Smart move, Mallory!* He was liking Libby's best friend more and more.

"Okay, this is weird. Where are we? Are we going cow tipping? You know how bad I feel after we do it."

Harland stifled his laugh.

"We're not going cow tipping. Chill out. Okay stand there and don't move. Got it?"

"Okay, but—"

The sound of Mallory's boots on the gravel caused Libby to turn, though she didn't reach for the blindfold. When the SUV revved to life, however, she yanked it off, but by then it was too late.

"Mallory! Mallory Robinson, you get yourself back here! You are *not* leaving me alone out here! Mallory!"

That was his cue. He tapped the switch for the lights with his booted foot, and suddenly, the darkness erupted into glowing light as if the stars had decided to fall around them, suspended in mid-air.

Libby gasped and turned as Harland came out from behind the small building. Her eyes took him in, then his guitar, then they continued around the area flitting over the office space, the pond, and all of the lights strung from the trees to the arena he'd had workers finish that very afternoon.

"I—what? Harland, what are you doing here?"

He began to strum the familiar chords, the melody begging to be released, but he held back until he was just a few feet from her. She wore a black button up shirt over light washed jeans with boots—always with boots—and her blonde hair cascaded in gentle waves around her shoulders. She'd even put on makeup, part of the ploy Mallory had woven to get her out of the house on a Friday night, no doubt.

She was stunning, but he thought he actually preferred her when she had no makeup and was working with horses. It was there that her best qualities shone.

"Harland, what is going on?" Her voice was uncharacteristically soft. Gone was the fiery woman who had told him off in no uncertain terms.

"I needed to apologize the right way."

An eyebrow quirked. "Oh?"

He strummed more boldly, the sound flowing out of the guitar to surround them in the stillness of the night. And then he sang.

I wrote you a love letter today
Had a lot of things I wanted to say
But as it turns out they are better
Better left said this way

I said it all in the letter
The one that you'll never see
About how I know you are the best
The best one for me

He stepped closer as he ramped up to the bridge, Libby's eyes shining with tears.

I'm not who you think I am
There's more beneath the surface just dying to get out
I'm not who you think I am
But if you'd stick around for while
I promise that I'll—open up

There was more to the song, but Harland could tell that he'd made his point with the first two verses and chorus, he let the last chord fade and then pulled his guitar strap off, placing the instrument back in the case.

When he turned, Libby was there, hands clasped in front of her like she wasn't sure what to do. Wasn't sure what to say.

"I know that just scrapes the surface, but every word is true." He ran a hand through his hair. "I came to Montana to run away, I guess. To escape the critical eyes of those in LA but also to find myself. There's so much in here." He tapped his chest. "And I want to let it out, but I'm afraid. I've been looking for something that's unattainable, when in reality what I needed—what's best—is standing right in front of me."

He closed the gap, taking her shaking hands in his, and entwined their fingers. The soft, sweet scent of sweet pea and hay reached him, and he smiled down at her, wanting her to see the commitment in his gaze.

"I don't deserve a woman like you, Libby Taylor. I don't deserve your dogged determination to stick up for what's right. I don't deserve your dedication. And I certainly don't deserve your love after how I've acted, but if there's any way you might see fit to forgive me, I'd like to try to earn your respect and your trust. To be the kind of man that you can walk alongside in this life."

He swallowed. It was everything on his heart and in his mind laid bare and resting at the feet of the woman before him. He didn't know what she'd say, but he was prepared to take it with dignity either way.

"Did you write that for me?"

Her question surprised him. "The song?" She nodded. "I did."

"It's beautiful." Tears trailed down her cheeks, just visible in the glow of the lights.

"Thanks." He grinned.

She drew in a breath. "I can forgive you, Harland, but I need to ask for the same kindness in return." She drew closer, their hands entwined between them still. "I pushed you because *I* was afraid. I wanted assurances that were unfair of me to ask for. I wanted to know that you weren't a risk, but that's not how life is." She sniffed and looked down. "My dad reminded me that, just like Vicky, I too can be impulsive. You gave me an inch that night on the bluff, and I tried to take a mile. Can you forgive me for that?"

"It's already done."

"And," she only let a beat of silence follow his forgiveness. "Can you forgive me for bringing Vicky to your house? I had no idea she'd taken those pictures, let alone sold them to the press. I—I know she's written you to apologize, and she's gotten an ear full from me, but I need you to know I would never, ever do anything that would hurt you like that. I know the video I took went against my NDA but you looked so peaceful and...it was just for me. I never meant for it to get out, and—"

He couldn't help it. The sweet apology and her vow to respect his privacy was just one of the many reasons he knew he already loved this woman, even if he wasn't quite prepared to tell her that yet. But he was prepared to show her.

He bent down and cut off her rambling words with a kiss. Instantly, her hands reached up around his neck to draw him closer. He encircled her waist, drawing her in, and he felt the same sense of home he had when he first saw Melody Ranch.

Libby was his homecoming. She was a safe place. A refuge in a world that tried to tear apart his best intentions. Sure, they had so much left to figure out, but he knew beyond a shadow of a doubt that she was the woman he wanted to take that journey with.

Thirty-Eight

Libby

When Harland finally pulled back from their kiss, she was breathless and elated. "I'm guessing that was a yes, you do forgive me?"

His laugh rumbled in his chest, and she relished their nearness. "That was most definitely a yes."

"I'm sorry, Harland, I just—" He silenced her with another kiss. "Okay, I get the hint. We're past the apologies."

He nodded, dropping his head down to look into her eyes. "I'm not sure what life looks like for," he paused, "for us."

"So you're saying there's an us?" She flashed a flirty grin, but his expression sobered.

"I am, if *you* want that." He licked his lips, the motion distracting to Libby. "I haven't dated anyone in a long time, and I'm more wary about press than anything. I don't want you to face the kind of harassment I get or the intrusion into our privacy, but I don't think those are things that should stop us."

"What changed?" Her tone was mild, but she was curious.

"First off, how I was so wrong about you." He grimaced. "I shouldn't have assumed you'd be the one to sell out my privacy like that."

"Yes, you should have known better." She laughed and was gifted with a responding smile.

"But secondly, I think I was faced with the reality that I've spent a good portion of my life writing songs about *the one*. You know, that mythical woman out there who's supposed to be perfect and who other women never can live up to." He sent her a worried look, but she kept her mouth closed, wanting to hear the rest of his explanation. "Ruth reminded me that sometimes real life doesn't look, or even feel, like my songs make it out to, but that doesn't mean real life is wrong—if anything, it's my perception that's off."

"So you're basically saying I'm nothing like the woman you've dreamed of, but I'll do?" She feigned mock hurt.

"Not at all." He was beginning to look frantic.

"I'm teasing you, Harland. Take a breath."

He did as she instructed. "What I mean is that I can create the perfect idea of someone, but when faced with what reality has brought me," he tugged her closer, "everything else pales in comparison. I couldn't have predicted you, Libby. I couldn't have known that I'd want to have someone unabashedly tell me what she thinks or who will call me out if I'm making a misstep. I couldn't have dreamed you up, but I can easily say reality is so much better than fantasy. You are perfect *for me* in every way."

She kissed him again, unable to help it when he was telling her such sweet things, but when she moved back, she cupped his cheek. "I feel the same about you. Believe it or not, I do need to learn when to say things and when to keep things inside. You are a great reminder to me of the beauty of thinking things through, and while I'll admit I'm not good at it, I want to learn."

"How about we grow together?"

"I like the sound of that." She pulled back and turned toward the arena. "Now tell me what in the world is going on here."

He laughed, taking her hand and gently tugging her toward the sanded area. "This is your new therapy space."

"I was supposed to sign papers on it tomorrow."

"Which is why a surprise investor stepped in at the last minute." He winked at her. "Just say this is my contribution to your dreams. What you do with it is your choice, but I wanted you to have what you needed. As much as I'm happy to have you come to the ranch, it's nice to have a business and a home separate."

Her stomach fluttered. Was he insinuating what she thought he was?

But it was too soon for that. Too soon to think of Melody Ranch as *her* home. Perhaps this was the perfect time to put into practice the concept of thinking on things before speaking them. She'd treasure the thought, but she'd let things play out as they would.

"It's perfect."

"I had Mallory and your dad help me figure out how you'd most likely want it set up. Did I get the placement of the office right?"

She turned and saw the small office space that she would definitely be calling the *She Shed*. "It's exactly how I envisioned it."

"We'll get someone out here for the pond—it smells more like a swamp at this point. But for now, you've got the space to work with your clients, a shaded area over there," he pointed to a roofed in area, "for the parents to sit and watch."

Overcome, Libby gave in to the tears for the second time in so many days. "I'm not one to cry, but this is literally my dreams coming true."

"Good." He pulled her against him, her back to his chest, and wrapped his arms around her. "I want to make your dreams come true. I want to help you, even though I know you don't need my help."

She laugh-sobbed. "I'm sorry I said that."

"Don't be. It was a good reminder that not everyone is after me for what I can do for them. I want more friends like that, more real relationships than business partnerships. More real life."

She spun around to face him. "I think Winter has just what you need."

"I couldn't agree more."

Thirty-Nine

Two Months Later

Harland

Harland stood at the window in his recording studio and watched the perfectly landscaped lawn fill up with guests. He felt the familiar twinge of anxiety in his gut. It wasn't stage fright; it was more a deep-seated fear of sharing his innermost thoughts through the form of song. He always felt this way before a performance, but it only confirmed that he was doing the right thing.

"It's getting full," Ruth said. She bustled into the room, holding out a glass of ice water and lemon. "Here."

"Thanks, Ruth." He took a refreshing sip and drew in a deep breath.

"You're not nervous, are you?"

He shot her a glance. "A little."

She made a *phhhsh* sound and shook her head. "Honey, you were made to live on the stage. Just because you've been away from it for a little while doesn't mean you won't slip right back into the groove once you sit down. Besides, I think the songs you've written since living here are some of your best ones yet. The town's going to eat them up."

He grinned. "And everything else is ready?"

"It sure is. That photographer, what's his name? He just showed up."

"Jamin." Harland nodded. "Good, he's exactly right for tonight."

"Need anything else?"

"No, you've got to go get your seat."

"James is saving one for me." She blushed, her tanned cheeks showing just a hint of color.

"Enjoy the show."

"You know we will." She went up on tip-toes and kissed his cheek, the feeling so reminiscent of how his mother had been there for him it caused his eyes to shine with tears.

He drew in a deep breath and flexed his fingers. The landscaping crew he'd hired had set up relaxed arena style seating on thick grass with a large deck-like stage at the base.

As he watched, he caught sight of Libby as she plugged in the myriad of white lights they'd hung up around the stage. She laughed, and while he couldn't hear it, he knew exactly what the sound was like.

Spending time with her over the last several months had been the highlight of his time in Winter. They'd gone horseback riding across his land, had a countless number of bonfires up on the ridge, he'd watched her lessons at the new property, they'd eaten at the diner weekly, and in general, they had slipped into an easy life together.

The type of life he'd always longed for but couldn't have imagined he'd find. Especially not in Winter. And yet, he couldn't imagine it anywhere else.

Dawson walked down the hillside, joining up with a few other friends he recognized from church. And there, on another blanket, he saw Vicky and some friends from school. She'd apologized every time she saw him for the first few weeks until he'd pulled her aside, and they had a talk to clear the air. It seemed to have worked, and now, he was happy to see her comfortable on his property.

He also caught sight of Sue with Ash and Sage, Gina from the diner, and a few of the older women from church who'd come with pies in tow. Even Winslow had made an appearance and sat near the Taylor family on his own blanket.

His chest warmed at the sight of so many new and old friends gathered together. It too was a change that had come about slowly in him due to his time with Libby. She'd made him see that Melody Ranch was his haven, but it didn't have to be a sanctuary. There was no point in walling himself off from Winter's residents. Instead, he'd found so much joy in opening himself up to them.

Tonight was the culmination of that, and so much more.

"It's time." Joshua, one of Dawson's friends and a sound engineer, popped his head into the studio. He'd helped set up the simple sound system for the night so everyone would be able to hear the acoustic set Harland had prepared.

"All right." Harland rose, pulling out his trusty Taylor guitar.

"Sir," Joshua still hadn't taken to calling him by his first name, "I've just got to say that what you're doing tonight is really cool. There are a lot of people out there that would never be able to afford going to one of your shows, and it's just really a nice thing to do. I'm glad I can be a part of it." The young man looked embarrassed to have spoken his thoughts out loud, but Harland merely slapped him on the back.

"I'm glad they can come too. How about you be my go-to sound guy when I do more house concerts like this?"

"I—I would love that," he stammered.

"Good. Then let's do this." Harland grinned and followed the young man out of the house.

Applause greeted him as he jogged easily down the hill to the stage. He climbed up and quickly held up a hand to silence the crowd, somewhat embarrassed by their enthusiasm.

"Thank you all for coming tonight," he said as he slid onto the high stool behind the lone mic. "I've got to say, for the first concert in over two years, this is by far my most anticipated one."

More applause and cheering.

His eyes found Libby. Her hands were clasped and pressed against her chest, and she wore the most beautiful, proud smile on her ruby red lips. She was wearing a sparkly black and silver top that was going to be a real distraction to him, so he pulled his gaze away and scanned the rest of the crowd.

"Tonight is about you, Winter. You welcomed me in when I wasn't sure where to go." His eyes met Reba and Hoyt's where they sat with a host of other people who, by the looks of it, he guessed were siblings to

Hoyt. "You stood by me when reporters tried to get any info they could." A loud voice called out "boo" in the back, and he laughed. "And you've supported my privacy in town every step of the way. Thank you. Thank you for not only letting me into your town, but also into your hearts."

The applause was thunderous this time, so much from such a small gathering, and all he could do was put a hand over his heart and bow his head for a moment in quiet thanks to their support.

When it quieted, he risked one more look at Libby. "This first song is for the woman I love, Libby Taylor."

Forty

Libby

She was crying again. In fact, it seemed all she did these days was weep, but this time, it was out of sheer happiness. Harland had worked tirelessly on a new set of acoustic songs he was hoping to produce in his almost-finished recording studio, and he'd brought the idea of a yard concert to her a few weeks back.

The fact he'd even suggested Melody Ranch for something like that was unbelievable, but also proof to her of how Harland had changed. Not in monumental ways. He was still thoughtful to the extreme, cautious when out in public—though much less so in Winter these days—and he valued his privacy just as much, but he was willing to trust that he could open up a part of him and not be afraid.

Jamin, the young photographer from the shoot so many weeks back, made his way quietly around the stage, capturing angles that Libby never would have thought of. He was unobtrusive, something she loved, but she had a feeling his shots of Harland would be some of her favorite yet.

She had a feeling Winslow would love that too. He was always after Libby to brush up on her phone camera taking ways, but she was happy to just be in the moment with Harland. Not everything was about promotion or building up his social media presence. Though, now that he was out of the clear on the lawsuit that had been dropped, she was determined to show off the most caring side of her boyfriend. She was going to show the world who he was at the core, and she knew they would love him for it.

He shifted to one of her favorite new songs and felt her dad swaying back and forth to it. "It's more country, right?" She whispered to him.

He grinned. "You've had an effect on him, I can see."

She giggled, turning her attention back to Harland. He was in his element, eyes closed, fingers eating up the fret board, and his strong voice belting out the melody of the chorus. She hummed along with him, knowing all the words, and simply enjoyed the moment.

When he finished, he paused for a drink of water while the applause died down, and she realized he was at the last song in his set. He'd made sure to play them through for her to get her opinion, something she still laughed over because she was the *least* musical person out there, but she'd been happy to listen even still.

How had the night gone so fast? Her eyes met his as he leaned toward the mic and smiled.

"I've got one more song for you all tonight, but I've decided to do the encore first. How about that?"

People clapped, but she could tell they were just as confused as she was.

"Libby, why don't you come on up here? You've got to help me with this one."

Her stomach twisted. She was more a *behind the scenes* type of girl, not one that went on stage. She shook her head.

"Oh, come on now." He turned to the crowd. "Maybe she needs some encouragement."

Whistles and cheers went up around the yard, and a few people called out her name. Face beet red, she pushed up from the blanket near the front and made her way toward Harland.

"Uh oh, I'm getting the "I'll kill you later" stare, folks. Pray for me?"

Laughter went around like a wave as she stepped onto the stage.

"What are you doing?" She whispered through clenched teeth.

"Come here." He pulled off his guitar, placing it on a stand behind him, and tugged her forward. "Folks, this woman right here is a great muse. If you heard a bit of country influence in the new songs, I blame her." Laughter followed his words. "But even more than with my music, Libby has shown me there is a lot more to life than I've allowed myself to see."

The awkwardness of being on stage with Harland lessened as his face took over her view. This was her Harland, a man she'd come to know more deeply than she'd thought possible. She trusted him, believed in him, and wanted nothing but the best for him.

"In fact, I think she is the true reason I'm here in Winter still. Her insistence that you good people would stand up for me convinced me to stay when it would have been easy to leave. But running from things, while easy, is never the best course forward."

Then, to her utter shock and that of the crowds, Harland knelt down on one knee. Audible gasps echoed around the crowd.

"Liberty Mae Taylor, I know we've only known each other a few months now, but I've seen enough of your heart to know who you are where it counts." His words went out to the crowd, though softly due to his distance from the mic. "You're fierce, loyal, and so beautiful."

Her insides melted with the look of pure adoration reflected in Harland's eyes. He held her hands in his, and she felt the slight tremor in his fingertips.

"I can't imagine going through this world without you by my side. Would you be my wife?"

The world went quiet, absolutely silent, as his words sunk into the depths of her heart. They were no longer in the midst of Winter residents, but alone on an island where only she and Harland existed. Head spinning, heart longing, she nodded. The motion grew as the tears fell, and finally, she shattered the silence with her answer.

"Yes!"

Harland erupted from his one kneed perch and enveloped her in his arms. His familiar woodsy, lemony scent surrounded her, and she knew her heart had found its resting place here on earth.

"I love you," he muttered into her hair.

"And I love you back." She pulled away to smile up at him, and then his lips were on hers, sealing their commitment with a kiss.

The cheers were deafening, but none as loud as the resounding yes her soul shouted with every breath.

There would be hardships in the future, she knew that. Mixing personalities like theirs always created rough patches, but if there was one thing Libby was sure of, it was that theirs was a love that would last. They would weather the storms together and come out stronger on the other side.

All they had to do was let the music of their love be reflected in the lyrics of their lives.

About the Author

Bell Renshaw, a pen name for Emilie Haney, grew up in the Pacific Northwest and has a love for the outdoors that matches her love for the written word. She turned her passion for stories toward writing at an early age and she's still getting lost in those worlds, but now they're of her own making. She believes that—no matter what—love fights for what's right.

Connect with her on her website: www.emiliehaney.com

Join her newsletter:
https://view.flodesk.com/pages/63d99e20b4f015f30446e5c0

facebook.com/AuthorEmilieHaney

Newsletter Signup

Don't miss the next release!

Sign up for the Two Dogs Newsletter to stay up-to-date on upcoming collections and releases, as well as news from our partner authors that have been included in previous releases!

Find and follow Two Dogs Publishing on Facebook to stay up to date on upcoming releases!

facebook.com/twodogspublishing

Made in the USA
Columbia, SC
09 August 2024

40264549R00390